Explorations in Bible Lands During
Hermann Vollrat Hilprecht and Immanuel Benzinger

Publisher's Note

The book descriptions we ask booksellers to display prominently warn that this is an historic book with numerous typos, missing text or index and is not illustrated.

We scanned this book using character recognition software that includes an automated spell check. Our software is 99 percent accurate if the book is in good condition. However, we do understand that even one percent can be a very annoying number of typos! And sometimes all or part of a page is missing from our copy of a book. Or the paper may be so discolored from age that you can no longer read the type. Please accept our sincere apologies.

After we re-typeset and design a book, the page numbers change so the old index and table of contents no longer work. Therefore, we usually remove them.

Our books sell so few copies that you would have to pay hundreds of dollars to cover the cost of proof reading and fixing the typos, missing text and index. Therefore, whenever possible, we let our customers download a free copy of the original typo-free scanned book. Simply enter the barcode number from the back cover of the paperback in the Free Book form at www.general-books. net. You may also qualify for a free trial membership in our book club to download up to four books for free. Simply enter the barcode number from the back cover onto the membership form on the same page. The book club entitles you to select from more than a million books at no additional charge. Simply enter the title or subject onto the search form to find the books.

If you have any questions, could you please be so kind as to consult our Frequently Asked Questions page at www. general-books.net/faqs.cfm? You are also welcome to contact us there.

General Books LLC™, Memphis, USA, 2012. ISBN: 9781459073104.

PREFACE

Nearly ten years ago Messrs. A. J. Holman & Co. approached me with a request to prepare, for the close of the century, a brief historical sketch on the explorations in Bible lands, which would convey to the intelligent English-reading public a clear conception of the gradual resurrection ot the principal ancient nations of Western Asia and Kgypt. After much hesitation, I consented to become responsible for the execution of their comprehensive plan, provided that I be allowed to solicit the cooperation of other specialists for the treatment of those subjects which did not lie directly within the sphere of my own investigations, as most of the books dealing with this fascinating theme suffer from the one serious defect that their authors are not competent authorities in every part of that vast field which thev attempt to plough and cultivate for the benefit and instruction of others. Several well-known German specialists, whose names appear on the title-page, were therefore accordingly invited to join the editor in the preparation of the volume, and to present to the reader sketches of their respective branches of science, with the historical development of which they have been prominently connected during previous years. At the close of 1900 the entire MS. was ready to be printed, when the results of a series of excavations carried on by the Babylonian Expedition of the University of Pennsylvania began to attract more than ordinary attention on both sides of the Atlantic. In view of the growing demand for a popular and authentic report of these important archaeological researches, the publishers deemed it necessary to modify their former plans by asking the editor to make the exploration of Assyria and Babylonia the characteristic feature of the uncompleted book, and, above all, to in-

corporate with it *the first full account of the American labors at Nuffar.* Thus it came about that the opening article of this collective volume, intended to give but a brief survey of a subject which at present stands in the centre of general interest, has grown far beyond its original limits.

As the results of Koldewey's methodical excavations and topographical researches at the vast ruin fields of the ancient metropolis on the Euphrates, belong chieflv to the twentieth century and, moreover, are not yet fully accessible to other scholars, their omission in these pages will scarcely be regarded as a serious deficiency, since the object of the present book was to set forth the work of the explorers of the previous century. If, however, the public interest in the material here submitted should warrant it, they will find their proper treatment in a future edition.

In preparing the first 288 pages of my own contribution I have had the extraordinary assistance of my lamented wife and colaborer, who, with her remarkable knowledge of the history of Assyriology and her characteristic unselfish devotion to the cause of science and art, promoted the work of the Babylonian Expedition of the Universitv of Pennsylvania (in charge of her husband) in many essential ways unknown to the public. The best passages in the following chapter on the " Resurrection of Assyria and Babylonia" are likewise due to her. She laid down her pen only when the approaching angel of death wrested it from her tired hand on March 1, 1902. The Board of Trustees of the University of Pennsylvania has since honored the memory of this great and gifted woman by resolving unanimously that the famous collections of tablets from the temple library at Nippur shall be known henceforth by her name. In view of her very extensive contributions to the present book, it was my desire to have her name associated with mine on its title-page. But when I asked for her consent the day previous to her final departure, — immediately after she had completed her last task, and had arranged with me for the next twenty years the details of the scientific publications of the American Expedition to Nuffar,— I received the memorable reply: "Why should the world learn to discriminate between your work and my work, your person and mv person? Was not your God my God, your country my countn, your labor my labor, your sorrow my sorrow, your name my name? Let it remain so even at my coffin and tomb." In the light of this sacred legacy, my reviewers will pardon me for appearing to appropriate more than is due to me.

More rapidly than I could have anticipated I was placed in a position to carry out my wife's lofty ideas with regard to the strictly scientific publications of the Philadelphia expedition. It seems therefore eminently proper for me in this connection to express publicly my deep gratitude to Messrs. F.dward W. and Clarence H. Clark of Philadelphia, the two widely known patrons of American explorations in Babylonia, who by their recent munificent gift of §100,000 have enabled the Board of Trustees of the University of Pennsylvania to establish the " Clark Research Professorship of Assyriology," the only chair of its kind in existence. As its first incumbent I am authorized to devote the rest of my life to the study and deciphering of those remarkable results which through the generosity and energy of a few Philadelphia citizens were obtained at the ruins of Nuffar, and which through the liberality and personal interest of Mr. Ecklev B. Coxe, Jr., will be printed and submitted to the public more rapidly than was hitherto possible.

From the very beginning I have been connected with the various Babylonian expeditions of the University of Pennsylvania. The farther we proceeded with our researches, the more it became necessary for me to spend my time almost regularly every year in three different parts of the world and to surrender completely the comfort of a fixed home. In consequence of this nomadic life I was often out of contact with my well-equipped library, — a disadvantage especially felt when certain passages were to be examined or verified from the earlier literature dealing with my subject. With warm appreciation of all the friendly assistance received, I acknowledge my great indebtedness to Messrs. Halil Bey, Director of the Imperial Ottoman Museum; Leon Heuzev, Director of the Louvre; L. King of the British Museum; Dr. A. Gies, First Dragoman of the German Embassy in Constantinople; F. Furtwaengler, H. Gebzer, F. Hommel, R. Kittel, V. Scheil, Eberhard Schrader, F. Thureau-Dangin, Karl Vollers, and not the least to mv friend and assistant, A. T. Clay, who not only read a complete set of proofs, and improved the English garment of all the articles here published, but in many other ways facilitated the preparation and printing of the entire volume.

As it was not always advisable to ship valuable photographic material to his temporary abode, the editor found it sometimes difficult to illustrate the articles of his colaborers in an adequate manner. In several instances it would have been almost impossible for him to obtain suitable illustrations had he not profited by the material kindly placed at his disposal by Mrs. Sara Y. Stevenson, Sc. D., Curator of the Egyptian Section of the Archaeological Museum of the L niversity of Pennsylvania; Miss Mary Robinson, daughter ot the late Professor Edward Robinson of New York; Mrs. T. Bent and Mrs. W. Wright of London; Mr. C. S. Fisher, ot the Babylonian Expedition of the University of Pennsylvania; Mr. T. Grotefend of Hanover; Professor J. Halevy of Paris; and Count Landberg of Munich; to all of whom are due his cordial thanks.

It is the hope of both authors and publishers that the present volume may help to fill a serious gap in our modern literature by presenting in a systematic but popular form a fascinating subject, equal in importance to the Bible student, historian, archaeologist, and philologist. The rich material often scattered through old editions of rare books and comparatively inaccessible journals has been examined anew, sifted, and treated by a number of experts in the light of their latest researches. It was our one aim to bring the historv of the gradual exploration of those distant oriental countries, which formed the significant scene and background of God's dealings with Israel as a nation, more vividly before the educated classes of Christendom. May the time and labor devoted to the preparation of this work contribute their small share towards arousing a deeper interest on the part of the public in excavating more of those priceless treasures of the past which have played such a conspicuous role in the interpretation of the Old

Testament writings.

THE EDITOR. Jena, December 2", 1902.

LIST OF ILLUSTRATIONS.

The asterisk () indicates that the illustration has been added by the Editor to the material furnished by the contributors.

Expedition of the University of Pennsylvania.

Minean Inscription from El-'Ola (Midian), mentioning two women

Levites (=Eut. 551 749

From J. H. Mordtmann, *Beitrage zur Minaiichen Efiigraphik.* THE HITTITES.

W. Wright 754

From a photograph in the possession of his widow.

Hittite Inscription from Ilamath 755

From W.Wright, "The Empire of the Hittites." second edition. (By permission of the publishers, Messrs James Nishet & Co., London)

Hittite Bowl from Babylon 757

From W. Wright, *l. c.* (By permission.)

The Hittite God of the Sky (Stele in dolerite, excavated by Dr. Koldewey in the palace of Nebuchadrezzar at Babylon, in 1S99). Opp. p. 758

From *U'iimukafUiche l'erijffenllirhungen der Deutsche Orient-CeselUcha/l,*

Hefl.

Page

Sculptures and Inscriptions near Ivriz 762

From *Rfcueil d. Travaux relatifs A la Philologie et A V Archtologie itgyptiennes et Assyriennes,* Vol. XIV.

The Pseudo-Sesostris (Carved on the rock in the pass of Karabel)

Opp. p. 762

From W. Wright, *l. c.* (By permission.)

Hittite Inscription on a Bowl from Babylon (Comp. p. 6).. 767

From W. Wright, *l. c.* (By permission.)

Bilingual Inscription on the Silver Boss of Tarkondemos... 769 From the "Transactions of the Society of Biblical Archarology," Vol. VII.

-The Inscribed Lion of Mar 'ash (Now in the Imperial Ottoman Museum,

Constantinople) Opp. p. 777

From W. Wright, *l. c.* (By permission.)

Hittite Relief, found near Malatya in 1894 (Now in the Imperial Ottoman Museum, Constantinople) Opp. p. 779

From a photograph in the possession of the Editor.

MAPS. (IN THE POCKET AT THE END OF THE BOOK.) No. I. Western Asia (with Plan of Ancient Jerusalem, according to J. Benzinger)

Drawn by L. Hirsch. architect, Jena, from material furnished by the Editor.

No. 2. Plan of Babylon, according to R. Koldewey.

Drawn bv L. Hirsch, architect, Jena, according to the drawing published in Friedrich Delitzsch. *Babylon,* second edition, Leipzig. 1901.

No. 3. Egypt.

Drawn by Hubert Kohler, Graph. Art Institute, Munich, from material furnished by the Editor.

No. 4. Arabia.

Drawn by Hubert Kohler, Graph. Art Institute, Munich, from material furnished by Professor Hommel.

THE RESURRECTION OF ASSYRIA AND BABYLONIA BY PROFESSOR H. V. HILPRECHT, PH.D., D.D., LL.D.

The history of the exploration of Assyria and Babylonia and of the excavation of its ruined cities is a peculiar one. It is a history so full of dramatic effects and genuine surprises, and at the same time so unique and farreaching in its results and bearings upon so many different branches of science, that it will always read more like a thrilling romance penned by the skilful hand of a gifted writer endowed with an extraordinary power of imagination than like a plain and sober presentation of actual facts and events.

Nineveh and Babylon! What illustrious names and prominent types of human strength, intellectual power, and lofty aspiration; but also what terrible examples of atrocious deeds, of lack of restraint, of moral corruption, and ultimate downfall!" Empty, and void, and waste " (Nah. 2:10); when "flocks lie down in the midst of her " (Zeph. 2: 14); when " the gates of the rivers shall be opened, and the palace shall be dissolved " (Nah. 2: 6) — was the fate of the queen in the North; and " How art thou fallen from heaven, O Lucifer, son of the morning! how art thou cut down to the ground, which didst weaken the nations " (Is. 14: 12) — rings like a mourning wail through Babylon's crumbling walls, and like the mocking echo of the prophetic curse from the shattered temples in the South.

Ignorant peasants draw their primitive ploughs over the ruined palaces of Qoyunjuk and Khorsabad; roaming Bedouins pasture their herds on the grass-covered slopes of Nimrud and Qal'at Shirgat; Turkish garrisons and modern villages crown the summits of Erbil and Nebi Yunus. Nothing reminds the traveller of the old Assyrian civilization but formless heaps and conical mounds. The solitude and utter devastation which characterize Babylonia in her present aspect are even more impressive and appalling. The whole country from 'Aqarquf to Qorna looks " as when God overthrew Sodom and Gomorrah" (Is. 13: 19; Jer. 50:40). The innumerable canals which in bygone days, like so many nourishing veins, crossed the rich alluvial plain, bringing life and joy and wealth to every village and field, are choked up with rubbish and earth. Unattended by industrious hands and no longer fed by the Euphrates and Tigris, they are completely "dried up " — "a drought is upon the waters of Babylon" (Jer. 50: 38). But their lofty embankments, like a perfect network, "stretching on every side in long lines until they are lost in the hazy distance, or magnified by the mirage into mountains, still defy the hand of time," hearing witness to the great skill and diligent labor which once turned these barren plains into one luxuriant garden. The proverbial fertility and prosperity of Babylonia, which excited the admiration of classical writers, have long disappeared. "Her cities are a desolation, a dry land, and a wilderness" (Jer. 51:43). The soil is parched and the ground is covered with fine sand, sometimes sparingly clad with *'arid* and *serim, qubbar,* and *tar/a,* and other low shrubs and plants of the desert.

And yet this is but one side — and not the most gloomy — of Chaldea's present cheerless condition. "The sea is come up upon Babvlon: she is covered with the multitudes of the waves thereof" (Jer. 51 142), savs the Old Testament seer, in his terse and graphic description of the future state of the unfortunate country. In the autumn and winter Babylonia is a "desert of sand," but during spring and summer she is almost a continuous marsh, a veritable "desert of the sea" (Is. 21: 1). While the inundations prevail a dense vegetation springs from the stagnant waters. Large flocks of birds with brilliant plumage, "pelicans and cormorants sail about in the undisputed possession of their safe and tranquil retreats." Turtles and snakes glide swiftly through the lagoons, while millions of green little frogs are seated on the bending rushes. Ugly buffaloes are struggling and splashing amongst the tall reeds and coarse grasses, " their unwieldy bodies often entirely concealed under water and their hideous heads just visible upon the surface." Wild animals, boars and hyenas, jackals and wolves, and an occasional lion, infest the jungles. Here and there a small plot of ground, a shallow island, a high-towering ruin, bare of every sign of vegetation, and towards the north large elevated tracts of barren soil covered with fragments of brick and glass and stone appear above the horizon of these pestiferous marshes. Half-naked men, women, and children, almost black from constant exposure to the sun, inhabit these desolate regions. Filthy huts of reeds and mats are their abodes during the night; in long pointed boats of the same material they skim by day over the waters, pasturing their flocks, or catching fish with the spear. To sustain their life, they cultivate a little rice, barley, and maize, on the edges of the inundations. Generally good-natured and humorous like children, these Ma'dan tribes get easily excited, and at the slightest provocation are ready to fight with each other. Practicing the vices more than the virtues of the Arab race, extremely ignorant and superstitious, they live in the most primitive state of barbarism and destitution, despised by the Bedouins of the desert, who frequently drive their cattle and sheep away and plunder their little property during the winter.

Restlessly shifting nomads in the north and ignorant swamp dwellers in the south have become the legitimate heirs of Asshur and Babel. What contrast between ancient civilization and modern degeneration! The mighty kings of yore have passed away, their empires were shattered, their countries destroyed. Nineveh and Babylon seemed completely to have vanished from the earth. Hundreds of years were necessary to revive the interest in their history and to determine merely their sites, while the exploration of their principal ruins, the deciphering of their inscriptions, and the restoration of their literature and art were achieved only in the course of the nineteenth century. The road was iong, the process slow, and many persons and circumstances combined to bring about the final result.

I

THE REDISCOVERY OF NINEVEH AND BABYLON

NINEVEH

Nineveh, the capital of the Assyrian empire, owed its greatness and domineering influence exclusively to the conquering spirit of its rulers and the military glory and prowess of its armies. As soon as the latter had been routed, her influence ceased, the city fell, never to rise again, and its very site was quickly forgotten among the nations. When two hundred years later Xenophon and his ten thousand Greeks fought their wav through the wilderness and mountains to the Black Sea, they passed the ruins of Nineveh without even mentioning her by name. But a vague local tradition, always an important factor in the East, continued to linger around the desolate region between Mosul and the mouth of the Upper Zab, where the final drama had been enacted.

Benjamin of Tudela, a learned Spanish Jew, who travelled to Palestine and the districts of the Euphrates and Tigris in the twelfth century, about the time when Rabbi Pethahiah of Ratisbon visited Mesopotamia, had no difficulty in locating the actual position of Nineveh. In speaking of Mosul he says: "This city, situated on the Tigris, is connected with ancient Nineveh by a bridge. It is

true, Nineveh lies now in utter ruins, but numerous villages and small towns occupy its former space." Comp. *Itintrarium Beniamini Tudelensis (ex Hebraico Latinum fac turn Bened. Aria Montano interpreted,* Antwerp, 1575, p. 58.

The German physician, Leonhart Rauwolff, who spent several days in Mosul at the beginning of 1575, writes ' in his attractive quaint style with reference to a high round hill directly outside the city (apparently Qoyunjuk): "It was entirely honevcombed, being inhabited by poor people, whom I often saw crawling out and in in large numbers, like ants in their heap. At that place and in the region hereabout years ago the mighty city of Nineveh was situated. Originally built by Asshur, it was for a time the capital of Assyria under the rulers of the first monarchy down to Sennacherib and his sons."

Sir Anthony Shirley, who sailed to the East at the close of the sixteenth century, is equally positive: "Nineve, that which God Himself calleth That great Citie, hath not one stone standing which may give memory of the being of a towne. One English mile from it is a place called Mosul, a small thing, rather to be a witnesse of the other's mightinesse and God's judgement, than of any fashion of magnificence in it selfe." In his *ltinerarium* or *Russsbuchlein,* which appeared in Laugingen, 1583, the author writes his name either Rauwolf", Rauwolff, or Rauchwolff, the middle being the most frequent of all. Interwoven with *allerhandt tvunderbarliche geschicht und Historien, die den gutherzigen leser erlustigen und hohcren sachen nach zudenken auffmundtcrn sollen,* this book contains much valuable information as to what Rauwolff has seen in the Orient during the three years of his perilous journey, which lasted from May I 5, 1 573, to February I z, 1576. Of especial importance are his observations on the flora of the regions traversed, a subject on which he speaks with greater authority. Comp. the statement of Tavcrnier, quoted on p. 10. P. 24.4: *Son it ersahe ich aueh ausscrhalb gleich vor der Stadt tin hohen runden Bihel, der schier gantz durchgraben und von armen leuten bea-rjhnet wirt, wie ichs dann offtermals hab in grosser anzahl (a/s die Ohnmay-sen in irtm hauffen) sehen iiuss und einkriechen. An der stet und in der geg-ne hierumb, ist vor Jarcn gelegen die mechtige Stutt Ninive, welche yon Assur erstlich erbawet) unter den Potcntatcn der ersten Monarchic eine zeitlang biss auf den Sennacherib und seine Sine die Hauptstatt in Assyrien gewesen,* etc. Comp., also, p. 214: *Mossel so vor Jar-cn Ninive gehaissen.*

From the beginning of the seventeenth century we quote two other witnesses, John Cartwright, an English traveller, and Pietro della Valle, an Italian noble-man, the latter being satisfied with the general statement: "Mousul, where pre-viously Nineveh stood," the former en-tering into certain details of the topog-raphy of the ruins, which, notwithstand-ing his assurance to the contrary, he cannot have examined very thoroughly. As a first attempt at drawing some kind of a picture of the city on the basis of personal observation, legendary infor-mation from the natives, and a study of the ancient sources, his words may de-serve a certain attention: "Ve set for-ward toward Mosul, a very antient towne in this countrey,... and so pitched on the bankes of the river Tigris. Here in these plaines of Assiria and on the bankes of the Tigris, and in the region of Kden, was Ninevie built by Nimrod, but finished by Ninus. It is agreed by all prophane writers, and confirmed by the Scriptures that this citty exceeded all other citties in circuit, and answer-able magnificence. For it seems by the ruinous foundation (which I thoroughly viewed) that it was built with four sides, but not equall or square; for the two longer sides had each of them (as we gesse) an hundredth and fifty furlongs, the two shorter sides, ninety furlongs, which amountcth to foure hundred and eighty furlongs of ground, which makes three score miles, accounting eight fur-longs to an Italian mile. The walls whereof were an hundredth foote up-right, and had such a breadth, as three Chariots might passe on the rampire in front: these walls were garnished with a thousand and five hundreth towers, which gave exceeding beauty to the rest, and a strength no lesse admirable for the nature of those times."' Comp. "His Relation of His Travels into Per-sia," London, 1613, p. 21, partly quoted by Felix Jones in "Journal ot the Royal Asiatic Society," Tol. xv., p. 333, foot-note 3; and the Dutch edition, Leydcn, 1706, p. 10.

1 quote from the German translation in my library (*Reise-Bfsehrfiiitag,* Gene-va, 1674), pan i, p. 193, b: *Mousul, an teelchem Ort vorzciten tittnden.*

Tavernier, who justly prides himself in having travelled by land more than sixty thousand miles within forty years, made no less than six different excursions into Asia. In April, 1644, he spent over a week at Mosul, and most naturally also visited the ruins of Nineveh, which were pointed out to him on the left bank of the Tigris. "They appear as a form-less mass of ruined houses extending almost a mile alongside the river. One recognizes there a large number of vaults or holes which are all uninhabit-ed," — evidently the same place which, seventy-five years before him, Rau-wolff had found frequented by poor people, and not unfittingly had com-pared to a large ant-hill. "Half a mile from the Tigris is a small hill occupied by many houses and a mosque, which is still in a fine state of preservation. Ac-cording to the accounts of the natives the prophet Jonah lies buried here."

During the eighteenth century men of business, scholars, and priests of differ-ent religious orders kept the old tradi-tion alive in the accounts of their trav-els. But in 1748 Jean Otter, a member of the French Academy, and afterwards professor of Arabic, who had spent ten years in the provinces of Turkey and Persia for the distinct purpose of study-ing geographical and historical ques-tions, suddenly introduced a strong ele-ment of doubt as to the value and con-tinuity of the local tradition around Mo-sul. He discriminates berween the state-ment of the Arabian geographer Abulfe-da, claiming the eastern bank of the Ti-gris tor the true site of Nineveh, and a tradition current among the natives, who identify Eski-Mosul, a ruin on the western side and considerably higher up the river, with the ancient city, himself favoring, however, the former view. For, "opposite Mosul there is a place called *Tell Et-tuba, i. e.,* 'Mound of Re-pentance,' where, they say, the Ninevites put on sackcloth and ashes to turn away the wrath of God." "The Preacher's Travels," London, 1611, pp. 89, *seq.* Comp., also, Rogers, " History of Babylonia and Assyria," vol. i., pp. 94, *seq.* -Comp. *Herrn Johnnn Baptis-ten Tavcrniers Vierzig-Jahrige ReiseBeschreibung,* translated by Menudier, Nuremberg, 1681, part 1, p. 74.

In his *Voyage en Turquie et en Perse,* Paris, 1748, vol. i., pp. 133, *seq.* Comp. , also, Buckingham, "Travels in Me-sopotamia," London, 1827, vol. ii., p. 17.

The old tradition which placed the ruin of Nineveh opposite Mosul was vindi-cated anew by the Danish scholar Carsten Niebuhr, who visited the place in 1766. Though not attempting to give a detailed description of the ruins in which we are chiefly interested, he states his own personal conviction very decidedly, and adds some new and im-portant facts illustrated bv the first sketch of the large southern mound of Nebi Yunus. Jewish and Christian in-habitants alike declare that Nineveh stood on the left bank of the river, and they differ only as to the original extent of the city.

Two principal hills are to be distin-guished, the former crowned with the village of Nunia (/'. e., Nineveh) and a mosque said to contain the tomb of the prophet Jonah (Nebi Yunus), the other known by the name of Qal'at Nunia (" the castle of Nineveh "), and occupied by the village of Cjoyunjuk. While liv-ing in Mosul near the Tigris, he was also shown the ancient walls of the city on the other side, which formerly he had mistaken for a chain of low hills. Niebuhr's account was brief, but it con-tained all the essential elements of a correct description of the ruins, and by its very brevity and terse presentation of facts stands out prominently from the early literature as a silent protest against the rubbish so often contained in the works of previous travellers.

Also reported ("and favored) by the Italian Academician and botanist Sestini, who in 1781 travelled from Constantinople through Asia Minor to Mosul and Basra, and in the following year from there via Mosul and Aleppo to Alexandria. Comp. the French translation of his account, *Voyagi de Constantinople a Bmsora,* etc., Paris, vi. (year of the Republic — 1798), p. I $2. Comp. C. *Niebuhrs Reisebeschrtibung nach Arabien und andern umlugenden Landern,* Copenhagen, 1778, vol. ii., p. 353, and Plates xlvi. and xlvii.. No. 2.

To a certain degree, therefore, D'Anville was justified in summing up the whole question concerning the site of Nineveh, at the close of the eighteenth century, by making the bold statement in his geographical work, " The Euphrates and Tigris ":' "We know that the opposite or left bank of the river has preserved vestiges of Nineveh, and that the tradition as to the preaching of Jonah by no means has been forgotten there." BABYLON

The case of Babylon was somewhat different. The powerful influence which for nearly two thousand years this great Oriental metropolis had exercised upon the nations of Western Asia, no less by its learning and civilization than by its victorious battles; the fame of its former splendor and magnitude handed down by so many different writers; the enormous mass of ruins still testifying to its gigantic temples and palaces; and the local tradition continuing to live among the inhabitants of that desolate region with greater force and tenacity than in the district of Mosul, prevented its name and site from ever being forgotten entirely. At the end of the first Christian century the city was in ruins and practically deserted. But even when Baghdad had risen to the front, taking the place of Babylon and Seleucia as an eastern centre of commerce and civilization, Arabian and Persian writers occasionally speak of the *VEupbrate et U Tigre,* Paris, 1779, p. 88.

two, and as late as the close of the tenth

century, Ibn Hauqal refers to Babel as " a small village."'

The more we advance in the first half of the second millennium, the scantier grows our information. Benjamin of Tudela has but little to say. His interest centred in the relics of the numerous Jewish colonies of the countries traversed and in their history and tradition. Briefly he mentions the ruins of the palace of Nebuchadrezzar, " to men inaccessible on account of the various and malignant kinds of serpents and scorpions living there." With more detail he describes the Tower of Babel (" built by the dispersed generation, of bricks called *al-aj&r* "), which apparently he identified with the lofty ruins of Birs (Nimrud). Other travellers, like Marco Polo, visited the same regions without even referring to the large artificial mounds which they must frequently have noticed on their journeys. Travelling to the valleys of the Kuphrates and Tigris, in those early days, was more for adventure or commercial and religious purposes than for the scientific exploration of the remains of a bygone race, about which even the most learned knew but little. In the following sketch I quote, in historical order, only those travellers who have actually furnished some kind of useful information concerning Babylon or other Babylonian sites.

A brief summary of the different ancient writers who refer to the gradual disappearance of Babylon, and of the more prominent European travellers who visited or are reported to have visited the ruins of Babylon (with extracts from their accounts in an appendix), is found in the introduction to the " Collection of Rich's Memoirs," written by Mrs. Rich. It rests upon the well-known dissertation on Babylon by De Ste. Croix, published in the *Mtmoires dc /' AcaJtmu Jti Inscriptions ft da Belles-Lettrci,* 1789. Of more recent writers who have treated the same subject, I mention only Kaulen (*Afrifn und Bjitnien,* jth ed., 1899) and Rogers (" History of Babylonia and Assyria," roL i., 1900*).* Much information on the early writers is also scattered through Ritter'i *Die ErdkunJe von*

Asien, especially vol. xi. of the whole series. *Itiatrarium Beniamini TuJe/ensis,* p. 7» *iff* The Latin translation has Lagzar (iTJSb). *Al-ajur* (comp. *lajur* in the Maghreb dialects) is used also by the present inhabitants of Babylonia as another designation for "baked brick" *(tabuq.* The word is identical with the Babylonian *agurru,* as was recognized by Rawlinson, "Journal of the Royal Asiatic Society," vol. xvii., p. 9.

From the latter part of the sixteenth century we have three testimonials, that of Rauwolff, the adventurous physician of Augsburg (travelling 1573-76), that of the Venetian jeweller, Balbi (1579-80), and that of the English merchant Eldred (1583), a contemporary of Queen Elizabeth, who descended the Euphrates in a boat, landed at Falluja (or Feluja, according to the popular Arabic pronunciation), and proceeded across 'Iraq to Baghdad. In vague terms they all speak of the ruins of "the mighty city of Babylon," the "Tower of Babel," and the " Tower of Daniel," which they beheld in the neighborhood of Falluja or on their way to Baghdad or " New Babylon." Their words have been generally accepted without criticism. It is, however, entirely out of question that a traveller who disembarked at Falluja, directing his course due east, and arriving at Baghdad after one and a half days' journey, could possibly have passed or even have seen the ruins of Babylon. From a comparison of the accounts given by Rauwolff", Eldred, and others with what I personally observed in 1889, when for the first time I travelled precisely the same road, there can be no doubt that they mistook the various ruin heaps and the many large and small portions of high embankments of ancient canals everywhere visible for scattered re Not having been able to examine his statement in the author's own book, I profited by the brief resume of his travel given by Mrs. Rich in her edition of her husband's " Collected Memoirs," p. 55, footnote .

' Rogers, in his " History of Babylonia and Assyria," vol. i.,pp. 89, *seqq.,* asserts that Eldred confused Baghdad and Babylon. But this is incorrect, for Eldred says plainly enough: "The citie of New Babylon Baghdad joyneth upon the aforesaid desert where the Olde citie was," *l'. e.*, the desert between Falluja and Baghdad which our author crossed. Possibly they included even the large ruins of Anbar, plainly to be recog mains of the very extended city of Babylon, and the imposing brick structure of 'Aqarquf for the "Tower of Babel" or "of Daniel." For 'Aqarquf, generally pronounced 'Agarguf, and situated about nine to ten miles to the west of Baghdad, is the one gigantic ruin which every traveller crossing the narrow tract of land from Falluja to Baghdad must pass and wonder at. Moreover, the description of that ruin, as given by Eldred and others after him, contains several characteristic features from which it can be identified without difficulty. We quote Eldred's own language: "Here also are yet standing the ruines of the olde Tower of Babell, which being upon a plaine ground seemeth a farre off very great, but the nearer you come to it, the lesser and lesser it appeareth: sundry times I have gone thither to see it, and found the remnants yet standing about a quarter of a mile in compasse, and almost as high as the stone work of Paules steeple in London, but it showeth much bigger. The brickes remaining in this most ancient monument be half a yard in the sense of our " foot" thicke and three quarters of a yard long, being dried in the Sunne only, and betweene every course of brickes there lieth a course of mattes made of canes, which remaine sounde and not perished, as though they had been layed within one yeere."

Master Allen, who travelled in the same region not many years afterwards, gives as his measurement of those bricks twelve by eight by six inches. Eldred's statement, however, is more correct. While visiting 'Aqarqüf, I found the average size of complete bricks from that ruin to be eleven inches square by four inches and a quarter thick. The layers of reed matting, a characteristic feature of the massive ruin, are not so frequent as stated by Eldred. They occur only after every fifth to seventh layer of bricks, at

an average interval of nearly three feet. What is now left of this high, towering, and inaccessible structure, above the accumulation of rubbish at its base, rises to a little over a hundred feet. If there is still any doubt as to the correctness of the theory set forth, a mere reference to the positive statement of Tavernier/ who visited Baghdad in 1652, will suffice to dispel it.

fuzed from Falluja, and only a few miles to the north of it. For all these travellers had a vague idea that ancient Babylon was situated on the Euphrates, and that its ruins covered a vast territory. Eldred's description is especially explicit: "In this place which we crossed over stood the olde (nightie cirie of Babylon, many olde ruines whereof are easilie to be scene by daylight, which I, John Eldred, have often behelde at my goode leisure, luring made three voyages between the New citie of Babylon *l. e.*, Baghdad and Aleppo." Hakluyt, "The Principal Navigations, Voiages, and Discoveries of the English Nation," London, 1589, p. 232. Comp. "Purchas his Pilgrimage," London, 1626, p. 50 (quoted in Rich's "Collected Memoirs," pp. 321, *tej.*, footnote).

Shirley's and Cartwright's references to Babylon, or rather to the locality just discussed, mav be well passed over, the former delighting more in preaching than in teaching, the latter largely reproducing the account of Eldred, with which he was doubtless familiar. Of but little intrinsic value is also what Boeventing, Taxeira, and a number of other travellers of the same general period have to relate.

Chesney, "The Expedition for the Survey of the Rivers Euphrates and Tigris," vol. ii., p. 605, practically gives the same measures (u inches square by 4 deep). I quote from the German edition before me *Vierzig-Jährige Reise-Beschreibung,* translated by Menudier. Nuremberg, 168 1, part 1, p. 91): *Ich muss noch a//hier beifügen, was ich wegen dessjenigen, das insgemein von dem Rest des Thurns zu Babylon geglaubet wird, in acht nehmen können, welcher Name Babylon) auch ordentlich der Stadt Bagdad gegeben wird, ungeachtet*

selbige davon über j Meilen entfernet liget. Man siehet also ... einen grossen von Erden aufgehäuften Hügel, den man noch heut zu Tage Nemrod nennet. Selbiger ist in mitten einer grossen Landschafft, und lasset sich ferne schon zu Gesichte fassen. Das gemeine Volk, wie ich bereits gedacht, glaubet, es seye solcher der Überrest des Babylonischen Thurns: Allein es hat eine besseren Schein, was die Araber ausgeben, welche es Agarcouf nennen. Comp., also, *C. Niebuhrs Reisebeschreibung,* Copenhagen, 1778, vol. ü., p. 305.

The first to examine the real site of ancient Babylon with a certain care was Pietro della Valle, who sent the first copy of a few cuneiform characters from Persepolis to Europe, at the same time stating his reasons why they should be read from the left to the right. This famous traveller also carried with him a few inscribed bricks — probably the first that ever reached Europe—from Babil, which he visited towards the end of 1616, and from Muqayyar (Ur of the Chaldees), which he examined in 1625 on his homeward journey. His description of Babil, the most northern mound of the ruins of Babylon, while not satisfactory in itself, stands far above the information of previous travellers. He tells us that this large mound, less ruined at those days than at the beginning of the twentieth century, was a huge rectangular tower or pyramid with its corners pointing to the four cardinal points. The material of this structure he describes as " the most remarkable thing I ever saw." It consists of sundriedbricks, something so strange to him that in order to make quite sure, he dug at several places into the mass with pickaxes. "Here and there, especially at places which served as supports, the bricks of the same size were baked."

Vincenzo Maria di S. Caterina di Sienna, procurator general of the Carmelite monks, who sailed up the Euphrates forty years later, like Pietro della Valle even made an attempt at vindicating the local tradition by arguing that the place is situated on the banks of the Euphrates, that the surrounding districts are fertile, that for many miles the land is covered with the ruins of magnificent buildings, and above all, that there still exist the remains of the Tower of Babel, "which to this day is called Nimrod's tower," — referring to Birs (Nimrud) on the western side of the Euphrates.

More sceptical is the view taken by the Dominican father Emmanuel de St. Albert, who paid a visit to this remarkable spot about 1700. In sharp contrast to the earlier travellers, who with but few exceptions were always ready to chronicle as facts the fanciful stories related to them by Oriental companions and interpreters in obliging response to their numerous questions, we here find a sober and distrustful inquirer carefully discriminating between " the foolish stories " current among the inhabitants of the country and his own personal observations and inferences. Near Hilla, on the two opposite banks of the river and at a considerable distance from each other, he noticed two artificial elevations, the one " situated in Mesopotamia," containing the ruins of a large building, " the other in Arabia about an hour's distance from the Euphrates," characterized by two masses of cemented brick (the one standing, the other lying overturned beside it), which "seemed as if they had been vitrified." "People think that this latter hill is the remains of the real Babylon, but I do not know what they will make of the other, which is opposite and exactly like this one." Convinced, however, that the ruins must be ancient, and much impressed by the curious " writing in unknown characters" which he found on the large square bricks, Father Emmanuel selected a few of the latter from both hills and carried them away with him.

In D'Anville's *Memoire lur la Position de Bukflone*, I 761, published as a paper of the *Mmoires de F Acadimie ties Inscriptions ct da Belles-Lfttrcs,* woL xxvfij., p. 256.

Travellers, whose education was limited, and missionaries, who viewed those ruins chiefly from a religious standpoint, have had their say. Let us now briefly discuss the views of such visitors who took a strictly scientific interest in the ruins of Babylon. In connection with his epoch-making journey to Arabia and Persia, Carsten Niebuhr examined the mounds around Hilla in 1765. Though furnishing little new information as to their real size and condition, in this respect not unlike the French geographer and historian Jean Otter, who had been at the same mounds in 1743, Niebuhr presented certain reasons for his own positive conviction that the ruins of Babylon must be located in the neighborhood of Hilla. He regarded the designation of " Ard Babel" given to that region by the natives, and the apparent remains of an ancient city found on both sides of the river, especially the numerous inscribed bricks lying on the ground, which are evidence of a very high state of civilization, as solid proof for the correctness of the local tradition. He even pointed out the large ruin heaps, " three quarters of a German mile to the north-northwest of Hilla and close by the eastern bank of the river Kl-Qasr," as the probable site of Babylon's castle and the hanging gardens mentioned by Strabo, while Birs (Nimrud), " an entire hill of fine bricks with a tower on the top " he regarded as Herodotus' " Temple of Belus," therefore as lying still within the precinct of ancient Babylon.

Our last and best informed witness from the close of the eighteenth century, who deserves, therefore, our special attention, is Abbe De Beauchamp. Well equipped with astronomical and other useful knowledge, he resided at Baghdad as the Pope's vicar-general of Babylonia for some time between 1780 and 1790. The ruins of Babylon, in which he was deeply interested, being only sixteen to eighteen hours distant from Baghdad, he paid two visits to the famous site, publishing the results of his various observations in several memoirs,' from which we extract the following noteworthy facts: "There is no difficulty about the position of Babylon." Its ruins are situated in the district of Hilla, about one league to the north of it (latitude 3 2 34'), on the opposite (left) side of the Euphrates, " exactly under the mound the Arabs call Babel." There are no ruins of Babylon proper on the western side of the river, as D'Anville in his geographical work assumes, making the Euphrates divide the city. The mounds which are to be seen "on the other side of the river, at about a league's distance from its banks, are called by the Arabs Bros meaning Birs." Among the ruins of Babylon, which chiefly consist of bricks scattered about, " there is in particular an elevation which is flat on the top, of an irregular form, and intersected by ravines. It would never have been taken for the work of human hands, were it not proved by the layers of bricks found in it.... They are baked with fire and cemented with *zepht zift* or bitumen; between each layer are found osiers." Not very far from this mound, "on the banks of the river, are immense heaps of ruins which have served and still serve for the building of Hillah.... Here are found those large and thick bricks imprinted with unknown characters, specimens of which I have presented to the Abbe Bartholomy. This place evidently El-Qasr and the mound of Babel are commonly called by the Arabs *Makloube* or rather *Muqailiba?* popularly pronounced *Mujeliba,* that is, overturned. " Further to the north Beauchamp was shown a thick brick wall, " which ran perpendicular to the bed of the river and was probably the wall of the city." The Arabs employed to dig for bricks obtained their material from this and similar walls, and sometimes even from whole chambers, "frequently finding earthen vessels and engraved marbles,.. .. sometimes idols of clay representing human figures, or solid cylinders covered with very small writing... and about eight years ago a statue as large as life, which was thrown amongst the rubbish." On the wall of a chamber they had discovered " figures of a cow and of the sun and moon formed of varnished bricks." Beauchamp himself secured a brick on which was a lion, and Com p. *Reiitbtsihreibung,* Copenhagen, 1778, vol. ii., pp. 287, *seq.: in der Gegend t'on Helle gelfgen hake, daran ist gar kein Za/ei* In *Jturnal dti Savants,* Mai, 1785, and Dec., 1790. For extracts see Rich' " Collected Memoirs," pp. 301, itq. In the Arabic dialect of modern Babylonia the diminutive (fa'ail) is frequently used instead of the regular noun formation. Comp. Oppert, *Expedition en Mesopotamie,* vol. i., p. 114.

others with a crescent in relief. He even employed two laborers for three hours in clearing a large stone which the Arabs supposed to be an idol, apparently the large lion of the Qasr recently set up again by the German expedition. I mperfect as the report of Beauchamp must appear in the light of our present knowledge, at the time when it was written it conveyed to the public for the first time a tolerably clear idea of the exact position and enormous size of the ruins of Babylon and of the great possibilities connected with their future excavation. It was particularly in England that people began to realize the importance of these cylinders and bricks covered with cuneiform writing " resembling the inscriptions of Persepolis mentioned by Chardin." The East India Company of London became the first public exponent of this rapidly growing interest in Great Britain, by ordering their Resident at Basra to obtain several specimens of these remarkable bricks and to send them carefully packed to London. At the beginning of the nineteenth century a small case of Babylonian antiquities arrived, the first of a long series to follow years later. Insignificant as it was, it soon played an important role in helping to determine the character of the third system of writing used in the Persian inscriptions.

There were other travellers at the close of the eighteenth century, who, like Edw. Ives and the French physician G. A. Olivier, also visited the ruins of Nineveh and Babylon, occasionally even contributing a few details to our previous knowledge. But they did not alter the general conception derived from the work of their predecessors, especially Niebuhr and Beauchamp. The first period of Also the opinion of Rich, " Collected Memoirs," pp. 36, 64, *iff.* Cotnp. "Journal from Persia to England," London, 1773, '-"» PP321, *iff.* (Nineveh), etc.

Comp. *I'eyagf dans F Empire Othuman, /'Egypt f et la Perse,* 6 vols., Piri», 1801-07, especially vol. ii.

Assyrian and Babylonian exploration had come to an end. Merchants and adventurers, missionaries and scholars had equally contributed their share to awakening Western Europe from its long lethargy by again vividly directing the attention of the learned and religious classes to the two great centres of civilization in the ancient Kast. The ruins of Nineveh, on the upper course of the Tigris, had been less frequently visited and less accurately described than those of Babylon on the lower Euphrates. The reason is very evident. The glory of the great Assyrian metropolis vanished more quickly and completely from human sight, and its ruins lay further from the great caravan road on which the early travellers proceeded to Baghdad, the famous city of Harun-ar-Rashid, then a principal centre for the exchange of the products of Asia and Europe. But the ascertained results of the observations and efforts of many, and in particular the better equipped missionaries and scholars of the eighteenth century, were the rediscovery and almost definite fixing of the actual sites of Nineveh and Babylon, which, forgotten by Europe, had seemed to lie under a doom of eternal silence, — the Divine response to the curses of the oppressed nations and of the Old Testament prophets.

II EXPLORING AND SURVEYING IN THE NINETEENTH CENTURY

The close of the eighteenth and the dawn of the nineteenth centuries witnessed a feverish activity in the workshops of a small but steadily growing number of European scholars. The continuous reports by different travellers of the imposing ruins of Persepolis, the occasional reproduction of sculptures and inscriptions from the walls and pillars of its palaces, the careful sifting and critical editing of the whole material by the indefatigable explorer Niebuhr, had convinced even the most sceptical men of science that there were really still in existence considerable artistic and literary remains of a bygone nation, whose powerful influence, at times, had been

felt even in Kgypt and Greece. Strong efforts were made in Denmark, France, and Germany to obtain a satisfactory knowledge of the ancient sacred language of the Zend-Avesta, to discover the meaning of the younger Pehlevi inscriptions on Sassanian seals and other small objects so frequently found in Persia, and to attempt even the deciphering of these strange wedge-shaped characters on the walls of Persepolis. Names like Anquetil-Duperron, Kugene Burnouf, Sylvestre de Sacy, Niebuhr, Tvchsen, M(inter, and others will always occupv a prominent position in the esteem of the following generations as the pioneers and leaders in a great movement which ultimately led to the establishment of the great science of cuneiform research, destined as it was to revolutionize our whole conception of the countries and nations of Western Asia. This new science, though the final result of many combined forces, sprang so suddenly into existence that when it was actually there, nobody seemed ready to receive it.

In the year 1802 the genius of a young German scholar, Georg Friederich Grotefend, then onlv twenty-seven years old, well versed in classical philology but absolutely ignorant of Oriental learning, solved the riddle, practically in a few days, that had puzzled much older men and scholars apparently much better qualified than himself. Under the magical touch of his hand the mystic and complicated characters of ancient Persia suddenly gained new life. But when he was far enough advanced to announce to the Academy of Sciences in Gottingen the epoch-making discovery which established his fame and reputation forever, that learned body, though comprising men of eminent mental training and intelligence, strange to say, declined to publish the Latin memoirs of this little known college teacher, who did not belong to the University circle proper, nor was even an Orientalist by profession. It was not until ninety years later (1893) that his original papers were rediscovered and published by Prof. Wilhelm Meyer, of Gottingen, in the Academy's

Transactions — a truly unique case of *post mortem* examination in science.

Fortunately Grotefend did not need to wait for a critical test and proper acknowledgment of his remarkable work until he would have reached a patriarchal age at the close of the nineteenth century. Heeren, De Sacy, and others lent their helping hands to disseminate the extraordinary news of the great historical event in the learned world of Europe. Afterwards it became gradually known that far away from Western civilization, in the mountain ranges of Persia, an energetic and talented officer of the British army, Lieutenant (later Sir) Henry Rawlinson (born on April 11, 1810), had almost independently, though more than thirty years later, arrived at the same results as Grotefend by a similar process of combination.

Niebuhr had already pointed out that the inscriptions of Persepolis appeared always in three different systems of writing found side by side, the first having an alphabet of over forty signs, the second being more complicated, and the third even more so. Grotefend had gone a step farther by insisting that the three systems of writing represented three different languages, of which the first was the old Persian spoken by the kings who erected those palaces and inscribed their walls. The second he called Median, the third Babylonian. The name given to the second language, which is agglutinative, has later been repeatedly changed into Scythian, Susian, Amardian, Elamitic, Anzanian, and Neo-Susian. The designation of the third language as Babylonian had been made possible by a comparison of its complicated characters with the Babylonian inscriptions of the East India House in London, published, soon after their arrival in i8oi,bv Joseph Hager. This designation was at once generally accepted, and has remained in use ever since.

For the time being, however, little interest was manifested in the last-named and most difficult system of writing, which evidently contained only a Babylonian translation of the corresponding Persian inscriptions. More material, written exclusively in the third style of cuneiform writing, was needed from the Babylonian and Assyrian mounds themselves, not only to attract the curiosity but to command the undivided attention of.scholars. This having been once provided, it would be only a question of time when the same key, which, in the hands of Grotefend, had wrought such wonders as to unlock the doors to the history of ancient Persia, would open the far more glorious and remote past of the great civilization between the Euphrates and Tigris. But in order to obtain the inscriptions needed, other more preparatory work had to be undertaken first. The treasure-house itself had to be examined and studied more carefully, before a successful attempt could be made to lift the treasure concealed in its midst. A survey of Babylon and Nineveh and other prominent ruins in easy access, and more authentic and reliable information concerning the geography and topography of the whole country in which they were situated, was an indispensable requirement before the work of excavation could properly begin.

So far England had been conspicuously absent from the serious technical work carried on by representatives of other nations in the study and in the field. And yet no other European power was so eminently qualified to provide what still was lacking as the "Queen of the Sea," through her regular and well-established commercial and political relations with India and the Persian gulf. The sound of popular interest and enthusiasm, which had been heard in Great Britain at the close of the eighteenth century, never died away entirely. Englishmen now came forward well qualified to carry out the first part of this scientific mission of the European nations in the country between the Euphrates and Tigris, where for many years they worked with great energy, skill, and success.

CLAUDIUS JAMES RICH

The first methodical explorer and surveyor of Babylonian and Assyrian ruins and rivers was Claudius James Rich. Born in 1787 near Dijon, in France, educated in Bristol, England, he developed, when a mere child, such a decided gift for the study of Oriental languages that at the age of sixteen years he was appointed to a cadetship in the East India Company's military service. Seriously affected by circumstances in the carrying out of his plans, he spent more than three years in the different parts of the Levant, perfecting himself in Italian, Turkish, and Arabic. His knowledge of the Turkish language and manners was so thorough that while in Damascus not only did he enter the grand mosque " in the disguise of a Mameluke," but his host, "an honest Turk, who was captivated with his address, eagerly entreated him to settle at that place, offering him his interest and his daughter in marriage." From Aleppo he proceeded by land to Basra, whence he sailed for Bombay, which he reached early in September, 1807. A few months later he was married there to the eldest daughter of Sir James Mackintosh, to whom we owe the publication of most of her husband's travels and researches outside of the two memoirs on Babylon published by himself. About the same time he was appointed Resident of the East India Company at Baghdad, a position which he held until his sudden and most lamented death from cholera morbus in Shiraz, October 5, 1821.

The leisure which Rich enjoyed from his public duties he spent in pursuing his favorite historical, geographical, and archaeological studies, the most valuable fruits of which are his accurate surveys and descriptions of the ruins of Babylon and Nineveh. In December, 1811, he made his first brief visit to the site of Babylon. It lasted but ten days, but it sufficed to convince him that no correct account of the ruins had yet been written. Completely deceived " by the incoherent accounts of former travellers," instead of a few " isolated mounds," he found " the whole country covered with the vestiges of building, in some places consisting of brick walls surprisingly fresh, in others merely a vast succession of mounds of rubbish of such indeterminate figures, variety, and extent as to involve the person who should have formed any theory in inextricable confusion and contradiction.

" He set to work at once to change this condition.

His two memoirs on the ruins of Babylon (especially the first) are a perfect mine of trustworthy information radically different from anything published on the subject in previous years. He sketches the present character of the whole country around Babylon, describes the vestiges of ancient canals and outlying mounds, and " the prodigious extent " of the centre of all his attention,— the ruins of Babylon itself. And to all this he adds his personal observations on the modern fashion of building houses, and the present occupations and customs of the inhabitants of 'Iraq, interwoven with frequent references to the legends of the Arabs and the methods of their administration under Turkish rule, correctly assuming that " the peculiar climate of this district must have caused a similarity of habits and accommodations in all ages." But valuable as all these details are, they form, so to speak, only the framework for his faithful and minute picture of the ruins of Babylon, which we now reproduce, as far as possible with his own words: — Rich's first " Memoir on the Ruins of Babylon " was written in 1812 in Baghdad, and published (with many typographical errors and unsatisfactory plates) in the *FunJgrubcn des Orients*, Vienna, 1813. To make it accessible to English readers, Rich republished this memoir in London (1816), where also his second memoir appeared in 1818. Both memoirs were later republished with Major Renncl's treatise ' On the Topography of Ancient Babylon," suggested by Rich's first publication, and with Rich's diaries of his first excursion to Babylon and his journey to Persepolis, accompanied by a useful introduction and appendix, all being united by Mrs. Rich into a collective volume, London, 1839. His widow also edited his "Narrative of a Residence in Koordistan and on the site of Ancient Nineveh," London, Comp. Map, No. 2 (Plan of Babylon).

"The whole of the area enclosed by the boundary on the east and south, and the river on the west, is two miles and six hundred yards in breadth from E. to W., and as much from Pietro della Valle's ruin /'. e., Babil in the north, to the northern part" of the southern city wall, "or two miles and one thousand yards to the most southerly mound of all. This space is again longitudinally subdivided into nearly half, by a straight line of the same kind with the boundary, but much its inferior in point of size.... These ruins consist of mounds of earth, formed by the decomposition of buildings, channelled and furrowed by the weather, and the surface of them strewed with pieces of brick, bitumen, and pottery."

The most northern mound is Babil, called by the natives *Mujeliba?* "Full five miles distant from Hilla, and nine hundred and fifty yards from the river bank, it is of an oblong shape, irregular in its height and the measurement of its sides, which point to the cardinal points. The elevation of the southeast or highest angle, is one hundred and forty-one feet. The western face, which is the least elevated, is the most interesting on account of the appearance of building it presents." Rich regarded this conspicuous mound as part of the royal precincts, possibly the hanging gardens. -Like Bcauchamp, Rich states correctly that this term is sometimes also applied to the second mound, El-Qasr.

"A mile to the south of Babil is a large conglomeration of mounds, the shape of which is nearly a square of seven hundred yards in length and breadth. " It was designated

B-O.asr, East Face by Rich F.l-Qasr (" the palace ") from a very remarkable ruin, "which being uncovered, and in part detached from the rubbish, is visible from a considerable distance.... It consists of several walls and piers, eight feet in thickness, in some places ornamented with niches, and in others strengthened by pilasters and buttresses, built of fine burnt brick (still perfectly clean and sharp), laid in lime-cement of such tenacity, that those whose business it is to find bricks have given up working on account of the extreme difficulty of extracting them whole." Here stood, as we now know, the palace of Nebuchadrezzar, in which Alexander the Great died after his famous campaign against India.

The height as measured by Rich differs considerably from that given by the later surveyors. This difference, while doubtless to a large extent the result of Rich's inaccurate estimation, must also be explained by the fact that in course of time the Arab brick-diggers have reduced the height of Babil. Most of the numbers given by Rich have been later on more or less modified by the different surveyors, who had more time and were better equipped with instruments. Separated from the previous mound by a valley of five hundred and fifty yards in length, "covered with tussocks of rank grass, there rises to the south another grand mass of ruins, the most elevated part of which is only fifty or sixty feet above the plain. From the small dome in the centre dedicated to the memory of a spurious son of 'Ali, named 'Omran ('Amran), it is called by the Arabs, Tell 'Omran ibn 'Ali. It has been likewise considerably dug into by peasants in search of bricks and antiquities.

The most southern point is connected with the large embankment here traceable and with a flourishing village, near which the luxurious date groves of Hilla commence. Both are called Qumquma (Sachau), now generally pronounced Jumjuma (regarded by Rich as original, meaning " skull ") or Jimjime. Here terminate the ruins of ancient Babylon.

It was to be expected that Rich, in connection with his topographical work on the ruins of Babylon, would also examine "the most interesting and remarkable of all the Babylonian remains," *viz.*, Birs (Nimrud), of which he likewise left us an accurate description, in several details soon afterwards supplemented by that of Buckingham. Like his successor he recognized the general character of the ruins as a stage tower, doubtless influenced by his endeavor to identify it with the Tower of Belus, and by the deep and lasting impression which this gigantic ruin, still one hundred and fifty-three feet high, made upon him at his first visit. I quote his own language:

"The morning was at first stormy, and threatened a severe fall of rain, but as we approached the object of our journey, the heavy clouds separating, discovered the Birs frowning over the plain, and presenting the appearance of a circular hill, crowned by a tower, with a high ridge extending along the foot of it. Its being entirely concealed from our view, during the first part of our ride, prevented our acquiring the gradual idea, in general so prejudicial to effect, and so particularly lamented by those who visit the Pyramids. Just as we were within the proper distance, it burst at once upon our sight, in the midst of rolling masses of thick black clouds partially obscured by that kind of haze whose indistinctness is one great cause of sublimity, whilst a few strong catches of stormy light, thrown upon the desert in the background, served to give some idea of the immense extent and dreary solitude of the wastes in which this venerable ruin stands." According to Felix Jones's survey of 1855, this is the exact vertical distance of Birs (Nimrud) from the water level of the plain to the highest point of the ruin at the summit of the mound, as over against the 235 feet strangely given by Rich.

The impression which the ruin left upon the mind of an otherwise sober observer and unbiassed man of facts was so profound that it deflected his judgment and blinded his eyes as to the great incongruity between his favorite theory and all the topographical evidence so minutely and accurately set forth by himself, — another illustration of the truth how detrimental to scientific investigation any preconceived opinion or impression must be.

In addition to all his valuable topographical studies Rich directed his attention to other no less important subjects of an archaeological character. We refer to his remarks on the hieratic and demotic styles of cuneiform writing (" Memoirs," pp. 184, *seqq.);* his observation that inscribed bricks, when found *in situ,* are "invariably placed with their faces or written sides downwards" (pp. 162, *seqq.),* a fact which he at once employed skilfully against his opponent,

Rennell, to vindicate the Babylonian origin of the "surprisingly fresh" looking ruin of the Qasr; furthermore, his discussion of the different kinds of cement (bitumen, mortar, clay, etc.) used in ancient and modern Babylonia (pp. 100, *seqq.* later supplemented by Colonel Chesney;' and his endeavor " to ascertain in what particular part of the ruin each antique is found" (pp. 187, *seqq.),* —the fundamental principle of all scientific excavations, against which later excavators have sinned only too often.

Comp. Rich's " Collected Memoirs," edited by his widow, p. 74.

He spared neither personal exertion nor expenses to acquire every fragment of sculpture and inscribed stone of which he had got information. To his efforts we owe the barrel cylinder, with Nebuchadrezzar's account of his work on the famous canal, *Libil-khegal.* It was Rich who collected the first contract tablets and account lists discovered in the lower parts of the Qasr (/. c., p. 187), and it is Rich again who obtained the first fragment of a clay tablet from Ashurbanapal's library at Nineveh.

But in mentioning the latter, we have approached another field of the indefatigable explorer's labors and researches, which we now propose to sketch briefly.

In 1820 and 1821, on his return from a trip to Persia and Kurdistan, Rich made an exploring tour to some of the most prominent ruins of ancient Assyria, Erbil (ancient Arbela), Qoyunjuk,Nebi Yunus (Nineveh), and Nimrud. The modern town of Erbil is situated partly on the top and partly at the foot of an artificial mound "about 150 feet high and 1000 feet in diameter." A Turkish castle, which up to the present day has been the chief obstacle to systematic excavations, crowns its flat top. Rich spent two and a half days at the place taking measurements, and trying hard to obtain satisfactory information as to the contents of these ruins and their early history.. But he could learn very little beyond the fact that some time before his arrival a man by the name of Hajji 'Abdullah Bey had dug

up a sepulchre, in which was a body laid in state, that fell to dust after it had been exposed to the air, and that large bricks without inscriptions had been taken by another man from a structure below the cellar of his house standing inside the castle.

In "The Euphrates and Tigris Expedition," vol. ii., pp. 625, *itqq.* Whoever has had one of these finest specimens of cuneiform tablets in his hands will readily recognize the character and origin of Rich's fragment from his short description (/. c., p. 188).

He was more fortunate at the ruins of Nimrud, which he visited in March, 1821. Though he could devote but a few hours to their examination, he was able to sketch and measure the chief mounds, to furnish a brief description of their actual condition, and to determine their generaj character from scattered fragments of burnt bricks with cuneiform inscriptions. In the large village of Nimrud, about a quarter of a mile from the west face of the platform, he even procured a whole brick covered with cuneiform writing on its face and edge, and containing the name and title of King Shalmaneser II., as we now know, since the deciphering of the Assyrian script has long been an accomplished fact.

Of still greater importance and of fundamental value for the archaeological work of his successors was his residence of four months in Mosul. It fell between his visits to Erbil and Nimrud, and was onlv interrupted bv an absence of twelve davs, during which he paid a visit to the Yezidi villages and the Christian monasteries of Mar Matti and Rabban Hormuzd, to the northeast and north of Mosul, surveying the country, gathering Syriac manuscripts, and studying the manners and customs of the people. The great facilities and freedom or movement which he enjoyed in consequence of his official position and the pleasant relations established with the Turkish authorities at three previous visits to this neighborhood were now utilized by Rich to satisfy his curiosity and scientific interest in the large mounds on the eastern side of the Tigris, opposite Mosul.

Tradition identified them with ancient Nineveh, as stated above (pp. 7-12). Yet doubts as to the correctness and continuity of the local tradition, as already expressed by Jean Otter, were justified, as long as the latter had not been corroborated by convincing facts. They were first adduced by Rich, who, by a careful topographical survey of the ruins here grouped together and by a close examination of all the large hewn stones, inscribed slabs, burnt bricks, and other smaller antiquities accidentally found by the natives, demonstrated beyond doubt that all these vestiges were of the same general age and character; that they belonged to a powerful nation, which, like the Babylonians, employed cuneiform script for its writing; and that the original area of the ancient city, represented by the two large mounds, Qoyunjuk and Nebi Yunus, and enclosed by three walls on the east and by one wall each on the three other sides, was "about one and a half to two miles broad and four miles long" — strong reasons, indeed, in support of the local tradition and the general belief expressed by so many travellers.

Twenty-eight years later his famous countryman, Layard, was enabled to excavate this site methodically and to make those startling discoveries which restored the lost civilization of the Assyrian empire to the astonished world. But it will always remain the great merit of Rich to have placed the floating local tradition upon a scientific basis, to have determined the real significance of the large Assyrian mounds in general, and to have prepared the way for their thorough exploration by his important maps and accurate description.

In returning from Mosul to Baghdad Rich used the ke/ek, as on two previous occasions, in order to obtain more ' A native raft composed of goat-skins inflated with air, and by reeds ot exact bearings of the frequent windings of the river, to fix the situations of ruins and other places on its embankments, and to correct and supplement his former measurements. On the basis of the rich material thus brought together personal-

ly, he drew the first useful map of the course of the Tigris from Mosul to a point about eighteen miles to the north of Baghdad, a map in every way far superior to that of Carsten Niebuhr, which rests entirely upon information, and that of Beauchamp, which in all essential features must be regarded as a mere copy of the latter's.

Previously he had surveyed a considerable portion of the Euphrates, Z'f'z. jfrom Hit to about the thirty-third degree north latitude. All his material was later incorporated into the results obtained by the British Euphrates expedition, and in 1 849 edited by Colonel Chesnev, its commander, as sheets VI. and VII. of his magnificent series of maps of the Euphrates and Tigris vallevs.

After the untimely death of Rich in the fall of 1821, his Oriental antiquities, coins, and an extraordinary collection of eight hundred manuscripts' were purchased by the English Parliament for the use of the British Museum. The fragments of clay and stone which he had gathered so scrupulously from Babylonian and Assyrian ruins filled a comparatively small space, and for the greater part at present have little but historical value. But these small beginnings contained in them the powerful germ which in due time produced the rich treasures now filling the halls of the London Museum.

ropes fastened close together to a frame of rough logs. On one part of this very ancient means of navigation a kind of hut covered with matting is generally raised as a necessary shelter against rain and sun. According to Forshall, 3 of these are in Greek, 59 in Syriac, 8 in Car-hunk, 389 in Arabic, 231 in Persian, 108 in Turkish, 2 in Armenian, and I in Hebrew. A list of the Syriac MSS. , accompanied by a brief description, is given by Forshall on pp. 306-311 of vol. ii. of Rich's " Narrative of a Residence in Koordistan."

Kelek or Native Raft composed of Goat-Skins

After the fundamental work of Rich little was left for the average European traveller to report on the ruins of Babylon and Nineveh, unless he possessed

an extraordinary gift of observation and discrimination, combined with experience and technical training, archaeological taste, and a fair acquaintance with the works of the classical writers and the native historians and geographers. Among the men to whom in some wav or other we are indebted for new information concerning the geography and topography of ancient Assyria and Babylonia at the very time when Rich himself was carrying on his investigations, the two following deserve our special attention.

J. S. BUCKINGHAM

It was in the year i 8 i 6, when, on his way to India, after a long and adventurous journey from Egypt through Palestine, Syria, and the adjacent districts east of the Jordan, Buckingham had arrived at Aleppo. Soon afterwards he joined the caravan of a rich Moslem merchant, with whom by wav of Urfa and Mardin he travelled to Mosul," adopting the dress, manners, and language of the country " for the sake of greater safety and convenience. A few days before the caravan reached the Tigris, it was overtaken by two Turkish Tartars in charge of papers from the British ambas sador in Constantinople to Mr. Rich, then English Resident at Baghdad. Buckingham decided at once to profit by the opportunity, so unexpectedly offered, of travelling in comparative safety through a country in which he had met with so much lawlessness and interference. Sacrificing, therefore, his personal comfort to speed and safety, he completed his journey in the company of the two Tartars. In consequence of the new arrangement, however, he could spend only two days at Mosul, and devote but a few morning hours immediately before his departure to a hasty inspection of the ruins of Nineveh, which for this reason contributed nothing to a better understanding of the site of this ancient city. In the oppressive heat of a Mesopotamian summer, and deserted on the road by one of his Tartars, he finally arrived at Baghdad, where, in the congenial atmosphere of Rich's hospitable house, he found the necessary encouragement and assistance in executing his plan of paying a visit to some of the principal mounds of ancient Babylonia.

Accompanied by Mr. Bellino, the weli-informed secretary to the Residency, he at first examined the ruins of 'Aqarquf of which' he has left us a more critical, correct, and comprehensive account than any of the preceding travellers, even Niebuhr and Olivier not excluded. From the numerous fragments of brick and pottery and other vestiges of former buildings scattered around the shapeless mass of the detached ruin he recognized with Olivier that near this socalled " Tower of Nimrod" ' there must have stood a city to which a large canal (the 'Isa), uniting the two great rivers, conveyed the necessary supply of water. To judge from the materials and the style of the principal building the whole settlement is of Babylonian origin. Accordingly, the theory of Niebuhr, who believed the lofty ruin to be an artificial elevation on which one of the early caliphs of Baghdad, or even one of the Persian kings of El-Mada'in, had erected a country house, to enjoy from such a height a breeze of cool and fresh air during the sultry summer months in the Babylonian plain, is improbable. It was rather Buckingham's firm conviction that the building represents the " remains of some isolated monument either of a sepulchral or religious nature." From the fact that the "present shapeless form having so large a base, and being proportionately so small at the top, seemed nearer to that of a much worn pyramid than any other," and from his observation that a much larger mass of the fallen fragments of the top would be visible around the base if it had been a square tower, he inferred correctly that the often described ruin was originally a step pyramid similar to that found at Saqqara in Egypt.-' Though the interior of the solid ruin of 'Aqarquf is composed of unbaked bricks, " its exterior surface seems to have been coated with furnace-burnt ones, many of which, both whole and broken, are scattered about the foot of the pile." The real character of Babylonian stage-towers at that time having

not yet been disclosed by the excavations, it was only natural that Buckingham, well acquainted with the pyramids of Egypt as he was, and once having recognized the original form of the structure at 'Aqarquf as a step-pyramid or stage-tower, should have regarded the latter as an ancient royal tomb rather than as the most conspicuous part of a Babylonian temple. According to inscribed bricks later discovered all around the central ruin by Sir Henry Rawlinson, the city whose stage-tower is represented by 'Aqarquf was called DurKurigalzu. One of the designations commonly given to this ruin by the Arabs (comp. above, p. 16, note 2, and Rich's "Memoirs," p. 80). 'Aqarquf has no satisfactory etymology in Arabic. Possibly it is only the badly mutilated old Babylonian name of the city. Comp. Buckingham, " Trav.," vol. ii., p. 226, footnote, and Ker Porter, "Travels," vol. ii., pp. 276, 279. A learned Arab of Baghdad, whom Buckingham consulted (7. -., p. 239), did not hesitate to explain it as " the place of him who rebelled against God." Two other etymologies are quoted by Yaqut in his geographical dictionary.

Comp. the four different views given by Ker Porter on p. 227 of his richly illustrated work quoted below, and the illustration facing p. I J above. See the illustration given below under Egypt.

Two davs later Buckingham and Bellino — the former in the disguise of a Bedouin acting as the guide of the latter — were on their way to the ruins of Babylon. As soon as the Mujeliba came into view, they turned away from the regular caravan road to Hilla, subjecting the whole complex of mounds along the eastern bank of the Euphrates to a care Bjl-ii. Writ Face, a it appeared in 1811 ful examination. In every detail Buckingham was able to corroborate the description and measurements of Rich, also sharing his view that this most northern pile of-ruins could never have represented the tower of Belus, as had been so vigorously maintained by Major Rennell. He pointed out that the appearance of walls and portions of buildings on its summit apparently con-

structed at different periods, the small quantity of rubbish accumulated around its base, and the remains of brickwork and masonry visible near the surface on the northern and western sides at the foot of the heap, proved beyond doubt that this mound " was never built on to a much greater height than that at which its highest part now stands," and for this very reason could not in any respect correspond to the famous tower for which it had been frequently taken. These features just mentioned, "added to the circumstance of its being evidently surrounded by ditches, and perhaps walls, with its situation within a quarter of a mile of the river, are strong arguments in favour of its being the castellated palace described" by Diodorus Siculus.

For a brief sketch of the history of exploration of the ruins of 'Aqarquf, ec Ritter, *Die-Erdkundt,* vol. xi., pp. 847-852.

After a satisfactory inspection of all the details connected with the second mound, called Kl-Qasr, Buckingham came to the conclusion arrived at by Rich that this ruin represented the remains of an (other) "extensive palace;" but differing somewhat from the view of his predecessor, he was inclined to identify the hanging gardens with a part of the ruins of El-Qasr, or possibly even 'Omran ibn 'All. The neighborhood of the river, a peculiar brick here discovered by Rich, and the famous single tree called Athla standing close to the broken walls and piers of El-Qasr, seemed to him favorable to his theory of locating the hanging gardens not very far from the latter.

Not satisfied with a mere examination of the principal mounds of Babylon, the two companions set out towards the east to search for the original walls of the great metropolis. In order to fully understand their efforts and to judge Buckingham's final and serious mistake in the proper light of his period, we must remember that the two most able geographers — D'Anville and Major Rennell — who had previously ventured to express an opinion on the original size of Babylon, as described by the classical writers, had differed so radically in their conclusions that new material was required to establish the entire correctness of Herodotus's measures, in which Rennell and Buckingham firmly believed. In favor, therefore, of giving to Babylon the full extent assigned to it bv its earliest historian, Buckingham found no difficulty in reclaiming the great network of ancient canals to the east of Babylon, flanked by very high embankments and often filled with mud and sand far above the level of the surrounding plain, as " the remains of buildings originally disposed in streets, and crossing each other at right angles, with immense spaces of open and level ground on each side of them." Engraved with a certain religious symbol, a kind of upright pole with pointed top, often found in bas-reliefs and seal-cylinders, but by Buckingham and others mistaken fora spade. Comp. Rich's " Memoirs," p. 60, note, and Ker Porter, "Travels," vol. ii., pi. 77, c.

If not a distinct species, at least a beautiful variety of *Tamarix Oriottalii (tarfa)* according to the Arabic *Materia Medica* of Ibn Kibti, the Baghdad! (A. H. 711). Comp. Mignan, "Travels," p. 258; Sonini, "Travels in Egypt," pp. 247, *ieq. ;* Forskal, *Flora jfcgyptiaco-Arnbica,* p. 206.

For more than two hours, in pursuit of their phantom, the two travellers had been riding over the parched and burning plain covered with burnt brick and pottery and an occasional detached heap of rubbish. The heat of the atmosphere had meanwhile become so intense and the air so suffocating and almost insufferable that Bellino, completely exhausted with thirst and fatigue, declined to proceed any farther. Buckingham left his companion in the shade of a Mohammedan tomb, himself pushing ahead, determined to reach a pyramidal mound called Kl-Ohemir, and previously visited only by Dr. Hine and Captain Lockett, of the British Residency at Baghdad, which he regarded as of the most importance for the final solution of his problem. Half an hour after quitting Bellino he reached the foot of the steep mound of which he had been so

eagerly in search. But he could remain only a few minutes. Clouds of dust and sand filling his eyes, mouth, ears, and nostrils, and rendering it difficult and painful to look around, drove him soon from the summit, which he judged to be seventy to eighty feet high. Yet this brief examination of the conical red mound and its surroundings had sufficed to enable him to furnish a general description of the size and character of the ruins and to state his conviction that this elevated pile, though nearly eight miles distant from the Euphrates, was the extreme eastern boundary of ancient Babylon, and itself a portion of its celebrated wall. In support of his extraordinary theory, which rested entirely upon the partly misunderstood statements of Herodotus, he endeavored to show that the peculiar white layers of ashes, occurring at certain intervals in the principal ruin of baked bricks, corresponded precisely to " the composition of heated bitumen mixed with the tops rather stems! of reeds," so particularly mentioned by the Greek historian as the characteristic cement used in the construction of the ditch and walls of Babylon.

Differently rendered by the travellers as *Al Hheimar* (Rich, Buckingham), *Al-Hymer* (Ker Porter), *El-Hamir* (Mignan), *(El-)Ohcmir* (Frazer), *Uhaimir* (lit. transl.), in accordance with a more or less successful endeavor to reproduce the present Arabic pronunciation of the word. The name, derived from Arabic *ahmar, "* red," designates the hill as *" the reddish one" (*diminutive) from its most characteristic feature, the deep red brickwork crowning it summit. A similar name is El-Homaira (dimin. of the fern. *humra),* one of the smaller mounds of Babylon, east of El-Qasr.

After their late arrival at Hilla, the two travellers presented a letter of introduction received from Rich to a powerful Arab residing in the same town. Through his assistance they were enabled to pay a visit to the lofty ruins on the western side of the Euphrates, which had been "identified" by Niebuhr and Rich with the "Tower of Belus," so often described by the classical writ-

ers. With regard to the name of this ruin Buckingham states correctly' that, though generally referred to as Birs Nimrud by the different travellers, it should properly be called only El-Birs. "Whenever Nimrud is added, it is merely because the inhabitants of this country are as fond of attributing everything to this mighty hunter before the Lord,' as the inhabitants of Egypt are to Pharaoh, or those of Syria to Solomon. " Both Rich and Buckingham assumed with good reason that the word *Birs* has no satisfactory etymology in Arabic, — the latter, for very apparent reasons, proposing to regard it as a corruption of " Belus, its original name," which of course is out of the question. Since the extensive ruins of El-Birs have been identified with the remains of the Babylonian city of Borsippa, we can safely assert that Birs or Burs — as it is pronounced occasionally — is nothing but a local corruption of Borsippa, just as the first half of the modern Egyptian village of Saft el-Henne has preserved the name of the ancient Egyptian god Sopt, whose sanctuary, Per-Sopt, was situated there.

As I personally have been able to verify repeatedly in that neighborhood in recent years. Comp., also, Abbe De Beauchamp, above, p. 20. The same name, El-Birs, is the only one given by Mas'udi in the chapter where he describes the course of the Euphrates. Similarly the Qamus gives Sirs as the name of a town or district between Hilla and Kufa still known.

On the basis of a careful study of the memoirs of Rich and Rennell, and after a close personal inspection of the ruins, Buckingham at once recognized the original building represented by the mound, on which the vitrified wall occupies such a conspicuous place, as a stage-tower. He went even farther than Rich by pointing out that four stages, "receding one within another, are to be distinctly traced, on the north and east sides, projecting through the general rubbish of its face." Determined as he was to prove the accuracy of Herodotus' account of the enormous area of Babylon, and not less influenced than Rich bv the magnitude of the lofty ruin, which, according to his idea, could not possibly have been excluded by the walls from the territory of the ancient city, he did not hesitate for a moment to take the ruin of El-Birs for its western extreme, as he had taken the ruin at El-Ohemir for its eastern. At the same time he accepted and strengthened the theory of Rich, who had identified El-Birs with the famous Tower of Babel, however contrary to the very explicit statement of Arrian: "The Temple of Belus is situated in the heart of Babylon." Already recognized as such by Captain Mignan, " Travels in Chalda," London, 1829, pp. 258, *ieq.* SIR ROBERT KER PORTER

One of the greatest mines of information concerning the life and manners of the people of Western Asia at the beginning of the last century, and also with regard to the monuments, inscriptions, and other antiquities then known to exist in Persia and Babylonia, is the magnificent work of Sir Robert Ker Porter," Travels in Georgia, Persia, Armenia, Ancient Babylonia, etc., etc., during the years 181720," ' equally remarkable for the " truth in what the author relates," and the " fidelity in what he copies " and illustrates by his numerous drawings, portraits, and sketches. From childhood loving and practising the arts, he had become a famous painter of international reputation, whose eminent talents, striking personality, and final marriage with a Russian princess had secured for him a social standing which enabled him, by his pen and brush, to reach circles hitherto but little influenced by the books of ordinary travellers and the scientific and often dry investigations of men of the type of Otter, Niebuhr, Beauchamp, and Rich. In his popularization of a subject which so far had stirred the minds of only a limited class of people, and in appealing, by his religious sentiment, the manner of his style, and the accurate representation of what he had observed, not less to the men of science and religion than to the aristocratic circles of Europe, on whose interest and financial support the resurrection of Assyria and Babylonia chiefly depended, lies the significance

of Ker Porter as a Babylonian explorer. Two volumes, London, 1821, 1822.

After extensive travels through Georgia and Persia, in the course of which the great monuments of Naqs-i-Rustam and Persepolis had received his special attention, Porter arrived at Baghdad in October, 1818. About two. years previously Buckingham had visited the same region, though by reason of peculiar circumstances' the latter's work could not be published until eleven years later. Compared with the clear statements and sober facts presented by his predecessors, Porter's book is sometimes deficient in definite information, — pious meditations and personal speculations occasionally becoming the undesirable substitutes for an intelligent description, judicial discrimination, and logical reasoning. Yet, with all these defects, due less to his lack of good will and personal devotion than to his unfamiliaritv with the Oriental languages and the absence of a proper technical training, Porter will always hold his distinct place in the history of Babylonian exploration.

During the six weeks which he spent under the inspiring influence of Rich at the British Residency in Baghdad, he examined the four Babylonian ruins at that time standing in the centre of public interest: 'Aqarquf, Kl-Birs, Babil, and Kl-Ohemir. As in the case of Buckingham, Bellino became his regular companion on his excursions to the ruins just mentioned. What his description of 'Aqarquf lacks in new elements and successful combination is made good by the four excellent drawings which he has left us of the four different sides of that conspicuous landmark at the northern boundary of ancient Babylonia. Of interest also is his remark as to the original purpose of the ruin in question, as coming nearer to the truth than that of any previous traveller: "I should suppose the mass we now see to be no more than the base of some loftier superstructure, probably designed for the double use of a temple and an observatory; a style of sacred edifice common with the Chaldeans, and likely to form the principal object in every city and town de-

voted to the idolatry of Belus and the worship of the stars." Arising from the scandalous and malicious accusations *of* Buckingham's former travelling companion, W. . Bankes, who in the most contemptible manner prevented the publication of his book, at the same time endeavoring to ruin the literary character of the author, as he had ruined him socially and financially in India.

Protected by more than a hundred well-armed horsemen of the Turkish army against any possible molestation from the marauding Bedouins, who were at open war with the governor of Baghdad, Porter had the rare opportunity of inspecting the huge mass of buildings known as El-Birs or Birs Nimrud, with a feeling of absolute security and comfort. Rich and Buckingham having described the more essential features of this grandest of all Babylonian ruins before, our traveller had nothing to add, but the more to speculate on the probable age and cause of the destruction of this " Tower of Belus," of which again he left us four fairly good drawings, though in certain prominent details decidedly inferior to the pen-and-ink sketch published by Rich. It was Porter's firm conviction that the extraordinary ruin as it now stands, " and doubtless representing the Tower of Babel," is the work of three different periods and builders. As over against the fundamental investigations of his two contemporaries, who by their accurate description and sober judgment of Babylonian ruins so favorably contrasted with the uncritical method of the early travellers, we find in Porter's account of Birs (Nimrud) a certain inclination to fall back into the outlived fashion of previous centuries. According to his view, the original tower built by Nimrod and "partially overturned by the Divine wrath," is still to be recognized in the four lowest stages of the present remains. "In this ruinous and abandoned state most likely the tower remained till Babylon was refounded bv Semiramis, who, covering the shattered summit of the great pile with some new erection, would there place her observatory and altar to Bel." Nebuchadrezzar, finding " the stupendous monument of Babel " in the manner in which it was left by the " Assyrian queen," and " constituting it the chief embellishment of his imperial city," restored the temple " on its old solid foundations." But as " it can hardly be doubted that Xerxes, in his destruction of the temple, overturned the whole of what had been added by the Babylonian monarchs, it does not seem improbable that what we now see on the fire-blasted summit of the pile, its rent wall, and scattered fragments, with their partially vitrified masses, may be a part ot that very stage of the primeval tower which felt the effects of the Divine vengeance." Not many years afterwards poor Porter's fantastic speculations were reduced to what they were really worth by the discovery that most of the vitrified bricks bear the common inscription of Nebuchadrexzar.

Ten days later, when Ker Porter paid a second visit to the Birs, he had the unique spectacle of seeing " three majestic lions taking the air upon the heights of the pyramid" — a veritable illustration of Isaiah's prophetic word: "Wild beasts of the desert shall lie there; and their houses shall be full of doleful creatures" (13: 21). But this time his stay did not last very long. While leisurely surveying the boundless desert from the sublime eminence on which he stood, a dark mass came up like a cloud from the horizon. It was soon discovered that a body of Bedouins was rapidly moving towards their place of observation, which they now hastily left, chased by the Arab pursuers to the very walls of H i'lla.

Ouite different from what he has to relate of Birs (Nimrud) is Porter's account of the ruins of Babylon. His eye seems sharpened to discover the slightest peculiarity; with a judicious discrimination he sets forth all the characteristic features of the bewildering mass; his expression is clear, his language precise, and yet betraying all the enthusiasm with which he approaches his subject. In this regard and in his earnest endeavor to define the enormous extent of these ruins on both banks of the river with accuracy, his graphic description

may well be placed alongside those of Rich and Buckingham, which in several details our author even supplements. Like his predecessors he adduces ample proof that the Mujeliba can never be taken for the remains of the " Tower of Babel." The absence of any trace of a sacred enclosure on its southern side, and of any considerable rubbish to represent the remains of the temple and residences of the priests around its base, the comparatively low elevation of the whole platform, the ruins of extensive buildings on its summit, the discovery of certain subterranean passages and objects in its interior, its very commanding position and strategic importance for the defence of the city, — in fact the whole situation and peculiar style of this gigantic mass of brick-formed earth "mark it out to have been the citadel of the fortified new palace of the ancient authors."

He traced Nebuchadrezzar's ancient embankments to a considerable length along the steep eastern shore; he noticed the peculiarities of the edge-inscribed bricks on the lofty conical mound of El-Homaira; he dwelt upon the remarkable changes which had recently taken place in the appearance of the Qasr " from the everlasting digging in its apparently inexhaustible quarries," and he expressed his strong belief that this latter mound with its adjoining ridges contained nothing else than the " more modern and greater palace " and the hanging gardens.

With Rich and Buckingham, Porter believed Babylon to have extended considerably on the western side of the Euphrates, as far as Birs (Nimrud). In the expectation of finding traces of the "lesser palace," he spent a whole day in examining the ground to the north and west of Hilla, finally inclined to regard a group of mounds half-way between Kl-Qasr and the Birs as the possible remains of Alexander the Great's temporary abode, from which in the course of his illness he was removed to the palace on the other side, only to die.

In order to ascertain, if possible, the exact boundary line of the metropolis on the eastern side of the river, he visit-

ed Kl-Ohemir and a number of mounds in its neighborhood. Accompanied by Bellino and his usual strong escort, and provided with all the necessities of life, he set out on a fine November morning and examined the whole district at his leisure, so that he could leave us a much more satisfactory description than that of Buckingham, who had been at the same ruins but a few minutes under the most trying circumstances. To Ker Porter we are likewise indebted for the first inscribed brick' taken from the pyramidal mound of Kl-Ohemir, from which we learn that the god Zamama had his temple here restored by a Babylonian king, probably Adad-apal-idin-nam of the Fashe dynasty, who lived about 1065 B. c. The principal ruin, covered with a mass of red brickwork, and exhibiting " four straight faces, but unequal and mutilated, looking towards the cardinal points," apparently represents the original stage-tower or *ziggur-rat* of this temple. From a marble fragment picked up by Bellino, it becomes evident that the place must have occupied a prominent position as early as the time of Hammurabi, about one thousand years earlier. There can be little doubt that the city buried here is no other than Kish, with its famous sanctuary, playing such an important role at the verv beginning of Babylonian history. Though at the time unfamiliar with the details mentioned, which are but the product of subsequent investigations, Forter clearly recognized the general character of El-Ohemir and its neighboring ruins, and, contrary to Buckingham's untenable theory, regarded it as entirely out of question to suppose that these mounds "could have ever stood within the limits of Babylon or even formed any part of its great bulwarked exterior wall." Published in his " Travels," vol. ii., pi. 77, a.

Ker Porter had spent nearly a fortnight in examining the ruins of Babylon and their environments. After his return to Baghdad he illustrated what he had seen, not only by drawings of the most interesting mounds visited and objects discovered, but, profiting from the assistance of Bellino, by several plates of cuneiform inscriptions, among them the fragment of a large barrel-cylinder, which he had found in the ruins of the Qasr.

It is not within the scope of our present sketch to mention all the different travellers who during the first half of the last century visited the sites of Nineveh and Babylon and a few other prominent mounds of the two ancient empires on the Tigris and Euphrates. As a rule their accounts are little more than repetitions of facts and conditions even then well established. Men like Colonel Macdonald Kinneir (1808 and i8i3)and Edward Frederick (1811) had formed the necessary link between the old school of travellers in the eighteenth century and the accurate observers and topographical students of the nineteenth century. The time was now drawing rapidly near when instead of the text of the classical writers so ably interpreted by Rennell and others, or the measuring rod and compass so well used by Rich and his immediate successors, to whom we may still add Captain Keppel (1824),` spade and pickaxe would be called upon to speak the final word and settle those much discussed topographical questions. At the threshold which separates this last chapter of Assyrian and Babylonian exploration from the earlier period just treated, stand two men, who while properly speaking they added but few positive facts to our knowledge of ancient Babylonian ruins, yet instinctively felt the pulse of the coming age, and through their own personal courage and enterprising spirit entered upon the very road which ultimately led to success.
Now in the British Museum. In its preserved portions it is a NeoBabylonian duplicate of certain sections (col. iii., 15—63, and col. vi., 44, to col. vii., 20) of the so-called East India House Inscription of Nebuchadrezzar, giving a summary of his building operations in Babylon and Borsippa. "Geographical Memoir of the Persian Empire," together with Frederick's " Account of the present compared with the ancient state of Babylon," published in the " Transactions of the Bombay Society," Bombay,

1813, pp. 273-295, and pp. 120—139 respectively. Comp., also, Kinneir's "Travels in Asia Minor, Armenia, and Kurdistan," the account of his journey from Constantinople to Basra, in the year 18 1 3. CAPTAIN ROBERT MIGNAN
In the years 1826-28, when Major Taylor was the East India Company's political representative at Basra, Captain Robert Mignan, in command of the escort attached to the Resident, made several archaeological excursions into the little known districts of Persia, 'Iraq el-'Arabi, and northern Mesopotamia. While each of these little expeditions claims the attention of the historian of ancient geography to a certain degree, in this connection it will be sufficient to sketch briefly his share in the exploration of ancient Babylonia.

In consequence of the constant quarrels which the different Arab tribes were carrying on among themselves or against their common enemy, the Turkish government, only few travellers had ventured to leave the regular caravan road and to extend their researches beyond a very limited radius around Baghdad and Hilla. Kinneir and Keppel had thrown some light on certain remarkable vestiges on the banks of the Lower Tigris, but the whole region adjoining the two rivers between Qorna and Babylon on the one side, and Ctesiphon and Sclcucia on the other, needed a much closer investigation, before it could lay claim to another title than that of a *terra incognita*. Determined to prosecute his studies on a line different from those previously followed, Mignan decided to proceed on foot from Basra to Baghdad and Hilla, " accompanied by six Arabs, completely armed and equipped after the fashion of the country, and by a small boat, tracked by eight sturdy natives, in order to facilitate his researches on either bank of the stream." Accordingly he set out on his novel tour towards the end of October, 1827. Many years afterwards, when exploring the interior of Southern Babylonia, though then still unacquainted with Mignan's travels, I adopted the same method of alternate walking and riding in a native canoe *(turrdda)*. On the basis of my

own past experience, I am convinced that the method described is the only one which in the end will accomplish a thorough exploration of the marshy interior of Babylonia.
Personal Narrative of Travels in Babylonia, Assyria, Media, and Scythia," jd ed., London, 1827, 2 volumes. Comp. his " Travels in Chalda," London, 1829. The independence which Mignan thus enjoyed in all his movements was utilized especially to satisfy his curiosity concerning the early remains occasionally met on both sides of the Tigris. Often, when an old wall or an especially promising mound attracted his attention, he stopped a few hours to investigate the place or to cut a trench into the ruin, with a view of ascertaining its age or discovering its character. Sixteen days after his departure from Basra, and unmolested on his way by the Arabs, he reached the city of the caliphs. Under the heavy showers of an early November rain, he examined the tower of 'Aqarquf, in a few subordinate points even correcting the accounts of previous travellers. Then he turned his attention to the ruins of Babylon, Birs, and Ohemir, to which he devoted nearly a week of undivided attention. After all that had been written on them, we cannot expect to find extraordinary new discoveries in his description. Once more he summed up the different reasons, from which it may be safely concluded that the great metropolis stood in the place assigned to it, referring particularly to " the distances given by Herodotus from Is or Hit, and by Strabo and the Theodosian tables from Seleucia." With Buckingham he believed that Birs and Ohemir are probably to be included in the original territory of Babylon; but contrary to the generally expressed opinion of his predecessors, he asserted emphatically that Birs (Nimrud) cannot be identified with the Tower of Belus, as "all ancient authors agree in placing it in the midst of the city; " and with good reason he disclosed as the real cause for the universal mistake the fact that "it more nearly resembles the state of decay into which we might suppose that edifice to have fallen, after the

lapse of ages, than any other remains within the circumference of Babylon." Yet while thus judiciously protesting against a serious topographical error of his predecessors, he himself fell into another. Notwithstanding all the strong evidence presented against an identification of the Mujeliba with the famous tower, he clung to the exploded theory of Rennell, at the same time transferring the so-called lesser palace to the reddish mound of Homaira. He agreed with his predecessors only in the identification of the Qasr with the castellated palace of Nebuchadrezzar.

But Mignan's new departure from the method of research hitherto employed was not so much due to the circumstance that he again went on foot over the whole field from the Birs to Ohemir, in order to comprehend all the topographical details more thoroughly, as rather to the fact that he endeavored by actual small excavations at the principal mounds to discover their contents and to find new arguments for his proposed identifications. Sometimes he was successful beyond expectation. At the Qasr, *e.g.*, he employed no less than thirty men to clear away the rubbish along the western face of a large pilaster. A space of twelve feet square and twenty feet deep was soon removed, when he suddenly came upon a well-preserved platform of inscribed bricks, each measuring nearly twenty inches square — the largest which so far had been discovered. From the same clearing he obtained four seal-cylinders, three engraved gems, and several silver and copper coins, one of Alexander the Great being among them; while in a small recess near a well-preserved wall of an unexplored passage on the eastern side of the Qasr, he even found a large and beautiful inscribed barrel cylinder *in situ*, the first thus excavated by any European explorer.

What Mignan had done with regard to our knowledge of the eastern border of ancient Babylonia was attempted for the interior of the country by another Englishman.

G. BAILLIE FRASER

In connection with his travels in Kur-distan and Persia, which in no small degree helped to shape the future life and career of a Layard, Fraser made a hasty tour through the unexplored regions of the interior of Babylonia. The whole trip, on which he was accompanied by Dr. Ross, physician of the English Residency at Baghdad, lasted but one month, from December 24, 1834, to January 22, 1835. Naturally the information gathered and the impression gained had to be one-sided and inaccurate; but nevertheless his vivid account was of considerable value for the time being, as the greater part of the country traversed had never been visited by any European before. Names of ruins now so familiar to every student of Assyrian are found for the first time in Fraser's " Travels in Koordistan, Mesopotamia, etc." London, 1840, two volumes. For Babylonia comp. vol. ii., pp.

After a brief visit to the ruins of Cte-siphon and Seleucia, the little cavalcade, numbering fifteen persons, all the servants included, proceeded to Babylon and Birs (Nimrud), whence by way of El-Ohemir they turned back to the Tigris, which they reached not very far from Tell Iskharie, a peculiar and most interesting group of stonecovered mounds extending for about two miles on both sides of the bed of an ancient canal. With the assistance of two ill-qualified Arab guides, they pushed from there through the Babylonian plain, to-day often included in the general term of Jezire (" island "), passed Tell Jokha and Senkere at some distance, crossed the Shaft el-Kar, and, soon afterwards, the Euphrates with considerable difficulty, examined the conspicuous mounds of Muqayyar, which had attracted their attention as soon as they reached the western bank of' the great river" (the so-called Shamiye), and finally arrived at Suq esh-Shiyukh, the most southern point of their remarkable travels. After an unpleasant stay of several days with the shaikh of the Munte-fik(j), the party returned to Baghdad in nine days, for the greater part nearly following their old track, but stopping at Senkere for a little while, passing War-ka on their left, and observing the lofty ruin of Tell (J)ide far away in the distance. Before his final departure from Baghdad, Fraser also paid a visit to the imposing ruin of 'Aqarquf, which had been so often described by previous travellers.

Fraser was the first who boldly entered the then unknown regions of the Babylonian marshes and pasture grounds occupied by roaming Bedouins and the half-settled thievish and uncouth Ma'dan tribes. In this fact lies his importance for the history of Babylonian exploration. From his graphic account of the character and manners of the present Arabs and the nature of their desolate country, from his constant references to the many ancient canals often interfering with his progress, and the numerous sites of former cities, towns, and villages, of which he found important traces everywhere, we gained a first general idea of what ancient Babylonia must have been in the days of her splendor, and also what had become of this small but fertile country in the course of two millenniums. The picture which he draws is anything but pleasing. Where apparently a dense population and a high grade of civilization had formerly existed, there prevails at present nothing but utter ruin, lawlessness, and poverty. Even the characteristic virtues of the Arabs of the desert, proclaimed by so many songs and noble examples, seemed almost unknown or regarded as a mere farce in the interior of Babylonia. What wonder, then, that Fraser, little acquainted as he had been with Arab life and manners before, and suffering considerably from cold and exposure, lack of food and water during a severe Babylonian January, sums up his description of the country and of " all Arabs and Shaikhs, jointly and severally," with the words of Burns, *mutato nomine:* —

"There 's nothing here but Arab pride
And Arab dirt and hunger;
If Heaven it was that sent us here,
It sure was in an anger!"

So far the exploration of Assyria and Babylonia had been exclusively in the hands of private individuals who possessed great courage and the necessary means for travelling in districts which through their geographical position and the notoriously lawless habits of their inhabitants had offered most serious obstacles to an accurate scientific investigation. It is true, since the time of Niebuhr and Beauchamp a number of valuable geographical and topographical data had gradually been gathered, and careful measurements, trigonometrical angles, and astronomical calculations had more and more taken the place of former vague statements and general descriptions. A few attempts had even been made at drawing maps of the countries traversed, with the courses of rivers, the ranges of mountains, and the relative positions of the places and ruins examined. But no two maps could have been found which agreed with each other even in the most essential and characteristic features. It was therefore very evident that government support was needed, and the methodical survey by a well-equipped staff of experts required, in order to change this unsatisfactory condition. Most naturally the eyes of all who were interested in the resurrection of Assyria and Babylonia turned to England, where at this very moment peculiar constellations had arisen which were prognostications of systematic action.

THE EUPHRATES EXPEDITION

Under the especial patronage of King William IV., in the years 1835-37, an expedition was organized by the British government, in order to survey the northern part of Syria, to explore the basins of the rivers Euphrates and Tigris, to test the navigability of the former, and to examine in the countries adjacent to these great rivers the markets with which the expedition might be thrown in contact. The Suez Canal not yet existing, England, jealously watched by France and Russia, advanced this important step, apparently in the hope of stirring the national energy and enterprise by the results to be achieved to such an enthusiasm as to lead to establishing regular railway or steamer communications with the far East by way of the Euphrates valley, and to restoring life and prosperity to a region renowned for its fertility in ancient times and generally regarded as the seat of the earliest civilization.

This expedition, then, owed its origin mainly to commercial and political considerations, with the ultimate view of securing the Euphrates valley as a highway to India. But though its purpose was a practical one, it deserves a more prominent place in the history of Babylonian exploration and surveying than is generally accorded to it in Assyriological publications, alike for the novelty and magnitude of the enterprise, for the grand scale upon which it was got up, for the difficulties it had to encounter, and for the importance of the scientific results obtained.

Fifteen officers, including Captain H. B. Lynch and William F. Ainsworth, surgeon and geologist to the expedition, formed the staff of this great military undertaking commanded by Colonel (afterwards Major-General) Francis Ravvdon Chesney, who had travelled extensively in Western Asia before. The members of the expedition left Liverpool in February, 1835. Large provisions and the material of two iron steamers accompanied them to the bay of Antioch, whence under the greatest difficulties they were transported over land to the Upper Euphrates. Somewhat below the ferry and castle of Birejik (but on the west bank of" the great river ") light field works were thrown up, and a temporary station established under the name of Port William. Long delays in the transport of the material, carried by 841 camels and 160 mules from the seashore to the Euphrates, heavy rains and consequent inundations, the difficult task of putting the boats together, and the severity of the fever, which seized so many of the party, consumed almost the whole first year. As it was found impossible to descend the river during the winter, the greater portion of this season was spent in reconnoitring the Taurus and the country between the Euphrates and the river Balikh-Su as far north as Sammosata, the ancient capital of Commagene, and including Urfa (Edessa) and the ruins of Haran. Comp. Chesney, "The Expedition for the Survey of the Rivers Euphrates and Tigris," 2 vols., London, 1850; Chesney, "Narrative of the Euphrates Expedition," London, 1868; and a volume of twelve sections of a large map, and two additional maps of Arabia and adjacent countries, London, 1849. Also W. F. Ainsworth,' Researches in Assyria, Babylonia, and Chaldaea, forming part of the Labours of the Euphrates Expedition," London, 1838, and the same author's "A Personal Narrative of the Euphrates Expedition," 2 vols., London, 1888.

About a year after the expedition had left Kngland, the descent of the Euphrates was commenced, on the i6th of March, 1836. It was a memorable day when the first two steamboats brought to these regions, "Euphrates" and "Tigris," left their moorings. The whole Christian and Mohammedan population of the small town had turned out "to see an iron boat swim, and, what was more, stem the current of the river." For according to Chesney and Ainsworth, there was a tradition familiar at Birejik, which

The Steamen " Euphrates" and "Tigris" descending the Euphrates accompanied the expedition down the whole river, that when iron should swim on the waters of the Frit, the fall of Mohammedanism would commence.

The descent was made in the following manner. The day before the steamers started, a boat was sent ahead to examine and sound the river for a distance of twenty to thirty miles. "The officer who had accomplished his task became the pilot on the occasion of the first day's descent, while another was despatched in advance to become the pilot on the second day. Thus the naval officers took it by turns to survey the river and tc pilot the vessel." The detailed bearings of the river were taken by Colonel Chesney from the steamer itself. At times exploring tours and explanatory missions were sent to the neighboring districts of the Arabs, while at the same time the survev was carried on ashore by a chain of ground trigonometrical angles across the principal heights as they presented themselves.

In the early afternoon of May 21, 1836, the expedition suffered a most serious loss, almost at the same spot where many centuries before the apostate emperor Julian had met with a similar misfortune. The weather suddenly changed, " accompanied by a portentous fall of the barometer.... In the course of a few minutes dense masses of black clouds, streaked with orange, red, and yellow, appeared coming up from the W. S. W., and approached the boats with fearful velocity." Not far below the junction of the river Khabur (the biblical Habor) with the Euphrates, during a brief but fearful hurricane or simoom of the desert, which, turning day into night, struck the two boats with terrible force, the "Tigris," for the time being the flagship of the little squadron, was capsized, and rapidly went to the muddy bottom of the foaming river. Twenty men, including Lieutenants Cockburn and R. B. Lynch (brother of the commander of the " Tigris "), were drowned in the Euphrates. Only fourteen of the crew were washed by the high waves over the bank into a field of corn, Colonel Chesney, the gallant leader, fortunately being among the survivors. Few of the bodies, mostly disfigured by vultures beyond recognition, were recovered and buried. Among other things picked up "was Colonel Chesney's Bible, to which great interest attached itself, as it had already gone to the bottom of the river when the Colonel was first navigating the river on a raft, and had been washed ashore in a similar manner."

The " Euphrates " having descended the rest of the river alone, ascended also the Tigris as far as ancient Opis. But on October 28, in connection with an attempt to ascend the Euphrates, — the second part of the task assigned to the expedition, — upon entering the Lamlun marshes of Babylonia, the engine of the steamer broke down; and the crew, after making every possible effort to repair it temporarily, was obliged to drop down the river with the current, occasionally assisted by the sails. This breakdown was the beginning of the end. The funds of the expedition were exhausted; and Russia having reproached the Porte "for allowing steam navigation in the interior rivers of the empire to a nation whose policy was avowedly opposed to her own," the British government gradually lost its interest in an undertaking begun with such energy and enthusiasm, and the results of which up to that time had been fully adequate to the money and labor spent.

At the close of the nineteenth century, the old scheme of connecting the Persian Gulf with the Mediterranean by rail or boat has been vigorously taken up again by Germany, with an apparently greater prospect of ultimate success. A regular steamboat line, however, as it seems at present, will scarcely ever be established on the Euphrates, because of the enormous outlay of capital necessary to secure a certain depth of water at all seasons within a well-regulated channel, and to prevent the Arabs from building their dams into the stream or digging new canals for the purpose of irrigation.

Among the incomplete scientific results obtained by the Euphrates Expedition, the series of twelve maps, published by Colonel Chesney twelve years later (1849), ranks first. Even to-day, when for some time more accurate maps of certain sections of the Euphrates and Tigris basins have been in our hands, it is still of inestimable value, forming, as it does, the only source of our topographical knowledge for by far the larger part of the course of the two rivers. Naturally the accuracy attainable for any map prepared from a survey by water can only be relative. Rich's survey of the middle course of the Tigris, carried on from a primitive raft on a "swift-flowing" river, afterwards incorporated in Colonel Chesney's fundamental work, must therefore be even less accurate than that of the staff of the Euphrates Expedition, conducted from a well-equipped steamer on a river with considerably less current.

The great influence which these maps exercised upon future archaeological explorations in the countries between the Euphrates and the Tigris, lies in the fact that for the first time they showed the enormous wealth of ancient ruins, canals, and other remains of former civilizations along the entire embankment of both rivers. Ainsworth, who manifested a particular interest in the archaeology and history of the country, described carefully what he saw on his daily excursions, thus enabling us to form a first correct idea of the difference between the numerous barren hills crowned with the ruins of extensive castles, temples, and towers, along the upper course of the Euphrates, and the thousands of ancient and modern canals, numberless mounds of baked and sun-dried bricks, half buried under the sands of the desert or submerged under the encroaching water of the rivers, turning the country into immense swamps for many miles, along the lower course of both the Euphrates and Tigris. Through his " Researches in Assyria, Babylonia, and Chaldam " the same scholar added not only considerably to our knowledge of the general features of Mesopotamia and 'Iraq el-'Arabi (climate, vegetation, zoology, and natural history), but he also furnished the first scientific treatment of the latest deposits by transport, of the physical geography and geology of the alluvial districts of Babylonia, The name of the Tigris signifies "swift-flowing." and of the geological relations of the bitumen and naphtha springs characteristic of the adjacent regions.

The work of the Euphrates Expedition had been practically confined to a survey of the two great rivers. The next step needed for the exploration of Babylonia and Assyria proper was to proceed from the base established by Colonel Chesney and his staff into the interior of the neighboring districts, of which little or nothing was known, surveying section after section until all the material was gathered for constructing a trustworthy map of the whole country. This preliminary task has not yet been finished, even at the close of the nineteenth century. The most essential progress so far made in this regard is closely connected with the first great classical period of Assyrian and Babylonian excavations, during which Sir Henry Rawlinson, equally prominent as a soldier and explorer, decipherer and linguist, comparative geographer and archaeologist, occupied the influential position of British Resident and ConsulGeneral in Baghdad, to the greatest advantage of the scientific undertakings carried on in the regions of the Euphrates and Tigris during his administration (i 843-55)'

JAMES FELIX JONES

Among the technically trained men of that time who in no small part assisted by their work and interest in building up the young science of Assyriology, Commander James Felix Jones will always hold an especially conspicuous place. His excellent topographical material, for the greater part unfortunately buried in the " Records of the Bombay Government," from which twenty-five years later Heinrich Kiepert excavated it for the benefit of Oriental students, deserves a few words also in this connection.

After a residence of five years in Persia, Rawlinson had spent the greater portion of 1839 in Baghdad, when in consequence of the great war in Afghanistan he was appointed Political Agent at Candahar, where he distinguished himself greatly until 1843, when he was sent back to Baghdad as " Political Agent and Consul-General in Turkish Arabia."

Being stationed with his armed boat "Nitocris" at Baghdad, Jones naturally made this city the base of his operations. His attention was first directed to a re-examination of the course of the Tigris above the point where the Shatt el-Adhem empties into the former. In April, 1846, when the annual rise of the river had provided the necessary water for his steamer, he advanced northward. Notwithstanding the increased force of the current, which at times almost equalled the power of the machine, seriously interfering with his progress, Jones reached the rapids of the Tigris above Tekrit, and by his measurements and triangulations greatly improved the earlier map of Rich and furnished considerable new information.

In the years 1848-50, during the months of March and April, when the lack of water and the absence of a settled population did not yet prove too great an obstacle to topographical work in regions where every accommodation was wanting, he made three exploration tours into the districts to the east of the Tigris. His intention was to determine the tract of the ancient Nahrawan Canal, which, leaving the Tigris about halfway between Tekrit and Samarra, had once brought life and fertility to the whole territory as far down as Kud(t) el-Amara, to-day almost entirely covered with the sand of the desert or with large brackish water pools.

Of even greater importance from an Assyriological standpoint are his " Researches in the vicinity of the Median Wall of Xenophon and along the old course of the River Tigris," carried on in March, 1850, shortly before he closed his investigations on the eastern side of the river just mentioned. Although he succeeded as little in discovering the "Median Wall" as his predecessors, Ross and Lynch (i86), or his successor Lieutenant Bevvsher, all of whom endeavored in vain to locate it, yet, in addition to all the valuable discoveries of Babylonian and later Mohammedan ruins and canals which he carefully fixed and described on this journey, Jones proved conclusively that, contrary to previously held opinions, the site of the influential and powerful Babylonian city of Opis, better known from Xenophon's and Alexander's campaigns, is identical with the enormous Tell Manjur, on the southern or right side of the present bed of the Tigris; and that, moreover, this location is entirely in accordance with ancient tradition, which places it on the northern or left bank of that river, in so far as the ancient bed of the Tigris, still called by the natives " the little Tigris" (Shtet and Dijel), with numerous traces of canals once proceeding from the latter, could be established by him beyond any doubt to the S.W. of Opis. It was with great difficulty and only after long searching that I finally procured a copy of his "Selections from the Records of the Bombay Government," No. xliii., 1857, for my own library.

But the crowning piece of Jones's numerous contributions to the general and comparative geography of the countries adjacent to the Tigris was his excellent plan of Nineveh and his survey of the whole district intermediate between the Tigris and the Upper Zab. The new impulse given to science by the epoch-making discoveries of Botta and Layard in the Assyrian mounds had turned the eyes of the civilized world again to the long-forgotten country in which those historical places were situated. Yielding to a general desire of seeing a complete picture of Assyria in her present desolation, the East India Company, at the request of the Trustees of the British Museum, despatched Commander Jones in the spring of 1852 to proceed with the construction of the necessary map. Assisted by Dr. Hyslop of the British Residency in Baghdad, chiefly interested in the flora of the Nineveh region, the work was accomplished within a month and a half, at that great time when Victor Place was still excavating at Khorsabad, and Rawlinson inspecting the work of the Assyrian explorers, while Fresnel and Oppert had just arrived in that neighborhood from Paris, previous to their excavations in Babylon.

In June, 1900, when I examined that whole region, I heard both names from the Arabs. Comp. on this whole question Kiepert, *Begleitworte zur Karte der Ruinenftlder von Babylon,* Berlin, 1883, pp. 24, *seq.* Comp. his report in the "Journal of the Royal Asiatic Society of Great Britain and Ireland," vol. xv. (London, 1855), PP-97397

In three large sheets, which up to this day are the standard work for the geography of ancient Assyria, the results of the survey were published. Before closing his interesting report on the topography of Nineveh, Jones paid a warm tribute to the work of Rich, " the first real laborer in Assyrian fields," by writing the following memorable words: "His survey (of Nineveh and Nimrud) will be found as correct as the most diligent enthusiast can desire; indeed, were it not for the renewed inquiry into Assyrian subjects, the present survey we have the honor of submitting to the public might have been dispensed with, for its value chiefly consists in corroborating the fidelity of his positions, and otherwise, though quite unnecessary, stamping his narrative with the broad seal of truth." LYNCH, SELBV, COLLINGWOOD, BEWSHER

In the mean while the way was being gradually prepared for a similar kind of work in Babylonia. Fraser, Loftus, and Layard had boldly entered the swamps of 'Iraq and examined the interior of the country, the former two traversing this great alluvial plain almost its entire length, and bringing back the startling news that the whole surface was literally covered with large towers, extensive mounds, snd numerous smaller ruins, with frequent traces of ancient canals, fragments of bricks, statuary, and many other objects of a high antiquity. Fully convinced of the character and age of these remains of a former civilization, Sir Henry Rawlinson at once conceived the idea of having the whole of Babylonia surveyed after the manner so admirably followed by Jones and Hyslop in Assvria. Prior to his return to England (1855), he requested the two last-named experienced men, assisted by T. Kerr Lynch, to make an accurate survey also of the ruins of Babvlon and its environments, an order which they executed in 1854-55. Finally, after the lapse of some time, through Rawlinson's efforts a special committee was appointed bv the British government of India for the purpose of carrying out his more comprehensive plan. It consisted of Commander William Beaumont Selby and Lieutenants Collingwood and Bewsher. But notwithstanding the fact that this commission spent the years 1861-65 Babylonia executing the orders received, and that the most difficult part of the work, the surveying of the swampy district from Musayyib to Shenafiye, on the west side of the Euphrates, was finished in the very first year (1861), yet at the end of the period mentioned only about the fourth part of the entire area was on paper.

Who had succeeded Dr. Ross as physi-cian, after the former's untimely death. Comp. above, pp. 54, *seqq.* Comp. below, pp. 139, *seqq.* Comp. below, pp. 157, *seqq.*

When contrasted with the large amount of work done by Jones within such a short time and often under trying circumstances, one cannot but realize that the old fiery enthusiasm, which inspired the first Babylonian and Assyrian explorers willingly to risk everything, in order to break unknown ground and recover an ancient country, was strongly on the wane. And the American Expedition of the University of Pennsylvania had not yet demonstrated that, notwithstanding the excessive heat and the often almost incredible swarms of vermin and insects, it was possible to work ten to fourteen hours every day during the whole year at the edge of one of the most extensive Babylonian swamps, infested with unruly Arabs and troublesome deserters from the Turkish army, without any considerable increase of danger to the health and life of its members. Commander Selby and his party, however, spent only a few weeks out of every twelve months in actual work in the field, so that in 1866 the Indian government suspended the slowly proceeding and rather expensive work. In 1871 the results obtained by the commission of three were published under the title " Trigonometrical survey of a part of Mesopotamia with the rivers Euphrates and Tigris" (two sheets), comprising the land between 33 and 32 degrees north latitude. Even in its incomplete condition this map of Babylonia, thoroughly scientific, denotes a new epoch in the study of ancient Babylonian geography. A third sheet gives the regions west of the Euphrates, as mentioned above, while a fourth contains a most accurate survey of the city of Babylon. From all the material which since the time of Rich had been gathered together, in 1883 Heinrich Kiepert constructed his own excellent and much consulted map of Northern Babylonia, until the present day our only trustworthy guide through all the ruins to the south of Baghdad. No attempt has as yet been made to survey Central and Southern Babylonia.

How long will this unsatisfactory condition last? A single man, or even two or three, while in charge of an expedition at one of the Babylonian ruins, cannot survey the remaining three quarters of the whole land to the south of NufFar within a reasonable space of time. An especial expedition must be organized to execute the work properly and scientifically, under a firman which should grant the members of this expedition the necessary right to dig enough at the most prominent ruins to identify the early Babylonian cities buried below them.

Ruinenfelder der UmgegenJ von Babylon, Berlin, 1883.

In the year 1893, when the organization of the Babylonian Section of the Imperial Ottoman Museum was entrusted to the present writer, he was also requested to submit a report to the Minister of Public Instruction on the steps necessary for an effective preservation of the Babylonian ruins and their future methodical exploration. The report was written and certain measures proposed. A serious effort was even made to have the plan as outlined above adopted and executed by the Ottoman government, at whose disposal were a number of excellent officers trained in Germany and in France. For several years I had hoped to carry out the work myself with Halil Bey, Director of the Ottoman Museum, a high Danish military officer, and a number of engineers and architects from England and America. But pressing duties in Philadelphia, Constantinople, and Nuffar prevented me from realizing the long cherished plan.

The time, as it seemed, was not yet ripe for such an enterprise. It has considerably matured since. In connection with the preliminary survey for the recently planned railroad from Baghdad to Quwait, an accurate map of Central and Southern Babylonia could be easily prepared by Germany without any great additional expense. At a time when fresh zeal and activity for the organization of new expeditions to the land of the earliest civilization are manifested everywhere, may this grand opportunity, almost providentially given to Germany, not be lost but be seized with characteristic energy and perseverance and utilized for the benefit of Babylonian research at the dawn of the twentieth centurv.

III EXCAVATIONS AT THE PRINCIPAL SITES OF ASSYRIA AND BABYLONIA

In the fall of 1843, after a distinguished service in Afghanistan (1839-42), Rawlinson, as we have seen above (p. 63, note 1), was transferred to Baghdad as "British Political Agent in Turkish Arabia." The young "student-soldier," then occupying the rank of major, had requested Lord Ellenborough, Governor-General of India, to appoint him to this particular post (just about to be vacant) rather than to the much more dignified and lucrative "Central India Agency" offered him, because of his strong desire "to return to the scene of his former labors and resume his cuneiform investigations, in which he had found the greatest pleasure and satisfaction." In accepting a far inferior position with its lighter political duties, which allowed him ample leisure for his favorite studies, Rawlinson, with great perspicacity, chose a life for which he was peculiarly fitted, and entered upon a road which soon brought him fame and recognition far beyond anything that he could ever have achieved in governing half-civilized tribes or fighting victorious battles. The twelve years during which Rawlinson held his appointment in Baghdad mark the first great period of Assyrian and Babylonian excavations. It is true he undertook but little work in the trenches himself, but he influenced and supervised the excavations of others, and personally examined all the important ruins of Assyria and Northern Babylonia. His advice and assistance were sought by nearly all those who with pick and spade were engaged in uncovering the buried monuments of two great empires. While Continental explorers won their laurels on the mounds of Khorsabad and Nimrud, Rawlinson forced the inaccessible rock of Behistun to surrender the great trilingual inscription of Darius, which, in the quietude of Comp. "A Memoir of Major-General Sir Henry Creswicke Rawl-

inson," by his brother, Canon George Rawlinson, London, 1898, pp. 139, *seqq.*

The Rock of Behisrun with the Great Trilingual Inscription his study on the Tigris, became the "Rosetta Stone" of Assyriology, and in his master hand the key to the understanding of the Assyrian documents.

So far the leading explorers of Assyrian and Babylonian ruins in the nineteenth century had been British officers and private travellers. In no small degree, the East India Company, through its efficient representatives at Baghdad and Basra, had promoted and deepened the interest in the ancient history and geography of the Euphrates and Tigris valleys; and as long as this company existed, it never ceased to be a generous patron of all scientific undertakings carried on in regions which, through their close connection with the Bible, have always exercised a powerful influence upon the mind of the English public. Under Rawlinson's energetic and tactful management of British interests in" Turkish Arabia," the old traditional policy of the company was kept alive, and such a spirit of bold progress and scientific investigation was inaugurated in England as had never been witnessed before in the Oriental studies of that country. And yet, through a peculiar combination of circumstances and events, the first decisive step in the line of actual excavations was made not by an English explorer, but by an Orientalist of France, Professor Julius von Mohl, one of the secretaries of the French Asiatic Society, who, born and educated in Germany, had gained the firm conviction that those few but remarkable bricks which he had recently seen in London were but the first indication and sure promise of a rich literary harvest awaiting the fortunate excavator in the mounds of Babylonia and Assyria. No sooner, therefore, had the French government established a consular agency in Mosul and selected a suitable candidate for the new position, than Mohl urged him most strongly to utilize his exceptional opportunity in the interest of science, and to start ex-

cavations in the large mounds opposite Mosul.

The two fundamental and epoch-making publications in which Rawlinton submitted the first complete copy and his decipherment of the second (Persian) and third (Babylonian) columns of the Behistun inscription to the learned world, appeared in the "Journal of the Royal Asiatic Society of Great Britain and Ireland," vols. x. (1846-47), xi. (1849), xii. (1850), ind xiv. riSjl). 1

THE DISCOVERY OF ASSYRIAN PALACES FRENCH EXCAVATIONS AT KHORSABAD BY BOTTA AND PLACE

The man whom France had so judiciously sent as consular agent to Mosul in 1842 was the naturalist Paul Emil Botta, a nephew of the celebrated historian of Italy, and himself a man of no small gifts and of considerable experience in the consular service at Alexandria. A long residence in Egypt, Yemen, and Syria, " undertaken regardless of difficulties or the dangers of climate, solely to further his scientific pursuits, had eminently adapted him for an appointment in the East. He could assimilate himself to the habits of the people; was conversant with their language; possessed energy of character; and was besides an intelligent and practised observer. With such qualifications, it was obvious that his residence in the vicinity of a spot that history and tradition agreed in pointing out as the site of Nineveh could not but be productive of important results." Botta was then only thirty-seven years of age. Though very limited in his pecuniary resources, he commenced his researches immediately after his arrival at Mosul with the full ardor of youth, yet in the cautious and methodical manner of the scholar. He first examined the whole region around Mosul, visited the interior of many modern houses, and tried to acquire every antiquity in the hands of dealers and other persons, with the fixed purpose of tracing the place of their origin, and selecting if possible a suitable ruin for the commencement of his own operations. He soon came, however, to the conclusion that, unlike Hilla and other Babylonian places, Mosul had not been constructed with ancient Assyrian material. Of the two conspicuous mounds on the other side of the Tigris, which alone seemed to indicate a higher antiquity, the southern one, called Nebi Yunus, and partly covered with a village of the same name, attracted his first attention; for it was there that Rich had reported the existence of subterranean walls and cuneiform inscriptions. But the religious prejudice of the inhabitants, and the large sum necessary for their expropriation, excluded from the beginning any attempt on his part at excavating here. There remained, then, nothing else for him but to start operations at the northern *tell* Qoyunjuk (generally written K(o)uyunjilc, and meaning " Lamb" in Turkish), which doubtless was an artificial mass, and, to all appearance, contained the remains of some prominent ancient building. Here Botta commenced his researches on a very moderate scale, in the month of December, 1842. The results of his first efforts were not verv encouraging. Numerous fragments of bas-reliefs and cuneiform inscriptions, through which the Assyrian origin of the mound was established beyond question, were brought to light, but " nothing in a perfect state was obtained to reward the trouble and outlay " of the explorer. Though greatly discouraged by the absence of striking finds, he continued his excavations till the middle of March, 1843.

Comp. Joseph Bonomi, "Nineveh and its Palaces," London, 1852, As Rich had regarded as very likely.

During all the time that Botta was occupied at Qoyunjuk, superintending his workmen, and carefully examining every little fragment that came out of the ground, the curious natives of' the neighboring places used to gather around his trenches, gesticulating and discussing what this strange proceeding of the foreigner meant, but realizing that apparently he was in quest of sculptured stones, inscribed bricks, and other antiquities which he eagerly bought whenever they were offered. One day, as far back as December, 1842, an inhabitant of a distant village, a dyer of Khorsabad, who built his ovens of bricks obtained from the mound on which his village stood, happened to pass by Qoyunjuk and to express his astonishment about Botta's operations. As soon as he had learned what was the real purpose of all these diggings, he declared that plenty of such stones as they wanted were found near his village, at the same time offering to procure as many as the foreigner wished. Botta, accustomed to the Arab endeavor of appearing as bearers of important and pleasing news, did not at first pay much attention to what the man had reported, even after the latter had been induced to bring two complete bricks with cuneiform inscriptions from Khorsabad to Mosul. But finally, weary with his fruitless search in the mound of Qovunjuk, Comp. the Plan of the Ruins of Nineveh, published in a subsequent chapter, "Temporary Revival of Public Interest in Assyrian Excavations" *(sub* "George Smith").

Mound and Village of Khorsabad, from the West he abandoned the scene of his disappointing labors, and remembering the Arab dyer with his bricks and his story, he despatched a few of his workmen to Khorsabad on March 20, 1843, to test the mound as the peasant had advised.

The village of Khorsabad, situated about five hours to the northeast of Mosul, on the left bank of the same little river Khosar which flows through Nineveh, is built on the more elevated eastern part of a long-stretched mound. The gradually descending western half of the same *tell* ends in two ridges which are both unoccupied. It was in the northern ridge of the latter section that Botta's workmen began to cut their trenches. They came almost immediately upon two parallel walls covered with the mutilated remains of large bas-reliefs and cuneiform inscriptions. A messenger was despatched to Mosul in order to inform their master of the great discovery. But well acquainted with the rich phantasy and flowery speech of the Arab race, Botta seriously doubted the truth of the extraordinary news so quickly received, and at first ordered a servant to the scene of excavations with instructions to inspect the work and bring him a more intelligent account of the actual finds. The required evidence was soon in Botta's possession. There could be no longer any doubt that this time the Arabs had spoken the full truth, and that most remarkable antiquities of a genuine Assyrian character had been brought to light. He now hastened at once to Khorsabad himself. His consular duties allowed him to remain only one day. But the few hours which he could spend in the trenches were well employed. Though the first sight of these strange sculptures and witnesses of a long-forgotten past which, out of the depth of a buried civilization, suddenly rose like the *fata morgana* before his astonished eyes, must have filled his soul with great excitement and rare delight, yet he could calm himself sufficiently to sit down among his Arab workmen, and sketch the most important reliefs and inscriptions for his friend in Paris.

On April 5, 1843, Botta wrote the first of a series of letters to Mohl, in which he briefly described what he had just seen, and expressed the hope that some way might be found for the safe transport and final preservation of the excavated treasures. His ardent desire was soon to be realized beyond expectation. It was a memorable day when his letter was submitted to the members of the *Societe Asiatique,* and the explorer's statement was read: "I believe myself to be the first who has discovered sculptures which with some reason can be referred to the period when Nineveh was flourishing." What could have appealed more strongly to the French nation! The impression which these simple and yet so significant words created in the scientific circles of France was extraordinary. The Academy of Paris at once requested the minister to grant the necessary funds for a continuation of the excavations (so far chiefly carried on at Botta's personal expense), and for the transport of all the objects recovered to Europe. With its old traditional spirit of munificence, and always ready to encourage and support undertakings which by their very nature were to shed

new lustre upon the name of France, the government granted the required sum, and a few months later despatched E. Flandin, well prepared by his work in Persia, to the assistance of Botta, in order to sketch all such monuments as could not safely be removed from Khorsabad. But half a year elapsed before the artist arrived at the ruins, and in the meanwhile Botta had to fight his way, blocked with numerous obstacles, to the best of his ability.
Published in *Journal Asiatique*, series iv., vol. ii., pp. 61-72 (dated
Many of the excavated sculptures had suffered considerably at the time when the great building was destroyed by fire. Resting only on the earth of the mound, they began to crumble as soon as the halls were cleared of rubbish and

April 5, 1843), with 12 plates; pp. 201-214 (May 2, 1843), with 9 plates; vol. iii., pp. 91—103 (June 2, 1843) and pp. 424-435 (July 24, 1843), with 17 plates; vol. iv., pp. 301-314 (Oct. 31, 1843), with 11 plate. Comp., also, his report to the Minister of the Interior (March 22, 1844) in vol. v., pp. 201-207.
exposed to light. He ordered large beams to prevent the collapse of the walls. But scarcely had he turned his back when the unscrupulous inhabitants of the village, always in need of wood, pillaged his supports, thus causing destruction. The heat of the summer and the rains of the winter interfered seriously with his progress, often damaging beyond recognition what with great labor and patience had just been rescued from the ground, sometimes even before he was able to examine the sculptures. The malarious condition of the whole region caused illness and death among his workmen, proving nearly fatal to his own life. The peasants of Khorsabad, suspicious beyond measure, and unwilling to aid his researches, refused to work and sell him their houses, which occupied the most important part of the ruins. In addition to all these constant worriments, necessarily affecting his mind and body, the governor of Mosul, with ever-increasing jealousy and cunning, tried in many ways to disheart-

en the explorer. He shared the general belief of his people that the foreigner was searching for treasures. Anxious to appropriate them himself, he frequently threw Botta's workmen into prison in order to extract a confession, or he appointed watchmen at the trenches to seize every piece of gold that might be discovered. When all this failed to have the desired effect, he closed the work altogether, on the pretext that Botta was evidently establishing a military station to take the country by force of arms from the sultan. At Paris and Constantinople everything was done by the French government and its representative to counteract these miserable machinations, and to prove the utter baselessness of the malicious accusations. Finally, well-directed energy, tact, and perseverance triumphed over all the obstacles and animosity of the native population. Botta gradually induced the chief of the village to abandon his house on the summit of the mound temporarily for a reasonable price, and to move down into the plain, where later the rest of the inhabitants followed, after the explorer's promise to restore the original contour of the mound as soon as the latter had been fully examined. Even before this agreement was entered into with the villagers, Botta had found it necessary to fill his trenches again after he had copied the inscriptions, drawn the sculptures, and removed those antiquities which could be transported, as the only way in which the large mass of crumbling reliefs could be saved for future research from their rapid destruction by the air. But it was not until the beginning of May, 1844, after the excavations had rested almost completely during the winter, that Flandin finally brought the necessary firman from Constantinople allowing the resumption of the excavations. Notwithstanding the approaching heat, no more time was lost. Three hundred Christian refugees were gradually engaged to excavate the unexplored part of the mound, Botta copying the inscriptions and Flandin preparing the drawings of the sculptures as soon as they had been exposed. Both

men worked with the greatest harmony, energy, and devotion during the whole oppressive summer, until, in October, 1844, after most remarkable success, the excavations were suspended temporarily.
A large mass of material was packed for shipment by raft down the Tigris to Basra, whence the Cormorant, a French man-of-war, in 1846, carried it safely to Havre. Flandin was the first to leave Khorsabad (November, 1844) and to return to Paris. His large portfolio of beautiful sketches and drawings had fairly prepared the way for the arrival of the originals. But when now these extraordinary monuments themselves had found a worthy place in the large halls of the Louvre, constituting the first great Assyrian museum of Europe; when these gigantic winged bulls, with their serene expression of dignified strength and intellectual power, and these fine reliefs illustrating the different scenes of peace and war of a bygone race before which the nations of Asia had trembled, stood there again before the eyes of Only interrupted by a short visit to Khorsabad in company with a few travellers, among them Mr. Dittel, sent by the Russian Minister of Public Instruction to inspect the excavations. In connection with this visit Botta even made a slight excavation in order to satisfy the curiosity of his guests.
the whole world, as a powerful witness to the beginning of a resurrection of an almost forgotten empire, the enthusiasm among all classes of France knew no bounds. By order of the government, and under the auspices of the Minister of the Interior, the most prominent members of the Institute of France were at once appointed a commission, under whose advice and cooperation Botta and Flandin were enabled to publish the results of their combined labors in a magnificent work of five large volumes. The excavations of the two explorers had penetrated into the interior of the mound of Khorsabad until all traces of walls disappeared. But a careful study of the plan drawn by Flandin had enabled them to infer that the great structure which yielded all these bas-reliefs

and inscriptions must formerly have extended considerably farther. From certain indications in the ground it became evident that a part of the monumental building had been intentionally destroyed in ancient times, but it was to be expected that another considerable part was still preserved somewhere in the unexplored sections of the mound. Stimulated by the hope of finding the lost trace again, Botta himself opened a number of trial trenches at various points. But all his exertions having failed, he came to the conclusion that everything that remained of the palace at Khorsabad had been excavated, and therefore he put a stop to the work on this ruin.

In the vear 1851 the French Assembly voted a sum of money for an expedition to be sent to Babylonia (which we shall discuss later), and another for the resumption of the suspended excavations at Khorsabad, to be directed by Victor Place, a skilful architect and Botta's successor as French consular agent at Mosul. Technically well prepared for his task, and faithfully supported in the trenches by Botta's intelligent foreman, Nahushi, who with many other former workmen had gladly reentered French employment, Place completed the systematic examination of the great palace and restored its ground-plan during the years 1 851-55. Under his supervision the excavations exposed all the remaining buildings and rooms attached to the sculptured halls, — a space about three times as large as that explored by his *Moniimint de Ninive detouvert it decrit par M. P. E. Botta, mesurl tt destine par M. E. Flandin,* 5 volumes with 400 plates, Paris, 1849-50.

Wall Decoration in Enamelled Tiles, Khorsabad predecessor, and successfully extended even to the walls of the town. In these outlying mounds he unearthed four simple and three very fine gates, flanked by large winged bulls and other sculptures, and their arches most beautifully decorated with friezes of blue and white enamelled tiles representing winged genii and animals, plants and rosettes, in excellent design and execution. At the angle formed by

two of the walls of the palace he made an especially valuable discovery in the form of an inscribed box serving as corner-stone, and containing seven tablets of different size, in gold, silver, copper, lead, lapis lazuli, magnesite, and limestone. They all bore identical cuneiform records pertaining to the history of these buildings.

It was not always very easy for Place to trace the rooms of the "harem" and the other smaller structures, as no sculptures like those discovered by Botta had adorned their walls and sustained the crumbling mass of unbaked bricks. But gradually his eyes became sharpened and were able to distinguish the faint outlines of walls from the surrounding earth and rubbish. Though his excavations did not yield Comp. Oppert, *Expedition en Mesopotamie,* vol. i., p. 349, note 2.

anything like the rich harvest in large monuments of art reaped bv his predecessor, as we have just seen, they were by no means deficient in them. But they were especially productive in those small objects of clay and stone, glass and metal, which in a welcome manner supplemented our knowledge of the life and customs and daily needs of the ancient Assyrians. Place discovered no less than fourteen inscribed barrel cylinders with historical records. He found a regular magazine of pottery, another full of colored tiles, and a third containing iron implements of every description in such a fine state of preservation that several of them were used at once by his Arab workmen. He unearthed even the waterclosets, the bakery and the "wine-cellar" of the king, the latter easily to be identified by a number of pointed jars resting in a double row of small holes on the paved floor, and discharging a strong smell of yeast after the first rain had dissolved their red sediments.

Unlike Botta, who, after his great discovery, most naturally had concentrated all his energy upon a systematic exploration of the mound of Khorsabad, Place made repeated excursions into the regions to the east and south of Mosul, examining many of the smaller mounds

with which the whole country is covered, and excavating for a few months without success at Qal'at Shirgat, the large Tell Shemamvk (about halfway between the Upper Zab and Krbil, to the southwest of the latter) and even in the neighborhood of Nimrud, which had yielded such extraordinary treasures to Layard. About the same time Knglish excavations were carried on bv Rassam, in the ruins just mentioned, under Rawlinson's direction, the Ottoman firman having granted to both the French and British governments the right of excavating "in anv ground belonging to the state." In consquence of this peculiar arrangement, the interests of the two European nations threatened frequently to clash against each other, a pardonable rivalry existing all the while between the different excavators, accompanied by a constant friction and illfeeling among their workmen. This was particularly the case at Qal'at Shirgat, where Rawlinson "made a distinct and categorical assertion of the British claims," and at Qoyunjuk, where, at Place's request, he had apportioned the northern half of the mound to the French representative— a compact which was later entirely ignored by Rassam on the ground that this mound was not state propertv, and that Rawlinson accordingly had no power to give away what did not belong to him. musicians, or attacking strong cities and castles, subduing foreign nations, punishing rebels, and leading back thousands of captives and innumerable spoil of every description. The private apartments of the monarch, which were much smaller and simpler, occupied the southeast wing, close to the harem or women's quarter. The latter was entirely separated from the other two sections, even its single rooms, as the traces of discovered hinges indicate, being closed by folding doors, while everywhere else the entrances appear to have been covered with curtains.

Comp. *Lettre it M. Place a M. Mohl sur une Expedition faite a Ar biles* (dated Mosul, Nov. 20, 1852) in the *Journal Asiatique,* series hr., vol. xx. (1852), pp. 441-470.

Unfortunately, a large part of the antiquities excavated by Victor Place at Khorsabad met with a sad fate. Together with sixty-eight cases of the finest bas-reliefs from Ashurbanapal's palace at Qoyunjuk, which Rawlinson had allowed him to select for the Louvre, and including all the results of Fresnel's expedition to Babylon, they were lost on two rafts in the Tigris on their way from Baghdad to Basra in the spring of 1855. But notwithstanding this lamentable misfortune, Place was enabled to submit to the public all those results which he had previously brought on paper in another magnificent work published by his liberal government.

The importance of all the discoveries at Khorsabad, brought about by the united efforts of Botta, Flandin, and Place, cannot be overrated. The mounds under which the monuments had been buried for twenty-five hundred years represented a whole fortified town, called after its founder, Comp. the interesting story of these quarrels as told by Rassam, "Asshur and the Land of Nimrod," New York, 1897, pp. 7, 12-27; d George Rawlinson, "Memoir of Major-General Sir Henry Creswicke Rawlinson," pp. 178, *seqq.* Victor Place, *Nitlive ct I' Assyrie, avec des essais de restauration par F. Thomas,* 3 volumes, Paris, 1866-69.
Sargon, the conqueror of Samaria (722 B. C), DGr-Sharruken or "Sargon's Castle." The walls by which the town was protected were found intact at their bases. They constituted a rectangular parallelogram, or nearly a square, pointing with its four corners to the cardinal points, and enclosing a space of a little over 741 acres. Its northwest side was interrupted bv the royal palace, which, like a huge bastion, protruded considerably into the plain, at the same time forming part of the great town-wall. The latter was provided with eight monumental gates, each of which was named after an Assyrian deity.

The royal residence was erected on a lofty terrace, nearly forty-five feet high and built of unbaked bricks cased with a wall of large square stones. At the northern corner of this raised platform, covering an area of nearly twenty-five acres of land, was an open place; near the western corner stood a temple, and at the centre of the southwest side rose the stage-tower belonging to it and used also for astronomical observations; the rest was occupied by the palace itself. This latter was divided into three sections, the seraglio occupying the centre of the terrace and extending towards the plain; the harem, with onlv two entrances, situated at the southern corner, and the domestic quarters at the eastern corner, connected with the store and provision rooms, the stables, kitchen, and bakerv, at the centre of the southeast side. The seraglio, inhabited by the king and his large retinue of militarv and civil officers, like the other two sections of the extensive building, consisted of a great many larger and smaller rooms grouped around several open courts. The northwest wing contained the public reception rooms, — wide halls, elaborately decorated with winged bulls, magnificent sculptures and historical inscriptions, glorifying the king in his actions of peace and war. We see him hunting wild animals, doing homage to the gods, sitting at the table and listening to the singers and

The floor of the different chambers as a rule was only stamped clay, upon which in many cases doubtless precious rugs had been spread. Here and there it was overlaid with tiles or marble blocks, which were especially employed for pavements in connection with courts and open spaces around the palace. The walls of the rooms, serving to exclude the intense heat of the summer, and to protect against the severe cold of the winter, were exceptionally thick. They varied between nine feet and a half and sixteen feet, and in one case reached the enormous thickness of even twenty-five feet and a half. Apart from the large reception rooms and gateways, which displayed all the splendor that Assyrian artists were able to give them, the inner walls were generally covered only with a white plaster surrounded by black lines, while the women's apartments were adorned more tastefully with fresco paintings and white or black arabesques. Marble

statues as a decorative element were found exclusively in the principal court of the harem. The exterior of the palace walls exhibited a system of groups of half-columns, separated bv dentated recesses or chasings, — the prevailing type of ancient Babylonian external architecture, as we shall see later.

It is impossible to enter into all the characteristic features which this remarkable complex must have presented to Sargon and his people, and as a careful study of the whole monument allowed Place and others gradually to restore it. The Assyrian architecture, previously completely unknown, appeared suddenly before us in all the details of a sumptuous building, adorned with sculptures and paintings which lead us back into the midst of Assyrian life during the eighth pre-Christian century. We get acquainted with the occupations of the king and his subjects, their customs, their pleasures, their mode of living, their religion, their art, and part of their literature. With great astonishment, artists and scholars began to realize how high a standard this people in the East had reached at a time when Europe as a whole was still in a state of barbarism. With extraordinary enthusiasm, students of philology and history welcomed the enormous mass of authentic material, which, in the hands of Rawlinson, Hincks, and Oppert, was soon to shed a flood of new light upon the person and reign and language of that great warrior, Sargon, so far known only by name from a statement in Isaiah (20: 1), and upon the whole history and geography of Western Asia shrouded in darkness, and which, bv its constant references to names and events mentioned in the Bible, was eagerlv called upon as an unexpected witness to test the truthfulness of the Holy Scriptures. There have been made other and even greater discoveries in Assyrian and Babvlonian ruins since Botta's far-reaching exploration of the mounds of Khorsabad, but there never has been aroused again such a deep and general interest in the excavation of distant Oriental sites as towards the middle of the last centurv, when Sargon's palace rose suddenly out of the ground, and furnished the first faithful picture of a great epoch of art which had vanished completely from human sight.

ENGLISH EXCAVATIONS AT NIMRUD, QOYUNJUK, AND QAL'AT SHIRGAT BY LAYARD, RASSAM, AND LOFTUS

The eagerness and determination of the scholar to decipher and understand those long cuneiform inscriptions which, like a commentary, accompanied the monuments of Khorsabad, could be satisfied only after the whole material had arrived and been published. In the meanwhile the new impulse given to archaeological studies by the announcement of Botta's success manifested itself at once in influencing a young Englishman to imitate the latter's example, and to start excavations at one of the most prominent Assyrian mounds, which, even two years before Botta's arrival at Mosul, he had viewed "with the design of thoroughly examining them whenever it might be in his power." The man who now, as England's champion, stepped forth into the international contest for great archaeological discoveries was so exceptionally qualified and prepared for his task by natural gifts and the experience of his past life, and at the same time so eminently successful in the choice of his methods and men, in the overcoming of extraordinary obstacles and difficulties, in the rapid obtaining of the most glorious results, and in the forcible and direct manner with which through the remarkable story of his rare achievements he appealed to the heart of his countrymen and to the sentiment of the whole educated world, that he at once became, and during the whole nineteenth century remained, the central figure of Assyrian exploration.

Sir Austen Henry Layard, the descendant of a Huguenot refugee who had settled in England, was born in Paris on March 5, 1817. In consequence of his father's illness, which frequently necessitated a change of climate, he spent much of his boyhood in France, Switzerland, and Italy, where, with all the deficiencies of a desultory and highly cosmopolitan education, he acquired a taste for the fine arts and archaeology, and that characteristic love for travel and adventure which prepared him so well for his later nomadic life and career as an explorer. When about sixteen years ot age he was sent to the house of his uncle in London to study law. But, to quote his own words, "after spending nearly six years in the office of a solicitor, and in the chambers of an eminent conveyancer, I determined for various reasons to leave England and to seek a career elsewhere." From his childhood well acquainted with several European languages, and familiar with the manners of men in various European lands, he now longed to see the fascinating Orient itself, the land of the "Arabian Nights," which had often inflamed his youthful mind. With the greatest eagerness he had devoured every volume of Eastern travel that fell in his way. The reading of the works of Morier, Malcolm, and Rich, and the personal acquaintance with men like Baillie Fraser (comp. pp. 54, seqq., above) and Sir Charles Fellowes, favorably known from his discoveries among the ruined cities of Asia Minor, had inspired him with an ardent desire to follow in their footsteps. In order to prepare himself for his journey, he had mastered the Arabic letters, picked up a little of the Persian language, taken lessons in the use of the sextant from a retired captain of the merchant service, and even hastily acquired a superficial medical knowledge of the treatment of wounds and certain Oriental diseases.

In the company of another enthusiastic traveller, E. L. Mitford, who, like Layard himself, has left us a narrative of this first interesting journey, the latter finally set out upon his "Early Adventures" in the summer of 1839, "with the intention of making his way through Turkey, Asia Minor, Syria, Persia, and India to Ceylon," where he expected to establish himself permanently. Not without difficulties and troublesome incidents the two associates reached Jerusalem in January, 1840, where they separated for a little while, Mitford declining to join in the perilous excursion to the ruins of Petra, Ammon, and Jerash, which Layard, passionately fond of adventures, undertook alone. Two months later he reached Aleppo, whence, together with Mitford, he travelled to Mosul and Baghdad. During their brief stay at the former place, the two travellers met Ainsworth, a prominent member of the British Euphrates Expedition, and Christian Rassam, brother of the later faithful friend and assistant of Layard, with both of whom they visited the ruins of Nineveh, Hammam 'All, Qal'at Shirgat, and El-Hadhr. It was in the month of April, 1840, in connection with this excursion down the western bank of the Tigris, that Layard, from an artificial eminence, for the first time looked upon the line of lofty mounds on the other side of the river, called Nimrud, where but shortly afterwards he was to raise " a lasting monument to his own fame." Comp. Layard, " Early Adventures in Persia, Susiana, and Babylonia, including a Residence among the Bakhtiyari and other Wild Tribes before he Discovery of Nineveh," ist cd., London, 1887, 2 vols. The second edition (London, 1894, I vol.), an abridgment of the first, and omitting a description of the countries through which Layard and Mitford travelled Together, has an introductory chapter on the author's life and work by his surviving friend, Lord Aberdare.

Mitford and Layard travelled together as far as Hamadan, whence on August 8 of the same year they finally parted, the former to continue his long and difficult journev to Kandahar, and the latter to engage in his adventurous life and perilous wanderings among the wild tribes of Persia and 'Iraq, until two years later, when we find him again at Mosul, stopping there for a little while on his way from Baghdad to Constantinople. Botta had meanwhile been appointed French consular agent, and tentatively cut a trench or two in the mound of Qoyunjuk. The two famous explorers met then and there — June, 1842 — for the first time, the one on the fair road to a great discovery, the other so far disappointed in his efforts to raise the necessary funds for similar excavations. Brief as this first meeting was, it formed the beginning of a friendly intercourse between the two great men, Layard, free from envy and jealousy, always encouraging Botta in his labors, and particularly calling his attention to Nimrud, the one place above others which he himself so eagerly desired to explore, when the paucity of results at Qoyunjuk threatened to dishearten his lonely friend.

Edward Ledwich Mitford, "A Land-March from England to Ceylon Forty Years Ago, through Dalmatia, Montenegro, Turkey, Asia Minor, Syria, Palestine, Assyria, Persia, Afghanistan, Scinde, and India," London, 1884, 2 vols. Comp. pp. 57, *seqq.,* above.

Robbed as he frequently was, and exposed to hardships and dangers of every kind, repeatedly even at the point of losing his life, Layard never ceased to "look back with feelings of grateful delight to those happy days when, free and unheeded, we left at dawn the humble cottage or cheerful tent, and lingering as we listed, unconscious of distance and of the hour, found ourselves as the sun went down under some hoary ruin tenanted by the wandering Arab, or in some crumbling village still bearing a wellknown name. No experienced dragoman measured our distances and appointed our stations. We were honored with no conversations by pashas, nor did we seek any civilities from governors. We neither drew tears nor curses from villagers by seizing their horses, or searching their houses for provisions: their welcome was sincere; their scanty fare was placed before us; we ate and came and went in peace."

At a time when every moment the chronic dispute as to the actual boundary line between Turkey and Persia threatened to lead to a serious war which might prove detrimental to British interests in those countries, Layard's intimate knowledge of the territory in dispute proved of great value to Sir Stratford Canning (afterwards Lord Stratford de Redcliffe), then British ambassador at the Porte in Constantinople, whither our traveller had hastened. Though for apparent political reasons the Russian point of view was finally

accepted by England, much against Canning's protest and his own very decided conviction, Layard had found in this man of influence a liberal patron, who during the following years entrusted him with many important missions, endeavoring all the time to have him definitely attached to his staff. While thus waiting at the shore of the Bosphorus for a much coveted position, Layard remained in regular correspondence with Botta, whose reports and drawings he received before they were published. The latter's unexpected brilliant success at Khorsabad brought him new encouragement for his own plans, and increased his hope and desire to return on some future day to Mesopotamia and excavate the ruins of Nineveh. With his mind firmly fixed upon this one object of his life, he commenced "the study of the Semitic languages, to which I conjectured the cuneiform inscriptions from the Assyrian ruins belonged."' But when he saw Sir Stratford making arrangements for a temporary return to England, he became tired of waiting longer for his promised attacheship, and one day spoke to the latter of his ardent desire to examine the mounds near Mosul. To his great delight, his generous patron not only approved of his suggestion, but offered *j.6o* (=$300) towards the expenses which would be incurred in making tentative Comp. "Early Adventures," 2d edition, p. 409. We quote the above statement literally, in order to *show* that Layard, with his well-known intuition, divined the truth later established, even before Lowenstein expressed the same thought in his *Essai dt dechifrement de l' Etriture Assyriennt pour servir a P explication du Monument de Khonabad,* Paris and Leipzig, 1845, pp. 12, *ieq.* excavations. Who was happier than Layard! Without a servant, and without any other effects than a pair of large saddle-bags, but with a cheerful heart, and, above all, with this modest sum in his pocket, increased by a few pounds from his own meagre resources, he started in October, 1845, / to excavate Nineveh. How eagerly Layard turned his face towards the place in which all his hopes had centred for the

past five years we may easily infer from the fact that, like a Tartar, he travelled by day and night without rest, crossing the mountains of Kurdistan and galloping over the plains of Assyria, until he reached Mosul, twelve days after his departure from Samsun.

First Expedition, 1845-1847. Profiting by the experience of Botta, Layard deemed it best for the time being to conceal the real object of his journey from the ill-disposed governor and the inhabitants of Mosul. On the 8th of November, having secretly procured a few tools, he left the town with "guns, spears, and other formidable weapons," ostensibly to hunt wild boars in a neighboring district. Accompanied by Mr. Ross, a British resident merchant, who in many ways facilitated the work of our explorer during his long stay in Assyria, and by a mason and two servants, he floated down the Tigris on a small raft, reaching Nimrud the same night. With six untrained Arabs, he commenced work at two different points of the ruins on the following morning. Like the mounds of Khorsabad, the ruins of Nimrud represent a clearly defined rectangular parallelo-"' gram, rising above the ground as a plateau of considerable height and extent, and pointing with its two smaller sides to the north and south respectively. A lofty cone, from the distance strikingly resembling a mountain of volcanic origin, and constituting the most characteristic feature of this conglomeration of furrowed hills, occupies their northwest corner. During the early spring the whole mound is clothed with a luxuriant growth of grass and many-colored flowers. Black Arab tents and herds of grazing sheep, watched by the youngest members of some Bedouin tribe, are scattered over the ruins, relieving the monotony of the region for a few months. But when the rays of the sun and the scorching winds from the desert have turned the pleasant picture of a short but cheerful life again into a parched and barren waste, the human eye wanders unobstructed over the whole plateau, meeting numerous fragments of stone and pottery everywhere. The absence of all vegetation in

November enabled Layard to examine the remains with which the site was covered without difficulty. Following up the result of this general survey, which convinced him " that sculptured remains must still exist in some part of the mound," he placed three of his workmen at a spot near the middle of the west side of the ruins, and the other three at the southwest corner. Before night interrupted their first day's labors, they had partly excavated two chambers lined with alabaster slabs, all of which bore cuneiform inscriptions at their centres. The slabs from the chamber in the northwest section of the mound were in a fine state of preservation, while those from the southwest corner evidently had been exposed to intense heat, which had cracked them in every part. Remains of extensive buildings had thus been brought to light within a few hours. Soon afterwards it became apparent that Layard had discovered two Assyrian palaces on the verv first day of his excavations.

Exceedingly pleased with these unexpected results, Layard established his headquarters at once in the least ruined house of a deserted village which was only twenty minutes' walk from the scene of his labors. On the next morning he increased his force by five Turcomans from Selamtye, situated three miles farther up the river, a place to which he had soon to remove himself in consequence of the hazards of the region around Nimrud. On the third day he opened a trench in the high conical mound at the northwest corner, but finding nothing but fragments of inscribed brick, little appreciated in those early days of Assyrian exploration, he abandoned this section again, and concentrated his eleven men for the next time upon the southwest corner of the ruins, " where the many ramifications of the building already identified promised speedier success." A few days later he hurried to Mosul to acquaint the pasha with the object of his researches. A tiny piece of gold-leaf, recently discovered at Nimrud, had already found its way into the writing-tray of the latter, and roused his suspicion. Other signs indicated that a formidable opposition was gradually forming to prevent Knglish excavations. Layard, not protected by a firman from the Sultan, recognized what was coming. But as the governor, whose greediness had reduced the whole province to utter poverty and lawlessness, had not as yet openly declared against his proceedings, our explorer lost no time to push his researches as much as possible. He sent agents to several conspicuous ruins between the Tigris and the Zab, " in order to ascertain the existence of sculptured buildings in some part of the country," at the same time increasing his own party to thirty men at the southwest corner of Nimrud. It was soon found that the inscriptions on all the slabs so far exposed were identical with those unearthed in the northwest building, and that in everv case a few letters had been cut away at the edges in order to make the stones fit into the wall. "From these facts it became evident that materials taken from another building had been used " in the construction of the one which Layard was exploring. No sculptures, however, had so far been disclosed.

Winter rains were now setting in, and the excavations proceeded but slowly. The hours given to rest in the miserable hovel at Selamiye were spent most uncomfortably. The roofs of the house were leaking, and a perfect torrent descended on the floor and the rug on which the explorer was lying. "Crouched up in a corner, or under a rude table," which was surrounded by trenches to carry off" the accumulating water, he usually passed the night on these occasions. Finally, on the 28th of November, after he had ordered to clear the earth away from both sides of newlv exposed slabs, the first bas-reliefs were discovered. Layard and his Arabs were equally excited, and notwithstanding a violent shower of rain, they worked enthusiastically until dark. But their joy did not last very long; the next day the governor of Mosul closed the excavations at Nimrud. French jealousy, Mohammedan prejudices, and the pasha's own ill-will were equally responsible for this unfortunate result. There remained nothing for Layard but to acquiesce. At his own request, however, a *qawwas* was sent to the mounds as representative of the Ottoman government, while he pretended only to draw the sculptures and copy the inscriptions which had already been uncovered. It was not difficult for him to induce this officer to allow the employment of a few workmen to guard the sculptures during the day. In reality, they were sent to different sections of the mound to search for other sculptures and inscribed monuments. The experiment was very successful. Without being interrupted in his attempt, Layard uncovered several large figures, uninjured by fire, near the west edge, a crouching lion at the southeast corner, the torsos of a pair of gigantic winged bulls, two small winged lions, likewise mutilated, and a human figure nine feet high, in the centre of the mound. Though only detached and unconnected walls had been found so far, "there was no longer any doubt of the existence not only of sculptures and inscriptions, but even of vast edifices, in the interior of the mound of Nimrud." Nearly six weeks of undivided attention and constant exposure to hardships had been devoted to the exploration of the ruins. Layard now decided to lose no more time in opening new trenches, but to inform Sir Stratford Canning how successfully the first part of his mission had been carried through, and to urge "the necessity of a firman, which would prevent any future interference on the part of the authorities or the inhabitants of the country."

Towards the end of 1845 — about the time when this letter was written — one of the chief obstacles to archaeological research in Assyria for the time being was suddenly removed. The old governor was replaced by an enlightened, just, and tolerant officer of the new school. With a view of quietly awaiting the beneficial result of this radical change in the administration for the province as a whole, and for his own work at Nimrud, Layard covered over the sculptures brought to light, and withdrew altogether from the ruins. He descended the Tigris on a raft, and spent Christmas with Major Rawlinson, whom he desired to consult concerning the arrangements to be made for the removal of the sculptures at a future period. The two great English pioneers met then for the first time. "It was a happy chance which brought together two such men as Lavard and Rawlinson as laborers at the same time and in the same field, but each with his special task — each strongest where the other was weakest — Layard, the excavator, the effective task-master, the hard-working and judicious gatherer together of materials; and Rawlinson, the classical scholar, the linguist, the diligent student of history, the man at once of wide reading and keen insight, the cool, dispassionate investigator and weigher of evidence. The two men mutually esteemed and respected each other, and they were readv to assist each other to the utmost of their power."'

At the beginning of January, i 846, Layard returned to Mosul. The change since his departure had been as sudden as great. A few conciliatory acts on the part of the new governor had quickly restored confidence among the inhabitants of the province. Even the Bedouins were returning to their old camping grounds between the Tigris and Zab, from which for a long while they had been excluded. The incessant winter rains had brought forward the vegetation of the spring, and the surface and sides of Nimrud were clothed in a pleasing green. Security having been established in this part of the country, the mound itself now offered a more convenient and more agreeable residence to Layard than the distant village of Selamiye. Accompanied by a number of workmen and by Hormuzd Rassam, an intelligent Chaldean Christian and brother of the British viceconsul at Mosul, who henceforth acted as his reliable agent and overseer, he therefore moved at once to his new dwelling-place at Nimrud. The polite governor had offered no objection to the continuation of his labors, but another month elapsed before he could venture to resume his excavations. For the *qadi* of Mosul once

more had stirred up the people of the town against the explorer, so that it was found necessary to postpone work until the storm had passed away.

Comp. George Rawlinson, ' A Memoir of Major-General Sir Henry Creswicke Rawlinson," London, 1898, p. 152.

It was near the middle of February before Layard could make some fresh experiments at the southwest corner of the mound. Slab after slab was exposed, by which it was proved that "the building had not been entirely destroyed by fire, but had been partly exposed to gradual decay." But in order to arouse the necessary interest in England, he needed much better preserved sculptures. Abandoning, therefore, the edifice, which until then had received his principal attention, he placed the workmen at the centre of a ravine which ran far into the west side of the mound, near the spot where he had previously unearthed the first complete monuments. His labors here were followed by an immediate success. He came upon a large hall, in which all the slabs were not only in their original position, but in the finest state of preservation. It soon became evident that he had found the earliest palace of Nimrud, from which'" manv of the sculptures employed in the construction of the southwest building had been quarried.

On the morning following these discoveries he rode to the encampment of a neighboring shaikh, and was returning to his trenches, when he observed two Arabs of the latter's tribe "urging their mares to the top of their speed. On approaching him they stopped. 'Hasten, O Bey,' exclaimed one of them; 'hasten to the diggers, for thev have found Nimrod himself. Wallah, it is wonderful, but it is true! we have seen him with our eyes. There is no God but God;' and both joining in this pious exclamation, thev galloped off without further words in the direction of their tents." On reaching the ruins, he ascertained that the workmen had discovered the enormous human., head of one of those winged lions which now adorn the'/ British Museum. An equally well preserved corresponding figure was disclosed before nightfall

about twelve feet away in the rubbish, both forming the southern entrance into a chamber. Unfortunately " one of the workmen, on catching the first glimpse of the monster, had thrown down his basket and run off towards Mosul as fast as his legs could earn him.... He had scarcely checked his speed before reaching the bridge. F.ntering breathless into the bazaars, he announced to every one he met that Nimrod had appeared. " The result of this unexpected occurrence became quicklv apparent. The governor, "not remembering very clearly whether Nimrod was a true-believing prophet or an infidel," sent a somewhat unintelligible message "to the effect that the remains should be treated with respect, and be bv no means further disturbed, and that he wished the excavations to be stopped at once." This was practically the last interference with Layard's work on the part of the Mohammedan population. In accordance with the official request, the operations were discontinued until the general excitement in the town had somewhat subsided. Only two workmen were retained, who by the end of March discovered a second pair of winged human-headed lions, differing considerably in form from those previously unearthed, but likewise covered with very fine cuneiform inscriptions. Not many days afterwards, the much desired firman was finally received from Constantinople. It was as comprehensive as possible, "authorizing the continuation of the excavations, and the removal of such objects as might be discovered."

One of the greatest difficuMes so far encountered had now disappeared completely. Still; the necessary financial support was wanting, and Layard had to pursue his researches as best he could with the rapidly decreasing small means at his disposal. But bold as he was, and thoroughly enjoying the newly obtained privilege, he began at that very time to cut his first tentative trenches into the mound of 0yyjTJuk, opposite Mosul. Notwithstanding all his poverty, and regardless of the French consul's unwarranted opposition, he continued his excavations on the southern face, where the mound was highest, for about a month, until he had convinced himself, from fragments of sculptures and inscribed bricks, " that the remains were those of a building contemporary, or nearly so, with Khorsabad, and consequently of a more recent epoch than the most ancient palace of Nimrud." Meanwhile, the almost intolerable heat of the Assyrian summer had commenced. Hot winds and flights of locusts soon destroyed what had been left of the green plants of the desert and the few patches of cultivation along the river. Yet Layard felt little inclined to yield to circumstances which drove even the Bedouins into more northern districts. He was still under the refreshing influence of a brief visit which, with a cheerful party of Christian and Mohammedan ladies and gentlemen from Mosul, he had paid to the principal shaikh of the Shammarand to the lonely ruins of El-Hadhr, on the west side of the Tigris, during the recent suspension of his work. No wonder, then, that, after his excavations at Qoyunjuk, he returned to Nimrud again, and with about thirty men resumed his examination of the contents and extent of the large northwest building, which had previously furnished the well-preserved monuments. His Arabs, standing completely under the spell of his personal magnetism, seemed to feel as much interest in the objects disclosed as their enthusiastic master. As each head of all these strange figures was uncovered, "they showed their amazement by extravagant gestures or exclamations of surprise. If it was a bearded man, they concluded at once that it was an idol or a *jin,* and cursed or spat upon it. If a eunuch, they declared that it was the likeness of a beautiful female, and kissed or patted the cheek."

By the end of July so many fine bas-reliefs had been discovered in this building that Layard decided to make an effort to send a representative collection to England. Rawlinson's attempt at despatching the small steamer Nitocris, commanded by Felix Jones, directly to Nimrud for their embarkation to Baghdad, failed. Layard was therefore oblig-

ed to follow Botta's example and forward the smaller sculptures, the weight of which was reduced by cutting from the back, on a raft to Basra, which they reached safely some time in August. The explorer's health began now visibly to suffer from continual exposure to the excessive heat. A week's stay at Mosul, during which he discovered a gateway flanked bv two mutilated winged figures and cuneiform inscriptions with the name of Sennacherib in the northern boundary wall of Qoyunjuk, seemed to have refreshed him sufficiently to warrant his return to Nimrud. He uncovered the tops of many more slabs, bearing either similar sculptures or having only the usual inscription across them; but before August was over it was very evident that he required a cooler climate to regain his former vigor. Leaving, therefore, a few guards at the mound to protect his antiquities, and accompanied by Rassam and a few servants and irregular soldiers, he departed to the Tiyari Mountains, to the north of Mosul. The next two months were given entirely to rest and to his old favorite wanderings among the mountains and valleys of Kurdistan. The beautiful scenery and the exhilarating climate of these romantic districts, in which Kurdish tribes, Chaldean Christians, and the remarkable sect of the Yezidis or "Worshippers of the Devil," followed each their peculiar habits and interesting customs, soon completely restored him to health.

Towards the end of October, after his return from an expedition into the Sinjar Mountains, on which he had accompanied the pasha of Mosul and his soldiers, we find him again in the trenches of Nimrud. Important changes had taken place during his absence with regard to the character of his excavations. So far they had been conducted as a private undertaking for the account of Sir Stratford Canning. Letters were now received from England advising him that the latter had presented the sculptures discovered in Assyrian ruins, together with all the privileges connected with the imperial firman, to the British nation. In consequence of this generous act of the ambassador, a grant of funds

had been placed at the disposal of the British Museum " for the continuation of the researches commenced at Nimrud and elsewhere." This part of the news was encouraging, but, alas, the grant was very small, considerably smaller than the sum given by the French government to Botta for the exploration of Khorsabad. And the British grant was to include even " private expenses, those of carriage, and many extraordinary outlays inevitable in the East." But though the funds were scarcely adequate to the objects in view, Layard accepted the charge of superintending the excavations, and made every exertion to procure as many antiquities as possible. In the interest of science it remains a cause of deep regret that after his great discoveries, Layard did not at once find the same hearty support in England as his more fortunate French colleague so speedily had obtained in Paris. Not even an artist was despatched to draw the sculptures and copy the inscriptions, though many of the monuments "were in too dilapidated a condition to be removed," and though Layard " had neither knowledge nor experience as a draughtsman, — a disqualification which he could scarcely hope to overcome." He was thus practically prevented by his own government from making a methodical exploration of Nimrud. And this lack of method, system, and thoroughness unfortunately remained a characteristic feature of most of the following / Knglish excavations in Assyrian and Babylonian ruins, — a lack felt by nobody more keenly than by Layard, Loftus, and all the other great British explorers. Let us hear what Layard himself has to say on this system of unscientific pillage, justified to a certain degree only at the beginning of his excavations, but entirely to be condemned as soon as they were carried on under the auspices of a great nation. "The smallness of the sum placed at my disposal compelled me to follow the same plan in the excavations that I had hitherto adopted — *viz.,* to dig trenches along the sides of the chambers, and to expose the whole of the slabs, without removing the earth from the centre. Thus, few of the chambers were fully explored, and many small objects of great interest may have been left undiscovered. As I was directed to bury the building with earth after I had explored it, to avoid unnecessary expense I filled up the chambers with the rubbish taken from those subsequently uncovered, having first examined the walls, copied the inscriptions, and drawn the sculptures." From many other similar passages in his books we quote only the following two, in which he complains: "As the means at my disposal did not warrant any outlay in making more experiments without the promise of the discovery of something to carry away, I felt myself compelled, much against my inclination, to abandon the excavations in this part of the mound, after uncovering portions of two chambers." Or again: "If, after carrying a trench to a reasonable depth and distance, no remains of sculpture or inscription appeared, I abandoned it and renewed the experiment elsewhere."

In view of the unsatisfactory manner in which the excavations at Nimrud were now conducted, it would be an exceedingly unpleasant task to follow Layard into all the different trenches which he cut at many parts of the mound for no other purpose than to obtain the largest possible number of well-preserved objects of art at the least possible outlay of time and money. The winter season was fast approaching. In order to protect himself sufficiently against the dangers of the climate and the thievish inclinations of the marauding Bedouins, he constructed his own house in the plain near the ruins, and settled the Arab workmen with their families and friends around this temporary abode. Fifty strong Nestorian Christians, who wielded the pickaxe in the trenches, were quartered with their wives and children in a house on the mound itself. By the first of November the excavations were recommenced on a large scale at different sections: at the northwest and southwest buildings, in the centre of the mound, near the gigantic bulls mentioned above; in the southeast corner, where no walls as yet had

been discovered, and in other parts of the ruins hitherto unexamined. The first six weeks following this new arrangement " were amongst the most prosperous and fruitful in events" during all his researches in Assyria. Scarcely a day passed by without some new and important discovery. The trenches carried to a considerable depth in the southeast corner yielded at first nothing but inscribed bricks and pottery and several clay coffins of a late period; but those in the southwest palace brought to light a number of very valuable antiquities. Among other relics of the past, Layard found a crouching lion in alabaster, a pair of winged lions in a coarse limestone, the bodies of two lions carved out of one stone and forming a pedestal; the statues of two exquisite but crumbling sphinxes, and several interesting bas-reliefs uniting the head of an eagle or a lion with the body and arms of a man. He could now definitely prove that the slabs hitherto found in this section of the mound, and originally chiefly brought from the northwest edifice, were never meant to be exposed to view in the later palace. "They were, in fact, placed against the wall of sun-dried bricks, and the back of the slab, smoothed preparatory to being resculptured, was turned towards the interior of the chambers." In order to ascertain, therefore, the name of the king who built this palace, he had to dig behind the slabs. By continuing his researches in this new light, he soon found cuneiform inscriptions which bore the name of Ksarhaddon, king of Assyria (2 Kings 19:37).

Important as all these discoveries turned out to be, they were far surpassed by his finds in two other sections of the ruins. In the largest room of the northwest palace, which apparently had served as the royal reception hall, a series of the most beautiful and most interesting sculptures were brought to light, glorifying King Ashurnasirapal (885-860 B. c.) in war and peace. All the scenes are realistic and full of life, executed with great care and spirit. Here the monarch is followed by his warriors, himself standing in a chariot and dis-

charging arrows, while enemies are tumbling from their horses or falling from the turrets of a besieged city; there, in a boat, he is crossing a river full of tortoises and fishes, and lined with date-groves and gardens; then, again, he receives the prisoners, led by warriors and counted by scribes, or he is returning victoriously in procession, followed by his army and preceded by musicians and standard-bearers, while above them fly vultures with human heads in their talons. In other smaller chambers close by the principal hall, Layard found a number of bottles in glass and alabaster, bearing the name and titles of Sargon, who lived 150 years later, and, furthermore, he rescued from the rubbish sixteen copper lions, having served as weights, and a large quantity of iron scales of Assyrian armor and several perfect helmets in copper, immediately falling to pieces, which in a welcome manner helped to interpret the sculptures on the walls.

It was in the central building, however, that one of the most remarkable and important discoveries awaited the explorer. From a brick which apparently contained the genealogy of the builder, he concluded correctly at once that this third palace had been constructed by " the son of the founder of the earlier northwest edifice." He next came upon slabs with gigantic winged figures, and upon the fragments of a large winged bull in yellow limestone. The trench had reached the considerable length of fifty feet without yielding any valuable antiquity, and Layard was already planning to abandon his researches in this part of the mound as fruitless, when suddenly an obelisk of black marble, nearly seven feet high, lying on its side, but in admirable preservation, was unearthed by his workmen. y It was the famous obelisk of King Shalmaneser II. (860— 825 B. c), who had erected this stele of victory in his palace to commemorate the leading military events of his government. Sculptured on all four sides, it shows twenty small bas-reliefs, and above, below, and between them 210 lines of cuneiform inscription, containing the interesting passage above the second series of reliefs: "I received the tribute of Jehu, son of Omri, silver, gold, etc." (comp. 1 Kings 19:16, *sec/.;* *1 Kings,* chaps. 9 and 10). Until the present day this black obelisk has remained one of the choicest historical monuments ever rescued from the mounds of Assyria. Layard was not slow in recognizing the exceptional value of this precious relic. It was at once packed carefully, and a gang of trustworthy Arabs were placed near it at night, until shortly afterwards, on Christmas day, 1846, with twenty-two other cases of antiquities, it could be safely sent to Rawlinson, who, a few months later, wrote the first tentative exposition of the contents of its inscription. As Layard was able to determine from the repeated occurrence *of* the two cuneiform signs for "son" and "king," which even then had been recognized as such by the decipherers.

The first four months of 1847 were devoted principally to the exploration of the large northwest palace of Ashurnasirapal, where the sculptures and inscriptions, not having been exposed to a conflagration, as a rule were found in admirable preservation. By the end of April, Layard had explored twenty-eight halls and chambers, sometimes painted with figures and ornaments on a thin coating of plaster, but more frequently cased with alabaster slabs representing the monarch's wars and hunting expeditions, large winged figures separated by the sacred tree, various religious ceremonies, and elaborate scroll-work. Besides these larger monuments, he discovered numerous smaller objects of art, such as ivory ornaments betraying Egyptian origin or influence, three lions' paws in copper, different vases in clay and metal, and many baked bricks elaborately painted with animals, flowers, and cuneiform characters, which apparently had decorated the walls above the sculptures.

In a letter addressed to the Royal Asiatic Society, dated June 19, 1847.

In the ruins of the central edifice, which, with the northwest palace, had been used as a quarry to supply material for the southwest palace, he uncovered over one hundred sculptured slabs "packed in rows, one against the other," and "placed in a regular series, according to the subjects upon them." Nearly all the trenches which he opened in different parts of the mound, particularly, also, in the southeast corner and near the west edge, exposed to view traces of buildings, brick pavements, remains of walls and chambers, and fragments of sculptures. In his endeavor "to ascertain the nature of the wall surrounding the inner buildings," he found it to be nearly fifty feet thick, constructed of sun-dried bricks, and in its centre containing the first Assyrian arch ever discovered.

Until the end of April, thirteen pairs of the gigantic winged bulls and lions and several fragments of others had rewarded his labors. The authorities in London, not contemplating the removal of any of these enormous sculptures for the present, had determined that they " should not be sawn into pieces, to be put together again in Europe, as the pair of bulls sent from Khorsabad to Paris," but that they were to remain at Nimrud covered with earth, " until some favorable opportunity of moving them entire might occur." But Lavard was not the man to leave behind the most imposing of all the monuments unearthed, without making a serious effort to ship them. Accordingly he selected one of the best-preserved smaller bulls and a similar lion, and strained his brain and resources to the utmost to move them. With infinite toil and skill he succeeded. On the 22d of April, the two large monuments, with the finest bas-reliefs and above thirty cases of smaller objects found in the ruins, as a third cargo, left the mound on rafts for Basra, where they arrived safely, and were transshipped later to England. According to the instructions received from the trustees of the British Museum, the Assyrian palaces, which for a short while had been exposed to the light of day, as the last remains of the Biblical city of Calah (Gen. 10: n), telling their wonderful stories of human glory and decay, were soon reburied.

By the middle of May, Layard had finished his work and left Nimrud. But he did not quit the banks of the Tigris without having opened trenches at two other ruins. In the course of the first months of 1847, he had found an opportunity to visit the mound of Qal'at Shirgat, notoriously dangerous as "a place of rendezvous for all plundering parties. " A first general description of the ruins had been given by Ainsworth, with whom he had explored this neighborhood seven years before. The large extent of the mounds, which in size compare favorably with those of Nimrud and Qoyunjuk, and "a tradition current amongst the Arabs that strange figures carved in black stone still existed among the ruins," had excited his curiosity anew. He therefore sent a few gangs of Arab workmen down the river to excavate at the most promising points. Shortly afterwards he himself followed, spending two davs at the ruins in company with a shaikh of the Jebur, who was in search of fresh pastures for the flocks of his tribe. The hasty excavations, carried on principally on the western side of the mound, brought to light only a mutilated but very interesting sitting figure in black basalt, of life size, and on three sides covered with a , cuneiform inscription of Shalmaneser II., inscribed bricks of the same ruler, bits of boundary stones, fragments of slabs with cuneiform characters, and a few tombs with their usual contents belonging to a late period. Layard tried to have researches at this much exposed site continued under the superintendence of a Nestorian Christian, even after his departure, but repeated attacks from the Bedouins forced his workmen soon to withdraw. The sitting figure, as the first Assyrian statue discovered, was later sent by Mr. Ross, whom we have mentioned above, to London.

Comp. the illustration facing p. 93. "The present surface of Nimrud is a picture of utter destruction," many of the slabs and sculptures which could not be removed being only half buried. Comp. Sachau, *Am Euphrat und Tigris,* Leipzig, 1900, p. 105. In the "Journal of the Royal Geographical Society," vol. xi.

A small sum of money still remained after Layard had closed his trenches at Nimrud. He proposed, therefore, to devote it to a renewed personal search for the ruins of Nineveh in the mounds opposite Mosul. The prejudices of the Mohammedan population forbidding explorations at Nebi Yunus, as we have seen in connection with Botta's attempts, he devoted a month of concentrated attention to the mound of Qoyunjuk, where he had cut a few trenches in the previous year. His Arab basket men pitched their tents on the summit of the mound, the Nestorian diggers at its foot, while he himself spent the nights in the town and the days in the field. Well acquainted with the nature and position of Assyrian palaces as he was from his experience at Nimrud, he now set to work at first to discover the platform of sundried bricks upon which large edifices were generally constructed. At a depth of twenty feet he reached it, as he had expected. His next move was to open long trenches to its level in different directions near the southwest corner, until one morning the workmen came upon a wall, and following it, found an entrance formed by winged bulls, and leading into a hall. After four weeks' labor, nine long and narrow chambers of a large building destroyed by fire had been explored. In consequence of the conflagration most of the bas-reliefs, about ten feet high and from eight to nine feet wide, and four pairs of human-headed winged bulls, all of which had lined the walls, were reduced to lime. Perfect inscriptions were not very numerous, except on the bricks. But enough of the writing remained to show that Layard had discovered the t Assyrian palarp in the long-forgotten and ruined city of Nineveh. The monuments were too much destroyed to think of their removal. "A fisherman fishing with hook and line in a pond " was almost the only fragment of sculpture which Layard could send home as a first specimen of Assyrian art from Sennacherib's palace at Nineveh. Two more chambers, several other slabs, and a fairly preserved boundary stone with a long inscription were soon afterwards discovered by Ross in another wing of the same building.

On the 24th of June, 1847, Layard,

accompanied by Rassam, left Mosul to return to Constantinople and England. The ruins which he had examined were, to quote his own words," very inadequately explored." But with all his enthusiasm, energy, and constant exposure to dangers, he could do no better, considering the very small means at his disposal and the demands made upon him. After nearly two years of solid labor the tangible results were enormous. _ He had identified the sites of the Biblical Calah (Nimrud) and Nineveh, the capital of the Assyrian empire (in part represented by Qoyunjuk), as the inscriptions unearthed soon taught us. Moreover, he had discovered remains of no less than eight Assyrian palaces. At Nimrud, he found the northwest palace constructed by Ashurnasirapal 1. (885-860 B. c),and, in part at least, restored and reoccupied by Sargon (722-705 B. c.); the central palace erected by Shalmaneser II. (860-825 --'» rebuilt almost entirely by the Biblical Pul or Tiglath-Pileser III. (745-727 B. c.);' The great inscribed bulb and the black obelisk belonged to the older between these two, at the west edge of the mound, a smaller palace of Adadnirari III. (812-783 B.c.); in the southwest corner the palace of Esarhaddon (681-668 B. c.), who largely employed older materials from the northwest and central palaces; and in the southeast corner the insignificant remains of a building of Ashuretililani (after 626 B. c.), grandson of Esarhaddon and one of the last rulers of the Assyrian empire. And in addition to these seven palaces at Calah, he had discovered and partly excavated the large palace of Sennacherib (705-681 B.c.) at Nineveh. Indeed, he had accomplished a glorious work —and a munificent gift from the British nation awaited him at home. "As a reward for my various services and for my discoveries, I was appointed an unpaid attache of Her Majesty's Embassy at Constantinople."

It was not until the spring of 1848 that Layard received orders to proceed to his new post in Turkey. The halfyear immediately preceding his departure for the Bosphorus was principally devoted to the preparation of the narrative of his

first expedition, and to supervising the printing of the illustrations of the monuments and of the copies of the inscriptions recovered. These books, published during his absence from England, created an extraordinary impression throughout Europe, far beyond anything he could ever have dreamed of. It was in particular his popular narrative, king, while the series of over one hundred slabs, representing battles and sieges, and arranged as if" ready for removal (comp. p. 108), formed part of the decorations of the palace of Tiglath-Pileser III.

Comp. Austen H. Layard, "Early Adventures in Persia, Stisiana, and Babylonia," zd ed., London, 1894, p. 426 (the closing words of the whole book). Layard, " Nineveh and its Remains, a Narrative of a First Expedition to Nineveh," London, 1848. Layard, "The Monuments of Nineveh, from Drawings Made on the Spot," series i., 100 plates, London, 1849. Layard, "Inscriptions in the Cuneiform Character from Assyrian Monuments," 98 plates, London, 1851. written almost in the style of a fascinating novel, enlivened by the numerous stories of his difficulties and adventures, and interwoven with faithful accounts of the habits and customs of many different tribes, which had a marvellous success with the public. Though entirely unfamiliar with the contents of the cuneiform inscriptions, he had a rare gift of combination, and he understood in a masterly manner how to interpret the sculptures on the walls of the Assyrian palaces, and to illustrate the Scriptures and profane writers from these long-buried sources. The pressure of public opinion was now brought to bear upon the British government. Before many months had passed, Layard received an urgent request from the British Museum to lead a second expedition to Nineveh, and he readily consented to go. *Second Expedition, 1849-1851.* This time, Layard was better assisted and equipped with funds than previously. F. Cooper, a competent artist, had been selected to draw those bas-reliefs and sculptures which injury and decay had rendered unfit for removal, and Dr. Sandwith, a physician, who was on a visit to the East, was soon induced to join his party. Accompanied by these two Englishmen and by Hormuzd Rassam, his former faithful companion, he left Constantinople on the 28th of August, 1849, by a British steamer bound for the Black Sea. Three days later they disembarked and took the direct land route to Mosul *via* Erzerum and Lake Wan. On the first of October they were at Qovunjuk again. Since Layard's return to Europe in 1847, little had been done at these ruins. For a short while Mr. Ross, an English merchant of Mosul, had conducted excavations on a small scale, as mentioned above, and after his departure from the town, Christian Rassam, the British vice-consul, had placed a few workmen in the abandoned trenches at the request of the trustees of the British Museum, "rather to retain possession of the spot, and to prevent interference on the part of others, than to carry on extensive operations." By the middle of October, Layard had finished the necessary preparations and resumed active work at the mound with a force of about one hundred men. In order to save time and labor he changed the method of excavating formerly employed. Instead of carrying away all the rubbish from the surface down to the platform, he began to tunnel along the walls, sinking shafts at intervals to admit light, air, and the descending workmen, and "removing only as much earth as was necessary to show the sculptured walls." It is clear that under such circumstances the examination of the buried halls and chambers was even less thorough than it had been previously at Nimrud, as their centres had to be left standing to prevent the narrow subterranean passages from collapsing under the pressure from above. Small objects of art were accordingly found very rarely, their discovery being due more to a fortunate accident than to a methodical search.

As soon as the excavations in the mounds opposite Mosul had been fairly started, Layard and Hormuzd Rassam hurried to Nimrud, where operations were simultaneously conducted until the end of spring, 1850. Work was resumed in the four principal sections of the mound which had yielded so many antiquities during the first expedition, but trenches were now also opened in the remaining parts of the ruins. It was particularly the high conical mound at the northwest corner and the adjacent northern edge of the large plateau which received greater attention than had hitherto been possible. One morning, shortly after his arrival, while ascending the mound, Layard found an unexpected visitor in his trenches. In glancing downward from the summit of the ruins, he discovered Rawlinson on the floor of an excavated chamber, "wrapped in his travelling cloak, deep in sleep, and wearied by a long and harassing night's ride." After an absence of more than twenty-two years from England, this gallant officer was on his way home. Accompanied by a single servant, he had made the trip from Baghdad to Mosul, generally counted eight to twelve days, in less than seventy-two hours, a feat reminding us vividly of his famous ride between Poonah and Panwell, when still a young and ambitious lieutenant in India (1832). Unfortunately, in the present case, Rawlinson's extraordinary exertion, at a time when his health had suffered considerably from hard mental work and the effect of a semi-tropical climate, proved too much for his weakened constitution. For several days he was seriously ill at Mosul, unable to do more than to pay a hasty visit to Layard's excavations before his departure.

The work at Qoyunjuk and Nimrud proceeded regularly under the supervision of efficient native overseers. No longer embarrassed by those difficulties and molestations from the governor and the inhabitants of the country which had taxed their patience and energy so often during the previous campaign, Layard and Rassam spent their time generally between the two places, unless absent on one of their numerous exploration tours to the Sinjar and the banks of the Khabur, to Khorsabad and Bavian, to the rock sculptures of Gunduk, and the cuneiform inscriptions of Wan, to the ruins of Babylon and Nuffar, or to any of the different Assyrian sites in their immediate neighborhood. Following the example of Layard, who wisely abstained from relating, day by day, the further progress of his labors, we will now sketch briefly the principal discoveries which characterized the English operations in the two great ruins of Nineveh and Calah during the years 1849-51.

The ruins of Qovunjuk had practically been only scratched by Botta and Layard in their nervous attempts at disclosing sculptured remains in some part of the large mound. It was now decided to submit the whole complex to an Distance, 72 miles; time occupied, 3 hours, 7 minutes.
examination by experimental shafts and trial trenches, and to make the excavation of the southwest palace of Qoyunjuk the chief object of the present campaign. Like the southwest edifice at Nimrud, the latter had been destroyed by fire, when the Median armies, murdering and pillaging, entered the gates of Nineveh (606 B. C). Consequently, hundreds of the most elaborate sculptures were found cracked and broken, or almost entirely reduced to lime. Yet many had more or less escaped the results of the great conflagration, thus allowing the explorer to determine the spirited scenes which once adorned the walls of the principal chambers. Battles and victories, sieges and conquests, hunting scenes and sacrifices to the gods, were again the leading representations. But in the general conception of the subject, in the treatment of the costumes worn by the Assyrian
The Ruins of Nineveh, from the North warriors, as well as by the subdued nations, in the character of the ornaments, in the arrangement of the inscriptions, and in many other important details, there is a marked difference between the bas-reliefs in the palace of Sennacherib and those of the older palaces at Nimrud. There the sculptured slabs showed large figures or simple groups, divided into two friezes, an upper and a lower one, by intervening inscriptions, " the subject being frequently confined to one

tablet, and arranged with some attempt at composition, so as to form a separate picture." Here the four walls of a chamber were generally adorned "by one series of sculptures, representing a consecutive history, uninterrupted by inscriptions, or by the divisions in the alabaster panelling." Short epigraphs or labels, as a rule placed on the upper part of the stones, give the names of the conquered country, city, and even of the principal prisoners and historical events pictured below. Hundreds of figures cover the face of the slabs from top to bottom. We become acquainted with the peculiarities, in type and dress, of foreign nations, and the characteristic features and products of their lands; we are introduced into the very life and occupations of the persons represented. The sculptor shows us the Babylonian swamps with their jungles of tall reeds, frequented bv wild boars, and barbarous tribes skimming over the waters in their light boats of wicker-work, exactly as they are used to-day by the inhabitants of the same marshes; or he takes us into the high mountains of Kurdistan, covered with trees and crowned with castles, endeavoring even to convey the idea of a valley by reversing the trees and mountains on one side of the stream, which is filled with fishes and crabs and turtles. He indicates the different headgear worn by female musicians, or by captive women carried with their husbands and children to Nineveh. Some wear their hair in long ringlets, some platted or braided, some confined in a net; others are characterized by hoods fitting close over their heads, others by a kind of turban; Elamite ladies have their hair in curls falling on their shoulders, and bound above the temples by a band or fillet, while those from Syria wear a high conical headdress, similar to that which is frequently found to-day in those regions. It is impossible to enter into all the details so faithfully represented. Without the knowledge of a single cuneiform character, we learned the principal events of Sennacherib's government, and from a mere study of those sculptured walls we got familiar with the customs and habits

of the ancient Assyrians, at the same time obtaining a first clear glance of the whole civilization of Western Asia.

How much the interpretation of the Old Testament books profited from Layard's epoch-making discoveries, we can scarcely realize fully after we have been under the powermi influence which went forth from the resurrected palaces of Qoyunjuk since the earliest days of our childhood. Being written in a language closely akin to Assyrian, and compiled by men brought up in the same atmosphere and surroundings, they frequently describe the very institutions, customs, and deeds so vividly portrayed on the alabaster slabs of Nineveh. But it was not only through analogy and comparison that so many obscure words and passages in the Scriptures received fresh light and often an entirely new meaning, — sometimes the very same persons and events mentioned in the historical and prophetical books of the Bible were depicted on those monuments or recorded in their accompanying inscriptions. We refer only to the fine series of thirteen slabs adorning the walls of a room nearly in the centre of the great southwest wing of Sennacherib's palace. Seated upon his throne in the hilly districts of Southern Palestine, and surrounded by his formidable army, is the Assvrian king, attired in his richly embroidered robes. In the distance severe fighting is still going on, archers and slingers and spearmen attack a fortified city, defended bv the besieged with great determination. But part of the place has been taken. Beneath its walls are seen Assyrian warriors impaling their prisoners or flaying them alive, while from the gateway of a tower issues a long procession of captives, camels and carts laden with women and children and spoil, advancing towards the monarch. Above the head of the king we read the inscription: "Sennacherib, king of the Universe, king of Assyria, sat upon a throne and reviewed the spoil of the city of Lachish."

The discovery of so many priceless sculptures in more than seventy rooms, halls, and galleries of the palace of one

of the greatest monarchs of the ancient East forms a most striking result of Layard's second expedition to Nineveh. Indeed these bas-reliefs alone would have sufficed to make his name immortal, and to place his work in the trenches of Qoyunjuk far above the average archaeological explorations in Assyrian and Babylonian mounds. And yet they represent only half of what was actually obtained. No less remarkable, and in many respects of even greater importance for the founding and developing of the young Assyriological science, was another discovery, which at first may have seemed rather insignificant in the light of those magnificent sculptures. We know from the cuneiform inscriptions of Sennacherib's grandson, Ashurbanapal, that the southwest palace of Nineveh, which thousands of captives from all the conquered nations of Western Asia, under the rod of their merciless taskmasters, had erected on the gigantic platform at the confluence of the Tigris and the Khosar, was largely repaired and for some time occupied by this last great ruler of a great empire. So far as Layard's excavations, however, went to show, there remained very few complete sculptures of this monarch which escaped the general destruction, while many fragments of inscribed slabs testified to his extensive work at that building. But though the bas-reliefs which once announced his battles and victories to the people have long ago crumbled away, there were found in another section of the same southern wing of Sennacherib's palace those precious relics which will hand down from generation to generation the name of Ashurbanapal as that of a great patron of art and literature, and as the powerful monarch "instructed in the wisdom of the god Nebo." Comp. z Kings 18: 13, *sff.,* 19:8, and the parallel passages, Is. 36: I, *ieq.,* 27: 8.

Prominent among them are six fossiliferous limestone slabs adorned with scenes of his Elamitic war. These slabs, however, belonged originally to the older palace, as the name and titles of Sennacherib on the back of each bas-relief indicate. Ashurbanapal therefore adopted the same method in repairing his grandfather's building as was followed by his father, Esarhaddon, with regard to his own palace at Calah, almost entirely constructed of older material. Comp. Layard, "Nineveh and Babylon," p. 459.

One day Layard came upon two small chambers, opening into each other, and once panelled with sculptured slabs, most of which had been destroyed. But in removing the earth and rubbish from their interior he recognized that "to the height of a foot or more from the floor they were entirely filled with cuneiform tablets of baked clay, some entire, but the greater part broken into many fragments." He had discovered part of the famous royal library of Nineveh founded and maintained by the kings of the last Assyrian empire (about 720-620 B. c), the other half being later unearthed by Rassam in Ashurbanapal's north palace at Qoyunjuk. It was especially the last-mentioned king (668-626 B. C.) who "enlarged and enriched the collection of tablets which his predecessors had brought together, in such a way as to constitute them into a veritable library, by the addition of hundreds, even thousands of documents... dealing with every branch of learning and science known to the wise men of his day."' These tablets, when complete, varying in length from one inch to fifteen inches, were made of the finest clay, and inscribed with the most minute but singularly sharp and well defined cuneiform writing. Their contents are as varied and different as the forms and sizes of the fragments themselves. There are historical records and chronological lists which make us acquainted with the chief events and the number of years of the governments of many Assyrian kings; there are astronomical reports and observations, mathematical calculations, tables of measures of length and capacity, which reveal to us a branch of science in which the Babylonians and Assyrians excelled all other nations of the ancient world; there are hundreds of hymns and psalms, prayers and oracles, mythological texts and incantations, in their poetical expression and depth of

religious feeling often not inferior to the best Hebrew poetry; there are letters and addresses from kings and ministers, officers, and private persons, which deal with military expeditions, the revolts of subdued enemies, the payment of tribute, the administration of provinces, the repairing of buildings, the digging of canals, the purchase of horses, the complaints of unjust treatment or taxation, the transport of winged bulls, the calling in of a physician to prescribe for a lady of the court, and many other interesting details. By far the larger mass of the tablets discovered treat of astrology, and of the subjects of medicine and religious observations so closely connected with this pseudo-science. Not the least important tablets in the whole collection are those lists of cuneiform signs and syllabaries, lists of months, plants, stones, animals, temples, gods, cities, mountains and countries, etc., lists of synonyms, verbal forms, and other grammatical exercises, and a large number of bilingual texts which formed and still form the chief source for the reconstruction of the Assyrian and Sumerian grammars and lexicons. In view of such important and startling discoveries, the many smaller results which crowned Layard's archaeological researches at Nineveh— I refer only to his large collection of fine seals and seal-impressions, to his determination of the northwest city gate, and to his accidental discovery of chambers of Ksarhaddon's palace at the southern mound of Nebi-Yunus — may well be passed over.

Comp. Bezold, "Catalogue of the Cuneiform Tablets in the Kouyunjik Collection of the British Museum," vol. v. (London, 1899), p. xiii. The statement made by Bezold on p. xiv. of this volume, "that in 1849 and 1850 Layard discovered the palace of Ashurbanapal," though found in other Assyriological publications, is as erroneous as another view found, e.g., in Delitzsch's writings (comp. *Murdter" s Geschichte Babyloniens und Assyritns,* Calw and Stuttgart, 2nd ed. 1891, p. 5, or *Ex Oriente Lux,* Leipzig, 1898, p. 6) that it was only Rassam who discovered Ashurbanapal's library. This library was

stored in two palaces and discovered by both Layard (southwest palace) and Rassam (north palace).

The excavations at Nimrud, started at the high conical mound in the northwest corner, were also accompanied by results of considerable interest and value. By means of tunnels the workmen had soon reached a part of solid masonry, forming the substructure for the upper part of a massive building. From a comparison of this ruin with the similar high-towering mounds at Khorsabad, El-Birs, and other Babylonian sites, it is evident that Layard had found the remains of the *ziggurrat* or stage-tower of Calah, at first wrongly regarded by him and Rawlinson as "the tomb of Sardanapalus." Immediately adjoining this tower were two small temples erected by Ashurnasirapal II., and separated from each other by a staircase or inclined passage leading up to the platform from the north. They were built of sundried brick coated with plaster, and besides clay images and fragments of other idols contained a number of valuable sculptures, bas-reliefs, and inscribed slabs, which had adorned their principal entrances. One of the recesses at the end of a chamber was paved with one enormous limestone slab measuring no less than 21 feet by 16 feet 7 inches by 1 foot 1 inch, and completely covered with cuneiform inscriptions recording the wars and campaigns of the ruler, and full of geographical information, but also of disgusting details of the cruel punishments inflicted upon the unfortunate conquered nations. A similar great monolith was found in the second temple, and in the earth above it the entire statue of the monarch, with the following self-glorifying inscription, running across his breast: "Ashurnasirapal, the great king, the powerful king, king of the Universe, king of Assyria, son of Tuklat-Ninib, the great king, the powerful king, king of the Universe, king of Assyria, son of Adadnirari, the great king, the powerful king, king of the Universe, king of Assyria, the conqueror from beyond the Tigris to the Lebanon and the Great Sea Mediterranean — all the countries from the rising of the sun to the setting thereof he subdued under his feet." The well-known Hittite, Egyptian, and Aramcan seal-impressions on clay being among them. Comp. Layard, /. c, pp. 1 53-161.

Where he had offered to a Moslem property owner to dig underground summer apartments for him, through one of his agents, on condition that he should have all the antiquities discovered during the excavations.

Of no less importance, though of a different character, was a discovery in the northwest palace. Near the west edge of the mound the workmen came accidentally upon a chamber built by Ashurnasirapal, which probably served as a storeroom. In one corner was a well nearly sixty feet deep, while in other parts of the room there were found twelve huge copper vessels partly filled with smaller objects. Beneath and behind these caldrons were heaped without order large masses of copper and bronze vessels, arms (shields, swords, daggers, heads of spears and arrows), iron implements, such as picks, saws, hammers, etc., glass bowls, ivory relics, and several entire elephants' tusks. In another corner of this interesting chamber had stood the royal throne, carved in wood and cased with elaborate bronze ornaments. It was badly decayed, but enough remained to ascertain that it resembled in shape the chairs of state represented on the slabs of Khorsabad and Qoyunjuk, and particularly that on which Sennacherib is seated while reviewing the captives and spoil of the city of Lachish. About one hundred and fifty bronze vessels of different sizes and shapes, and eighty small bells in the same metal, could be sent to the British Museum. As many of the former were in a fine state of preservation and remarkable for the beauty of their design, being ornamented with the embossed or incised figures of men, animals, trees, and flowers, they constitute a most valuable collection of representative specimens of ancient metallurgy. A great many of the objects discovered are doubtless of Assyrian origin; others may have formed part

Bronze Plate from Nimrud (Calah) of

the spoil of some conquered nation, or perhaps they were made by foreign artists brought captive to the banks of the Tigris.

Omitting an enumeration of the numerous fragments of interesting sculptures and of other minor antiquities ' excavated at Nimrud during the second expedition, we mention only the fact that in the southeast corner of the mound Layard disclosed the remains of an earlier building and a solitary brick arch beneath the palace or temple constructed by Ashuretililani, while in the ramparts of earth marking the walls of Calah, he traced fifty-eight towers to the north, and about fifty to the east, at the same time establishing the existence of a number of approaches or stairways on the four different sides of the enclosed platform.

E. g., a weight in the shape of a duck discovered in the northwest palace, and bearing the inscription: "30 standard mana, palace of Erba-Marduk, king of Babylon " —a Icing otherwise unknown.

In addition to his successful excavations at Nineveh and Calah, and to his less fortunate operations at Babylon and Nuffar, about which we shall have to say a few words later, Layard, either himself or through one of his native agents, cut trial trenches into various other mounds, extending his researches even as far west as the Khabur. Most of these examinations were carried on too hastily and without method, and therefore have little value, while others, like those carried on in the mounds of Bahshiqa, Karamles, Lak, Shemamyk, Sherif Khan, Abu Marya, and 'Arban, yielded inscribed bricks or slabs from which the Assyrian origin of these ruins could be established. At Sherif Khan, on the Tigris, three miles to the north of Qoyunjuk, he discovered even remains of two Assyrian temples and inscribed limestone slabs from a palace which Esarhaddon had erected for his son, Ashurbanapal, at Tarbisu; at Qal'at Shirgat he gathered fragments of two large octagonal terra-cotta prisms of Tiglath-Pileser I. (about 1100 B. C.); and at 'Arban, on the Biblical Habor,

he conducted personal excavations for three weeks, bringing to light two pairs of winged bulls, a large lion with extended jaws, similar to those found in one of the small temples at Nimrud, and pieces of carved stone and painted brick — all belonging to the " palace " of a man otherwise unknown, who, to judge from his style of art, must have lived about the time of Ashurnasirapal II. Constructed by Shalmaneser II., as was proved by George Smith more than twenty years later. Comp. his "Assyrian Discoveries," 3d ed., New York, 1876, pp. 76-79.

During this second expedition Layard and the other members of his staff suffered from fever and ague considerably more than previously. Before the first summer had fairly commenced, both Dr. Sandwith and Mr. Cooper were seriously ill and had to return to Europe. Another artist was sent by the British Musem, but a few months after his arrival he was drowned in the Gomal at the foot of Sennacherib's sculptures at Bavian (July, 1851). Layard and Rassam alone braved and withstood the inhospitable climate until their funds were exhausted. More than one hundred and twenty large cases of sculptures, tablets, and other antiquities had been sent down to Baghdad, awaiting examination by Rawlinson previous to their shipment to England. Finally, on April 28, 1851, the two explorers themselves turned from the ruins of Nineveh, rich in new honors and yet "with a heavy heart." Two years later Layard submitted the results of his latest researches to the public, and for the first time was able to interweave the fascinating story of his work and wanderings with numerous quotations from the Assyrian inscriptions so admirably interpreted by Rawlinson and by Hincks. His nomadic days had now come to an end. He did not visit again the mounds of Nineveh and Babylon. The enthusiastic reception of his books all over Europe, and the extraordinarv services which he had rendered to the cause of science and art in his own country, secured for him at last that recognition from his government to which he was entitled. But though no longer active in the field of Assyrian exploration, where he occupies the foremost position, he never lost his interest in the continuation of this work by others, and twenty-four years later (1877), as Her Majesty's ambassador at Constantinople, he supported Rassam with the same sympathy and loyalty which once, when an unknown adventurer, he himself had experienced there at the hand of his predecessor and patron.

Comp. Layard, "Discoveries in the Ruins of Nineveh and Babylon," London, 185; and the sanie author's "The Monuments of Nineveh," series ii., 71 plates, London, 1853.

During the two years which Rawlinson spent in England (1850-51) for the restoration of his health and to superintend the publication of his famous second memoir "On the Babylonian Translation of the Great Persian Inscription at Behistun," through which he announced to the world that the deciphering of the Babylono-Assyrian cuneiform writing was an accomplished fact, he entered into closer relations with the British Museum. The trustees of this large storehouse of ancient art-treasures were anxious to resume their researches in the ruins on the banks of the Tigris and the Euphrates, which hitherto had been conducted with such marvellous success by Layard. Who was better qualified to carry out their plans and to take charge of the proposed excavations than Rawlinson, with his unique knowledge of the cuneiform languages, his rare experience as a soldier and traveller, and his remarkable influence in the East as the political representative of a great nation at Baghdad! And he was at once ready to add the labors of an explorer and excavator to those of a diplomat and decipherer. Before he departed from England, he was entrusted with the supervision of all the excavations which might be carried on by the British Museum in Assyria, Babylonia, and Susiana, and was authorized to employ such agents as he thought fit in excavating and transporting the best-preserved antiquities to the national collections in London. Well provided with the necessary funds furnished by the government

and private individuals, he entered upon his second official residence in Baghdad in the fall of 1851. But intelligent men who could be relied upon, and at the same time were able to manage the work properly in the trenches, far away from the place to which he was generally bound by his principal duties, were very rare in those regions. He was about to send Loftus, of the Turco-Persian Boundary Commission, who had excavated for him at the large mound of Susa, to the Assyrian ruins, when the trustees of the British Museum came unexpectedly to his assistance. The manifest interest among the religious and scientific circles of England in the historical and literary results of Layard's discoveries, daily increased by Rawlinson's own letters and instructive communications on the contents of the unearthed cuneiform inscriptions, influenced that administrative body to despatch a third artist to the scene of the old excavations, soon followed by Hormuzd Rassam, as chief practical excavator. Their choice could not have fallen upon a better man. In the school of Layard excellently trained and prepared for his task, as a native of Mosul entirely familiar with the language and character of the Arabs, through his previous connections deeply interested in the undertaking, and after a long contact with Western civilization thoroughly impregnated with the English spirit of energy, he was an ideal explorer, the verv man whom Rawlinson, the scientific leader and real soul of all these explorations, needed to carry the work in the Assyrian ruins to a successful conclusion. But Rassam's position was not very easy. For several years his predecessor, profiting by every hint which the appearance of the ground afforded, had tunnelled through the most promising spots of the Assyrian mounds, and what remained unexplored of Qoyunjuk had been transferred by Rawlinson to Victor Place, in generous response to the latter's request. Yet Rassam was shrewd and determined, and knew how to overcome difficulties.

Comp. George Rawlinson, "A Memoir of Major-General Sir Henry Creswicke

Rawlinson," London, 1898, pp. 172, *seqq.* By the name of Hodder, to succeed the lamented Mr. Bell, who was drowned in the Gomal. Hodder remained in Mesopotamia until the beginning of 1854, when he fell seriously ill, and was supplanted by William Boutcher. *Rassam's Excavations, 1852-54.* In the fall of 1852 operations were commenced under his superintendence, and continued till the beginning of April, 1854. Following Layard's example, he placed his workmen at as many different sites as possible, anxious also to prevent his French rival from encroaching any further upon what he regarded as the British sphere of influence. But more than a year elapsed without any of those startling discoveries to which the English nation had got accustomed through Layard's phenomenal success. At Qal'at Shirgat, where he excavated twice in the course of 1853, he obtained two terra-cotta prisms, inscribed with the annals of Tiglath-Pileser I. They were only duplicates of others unearthed by his predecessor two years before;' but, unlike those, they were complete and in a fine state of preservation, found buried in solid masonry, about thirty feet apart, at two of the corners of an almost perfect square, which originally formed part of the large temple of the city of Ashur. Soon afterwards their long text of 811 lines played a certain role in the history of Assyriology, being selected by the council of the Royal Asiatic Society of Great Britain and Ireland for a public test as to the correctness of the deciphering of the Assyrian cuneiform writing.

At the southeast corner of Nimrud, Rassam discovered Ezida, the temple of Nebo, and six large statues of the god, two of which had been set up by a governor of Calah "for the life of Adadnirari III., king of Assyria, his lord, and for the life of Sammuramat generally but wrongly identified with Semiramis, lady of the palace, his mistress." In another room of the same building he came upon the well-preserved stele of Samsi-Adad IV. (825812 B. c), father of the former and son of Shalmaneser II.; while among heaps upon heaps of broken sculptures in the so-called central palace he unearthed fragments of an inscribed black obelisk of Ashurnasirapal II., which when complete must have exceeded any other Assyrian obelisk so far discovered in size. But his principal work was carried on at Qoyunjuk. Shaft after shaft was sunk in the ground to find traces of a new palace — the one *desideratum* above others in those early days of exploration. As Victor Place never excavated in the northern half of the mound, so liberally allotted to him by Rawlinson, Rassam profited by his absence, and placed some of his Arabs very close to the line of demarcation drawn by his chief, in order to obtain some clue as to the probable contents of that forbidden section. But his endeavors did not prove very successful. Meanwhile he had also opened trenches in the English southern half of the mound, which yielded a white obelisk nearly ten feet high, covered with bas-reliefs, and an inscription of Ashurnasirapal II., the upper half of a similar monument, and the torso of a female statue from the palace of Ashurbelkala, son of Tiglath-Pileser I.

Comp. p. i 26. The real facts concerning the discovery of these important prisms as set forth above are generally misrepresented, their discovery being ascribed either to Layard or Rassam. The inscription was sent to four prominent Assyrian scholars, Rawlinson, Hincks, Oppert, and Talbot, at the latter's suggestion, for independent translations, which in all essential points agreed, and were published in the journal of that society, vol. xviii., pp. 150-219, London, 1857. Valuable as all these and other recovered antiquities were in themselves, they shrank almost into insignificance when compared with the character and mass of Layard's accumulated treasures. Rassam felt this very keenly, and was dissatisfied, particularly as the time rapidly drew near when the funds available for his work would cease. His only hope lay in the northern part of Qoyunjuk, over which he had no control, but which he longed to examine. How could he explore it "without getting into hot water with Mr. Place "? If anything was

to be done, it had to be done quickly. He decided upon an experimental examination of the spot by a few trustworthy Arabs at night. A favorable opportunity and a bright moonlight were all that was required for his nocturnal adventure, and they presented themselves very soon. Let us hear the story of this daring attempt, and of his subsequent discovery, in Rassam's own language. That even Shalmaneser II. himself built at the temple of Nebo was shown later by George Smith, " Assyrian Discoveries," 3d ed., New York, 1876, pp. 73, *seq.* Who, after Botta's and Layard's fruitless attempts, very evidently did not regard that section worth keeping. For on other occasions he took quite a different attitude both against Place and Loftus in his vigorous defence of the interests of the British Museum.

"It was on the night of the 20th of December, 1853, that I commenced to examine the ground in which I was fortunate enough to discover, after three nights' trial, the grand palace of Ashurbanapal, commonly known by the name of Sardanapalus. When everything was ready I went and marked three places, some distance from each other, in which our operations were to be commenced. Only a few trenches had been opened there in the time of Sir Henry Layard; but on this occasion I ordered the men to dig transversely, and cut deeper down. I told them they were to stop work at dawn, and return to the same diggings again the next night. The very first night we worked there, one of the gangs came upon indications of an ancient building; but though we found among the rubbish painted bricks and pieces of marble on which there were signs of inscriptions and bas-reliefs, I did not feel sanguine as to the result. The next night the whole number of workmen dug in that spot; and, to the great delight of all, we hit upon a remnant of a marble wall, on examining which I came to the conclusion that it belonged to an Assyrian building which had existed on that spot. The remnant of the basrelief showed that the wall was standing in its original position, and, though the upper part of it had been de-

stroyed, I was able to judge, from experience, that it had not been brought thither from another building. The lower part of the slab, which contained the feet of Assyrian soldiers and captives, was still fixed in the paved floor with brick and stone masonry, intended to support it at the back. To my great disappointment, after having excavated round the spot a few feet, both the remnant of the bas-relief and the wall came to an end, and there was nothing to be seen save ashes, bones, and other rubbish.... This put a damper on my spirits, especially as I had on that day reported to both the British Museum authorities and Sir Henry Rawlinson the discovery of what I considered to be a new palace, as I was then fully convinced of its being so. I knew, also, that if I failed to realize my expectations I should only be found fault with and laughed at for my unrewarded zeal. However, I felt that as I had commenced so I must go on, even if only to be disappointed. The next night I superintended the work in person, and increased the number of men, placing them in separate gangs around the area, which seemed the most likely place for good results. The remnant of the sculptured wall discovered was on a low level, running upward, and this fact alone was enough to convince an experienced eye that the part of the building I had hit upon was an ascending passage leading to the main building. I therefore arranged my gangs to dig in a southeasterly direction, as I was certain that if there was anything remaining it would be found there. The men were made to work on without stopping, one gang assisting the other. My instinct did not deceive me; for one division of the workmen, after three or four hours' hard labor, were rewarded by the first grand discovery of a beautiful bas-relief in a perfect state of preservation, representing the king, who was afterwards identified as Ashurbanapal, standing in a chariot, about to start on a hunting expedition, and his attendants handing him the necessary weapons for the chase.... The delight of the workmen was naturally beyond description; for as soon as the word *suwar* ('images') was uttered, it went through the whole party like electricity. They all rushed to see the new discovery, and after having gazed on the bas-relief with wonder, they collected together, and began to dance and sing my praises, in the tune of their warsong, with all their might. Indeed, for a moment I did not know which was the most pleasant feeling that possessed me, the joy of my faithful men or the finding of the new palace."'

After this unmistakable success had rewarded his clandestine efforts, Rassam was no longer afraid of French or Turkish interference, and accordingly ordered the work to be continued in broad daylight. For " it was an established rule that whenever one discovered a new palace, no one else could meddle with it, and thus, in my position as the agent of the British Museum, I had secured it for England." The large edifice once having been discovered, one cannot help wondering how Botta and Layard could have missed coming upon some of its walls, which in many places were only a foot below the surface, and indeed in one or two instances so close to it that" a child might have scratched the ground with his fingers and touched the top of the sculptures." Before the first day was over, Rassam had cleared the upper parts of all the bas-reliefs which adorned the long but narrow hall, known as the " lion-room," because the subject here represented is the royal lion-hunt. The sculptures gathered from this and other chambers of the palace belong to the finest specimens of Assyrian art. The change from the old school of the tenth century to that of the later period referred to above (p. 117), both in the design and in the execution of single objects and persons and of whole groups, Comp. Rassam, "Asshur and the Land of Nimrod," New York, 1897, pp. 24, seqq. is even more pronounced in the sculptures of the palace of Ashurbanapal than in those from the reign of his grandfather. They are distinguished by the sharpness of the outline, their minute finish, and the very correct and striking delineation of animals, especially lions and horses, in their different motions and positions. In looking at these fine bas-reliefs we gain the conviction that the artist has carefully studied and actually seen in life what he has reproduced here so truthfully in stone on the walls. The furious lion, foiled in his revenge, burying his teeth in the chariot wheels; the wounded lioness with her outstretched head, suffering agony, and vainly endeavoring to drag her paralyzed lower limbs after her; or the king on his spirited horse with wild excitement in his face, and in hot pursuit of the swift wild ass of the desert, — all these scenes are so King Ashurbinapal Hunting realistic in their conception, and at the same time so beautifully portrayed, that from the beginning they have found a most deserved admiration.

This lion-room was a picture gallery and library at the same time. For in the centre of the same hall Rassam discovered the other half of Ashurbanapal's library, several thousand clay tablets, mostly fragmentary, in character similar to those rescued by Layard, and including the Assyrian account of the Deluge. It is impossible to follow Rassam into all the chambers which he laid open, and which were generally lined with bas-reliefs illustrating the king's wars against Elam, Babylonia, the Arabs, etc. While breaking down the walls of one of these rooms, he found a large terracotta prism, unfortunately crumbling to pieces when exposed to the air, but soon afterwards replaced by the fragments of a second. They were duplicates, and contained the annals of Ashurbanapal, equally important for our knowledge of the history and for a study of the language and grammar of that prominent period of Assyrian art and literature.

During the first three months in 1854 the fortunate explorer was busy in excavating the palace as far as he could. But his funds were limited and quickly exhausted. At the beginning of April he was obliged to dismiss the different gangs of workmen employed at Qoyunjuk and Nimrud and to return to England. The acceptance of a political appointment at Aden prevented him from going out to Nineveh again in the same year, as the British Museum had planned. His place was filled by Loftus and by Boutcher, who acted as the artist of the former. They had been for some time in Southern Babylonia, carrying on excavations at a moderate rate on behalf of the Assyrian Excavation Fund. This was a private society organized for the purpose of enlarging the field of English operations in Assyria and Babylonia, as the parliamentary grant secured by the British Museum was considered quite inadequate for the proper continuation of the national work so gloriously initiated by Layard. The thought and spirit which led to the founding of this society were most excellent and praiseworthy, but the method and means by which its representatives endeavored to reach their aim were neither tactful nor wise, and finally became even prejudicial to the very interests they intended to serve. Instead of placing their contributions and funds with a statement of their desired application at the disposal of the British Museum, that great national agency for all such archaeological undertakings, the managers of the new corporation proceeded independently. The expedition which they sent out appeared as a competitor rather than as a helpmate of the other, and was about to risk serious collisions between the rival workmen of the two parties by occupying the same mound of Qoyunjuk after Rassam's departure, when upon the energetic representation of Rawlinson, who naturally did not look very favorably on the proceedings of this new society, an arrangement was concluded in London which placed matters on an entirely satisfactory basis. The Assyrian Excavation Fund transferred its remaining property to the British Museum, and decided that Loftus and Boutcher should henceforth receive their directions from Rawlinson.

The examination of the north palace of Ashurbanapal at Nineveh was resumed with new vigor under these two men, who had gathered considerable experience in the trenches of Warka and Senkere. While Boutcher drew the numerous sculptures and copied the monumental inscriptions, Loftus continued the excavations where Rassam had left them, trying first of all to determine the precise extent of the new building. But he also cleared a portion of its interior, and laid bare the whole ascending passage and a portal with three adjoining rooms at the western corner. Being deeply interested in the edifice as a whole, and in the determination of its architectural features, somewhat neglected by his predecessor, he did not confine himself to digging for new sculptures, though appreciating them whenever thev were found. The bas-relief representing the king in comfortable repose upon a couch under the trees of his garden, and the queen sitting on a chair beside him, both drinking from cups while attendants with towels and fans stand behind them, was with many other interesting monuments discovered by Loftus. Unfortunatelv, however, the British Museum had not the means or did not care to continue the excavations at Nineveh and Calah after Rawlinson's final departure from Baghdad, for Loftus and Boutcher were soon recalled. Repeated attempts have been made since to resume the work at Qoyunjuk, but a Layard was not found to remove the obstacles in the field and to stir the masses at home to provide the financial support. Neither of the two large buildings which occupy the platform of Qoyunjuk has as yet been thoroughly explored, and much more remains to be done before the grand palace ofAshurbanapal with its hidden treasures will rise before our eyes as completely as that excavated in a methodical manner by Botta and Place at Khorsabad.

FIRST SUCCESSFUL ATTEMPTS IN BABYLONIA

During the first four years of the second half of the last century the proverbial solitude of the Babylonian ruins seemed to have disappeared temporarily under the powerful influence of some magical spell. Fraser's intrepid march across the desolate plain and extensive swamps of Iraq, followed by his intelligent report of the innumerable mounds and other frequent traces of a high civilization which he had met everywhere in the almost forgotten districts of the interior of Babylonia, had directed the gen-eral attention again to the vast ruins of ancient Chaldea. Botta's and Layard's epoch-making discoveries in the royal palaces of Khorsabad and Nimrud had created an extraordinary enthusiasm throughout Europe. As a result of both, scholars began to meditate about the possibilities connected with a methodical exploration of the most conspicuous ruins in Babylonia. The earlier accounts and descriptions of Rich and Ker Porter and Buckingham were eagerly devoured and reexamined with a new zeal, stimulated by the hope of finding other indications that the soil of the country in the south would contain no less important treasures than those which had just been extracted from the Assyrian tells in the north. But neither scientific nor religious interest was the immediate cause of these tentative but fundamental researches in Babylonia with which we will now occupy ourselves in the following pages. The first successful explorations and excavations in the interior of Babylonia were rather the indirect result of certain political difficulties, which in 1839-40 threatened to lead to serious complications between Turkey and Persia. The chief trouble was caused by the extensive frontier between the two Mohammedan neighbors continually changing its limits as the strength of either government for the time prevailed. Under the influence of the cabinets of England and Russia, which offered their friendly mediation in order to maintain peace in regions not very far from their own frontiers in India and Georgia, a joint commission with representatives from the four powers was finallv appointed and instructed " to survey and define a precise line of boundary between the two countries in question which might not admit of future dispute." The work of this "Turco-Persian Frontier Commission," after meeting with extraordinary difficulties and delays, lasted from 1849 to 1852.

WILLIAM KENNETT LOFTUS

To the stafF of the British commissioner, Colonel Williams, "the Hero of Kars," was attached, as geologist, William Kennett Loftus, who utilized the rare facilities granted to him as a mem-ber of that commission to satisfy "his strong desire for breaking new ground " in an unexplored region, " which from our childhood we have been led to regard as the cradle of the human race."

After a short trip to the ruins of Babylon, Kl-Birs, Kefil (with "the tomb of the prophet Kzekiel "), Kufa, famous in early Moslem history, and the celebrated Persian shrines of Meshhed 'Ali and Kerbela, — all but the first situated on the western side of the Euphrates, — Loftus decided to examine the geology of the Chaldean marshes and to explore the ruins of Warka, which, previous to the discovery of the Muqayyar cylinders, on the basis of native tradition, Sir Henry Rawlinson was inclined to identify with Ur of the Chaldees, the birthplace of the patriarch Abraham. An opportunity presented itself towards the end of December, 1849, when the representatives of the four powers, for nearly eight months detained at Baghdad, were at last ordered to proceed to the southern point of the disputed boundary line. While the other members of the party were conveyed to Mohammera by the armed steamer Nitocris, under the command of Captain Felix Jones, mentioned above in connection with his excellent maps of Nineveh, Loftus, accompanied by his friend and comrade, H. A. Churchill, and a number of irregular Turkish horsemen, took the land route between the Euphrates and Tigris, hitherto but once trodden by European foot.

Notwithstanding the great difficulties and dangers then attending a journey into Babylonia proper, the two explorers, " determined on being pleased with anything," overcame all obstacles with courage and patience, reaching the camp of the frontier commission on the eastern bank of the Shatt el-'Arab safely after an absence of several weeks. They had crossed the unsafe districts of the Zobaid Arabs and their tributaries, regarded as perfectly wild and uncontrolled in those days; they had visited the filthy reed huts of the fickle and unreliable 'Afej tribes, inhabiting the verge and numerous islands of the immense swamps named after them; and riding parallel with the course of the ancient bed of the Shatt el-Kar, they had established friendly relations with the wildest and poorest but good-natured Ma'dan tribes in Southern Babylonia. Everywhere, like Fraser, they had found traces of an early civilization and a former dense population, and for the first time they had closely examined these lofty and massive piles covered with fragments of stone and broken pottery, which loom up in solitary grandeur from the surrounding plains and marshes of ancient Chaldea. The ruins of Nuffar, Hammam, Tell (J)ide, Warka, Muqayvar, and others became at once centres of general interest, and were rescued forever from the oblivion of past centuries.

Loftus' enthusiastic report of all the wonderful things which he had seen, illustrated bv careful sketches and plans and by a number of small antiquities picked up on the surface of the various mounds, or purchased for a trifle from the neighboring Arabs, impressed Colonel Williams so favorably that he readily listened to the suggestions of the bold explorer "that excavations should be conducted on a small scale at Warka. " After a few davs' rest, we find Loftus again on his way to the ruins, supplied with the necessary funds by his patron, and " with instructions more especially to procure specimens of the remarkable coffins of the locality, and seek objects as might be easily packed for transmission to the British Museum." His whole caravan consisted of four servants, three muleteers, two Arab guides, and fifteen horses and mules.

Under the protection of the powerful Muntefik(j) shaikh Fah(a)d (" Leopard," " Panther"), Loftus proceeded to the Arab encampment nearest to the ruins of Warka. It was fully six miles away from the scene of his labors, a distance soon afterwards increased even to nine miles, when, in consequence of the frequent desertions of his Tuwaiba workmen, he was forced to decamp to Durraji on the Euphrates, in order to ensure greater safety to his little party.

His work of three weeks was harassing in the extreme. "At sunrise," to quote his own words, " I set out with the Arabs for the mounds,... and never left them during the whole day. The soil was so light that, in walking from trench to trench, my feet were buried at each step. The Arabs required constant directions and watching. It was usually long after sunset ere we returned to camp, stumbling every instant over the broken ground. A few minutes sufficed for me to swallow the food my cook had prepared, when, almost tired to death, I was obliged to lay down plans from my rough notes, write myjournal, and pack the objects procured in the course of the day. On many occasions it was two o'clock in the morning before I retired to rest, perfectly benumbed from the intensity of the cold, which even the double walls of my little tent could not exclude."

After many fruitless trials and the demolition of perhaps a hundred specimens, Loftus succeeded in finding a method by which some of the fragile but heavy slipper-shaped coffins so abundantly found at Warka could be removed without breaking. The surface of the coffin having been carefully cleaned, inside and out, thick layers of paper were pasted on both sides. When thoroughly dried, this hard mass became like a sheath, strengthening and protecting the enclosed coffin, which now could be lifted and handled without difficulty. Many years later, in connection with the University of Pennsylvania's excavations at NufFar, the same method was often employed with the same general result, and more than fifty coffins were carried away "whole" to Kurope and America. Yet after a long experience I have definitely abandoned this method as unsatisfactory and most damaging to the blue enamel of the object thus treated. It is by far wiser to save and pack all the fragments of glazed coffins separately and to put them together at home in a strictly scientific manner. Yet for the time being Lottus might well feel proud of having been able to secure the first three complete Babvlonian coffins, then still unknown to European scholars. Under the dances and yells of his Tuwaiba Arabs, frantic with delight and excitement, they were carried with numerous other antiquities to the river, whence thev were shipped to the British Museum.

Towards the end of 1853 Loftus returned to the ruins of Babylonia for the last time, in charge of an expedition sent out by the " Assyrian Excavation Fund " of London and accompanied by his two friends, W. Boutcher and T. Kerr Lynch. In order to secure him greater facilities, he was soon afterwards appointed by his government an attache of the British Embassy at Constantinople. It was his intention to commence operations at the conspicuous mound of Hammam, where in connection with a former visit he had found the large fragments of a fine but intentionally defaced statue in black granite. But the utter lack of water in the Shatt el-Kar interfered seriously with his plans. Compelled, therefore, to seek another locality, he decided at once to resume the excavation of Warka, where he had won his first laurels. And it was in connection with this last visit to the place so dear to him that he effected the principal discoveries which established his name as a Babylonian explorer.

The first three months of the year 1854 he devoted to his difficult task. Conditions around Warka had completely changed during his absence. The Tuwaiba tribe had been driven out of Mesopotamia, and it was no small matter to obtain the necessary gangs of workmen from his distant friends and the exorbitant shaikh of El-Khidhr. In consequence of the river having failed to overflow its natural banks in the previous years, extreme poverty prevailed among the Arabs of the Lower Euphrates, and it became necessary to order all the supplies for men and beasts from Suq esh-Shiyukh, a distance of sixty miles, while every day a number of camels were engaged to carry water from the river to the camp, which he had pitched halfway between El-Khidhr and the ruins, and to the Arabs working in the trenches of Warka, nine miles away. To make the situation even more disagreeable, frequent sand-storms, especially characteristic of the regions of Warka and Jokha and Tell Ibrahim

(Cuthah), at the slightest breath of air enveloped the mounds " in a dense cloud of impalpable sand," driving from their places the workmen, who often lost their way in returning to camp. Loftus, however, was not to be discouraged by all the difficulties, and with determination he tried to accomplish his task.

The ruins of Warka, the largest in all Babylonia, are situated on an elevated tract of desert soil slightly raised above a series of inundations and marshes caused by the annual overflowing of the Euphrates. When this inundation does not occur, the desolation and solitude of Warka are even more striking than at ordinary seasons. There is then no life for miles around. "No river glides in grandeur at the base of its mounds; no green date groves flour At least twice or thrice a week.
ish near its ruins. The jackal and the hyama appear to shun the dull aspect of its tombs. The king of birds never hovers over the deserted waste. A blade of grass or an insect finds no existence there. The shrivelled lichen alone, clinging to the withered surface of the broken brick, seems to glory in its universal dominion upon these barren walls." No wonder that ot alT the deserted pictures which Loftus ever beheld, that of Warka incomparably surpassed them all. The ruins represent an enormous accumulation of long stretched mounds within "an irregular circle, nearly six miles in circumference, defined by the traces of an earthen rampart, in some places fifty feet high. " As at NufFar, a wide depression, the bed of some ancient canal, divides this elevated platform of debris into two unequal parts, varving in height from twenty to fifty feet, above which still larger mounds rise. The principal and doubtless earliest edifices are found in the southwest section, and to this Loftus verv naturally directed his attention. Most conspicuous among them is a pyramidal mound, about a hundred feet high, called by the Arabs Buweriye, /. e., " reed matting," because at certain intervals reed mats are placed between the layers of unbaked brick. It represents the stage tower or *ziggurrat* of the ancient Babylonian city Uruk or Krech (Gen. 10: 10), forming part of the famous temple *E-anna,* sacred to the goddess Ninni or Nana. The mass of the structure, which, unlike the similar towers of Muqayyar and Nuffar, at present' has no external facing of kiln-baked brickwork, is at least as old as King Ur-Gur (about 2700 B. c.), whose name is stamped upon the baked bricks of the water courses built in the centre of its sides. Singashid, a monarch living somewhat later, left traces of his restoration at the summit of the Buweriye. The lowest stage was apparently not reached by Loftus, who after a fruitless attempt to discover a barrel cylinder in the west corner of the building, and unable to carry on any extensive excavation, left this mound to future explorers.

Another interesting structure at Warka is a ruin called Wuswas, said to be derived from a negro of this name who hunted here for treasures. It is situated less than a thousand feet to the southwest of the Buweriye, and, like the latter, though much smaller in size, contained in a walled quadrangle, including an area of more than seven and a half acres. Its corners again are approximately toward the four cardinal points. The most important part of this great enclosure is the edifice on the southwest side, which is 246 feet long and 174 feet wide, elevated on a lofty artificial platform fifty feet high. This building at once attracted Loftus' attention. By a number of trenches he uncovered a considerable portion of the southwest facade, which in some places was still twenty-seven feet high. The peculiar style of exterior decoration here exhibited afforded us the first glimpse of Babylonian architecture. On the whole, this facade shows the same characteristic features — stepped recesses with chasings at their sides, repeated at regular intervals — as the exterior of Sargon's palace at Khorsabad, excavated by Victor Place about the same time, or the ancient southeast wall of the temple enclosure at Nippur, uncovered during our latest campaign in 1899-1900, and many other Babylonian public buildings examined by various explorers.

From a number of indications and details in Loftus' description it follows almost with certainty that the stage tower of Erech originally also had the usual facing of brickwork. It evidently, however, furnished welcome building material to the later inhabitants of Erech. More extensive and deeper excavations would doubtless reveal traces enough in the lower stage. Mistaken by Loftus for buttresses "erected for the purpose of supporting the main edifice " (p. 167). Comp. Hilprecht, "The Babylonian Expedition of the University of Pennsylvania," series A, vol. i., part *2,* p. 18. I doubt whether Loftus examined all the four sides ot the building (" on the centre of each side"). As the tower must have had an entrance, possibly on the southwest side, it is impossible to believe that this side should have had a drain on its centre. My own view is that, like the *ziggurrat* at Nuffar, the tower at Warka had such "buttresses" only on two sides (the number "three," given in my publication, p. 18, was due to Haynes' erroneous report).

Loftus found an entrance to this remarkable complex at its northeast side, leading into a large outer court flanked by chambers on either side. He also traced and partly excavated a number of halls and smaller rooms along the southwest facade, which had neither door nor window; he could ascertain the extraordinary thickness of the walls as compared with the size of the enclosed chambers, and the lack of uniformity in size and shape noticeable in the latter, — another characteristic feature of Babylonian architecture; he found that the bricks used in the construction of this edifice were either marked with a deeply impressed triangular stamp on the under side — something altogether unknown from early Babylonian ruins — or were stamped with "an oblong die bearing thirteen lines of minute cuneiform characters," which has not vet been published. But Loftus was unable to determine the real character of this structure. In consideration of the small funds at his disposal, and apparently disappointed by his failure to discover sculptured bas-reliefs and other works of art, similar to those which had repaid the labors of Botta, Place, and Layard in the Assyrian mounds, he abandoned his trenches at Wuswas, as he had done at the Buweriye, trying another place where he might find the coveted treasures. From all the indications contained in Loftus description of his work at Wuswas we may infer that the remaining walls of the excavated building cannot be older than 1400 B. C, and possibly are about 800 to 1000 years later, apparently being a temple or the residence of some high-ranked person.

To the south of Wuswas there is a second immense structure, resembling the former in area and general disposition of its plan, but having no court and being more lofty and therefore more imposing in the distance. The bricks bearing the same peculiarities as those of Wuswas, it seems to be of about the same age. Loftus accordingly abstained from examining this edifice, turning his attention rather to a doubtless earlier building situated nearly on a level with the desert, close to the southern angle of the Buweriye. He unearthed part of a wall, thirty feet long, entirely composed of small yellow terra-cotta cones, three inches and a half long. They were all arranged in half circles with their rounded bases facing outwards. "Some had been dipped in red and black color and were arranged in various ornamental patterns, such as diamonds, triangles, zigzags, and stripes, which had a remarkably pleasing effect." Large numbers of such cones, frequently bearing votive inscriptions, have been found in most of the early Babylonian ruins where excavations were conducted, thus proving the correctness of Loftus' theory that "they were undoubtedly much used as an architectural decoration " in ancient Chaldea.

Another extraordinary mode of decoration in architecture was found in a mound near Wuswas. Upon a basement or terrace of mud-brick there rose a long wall entirely composed of unbaked bricks and conical vases, fragments of the latter being scattered all about the surface in its neighborhood. The

arrangement was as follows: "Above the foundation were a few layers of mud-bricks, and superimposed on which were three rows of these vases, arranged horizontally, mouths outward, and immediately above each other. This order of brick and pot work was repeated thrice, and was succeeded upwards bv a mass of unbaked bricks. The vases vary in size from ten to fifteen inches in length, with a general diameter at the mouth of four inches. The cup or interior is only six inches deep, consequently the conical end is solid." One can easily imagine the very strange and striking effect produced by these circular openings of the vases, the original purpose and age of which Loftus was unable to ascertain.

On the east side of the Buweriye he excavated a terrace paved with bricks " inscribed in slightly relieved cuneiform characters " containing the name of Cambyses, while half a mile southeast of the former, in a small detached mound, he found a large mass of broken columns, capitals, cornices, and many other relics of rich internal decoration — all belonging to the Parthian period.

Important portable antiquities of early Babylonian times were unfortunately not disclosed by the explorer. Yet his excavations were by no means entirely lacking in literary documents and other valuable archaeological objects, though mostly of a comparatively late period. As most conspicuous among them mav be mentioned less than a hundred so-called contract tablets of the Neo-Babylonian, Persian, and even Seleucide dynasties, the latter at the same time proving that at least as late as the third pre-Christian century cuneiform writing was in use in Babylonia; a few syllabaries and two large mushroom-shaped cones of baked clay covered on their flat tops and stems with cuneiform legends; an interesting small tablet in serpentine with pictures on the one side and four lines of early cuneiform characters on the other; a limestone slab with an imperfect inscription in South-Arabian writing — the first of the kind discovered in Babylonian ruins; a brick with stamp in relief of an elevated altar

surmounted by a seven-rayed sun; several terracotta figurines; a thin silver plate embossed with a beautiful female figure; fragments of a bivalve shell *(tridacna squamosa)*, the exterior of which shows fine carvings of horses and lotus flowers, etc.

The chief results ot our explorer's rather superficial diggings at Warka being for the greater part due to a fortunate accident rather than to a clearly defined method and logical planning, were of real importance only for the history of architecture and for a study of the burial customs prevailing during the Persian, Parthian, and later occupations of Babylonia. Loftus is therefore correct in summing up his labors with the statement that " Warka may still be considered as unexplored." Within the three months at his disposal he scratched a little here and there, like Lavard at Babylon and Nuffar, filled with a nervous desire to find important large museum pieces at the least possible outlav of time and money. Warka, however, is not the place to yield them readily. Objects of art and business archives and libraries with precious literarv documents are doubtless contained in the enormous mounds. But in what condition they will be found is another quite different question. As we know from cuneiform records, the Elamite hordes invading Babylonia towards the end of the third pre-Christian millennium sacked and looted the temples and palaces of ancient Erech above others, establishing even a kingdom of their own in those regions. The large stratum of intentionally broken inscribed vases, statues, reliefs, and other objects of art of the earliest Babylonian period surrounding the temple court of Nippur, which 1 have shown to be the results of revengeful Elamite destruction, indicates what we may expect to find in the middle strata of Warka. In order to reach these deeper strata, a heavy superincumbent mass of rubbish and funereal remains, representing a period of about one thousand years after the fall of the Neo-Babylonian empire, has to be examined and removed.

In itself, any ancient city continuously inhabited for at least 5000 years, and repeatedly occupied by hostile armies, as Erech was, must be regarded as a site most unfavorable to the discovery of large and well preserved earlier antiquities. As a rule these latter, if escaping the vicissitudes of war, have been transferred from generation to generation until they were consumed or damaged in their natural continued use, while others, perhaps intact at the time when they were hidden under collapsing walls, have been frequently afterwards brought to light in connection with the thousands of later burials. No longer understood or appreciated by the inhabitants of a subsequent age, and frequently also of another race and religion, they were often intentionally broken and employed in a manner quite different from their original purpose.

In addition to the points just mentioned, the natural conditions around Warka are even worse than at Nuffar. From February or March to July the inundations of the Euphrates extend frequently almost to the very base of the ruins. The swamps thus formed are swarming with innumerable mosquitoes, which, with the even more dreaded sand-flies of the surrounding desert, render the life of the explorer extremely miserable. Towards the latter part of the summer the waters recede. The human system, being worn out by the heat and fatigue of the summer, is liable to fall a victim to the severe fevers now following, which have constantly proved to be the greatest real danger to our own expeditions at Nuffar. At other times, particularly when the Kuphrates fails to inundate those regions, fresh water is not to be had for miles in the neighborhood, while at the same time the frequent sand-storms, of which Warka is one of the most characteristic centres, increase the general discomfort and render work in the trenches often absolutely impossible. No expedition should ever resume excavations at Warka unless it fully understands all these difficulties beforehand, and, in contrast with the superficial scratchings of Loftus, is prepared to excavate these largest of all Babylonian mounds in a strictly methodical manner for a period of at least

fifty years, assured of a fund of no less than $500,000. By the mere " digging" for a few vears at such an important place as Warka, Assyriology would irreparably lose more than it ever could gain by the unearthing of a number of antiquities, however valuable in themselves.

After three months of brave battling against odd circumstances Loftus instinctively began to realize the grandeur of the task with which he was confronted, and the utter insufficiency of the means at his disposal and the methods hitherto employed. Accordingly he decided to quit Warka, leaving its thorough exploration to an adequately equipped future expedition. Under the protection of a friendly shaikh of the Shammar Bedouins, then encamped near the ruins of Warka, he moved to Senkere, on the western bank of the Shaft el-Kar, situated about fifteen miles southeast of the former and plainly visible on a clear day from the summit of the Buweriye. These mounds had previously been visited only by Fraser and Ross in the course of their hasty journey through the Jezire, briefly described above (pp. 54-56)

As over against the lofty ruins of Warka, covering a city which continued to be inhabited for centuries after the commencement of the Christian era, Senkere, rather smaller in height and extent than the former, shows no trace of any considerable occupation later than the Neo-Babylonian and Persian periods. From the very beginning it was therefore evident that Loftus' labors at this site would be repaid by much quicker and more satisfactory results than at Warka. The two principal mounds of the ruins, which measure over four miles in circumference, were first examined. They contained the remains of the temple and stage-tower of the Sun-god, as was readily ascertained by a few trenches cut into their centre and base. The stage-tower, about four hundred paces to the northeast of the temple ruins proper, shows the same peculiarities as the Buweriye at Warka and other similar buildings. From inscribed

bricks taken from this mound it was proved that Hammurabi, of the so-called First Dynasty of Babylon (about 2250 B. c.),and Nabonidos, the last king of the Neo-Babylonian dynasty (556-539 B. a), were among those who repaired this verv ancient structure. It was of course out of the question for Loftus to make an attempt to uncover the temple of the Sun-god completely, in order to restore its original plan, within the few weeks which he was able to devote to the excavations at Senkere. However, he showed that upon a large platform or terrace constructed six feet above another larger one, from which the former receded seventy-four feet, there stood a large hall or chamber entirely filled with rubbish. The walls of this building, which doubtless formed the main feature of the whole oval mound, were in part preserved, being still four feet high. While cleaning its characteristic entrance, formed by ten stepped recesses, Loftus was fortunate to discover two barrel-shaped clay cylinders. They were duplicates, bearing the same inscription. A third copy was soon afterwards discovered at a distant part of the ruins. From these cuneiform records and from numerous bricks taken from the upper building and the enclosing temple wall, it was ascertained that, in accordance with a reference on the cylinder brought by Rich's secretary Bellino from Babylon, Nebuchadrezzar had devoted considerable time and labor to the restoration of this ancient sanctuary. It became furthermore evident that the ancient Babylonian city buried under the ruins of Senkere was no other than Larsam, sacred to Shamash and identical with the Biblical Ellasar (Gen. 14: i). From a single brick of sixteen lines, also taken from these ruins, Sir Henry Rawlinson obtained the name of a new king, Burnaburiyash (about 1400 B. c.), one of the powerful rulers of the Cassite dynasty, while the lower strata of the mound furnished ample evidence that King Ur-Gur of Ur (about 2700 B. c.), the great builder of Babylonian temples, had also been very active at Larsam.

In addition to these very important discoveries, by which the name of the ancient city was identified and the first glimpses of its long history obtained, Loftus furnished material for us to show that in later years, when the temple was in ruins, the ground of the destroyed city of Larsam, like the other more prominent mounds of Babylonia, was used as a vast cemetery. Contrary, however, to the views of Loftus and other writers who followed him without criticism, the numerous clay tablets, which he continually found scattered through the upper layers partially burned, blackened and otherwise damaged by fire, and disintegrating from the nitrous earth composing or surrounding them, in most cases have nothing to do with the tombs in and around which they occur. Belonging to the period of about 2400 to 500 B. c., these tablets as a rule considerably antedate those burials. It has not yet been proved that in real Babylonian times Larsam was a cemetery, and in fact many strong reasons speak against such an assumption. On the other hand it is only natural to infer that when Larsam finally was no more, later grave-diggers, frequently disturbing the deserted mounds to a considerable depth, should accidentally have struck hundreds of clay tablets and sealcvlinders, which they moved out of their original resting places to an upper stratum, thus filling the burial ground with the literary and artistic remains ot an older period, and creating the impression upon the uninitiated or careless observer that the burials are contemporary with those antiquities, and that the latter furnish us a real clue for determining the age of the former. In the first years of our own excavations at Nuffar I was frequently misled by the positive statements of those in the field, occasionally quoting Loftus and Taylor as their authorities, until by personally taking charge of the expedition, I definitely determined that with but few exceptions, which can easily be explained, the large mass of tombs at Nuffar is later than 400 B. C, though often found thirty feet and more below the surface. Many of the tablets discovered by Loftus were wrapped in thin clay envelopes, similarly inscribed, and like the enclosed document covered with the impressions of seal cylinders. Others, also bearing the impressions of cylinders, were triangular in shape. From the fact that at their corners there are holes through which cords must have passed, it became evident, even without deciphering their inscriptions, that they were used

Somewhat like labels attached tO Clay Tablet with Envelope, Nuffar an object. As a rule I have found Babylonian documents of this class to belong to the second half of the third pre-Christian millennium. Of especial value and interest was a certain tablet which proved to be a table of squares from one to sixty, both numbers i and 60, being rendered by the same perpendicular wedge, thus confirming the statement of Berosus that the Babylonians employed a sexagesimal system of calculation.

Among the stray clay reliefs taken from the upper layers of Senkere, but doubtless belonging to a much earlier period of Babylonian civilization, are some tablets with a religious representation, others showing persons employed in their every-day life. One of the latter, for example, exhibits two persons boxing, while two others are occupied over a large vase; another reproduces a lion roaring and furiously lashing his tail because of being disturbed in his feast of a bullock by a man armed with a hatchet and a club.

Larsam is one of those mounds easily excavated and sure to repay the labors of the systematic explorer quickly. Representing one of the earliest and most famous Babylonian cities, with a sanctuary in which the kings of all ages down to Nabonidos were prominently interested, it will furnish literary and artistic monuments of importance for the early history and civilization of Babylonia.

While engaged in his work at Senkere, Loftus sent a few gangs of workmen to the ruins of Tell Sifr and Tell Medina, on the east of the Shaft el-Kar. The trenches cut into the desolate mound of Medina, situated on the border of extensive marshes and inhabited by lions and other wild animals, yielded no results beyond a single stray clay tablet, a number of tombs, and the common types of pottery. But the excavations carried on for a few days at Tell Sifr (" Copper") were most encouraging, bringing to light about one hundred mostly well-preserved case tablets, dated in the reigns of the kings of the First Dynasty of Babylon (Samsu-iluna, previously unknown, being among them), and a large collection of caldrons, vases, dishes, hammers, hatchets, knives, daggers, fetters, mirrors, and other instruments and utensils, all in copper, and evidently likewise belonging to the second half of the third pre-Christian millennium.

Unfortunately the excavations so successfully begun at Senkere and Tell Sifr came to a sudden end. The continued advance of the marshes from the overflowing of the Shaft el-Kar indicated very plainly that in a few weeks the whole of Southern Babylonia would be covered with inundations. The Arabs, who for several successive years had terribly suffered from lack of water and food, and therefore were anxious to cultivate their patches of land, rapidly decreased the necessary forces in the trenches by their frequent desertions. In order not to be finally left alone with his excavated treasures on an isolated mound surrounded by the Chaldean swamps, Loftus was forced to sacrifice his personal wishes and return to the Euphrates, much to his regret quitting the South Babylonian mounds, the real character and contents of which he had been the first to disclose to the public.

SIR AI'STEN HENRY LAYARD

The next to appear on the unexplored ground in the South was Henry Lavard. A long experience in the trenches of Nimrud and Qoyunjuk had qualified him above others for the exploration of the mounds in ancient Babylonia. Besides, he was well acquainted with the life and manners of the Arabs, and not unfamiliar with the peculiarities of 'Iraq el-'Arabi as a whole. For in connection with his early adventures in Luristan and Khuzistan he had visited Baghdad repeatedly, and in Arab or Persian disguise he had travelled even among the lawless tribes of the districts adjoining the two rivers to the east and west as far down as Qorna and Basra. Prevented hitherto by lack of means from carrying out his old and comprehensive scheme of" excavating many remarkable sites both in Chaldea and Susiana," he was finally enabled to gratify his ardent desire to a limited extent. Apparently influenced in their decision by the encouraging results of Loftus' first tentative work at Warka, the trustees of the British Museum granted him permission to excavate some of the more prominent Babylonian mounds.

Accompanied by his trusted comrade Rassam and by about thirty of his most experienced workmen from Mosul, he descended the Tigris on a raft, reaching Baghdad October 26, 1850. But the time was ill chosen for his exploring tour. His old friend Dr. Ross had died a year before; Colonel Rawlinson, the British resident, was on a leave of absence in England; Hormuzd Rassam fell seriously ill soon after their arrival, and the whole country around the city was swarming with Bedouins in open revolt against the Ottoman government, so that it was next to impossible to leave for the ruins of Babylon.

Not to lose time, he began operations at Tell Mohammed, a few miles to the southeast of Baghdad, where Captain Jones' crew had discovered inscribed bronze balls, from which it became evident that at some previous time a royal Babylonian palace (of Hammurabi) had occupied this site. Beyond several insignificant finds Layard's excavations proved unsuccessful. After a delay of nearly six weeks he moved to Hilla. Owing to the disturbed state of the country he could do no more than pay a hurried visit to the conspicuous mound of Kl-Birs, which, like his predecessors, he recognized at once as the remains of a stage tower, "the general type of the Chaldean and Assyrian temples."

As soon as he had established friendly relations with the most influential inhabitants of the town, he commenced excavations at Babil. The subterranean passages opened by Rich forty years previously were quickly discovered and followed up, but without results. By

means of a few deep trenches he arrived at the doubtless correct conclusion that the coffins here found must belong to a period subsequent to the destruction of the edifice which forms the centre of the mound, and that in all probability long after the fall of the Babylonian empire a citadel had crowned its summit. He exposed at the foot of the hill enormous piers and buttresses of brickwork, frequently bearing the name of Nebuchadrezzar, but he could find no clue as to the original character of the gigantic structure which had left such vast remains.

Next he turned to the shapeless mass of shattered walls, known since the time of Rich under the name of Kl-Qasr ("The Palace"), but like Babil also frequently called Mujeliba (" Overturned ") by the Arab population. Again his labors were deficient in positive results. He gathered nothing but a few specimens of the well-known enamelled bricks of various colors, and excavated some rudely engraved gems and the fragment of a limestone slab containing two human figures with unimportant cuneiform characters.

No better antiquities were discovered at Tell 'Omran ibn 'Ali and several smaller mounds included in the territory of ancient Babylon. After a month of nearly fruitless digging in the extensive ruins of the famous metropolis he decided to leave a small gang of workmen at these disappointing mounds and to depart with his Mosul Arabs for Tell NufFar, the only place in the interior of the country to which he devoted a few weeks of concentrated attention. At the head of a good-sized caravan of fifty men he arrived at the marshes of NurTar on January 17, 1851. He was received in the most friendly mariner by the shaikh of the 'Afej, whose protection he had solicited before he left the banks of the Euphrates. But much to his disappointment and personal discomfort he felt obliged to comply with the shaikh's request and to pitch his tent at Suq el-'Afej, "the market place" of the tribe and the residence of his newly acquired patron. The conglomeration of filthy reed huts which had received this high-

sounding name was situated at the southeast edge of the unhealthy marshes and nearly three miles away from the ruins of Nuffar. In order to reach the latter with his Arabs of Mosul and a number of 'Afej, it was necessary to cross the swamps every

'Afej Reed-Huts near Nurfar day by means of the *turrada,* a long narrow and shallow boat of the natives consisting of a framework of bulrushes covered with bitumen.

The imposing ruins of NufTar, with Babylon and Warka the largest in Babylonia, are situated at the northeastern boundary of these marshes, which varv in size according to the extent of the annual inundations of the Euphrates. A large canal, now dry and for miles entirely filled with sand and rubbish, divides the ruins into two almost equal parts. It is called by the surrounding tribes Shatt en-Nil, supposed to be a continuation of the famous canal which, branching off from the Euphrates above Babylon, once carried life and fertility to the otherwise barren plains of Central Babylonia. On an average about fifty to sixty feet high, the ruins of Nuffar form a collection of mounds torn up by frequent gulleys and furrows into a number of spurs and ridges, from the distance not unlike a rugged mountain range on the banks of the upper Tigris.

In the Babylonian language the citv buried here was called Nippur. Out of the midst of collapsed walls and broken drains at the northeastern corner of these vast ruins there rises a conical mound to the height of about ninety-five feet above the present level of the plain. It is called Bint elAmir (" The Princess ") by the Arabs of the neighborhood, and covers the remains of *Imgharsag,* the ancient stage-tower of *Ekur,* the great sanctuary of Bel. An almost straight line formed bv two narrow ridges to the northeast of the temple towards the desert indicates the course of *NlmitAfarduk,* the outer wall of the city. The surface of this whole mass of ruins is covered with numerous fragments of brick, glazed and unglazed pottery, stone, glass and scoria, which generally mark the sites of Babylonian cities.

Lavard spent less than a fortnight at these ruins, to examine their contents, devoting considerable time to the fruitless search of " a great black stone" said by the Arabs to exist somewhere in the mounds of Nuffar. But a last time his hopes and expectations connected with the ruins of Babylonia were bitterly disappointed. Though opening many trenches in different sections of the ruins, and especially in the conical mound at the northeastern corner, where forty years later the present writer still found their traces, he discovered little of the true Babylonian period beyond massive walls and stray bricks inscribed with a cuneiform legend of King Ur-Gur. All the mounds seemed literally filled with the burials of a people inhabiting those regions long after the ancient city was covered with rubbish and the sand of the desert. He unearthed and examined nearly a hundred slipper-shaped clay coffins similar to those which Loftus had recently sent from Warka to England. Frequently they contained small cups and vases with blackish deposits of unknown liquids and crumbling remains of dates and bones, occasionally a few beads and engraved stones, but in no case ornaments of gold and silver.

Somewhat disheartened by this lack of success which everywhere characterized his brief and superficial work among the Babylonian ruins, differing from those in Assyria by the natural conditions of the soil, their long and varied occupation and the peculiarity of the material employed in constructing palaces and other large edifices, Layard's opinion of the character of the mounds examined was naturally faulty and colored by his unfortunate experience. "On the whole I am much inclined to question whether extensive excavations carried on at Niffer would produce any very important or interesting results," was the verdict of the great explorer at the middle of the last century. "More than sixty thousand cuneiform tablets so far rescued from the archives of Nippur, temple library definitely located, and a large pre-Sargonic gate discovered below the desert," was another message which fifty years later the pre-

sent writer could despatch to the committee of the Philadelphia expedition from the same mounds of Nuffar. In consequence of the state of anarchy which prevailed everywhere in Babylonia, and influenced by what has been stated above, Layard abandoned his original plan of visiting and exploring the ruins of Warka. His physical condition had also suffered considerably during his brief stay among the 'Afej. The dampness of the soil and the unwholesome air of the surrounding marshes had brought on a severe attack of pleurisy and fever. It was therefore with a feeling of joy and relief that soon after the arrival of Rassam, who had just recovered from his long and severe illness at Baghdad, Layard quitted the unhospitable and malarious regions around Nuffar forever.

We cannot close the brief description of Layard's fruitless efforts in Babylonia without quoting a remark which, on the authority of Fresnel, he is said to have made to his English friends after his return to Baghdad. "There will be nothing to be hoped for from the site of Babylon except with a parliamentary vote for,£25,000 (= $ 125,0x50), and if ever this sum should be voted, I would solicit the favor of not being charged with its application." THE FRENCH EXPEDITION UNDER FRESNEL, OPPERT AND THOMAS

The continued activity of the English explorers among the ruins of Assyria and Babylonia, the encouraging news of the results of Loftus' first tentative work at Warka, and the general conviction of European scholars that the kings of Babylon must have left similar and even earlier monuments than those excavated by Botta and Lavard in the Assyrian mounds moved the French government to a decisive step. In August, 1851, Leon Faucher, then minister of the interior, laid a plan for the organization of " a scientific and artistic expedition to Mesopotamia and Media" before the National Assembly, accompanied by the urgent request for acredit of70,000francs (= $14,000). The necessary permission was soon granted. On October 1, the members of the expe-

dition left Paris, and Marseilles eight days later. Fulgence Fresnel, formerly French consul at Jidda and thoroughly acquainted with the language and manners of the Arabs, was the director, ably assisted by Jules Oppert as Assyriologist, a voung naturalized German scholar of great talents and independence of judgment, and Felix Thomas as architect.

In *Journal Asiatique,* Series v., vol. vi. (1856), p. 548.

Adverse circumstances and unavoidable delavs kept the members of the expedition three months on their way from France to Alexandretta, a time which they employed to the best of their ability in examining the ancient remains at Malta, Alexandria, Baalbek, and the Nahr el-Kelb above Beirut. With forty mules they finally left Aleppo, and after an interesting journey via Diarbekr, Mardin, and Nisibin, on March i, 1852, reached Mosul, where Victor Place had succeeded Botta as vice-consul and archaeological representative of France, while Layard, having finished his second successful campaign at)oyunjuk, had returned to Europe in the previous year. The very next day after their arrival on this historical ground the enthusiastic French commission visited Place at Khorsabad, who had but recently commenced his operations there. For three weeks they remained at Mosul, occupying themselves with a study of the history of the city, examining the ruins of Nineveh on the other side of the river, taking squeezes, copying cuneiform inscriptions, and preparing themselves in many other ways for their impending task at Babylon. As soon as their large raft of three hundred goatskins was finished, they embarked and descended the Tigris, arriving at Baghdad five days later.

As we have seen above in connection with Layard's visit to Babylonia, there prevailed at the middle of the last century a general state of anarchy in the northern part of that country. Large parties of roaming Arabs, defying the authority of the Turkish governor, were constantly plundering pilgrims and caravans, and even made the neighborhood of Baghdad very unsafe. The French expedition was not slow in recognizing its unfavorable position. Men like Rawlinson, who were thoroughly familiar with the country and its inhabitants, advised the three members strongly to devote their first attention rather to the Median ruins, Oppert himself proposing to explore the site of ancient Kcbatana. But the cool political relations then existing between France and Persia seemed to Fresnel a serious obstacle to any successful work in that direction. After a repeated discussion of the whole situation, it was decided to remain at Baghdad, waiting for the first opportunity to proceed to Hilla.

This decision did not turn out to be very wise; for it soon became evident that the dangers had been greatly exaggerated, in order to keep the expedition from the ruins. Over three months the members were thus practically shut up within the walls of the city. Spring passed away, and it was summer when a foolish rumor of the discovery of the golden statue of Nebuchadrezzar at Babvlon, which spread rapidly all over Asia Minor, finding its wav even into the American papers, finally roused Fresnel to new activity. In the company of two regiments of soldiers, who happened to leave for Hilla, the French expedition quitted Baghdad, established its headquarters at Jumjuma or Jimjime, and began actual excavations at the Qasr on Julv 15, 1852.

The commencement of their work was most discouraging. The mass of masonry and rubbish to be removed was enormous and far beyond the time and means at their disposal. Owing to the great danger connected with cutting trenches into the loose fragments, thev had to confine their labors to certain sections of the large ruin. The results, accordingly, were as modest as possible. Like Layard, they found the ordinary bricks inscribed with the well-known legend of Nebuchadrezzar, of which Oppert made the best by showing that nearly forty different stamps had been employed in their manufacture. They gathered a large number of varnished tiles representing portions of

men, animals, plants, ornaments, and cuneiform characters, as often noticed before, and they discovered even some fragments of a barrel cylinder of Nebuchadrezzar, a duplicate of the complete cylinder published by Rich.

Shortly before their final departure for Babvlon, Oppert and Thomas made a brief excursion by water to the ruins of Ctesiphon and Scleucia (June 23)1 and also paid a visit to Kadhimen, a little above Baghdad. While in his recent publication, *Am Euphrat undam Tigris* (p. 37), Sachau regards *iVumtjuma* as the original word, Oppert *Expedition en Mesopotamie*, vol. i., p. 141) following Rich (comp. p. 30, above) and the Turkish geographer (Rich's "Collected Memoirs," p. 61), retained *Jumjuma*, meaning "Skull, Calvary."

Of no greater importance were the excavations conducted in Tell 'Omran ibn 'All (to the south of the Qasr), which Oppert firmly believed to represent the site of the famous hanging gardens, and which he examined alone, as his two companions Fresnel and Thomas had fallen ill. He showed that the whole upper part of the ruin contained tombs of a very late period. They were particularly numerous at the extreme ends and in the ravines of the mound, but in no case were found at any great depth in the centre, which contained many inscribed bricks of Nebuchadrezzar. These tombs clearly betrayed their Parthian origin. They were generally constructed in the form of coffins of Babylonian bricks, which sometimes bore cuneiform inscriptions of Esarhaddon, Nebuchadrezzar, Neriglissar, and Nabonidos. Though for the greater part previously pillaged, these burial places yielded a quantity of smaller antiquities, such as terra-cotta vases, simple and ornamented, clay figurines and playthings, glass vessels, instruments in copper and iron, and a few gold objects. As the lower strata, apparently concealing structures from the time of Nebuchadrezzar, could not be examined satisfactorily, unfortunately no definite information was obtained as to the character of the large edifice which once occupied this prominent site. Oppert's the-

ory as set forth above, and defended by him with much vigor, has recently been proved by Dr. Koldewey's researches to be erroneous.

The most imposing mound of the ruins of the ancient metropolis is Babil, situated at the extreme northern end of the vast complex. Its summit, forming an irregular plateau of considerable extent, had been described by Rich, Buckingham, Porter and other earlier explorers as covered with numerous remains of buildings. When Oppert examined this site, all these walls had disappeared under the industrious hands of the Arab brick-diggers, who had begun to start excavations even in the interior of the enormous tumulus. Since then Babil has again completely changed its aspect, BJbil, Sciuth-East Face, as it appeared in 1853 so that if three pictures of the same mound taken at the beginning, middle and end of the last century were placed alongside of one another, nobody would recognize one and the same ruin in them. The French excavations undertaken on a very limited scale at the top and base of this mound brought to light only the common bricks and fragments of stone and glass and part of a Greek inscription, without furnishing any clue as to the building which originally stood here. Interpreting the classical writers in the light of his own theories concerning the topography of Babylon, Oppert came to the conclusion that Babil represents the ruins of the pyramid called by Strabo the "Sepulchre of Bel," which according to his view was a building entirely distinct from the " Temple of Bel " with its stage-tower.

Comp. Rich's sketch of 1811 (sec page 39, above) with that made by the French architect Thomas in 1853, and reproduced on the present

Considerable time was devoted to tracing the ancient quay of the river and the different walls of the city. Fully convinced that the capital of Nebuchadrezzar was about twenty-five times as large as the ancient city of Babylon' (previous to the fall of Nineveh), and that the latter was reserved exclusively for the royal quarter under the kings of the Neo-Babylonian dynasty, Oppert followed Buckingham's example and included El-Birs and Kl-Ohemir in the enormous territory of his "Greater Babylon." He examined these two extreme quarters and the territory lying between them personally, supplementing or correcting the statements of his predecessors in certain details. While himself occupied with the excavations at 'Omran ibn 'All, he even ordered a few trenches to be cut in Tell Ibrahim elKhalil, a large mound adjoining El-Birs, and with the latter forming the principal ruins of an ancient city. The finds were insignificant, with the exception of a small dated tablet found in a tomb and bearing the name of the place, Barsip, at the end. In the light of Sir Henry Rawlinson's fundamental discoveries at the Birs made a few years later, but published several years before Oppert's work appeared, this document, though as a stray tablet of little importance for the whole question in itself, could be claimed as the first cuneiform witness in support of the proposed identification of these ruins with ancient Borsippa. Having once set forth his theory on the enormous extent of the city of Babylon and having failed to find any trace of Herodotus' "Temple of Belus " among the ruins on the left side of the Euphrates, it was only natural that with most of the former travellers Oppert should decide upon the gigantic remains of the tower of Borsippa as the ruins of that great sanctuary.

According to Oppert, the great outer wall of Babylon enclosed a territory as large as the whole department *of* the Seine, or fifteen times as large as the city of Paris in 1859, or seven times the extent of Paris in 1860. Co'mp. Oppert, /. -., vol. i., p. 234. Comp. Oppert, /. c., vol. i., p. 204.

In October, 1852, Fresnel and Oppert excavated for a week at the group of mounds generally called El-Ohemir, and including the tumulus of El-Khazna (" The Treasure "), Fl-Bandar ("The Harbor ") and a number of lower elevations, several hours to the east of Babylon, near the old bed of the Shatt en-Nil. They uncovered a brick pavement of Nebuchadrezzar close by El-Ohemir,

and a piece of basalt bearing an archaic cuneiform inscription with manv smaller antiquities in the other two principal mounds just mentioned. The identification of this whole group "with one of the two cities of Cuthah" referred to by Arab writers was proposed by Oppert, but cannot be accepted. For the brick found and published by Ker Porter says clearly that Zamama, the chief deity of Kish, had his sanctuary, *E-me-teur-sag-ga,* there, while the god of Cuthah was Nergal.

The French explorers worked at Babylon and its environment for almost two years, extending their topographical researches on the west side of the Euphrates as far as Kerbela and Kefil, and locating and briefly describing a number of Babylonian and Mohammedan ruins previously unknown. At the beginning of February, 1854, after a visit to the ruins of'Aqarquf, Oppert finally left Babylonia, while Fresnel remained in Baghdad until his early death in November, 1855. The former returned to France by way of Mosul, where in the company of Victor Place he devoted six weeks to a thorough study of the ruins of Nineveh and Khorsabad, and their exposed monuments, many of which he could decipher at the places of their discovery before they were Comp. p. 49, above, with ii. *R.* 50, 12.

removed to Europe. On July i, 1854, Oppert arrived at Paris alone with his notes and plans and a few antiquities, waiting for the bulk of the results of his expedition, which had been ordered to be sent home by a French boat from Basra. But unfortunately they never reached their destination. It was about a year later when Oppert, while in London, learned the first news of the disaster from Sir Henry Layard. All the collections excavated and purchased, including even the valuable marble vase of Naram-Sin (about 3750 B. c.), the first and for a long while the only monument of the ancient Sargonides discovered, went down in the muddy waters of the Tigris, a few miles above its junction with the Euphrates, on May 23, 1855.

It was a long series of difficulties and adverse circumstances which the French expedition had to encounter from the beginning to the end. Owing to the very limited means at their disposal, Fresnel and Oppert had not been able to do much more than to scratch the surface of the vast mounds, without contributing anything of importance to our knowledge of the ancient topography of Nebuchadrezzar's metropolis. "The great city of Babylon" was practically still unexplored when the French expedition quitted the ruins. But notwithstanding all that has been said to the contrary, scientific results were by no means lacking. In a general way first communicated by Fresnel in the *Journal Asiatique,* they were methodically and neatly set forth by Oppert, the real soul of the whole undertaking, in a work of two volumes, illustrated by a number of sketches from the Comp. Fresnel's two letters to . Mohl, published in the *Journal Aiiatique,* Series v., vol. i. (1853), pp. 485-548, dated Hilla, December, 1852, and continued in vol. ii. (1853), pp. 5-78; and vol. vi. (1856), pp. 525-548, dated Hilla, end of June, 1853. Authorized by ministerial order in 1856, it appeared under the title *Expedition Scientifique en Mesupotamie,* two volumes, Paris, vol. ii. (published first), 1859: "Decipherment of the Cuneiform Inscriptions" (part hand of Thomas. This publication, written by one of the founders of the young Assyriological science, will always hold a prominent place in the history of exploration, alike for the manifold information it conveys on various archaeological topics, for the boldness with which our author attacks difficult topographical problems, and above all for the skill and brilliancy with which Oppert — in many cases for the first time—translates and analyzes the historical inscriptions from Assyrian and Babylonian palaces, thus contributing essentially to the restoration of the eventful past of two powerful nations.

J. E. TAYLOR

At the beginning of 1854, when Petermann, of Berlin, was studying the language and life of the Sabean Christians at Suq esh-Shivukh, and Loftus was engaged at Warkd for the "Assyrian Kxcavation Fund," at the request of Sir Henry Kawlinson excavations were also undertaken at Muqayyar for the British Museum by J. E. Taylor, Her Majesty's Vice-Consul at Basra. The ruins of Muqayyar" ("Bitumined" or "Cemented with Bitumen") are situated upon a slight elevation six to seven miles southwest from the modern town of Nasriye. The country all about is so low that frequently during the annual flood of the Euphrates, /. e. from March till June or July, the ruins form practically an island in the midst of a large marsh, unapproachable on any side except in boats. The ruins are then sometimes occupied as a stronghold by the Dhafir, a lawless tribe of the desert, which at certain seasons extends its camping-grounds far into the districts of the Jezire. Travellers who in recent years desired to visit Muqayyar were often obliged to do so at their own risk, the Turkish officials not only declining a military escort, but demanding even a written declaration in which it is stated that the person in question does not hold the Ottoman government iii. including inscriptions discovered by the French expedition); vol. i. 1863: "Report of the Journey and Results of the Expedition" (pp. 287— 357 containing a description of Assyrian ruins, illustrated by a translation of the largest and most important inscriptions then discovered).

Published as part ot an Atlas (21 plates) accompanying Oppert's two volumes. To-day generally pronounced *Mugayer* bv the Arabs. The various writers, with more or less success endeavoring to reproduce the name as it was heard by them, write it in many different ways, *Muqucijer, Mughycr, Mvgeyer, Mughair, Megheyer, Meghaiir, Umghser, Vmghcir,* etc. responsible for any accident that may befall him in a region outside of their real jurisdiction. The ruins of Mu qayyar consist of a *r* -T'Ows" '' *n A* series or low mounds of oval form, their whole circumference measuring nearly 3000 vards, and their largest diameter from north to south a little over 1000 vards. Previous to Taylor, they had been examined by PietrodellaValle (1625),

who took one of the inscribed bricks with him, and gathered some inscribed seal cylinders on the surface, bv Baillie Fraser (1835),' and by Loftus (1850), who again visited them shortly before he quitted Babylonia forever (1854). But our real knowledge of the character and contents of the ruins is based upon the excavations of the firstnamed explorer, who worked there in the beginning of 1854, and who opened a few additional trenches, in connection with a second visit, about a year later.

Plan of the Ruins of Muqayyar
(Ur of ike Chaldcet)

A French professor from Bordeaux, who had been my guest at NufFar in March, 1900, and whom I had advised to visit Muqayyar also, reported the same experience to me. The Dhafir allowed him only to walk around the ruins hurriedly. Since the fall of 1900, after the great troubles among the Arabs of those regions and to the south of them have been settled temporarily, conditions have improved somewhat.

Near the north end of the mounds stands the principal building of the whole site, about seventv feet high. It is a two-storied structure having the plan of a right-angled parallelogram, the largest sides of which are the northeast and southwest, being each 198 feet long, while the others measure only 133 feet. As in all other similar Babylonian buildings, one angle points almost due north. The lower story, twenty-seven feet high, is supported bv strong buttresses; the upper story, receding from thirty to forty-seven feet from the edge of the first, is fourteen feet high, surmounted by about five feet of brick rubbish. The ascent to this remarkable stage-tower, perforated with numerous air-holes, like those at 'Aqarquf and Kl-Birs, was on the northeast side. By driving a tunnel into the very heart of the mound, Taylor convinced himself first that " the whole building was built of sun-dried bricks in the centre, with a thick coating of massive, partially burnt bricks of a light red color with layers of reeds between them, the whole to the thickness of ten feet being cased by a wall of inscribed kilnburnt bricks."

Next he turned his attention to the four corners. While excavating the southwest corner of the upper story, he found, six feet below the surface, a perfect inscribed clay cylinder, standing in a niche formed by the omission of one of the bricks in the layer. A similar cylinder having been discovered in the northwest corner, the fortunate explorer naturally concluded that corresponding objects would be found in the remaining two corners. A shaft sunk in each of them proved his theory to be correct, at the same time bringing out the important fact that the commemorative cylinders of the builders or restorers of Babylonian temples and palaces were generally deposited in the four corners. Fragments of another larger and even more interesting barrel cylinder were rescued from the same mound and from a lower elevation immediately north of it.

Pietrodella Valle (comp. p. 17, above) not only gave the correct etymology of the name of the ruins, but recognized even the peculiar signs on the bricks and seal cylinders as *unbektinnte una uhralte Buchstaben. Unter anderen Buchstaben habe ich iher ztceen an vie/ en Orten tcahrgenommen, worunter der tine viie eine liegende Pyramid oder Flamm-saule (£), der andere aber tcie ein Stern mil acht Strahlen ($fc)* — the sign for "God" — *geteeit.* Comp. the German translation of his work, *Reiss-Beschreibung,* Geneva, 1674, part 4, p. 184. Comp. his "Travels in Koordistan, Mesopotamia," etc., vol. ii., pp. 90— 94, and p. 5 5, above. "Travels and Researches in Chaldxa and Susiana," pp. 127-135. Comp., also, p. 141, above.

The massive structure thus examined by Taylor turned out to be the famous temple of the Moon-god Sin. It is "the only example of a Babylonian temple remaining in good preservation not wholly covered by rubbish." From the fine barrel cylinders and the large inscribed bricks differing as to size and inscription in the two stories, Rawlinson established soon afterwards that the site of Muqayyar represents the Biblical Ur of the Chaldees (Gen. 11:28; 15:7). The temple was constructed by King Ur-Gur (about 2700 B. c.), repaired by his son

Dungi, and more than 2000 years later was for the last time restored by the last king of Babylon, Nabuna'id (Nabonidos), who deposited the account of his work inscribed upon these clay cylinders in the corners of the stage-tower.

After him Mount Sinai is called, the name meaning "Sacred to Sin." Comp. Loftus, *l. c.,* p. 128.

The discovery of these documents was of the greatest importance for Biblical history in another way. The inscriptions upon all of them closed with a poetical prayer for the lite of the king's oldest son, Bel-shar-usur, who is no other than the Biblical Belshazzar (Dan. 5), appointed by

Ruins of the Temple of Sin at Muqayyar his father as co-regent, defeated by Cyrus near Opis, and murdered soon after the conquest of Babylon.

In a small hill close to the southeast corner of the large ruin Taylor unearthed a regular house built of large inscribed bricks upon a platform of sundried bricks. Some of the burnt bricks were remarkably fine, having a thin coating of enamel or gypsum on which the cuneiform characters had been stamped, — the first example of this kind known. From the northwest corner of the mud wall he obtained a small black stone inscribed on both sides, from which it can be inferred that the building dates back to the third millennium.

At a depth considerably below this building, he came upon a pavement consisting of bricks fourteen inches long, eight and a half wide, and three and a half thick, " most of them having the impressions of the tips of two fingers at the back; none were inscribed, the whole imbedded in bitumen." From what the present writer has pointed out in 1896 as a characteristic feature of the earliest Babylonian bricks,' it is very evident that here Taylor had reached the pre-Sargonic period (about 4000 B. C).

He mentions other interesting bricks found upon the same mound, which were " painted red, and had an inscription over nearly the whole length and breadth in a small neat character," while "on one portion of them was the symbol of two crescents, back to back." But his statements here and in other places are so vague that our curiosity is only raised without any chance of being satisfied.

The rest of the mounds of Muqayyar, so far as Taylor was able to dig into them, seemed to represent a vast cemetery of the early Babylonians, yielding clay coffins and

Clay Coffin from Muqayyar vases of different size and shape, numerous drains, and many smaller objects in stone, metal, and clay valuable for illustrating the life and customs of the former inhabitants, especially those of the later periods.

All around the graves in the different parts of the ruins he came across many fragments of inscribed cones. In the long west mound he found two whole jars filled with clay tablets placed in envelopes of the same material, and frequently bearing seal impressions, in addition to over thirty stray tablets and fragments.

Comp. Hilprecht, "The Babylonian Expedition of the University of Pennsylvania," Series A, vol. i., part 2, p. 45.

Notwithstanding the insignificant funds and the short time placed at the disposal of our explorer, and notwithstanding the lack of a proper archaeological training so seriously felt by himself, and through which a large portion of the scientific results have been lost, Taylor's patient labors and attempts at disclosing the contents of Muqayyar were successful beyond expectation. Different travellers have since visited the ruins, taking measurements and picking up a few objects here and there on the surface; but they all have added practically nothing to our knowledge of those mounds, which is derived exclusively from the reports of Loftus and Taylor written nearly fifty years ago. The methodical exploration of Muqayyar and a complete restoration of its history belong still to the desirable things expected from the future. There is hope, however, that even before the German railroad line from Baghdad to Basra has been constructed, an American expedition will start excavations at these ruins in the beginning of the twen-

tieth century. Owing to the lawlessness of the Arab tribes roaming over that part of the desert, and no less to the swampy condition of the neighborhood of Muqayyar during the annual inundations, there are peculiar difficulties to be overcome here, similar to those prevailing at Nippur and Warka. But with the necessary tact and determination they can be overcome, and the mounds, considerably smaller in extent than either of the two ruins mentioned, can be thoroughly explored at an expense of $200,000 within a period of twenty-five years. The results, though scarcely ever furnishing a document referring to the life and person of Abraham,— as has been expected, — will doubtless add many fresh stones to the rising building of the early history of Babylonia.

According to information received by cable from Dr. Banks, the director of the planned Expedition to Ur, at the beginning of October, 1901, the Ottoman Government has declined to grant him a firman for the excavation of Muqayyar. Previous to his second visit to Muqayyar, early in 1855, Taylor excavated for a few days at two other ruins, called Tell el-Lahm and Abu Shahrain. The former ruin, consisting of two mounds of some height surrounded by a number of smaller ridges and elevations, is situated three hours to the south of Suq esh-Shiyukh, near the dry bed of an ancient canal, and does not exceed half a mile in circumference. Nothing of especial interest was discovered. But Taylor exhumed numerous coffins formed of two large jars joined together by a bitumen cement, traced several pavements constructed of baked bricks, occasionally bearing defaced cuneiform characters, and found a perfect clay tablet, so that the Babylonian origin, though not the early name of the site, could be established beyond any reasonable doubt.

Of greater importance were Taylor's excavations at Abu Shahrain, situated in the desert beyond the sandstone bluffs which separate it from Ur and the valley of the Euphrates, but — strange to say — very generally placed wrongly by Assyriologists on the left side of "the great river," somewhere opposite Suq esh-Shiyukh, though its correct situation might have been inferred from several cuneiform passages in which Kridu is mentioned. "The first aspect of the mounds is that of a ruined fort, surrounded by high walls with a keep or tower at one end," placed on an eminence nearly in the centre of the dry bed of an inland sea. They are half concealed in a deep valley about fifteen miles wide, and only towards the north open to the Euphrates. For the greater part this depression is "covered with a nitrous incrustation, but with here and there a few patches of alluvium, scantily clothed with the shrubs and plants peculiar to the desert." To the northwest and southeast of the principal mounds are "small low mounds full of graves, funeral vases, and urns." Paint traces of an ancient canal, six yards broad, were discovered at no great distance to the northwest of the ruins.

With whom this error started I do not know. We find it in Menant, *Baby lone et la Chaldee* (1875), and Delitzsch, *Wo lag das Parodies?* (1881)—notwithstanding Taylor's very explicit statements to the contrary. George Rawlinson, "Five Great Monarchies," 4th ed., London, 1879, vol. ii., f" Map of Mesopotamia," etc.) places Abu Shahrain correctly, on the right side of the river, hut too far to the south. About where Tell el-Lahm is situated is Abu Shahrain, and where he has Abu Shahrain is Tell el-Lahm. The ruins of Abu Shahrain, situated as they are in a deep valley, cannot be seen from Muqayyar, nor are they identical with Nowawis, as assumed by Peters ("Nippur," vol. ii., pp. 96 and 298, *r(f.)* S.cheiPs recent statement concerning them (*Recueil*, vol. xxi., p. 126) evidently rests on Arab information. It is correct, but only confirms facts better known from Taylor's own accurate reports, which, however, do not seem to have been read carefully by Assyriologists during the last twenty-five years. These latter, which are considerably smaller than those of Muqayyar, " rise abruptly from the plain, and are not encumbered with the masses of rubbish usually surrounding similar places."

Consisting of a platform enclosed by a sandstone wall twenty feet high, the whole complex is divided into two parts of nearly equal extent. As in most of the larger Babylonian ruins so far examined, the northern part of Abu Shahrain is occupied by a pyramidal tower of two stages, constructed of sun-dried brick cased with a wall of kiln-burnt brick, and still about seventy feet high.

The summit of the first stage of this building is reached by a staircase fifteen feet wide and seventy feet long, originally constructed of polished marble slabs, now scattered all over the mound, and at its foot flanked by two columns of an interesting construction. An inclined road leads up to the second story. "Pieces of agate, alabaster, and marble, finely cut and polished, small pieces of pure gold, goldheaded and plain copper nails, cover the ground about the basement" of the latter — sufficient to indicate that a small

Temple Ruin at Abu Shahrain from the South but richly embellished sacred chamber formerly crowned the top of the second stage. Around the whole tower there is a pavement of inscribed baked brick placed upon a large laver of clav two feet thick.

From several trenches cut in various parts of these remarkable mounds, Taylor reached the startling conclusion that all the ruined buildings he met with, including the ponderous mass of the stage-tower, rested on the fine sand of the desert confined by a coating of sun-dried brick, upon which the above-mentioned sandstone wall rises. In contrast to all the other Babvlonian ruins, where natural stone is almost entirelv unknown as building material, we find sandstone and granite and marble liberally employed in Abu Shahrain, a fact which illustrates and proves the correctness of the theory that the extensive use of clay in ancient Babylonia is due only to the complete absence of any kind of stone in the alluvial ground of the country.

A number of chambers, which the explorer excavated, yielded but little. But the inscribed bricks gathered from the temple enclosure told us the important

news that the city here buried was Eridu, sacred to the early inhabitants of Babylonia as the seat of a famous oracle so frequently mentioned in the inscriptions of the third pre-Christian millennium and later. A peculiar structure partly unearthed at the south-east section of the ruins, the precise character of which has hitherto not been recognized, also testifies to the great age of the place. The uninscribed bricks were laid in bitumen, and by their curious shape (" thin at both ends and thick in the middle, as in the margin, the under part perfectly flat") naturally attracted the attention of Taylor. From what we now know about the history of Babylonian brick-making, it becomes evident that Taylor had hit a preSargonic structure of about 4000 B. C, the southern gateway of the large temple complex. If instead of "a few feet" he had dug about fifteen to twenty feet on either side along the stone wall adjoining it, he probably would have found another similar pair of bastions, thereby obtaining the characteristic three divisions of a Sumerian gateway with a central passage for beasts and chariots and two narrower side entrances, reached by means of steps, for the people.

With regard to portable finds, Tavlor's work at Abu Shahrain was unproductive of important results. But the discovery' and brief description of those large ruins and of so many inscribed bricks, through which it was possible to restore the old Babylonian name of the city buried there, was in itself a most valuable contribution to our knowledge of ancient comparative geographv, especially when it is remembered that, owing to the seclusion of the spot and the insecurity of its neighborhood, Abu Shahrain has never been visited again by any European or American explorer. Taylor's reports are published in the "Journal of the Royal Asiatic Society of Great Britain and Ireland," vol. xv. (1855), under the titles SIR HENRY RAWLINSON

The first period of Babylonian excavations was well brought to an end by Sir Henry Rawlinson himself. For a long while the Birs (Nimrud) with its high towering peak had been the one ruin above all which he desired to subject to a more careful examination than had been hitherto the case. During the months of September and October, 1854, shortly before he closed his memorable career in the Orient entirely, his desire could be finally gratified.

On behalf of the British Museum, he sent an intelligent young man, Joseph Tonietti, apothecary in the Ottoman army, to the ruins of Birs with instructions to ascertain the general features of the building through a number of specified trenches, and in particular to run a trench along the whole line of one of the walls " until the angles were turned at the two corners, so as to expose the complete face of one of the stages " of which Rawlinson had no doubt the

"Notes on the Ruins of Muqeyer," pp. 260-276, and "Notes on Abu Shahrain and Tel-el-Lahm," pp. 404.-415.

original building had been formed. His orders were carried out "with care and judgment" within a little more than two months, when the director, who had been encamped for ten days at the foot of the ruins of Babylon, occupied with questions of their topography, appeared personally on the ground, in order to apply his knowledge and critical discrimination to the partly exposed structure.

Having satisfied himself from an inspection of the various trenches in progress that the outer wall of the southeastern face of the third stage had been completely uncovered, he "proceeded on the next morning with a couple of gangs of workmen to turn to account the experience obtained from the excavations of Qal'at Shirgat (in Assyria) and Muqayyar (in Babylonia) in searching for commemorative cylinders. Accordingly he " placed a gang at work upon each of the exposed angles of the third stage, directing them to remove the bricks forming the corner carefully, one after the other," until " they had reached the tenth layer of brick above the plinth at the base." Half an hour later Rawlinson was summoned to the southern corner, where the workmen had reached the limit which he had marked out for their preliminary work. On

reaching the spot, he was first "occupied for a few minutes in adjusting a prismatic compass on the lowest brick now remaining of the original angle, which fortunately projected a little," and he then ordered the work to be resumed. The excitement which immediately followed we describe better in his own language.

"No sooner had the next layer of bricks been removed than the workmen called out there was a *Khazeneh khazna,* or treasure hole;' that is, in the corner at the distance of two bricks from the exterior surface, there was a vacant space-filled half up with loose reddish sand. 'Clear away the sand,' I said, 'and bring out the cylinder;' and as I spoke the words, the Arab, groping with his hand among the debris in the hole, seized and held up in triumph a fine cylinder of baked clay, in as perfect a condition as when it was deposited in the artificial cavity above twentyfour centuries ago. The workmen were perfectly bewildered. They could be heard whispering to each other that it was *sihr,* or 'magic,' while the greybeard of the party significantly observed to his companion that the compass, which, as I have mentioned, I had just before been using, and had accidentally placed immediately above the cylinder, was certainly *'a wonderful instrument.'"*

Soon afterwards an exact duplicate of the cylinder was discovered near the eastern corner of the same stage, while a search for the remaining cylinders at the northern and western corners proved fruitless, because the greater portion of the wall at these angles had been already broken away. But from the debris which had rolled down from the upper stages, Rawlinson gathered two more fragments of a third cylinder with the same inscriptions, and a small fragment of a much larger new cylinder. All these documents are commemorative records of the time of Nebuchadrezzar, by whom they were placed there after his restoration of the old tower of Borsippa, called *E-ur-imin-an-ki, i. e.,* "Temple of the Seven Directions (Spheres) of Heaven and Karth," while the last-mentioned fragment "in some detail con-

tains a notice of Nebuchadrezzar's expedition to the Mediterranean and his conquest of the kings of the West."

In entire accordance with the peculiar Babylonian name of the tower which formed the most conspicuous part of the temple Kzida, dedicated to Nebo, son of Merodach, were Rawlinson's remarkable findings in the trenches. There could not be any doubt that the six or seven stages of the huge temple tower still to be recognized had been differently colored, and that " the color black for the first stage, red for the third, and blue for what seemed to be the sixth, were precisely the colors which belonged to the first, third, and sixth spheres of the Sabatan planetary system... or the colors which appertained to the planets Saturn, Mars, and Mercury." The bricks of this stage are the only ones laid in bitumen, and the face of the exposed southeastern wall "to a depth of half" an inch was coated with the same material, so as to give it a jet-black appearance."

Down to the present time the large vitrified masses of brickwork on the top of the Birs have given rise to much speculation and to the wildest theories concerning their origin, prominent among which is the common belief that they are fragments of the upper stage of the original " Tower of Babel," destroyed by lightning from heaven (Gen. 11), which rather must have formed a prominent part of Babylon proper on the other side of the Euphrates. While examining these upright and scattered remains of ancient walls on the summit of the mound, the present writer, with other explorers, often recognized the well preserved name of Nebuchadrezzar on many of the clearly defined bricks which had undergone this vitrification.

Among all the theories proposed to explain this remarkable phenomenon at such an elevation, that of Sir Henry Rawlinson, though not entirely removing all the difficulties, seems still to be the most plausible. He assumes that previous to the erection of the culminating stage, of which the remains exist in the solid pile at the summit, by the action of fierce and continued heat the bricks of the second highest stage of the temple were artificially vitrified, in order to give them the color of the corresponding sphere of Mercury by the solid mass of dark blue slag thus obtained. And "it was owing to the accidental use of an imperishable material like slag so near the summit of the Birs, that we are indebted for the solitary preservation of this one building among the many hundreds of not inferior temples which once studded the surface of Babylonia." Built of bricks of red clay and only half burned. They were laid in crude red clay, mixed up with chopped straw. Comp., *f. g.*, Ker Porter, pp. 46, *seq.*, above.

After a careful study of all the details offered by the trenches, the inscriptions, and other outside facts, Rawlinson gave a tentative picture of the original design of the temple at Borsippa: "Upon a platform of crude brick, raised a few feet above the alluvial plain, and belonging to a temple which was erected probably in the remotest antiquity by one of the primitive Babylonian kings, Nebuchadrezzar, towards the close of his reign, must have rebuilt seven distinct stages, one upon the other, symbolical of the concentric circles of the seven spheres, and each colored with the peculiar tint which belonged to the ruling planet." The first stage was black, sacred to Saturn; the second redbrown or orange, sacred to Jupiter; the third, red, belonged to Mars; the fourth, gold-plated, to the sun; the fifth, yellowish white, to Venus; the sixth, dark blue, to Mercury (Nebo); the seventh, silver-plated, to the moon. The entrance to this grand structure was on the northeast side, as in the temple of Sin at Ur. The lowest stage was two hundred and seventy-two feet square, and probably twentysix feet high. As the successive stages rose to the height of about one hundred and sixty feet, they gradually receded, becoming smaller and smaller, the seventh stage being occupied by the richly decorated shrine of the god Nabu (Nebo), "The Guardian of Heaven and Earth," to whom the temple was dedicated. Rawlinson's first paper " On the Birs Nimrud, or the Great Temple of Borsippa," was published in the "Journal of" the Royal Asiatic Society," vol. xvii. (1860), pp. 1-34.

TEMPORARY REVIVAL OF PUBLIC INTEREST IN ASSYRIAN EXCAVATIONS

A large amount of cuneiform material had been gradually stored in the halls of the Louvre and of the British Museum towards the middle of the last century. Before other funds were likely to be granted by governments and liberal-minded individuals for the continuation of the excavations in Assyrian and Babylonian mounds, it became necessary to satisfy the learned, and to prove to the public at large that the numerous monuments and broken clay tablets unearthed could really be read, and that their intrinsic value or the contents of their inscriptions were well worth the capital and time spent in their rediscovery. The number of scholars ready to make the study of cuneiform inscriptions their chief occupation, or at least part of their life's work, was exceedingly limited, and those who had manifested any deeper interest in their interpretation were concerned more with the Persian inscriptions than with those of Assyria. Grotefend had tried repeatedly to elucidate the meaning of the most complicated of all cuneiform writings, — the so-called third system of the Persian monuments, but he had made little progress. In 1845, Loewenstern of Paris had guessed the Semitic character of the Assyrian language correctly. Soon afterwards De Longperier had recognized a few proper names often occurring in the titles of the Khorsabad inscriptions. Botta had published important collections of the different cuneiform signs found in the same texts, from which it was proved beyond doubt that the Assyrians could never have employed an alphabet. And following in the footsteps of his predecessors, De Saulcy had even gone so far as to undertake boldly the translation of an entire Assyrian inscription. But valuable as all these attempts were as public expressions of the growing interest in Assyrian literature and civilization, and of the constant efforts made to solve a difficult problem, the positive gain derived from them was very moderate. There was too much chaff mixed with the few grains of wheat which remained after sifting. To have finally accomplished the gigantic task in all its essential features, and at the same time to have laid that solid grammatical foundation upon which the young science of Assyriology gradually rose like a magnificent dome, and as a grand monument of the penetrating acumen and the conquering force of the human mind, is the lasting merit of Edward Hincks, an Irish clergyman, and of Colonel Rawlinson.

The combined labors of these two great British geniuses shed a flood of light upon a subject where previously nothing but darkness and utter confusion prevailed. But the results at which they had arrived by strictly scientific methods and through sound reasoning, appeared so extraordinary and strange even to those who were occupied with the study of ancient nations, and their manner of thinking and writing, that twenty-five years were necessary to secure for Assyriology the general recognition of the educated classes of Europe.

The detailed investigations of the many new questions raised by the successful determination of the numerous polyphone characters which constitute the Assyrian writing were, however, carried on vigorously by a few enthusiastic scholars of England and France, until, in 1857, a peculiar but impressive demonstration on the part of the Royal Asiatic Society led to a public acknowledgment in England of the correctness of the principles of Assyrian deciphering and to a general acceptance of its startling conclusions. Soon afterwards (1859) Oppert's fundamental discussion of the whole problem, accompanied by a thorough Comp. p. 130, above. analysis and a literal translation of representative inscriptions,' produced a similar effect in France, while it took ten to twenty years longer before German scepticism was fully overcome through Eberhard Schrader's renewed critical examination of the elaborate system of Assyrian writing, and his convincing proofs of the perfect reliability of the achieved philological and historical results.

Meanwhile the rich cuneiform material previously gathered began to be made accessible to all those who were eager to participate in the fascinating researches of the newly established science. Rawlinson himself became the originator of a comprehensive plan, the execution of which was entrusted to him, in i860, by the trustees of the British Museum. Ably assisted by Edwin Norris, Secretary of the Royal Asiatic Society, to whom we are indebted for the first attempt at compiling an Assyrian dictionary, and by George Smith, a talented engraver, who "was employed to sort the fragments, and tentatively to piece together such as seemed to him to belong to each other," the "father of Assyriology " — as Rawlinson has been well styled — undertook to publish the most important texts of the English collections in an accurate and trustworthy edition. In the course of twentv-four years five large volumes of " The Cuneiform Inscriptions of Western Asia " were prepared by the united efforts of these three men and of Theophilus Pinches, who later took the places of Norris and Smith. Notwithstanding the numerous mistakes occurring on its pages, which must be attributed as much to the frequently unsatisfactory condition of the originals as to the defective knowledge of the laws of palaeography and philology in these early days of Assyrian research, this English publication has remained the standard work from which our young science has drawn its chief nourishment until the present day.

Comp. Oppcrt, *Expedition Scientijique en Mesopotamie,* vol. ii., p. 1859, and p. 171, above. Comp. E. Schrader, *Die Basis tier Entzifferung der assyrisch-babylonischen Krilinschriften,* in *Zeitschrift der Deutschcn MorgenlanJischen Gcsellschaft,* vol. xxiii., Leipzig, 1869, and *Die assyrisch-babylonischcn Kcrlinschriften. Kritische Untersuchung der Grundlagen Hirer Entzifferung, nebst dcm Babylonischen Texte der Tri/inguen lnschriften in Transscription somt Ubersetzung and Glossar, ibidem,* vol. xxvi., Leipzig, 1872, and furthermore, *Keilimchriften und Gesehichts-*

forschung, Giessen, 1878. Comp. George Rawlinson, "A Memoir of Major-General Sir Henry Crcswicke Rawlinson," London, 1898, p. 240. Vol. i., London, 1861; vol. ii., 1866; vol. iii. , 1870; vol. iv., 1875; 2d edition (prepared by Pinches), 1891; vol. v., Part I, 1880 (Pinches); Part 2, 1884 (Pinches).

GEORGE SMITH (1873-76)

In connection with his duties as Rawlinson's assistant George Smith manifested a decided gift for quickly recognizing the characteristic peculiarities of the many and often very similar cuneiform signs, which soon enabled him to acquire an extraordinary skill in finding missing fragments of broken tablets. Natural talents and personal inclinations, fostered by the frequent intercourse and conferences with the acknowledged master in the field of Assyriology, encouraged him to make strong efforts to overcome the disadvantages resulting from the lack of a proper education, and to occupy himself seriously with the language and writing of a people whose relics he was handling daily. It was particularly his earnest desire to contribute something towards a better understanding of the Old Testament which influenced him to devote his whole time to the study of the Assyrian monuments. After he had gone over the originals and paper casts of most of the historical inscriptions, especially of Ashurbanapal, whose annals he was the first to edit and to translate entirely, he began a methodical search for important texts among the thousands of fragments from the famous library of the same monarch. While unpacking the numerous boxes, and cleaning their contents, his eye used to glance over the cuneiform characters, as they gradually appeared under his brush upon the surface of each tablet. To facilitate his later studies, he divided the whole material into six divisions. Whenever anything of interest attracted his attention, he laid the fragment aside, endeavoring to find the other parts and trying every piece that seemed to join or to throw some light on the new subject. One day, in the fall of 1872, he picked up a very large fragment of the "mythological di-

vision," which occupied his mind completely as soon as he commenced to decipher. He read of a destructive flood and of a great ship resting on the mountain of Nisir. A dove was sent out to try if the water had subsided. A swallow came next; but it found no resting place, and returned likewise. A raven followed, which noticed the receding waters, discovered something to eat, flew away and did not return.

Smith had discovered the Babylonian account of the Deluge, which in salient points agreed most strikingly with the Biblical narrative. He immediately made a brief announcement of what he had found. The general interest was roused. With renewed zeal he began to search for the missing pieces. After infinite toil he discovered portions of two other copies and several minor parts of the first fragment, at the same time recognizing that the Babylonian account of the Deluge formed the eleventh chapter of a series of probably twelve tablets containing the legends of the great national hero Gilgamesh, commonly known by the name of Izduharfrom Smith's first provisional reading, and regarded as identical with the Nimrod of the Bible (Gen. 10). On December 3 of the same year Smith gave a public lecture before a large meeting of the Society of Biblical Archaeology at which Rawlinson presided, while Gladstone and other prominent men took part in the discussion. He sketched the principal contents of the Gilgamesh legends, accompanied by a first coherent translation of the fragmentary account of the Deluge. The sensation created by this paper in England and elsewhere was extraordinary. Scientific and religious circles were equally profuse in their comment upon the value of the new discovery, and loud voices were heard pleading for the early resumption of the excavations in the mounds of Nineveh.

Before the government could act, the proprietors of the London "Daily Telegraph" seized this opportunity to make themselves, through Edwin Arnold, their editor-inchief, the eloquent interpreters of the public sentiment. They offered to advance one thousand guineas for a fresh expedition to the East, if Smith would go out personally to search for other tablets of the interesting legends, and from time to time would send accounts of his journeys and discoveries to their paper. The British Museum accepted the generous proposition and granted the necessary leave of absence to its officer. On the 20th of January, 1873, George Smith left London, reaching Mosul, " the object of so many of his thoughts and hopes," six weeks later. But on his arrival in Assyria he learned that no firman had yet been granted in Constantinople. Unable to obtain any favors from the local government, he started for Baghdad, on his way down the Tigris examining the mounds of Nimrud and Qal'at Shirgat, as far as winter storms and rains would permit. He could spend only a fortnight in northern Babylonia, but it was profitably employed in buying antiquities and visiting the mounds of Babylon, El-Birs, Ohemir and Tell Ibrahim in rapid succession. The more he looked upon these enormous heaps of rubbish gradually formed by the crumbling works of former generations, the more he realized the necessity of their methodical exploration. He would himself have preferred excavating in " the older and richer country " to searching for the fragmentary copies of Babylonian originals in the palaces of Assyrian kings. But it mav well be doubted whether he would have been so successful in the South as he was with his clearly denned task and his limited time in the North. Most curious is his attempt at rearranging the principal ruins of Babvlon in accordance with his own notions of the topography of the ancient metropolis. Notwithstanding his superior knowledge of the cuneiform inscriptions, and though contrary to all evidence adduced by the early explorers of the nineteenth century, he revived the old theory of Rennell and Mignan, believing the lofty mound of Babil to represent the remains of the temple of Belus. The hanging gardens were placed on the western side of the Qasr, between the river Euphrates and the palace of Nebuchadrezzar, and the fine yellow piers and buttresses of

the latter regarded as part of them; while 'Omran ibn 'Ali, " which promises little or nothing to an explorer," only marks "the spot, where the old city was most thickly inhabited." It was fortunate for Smith and for science that he had no time to imitate Layard's example at Babvlon and Nippur, the final grant of the firman calling him away to the mounds of Assyria.

On the 3d of April he was back in Mosul. Six days later he started his excavations at Nimrud, which he continued for a whole month. There was no longer a chance of lighting on any new sculptured palaces or temples like those discovered by Botta and Layard. The " day of small things," announced long before by Rawlinson as "certain to follow on the rich yield of the earlier labours," had commenced. "New inscriptions and small objects of art are all that I expect to obtain from continual excavations either in Assyria or Babylonia," he had written to Sir Henry Ellis in 1853, and the proceeds of the later operations fully justified his prediction. Smith opened trenches at nearly all the different places of Nimrud, where Layard and Rassam had won their laurels, but on the whole he found nothing but duplicates of texts and other antiquities previously known. His entire fresh harvest from the ruins of Calah consisted in part of an inscribed slab of Tiglath-Pileser III.; three terra-cotta models of a hand embedded in the walls — one of them bearing a legend of Ashurnasirapal II.; fragments of enamelled bricks representing scenes of war; and a receptacle discovered in the floor of a room of the S. K. palace and filled with six terra-cotta winged genii. These figures apparently were placed there to protect the building and to secure fertility to its inmates. From the ornamentation of the palace, the nature of the few objects gathered from its chambers, and inscribed bricks taken from the drains surrounding it, Smith was enabled to conclude that it originally must have been a private building for the wives and families of King Shalmaneser II. (later restored by Ashuretililani).

Comp. George Rawlinson, "A Memoir

of Major-General Sir Henry Crcswicke Rawlinson," London, 1898, pp. 117, *seq.*

On the yth of May he moved to Qoyunjuk to begin his search for the remaining tablets of the royal library. He superintended the work in person, with the exception of a brief absence caused by his visits to the ruins of Hammam 'Ali and Khorsabad. The excavations proceeded but slowly. The whole ground had been cut up by former explorers and by the builders of the Mosul bridge, who extracted their materials from the foundation walls of the Assyrian palaces. Many of Layard's subterranean passages had collapsed, and small valleys and hills had been formed, changing the old contour of the mound entirely. Wherever the eye glanced, it saw nothing but pits and gulleys partly filled with rubbish, crumbling walls of unbaked clay threatening to fall at the slightest vibration, heavy blocks of stones peeping out of the ground, large pieces of sculptured slabs jammed in between heaps of fragments of bricks, mortar, and pottery— a vast picture of utter confusion and destruction. To secure good results it would have been necessarv to remove and to sift this whole mass of earth. All that Smith could do was to select the library spaces of the two ruined buildings and to examine that neighborhood once more for fragments of tablets, leaving their discovery chiefly to good luck and to fortunate circumstances. But after all, the mission for which he had Not merely "to preserve the building against the power of evil spirits;" Smith, "Assyrian Discoveries," 3d ed., New York, 1876, p. 78.

been sent out was accomplished more quicklv than he could have expected. On the 14th of May, on cleaning one of the fragments of cuneiform inscriptions from the palace of Ashurbanapal, the result of that dav's digging, he found to his surprise and gratification " that it contained the greater portion of seventeen lines of inscription belonging to the first column of the Chaldean account of the Deluge, which

The Ruins of Nineveh *A North gate.*

B North palace of Ashurbanapal). C Southwest palace of Sennacherib'). D Pillage of Neb's Tunus. E Burial ground. F Large east gate. Roads are marked thus: fitted into the only place where there was a serious blank in the story."' The cheerful news was soon cabled to London, in the expectation that the proprietors of the " Daily Telegraph" would feel encouraged to continue the excavations still longer. But considering " that the discovery of the missing fragment of the deluge text accomplished the object they had in view," they declined to authorize new explorations. Disappointed as Smith felt at the sudden termination of his work, he had to obey. On the 9th of June he withdrew his Arabs from the mound, leaving the same day for England, which country he reached forty days later, after his antiquities had been seized by the custom house officials in Alexandretta.

Through the representations of the British ambassador at Constantinople, the precious fragments of the library, which formed the principal result of his expedition, were soon released. Upon their arrival in London they received Smith's immediate attention. Before long he could report on the variety and importance of their contents. The trustees of the British Museum, realizing the value of the recent additions, decided to profit by the old firman as long as it lasted, and, setting aside a sum of 1000, directed their curator to return to Nineveh at once and search for other inscriptions at the mound of Qoyunjuk. On the 25th of November, 1873, Smith was on the road again, arriving at Mosul on the first day of the new year. During the few months of his absence from the field things had changed considerably. Another governor, to whom the pasha of Mosul was subordinate, had been appointed at Baghdad. He now issued orders to watch the movements of the foreigner, to question his superintendents, and to place a scribe as spy over his excavations. Greatly annoyed as Smith naturally felt by constant false reports and many other impediments thrown in his way, he conducted his labors with characteristic determination, gradually

increasing the number ot his workmen to almost six hundred. The peculiar task of his mission requiring, as it did within the short period of two months, the examination of as wide an area as possible and the removal of an enormous amount of rubbish thrown upon the surface of the mound by the former excavators, explains sufficiently why he employed such a large body of men over which it was impossible to exercise a proper control. About the middle of March his firman ceased. A few days previously he closed his researches. But a new embarrassment appeared. The local authorities refused to let him go, unless he delivered half of all the antiquities found as the share of the Ottoman Museum. Telegraphic communications were opened with the British ambassador at Constantinople, which subsequently led to a satisfactory arrangement with the Porte. Leaving only half of the duplicates in the hands of the Turkish officials, Smith could finally depart from Mosul on the 4th of April, 1874.

The divine command to construct and to fill the ark with all kinds of living creatures.

In examining the fruit of our explorer's two visits to the East, we are forcibly reminded of a word of Rawlinson. The immediate results of his excavations were " not such as to secure popular applause, or even to satisfy the utilitarian party; " they had to be studied at first to prove that they constituted a very decided gain for science. Under peculiar difficulties Smith had worked only three months altogether in the rich mines of antiquities at Oovunjuk. But in this limited space of time he had obtained over 000 inscriptions from the royal library of Nineveh, including mythological, astronomical, chronological, and grammatical texts, prayers, hymns, and litanies, syllabaries, and bilingual tablets of the utmost importance. Moreover, the majority of the fragments rescued formed parts of inscriptions, the other portions of which were already in the British Museum, thus completing or greatly enlarging representative texts of nearly all the different branches of Assyrian literature. Among the new in-

scriptions which he brought home, there were fragments of the Chaldean stories of the Creation, of the Fall of Man, of the Deluge, and portions of the national epics of Gilgamesh; the legend of the seven evil spirits; the mythical account of the youth of Sargon of Agade; a "tablet for recording the division of heavens according to the four seasons and the rule for regulating the intercalary month of the year "; the report of an eclipse of the moon and its probable meaning for Assyria; an officer's communication to the king as to repairs necessary at the queen's palace at Kabzi (= Tell Shemamyk); a beautiful bilingual hymn to Ishtar, as " the light of heaven "; an invocation to the deified hero Gilgamesh; explanations of the ideographs of prominent Assyrian and Babylonian cities; directions to the workmen as to what inscriptions are to be carved over the various sculptures in the palace, and many other tablets of equal interest and importance. His new acquisitions added no less to our knowledge of the general history of Assyria and its neighboring countries. I mention only the fine stone tablet of Adadnirari I. (about 1325 B. c.), purchased from the French consul at Mosul; the votive dishes and bricks of his son, Shalmaneser I., from a palace and temple at Nineveh; the first inscription of Mutakkil-Nusku (about 1175 B. c.); the Assyrian copy of the genealogy and building operations of the Cassite king, Agumkakrime (about 1600 B. c.); a new fragment of the synchronous history of Assyria and Babylonia in the thirteenth century; the expedition of Sargon against Ashdod (Is. 20: i) from a new octagonal prism; a large number of texts to complete the annals of Sennacherib, Esarhaddon, and Ashurbanapal, and part of a barrel cylinder of Sinsharishkun, the last Assyrian ruler — all of which were discovered at the mound of Which had been discovered in the ruins of Qal'at Shirgat on the Tigris.

Qovunjuk. Compared with former expeditions the excavations of Smith furnished but little on the subject of art and architecture. This cannot surprise us, for he was sent out not to find sculptures and palaces, but to search for those small fragments of inscriptions which others had neglected to extract from their trenches.

After his return to England in June, 1874, George Smith was occupied for some time with a renewed examination of the Qovunjuk collection of tablets, in order to gather and to translate all those texts which dealt with the earliest Babylonian legends, and through their frequent remarkable coincidence with similar stories in the Old Testament were likely to throw new light upon the first chapters of the Pentateuch, and to illustrate the origin and development of ancient Hebrew traditions. In rapid succession he published his "Assyrian Discoveries" (London, 1875), which gave the history and principal results ot his two expeditions, and "The Chaldean Account of Genesis" (London, 1876), containing the translations of Babylonian legends and fables from the cuneiform inscriptions discovered by Lavard, Rassam, and himself. Both books were received enthusiastically by the public, the latter witnessing no less than five editions within a few months. It was doubtless in no small part due to this great popularity, which the researches of Smith found again in consequence of their bearing upon the Bible, that, in the fall of 1875, the British Museum decided to resume its excavations at Nineveh. In March, 1876, after the necessarv firman had been granted again, Smith could start for the East a third time. A collection of antiquities unearthed by the Arabs at Jumjuma the previous winter, and offered for sale to Rawlinson, led him at first to Baghdad. But on his arrival he found himself seriously embarrassed. The whole population was in a state of great excitement. Cholera and plague had appeared and played terrible havoc among the inhabitants of the towns and the wandering tribes of the desert. Order and discipline had become words without meaning, the regular channels of communication with the officials were frequently interrupted, and the laws of hospitality were no longer respected. Smith tried in vain to fight against unfortunate circumstances and superior forces. As long as

the dreaded maladies kept their iron rule in the country, there was no possibility for him to begin excavations. Unmindful of the dangers from climate and constant exposure, working too much and resting too little, often without food and finding no shelter, he gradually broke down on the road. With difficulty he dragged himself to Aleppo, where on the i 9th of August he died in the house of the English consul, having fallen a staunch fighter in the cause of science.

In looking back upon the short but eventful life of George Smith as a scholar and as an explorer, we cannot but admire the man who by his extraordinary zeal and power of will became one of the most remarkable interpreters of cuneiform inscriptions whom England has produced. Without the advantage of a well directed instruction, and in his early davs debarred from those beneficial associations with inspiring men which essentially help to color our life and to shape our character, he was left to his own inclinations until he attracted the attention of Rawlinson. With the latter as a guide, and supported by natural gifts, he worked hard to train his mind and to fill out those gaps which separated him from the republic of letters. But notwithstanding all his serious exertions, he did not succeed entirely in effacing the traces of a desultory self-education, and the obnoxious influences of an unguarded youth. As an explorer he did not possess that linguistic talent, that congenial manner of adapting oneself to the customs and laws of the East, that loving sympathy with the jovs and sorrows of the children of the desert, which won for Lavard the respect and confidence of the natives, and made him a welcome guest at every camp-fire and tent of the Arabs. And as a scholar he did not acquire that depth and extent of knowledge, that independence of judgment and bold selfreliance which permeate the writings of Rawlinson, nor could he ever boast of Hinck's mental brilliancy and that subtle understanding of grammatical rules which characterize the latter's works. But stern in the conception of his duties, always thinking of his task and never of his person, pro-

vided with an astonishing memory, and a highly developed sense for the differences of form, he stands unexcelled in his masterly knowledge of the cuneiform inscriptions of the British Museum, while his numerous contributions to science testify to that rare intuition and gift of divination which enabled him often to translate correctly where others failed to grasp the meaning.

Comp. the notices of his death in " The Academy," vol. x., pp. 265, *seq.,* and "The Athens-urn" of Sept. 9, 1876, p. 338. Extracts from Smith's last diary were published by Delitzsch, *Wo lag das Paradics 'f* Leipzig, 1881, pp. 266, *seq.*

Rassam (1878-82).

Upon the sudden death of George Smith the trustees of the British Museum requested Hormuzd Rassam to take charge again of the excavations in the Assyrian mounds. Although in 1869 the latter had resigned his political appointment at Aden and retired to private life in Kngland, after manv hardships experienced as prisoner of King Theodore of Abyssinia, he accepted the proffered trust at once and started for Constantinople in November, 1876, in order to obtain a more satisfactory firman than had been granted to his predecessor. But all his efforts in this direction proved without result. Certain grave political complications which soon led to the Turco-Russian war, and the unexpected termination of the International Conference at Pera which tried to prevent it, had created a situation most unfavorable to the resumption of archaeological researches in the Ottoman empire. Edhem Pasha, father of Hamdy Bey, the present director-general of the Imperial Museum at Stambul, was then Grand Vizier. He was not ill disposed towards England, but as one of Turkey's most eminent and enlightened statesmen, he considered it his first duty to protect and promote the interests of his own country. Accordingly, he suggested that "a convention should be entered into between the British government and the Porte, giving the sole privilege to England of making researches in Turkey, similar to that which had been agreed upon between Germany and Greece." Such an arrangement, however, was to be based upon the condition that Turkey retained all the antiquities discovered, with option of giving only duplicates to the British Museum. But Rassam did not consider himself authorized to spend public money without the prospect of some material compensation. Looking upon the mere right of publishing the scientific results as "an empty favor," for which he had little understanding, he declined the proposition of the Grand Vizier as a one-sided agreement, and returned to England after having waited nearly four months in a vain effort to accomplish his purpose.

All the ambassadors had left Constantinople before, as a last protest against Turkey's stubborn and most unfortunate attitude towards the conciliatory measures proposed by the great European powers. But England deemed it soon necessary to dispatch a special representative to the Turkish capital, who was well versed in Oriental matters and publicly known as a warm friend of the Ottoman empire. The choice of the British government fell upon Sir Henry Layard, who at that time occupied a similar position at the court of Spain. No better appointment could have been made for realizing the plans of the British Museum. Two months after Layard's arrival at Constantinople (April, i 877), we find Rassam again on the shore of the Bosphorus, inspired with fresh enthusiasm by the hope of attaining the object of his mission under the more favorable new constellation. Deeply interested as the ambassador still was in the Assyrian researches of his nation, which more than thirty years previously he had inaugurated so successfully himself, he addressed the Sultan personally for a renewal of the old concessions repeatedly accorded to the British Museum. The request was granted at once, but before the official document could be signed, Rassam " received orders from Sir Henry Layard, under direction of the Foreign Office," to visit the Armenians and other Christians in Asia Minor who were reported to be maltreated and in danger of being massacred bv their fanatic Kurdish neighbors. About the time when this diplomatic mission was completed, — towards the end of 1877, — Rassam was informed by cable that the Sublime Porte had formally sanctioned the resumption of his excavations in Assyria. A few weeks later he commenced that series of explorations which, with several short interruptions, generally caused by the ceasing of the necessary funds at home, were carried on with his well-known energy, in four distinct campaigns, for a period of nearly five years, from January 7, 1878, to the end of July, 1882.' *First Expedition:* He leaves England June, 1877, Constantinople a month later, begins operations at the Assyrian mounds Jan. 7, 1878, departs from Mosul May 17, returns to London July 12 of the same year.

Second Expedition: He leaves England Oct. 8, 1878, arrives at Mosul Nov. 16, descends the Tigris for Baghdad Jan. 30, 1879, excavates and explores Babylonian sites during February and March, returns to Mosul April 2, departs tor Europe May z, reaches London June 19 of the same year. *Third Expedition:* He leaves London April 7, 1880, arrives at Hilla May 24, superintends the excavations at Babylon and neighboring ruins for eight days, spends a week in Baghdad, leaves this city June 9, reaches Mosul a fortnight later, departs for Wan July 1 5, reaches the latter July 29, for a month resumes the excavations at Toprak Kale, which at his request an American missionary, Dr. Reynolds (later in conjunction with Captain Clayton, the newly appointed British consul), had carried on for him since 1879. He leaves Wan Sept. 10, returns to Mosul Sept. 27, superintends the Assyrian excavations for six weeks, leaves Mosul by raft Nov. I i, excavates at Babylon and El-Birs during the first three weeks in December. Then he proceeds northward to explore other Babylonian ruins and to search for the site of ancient Sippara, begins his excavations at Abu Habba and tries Tell Ibrahim and other neighboring mounds during the first four months of 1881, departs from Abu Habba for the Mediterranean May 3, 1881, reaching England about two months later.

As long as Layard occupied his influential position at the Turkish capital (1877-80) there was no difficulty in obtaining new grants, and the special recommendation of his excavator to all the local authorities in the different provinces of the Ottoman empire. The first firman lasted only one year. It gave Rassam the right to explore any Assyrian ruin not occupied by Moslem tombs, and allotted one third of the antiquities discovered to the British Museum, one third to the owner of the mound, and the rest to the Archaeological Museum at Constantinople, the share of the latter naturally being doubled in case the site was crown property. An imperial delegate, who was appointed at first to guard the interests of the Ministry of Public Instruction in the trenches, was soon afterwards withdrawn on the representation of the British ambassador. The second finnan, written in the name of Layard, must be regarded as a gracious compliment paid to him by the Sultan. It was granted for two years (until Oct. 15, 1880), with the promise of a further term (till 1882), if required, and invested Layard with the exceptional power of carrying on excavations simultaneously in the various ruins of the vilayets of Baghdad, Aleppo, and Wan (Mosul being included in the first-named pashalic), giving him, in addition, the privilege of retaining all the antiquities found except duplicates, after their mere formal inspection by an imperial commissioner.

Fourth Expedition: He leaves England March 7, 1882, reaches Baghdad April 21, superintends the excavations at Abu Habba until the end of July, waits nearly three months longer at Baghdad for a renewal of the firman, but, disappointed in his hopes, departs for Basra Oct. 22, 1882, leaves the latter port Nov. i i by steamer, reaching London again in December, 1882.

It was a comparatively easy task for Rassam to excavate under such favorable conditions and supported by a powerful friend. The remarkable results which accompanied his labors in Babylonia will be treated later. The method followed was everywhere the same. Owing to the large geographical area included in his permit it was impossible for him to superintend all the excavations in person. As a rule he directed them only from the distance, sometimes not visiting the same ruin for weeks and months, and in a few cases even for a whole year. During his absence from 'Iraq, the British Resident at Baghdad undertook a general control of his excavations in Babylonia, while at Mosul his nephew, Nimrud Rassam, acted most of the time as his agent in connection with the operations conducted on several Assyrian sites. A number of intelligent native overseers, among whom a certain Daud Toma played a conspicuous role as his representative at Babylon, carried on the work as well as they could and as far as possible in accordance with their master's instructions. One can easily imagine how unsatisfactory such an arrangement must prove in the end, as diametrically opposed to all sound principles of a strict scientific investigation and in part as contrarv to the very explicit instructions received from the British Museum. It was the old system of pillage in a new and enlarged edition. Nobody recognized and felt this more than Hamdv Bey, to whom we must be truly grateful for sparing no efforts to stop this antiquated and obnoxious system immediately after the termination of Rassam's concession in 1882. Through his energetic measures, which led to a complete reorganization of the Ottoman laws of excavation, henceforth no person received permission to explore more than one ancient ruin at the same time, and this only with the express stipulation that all the antiquities recovered became the exclusive property of the Imperial Museum in Constantinople.

Before Rassam left England in 1877, his duties had been clearly defined by the trustees of the great London Museum. In continuing the work of his lamented predecessor, he was ordered to concentrate his activity upon the mounds of Nineveh, and to try to secure as many fragments as possible from the library of Ashurbanapal. But such a task was very little to the liking of Rassam, whose personal ambition was directed to sensational finds rather than to a careful search for broken clay tablets which he could not read, and the importance of which he was not educated enough to realize. We cannot do better than to quote his own words: "Although that was the first object of my mission, I was, nevertheless, more eager to discover some new ancient sites than to confine my whole energy on such a tame undertaking.... My aim was to discover unknown edifices, and to bring to light some important Assyrian monument." His ambition was soon to be gratified.

A year before he was commissioned to renew the British explorations in Assyria, a friend of his, employed as dragoman in the French consulate at Mosul, had sent him two pieces of ancient bronze adorned with figures and cuneiform signs, in which Savce recognized the name of Shalmaneser. Upon the latter's advice, Rassam endeavored to determine, immediately after his return to the banks of the Tigris, where these relics had been found. It did not take him long to learn that the two pieces presented to him were part of a large bronze plate accidentally unearthed by a peasant in the mound of Balawat(d), about fifteen miles to the east of Mosul. On examining this ruin he observed that the whole site had been largely used as a burial ground by the native population of that district, and was therefore excluded from the sphere of his firman. But feeling that the exceptional character of the desired monument " was well worth the risk of getting into hot water with the authorities, and even with the villagers," he troubled himself concerning the restrictions imposed upon him by law or etiquette just as little then, as he had done twenty-four years previously, when he tore down the barrier erected by Rawlinson, and occupied the French territory of Qoyunjuk. However, it cost him considerable time and anxiety and frequent disappointment before he obtained the much coveted prize. The excitement and disturbance among the Arabs of the neighboring tribes subsequent to his first attempts at cutting trenches in the promising mound were extraordinary, and at times threatened to end in serious conflicts and bloodshed. There even were moments when he himself lost all hope of ever reaching the object of his desire and efforts. But by profiting from every temporary lull in the storm, by distributing occasional small gifts among the dissatisfied workmen, and by superintending the excavations, as far as possible, himself, he overcame the chief opposition, and the strong prejudices of the owners of graves, so far as to enable him to ascertain the general contents of the mound, and to make some most valuable discoveries.

Comp. Rassam, "Asshur and the Land of Nimrod," New York, 1897, p. zoo.

Shortly after the commencement of their operations the workmen came upon several scrolls or strips of bronze, in form and execution similar to those in his possession. Originally about four inches thick, thev had suffered greatly from corrosion and other causes, and no sooner had thev been exposed to the air, when they began to crack and to crumble, offering no small difficulty to their safe removal to Mosul. Within five days the whole twisted and bent mass was uncovered and packed in proper cases large enough to take in the full length of this remarkable monument. Sixty feet away to the northwest a second set of bronze strips was disclosed, halt the size of the former, and in several other characteristic features differing from it. It was, however, so much injured from the dampness of the soil in which it had been hidden for more than 2500 years, that it fell to pieces immediately after its discovery. These ornamented bronze plates had once covered the cedar gates of a large Assyrian building. Each leaf of the first-mentioned better-preserved monument consisted of seven panels eight feet long, and

Part or" a Bronze Panel from the Great Palace Gate or Balawit richly embossed with double rows of figures surrounded by a border of rosettes. The plates represent a variety of subjects taken from the life and campaigns of a king, who according to the accompanying inscription was no other than Shalmaneser II. The ancient town buried under the rub The publication of this important monument was undertaken in I 881 by the Society of Biblical Archeology, but for some reason it has never been finished. Comp. "The Bronze Ornaments of the Palace Gates of Balawat," edited, with an introduction, by Samuel Birch, with descriptions and translations by Theophilus G. Pinches, parts i.-iv., 72 plates, London.

bish heap of Balawat was called Imgur-Bel. It had been chosen by Ashurnasirapal II. as the site for one of his palaces, restored and completed by his son and successor, Shalmaneser.

Bv means of tunnels Rassam extended his excavations to various sections of the interesting mound, at one place coming upon the ruins of a small temple, at the entrance of which stood a huge marble coffer. The latter contained two beautiful tablets of jhe same material covered with identical inscriptions of Ashurnasirapal; a similar third tablet was lying upon an altar in its neighborhood, and fragments of others were scattered among the debris. Kxaggerated rumors of this "great find" spread rapidly. Some credulous people insisted that a treasure-chest full of gold had been brought to light, while others believed that the very stone tablets of Moses inscribed with the Ten Commandments had been discovered. Great excitement was the result in the trenches, and new riots broke out in the villages. The large quantity of human bones constantly unearthed tended only to increase the general irritation, and to inflame all slumbering passions. After a little while Rassam found it useless to contend longer against ignorance and fanaticism. As soon as he had cleared the little chamber entirely, he abandoned his trenches at Balawat, convinced that a thorough examination of the whole remarkable site was an absolute impossibility for the time being.

The discovery of such a unique specimen of ancient metallurgy as the bronze

gates of Imgur-Bel had well inaugurated the resumption of Rassam's researches in the Assyrian mounds. Neary 500 workmen were occupied at the same time, to continue the British excavations at Qoyunjuk and Nimrud. The most promising space of the palaces of Sennacherib and Ashurbanapal, practically stripped of only their bas-reliefs and larger objects of art by the early explorers, had been subjected by Smith to a more careful examination. The quick results of his labors have been treated above. To extricate more of the precious fragments from the royal library, it became necessary to remove all the debris thrown in the excavated halls, or without system heaped upon some unexplored part of the ruin..The large pillars of earth left untouched by Layard and Rassam in the centres of the different rooms (comp. p. i 15) and every enclosing wall likely to contain relics of the past were torn down. The number of tablets obtained in the end were not as great as Smith had expected. Instead of the 20,000 fragments calculated by him to remain buried in the unexcavated portions of the palace of Sennacherib, scarcely 2000 were gathered by Rassam from the two buildings after five years' labors. But an important and nearly perfect decagon prism in terra-cotta inscribed with the annals of Ashurbanapal' was found in a solid brick wall of the north palace, and no less than four fine barrel-cylinders of Sennacherib, covered with identical records, were taken from the southwest palace in rapid succession.

The results from the trenches of Nimrud were rather meagre. In resuming the exploration of the two temples discovered by Layard near the northwest edge of the elevated ruin, Rassam unearthed a marble altar, and several inscribed marble seats still standing in their original positions; he gathered a few bas-reliefs, a number of carved stones, and clay tablets, and filled more than half a dozen baskets with fragments of enamelled tiles. But here as well as in other parts of the country his work bore more the character of a gleaning following the rich harvest which he with Layard

had gathered from the same ruin fields a quarter of a century before. Notwithstanding all his serious efforts to make other startling discoveries like that which had crowned his first year's labors at Balawat, and notwithstanding the fact that the excavations at Nimriad and Qoyunjuk, at Qal'at Shirgat, and other Assyrian mounds, never ceased entirely during the five years which he spent again in the service of the British Museum, his great expectations were not to be realized. For a little while, in 1879, it had seemed as if Rassam would be able to accomplish what all the great Assyrian excavators before him had tried in vain — the partial exploration of Nebi Yunus. Layard had managed through one of his overseers to dig for a few days in the courtyard of a Moslem house, proving the existence of buildings and monuments of Adadnirari III., Sennacherib and Ksarhaddon in the interior of this second large ruin of Nineveh. In 1852, Hilmi Pasha, then governor of Mosul, had excavated there eight or nine months for the Ottoman government, discovering two large winged bulls, several bas-reliefs, and an important marble slab, commonly known among Assyriologists as "Sennacherib Constantinople."' But since then nobody had made another move to disclose the secrets of Nebi Yunus. Rassam went quietly and cautiously to work by making friends among the different classes of the inhabitants of the village, which occupied nearly the whole mound. With infinite patience and energy he gradually overcame the opposition of the most influential and fanatic circles, succeeding even in winning the confidence and assistance of the guardians of the holy shrine dedicated to the memory of the prophet Jonah. Well-to-do landowners began to offer him their courtyards for trial-trenches without asking for an indemnity or remuneration; others, who were in poorer circumstances, were ready to sell him their miserable huts for a small sum. If he had possessed money enough, he "could have bought half of the village for a mere trifle." Many of the laborers whom he employed at Qoyunjuk had been prudently chosen from Nebi Yunus. It was only natural, therefore, that they should faithfully stand by their master, strengthening his hands in the new undertaking at their own village. One morning operations were hopefully started at the great ruin. In the beginning everything went on very well. But before his tentative examination could have yielded any satisfactory results, the jealousy and intrigues of some evildisposed individuals, who brought their influence to bear upon the local authorities of Mosul and upon the Minister of Public Instruction at Constantinople, caused the temporary suspension of his excavations, soon followed by the entire annihilation of all his dreams. All the tablets and fragments so far obtained by the British Museum from the royal library of Nineveh were made accessible to scientific research through C. Bezold's fine " Catalogue of the Cuneiform Tablets in the Kouyunjik Collection of the British Museum," : vols., London, 1889-99.

Two fragmentary and crumbling copies of this important monument had been discovered by Rassam in the same palace as early as 1854. Comp. p. I 6, above. One of them is preserved in the Imperial Ottoman Museum at Constantinople. This monument disappeared suddenly from the collections of the Imperial Museum between 187 and 1875 under Dethier's administration. Comp. Htlprecht in *Ztitschrift fur Assiriologie,* vol. xiii., pp. 322-326. Within the last few months I have been able to trace the lost marble slab to the shores of England, where at some future day it may possibly be rediscovered in the halls of the British Museum.

With Rassam's return to England, in 1882, the Assyrian excavations of the nineteenth century have practically come to an end. E. A. Wallis Budge of the British Museum has since paid repeated visits to the East (1888, 1889, 1891), looking after English interests also at Qoyunjuk and neighboring mounds. Other scholars and explorers (the present writer included) have wandered over those barren hills, meditating over Nineveh's days of splendor, gazing

at Calah's sunken walls, resting for a little while on Ashur's lonely site. But no expedition has pitched its tents again with the roaming tribes between the Tigris and the Zab; the sounds of pickaxe and spade have long ago died away. Only now and then a stray cuneiform tablet or an inscribed marble slab, accidentally found in the mounds when a house is built, or a tomb is dug, reminds us of the great possibilities connected with methodical researches in those distant plains. Much more remains to be done, before the resurrection of ancient Assyria will be accomplished. Hundreds of ruins scarcely yet known by their names await the explorer. It is true, not all of them will yield magnificent palaces and lofty temples, gigantic human-headed bulls and elaborate sculptures. But whether the results be great or small, every fragment of inscribed clay or stone will tell a storv, and contribute its share to a better knowledge of the life and history, of the art and literature, of that powerful nation which conquered Babylon, transplanted Israel, subdued Kgypt, even reached Cyprus, and left its monuments carved on the rocky shores of the Mediterranean.

Comp. Hormuzd Rassam, "Asshur and the Land of Nimrod," New York, 1897. This book contains a narrative of his different journeys in Mesopotamia, Assyria, and Babylonia, and the account of his principal discoveries in the ruins which he excavated. 4

METHODICAL EXCAVATIONS IN BABYLONIA

The large number of fine monuments of art which through the efforts of a few determined explorers had been sent from the districts of the Euphrates and Tigris to the national collections in Paris and London, came almost exclusively from the mounds of Assyria proper. Marble, so liberally used as a decorative element and building material in the palaces and temples of the empire in the North, seemed but rarely to have been employed by the inhabitants of the alluvial plain in the South, where from the earliest times clay evidently took the place of stone. The tentative excavations of Loftus and Taylor in ancient

Chaldea had indeed been of fundamental importance. They gave us a first glimpse of the long and varied history, and of the peculiar and interesting civilization of a country of which we knew very little before; they even revealed to us in Babylonian soil the existence of antiquities considerably older than those which had been unearthed at Nimrud and Qal'at Shirgat; but, on the whole, they had been unproductive of those striking artistic remains which without any comment from the learned appeal directly to the mind of intelligent people. The decided failure of Layard's attempts at Babylon and Nuffar, and the widely felt disappointment with regard to the tangible results of the French excavations under Fresnel and Oppert did not tend to raise the Babylonian mounds in the public estimation, or to induce governments and private individuals to send new expeditions into a country half under water, half covered with the sand of the desert, and completely in the control of lawless and ignorant tribes.

Marble, sandstone and granite as building materials in ancient Babylonia were found to any great extent onlv in the temple ruin of Abu Shahrain

But however seriously these and similar considerations at first must have affected the plans and decisions of other explorers, the chief obstacle to the commencement of methodical excavations in Babylonian ruins was doubtless the brilliant success of Botta, Layard, and Rassam in the North, which for a long while distracted the general attention from ancient Chaldea. Moreover, the epoch-making discovery of the royal library of Nineveh provided such a vast mass of choice cuneiform texts, written in an extremely neat and regular script on well-prepared and carefully baked (Eridu) situated in a depression of" the Arabian desert, where stone apparently was as easily obtained as clay. Conip. pp. 178, *seqq.,* above. In the Selcucidan and Parthian periods under foreign influence, stone was used considerably more all over Babvlonia.

material, and at the same time representing nearly every branch of Assyrian literature — precisely what the first pioneers of the young science needed to restore the dictionary and to establish the grammatical laws of the longforgotten language — that the few unbaked and crumbling tablets from the South, with their much more difficult writing and their new pala;ographical problems, with their unknown technical phrases and their comparatively uninteresting contents, naturally received but little attention in the early days of Assyriology.

It is true, the increasing study of the thousands of claybooks from Nineveh demonstrated more and more the fact that the great literary products with which they make us acquainted are only copies of Babylonian originals; and the subsequent comparison of the sculptured monuments of Assyria with the seal-cylinders and other often mutilated objects of art from the ruins and tombs of Chaldea again led scholars to the neighbourhood of the Persian Gulf as the real cradle of this whole remarkable civilization. But a new powerful influence was needed to overcome old prejudices entirely and to place the Babylonian mounds in the centre of public attention. The well-known archaeological mines in the North, which had seemed to yield an almost inexhaustible supply of valuable monuments, began gradually to give forth less abundantly and even to cease altogether. The sudden death of George Smith, who had stimulated and deepened the interest of the religious communities of his nation in cuneiform research, and thereby temporarily revived the old enthusiasm for British excavations at ()ovunjuk, marked the beginning of the end of that brief but significant period which bears the stamp of his personality as the great epigone of the classical age of Assyrian exploration.

FRENCH EXCAVATIONS AT TELLO UNDER DE SARZEC

It was the French representative at Mosul who in 1842 had successfully inaugurated the resurrection of the palaces and temples of Assyria; and it was another French representative at Basra who thirty-five years later made a no less farreaching discovery in the mounds of Chaldea, which opened the second great period in the history of Assyrian and Babylonian exploration, — the period of methodical excavations in the ruins of Babylonia proper. In January, 1877, Ernest de Sarzec, a man of tall stature and expressive features, then about forty years old, combining an active mind and sharp intellect with a pronounced taste for art and archaeology, and through his previous service in Egypt and Abyssinia well versed in Oriental manners and to a certain degree familiar with the life of the desert, was transferred to Basra as vice-consul of France.

This city, situated on a rich alluvial soil of recent formation and surrounded by luxuriant gardens and palmgroves, which for sixty miles on both sides accompany the grand but muddy river until it empties into the Persian Gulf near the light-house of Fao, is one of the hottest and most unhealthy places in the whole Turkish empire. The population is almost exclusively Mohammedan. The few European merchants and representatives of foreign governments, who live as a small colony by themselves along the west bank of the Shatt el-'Arab, outside the city proper, suffer more or less from fever and the enervating influence of the oppressive climate. An occasional ride into the desert, with its bracing air, and the hunting of the wild boar, francolin, and bustard are the general means by which the members of the European colony try to keep up their energy and vitality in the hot-house atmosphere of this tropical region. But such an aimless life was very little to the liking of De Sarzec, who longed for a more serious occupation to fill out the ample time left him by the slight duties of his consular position. Being stationed near the ruins of some of the great centres of ancient civilization, he decided at once to visit the sites of Babylon and Kl-Birs, and to devote his leisure hours, it practicable, to the exploration of a section of Southern Babylonia.

He was very fortunate to find a trustworthy councillor in J. Asfar, a prominent native Christian, and the present hospitable representative of the Strick-Asfar line of steamboats plying regularly between London and Basra. The latter had formerly dealt in antiquities and was personally acquainted with several Arab diggers, who continued to keep him well informed as to the most promising ruins between the Euphrates and the Tigris. The name of Tel 16 had recently become a watchword among them in consequence of the discovery of inscribed bricks and cones and the partly inscribed torso of a fine statue of Gudea in diorite, said to have come from these ruins.-It is Asfar's merit to have first directed the attention of De Sarzec to this remarkable site and to have urged him to lose no time in examining it more closely and in securing it for France. In order to avoid undesirable public attention, the French vice-consul deemed it wise for the present not to apply for the necessary firman at Constantinople, but to begin his operations as quietly as possible, somewhat in the manner followed by the first explorers of Assyria. Moreover, the whole of Southern Babylonia was then in a kind of semiindependent state under Nasir Pasha, the great chief of the Muntefik(j), who built the town of Nasriye called after him, and was appointed the first wali of Basra. It was therefore necessary to secure his good will and protection for any scientific undertaking that might be carried on in regions where the law of the desert prevailed, and Nasir's power was the only acknowledged authority. Immediately after his arrival on the Persian Gulf, De Sarzec entered into personal communication with the latter and established those friendly relations by means of which he was able to travel safely everywhere among his tribes and to excavate at Tello or any other ruin as long as Nasir retained his position.

Published by Lenormant, *Choix de Textes Cuneiformes inidits*, Paris, 1873—75, p. 5, no. 3, and in George Smith, "History of Babylonia," edited by A. H. Sayce, London, 1877. No sufficient reasons have been brought forward, however, to show that this torso actually came from Tello. Mr. Leonard W. King, of the British Museum, whom I asked for information as to its place of origin, was unable, to throw any light on this question. Comp. p. 221, note 1, below. For valuable information as to the immediate causes which led to De Sarzec's great discovery, I am obliged to his friend, Mr. Asfar, who had preserved his deep interest in Babylonian excavations as late as 1900, when the present writer spent nearly three weeks at Basra and its neighborhood, frequently enjoying his unbounded hospitality. In March of 1877, after a brief reconnoitring tour along the banks of the Shaft el-HaT, we find De Sarzec already in the midst of his work, commencing that series of brief but successful campaigns which were soon to surprise the scientific world, and to make Tello, previously scarcely known by name in Europe, the " Pompeii of the early Babylonian antiquity." For very apparent reasons De Sarzec did not write the history of his various expeditions extending over a considerable part of the last twenty-four years of the nineteenth century, so that it becomes extremely difficult for us to gather all the facts and data necessary to obtain a clear conception of the genesis and maturing of his plans, of the precise results of each year's exploration, of the difficulties which he encountered, and of the methods and ways by which he overcame all the obstacles, and in the end accomplished his memorable task.

Thus styled by Heuzcy in the introduction to his *Catalogue de la Sculpture Chaldeenne au Musee du Louvre,* Paris, 1901, the galley-proofs of which he kindly placed at my disposal in January, 1901, long before the book itself appeared.

His excavations were carried on in eleven distinct campaigns, generally lasting from three to four months in winter and spring. With regard to the three great intervals lying between them, they might be grouped together into four different periods, each of which is characterized by some more or less conspicuous discovery: i. 1877, 1878, 1880, 1881; ii. 1888, 1889; in. 1893, 1894, 1895; iv. 1898, 1900. But as the excavations conducted by De Sarzec at Tello in the later years con-

sisted mainly in deepening and extending the trenches previously opened at the two principal elevations of the ruins, a mere chronological enumeration of all his single discoveries would neither do justice to the explorer, nor enable us to comprehend the importance of the results obtained in their final totality, as well as in their mutual relation to each other. It will therefore be preferable to consider the excavations from an historical and a topographical point of view at the same time. In this way we shall be enabled to preserve the unity of the subject and to avoid unnecessary repetitions. Accordingly we distinguish three phases in the excavations of De Sarzec: i. His preliminary work of determining the character of the whole ruins by trial trenches, 1877-78; 2. The excavation of a Seleucidan palace and of ancient Babylonian remains, especially a fine collection of large statues at the principal mound of Tello, i 880-81; 3. The unearthing of constructions, sculptures and inscriptions of a still earlier civilization in another prominent mound of the same ruins, 1888-89, 1893-95, 1898, 1900.

i. The ruins of Tello, or more correctly Tell-Lo, are situated in a district which is half the year a desert and the other half a swamp, about eight miles to the northeast of Shatra, a small Turkish town and the seat of a *qaimmaqam,* or sub-governor. They include a number of higher and lower elevations stretching from northwest to southeast for about four English miles along the left bank of a large dry canal that represents either the ancient bed or a branch of the Shatt el-Ha'i, from which in a straight line they are distant a little over three English miles. The two principal mounds of the whole site are designated as mounds A and B in the following sketch. The former and smaller one (A) rises only fifty feet above the plain at the extreme northwest end of the ruins, while the latter (B) is nearly fifty-six feet high and about 650 feet to the southeast of it. These and the many other smaller mounds constituting the ruins of Tello consist as a rule of an artificial massive terrace of unbaked brick, upon and around

which the scattered remains of one or more ancient buildings once occupying the platform are mixed with the sand of the desert into one shapeless mass. The meaning and etymology of Tello is obscure. An attempt by the Ute Dr. Scheter ot Paris to explain the name is found in Heuzey, *Decouvtrtti en Chaldre far Erntit de Sarzec,* p. 8, note I.

In January, 1877, at his very first ride over the ruins, De Sarzec recognized the value of this large archaeological field, scarcely yet touched by the professional Arab digger, from the many fragments of inscribed cones and bricks, sculptures and vases which covered the surface. Among other objects of interest he picked up the magnificent piece of a large statue in dolerite inscribed on the shoulder. After a few minutes he had gathered evidence enough to convince him that he stood on a prominent site of great antiquity. The fragment of the statue was interpreted bv him as having rolled down from Mound A, at the foot of which it was discovered, thus serving as the first indication of an important building which probably was concealed in its interior. This starting point for his excavations once being given, he hired all the workmen whom he could obtain from the wandering tribes, and set to work to determine the character and contents of the hill in question. A few weeks of digging revealed the fact indicated above, that the whole mound consisted of a platform of unbaked bricks crowned bv an edifice of considerable size and extent. But he was not satisfied with this general result. Though the lack of drinking water in the immediate vicinity of the ruins and the proverbial insecurity of the whole region did not allow him to pitch his tents anywhere near the mounds, he was by no means discouraged. During all his several expeditions to Tello he established his headquarters at Mantar-Qaraghol, in the midst of the green fields embellishing the left bank of the Shatt el-Hai, whence he walked or rode every morning to the ruins, to return in the evening to the waters of the river. After seven months of successful excavations conducted during the springs of 1877 and 1878, he obtained a leave of absence from his duties at Basra, and sailed to France as the bearer of important news and with the first fruit of his archaeological researches.

By following a ravine ending at the point where the fine sculptured fragment was discovered, he had reached a kind of deep recess in the outer northeast wall of the building which stood on the platform. No sooner did the workmen begin to remove the debris with which it was filled, when the lower part of a great statue in dolerite, partly covered with a long cuneiform inscription, rose gradually out of the depth. It became at once evident that theshoulder piece bearing the name of Gudea, referred to above, was a portion of this extraordinary monument. De Sarzec having no means at his disposal to remove the heavy torso, took a squeeze of the inscription and buried the precious relic again for a future occasion. Two years later, when Rassam visited Tello, he found its upper part exposed again by the Arabs. Comp. Rassam, " Asshur and the Land of Nimrod," New York, 1897, p. 276, on the one side, and De Sarzec and Heuzey, *Decouvertes en Chaldcc,* p. 5, on the other. The British explorer asserts that this first statue unearthed by De Sarzec is identical with the one previously discovered and mutilated by the natives, who sold the bust and arm to George Smith. But this statement is wrong, as the inscription on the back of De Sarzec's statue is complete. In fact, it must be regarded as doubtful if the torso obtained by Smith belongs to any of the statues or fragments discovered by Dc Sarzec at Tello, as long Es this question has not been settled by means of casts of the pieces in the British Museum sent to Paris for examination.

After the French consul had ascertained the general character of Mound A and its probable contents, he devoted the rest of his time to an investigation of the other parts of the ruins by placing his workmen in long rows over the whole surface of the enormous site. This peculiar method, which would have utterly failed at Babylon, NurFar, Warka, and other similar mounds, pro-

duced important results at a ruin as little settled in later times as Tello subsequently proved to be. De Sarzec unearthed many fragments of inscribed vases and sculptures, several inscribed door-sockets, a large number of cuneiform tablets, the bronze horn of a bull in life-size, etc. He exposed large columns of bricks of the time of Gudea, and found not a few peculiar cubical brick structures generally concealing a votive tablet of Gudea or Dungi. The latter was placed over a small copper or bronze statue of a man or a bull, which often terminated in the form of a nail. Above all, he brought to light one of the earliest bas-reliefs of ancient Chaldea so far known, the first two fragments of the famous "stele of vultures " erected by King Eannatum, and two large terra-cotta cylinders of Gudea in tolerably good preservation. Each of the latter is nearly two feet long and a little over one foot in diameter, and is inscribed with about 2000 lines of early cuneiform writing, thus forming the longest inscriptions of that ancient period so far known.

Votive Statuette in Copper *Inscribed ivilh the name of Cuded, about 2700 B. C.*

On his arrival at home (July 28, 1878), De Sarzec was most fortunate in finding the precise man whom he needed in order to see his work placed upon a permanent basis. Waddington, well known in scientific circles for his numismatic researches, was then Minister of Foreign Affairs. Deeply interested as he was in the enthusiastic reports of his consul, he referred him for a critical examination of his excavated treasures to Leon Heuzey, the distinguished curator of the Department of Oriental Antiquities at the Louvre, who at once recognized that here were the first true specimens of that original, ancient Chaldean art to which De Longperier tentatively had ascribed two statuettes previously obtained by the National Museum of France. From this moment dates the archaeological alliance and personal friendship between De Sarzec and Heuzev which in the course of the next twenty years bore the richest fruit for

Assyriology and was of fundamental importance for the gradual restoration of a lost page in the history of ancient Oriental art and civilization.

On the recommendation of Heuzey the antiquities already discovered at Tello were deposited in the Louvre with a view of their final acquisition by the nation, while De Sarzec was requested to return quietly to the ruins and to develop his promising investigations at his own responsibility and expense, until the proper moment for action had come on the side of the government. At the same time the necessary steps were taken in Constantinople to secure the imperial firman which established French priority over a ruin soon to attract a more general attention. As we shall see later in connection with the contemporaneous British excavations in the vilayet of Baghdad, this cautious but resolute proceeding by a few initiated men, who carefully guarded the secret of De Sarzec's great discovery, saved Tello from the hands of Rassam, long the shrewd and successful rival of French explorers in Assyria and Babylonia. Comp. Heuzey, *Dicouvertes,* pi. I, no. I. The third one, the existence of which was dvined by Amiaud from certain indications contained in the cuneiform texts of the first two cylinders, has been found since by the Arabs. Comp. Scheil in Maspero's *Recueil,* vol. xxi 1 1899), p. 1 24. 2. On the 21st of January, 1880, De Sarzec was back again at his encampment near the Shatt el-Hai, this time accompanied by his young bride, who henceforth generally shared the pleasures and deprivations of her husband in the desert. During this and the following campaign (November 12, 1880, to March 15, 1881) he concentrated his energy on a thorough examination of the great building hidden under Mound A and of its immediate environments, discovering no less than nine' large statues in dolerite, besides several statuettes in stone and metal, fragments of precious bas-reliefs, an onyx vase of Naram-Sin, and numerous inscriptions and small objects of art. It is true, all the statues hitherto unearthed were previously decapitated, and in some instances otherwise mutilated, but three detached heads, soon afterwards rescued by De Sarzec from different parts of the ruins, enabled us to gain a clearer conception of the unique type of these priceless specimens of ancient Babylonian art. According to Heuzey, in the introduction to his *Catalogue de la Sculpture Chaldeenne tiu Musee du Louvre*, Paris, 1902. De Sarzec, in his brief description of his first four campaigns *(Decouvertes en C/ialdee*, p. 6) mentions the discovery of a tenth (or including the lower part of a statue unearthed in 1877, an eleventh) statue, and speaks of onlv two detached heads then found by him. This difference in counting is due to the size and fragmentary condition of some of the statues and objects discovered.

With the exception of the six hottest months of the year, which he spent in the cooler *serdabs*' of Baghdad, to restore his health affected by the usual swamp fevers of 'Iraq, he continued his labors at Tello until the spring of 188finding even older remains below the foundations of the abovementioned palace, when the threatening attitude of the Muntefik(j) tribes, and the growing insecurity of his own partv drove him away from the ruins. At the end of May in the following year he arrived at Paris a second time with a most valuable collection of antiquities, which by special *trade* from the Sultan he had been allowed to carry away with him as his personal property.

The first announcement of De Sarzec's fundamental discovery before the French Academy, and Oppert's impressive address at the Fifth International Congress of Orientalists at Berlin, opening with the significant words: "Since the discovery of Nineveh... no discovery has been made which compares in importance with the recent excavations in Chaldea," had fairly prepared the scientific world for the extraordinary character and the rare value of these ancient monuments. But when they were finally unpacked and for the first time exhibited in the galleries of the Louvre, the general expectation was far surpassed by the grand spectacle which presented itself to the eyes of a representative assembly. This first fine collection of early Babylonian sculptures was received in Paris with an enthusiasm second only to the popular outburst which greeted Botta's gigantic winged bulls from the palace of Sargon thirty-six years previously. On the proposition of Jules Ferry, then Minister of Public Instruction, the French Assembly voted an exceptional credit to the National Museum for the immediate acquisition of all the monuments from Tello, while the *Academic des Inscriptions et Belles Lettres* added a much more coveted prize to this pecuniary remuneration on the side of the government, by appointing the successful explorer a member of the Institute of France. An Oriental section was created in the Louvre, with Leon Heuzey, the faithful and energetic supporter of De Sarzec's plans and endeavors, as its director. Under the auspices of the Minister of Public Instruction, and assisted in the deciphering of the often difficult cuneiform inscriptions by Oppert, Amiaud, and lately by Thureau-Dangin, Heuzey began that magnificent publication" in which he made the new discoveries accessible to science, and laid the solid foundation for a methodical treatment of ancient Chaldean art, by applying fixed archaeological laws to the elucidation of the Assyrian and Babylonian monuments.

Subterranean cool rooms which are provided in every better house of Baghdad in order to enable the inhabitants to escape the often intolerable heat of the daytime during the summer months. Published in *Revue Archeologique*, new series, vol. xlii, Nov., 1881, pp. 56 and 259-272: *Les Fouilles de Chaldee; communication (Tune Icttre de M. de Sarzec par Leon Heuzey. Die franzisischen Ausgrabungen in Chaldaa*, pp. 235-248 of *Abhandlungen des Berliner Orientatisten-Congresses. A* useful synopsis of the early literature on De Sarzec's discoveries was given by Hommcl in *Die Semitischen Vi/ier und Sprachen*, Leipzig, 1883, p. 459, note 104, to which may be added an article by Georges Perrot in *Revue des Deux-Mon-*

des, Oct. I, 1882, pp. 525, *seqq.*

The palace excavated in Mound A does not belong to the Babylonian period proper. But in order to understand the topographical conditions and certain changes which took place in the upper strata of Tello, it will be necessary to include it in our brief description of the principal results obtained by De Sarzec at this most conspicuous part of the ruins. The massive structure of crude bricks upon which the building was erected forms an immense terrace over 600 feet square and 40 feet high. As certain walls discovered in it prove that this lofty and substantial base was not the work of one builder, we have to distinguish between an earlier *substratum* and later additions. The crumbling remains of the large edifice lying on the top of it form a rectangular parallelogram about 175 feet long and 100 feet wide. Only two of its sides, the principal and slightly curved northeast, and the smaller but similar northwest facade, exhibit any attempt at exterior ornamentation, consisting of those simple dentated recesses and half-columns with which we are familiar from Loftus' excavations at Warka. As to its ground plan, the building does not essentially differ from the principle and arrangement observed in the Assyrian palace of Khorsabad, or in the Seleucido-Parthian palace recently completely excavated bv the present writer at the ruins of NufFar. Here as there we have a number of different rooms and halls — in the latter case thirtv-six — around a grouped number of open courts and around as many different centres.

Comp. pp. 79, *seqq.*, above. *Decouvertes en ChalJefpar Ernest dt Sarzec*, published by Leon Heuzey, large folio, Paris, 1884, *seqq.* The work is not yet complete.

The walls of this edifice, in some places still ten feet high, are built of ancient Babylonian bricks, laid in mortar or bitumen and generally bearing the name and titles of Gudea, a famous ruler of that Southern district, who lived, however, about twenty-five hundred years prior to the days when his material was used a second time. Each of the four exterior walls, on an average four feet thick, has one entrance, but no trace of any window. The northeast facade originally had two gates, the principal one of which, for some unknown reason, was soon afterwards closed again. The inscribed bricks used for this purpose, and similar ones taken from certain constructions in the interior, are modelled after the pattern of Gudea's material, but bear the Babylonian name Hadad-nadinakhe(s) in late Aramean and early Greek characters, from which the general age of this building was determined to be about 300-250 B. c., a result corroborated by the fact that numerous coins with Greek legends of the kings of Characene were found in its ruins.

The palace of Tello has three courts of different dimensions. The smallest is nearly square, measuring about 20 by 18 feet, the second is 27 by 30 feet, while the largest is about 56 by 69 feet. Both the inside of the palace and the open space immediately before its principal facade were paved with burned bricks of the same size and make-up as those in the walls of the palace. These bricks did not rest directly upon the large terrace of crude bricks, but upon a layer of earth two to three feet deep mixed with sculptured fragments of an early period. In the centre of the platform before the palace there stood upon a kind of pedestal an ancient trough or manger, in limestone, about eight feet long, one foot and a half wide, and one foot deep. Being out of its original position it had apparently been used by the later architects to provide water for the guards stationed near the northeast entrance of the palace. Its two small sides had preserved traces of cuneiform writing of the style of the time of Gudea, to whom this unique monument doubtless must be ascribed. The two long sides, once exquisitely adorned with bas-reliefs, had likewise suffered considerably from exposure. But enough remained to recognize in them a living chain of female figures, a "frieze of veritable Chaldean Naiads through their union symbolizing the perpetuity of water." A number of women, in graceful attitude, hold, in their outstretched hands, magi-

cal vases which they evidently are passing one to another. A double stream of water gushing forth from each of these inexhaustible receptacles represents the two sacred rivers, the Tigris and the Euphrates, which, on another fine sculptured fragment rescued from the rubbish below the pavement of the same palace, are indicated with even greater detail by a plant growing out of the vase and by a fish swimming against the current in each river.

A district situated on the east bank of the Tigris, not very far from its junction with the Euphrates. Thus in his usual masterly manner characterized by Heuzey, *Decouvrrtej* p. 217 (comp. p. 43, note I, of the same work).

Close to the middle of the southwest wall of the palace just described, and extending considerably into its principal courts, there rose two massive structures, or terraces of baked bricks laid in bitumen, above the remains of the Parthian building. Both joined each other at one corner, but they were reached by separate stairs and differed from each other also as to their height. As they interfered greatly with the general plan and arrangement of the interior of the palace, it was evident from the beginning that they belonged to an older building, lifting, so to speak, its head out of a lower stratum into the post-Babylonian period, as the last witness of a by-gone age. The fact, however, that the inscribed bricks, so far as examined, bore the name of Gudea on their upper-sides, was in itself a proof that the visible portion of this ancient structure had in part been relaid and otherwise changed in accordance with its different use in the Seleucidan times. The two terraces, affording a grand view over the surrounding plain, must have been important to the late inhabitants from a military standpoint, while at the same time they served as a kind of elevated gallery or esplanade where the residents of the palace could enjoy a fresh breeze of air in the cooler evening hours of a hot Babylonian summer.

No sooner had De Sarzec commenced to examine the ground around the vertical walls of these peculiar struc-

tures than, to his great astonishment, he came upon other remains of the same building imbedded in the crude brick terrace. Unfortunately, the rebellion breaking out among the Muntefik(j) tribes, in 1881, brought the explorer's work to a sudden end, so that he was then unable to arrive at a definite conclusion concerning its true character. But in connection with his later campaigns he also resumed his excavations at the lower strata of Mound A, discovering that the remains which had puzzled him so much before belonged to the tower of a fortified enclosure. In digging along its base, he established that one side of the latter showed the same simple pattern as the two facades of the Parthian building, — in other words, those peculiar architectural ornaments which the ancient Babylonians and Assyrians reserved exclusively for exterior decoration. Soon afterwards he excavated a large gate with three stepped recesses, which on the one hand was flanked by the tower, while on the other side its wall was lost in the later building. Comp. *Demuvertes*, pi. zj, no. 6. Comp. the end of p. 31, above.

All the bricks taken from this fortified enclosure were in their original position, and bore the inscription: " To NinGirsu, the powerful champion of Bel, Gudea, patesi of *Shir-pur-la*, accomplished something worthy, built the temple *Eninnu-Imgig(-gu)frarbara* and restored it." This legend and similar statements occurring on the statues in dolerite and on other votive objects rescued from the same part of the ruins, the fact that Mound A represents the most extensive single hill of Tello, and several other considerations, lead necessarily to the conclusion that the ancient structure lying below the Seleucidan palace and partiv worked into it can only be *Eninnu*, the chief sanctuary of the Babylonian city, sacred to Nin-Girsu or Nin-Su(n)gir, the tutelary deity of Lagash. Comp. Heuzey in *Comptes Rcndus de /' Academie dcs Inscriptions*, 1894, pp. 34-42. The name of the temple appears either as *E-Ninnu*, "House of God Ningirsu" (Ninnu, " 50," being the ideogram of the god), or as *E-Imgtg(-*

gu)bara, i. c. the temple called *lmgig(-u)bara* (" Imgig is shining"), or as *E-Ninnu-Imgig(-gu)//arbara* (a composition of these two names). The divine bird Imgig was the emblem of the God Ningirsu and of his city *Shirpur-la Z. A.* xv, pp. 52 *seq.,* xvi, p. 357), according to Hommcl, originally a raven (jA/r-/«r(-«) = *ariiu.*)

This temple existed at Tello from the earliest times. But an examination of the inscription on the statue of UrBau, and the results of De Sarzec's explorations in the lower strata, would seem to indicate that this ruler abandoned the old site of Kninnu altogether, and rebuilt the temple on a larger scale at the place where its ruins are seen at present. However, it must not be forgotten that the displacement of a renowned sanctuary involved in this theory is something unheard of in the history of ancient Babylonia. It is contrary to the well-known spirit of conservatism manifested by the ancient inhabitants of Babylonia in all matters connected with their religion, and directly opposed to the numerous statements contained in the so-called building inscriptions and boundary regulations of all periods.

Unfortunately very little of the temple of Nin-Su(n)gir seems to have been left. De Sarzec had previously discovered a wall of Ur-Bau under the east corner of the palace. But besides it and the tower and gate of Gudea he brought nothing to light except layers of crude bricks from the artificial terrace. In the light of these negative results, how can the continuity of the sanctuary at one and the same place be defended? On the ground that in order to secure a stronger and larger foundation for his own new sanctuary, Ur-Bau mav have razed the crumbling terrace of the old temple entirely, as many other Babylonian and Assyrian monarchs did afterwards in other cities. And no less on the ground that according to all evidence furnished by the excavations, the present terrace, on which the local rulers of the Seleucidan age erected their castle, is considerably smaller than the platform of the patesis of Lagash. There can be no doubt therefore that a considerable part

of the earliest temple ruins, which in all probability included even those of a stagetower,' was intentionally demolished and removed by UrBau, or, if not by him, surely by the Parthian princes of the third century, who built their palace almost exclusively of the bricks of Gudea's temple. We have a somewhat similar case at Nippur. For it is a remarkable fact that the characteristic change from a Babylonian sanctuary into a Seleucido-Parthian palace observed at Tello is precisely the same as took place in the sacred precinct of Bel at Nuffar, so that the evidence obtained in the trenches of the latter, better preserved ruin goes far to explain the detached walls unearthed in the lower strata of Tello.

The *E-Niiigirsu* of Ur-Nina is practically the same name as *E-Ninnu,* both meaning " temple of Ninib." As far as I can see, the name *E-Ninnu* occurs for the first time in the inscriptions of Entemena, great-grandson of Ur-Nina, and in a text of Urukagina. That in the earliest days of ancient Babylonia practically the same spirit prevailed as in Semitic times with regard to the inviolable character of sacred enclosures, boundary lines, agreements (especiallv when made with gods, /. e., their territory, income, gifts) is clear from certain instructive passages engraved upon "the historical cone of Entemena," which doubtless came from Tello (comp. *Revue l'Asssriologie,* vol. iv, pp. 37, *seqq.*), and from the long curse attached to Gudea's inscription on Statue B. And in a recent letter to the present writer expressly confirmed by Heuzey. From the analogical case of Nippur (Fourth Campaign, below), where a central kernel of the huge *ziggurrat* descends tar down into the pre-Sargonic stratum, and from certain passages in the earliest inscriptions from Tello, I feel convinced that a stage-tower, the most characteristic part of every prominent Babylonian temple, must also have existed at Lagash — however modest in size — at the time of the earliest kings. Traces of it may still be found somewhere in the lowest strata of Mound A. For the pre-Sargonic *ziggurrat* at Nippur comp.

Helm and Hilprecht, *Mitteilung ubcr die chemisette Untersuchung von altbabylomschen Kitpfer-and Bronze Gegenstanden und deren Altersbatimmung,* in *l'erhatidlungen dcr Berliner anthropologisehen Gcsellschaft,* Febr. 16, 1901, p. I 59. As to a stage-tower probably mentioned in the Tello inscriptions, comp. Gudea D, col. ii, 1. 11: *E-pa e-ub-imin-na-ni mu-ita-ru,* and Jensen in Schrader's *Kfilinschriftliche Bibliothek,* vol. iii, part I, pp. 50, *seq.* Comp. also Ur-Nina's inscription published in *Decouvrtes,* pi. *2,* no. 2, col. ii, 1. 7—10, where *uruna-ni mu-ru,* "he built his (Ningirsu's) obscrvatorv," is immediately preceded by *E-fii'-mu-ru,* so that in view of the Gudea passage, we probably have to recognize a close connection between the *Efa* and the *uruna,* the latter being situated upon the top of the former. For stage-tower and observatory cannot be separated from each other in ancient Babylonia.

With the exception of the Seleucido-Parthian building just described, the few but important remains of Kninnu and the ingeniously constructed brick columns of Gudea above (p. 222) referred to, De Sarzec's excavations had so tar been comparatively unproductive of noteworthy architectural results. Thev were more interesting and truly epoch-making in their bearing upon our knowledge of the origin and development of ancient Babylonian art. For the rubbish which filled the chambers and halls of the palace not only contained the ordinary pottery, iron instruments, perforated stone seals in the forms of animals,-and other objects characteristic of the last centuries preceding the Christian era, but it also yielded numerous door-sockets of Gudea and Ur-Bau re-used later in part, inscribed vases and mace-heads, a large quantity of seal cylinders, principally taken from the mortar uniting the different layers of brick in a furnace, and not a few of those priceless fragments of bas-reliefs, statues, and statuettes which will always form the basis for a systematic study of earlier Chaldean art. The most valuable discoveries, however, awaited the explorer in the debris filling the large open court and the rooms and passages grouped around it, and in the layer of earth separating the pavement of the Parthian edifice from the crude brick terrace below it. No less than eight decapitated statues — four sitting and four standing— lay on the court in two distinct groups scarcely more than ten yards apart from each other. A detached shaved head, doubtless originally belonging to one of them, was found in their immediate neighborhood.

Comp. my " Report from Nuffar to the Committee of the Babvl. Exped. in Philadelphia," April 21, 1900, from which I quote: "The building described by Peters and Haynes as the temple of Bel is only a huge Parthian fortress lying on the top of the ancient temple ruin, and so constructed that the upper stages of the *ziggurrat* served as a kind of citadel." Found under the alabaster threshold in the inner gate of the southwest side of the palace, where, in accordance with a custom frequently observed in Assyrian buildings, they evidently had been placed as talismans. The tine Sommerville collection of talismans in the Archa"ological Museum of the University of Pennsylvania contains a large number of similar Parthian stone seals.

'Likewise serving as talismans against demons and their obnoxious influences. This interesting use of ancient Babylonian seal-cvlinders, cuneiform tablets, and other inscribed objects by the later inhabitants of the country explains why they occur so frequently in Parthian tombs (comp. my remarks on pp. 154, *seq.*, 168, above, and De Sarzec and Hcuzey, *Dfi'juvcrtes*, p. 73, note 1). But it also illustrates how impossible it is to ue such finds without criticism as material for determining the age of tombs in Babvlonian ruins, as unfortunately was done by Peters in his " Nippur," vol. ii, p. 219. Petc' classification of Babylonian coffins and pottery cannot be taken seriously, because it ignores the established laws of archeology and the principles of historical research.

Among the manv valuable antiquities which came from the adjoining halls

and from the earth below this whole section we mention one of the largest bas-reliefs discovered in Tello, representing a procession of priests and a musician playing a peculiarly decorated harp of eleven chords dating from the time of Gudea; a little fragment of sculpture of the same epoch, which rapidly gained a certain celebrity among modern artists for the exquisite modelling and fine execution of a naked female foot; a mutilated and halfcalcined slab showing a humped bull carved with a rare skill and surprising fidelity to nature; a small but well preserved head in steatite reproducing the type of the large shaved head with a remarkable grace and delicacy; a new piece of the "stele of vultures" previously mentioned;' and the first fragment of an inscribed tablet of Ur-Nina, exhibiting the lion-headed eagle with outspread wings victoriously clutching two lions in its powerful talons, — the well-known. coat of arms of the city *of Shir-pur-la."* Over four feet high, and, according to Heuzev, probably belonging to a four-sided altar, stele, or pedestal (*Decout'ertes*, pi. 23). Comp. *Decouvcrtes*, pi. 25.no. 6, identical with the fragment quoted on p. 229, above. Comp. *Decouvertes,* pi. 25, no. 4. Comp. *Decouvertes,* pi. 25, no. 1. Comp. *Decouvcrtes,* pis. 3 and 4, B.

The last-named monument enabled Heuzey to bring the earliest remains of Chaldean art, so scrupulously gathered by De Sarzec, into closer relation with the ancient kings of Tello. He ascertained that, contrary to what we know of the first princes of Assyria, the rulers who style themselves "kings of *Shir-pur-la "* are older than those who bear the title *patesi, i. e., "*priest-king," or more exactly "princepriest," in their inscriptions, — a result which allowed him at once to establish an approximate chronologv for the newly discovered rulers of Southern Babylonia in accordance with the progress in style to be traced in their sculptures and basreliefs. Furthermore, the French archa-ologist determined a number of general facts, on the basis of which he successfully defended the two following theses, — (i) that the style of the monuments of

7'ello is not a style of imitation, but a real and genuine archaism; (2) that quite a number of the monuments discovered antedate the remote epoch of King Naram-Sin (about 3750 B.c.), and lead us back to the very beginning of Chaldean art. These fundamental deductions and historical conclusions, so quickly drawn by Heuzey after his study of the archaeological details of the monuments, found their full corroboration through the deciphering of their accompanying inscriptions by Oppert and Amiaud, and through the present writer's paheographical and historical researches in connection with the Nuffar antiquities, which afforded a welcome means of controlling and supplementing the results obtained at Tello.

Comp. *Decouvcrtes,* pi. 1, no. 2. A very similar fragment is in the Imperial Ottoman Museum at Constantinople (no. 420). This statement has reference onlv to the two principal groups of rulers of Lagash then known. In all probability there was still an earlier dynasty at Tello, the members of which bear the title *patesi.* Comp. Thureau-Dangin in *Zeitschrift fur Assyriologie,* vol. xv, p. 403. Comp. Heuzey's subtle observations on Chaldean art in *Revue Arclttologique,* new scries, vol. xlii, 1881, p. 263, and in *Decouvcrtes,* pp. 77-86, 1 19-127, 186, *sea.* The date of NarSm-Sin's government was obtained from a cylinder of Nabonidos excavated by Rassam at Abu Habba about the same time. Comp. p. 273, below.

The magnificent collection of statues in diorite, or more exactly dolerite, will always remain the principal discovery connected with De Sarzec's name. With the exception of but one erected by Ur-Bau, they bear the name of Gudea, patesi of *Shir-pur-la* or Lagash, as the city at some time must have been called. Famous as the choicest museum pieces so far recovered from Babylonian soil, and remarkable for their unity of style and technique, and therefore occupying a most prominent place in the history of ancient art, they appeal to us no less through the simplicity and correctness of their attitude and through the reality and power of their expression, than through the extraordinary skill and ability with which one of the hardest stones in existence has here been handled by unknown Chaldean artists. The mere fact that such monuments could originate in ancient Babylonia speaks volumes for the unique character and the peculiar vitality of this great civilization, which started near the Persian Gulf thousands of years before our era, and fundamentally influenced the religious ideas and the intellectual development of the principal Semitic nations, and through them left its impression even upon Europe and upon our own civilization.

All the statues represent a human ruler — generally Gudea — whose name is found in a kind of cartouche on the right shoulder or in a long inscription engraved upon a conspicuous part of the body or garment; and they all have the hands clasped before the breast in an attitude of reverence. As over against the typical sobriety and conventional style of the early Egyptian sculptures, the Chaldean artist endeavors to express real life and to imitate nature within certain limits set by the peculiar material, " the routine of the studios and the rules of sacred etiquette." The swelling of the muscles of the right arm, the delicately carved nails of the fingers, the expressive details of the feet firmly resting on the ground, the characteristic manner in which the fringed shawl is thrown over the left shoulder, and the first naive and timid attempt at reproducing its graceful folds betray a remarkable gift of observation and no small sculptural talent on the part of these ancient Sumerians. Two of the sitting statues show Gudea as an architect with a large tablet upon his lap, while a carefully divided rule and a stylus are carved in relief near its upper and right edges. The surface of the one tablet is empty, while on the other the patesi has drawn a large fortified enclosure provided with gates, bastions and towers.

The great number and the artistic value of the monuments of Gudea point to an extraordinary prosperity and a comparatively peaceful development of the various resources of the city of Lagash

at the time of his government (about 2700 B. c). This natural inference is fully confirmed by the vast remains of his buildings at the ruins and by the unique contents ot his many inscriptions. The latter were greeted by Assyriologists as the first genuine documents of a period when Sumerian was still a spoken language, however much influenced already by the grammar and lexicography of their Semitic neighbors and conquerors. But aside from their linguistic and palæographical importance these inscriptions, though even at present by no means fully understood, revealed to us such a surprising picture of the greatness and extent of the ancient Sumerian This is the tablet seen in the illustration facing this page.

civilization and of the geographical horizon of the early inhabitants of Lagash that at first it seemed almost impossible to regard it as faithful and historical. Gudea fought victorious battles against Elam and sent his agents as far as the Mediterranean. He cut his cedars in Northern Syria and Idumea and obtained his dolerite in the quarries of Kastern Arabia (Magan). His caravans brought copper from the mines of the Nejd (Kimash),and his ships carried gold and precious wood from the mountains of Medina and the rocky shores of the Sinaitic peninsula (Melukh). What an outlook into the lively intercourse and the exchange of products between the nations of Western Asia at the threshold of the fourth and third pre-Christian millenniums, but also what an indication of the powerful influence which went forth from this little known race of Southern Babylonia, irresistibly advancing in all directions and affecting Palestine long before Abram left his ancestral home on the west bank of the Euphrates. And vet De Sarzec's excavations at Tello and the Philadelphia expedition to NufFar were soon to provide ample new material by means of which we were enabled to follow that remarkable civilization a thousand years and even further back. 3. De Sarzec's careful description of the many ancient remains unearthed by him, and Heuzev's admirable exposition of the age and im-

portance of the new material, prepared the way for an early resumption of the excavations at Tello. But in view of certain fundamental changes recently made in the archaeological laws of the Ottoman empire at Hamdy Bev's recommendation, the French minister deemed it wise at first to ascertain the future attitude of the Porte with regard to the ownership of other antiquities which might be discovered, before he sanctioned any further exploration in Southern Babylonia. After frequent and protracted negotiations a satisfactory understanding was finally reached between the two interested powers. De Sarzec had meanwhile been appointed consul at Baghdad. In 1888 he was authorized to proceed again to the scene of his former labors, which henceforth were deprived of their private character and conducted under the auspices and at the expense of the French government. Comp. Hommel's article " Explorations in Arabia," in this volume. Iron, however, was not among the metals brought by Gudea from Melukh, as was asserted by Hommel and (following him) by myself fin *VcrhanJIangen dtr Berliner anthrofologhchen Gcscllichaft,* session of 16 Febr., 1901, p. 164)So far no iron has been discovered in the earliest strata of cither NufFar or Tello. Indeed, I doubt whether it appears in Assyria and Babylonia much before 1000 B. C. The earliest large finds of iron implements known to us from the exploration of Assyrian and Babylonian ruins date from the eighth century B. C. and were made in Sargon's palace at Khorsabad (comp. p. 83, above) and in Ashurnasirapal's northwest palace at Nimrud (comp. p. 124, above). As we know, however, that Sargon (722-705 B. c.) also restored and for a while occupied the latter palace (comp. pp. 106 and 1 11, above) the iron utensils found in it doubtless go back to him and not to the time of Ashumasirapal.

Certain scattered fragments of sculptures and a few inscriptions previously gathered had made it evident that the mounds of Tello contained monuments considerably older than the statues of Ur-Bau and Gudea, and reaching back almost to the very beginning of Babvlonian civilization. The question arose, Which of the numerous elevations of the very extensive site most probably represents the principal settlement of this earlv period and is likelv to repav methodical researches with corresponding important discoveries? Remembering the very numerous ancientconstructionswhich ten years before had been brought to light by his trial trenches in Mound B, De Sarzec now directed his chief attention to the exploration of this section of the ruins, at the same time continuing his examination of the lower strata of Mound A, as indicated above. Comp. pp. 205, *stq.*, above. Among them inscribed monuments of Ur-Nina, Eannatum, Entemena, and Enannatum. Comp. the fragments of the bas-rclicfs of Ur-Nina and " the stele of vultures " previously referred to; furthermore *Duouzrrtfs*, pp. 59 and 68; and Heuzy, *La rois de Tello et la periods arehaique de Vart chaldeen*, in *Revue Archeologique*, Nov., 1885.

It was a comparatively easy task for the explorer to determine the character of the latest accumulation which covered the top of this tumulus. Upon a layer of crude bricks he found part of a wall which constituted the last remains of a building of the time of Gudea (2700 B. C), whose name was engraved on a door-socket and upon a small copper figurine discovered *in situ*. Another figurine of the type of the basket-bearers had a votive inscription of Dungi, king of Ur, who belonged to the same general epoch. But his greatest finds from this upper stratum of Mound B were two exquisite round trays in veined onyx and half-transparent alabaster, which, with the fragment of a third, bore the names of as many different patesis of Lagash, Ur-Ninsun, otherwise unknown, Nammakhani, the son-in-law and successor of Ur-Bau, and (Ga)lukani, a vassal of Dungi.

As soon as De Sarzec commenced to deepen his trenches, he came upon older walls constructed of entirely different bricks laid in bitumen. They were baked and oblong, flat on their lower and convex on their upper side, and without ex-

ception had a mark of the right thumb in the centre of the latter. A few of them bearing a legend of King Ur-Nina in large linear writing, it seemed safe to assume that here there were architectural remains which went back to the earliest kings of Lagash. With great care and expectation De Sarzec examined the whole building and its environment in the course of the next twelve years. Everywhere at the same level characterized bv a large pavement of bricks and reached at an average depth of only thirteen feet from the surface, he found inscribed stone tablets and door-sockets, Now in the Museum of Archsology at Constantinople, where with other Babylonian antiquities they were catalogued by the present writer.

Silver Vase of Entemcna, Hriest-King of Lagash, decorated with the Emblem of his God *About jgjo B. C.* weapons, — including a colossal spear-head dedicated to Ningirsu by an ancient king of Kish, and the elaborately carved macehead of the even earlier King Mesilim of the same city, — figurines in copper, the magnificent silver vase of Entemena, lion heads and bas-reliefs, — among them the famous genealogical bas-reliefs of Ur-Nina and three new fragments of " the stele of vultures," — besides many other precious antiquities which about 4000 B. C. had been presented as votive offerings to their gods by Ur-Nina, Kannatum, Entemena, Enannatum, etc., and several contemporaneous rulers of other Babylonian cities with whom this powerful dynasty of Lagash fought battles or otherwise came into contact.

But even Ur-Nina's edifice did not represent the earliest settlement of Mound B. In examining the ground below his platform, De Sarzec disclosed remains of a still older building imbedded in the crude bricks of the lofty terrace which served as a solid basis for the great king's own construction. Its ruined walls rose to the height of more than nine feet, and were made of bricks similar to those from the next higher stratum, but somewhat smaller in size and without their characteristic thumb marks. This very ancient building rested

upon a pavement of gypsum, lying nearly sixteen feet and a half below the platform of Ur-Nina and a little over twenty-six feet above the surrounding plain, occupying therefore about the centre of the whole artificial mound. The unknown ruler of Lagash who erected it must have lived towards the end of the fifth pre-Christian millennium. A number of votive statuettes in copper of a very aichaic type, and fragments of sculptured stones, including the lower part of a large military stele, which, owing to its weight and its unimportant details, remained on the ground,' repaid De Sarzec's researches in the rubbish that filled the interior of the structure and covered the adjacent platform.

In copper, over two feet and a halt" long. In limestone, over six and a half feet long, almost three feet high, and half a foot thick. Comp. *Decouvertes*, pp. 195, *scq.*, and pi. 56, no. *2.*

A new interruption in the French excavations at Telle was caused in 1889 by the explorer's failing health and h temporary transfer to a higher and more lucrative posit: in Batavia. When four years later he returned once m to Southern Babylonia, soon afterwards (1894) to be pointed consul-general, he extended his trenches i directions around these enigmatic architectural remain resumed his explorations at the other points pre' attacked. In order to ascertain especially, whether the lower strata of mound B concealed monuments greater antiquity than hitherto disclosed by him, hi his workmen to cut a trench through the soli.' bricks which had formed the basis for the diffc ings once crowning its summit. At a depth of; twenty-six feet he reached the virgin soil, w h continued his researches. With the exceptin ber of emptv receptacles made of bitumen in large jars and similar to others which had the walls of the archaic building, this expev yielded only a few rude mace-heads, ham 11 eggs, probably used by slingers in warfai and fragments of ordinary pottery, all a; poraneous with the first edifice for whic been erected.

On the west slope of Mound B De S wells and a water-course of the time manner peculiar to the earliest period 1' the two former were constructed ot marked with the impressions of two According to De Sarzcc and Heu/.cv. Paris, 1900, p. 63, these eggs were comnnis regarded as unknown. They occur tr Fourth Campaign, Temple Mound, Sectioi index—and in some instances bearing a long legend of the monarch just mentioned. After a brief reference to his reign and principal military expeditions, this ruler glorifies in having constructed " the great terrace ot the well,";'. e., in having extended the crude brick terrace of his predecessor so far as to include in it the mouths of these two water supplies which he raised from the plain up to the level of Ur-Nina's buildings. From the neighboring debris came some fine pieces of carved or incised shell, showing spirited scenes of men, animals and plants, and doubtless belonging to the same general epoch. A good many similar specimens of this important branch of ancient Chaldean art, a few of them colored, have been recently obtained from various other central and south-Babvlonian ruins by the present writer."

A rectangular massive building, remains of a gate, and several artificial reservoirs differing greatly in size and form were brought to light to the southeast and northeast of F.nannatuma's wells. A few inscribed bricks and a number of copper figurines carrying alabaster tablets upon their heads indicated sufficiently that most of these structures were the work of Kntemena, nephew of the last-mentioned patesi of *Shir-pur-la.* Some of them may have been rebuilt in subsequent times, but preceding the governments of Ur-Bau and Gudea. Not without good reason Heuzey proposed to identify the terrace to the southeast with the substructure of the *sfb(Es/i)-gi* mentioned on some of the inscribed bricks taken from the former, and the sacred enclosure to the northeast, which in part at least can be still defined bv means of the copper figurines found *in situ,* with the *Ab-bi-ru* of the alabaster tablets. Comp. De Sarzec and Heuzey, *Vne Ville Rosale Chaldetnne,* Paris, 1900, pp. 69-

75, especially p. 74. Comp. Hilprecht, ''The South-Bab) Ionian Ruins of Abu Hatab and Fara" (in course of preparation). Comp. De Sarzec and Heuzey, *Une Vilie R&tale Chaldetnne,* p. 79. Comp. De Sarzec and Heuzey, 1. c, pp. 87, *seqq.*

Though the precise meaning of both of these names is obscure, Heuzey is doubtless correct in trying to explain the significance of the two structures represented by them from the nature of the principal building occupying Mound B, from the character of the numerous antiquities excavated in their neighborhood, and from certain other indications furnished by the inscriptions. The large oval reservoir and three smaller rectangular ones, discovered within the enclosure marked by Entemena's figurines, have probably reference to the (temporary) storing of dates ' and to the preparation of date wine. Even to-day the date-growing Arabs of Babylonia, who have not been influenced by certain changes recently introduced in connection wijh the increased export of dates to Europe and America, use similar elevated receptacles, — the so-called *med-ibsa* — which have all the characteristic features of the ancient (oval) basin with its inclined pavement and outlet.

There are architectural remains which were unearthed in other parts of these ruins close to the large brick terrace erected by Ur-Nina and enlarged by his successors. But being too fragmentary in themselves and valuable chiefly as providing further evidence with regard to the real character of the whole complex of buildings concealed in Mound B, we may well abstain from enumerating them one by one and describing their peculiarities in detail.

What was the original purpose of all these separate walls and crumbling constructions, which at some time apparently constituted an organic whole? Certain pronounced architectural features still to be recognized in the central buildings of the two lowest platforms, and a careful examination of the different antiquities taken from the accumulated rubbish within and around them, will enable us to answer the question

and to determine the general character of the vast enclosure with reasonable certainty.

' Comp. the *khasiiru* of the Nco-Babylonian contracts.

For further details as to their construction and use, comp. Hilprecht, "The Babylonian Expedition of the University of Pennsylvania," series A, vol. x (in press).

We notice, first of all, that the most prominent structure discovered in the stratum of the period of Ur-Nina, about thirty-five feet long and twenty-four wide, shows no trace of a door or any other kind of entrance, though its walls, when excavated, were still standing to the height of nearly four feet. It is therefore evident that access to it must have been had from above by means of a staircase or ladder now destroyed, and that for this reason it could never have been used as a regular dwelling-place for men or beasts. A French Excavations at Tellu under De Sar«c

Scultitait facade of the Hordiouu of King Ur-Nina, about 4000 B. C.

similar result is reached by examining the more archaic but somewhat smaller building below, which presents even greater puzzles from an architectural standpoint.

The inner disposition of the upper edifice is no less remarkable than its external appearance. It consists of two rooms of different size, which, however, do not extend directly to the outer walls, but are disconnected by a passageway or corridor over two feet and a half wide, running parallel with the latter and also separating the two rooms from each other. These inner chambers likewise have no opening. With good reason, therefore, Heuzey regards this curious building as a regular store or provision house similarly constructed to those known in ancient Egypt. This view is strengthened by the fact that the inscriptions of UrNina, Enannatum, Urukagina, and especially those of Entemena repeatedly refer to such a magazine or depot of the god Nin-Su(n)gir. The ancient kings and *patesis* of Lagash used to fill it with grain, dates, sesame oil, and other produce of the country required for the maintenance of the temple servants, or needed as supplies for their armies, which fought frequent battles in the name of their tutelary deity. The double walls, which form a characteristic feature also of a number of chambers in the outer wall of the huge Parthian fortress at Nippur, were useful in more than one regard. They excluded the extreme heat of the summer and the humidity of the winter, while, at the same time, they insured the safety of the stored provisions against damage from crevices, thieves, and troublesome insects. A coat of bitumen covering the walls and floors of the rooms and corridor answered the same purpose.

At a distance of thirteen feet from the principal building De Sarzec discovered eight bases made of baked brick, two on each side, which originally supported as many square pillars, clearly indicated by the remains of charred cedarwood found near them. It is therefore apparent that a large gallery, a kind of portico or peristyle, as we frequently see it attached to the modern houses of Kurdish and Armenian peasants in Asia Minor, surrounded the ancient Babylonian edifice on all four sides, furnishing additional room for the temporary storage of goods, agricultural implements, and large objects which could not be deposited within. On this theory it is easy to explain the existence of so many artificial reservoirs, water-courses, and wells in the immediate neighborhood of this interesting structure. As indicated above, they served various practical purposes in connection with this large rural establishment, such as cleansing and washing, the storing of dates, the preparation of date wine, and the pressing of oil.

Comp. Thureau-Dangin in *Revue d'dayriologie,* vol. iii, pp. 119, *ifff.* Through Heuzcy, in *Revue d Assyriologie,* vol. iii, pp. 65-68.

Like the storerooms of the temple at Sippara so frequently mentioned in the later cuneiform inscriptions, this sacred magazine of the earliest rulers of Lagash was not exclusively a granary and oil-cellar. According to time and circumstances, it was turned into an ar-

mory or into a safe for specially valuable temple property, vessels and votive offerings of every description, as a small lot of copper daggers, fragments of reliefs, and two inscribed door-sockets.found on the floor of the rooms sufficiently demonstrate. Many other objects of art gathered from the debris around this building may therefore have formed part of the treasures which, previous to the final destruction of the city, were kept within its walls. Modest and simple as this whole temple annex appears to us from our present standpoint, it was in every way adapted to the needs of the ancient population *of Shir-purla,* on its lofty terrace equally protected against the annual inundations of the rivers and the sudden invasion of hostile armies.

Among the portable antiquities which rewarded De Sarzec's labors during the three campaigns conducted from 1893 to 1895, about 30,000 baked cuneiform tablets and fragments constitute his most characteristic discovery. In 1894 and 1895 they were found in a small elevation a little over 650 feet distant from the large hill which contained the buildings of the ancient princes of Lagash just described. The successful explorer informs us' that he came upon two distinct groups of rectangular galleries constructed of crude bricks, upon which these first large collections of clay tablets from Tello were arranged in five or six layers, one above another. Unfortunately, soon after their discovery, these interesting depots, which must be regarded as regular business archives of the temple, similar to others unearthed at Abu Habba and Nuffar, were plundered by the natives. Nearly all the leading museums of Europe and America have profited therefrom. But nevertheless it will always remain a source of deep regret that the French government does not appear to have succeeded in establishing regular guards at Tello. Even when De Sarzec was in the field, the ruins were not sufficiently protected at night, to say nothing of the frequent and long intervals in his work when no one was left on guard and those precious mounds remained at

the mercy of unscrupulous merchants and of the neighboring Arabs, who soon began to realize the financial value of these almost inexhaustible mines.' A large number of the stolen tablets are still in the hands of the antiquity dealers. At first greedily bought by the latter in the sure expectation of an extraordinary gain, this archaeological contraband began recently to disappoint them, the comparatively uninteresting and monotonous contents of the average clay tablet from Tello offering too little attraction to most of the Assvriological students.

As a rule they refer to the administration of temple property, to agriculture and stock-raising, to trade, commerce, and industry. There are lists of offerings, furniture, slaves, and other inventories, bills of entry, expense lists, receipts, accounts, contracts, and letters; there are even land registers, plans of houses, of fortifications, rivers, and canals. Especially numerous are the lists of animals (temple herds, and the like) and statements of the produce of the fields, testifying to the eminently agricultural and pastoral character of the ancient principality of Lagash. Among the more interesting specimens we mention the fragments of a correspondence between Lugal-ushumgal, *patesi* of *Shir-pur-la,* and a contemporaneous king of Agade (Sargon or NaramSin), his suzerain. Or we refer to a number of inscribed seal-impressions in clay, as labels attached to merchandise and addressed to various persons and cities. For we learn from a studv of these long-buried archives that northern Babylonia largely exported grain and manufactured goods to the south, while the latter dealt principally in cattle, fowl, wool, cheese, butter, and eggs — precisely the same characteristic products which the two halves of Babylonia exchange with each other to-day.

The ruins of NufFar, the neighborhood of which is as unsafe as that of Tello, and the property of the expedition of the University of Pennsylvania (house and gardens, and stores, furniture and utensils locked up in the former) were always entrusted to native guards during our absence from the field, the 'Afej shaikhs agreeing to guarantee their inviolability for a comparatively small remuneration. Thev have always kept their promise faithfully, notwithstanding the wars which they frequently waged against the Shammar or against each other in the meanwhile. Comp. Heuzey, *Catalogue de la Sculpture Chaldeenne au Musee du Louvre,* Paris, 1902, Introduction.

With regard to their age, these tablets cover a considerable period. Some of them antedate the dynasty of UrXina (40CX) B. c.); others bear the name of Urukagina, "king *of Shir-pur-la,"* whose time has not been fixed definitely; again others belong to the age of Sargon and Naram-Sin (3802 B. C.) and are of inestimable value for their dates, which contain important historical references; a few are the documents from the reign of Gudea (about 2700 B. c.); by far the largest mass of the tablets recovered belongs to the powerful members of the later dynasty of Ur, about 2550 B. c. Comp. Heuzey in *Comptes Ren J us da Seances de /' Academic des Inscriptions ct Belles-Lcttres,* 1896 (4th series, vol. xxiv), session of April 17, and in *Revue d' Assyriologie,* vol. iv, pp. 1-12.

According to Thureau-Dangin, he lived after Entemena. Comp. *Zeitschrift fur Assyriologie,* vol. xv, p. 404, note I. Babylon, written Ka-dincir-ra-ki, appears on one of these tablets — according to our present knowledge the first clear reference to the famous city known in history.

Numerous other inscribed antiquities of a more monumental character, such as statuettes with intact heads, truncated cones, stone cylinders, and, above all, the large pebbles of Eannatum, grandson of Ur-Nina, with their welcome accounts of the principal historical events occurring during his government, were taken from the clay shelves of the same subterranean galleries. Unique art treasures were found at different parts of the ruins as previously indicated, but they were especially numerous in the neighborhood of the storehouses and temple archives. Among those from Tello which exhibit the most primitive style

of art so far known, the fragments of a circular bas-relief representing the solemn meeting of two great chiefs followed by their retinues of warriors hold a very prominent place. It is contemporaneous with the earliest building discovered in mound B, while three excellent specimens of Old Babylonian metallurgy,'two bulls' heads in copper and a peculiarly formed vase in the same metal, belong to the more advanced period of Ur-Nina and his successors.

For many years to come the excavations of De Sarzec in and around mound B have furnished rich material for the student of ancient languages, history, and religion. Though none of the shrines and temples of the different local gods worshipped here has as vet been identified with certainty, the crumbling remains of so many buildings unearthed, the exceptionally large number of fine objects of art, and the mass of clay tablets and monumental inscriptions already recovered, enable us to form a tolerably fair idea of the general character and standard of civilization reached by the early inhabitants of the Euphrates and Tigris valleys at the threshold of the fifth and fourth millenniums before our era. This civilization is of no low degree, and is far from taking us back to the first beginnings of human order and society. Of course art and architecture, which developed in close connection with the religious cults and conceptions of the people, and were strongly influenced in their growth by the peculiarities of climate and the natural conditions of the soil, are simple, and in accordance with the normal development of primitive humanity. The alluvial ground around Lagash furnished the necessary material for making and baking bricks for the houses of the gods. During the first period of Babylonian history rudelv formed with the hand, small in size, flat on the lower and slightly rounded on the upper side, which generally also bears one or more thumb marks, these bricks looked more like rubble or quarry stones, in imitation of which they were made, than the artificial products of man. Gradually thev became larger in size, and under Ur-

Nina they frequently have even a short inscription in coarse linear writing on the upper surface. But still they continued to retain their oblong plano-convex form down to the reign of Kntemena, the great-grandson of the former, who was the first ruler at Lagash to employ a rectangular mould in the manufacture of his building material. As we learned from the results of the Philadelphia expedition to Nuffar, later confirmed by De Sarzec's own discoveries at Tello, the principle of the arch was well known in the earliest times and occasionally applied in connection with draining. There is much in favor of Heuzey's view that the origin of the arch may possibly be traced to the peculiar form of the native reed-huts called *sari/as* by the Arabs of modern Babylonia (comp. the illustration on p. 160). They are the regular dwelling places of the poor Ma'dan tribes which occupy the marshy districts of the interior today, and they doubtless represent the earliest kind of habitation in the " country of canals and reeds " at the dawn of civilization. The common mortar found in the buildings of the lowest strata is bitumen (comp. Gen. ii: 3), which was easily obtained from the naphtha springs of the neighboring regions, while at least three different kinds of cement were employed in later centuries (comp. p. 32, above).

Comp. especially Thureau-Dangin in *Comftes Rendus,* 1896, pp. 355361, and in *Revue d' Assyriologie,* vol. iii, pp. 1 18-146; vol. iv, pp. 1327 (also Oppert, *ibidem,* pp. 28-33), 69-84 (accompanied by 32 plates of representative texts). The latest inscribed cuneiform document so far obtained from Tello is an inscribed cone of Rim-Sin of Larsam, according to a statement of Hcuzey in *Compta Rendus,* 1894, p. 42. -Two fine heads of Markhur goats in the same metal and of the same period were obtained by the present writer from the pre-Sargonic mounds of Fara. Comp. Helm and Hilprecht in *Verhandlungcn der Berliner anthropohgiichen Gesellichuft,* February 16, 1901, pp. 162, *stqq.*

Vessels of different shapes and sizes

were made of terracotta and stone, sometimes even of shell handsomely decorated. It is a remarkable fact that in material, form, and technique the earliest Babylonian vases often strikingly resemble those found in the tombs of the first dynasties of Egypt. A kind of veined limestone or onyx geologically known as calcite appears as a specially favorite material in both countries. The art of melting, hardening, casting, and chasing metals, especially copper and silver, was well established. The chemical analysis of early metal objects by the late Dr. Helm has recently shown that the ancient Babylonian brass founders who lived about 4000 B. c. used not only tin but also antimony, in order to harden copper and at the same time to render it more fusible. Statues and bas-reliefs are less graceful and accurate in their design and execution than realistic, sober and powerful through their very simplicity. In order to give more life and expression to animals and men carved in stone or cast in metal, the eyes of such statues are frequently formed by incrustation, the white of the apple of the eye being represented by shell or mother of pearl and the pupil by bitumen, lapis lazuli, or a reddish-brown stone. Red color is also sometimes used to paint groups of figures, which with an often surprising grace and fidelity to nature are incised in thin plates of shell or mother of pearl, in order to set them off better from the background, somewhat in the same manner as the Phenician artist of the sixth century treated the two inscriptions of Bostan esh-Shaikh (above Sidon) recently excavated by Makridi Bey for the Imperial Ottoman Museum. Comp. Helm and Hilprecht in *I'erhandlungtn der Berliner antfirofo/fgischen Grsellschaft,* Feb. 16, 1901, pp. 157

We do not know when writing (which, contrary to Delitzsch's untenable theory, began as a picture writing) was first introduced into Babylonia. About 4000 B. C. we find it in regular use everywhere in the country. Moreover, the single linear characters are already so far developed that in many cases the original picture can no longer be recognized. Onlv a few short inscriptions of the earliest historical period, when writing was still purely pictorial, are at present known to us. The one is in the Archaeological Museum of the University of Pennsylvania, another in New York, a third in Paris. Owing to the scarcity of this class of inscribed stones, their precise date cannot yet be ascertained. They probably belong to the beginning of the fifth millennium.

These first few conclusions drawn from the architectural remains, the sculptures, and inscriptions of the period of Ur-Nina, incomplete as the picture obtained thereby naturally is, will be sufficient for our present purpose to show that the civilization represented by his dynasty must be regarded as a very advanced stage in the gradual development of man, and that thousands of years of serious striving and patient work had to elapse before this standard was reached. The political conditions in the country were by no means always very favorable to the peaceful occupations of its inhabitants, to the tilling of the ground, to the expansion of trade, to the advancement of art and literature. At the time of Ur-Nina, Babylonia was divided into a large number of petty states, among which now this one, now that one exercised a passing hegemony over the others. The three Biblical cities Erech, Ur, Ellasar (/'. e., Larsam), Nippur (probably identical with Calneh, Gen. 10: 10), Kish, Lagash, and a place written *Gis/i-K/iu,* the exact pronunciation of which is not yet known, are the most frequently mentioned in the inscriptions of this remote antiquity. Every one of these fortified cities had its own sanctuary, which stood under the control of a *patesi* or " prince-priest." The most renowned religious centre of the whole country was Nippur, with the temple of Enlil or Bel, " the father of the gods," while for many years the greatest political power was exercised by the kings of Kish, a city "wicked of heart," until Ur-Nina and his successors established a temporary supremacy of Lagash over the whole South.

A large number of such colored plates of mother of pearl obtained from Fara and other South-Babylonian ruins is in the possession of the present writer. Comp. Hilprecht in *Deutsche Litteraturzeitung,* Nov. 30, 1901, pp. 3030, *iff.,*-and in "Sunday School Times," Dec. 21, 1901, p. 857.

'Comp. Delitzsch, *Die Entstehung ties alteiten Schriftsystemi,* Leipzig, According to Scheil probablv represented by the ruins of Jokha.

The last-named place consisted of several quarters or suburbs grouped around the temples of favorite gods and goddesses. Sungir, generally transliterated as Girsu, and possibly the prototype of the Biblical Shinar (-is 3 27 Gen. 10: 10; Ii: *if* and of the Babylonian Shumer, which is only dialectically different from the former, was one of them, indeed the most important of all the quarters of the city. It furnished the new dynasty from its nobility and took the leading position in the fierce struggle against the powerful neighbors and oppressors. Nin-Sungir, " the Lord of Sungir," was raised to the rank of the principal god, and his emblem — the lion-headed eagle with its outspread wings victoriously clutching two lions in its powerful talons — became the coat of arms of the united citv and characterizes best the spirit of independence and bold self-reliance which was fostered in his sanctuary.

Comp. Hilprecht, "The Babylonian Expedition of the University of Pennsylvania," series A, vol. I, part 2 (1896), pp. 57, *seq.;* and Radau, "Early Babylonian History," New York, 1900, pp. 216, *seqq.*

According to all indications the dvnastv of Ur-Nina was one of the mightiest known in the earlv history of Babylonia. The founder himself seems to have devoted his best strength and time to the works of peace. The numerous temples and canals received his attention, statues were carved in honor of the gods, and new storehouses constructed to receive " the abundance of the country. " Caravans were sent out to obtain the necessary timber from foreign countries, and the walls of the city were repaired or enlarged in anticipation of future complications and troubles. It was, however, reserved to Kannatum, the most illustrious representative of the whole dynasty, to fight those battles for which his grandfather had already taken the necessary precautions. Like his ancestors he continued to develop the natural resources of the country by digging new canals and wisely administering the inner affairs of his city. But, above all, he was great as a warrior, and extended the sphere of his influence far beyond the banks of the Shatt el-Ha'i and the two great rivers, by defeating the army of Elam, subduing *Gish-khu*, carrying his weapons victoriously against Krech and Ur, destroying the city of Az on the Persian Gulf, and crushing even the power of the kings of Kish, the old suzerains and hereditary enemies of the princes of Lagash.

Comp. the illustration ("Silver Vase of Entemena") facing p. 241, above, and what has been said on p. 235.

'Comp. Heuzey, *Les armoiriei Chaldeennes de Sirpourla,* Paris, 1894.

More than once in my preceding sketch of De Sarzec's labors and results I have referred to his discovery of new fragments of the so-called " stele of vultures." This famous monument of the past, one of the most interesting art treasures unearthed in Tello, received its name from a flock of vultures which carry away the hands, arms, and decapitated heads of the enemies vanquished and killed by Eannatum and his soldiers. It was originally rounded at the top, about five feet wide and correspondingly high, and covered with scenes and inscriptions on both its faces. The representations on the front celebrate King Eannatum as a great and successful warrior, while those on the reverse, so far as preserved, are of a mythological character, showing traces of several gods and goddesses in whose names the battles were fought, and who seem to be represented here as assisting their pious servant in the execution of his great and bloody task. The stele of vultures, which indicates a very decided progress in its style of art and writing as over against the more primitive monuments of Ur-Nina, was erected by Eannatum to commemorate his victory over

the army of *Gish-khu,* and his subsequent treaty concluded with Enakalli, *patesi* of the conquered city, whom he made swear never again to invade the sacred territory of Nin-Sungir nor to trespass the boundary established anew between the two principalities.

During the early months of 1898 and 1900 De Sarzec conducted his last two campaigns at Tello. Little as yet has been published with regard to their results. Heuzey announced that among the precious monuments obtained through the excavations of the tenth expedition (1898) there are the first inscribed bricks of Ennatuma I., brother and successor of Eannatuma, and two carved oblong plates, In *Comptes Rcndus,* 1898, pp. 344-349.

or slabs, of Naram-Sin, in slate and diorite, apparently intended as bases for small statues or some other kind of votive objects. Both slabs are provided with square holes in their centres and engraved with inscriptions of considerable interest. We learn from the one legend that the conquests of the last-mentioned powerful king, whose empire extended from the mountains of Elam to the boundary of Kgvpt, included the country of Armanu. The other makes us acquainted with a son and with a granddaughter of Naram-Sin, who served as a priestess of Sin, so that practically we now know four generations of the ancient kings of Agade.

According to a personal communication from De Sarzec, his eleventh campaign, which lasted only twelve weeks, yielded no less than 4000 baked cuneiform tablets and fragments of the same general character as those described above, two exquisite new heads of statues in dolerite, and several other monuments of the period of Ur-Nina and his successors, the first description of which we must leave to the pen of Heuzev, the eloquent and learned interpreter of his friend's epoch-making discoveries in Southern Babylonia. The tablets have been studied very recently by Thureau-Dangin. According to his information they contain several new governors *(patesis) of Shir-pur-la* from that obscure period which lies between the

reigns of Naram-Sin (about 3750 B. c.) and Ur-Gur (at present read Ur-Engur by the French scholar), the probable founder of the later dynasty of Ur (about 2700 B. C.) Thev also give us an insight into the administrative machinery of the powerful kingdom of Ur, and are of especial importance for the long government of Dungi, son and successor of Ur-Gur, who occupied the throne of his father for about half a century. They instruct us concerning many valuable chronological, historical, and geographical details, among other things furnishing almost definitive new proof for the theory that Dungi, "king of Ur, king of the four quarters of the world," and Dungi, "king of Ur, king of Shumer and Akkad," are one and the same person.

Which can scarcely be separated from *Ar-tnan* mentioned v *R.* 12, No. 6, a,". Comp. Delitzsch, *It'0 lag das Paradies?* Leipzig, 1881, p. 205. Comp. *Cimptes Rendus,* 1902, session of Jan. 10, pp. 77-94.. *L. c.* p. 82, note 2.

Towards the middle of February, 1900, the French explorer descended the Tigris for the last time, in order to reach Kud(t) el-'Amara and the scene of his activity on the eastern bank of the Shatt el-Ha'i. At the same time the present writer ascended the river, being on his way to Baghdad and to the swamps of the 'Afej. A heavy thunderstorm was raging over the barren plains of 'Iraq, and the muddy waters of the Tigris began suddenly to rise, greatly interfering with my progress, when the two steamers came in sight of each other. I stood on the bridge of the English " Khalifa," intently looking at the approaching Turkish vessel, which flew the French colors from the top of its mast. A tall figure could be faintly distinguished on the passing boat, leaning against its iron railing and eagerly scanning the horizon with a field-glass. A flash of light separated the thick black clouds which had changed day into twilight, and illuminated the two steamers for a moment. I recognized the features of De Sarzec, the newly (1899) appointed minister plenipotentiary of France, who in an instant had drawn a handkerchief, which he waved lustily on his fast disappearing boat as a greeting of welcome to the representative of the Philadelphia expedition. A month later a cordial and urgent invitation was received from the French camp near Tello. I still regret that at that moment my own pressing duties at the ruins of Nuftar did not allow of an even short visit to Southern Babylonia, and that consequently I missed my last chance of seeing De Sarzec in the midst of his trenches and directing his famous excavations in person.

Towards the end of May we both were back in Baghdad, and for a whole week we met regularly at the hospitable house of the American vice-consul, communicating to each other the results of our latest expeditions, discussing our new plans and dwelling with especial pleasure on the bright prospect of methodical explorations in the numerous ruins of Shumer and Akkad. Seated on the flat roof of our temporary abode, we used to enjoy the refreshing evening hours of a Babylonian spring, — over us that brilliant sky in the knowledge of which the early inhabitants of the country excelled all other nations, below us the murmuring waters of the Tigris which gradually expose and wash away the tombs of by-gone generations, carrying their dust into the realm of the god Ka, "the creator of the Universe," and far away into the ocean to the island of the blessed. De Sarzec himself looked exceedingly tired and frequently complained of chills and fever. When we finally separated, he took the direct route to the coast of the Mediterranean by way or Der and Aleppo, while the present writer rode along the western bank of the Tigris and examined the ruins of Assyria and Cappadocia before he reached Europe at Constantinople. De Sarzec's hope of a speedy return to his Arabs and ruins was not to be realized. On May 30, 1901, at the age of sixty-four years, the great French explorer succumbed suddenly, at Poitiers, to a disease of the liver, which he had contracted during his long sojourn in the East. Only a few weeks later his faithful companion, who so often had dwelt with him in the tents of the desert, as-

sisting and encouraging him in the great task of his life, followed her husband on his last journev to "the land without return."

The French government, fully recognizing the extraordinary importance of De Sarzec's work and the necessity of its continuation, has taken steps at an early date to resume the exploration of Tello, so gloriously initiated and for nearly a quarter of a century carried on by its own representative. Great results doubtless will again be forthcoming. But significant and surprising as the success of future expeditions to this ancient seat of civilization may be, the name of De Sarzec, to whom science owes the resurrection of ancient Chaldean art and the restoration of a long forgotten leaf in the history of mankind, will always stand out as an illustrious example of rare energy, great intelligence, and indefatigable patience devoted to the cause of archaeology in the service and for the honor of his country.

ENGLISH EXCAVATIONS UNDER RASSAM AT BABYLON,

EL-BIRS, AND ABU HABBA

The exceptional terms and the wide scope of the firman granted to Sir Henry Layard in 1878, induced Hormuzd Rassam, then in charge of the British excavations in Assyria, to extend his operations at once to as many ruins as possible. In the interest of a strictly scientific exploration of the ancient remains of Asshur and Babel, this decision must be regretted, unless we regard the rapid working of new mines of antiquities and the mere accumulation of inscribed tablets the principal — not to say the only — object of archaeological missions to the countries of the Euphrates and Tigris. But whatever may be said against Rassam's strange methods, radically different from those of other recent Babylonian explorers, and largely responsible for the irreparable loss of many important data necessary for a satisfactory reconstruction of the topography and history of the different sites excavated by him, he deserves credit for his extraordinary mobility and devotion to what he regarded his duty, and by

which he was enabled to gather an immense number of cuneiform texts and to enrich the collections of the British Museum with many priceless treasures. Comp. Rassam, "Asshur and the Land of Nimrod," New York, 1897, p. 363.

Towards the middle of February, 1879, he commenced his excavations of Babylonian mounds, which for more than three years ' were carried on by native overseers under his general supervision. The first ruins to which he directed his attention were Babylon and Borsippa (El-Birs). Arab diggers, forming a secret and strong combination, were then engaged in extracting bricks from the walls and buttresses of Babil. As soon as they heard of the foreigner's intentions, they began to watch his movements with jealousy and suspicion. In order to protect himself against their unscrupulous machinations, and at the same time to secure their confidence and assistance for his own operations, Rassam proposed to them to enter his service on the promise that all the plain bricks which might be unearthed should become their property. Naturally they agreed readily to an arrangement which gave them regular wages besides their ordinary share in the excavated building material. During the two or three months which, in the course of his Babylonian excavations, he could spend in the trenches near Hilla, he examined and followed the excavations of the Arab brick-diggers at Babil with undivided attention. No sooner had they struck four exquisitely built wells of red granite in the southern centre of the mound, than he hurried to the scene and uncovered them entirely. They still were 140 feet high, and communicated with an aqueduct or canal supplied with water from the Euphrates. From the peculiarity of their material, which must have been brought from a great distance in Northern Mesopotamia; from the fine execution of the enormous circular stones," which had been bored and made to fit each other so exactly that each well appeared as if hewn in one solid block; from the numerous remains of huge walls and battlements built of kilnburned bricks, so eagerly sought by the Arabs; from the commanding position of the whole lofty mound, — details which agreed most remarkably with characteristic features of the hanging gardens, as described by Diodorus and Pliny, — Rassam came to the conclusion that this great wonder of the ancient world could only be represented by Babil, a view first held by Rich, and for various additional reasons also shared by the present writer.

Corap.' the summary of Rassam's activity on Assyrian and Babylonian ruins given on p. 203, *seq.*, footnote. He ceased his excavations July, 1882. Each stone was about three feet high.

On the assumption that the large basalt lion of the Qasr, so often mentioned by earlier explorers, must have flanked the gate of a palace in the days of the Babylonian monarchs, he searched in vain for "another similar monolith, which stood on the opposite side of the entrance." After cutting a few trial trenches into the centre of the mound, not far from the ruin where Mignan, Layard, and Oppert had left their traces, Rassam abandoned this unpromising site for other less disturbed localities in its neighborhood.

As long as he employed workmen on the ruins of the capital of Amraphel and Nebuchadrezzar, he concentrated his efforts at the two southern groups of the vast complex, known under the names of'Omran ibn 'Ali and Jumjuma. Though succeeding as little as those who excavated there before him in finding large sculptured monuments, Rassam was amply repaid for his labors at the last-named place, by discovering a great many of the so-called contract tablets, left by private individuals, or forming part of the archives of business firms, among which the famous house of Egibi played a most prominent role. Unfortunately not a few of these documents crumbled to pieces as soon as they were removed, the damp soil in which they had been lying being impregnated with nitre. The first great collection of this class of tablets had come from the same mound in the winter of 1875—76, when Arab brick-diggers unearthed a number of clay jars filled with

more than 3000 documents, which, shortly before his death, Comp. Map No. 2.

George Smith had acquired for the British Museum. They all belonged to the final period of Babylonian history, to the years when for the last time Nabopolassar and his successors restored the glory of the great city on the Euphrates. Their contents revealed to us an entirely new phase of Babylonian civilization. We became acquainted with the everv-dav life of the different classes of the population, and we became witnesses of their mutual relations and manifold transactions. We obtained an insight into the details of their households, their kinds of property and its administration, their incomes and their taxes, their modes of trading and their various occupations, their methods in irrigating and cultivating fields and in raising stocks, their customs in marrying and adopting children, the position of their slaves, and many other interesting features of the life of the people. Above all, these tablets showed us the highly developed legal institutions of a great nation, thus furnishing an important new source for the history of comparative jurisprudence. There is scarcely a case provided against by the minute regulations of the Roman law which has not its parallel or prototype in ancient Chaldea.

Valuable as all these small and unbaked tablets proved for our knowledge of the private life, the commercial intercourse, and the chronology of the time of the Chaldean and Persian dynasties, they did not constitute the entire harvest which Rassam could gather. There were other important documents of a literarv and historical character rescued from the same vicinity. We mention only the broken cylinder of Cvrus containing the official record of the conquest of Babylon (539 B. c), and in its phraseology sometimes curiously approaching the language of Isaiah. Comp. chaps. 44 (end) and 45 with my remarks on Pl. 33 of the "New Gallery of Illustrations" in Holman's "Self-pronouncing S. S. Teachers' Bible," Philadelphia, 1897. According to Rasam's own statement

(7. c, p. 267), the cylinder of Cyrus was not found in the ruins of the Qasr, as asserted, *e. g.* by Hagen, *Bcitrage zur ji-iSjriologit*, vol. ii, p. 204, and Delitzsch, *Babylon,* zd ed., Leipzig, 1901, p. 13, but in the mound of Jumjuma.

Rassam's excavations, conducted at the foot of El-Birs and in the adjoining mound of Ibrahim el-Khalil, which doubtless conceals some of the most conspicuous buildings of ancient Borsippa, were likewise productive of good results. A fine collection of inscribed tablets came from the latter ruin, while about eighty chambers and galleries of a large building were laid bare on the platform to the east of the stage-tower which in previous years had been partly explored by Rawlinson. This unique complex, mistaken by Rassam for "another palace of Nebuchadrezzar," turned out to be nothing less than the famous temple of Ezida, sacred to Nebo, the tutelar deity of Borsippa. All the rich property of the god and his priests, with the many valuable gifts deposited by powerful kings and pious pilgrims, had been carried away long before. Heaps of rubbish, broken capitals and fallen pillars, interspersed with pieces of enamelled tiles once embellishing its ceilings and walls, were all that was left of the former splendor. A small bas-relief, two boundary stones, an inscribed barrel cylinder, and the fragment of a heavy bronze threshold of Nebuchadrezzar, on the edge of which the first' six lines of a cuneiform legend had been wrongly arranged by an uneducated engraver, were the few antiquities of true Babylonian origin which, after infinite labor and pain, could be rescued from this scene of utter devastation. But the well-preserved terra-cotta cylinder proved of exceptional value in giving us the brief history of the final restoration of Nebo's renowned sanctuary, in 270 B. c, bv Antiochus Soter, " the first-born son of Seleucus, the Macedonian king. " So far as our present knowledge goes, it is the last royal document composed in the Old-Babvlonian writing and language.

There are remains of three cuneiform characters at the end of the broken edge, which is four inches thick, so that the inscription must have had at least nine lines. Properly speaking, the preserved portion ot the inscription consists of two columns, three lines each. But by disregarding the separating line between the two columns on the tablet from which he copied, the scribe changed the six short lines into one column with three long lines. A picture of the threshold, which, in its present state, measures a little over five feet by one foot eight inches, was published by Rassam in his first report, "Transactions of the Society of Biblical Archeology," vol. viii, p. 188.

There are many important finds connected with the name of Rassam as an Assyrian and Babylonian explorer. The discovery of Ashurbanapal's north palace, with its library and art treasures at (ovunjuk, and the unearthing of Shalmaneser's bronze gates at Balawat, will alone suffice to keep his memory fresh forever in the history of Assyrian excavations. But among all the remarkable results which through his skill and energy he wrested from the soil of Babylonia there is none greater and more far-reaching in its bearings upon the whole science of Assyriology than his identification and partial excavation of the site of Sippara. Every trace of this famous ancient citv, in connection with Agade or Akkad (Gen. 10: 10), so often mentioned in the cuneiform literature, and occasionally referred to even by classical writers, seemed to have vanished completely. Numerous attempts had been made to determine its ruins. Rassam himself had thought for a while of Tell Ibrahim, which Rawlinson identified with Cuthah (2 Kings 17: 24); others had hit upon Tell Shaishabar, about eighteen miles to the south of Baghdad; others again were fully convinced that it was represented by Tell Sifaira, between the Nahr 'Isa and the Euphrates; while modern geographers inclined generally to place it at the present Musayyib. This only seemed certain, that the citv must have been situated in Northern Babylonia, not far from the banks of the Euphrates. George Smith was the first to propose the ruins of Abu

Habba as its probable site. They extend to the south of the Nahr el-Malik (the Naarmalcha of Plinv), to-dav more commonly called the Nahr Yusufiye, about halfway between " the great river " and the caravan road which leads from Baghdad to Kerbelaand Hilla. Nobody, however, had apparently taken notice of his stray remark in the " Records of the Past," and Rassam, unfamiliar as he was with Assyriological publications, had surely never heard about it. He went to search for the site of the city in his own way.

It was in December, 1880. After half a year's absence from the plains of 'Iraq el-'Arabi he had returned from Kurdistan and Mosul to superintend his excavations at Babylon and Borsippa in person, and to examine the districts to the north and south of them with a view of locating other promising ruins for future operations. As soon as he had satisfied himself that in the immediate environments of Hilla and El-Birs there was no ruin to tempt him, he proceeded northward by way of Tell Ibrahim and Mahmudiye, " bent upon visiting every mound in the neighborhood, and seeing if he could not hit upon the exact site of Sippara to the north of Babylon." Dissatisfied with the results of various trials to locate it, he finally had arrived and settled temporarily z.t Mahmudiye. The number of his workmen from Jumjuma, soon increased from the ranks of passing pilgrims and wayfaring loiterers, were ordered to dig at some of the principal ruins around the village. Meanwhile he himself wandered from mound to mound, searching and hoping, only to be later disappointed.

On previous occasions he had repeatedly heard of three other conspicuous *tells* to the north and northwest of Mahmudiye, called by the Arabs F.d-Der, Abu Habba, and Harqawi. His way from Baghdad to Hilla had often led him close by them. But as the peculiar topographical and atmospheric conditions of Babylonia render it extremely difficult to judge the height of a mound correctly from a distance, or to distinguish it from the huge embankments of the numerous canals which intersect the alluvial plain

everywhere, Rassam had never paid much attention to the stories of the natives. This time, however, his interest was suddenly aroused. We quote from his own account: " One day, on returning to my host's house at Mahmudiye, his brother, Mohammed, showed me a fragment of kiln-burnt brick with a few arrow-headed characters on it, which he said he had picked up at the ruins of Der when he was returning from a wedding to which he had been invited. I no sooner saw the relic than I began to long for a visit to the spot, and 1 lost no time the next day in riding to it. It happened then that the Euphrates had overflowed its banks, and the Mahmudiye Canal, which is generally dry nine months in the year, was running and inundating the land between Der and the village of Mahmudiye; the consequence was we had to go a round-about way to reach that place. We had first to pass the Sanctuary of Seyyid 'Abdallah, the reputed saint of that country, situated about six miles to the northwest of Mahmudiye; and we then veered to the right and proceeded to Der in an easterly direction. In about half an hour's ride further, we came to an inclosure of what seemed to me an artificial mound, and on ascending it I asked my guide if that was the ruin in which he had picked up the inscribed brick. He replied in the negative, but said that we were then at Abu Hahha, and Der was about an hour further on. I could scarcely believe my eyes on looking down and finding everything under my horse's feet indicating a ruin of an ancient city; and if I had had any workmen at hand I' would have then and there placed two or three gangs to try the spot. I was then standing near a small pyramid situated at the westerly limit of the mound, which I was told contained a golden model of the ark in which Noah and his family were saved from the Deluge, and that the second father of mankind had it buried there as a memorial of the event," — apparently a faint and distorted reminiscence of the old Babylonian tradition preserved by Berossos, and according to which before the great flood Xisouthros (/. e., Noah), by order of his god, buried the tablets inscribed with " the beginning, middle, and end of all things," at Sippara.

From which they are distant not more than four miles in a direct line. Comp. Rassam, "Asshur and the Land of Nimrod," New York, 1897, p. 403. 1st ed., vol. v (London, 1875), p. 107, No. 56. Generally pronounced Hargawi in the modern dialect of the country, and situated to the west of Abu Habba, while Ed-Der is found to the northeast of the latter. Here, as well as in passages where I quote literally from R;istam, I have quietly changed his wretched spellings of Arabic and Turkish names in accordance with a more scientific method.

Though rising scarcely more than thirty to forty feet above the desert, the ruins of Abu Habba are of considerable extent. Except on the western side, where the conical remains of the stage-tower are situated near a dry branch of the Euphrates, they are surrounded by large walls, which on the northwest and northeast are almost perfect. The rectangular parallelogram thus formed encloses an area of more than 1,210,000 square yards, or about 250 acres, its longest side measuring more than 1400 yards. Only the third part of this whole space is occupied by an irregular conglomeration of mounds which conceal what is left of the ancient city. As soon as Rassam had taken a hasty survey of the prominent site, he lost no time in making the necessary preparations for immediate excavations. No Arab encampment being anywhere near the ruins, he established his headquarters at Seyyid 'Abdallah, where the guardian of the sanctuary and his near relatives lived in peaceful seclusion.

The 3500 square yards given by Rassam (" Asshur and the Land of Nimrod," New York, 1897, p. 399) tor the whole area are an evident mistake, the temple mound alone being considerably larger. The measurements quoted above are based upon my own calculations in connection with a personal visit to the ruins. They were recently confirmed by Scheil, who kindly sent me the following statement before the final proof was passed: 'The enclosure of Sippar is 1300 meters 1422 yards long, and 800 m. 875 yards wide. The temple enclosure is about 400 m. 437 yards square. " In other words the temple area represents about 190,969 square yards, or nearly 39 acres.

Operations were commenced near the pyramid in January, 1881. On the very first day the workmen dug up pieces of a barrel cylinder and fragments of inscribed bricks and bitumen. A little later they came upon the wall of a chamber svhich presented all the characteristic features of true Babylonian architecture. Soon afterwards they discovered similar rooms in different parts of the same mound. There could be no longer any doubt; Rassam had struck a large ancient building of great interest and importance. Encouraged by this rapid success of the first few days, he prosecuted his researches with redoubled energy. As he proceeded with his work, he entered a chamber which attracted his curiosity at once. Contrary to his previous experience, it was paved with asphalt instead of marble or brick. He ordered his men to break through the pavement and to examine the ground below. They had scarcely begun to remove the earth at the southeast corner, when three feet below the surface they discovered an inscribed terra-cotta trough or box closed with a lid. Inside lava marble tablet, eleven inches and a half long by seven inches wide, broken into eight pieces, but otherwise complete. It was covered with six columns of the finest writing, and adorned with a beautiful bas-relief on the top of the obverse. The subject represented is the following: A god seated in his shrine is approached by two priests and a worshipper, who is probably the king himself. The three persons stand before the disk of the sun, placed upon an altar and held with ropes by the two divine attendants of Shamash, Malik and Bunene, who, according to Babylonian mythology, as guides direct the course of the fiery orb "covering heaven and earth with lustre. " The cuneiform legend in front of the sanctuary is identical with the label inscribed on each side of the box in which the tablet was placed, and serves as an explanation of the pictorial representation: "Image of Shamash the Sungod, the great lord, dwelling in Kbabbara, situated in Sippar." The interpretation of the other two small legends written above and below the roof of the shrine has offered considerable difficulty. They are evidently also labels which, in the briefest possible form, indicate important and characteristic details of the golden image mentioned in the long inscription below, and of which the stone relief is a faithful reproduction. Similar to those found bv Smith on clay tablets in the royal librarv of Nineveh,-they are to be regarded as instructions and explanations for the artist' who in davs to come may be called upon to make another image. Two terra-cotta moulds, showing all the details of our bas-relief, were found in the box with the stone tablet. The Comp. iv R. 20, No. 2, 1. 4, and the beautiful hvmn to the Sungod, first published bv Pinches, in the " Transactions of the Society of Biblical Archeology," vol. viii, pp. 167, *seq.* Comp. p. 198, above, and George Smith, "Assyrian Discoveries," 3d

Marble Tablet of King Nabu-apal-iddina, about 850 B. c. *From the temple of the Sun-god at Sippar a* ed., New York, 1876, p. *n,uqa.* Comp., also, Bezold, "Catalogue of the Cuneiform Tablets in the Kouyunjik Collection of the British Museum," vol. v (London, 1899), pp. xix and xxvii, 5.

The upper inscription reads: *Sin, Shamash, hhtar ina pu-ut apsi ina bi-rit Siri ti-mi innadi (-ii), i. e., Sin, Shamash, and hhtar* (whose symbols are engraved below this inscription) *have been placed (on* the golden image, or *are to be placed* on a new image that may be made; the verbal form can be regarded as preterite or present tense) *opposite the ocean* (indicated at the lower end of the bas-relief by wavy lines; comp., also, v *R.* 63, col. ii, 5) *between the snake* (in the year 1887, when at the request of Dr. Hayes Ward I gave him my interpretation of this bas-relief at his house in Newark, I called his attention to the important fact generally overlooked, that the back and top of the shrine represents an immense snake, whose head can be clearly recognized over the column in front of the god) *and the rope* (= *timmi,* by which the altar and disk of the sun are suspended. But it is perhaps better to interpret *ti-mi* as a dialectical or inexact writing for *di-mi,* intended for *dimmi,* "column," which we see immediately before the god supporting the roof of his house).

The lower inscription, which stands as a label near the head-dress of the god, reads: *agu Shamash, mushshi agu Shamash,* which I interpret, *tiara of Shamash, make the tiara of Shamash bright (mashu = namaru,* ii *R.* 47, 58, and 59 e, f, here imperat. ii. This special order must be interpreted in the light of the difficult passage, v *R.* 63, col. i, 43 to col. ii, 40, especially col. ii, 36-39, "I made the golden tiara of Shamash anew and made it bright as the day "). The Sun-god was the bringer of light; rays *of* light therefore were supposed to go forth from his head and tiara, as they did from the head of Apollo on the coins of Rhodes. Even if *mushshi* be interpreted as a noun, it cannot refer to the wand and rod in the right hand of Shamash, as has been supposed, but it must refer to the tiara, of which then it possibly denotes a part, — a view supported by the fact that the two lines form but one label, and by the circumstance that in v *R.* 63, col. i, 43, *seqq.,* Nabonidos gives a detailed description as to how a correct tiara of the Sun-god has to look.

One of them, together with a cylinder of Nabonidos, is in the Ottoman Museum at Constantinople. golden image, just referred to, was the work of King Nabuapal-iddina. In connection with the pillaging of the temple by Sutean hordes in a previous war, the old image of the god had been destroyed. All efforts to find a copy of the famous representation had proved in vain. Finally, in 852 B. c, a terra-cotta relief was accidentally discovered on the western bank of the Euphrates, which enabled Nabu-apal-iddina to revive the ancient cult in its former glory. In order to secure its continuity, in case another national calamity should befall his country, the king had an exact copy of the original with

explanatory labels carved at the top of his memorial tablet, which was buried in the ground.

In unearthing this stone, Rassam had discovered the famous temple of Shamash and, at the same time, identified one of the earliest Babylonian cities. He stood in the very sanctuary in which Babylonian monarchs once rendered homage to the golden image of their god. In a room adjoining the one just described, the fortunate explorer found two large barrel cylinders of Nabonidos in a fine state of preservation, and " a curiously hewn stone symbol... ending on the top in the shape of a cross," and " inscribed with archaic characters." The text of these cylinders proved an historical source of the utmost importance. The royal archaeologist, to whom we are indebted for so many precious chronological data, delighted more in excavating ancient temples and reviving half-forgotten cults than in administering the affairs of his crumbling empire. Sippara, situated scarcely thirty miles to the north of Babylon, and renowned equally for its venerable cult and its magnificent library, naturally received his special attention. After a poetical description of the principal circumstances and events which led to the destruction and his subsequent restoration of the temple of Sin at Haran, Nabonidos proceeds to inform us how the temple of Shamash, " the judge of heaven and earth," had decayed in Sippar within less than fifty years after its reparation by Nebuchadrezzar. To the mind of the king there was only one reason which could account sufficiently for this alarming fact, — the displeasure of the god himself. His predecessor apparently had not followed the exact outline and dimensions of the oldest sanctuary, which, according to Babylonian conception, must be strictly kept to insure the favor of the god and the preservation of his dwelling place on earth. Nabonidos, therefore, ordered his soldiers to tear down the walls and to search for the original foundation stone. Kighteen cubits deep the workmen descended into the ground. After infinite labor and trouble the last Chaldean ruler

of Babylon succeeded in bringing to light the foundation stone of Naram-Sin, the son of Sargon of Agade, "which for 3200 years no previous king had seen," conveying to us by this statement the startling news that this great ancient monarch lived about 3750 B. C, a date fully corroborated by my own excavations at Nuffar.

Col. iii, 19, *scq.: usurti salmishu sirpu sha khasbi,* "the relief of his image in terra-cotta." For *sirpu sha khasbi,* "something in terra-cotta," a terra-cotta relief, figurine, etc., comp. the verb *sarapu,* "to burn, bake (bricks)," quoted by Meissner, *Suppl. zu den Assr. Wort-crbiihern,* p. 82.

No sooner had the rumor of Rassam's extraordinary discovery spread in the neighboring districts than new difficulties were thrown in his way by jealous property owners and intriguing individuals. But with his old pertinacity he held his own and stuck to the newly occupied field, the real value of which he had been the first to disclose. For eighteen months British excavations were carried on at Abu Habba without interruption. Rassam could remain at the ruins only the third part of all this time, — the expiration of the annual grant by the British Museum and his desire to have the old firman renewed as soon as possible requiring his journey to Europe. But, as usual, during his absences native overseers were entrusted with the continuation of the explorations under the general control of the British Resident at Baghdad.

'Comp. Hilprecht, *Assyriaca,* part I, Boston and Halle, 1894, pp. 54, *stq.*

In the spring of 1882, after many fruitless efforts to obtain again those former privileges, which the awakened Turkish interest in archaeological treasures could concede no longer, he returned to Babylonia for the last time. As long as his permit lasted (till Aug. 16, 1882) he worked with all his energy, deepening and extending his trenches at Babil and Abu Habba, and despatching whatever was found to England. It was particularly the temple complex at the latter place upon which he concentrated his personal attention. According to his calculation, the chambers and halls buried here must have amounted to nearly three hundred, one hundred and thirty of which he excavated. They were grouped around open courts, and apparently divided into two distinct buildings enclosed by breastworks. The one was the temple proper, and the other contained the rooms for the priests and attendants. That King Nabonidos had not cleared away all the rubbish of the older structure, became very evident from the fact that Rassam found the height of the original chambers and halls to be twenty-five feet, while the asphalt pavement, in the room described above, and the floors of the adjoining chambers rested upon debris which filled half their depth.

The number of inscribed objects and other antiquities rescued from the ruins of Abu Habba within the comparatively short period of a year and a half is enormous. About 60,000 inscribed clay tablets are said to have been taken from different rooms of the temple. Unfortunately they were not baked as those from Qoyunjuk; and though Rassam did his best to save their contents by baking them immediately after their discovery, thousands of them, sticking together or heaped upon one another, crumbled to pieces before they could be removed. For the greater part, these documents are of a business character, referring to the administration of the temple and its property, to the daily sacrifices of Shamash and other gods, to the weaving of their garments, the manufacture of their jewelry and vessels, the building and repairing of their houses, and to the execution of various orders given in connection with the worship of their images and the maintenance of their priesthood. At the same time they make us acquainted with the duties and daily occupations of the different classes of temple officers and their large body of servants, with the ordinary tithes paid by the faithful, and with many other revenues accruing to the sanctuary from all kinds of gifts, from the lease of real estate, slaves, and animals, and from the sale of products from fields and stables. As tithes were frequently paid in kind,

it became necessary to establish regular depots along the principal canals, where scribes stored and registered everything that came in. Among the goods thus received we notice vegetables, meat, and other perishable objects which the temple alone could not consume, and which, therefore, had to be sold or exchanged before they decayed or decreased in value. No wonder that apart from its distinct religious sphere the great temple of Shamash at Sippara in many respects resembled one of the great business firms of Babel or Nippur.

Apparently the bulk of the temple library proper lies still buried in the ruins of Abu Habba. Yet among the tablets excavated by Rassam there are many of a strictly literary character, such as signlists and grammatical exercises, astronomical and mathematical texts, letters, hymns, mythological fragments, and a new bilingual version of the Story of the Creation, which originally formed part of an incantation. The large monuments and artistic votive offerings deposited by famous monarchs and other prominent worshippers in the temple of Shamash had mostly perished or been carried away. But numerous fragments of vases and statues engraved with the names of Manishtusu and Urumush (Alusharshid), two ancient kings of Kish, the fine mace-head of Sargon I., the curious monument of Tukulti-Mer, king of Khana, the lion-head of Sennacherib, several well-preserved " boundary stones," including the so-called charter of Nebuchadrezzar I. (about 1130 B. C) and more than thirty terra-cotta cylinders bearing Sumerian or Semitic records of the building operations of Hammurabi, Nebuchadrezzar II., Nabonidos, and other Babylonian and Assyrian rulers testify sufficiently to the high antiquity of the sanctuary and to the great renown in which it was held by natives and foreigners alike from the range of the Taurus to the shores of the Persian Gulf. The proposed and much repeated identification of Sippara with the Biblical Sepharvaim is, however, a philological and geographical impossibility.

In accordance with his usual custom,

followed in Assyria and elsewhere, Rassam cut trial trenches into other conspicuous mounds whenever he was in Babylonia. But from the nature of the ruins and the superficial character of his work, it was to be expected that they would be barren of results unless a fortunate accident should come to his assistance. The principal sites selected by him for such tentative operations were the group of mounds called Dilhim, about ten miles to the south of Hilla, where he discovered a few inscribed clay tablets; the low but extensive ruins of El-Qreni, about four miles to the north of Babil, where nothing but bricks indicated their Babylonian origin; the numerous *tells* in the neighborhood of Mahmudiye mentioned above, especially Der, which yielded only the common bricks of Nebuchadrezzar; and above all, the enormous ruins of Tell Ibrahim, about fifteen miles to the northeast of Hilla, with the nest of mounds situated to the southeast of it. Under extraordinary deprivations caused by the absence of water and frequent sandstorms, several of his best gangs of workmen remained a month in the desert around Tell Ibrahim. But though they showed a rare energy and labored with all their might, opening no less than twenty different tunnels and trenches and penetrating deep into the mass of rubbish, nothing but stray bricks of Nebuchadrezzar, a few cuneiform tablets and terra-cotta bowls covered with Hebrew inscriptions had been brought to light when they finally quitted this inhospitable region.

According to 2 Kings 18:34; 9 ' '3 (comp. Is. 36: 19; 37:1 3) Sepharvaim must have been situated not in Babylonia, but in Syria. Comp. Halevy in *Journal Asiatique*, 1889, pp. 18, seqq.; *Zeitschrift fur Aisyriologie*, vol. ii, pp. 401, *seq*. Called by Rassam Daillum or Tell-Daillam; comp. his " Asshur and the Land of Nimrod," New York, 1897, pp. 26; and 347. Rassam, *l. c*, pp. 347, *scq*., where he spells the name *Algarainec* according to its modern pronunciation.

We cannot close this sketch of Rassam's archaeological work in Babylonia without referring briefly to his hasty visit to the southern districts of 'Iraq, which lasted from February 24 to March 13, 1879. The news of De Sarzec's secret proceedings at Tello had spread rapidly among the Arabs, and naturally reached the ear of Rassam immediately after his arrival at Baghdad, in the beginning of February, 1879. A faithful and jealous guardian of British interests, as he proved to be during his long career in the East, he decided at once to examine those remarkable ruins in person with a view of occupying them, if possible, for his own government somewhat in the same manner as he previously had obtained the palace of Ashurbanapal in the northern part of Qoyunjuk. His task seemed to be facilitated by the circumstance that De Sarzec had made his first tentative excavations at Tello " without any firman from the Porte." No sooner had he therefore established his workmen, under native overseers, upon the ruins of Babylon and Borsippa, than he hurried back to Baghdad, descended the Tigris on a Turkish steamer as far as Kud(t) el-'Amara, and sailed through the Shatt el-Hai' until he reached the object of his journey. But upon landing he found, to his consternation, that Tello was not within the sphere of British influence. Shortly before Sir Henry Layard had obtained his far-reaching permit for simultaneous excavations in the vilayets of Baghdad, Aleppo, and Wan, the Ottoman government had reduced the large province of Baghdad in size by creating a new and independent pashalic with Basra as capital, and including all the Turkish territory to the east and south of the Shatt el-Hai." For the time being Rassam had, therefore, no legal right to make any excavations at Tello. But having gone to the expense of a voyage thither, he did not intend to turn away from the ruins without having convinced himself whether " it would be worth while to ask the British ambassador at Constantinople to use his influence with the Porte, so that his license might be extended to that province." Accordingly he engaged a guide and some workmen, and walked for a few days every morning the three miles

from the embankment of the canal to the site of Tello. The large statue in dolerite discovered and reburied by the French explorer had been exposed again by the Arabs after De Sarzec's departure in the previous year. It naturally attracted Rassam's attention first. Having cleared it entirely, and taken a squeeze of its inscription for the British Museum, he opened trenches in different parts of the ruins. Antiquities were often found almost directly below the surface. The very first day he came upon the remains of a temple ? and discovered two inscribed door sockets of Gudea at its entrance. In another place he unearthed a large number of unbaked clay tablets, while still other trenches yielded several inscribed maceheads in red granite, and many of those mushroom-shaped clay objects *(phalli)* with the names of Ur-Bau and Gudea upon them, in which the ruins of Tello abound. If Rassam had continued his researches one day longer in the highest mound and driven his trenches only two or three feet deeper, he could not have missed those fine statues in dolerite which now adorn the halls of the Louvre. But *kismet* (fate) — to quote an Oriental phrase — was this time decidedly against him. The threatening attitude of the Arabs in the neighborhood, the inclemency of the weather, and his own conscience, which told him that he was "carrying on his work under false pretences," drove him away from the ruins after three days' successful trial. He expected to return later, as soon as he had managed to obtain the necessary permit from the Porte. But De Sarzec was on the alert and quicker of action than Victor Place. While Rassam was meditating and planning in Babylonia, the French representative took decisive steps at Paris and Constantinople which secured for his nation the much-coveted ruins of Tello, and through them those priceless treasures with which we have occupied ourselves in the previous chapter.

Rassam, *l. c,* pp. 398, *icqq.* Rassam, *l. c,* pp. 396, *seq., 409, seqq.* Rassam, *l. c,* pp. 272, *seqq.* According to information obtained through the kindness of Dr. H. Gies, first dragoman of the

German embassy in Constantinople, the military administration of the *kolemen* was brought to an end in 'Iraq in 1243 *(Rumi* = 1827 A. D.). Henceforth Basra was ruled by the Ottoman government directly through *mutesarrifi,* subject to the orders of the wali of Baghdad, or through independent walis. The first wali of Basra, appointed in 1875, was Nasir Pasha, the famous shaikh of the Muntefik(j). Comp. p. 218, above. In 1884 the province of Baghdad was again reduced in size by the creation of the vilayet of Mosul. For further details, see *Salria/nc ot' Basra* of the year 1309 *Hijraz*= 1307 *Rumi).* The line of demarcation is at Kud(t) el-Hai. Only generally speaking the Shatt el-Hai forms the natural boundary between the two vilayets, for certain portions to the west of it, as, *t. g.,* the ruins of Senkere, and other smaller sites as far north as Durra-ji, belong to the southern vilayet of Basra. GERMAN EXCAVATIONS AT SURGHUL AND EL-HIBBA, UNDER MORITZ AND KOLDEWEY

Long after English and French pioneers had established and considerably developed the science of Assyriology, German scholars began to remember their obligations towards a discipline the seed of which was sown in the land of Grotefend, and to occupy themselves seriously with those farreaching researches which later were to find their strongest representation at their own universities. The first Assyrian courses delivered in Germany were given privately at Jena, where Eberhard Schrader, appropriately called the father of German Assyriology, defended its principles and applied its results to the elucidation of the Old Testament Scriptures. His careful and critical examination of all that had been accomplished in the past, and his successful repelling of Alfred von Gutschmid's violent attack upon the very foundations of Assyrian deciphering, were the beginning of a great movement which soon led to the establishment of the Leipzig school of Assyriologists under Friedrich Delitzsch, and to the subsequent consolidation of the whole science by him and his pupils. The old loose and unsatisfactory manner of dealing with philological problems, to a large extent responsible for the discredit in which Assyriological publications were held in Germany, was abandoned, and exact methods and a technical treatment of grammar and lexicography became the order of the day. Theories proclaimed and accepted as facts had to be modified or radically changed, and the interpretation of Assyrian and Sumerian cuneiform inscriptions was placed upon a new basis.

Problems partly or entirely unknown to the older school came up for discussion, and representative scholars from other nations began to participate in a thorough ventilation of the interesting subjects. The Sumerian question arose, and with it a multitude of other questions. If one riddle was solved to-day, another more difficult presented itself tomorrow. Our whole conception of the origin and development of Assyrian art and literature, of the beginnings of cuneiform writing, of the historical position and influence of the primitive inhabitants of Babylonia, of the age and character of Semitic civilization in general, and of many important details closely connected therewith seemed to be in need of a thorough revision. The Assyriological camp was soon split into factions, often fighting with bitterness and passion against one another.

According to direct information received from Professor Schrader, of Berlin, by letter, these courses were given in the summer of 1873, when Friedrich Delitzsch attended his lectures on Genesis at the university, while at the same time he was introduced privately by him into the study of Assyrian.

The extraordinary results of De Sarzec's epoch-making excavations at Tello furnished a mass of new material which was eagerly studied at once and essentially helped to extend our horizon. But important as their influence proved to be on the gradual solution of the Sumerian problem, on the clearing of our views on Babylonian art and civilization, and on the many other questions then under consideration, being felt alike in palaeography and philology, archaeology, history, and ancient geography, their greatest significance lies, perhaps, in the fact that they gave rise to the methodical exploration of the Babylonian ruins and kindled fresh enthusiasm for the organization and despatch of new expeditions. The statues in dolerite and the inscribed bas-reliefs and cylinders from Tello had clearly shown that the ruins of Southern Babylonia conceal sculptured remains of fundamental value, and, moreover, that the period to which these discoveries lead us is considerably older than that which had been reached by the previous Assyrian excavations. Indeed, the marble slabs from the royal palaces of Dur-Sharruken, Calah, and Nineveh looked very recent when compared with the much-admired monuments of Lagash. All indications pointed unmistakably to the districts of the lower Euphrates and Tigris as the cradle of the earliest Babylonian civilization.

Started in 1874 by Professor J. Halevy of Paris. On the whole subject comp. Weissbach, *Die Sumeristhe Frage,* Leipzig, 1898, and Halevy, *Le Sumerism et T histoire Babyhniennc,* Paris, 1901.

The first attempt at imitating De Sarzec's example was made in Germany. And though in the end it proved to be unproductive of great tangible results, and barren of those startling discoveries without which an expedition cannot command the general support of the people, it was important, and a sure sign of the growing popularity of cuneiform studies in a land where only ten years previous even university professors kept aloof from the Assyriological science. Through the liberality of one man, L. Simon, who in more than one way became a patron of archaeological studies in Germany, the Royal Prussian Museums of Berlin were enabled to carry on brief excavations at two Babylonian ruins during the early part of 1887. These researches were in control of Dr. Bernhard Moritz and Dr. Robert Koldewey, faithfully assisted in the practical execution of their task by Mr. Ludwig Meyer, the third member of their mission. Leaving Berlin in September, 1886, they reached the scene of their activity in the beginning of the following year. The mounds which were selected for operation are called Surghul and Kl-Hibba, distant from each other a little over six miles, and representing the most extensive ruins in the large triangle formed by the Euphrates, the Tigris, and the Shaft el-Hai. Situated in the general neighborhood of Tello, and about twenty miles to the northeast of Shatra, Surghul, the more southern of the two sites, rises at its highest point to almost fifty feet above the flat alluvial plain and covers an area of about 192 acres, while the somewhat lower mounds of Kl-Hibba enclose nearly 1400 acres. The excavations conducted at Surghul lasted from January 4 to February 26, those at El-Hibba from March 29 to May 11, 1887. But in addition to this principal work in Southern Babylonia, the expedition occupied itself with the purchase of antiquities and the examination of other mounds in 'Iraq el-'Arabi, with a view to determine some of the more promising sites for future exploration.

It soon became evident to the German party that a thorough examination of the enormous ruins was far beyond the time and means at their disposal. Under these circumstances it was decided to confine themselves to ascertaining the general contents of the most conspicuous elevations by means of long trial trenches. When remains of buildings were struck, their walls were followed to discover the ground-plans, while the interior of the chambers was searched for archaeological objects. Deep wells constructed of terracotta rings, which abound in both ruins, were, as a rule, exposed on one side in their entire length in order to be photographed before they were opened. The results obtained from the different cuttings in the two sites were on the whole identical. The explorers found a large number of houses irregularly built of unbaked bricks, and intersected by long, narrow streets, which rarely were more than three feet wide. These edifices formed a very respectable settlement at ElHibba, where the passageways between them extended fully two miles and a half. As to size and arrangement the buildings varied considerably, some containing only a few rooms, others occupying a large space, — in one instance a house covering an area of 72 feet by nearly 51 feet, and containing 14 chambers and halls. The walls of most of these constructions had crumbled so much that generally their lower parts, often only their foundations, remained, which could be traced without difficulty after an especially heavy dew or an exceptional shower. Characteristic of many of these houses are the wells mentioned above, which, according to Koldewey's erroneous view, doubtless abandoned since, were intended to provide the dead with fresh water. One of the buildings examined had no less than nine such wells, another eight, four of which were in the same room, which was only 25 feet by about 8 feet.

Wherever the mounds were cut, they seemed to contain nothing but remains of houses, wells, ashes, bones, vases, and other burial remains. Koldewey therefore arrived at the conclusion that both ruins must be regarded as " fire necropoles," dating back to a period "probably older than that of the earliest civilizations;" that the houses were not dwelling-places for the living, but tombs for the dead, and that the whole mass of artificial elevations forms the common resting-place for human bodies more or less consumed by fire.

There were two kinds of burial, "body-graves" and "ash-graves," thus styled by Koldewey in order to indicate the manner in which corpses were treated after their cremation; for the characteristic feature of all these burials was the destruction of the body by fire previous to its final interment, though in later times the complete annihilation of the body by intense heat seems to have given way to a rather superficial burning, which in part degenerated to a mere symbolic act. The process " began with the levelling of the place, remains of previous cremations, if such had occurred, being pushed aside. The body was then wrapped in reed-mats (seldom in bituminous material), laid on the ground, and covered all over with rudely formed bricks, or with a layer of soft clay. The latter was quite thin in the upper parts, but thicker near the ground, so that as little resistance as possible was offered to the heat attacking the body from above, while at the same time the covering retained the solidity necessary to prevent too early a collapse under the weight of the fuel heaped upon it." In order to concentrate the heat, a kind of low oven was sometimes erected, "but, on the whole, it seems as though in the oldest period the complete incineration under an open fire was the rule." Comp. Koldcuey, *Die altbabyloitischilt Grater in Surghu! and El Hiliba,* in *Zeitschrift fur Assriologie,* vol. ii, 1887, pp. 403—430. To my knowledge no more complete report on these first German excavations in Babylonia has yet been published.

Weapons, utensils, jewelry, sealcylinders, toys, food, and drink were frequently burned with the body, and similar objects were generally deposited a second time in the tomb itself, where the charred remains found their final restingplace. Which of the two methods of burial referred to above (" bodygraves" or "ash-graves ") was chosen, depended essentially on the intensity of the cremation. If considerable portions of the body were afterwards found to be untouched or little injured by the fire, the remains were left where they had been exposed to the heat; in other words, the funeral pyre became also the grave of the dead person (so-called " bodygrave"). If, on the other hand, the cremation was successful, and the body reduced to ashes or formless fragments, the remains were generally gathered and placed in vases or urns of different sizes and shapes, which, however, were often too small for their intended contents. In many instances the ashes were merely collected in a heap and covered with a kettle-formed clay vessel. Burials of this kind, the socalled " ash-graves," are both the more common and the more ancient at Surghul and Fl-Hibba. The urns of ordinary persons were deposited anywhere in the gradually increasing mound, while the rich families had special houses erected for them, which were laid out in regular streets. It must be kept in mind, however, that cremation was practically the main part of the burial, the gathering of the ashes being more a non-essential act of piety.

Frequent sandstorms and the heavy rains of the SouthBabylonian fall and spring must often have ruined whole sections of these vast cemeteries, and otherwise greatly interfered with the uniform raising of the whole necropolis. From time to time, therefore, it became necessary to construct large walls and buttresses at the edges of the principal elevations in support of the light mass of ashes and dust easily blown away; to level the ground enclosed; to cover it with a thick layer of clay, and to provide the houses of the dead with drains to keep the mound dry and the tombs intact. The rectangular platforms thereby obtained were reached by means of narrow staircases erected at their front sides. Thus while most of these artificial terraces owe their origin to secondary considerations, the large solid brick structure of Kl-Hibba must be viewed in a somewhat different light, contrary to the theory of Koldewey, who is inclined to regard even this elevation as the mere substructure of an especially important tomb. It represents a circular stage-tower of two stories, resting directly on the natural soil, and in its present ruinous state still twenty-four feet high. The diameter of the lower story, rising 13 feet above the plain, is 410 feet, while that of the second story is only 315 feet. The entire building is constructed with adobes, and the second story, besides, encased with baked bricks laid in bitumen. The upper surfaces of both stories are paved with the same material to protect them against rain. Water was carried off by a canal of baked bricks, which at the same time served as a buttress tor the lower story. Remains ot a house and many of those uninscribed terra-cotta nails which, in large masses, were found at the base of the stage-tower at Nippur, were observed on the upper platform. With the exception ot its circular form, which, however, cannot be regarded as a serious objection to my theory, the solid brick structure of Kl-

Hibba presents all the characteristic features of a *ziggurrat,* with which I regard it as identical, the more so because I have recently' found evidence that, like the Egyptian pyramid, the Babylonian stage-tower (or step-pyramid) without doubt was viewed in the light of a sepulchral mound erected in honor of a god, and because it seems impossible to believe that a deeply religious people, as the early inhabitants of Shumer doubtless were, should have cremated and buried their dead without appropriate religious ceremonies, and should have left this vast necropolis without a temple. It is certainly no accident that the only remains of pictorial representations in stone discovered in the course of the German excavations (part of a wing, fragments of a stool, and a pair of clasped hands) were unearthed at the foot of this structure, and near the second large elevation of Kl-Hibba — the only two places which can be taken into consideration as the probable sites for such a sanctuary.

That the "wells" mentioned by Koldewey had this more practical purpose rather than to provide fresh water for the dead, becomes very evident from the fact that they are frequently constructed of" jars with broken bottoms joined to each other, that the terra-cotta rings of which they are usually composed, like the top-pieces covering their mouths, are often perforated, and — apart from many other considerations— that in no case the numerous similar wells examined by me at Nuffar descended to the water level. Real wells, intended to hold fresh water, doubtless existed in these two ancient cemeteries, but they are always constructed of baked bricks (arranged in herring-bone fashion in prc-Sargonic times), and have a much larger diameter than any of these terra-cotta pipes described by Koldewey. Evidently they had fallen from a building once crowning its summit. I am also inclined to see a last reminiscence of the Babylonian *ziggurrat* in the *meftul,* the characteristic watchtower and defensive bulwark of the present Ma'dan tribes ot Central Babylonia. Notwithstanding the etymology *of*

the Arabic word, a *meftul* is seldom round (against Sachau, *Am Euphrat und Tigris,* Leipzig, 1900, p. 43, with picture on p. 45), but like the *ziggurrat,* generally rectangular, and from forty to eighty feet high. Almost without exception these towers are built of clay laid up en masse. Throughout my wanderings in Babylonia I met with only one fine (rectangular) specimen constructed entirely of kiln-burnt bricks. It is situated on a branch of the Shatt el-Kar, a few miles to the west from the ruins of Abu Hatab and Fara, which I recently recommended for excavations to the German Orient Society. Comp. my later remarks in connection with the results of the excavations at Nufrar, Fourth Campaign, Temple Mound, section 3.

There can be no doubt that most of these tombs belong to the true Babylonian age. The entire absence of the slippershaped coffin, which forms one of the most characteristic features of the Parthian and Sassanian periods, enables us to speak on this point more positively. On the other hand, the thin terra-cotta cups, in form very similar to a female breast, which Koldewey mentions, betray late foreign influence. They cannot be older than about 300 B. c., and are probably somewhat younger, as they occur exclusively in the upper strata of Nutfar. It is more difficult to determine the time when these cemeteries came first into use. However, the scattered fragments of statues and stone vessels of the same type and material as those discovered at Tello and Nuffar (near the platform of Sargon and Naram-Sin), the inscribed bricks and cones referred to by various explorers, the characteristic situation of the two mounds in the neighborhood of the first-named ruin, the peculiar form and small height of the *ziggurrat,* the pre-Sargonic existence of which was recently proved by the present writer, certain forms of clay vessels which are regularly found only in the lowest strata of NufFar, and various other reasons derived also from the study of the inscriptions and bas-reliefs of Tello go far to show that the pyres of Surghul and El-Hibba already blazed when the Sumerian race was still in the

possession of the country.

Koldewey, *l. c.,* p. 418. Comp. p. 232, above, note 2. It is to be regretted that Koldewey did not give a description of the forms and sizes of the various bricks, which, as I have pointed out in my "Old Babylonian Inscriptions chiefly from Nippur," part ii, p. 45, are a very important factor in determining pre-Sargonic structures. The rudely formed bricks mentioned by him (comp. p. 284 above) point to the earliest kind of bricks known from Nuffar and Tello.

AMERICAN EXCAVATIONS AT NUFFAR UNDER THE AUSPICES OF THE UNIVERSITY OF PENNSYLVANIA.

The importance of the study of Semitic languages and literature was early recognized in the United States. Hebrew, as the language of the Old Testament, stood naturally in the centre of general interest, as everywhere in Europe; and the numerous theological seminaries of the country and those colleges which maintained close vital relations with them were its first and principal nurseries. But in the course of time a gradual though very visible change took place with regard to the position of the Semitic languages in the curriculum of all the prominent American colleges. The German idea of a university gained ground in the new world, finding its enthusiastic advocates among the hundreds and thousands of students who had come into personal contact with the great scientific leaders in Europe, and who for a while had felt the powerful spell of the new life which emanated from the class rooms and seminaries of the German universities. Post-graduate departments were organized, independent chairs of Semitic languages were established, and even archaeological museums were founded and maintained by private contributions. Salaries in some cases could not be given to the pioneers in this new movement. They stood up for a cause in which they themselves fully believed, but the value of which had to be demonstrated before endowments could be expected from the liberal-minded public. They represented the coming generation, which scarcely now realizes the difficulties and obstacles that had to be overcome by a few self-sacrificing men of science, before the present era was successfully inaugurated.

The study of the cuneiform languages, especially of Assyrian, rapidly became popular at the American universities. The romantic story of the discovery and excavation of Nineveh so graphically told by Layard, and the immediate bearing of his magnificent results upon the interpretation of the Old Testament and upon the history of art and human civilization in general, appealed at once to the religious sentiment and to the general intelligence of the people. The American Oriental Society and the Society of Biblical Literature and Exegesis became the first scientific exponents of the growing interest in the lands of Ashurbanapal and Nebuchadrezzar. The spirit of Edward Robinson, who more than sixty years before had conducted his fundamental researches of the physical, historical, and topographical geography of Syria and Palestine, was awakened anew, and the question of participating in the methodical exploration of the Babylonian ruins, to which De Sarzec's extraordinary achievements at Tello had forcibly directed the public attention, began seriously to occupy the minds of American scholars. "England and France have done a noble work in Assyria and Babylonia. It is time for America to do her part. Let us send out an American expedition," — was the key-note struck at a meeting of the Oriental Society which was held at New Haven in the spring of 1884. This suggestion was taken up at once, and a committee was constituted to raise the necessary funds for a preliminary expedition of exploration, with Dr. W. H. Ward of " The Independent" as director. The plan was sooner realized than could have been anticipated. A single individual, Miss Catherine Lorillard Wolfe of New York, gave the $5000 required for this purpose, the Archaeological Institute of America took control of the undertaking, and on September 6 of the same year Dr. Ward was on his way to the East. His party consisted of Dr. J. R. S. Sterrett, now

professor of Greek in Amherst College, Mr. J. H. Haynes, then an instructor in Robert College, Constantinople, who had served as photographer on the Assos expedition, and Daniel Z. Noorian, an intelligent Armenian, as interpreter. Before the four men could enter upon their proper task, Dr. Sterrett fell seriously ill on the way, so that he was obliged to remain at Baghdad. The others left the city of Harun ar-Rashid on January 12, and devoted nearly eight weeks to the exploration of the Babylonian ruins to the south of it. After a hurried visit to Abu Habba, Babylon, and El-Birs, they struck for the interior, and on the whole followed in the wake of Frazer and Loftus. Though, like the former, at times suffering severely from lack of proper food and water and from exposure to cold and rain, they executed their commission of a general survey of the country in a satisfactory manner, as far as this was possible within the brief period which they had set for themselves. They examined most of the principal sites of 'Iraq el-'Arabi down to Kl-Hibba and Surghul, Tello, and Muqayyar, recorded numerous angular bearings from the various mounds, took photographs and impressions of antiquities whenever an opportunity-presented itself, and worked diligently to gather all such information as might prove useful in connection with future American excavations in the plains of Shumer and Akkad. Upon his return, in June, 1885, Dr. Ward submitted a concise " Report on the Wolfe Expedition to Babylonia" to the Institute which had sent him, and continued in many other ways to promote the archaeological interests of his country. But it seemed as if the public at large was not yet prepared to contribute money for excavations in an unsafe foreign country, however closely connected with the Bible. Moreover, with the despatch of this preliminary expedition, the original committee of the Oriental Society very evidently regarded the work for which it was called together as finished, and accordingly passed out of existence.

We thus owe our only knowledge of one of the earliest Babylonian inscrip-

tions to a photograph taken by Dr. Ward at Samawa on February 17, 1885, and soon afterwards published by him in the " Proceedings of the American Oriental Society," October, 1885. This legend was engraved upon a stone, in the possession of Dr. A. Blau, a German, who had formerly served as a surgeon in the Turkish army, but was then engaged in trade at Samawa. All traces of the important monument have since been lost. His " Report" appeared in the " Papers of the Arch1eological Institute of America," Boston, 1886. Comp. "The Wolfe Expedition," by the same author, in "Journal of the Society of Biblical Literature and Exegesis," June to December, 1885, pp. 56—60, and his article "On Recent Explorations in Babylon" in "Johns Hopkins University Circulars," No. 49, May, 1886. A large portion of" Dr. Ward's abridged diary was published by Dr. Peters in " Nippur," vol. I, appendix F, pp. 318-375.

Among the Semitic scholars who in 1884 had met at New Haven to discuss the feasibility of independent American explorations in different sections of Western Asia, Rev. Dr. John P. Peters, Professor of Hebrew in the Episcopal Divinity School of Philadelphia, had been especially active in promoting that first expedition and in raising the funds required for it. He and others had quietly cherished the hope that the lady who so generously defrayed all the expenses of Dr. Ward's exploring tour would also take a leading part in future archaeological enterprises of the country. But for some reason or other their well-founded expectations were doomed to disappointment. If, therefore, the former comprehensive scheme of starting American excavations in one or more of the recommended Babylonian sites was ever to be realized, it became necessary above all things to arouse greater interest among the religious and educated classes of the people by public lectures on Semitic and archaeological topics, and to make especial efforts to win the confidence and cooperation of public-spirited men of influence and wealth, on whose moral and financial support the practicability of the intended undertaking chiefly depended; for direct assistance from the United States government was entirely out of the question. Such courses were given in the University of Pennsylvania in the winter of 18861887.

This circumstance is mentioned especially, because as late as 1900 Mr. Heuzey, director of the Oriental Department of the Louvre and editor of the monuments from Tello, assigns the origin of the Nuffar expedition of the University of Pennsylvania to a legacy left by Miss Wolfe to that institution for excavations in Babylonia. Comp. De Sarzec and Heuzey, *Une I'illt Royale Chaldeenne,* Paris, 1900, pp. 3 1 *seq.*

But where could a sufficient number of enlightened men and women be found who had the desire and courage to engage in such a costly and somewhat adventurous enterprise as a Babylonian expedition at first naturally must be, as long as there were more urgent appeals from churches and schools, universities and museums, hospitals and other charitable institutions, which needed the constant support of their patrons, and while there were plenty of scientific enterprises and experiments of a more general interest and of more practical value with regard to their ultimate outcome constantly carried on immediately before the eyes of the public at home? Indeed, the prospect for excavations in the remote and lawless districts of the Euphrates and the Tigris looked anything but bright and encouraging.. It was finally Dr. Peters' patient work and energy which secured the necessary funds for the first ambitious expedition to Babylonia through liberal friends of the University of Pennsylvania, where a short while before (1886) he had been appointed Professor of Hebrew, while the present writer was called to the chair of Assyrian.

The university was then ably managed by the late provost, Dr. William Pepper, a man of rare talents, exceptional working power, and great personal magnetism, under whom it entered upon that new policy of rapid expansion and scientific consolidation which under his no less energetic and self-sac-

rificing successor, Dr. C. C. Harrison, brought it soon to the front of the great American institutions of learning. The remarkable external growth of which it could boast, and the spirit of progress fostered in its lecture halls were, to a certain degree, indicative also of the high appreelation of scholarship and original investigation on the part of the educated classes of the city in which it is situated. It will therefore always remain a credit to Philadelphia that within its confines a small but representative group of gentlemen was ready to listen to Dr. Peters' propositions, and enthusiastically responded to a call from Mr. E. W. Clark, a prominent banker and the first active supporter of the new scheme, to start a movement in exploring ancient sites under the auspices of the University of Pennsylvania which is almost without a parallel in the history of archaeological research. The immediate fruit of this unique demonstration of private citizens was the equipment and maintenance of a great Babylonian expedition, which has continued to the present day at a cost of more than §100,000, and which was soon followed by the organization or subvention of similar enterprises in Egypt, Asia Minor, North and Central America, Italy and Greece. It has well been stated that no city in the United States has shown an interest in archaeology at all comparable with that displayed by Philadelphia within the last fifteen years.

The history and results of this Babylonian expedition of the University of Pennsylvania will be set forth in the following pages. Its work, which centred in the methodical exploration of one of the earliest Babylonian cities, the ruins of Nuffar, the Biblical Calneh (Gen. 10: 10), was no continuous one. Certain intervals were required for the general welfare and temporary rest of its members, for replenishing the exhausted stores of the camp, and, above all, for preparing, studying, and, in a general way, digesting the enormous mass of excavated material, in order to secure by preliminary reports the necessary means for an early resumption of the labors in the field. For as to the wealth

of its scientific results, this Philadelphia expedition takes equal rank with the best sent out from England and France, while it eclipses them all with regard to the number and character of the inscribed tablets recovered, four distinct campaigns were conducted before those priceless treasures of literature and art which are now deposited in the two great museums on the Bosphorus and the Schuylkill could be extracted from their ancient hiding places.

Each had its own problem and history, its special difficulties and disappointments, but also its characteristic and conspicuous results. The work of *the fir st expedition (1ss8S9)* was on the whole tentative, and gave us a clear conception of the grandeur of the task to be accomplished. It included an accurate survey of the whole ruins, the beginning of systematic excavations at the temple of Bel, the discovery of a Parthian palace, and the unearthing of more than two thousand cuneiform inscriptions representing the principal periods of Babylonian history, and including numerous tablets of the ancient temple library. *The second (isso-go)* continued in the line of research mapped out bv the first, explored the upper strata of the temple, and by means of a few deep trial trenches produced evidence that a considerable number of very ancient monuments still existed in the lower parts of the sacred enclosure. It resumed the excavation of the Parthian palace, discovered important Cassite archives, and acquired about eight thousand tablets of the second and third pre-Christian millenniums. *The third (/Sgj-g6)* also directed its chief attention to the temple mound, but at the same time made a successful search for inscribed monuments in other sections of the ruins, gathering no less than twenty-one thousand cuneiform inscriptions largely fragmentary. It removed the later additions to the stage-tower; revealed the existence of several platforms and other important architectural remains in the centre of the large mound, thereby enabling us to fix the age of its different strata with great accuracy; it excavated three sections of the temple court down to the water level, and discovered the first wellpreserved brick arch of pre-Sargonic times (about 4000 B. C), with numerous other antiquities, including the large torso of an inscribed statue in dolerite of the period of Gudea, and over five hundred vase fragments of the earliest rulers 'of the country. The *fourth expedition (1898-1900)* was the most successful of all. It explored the Parthian palace completely, and examined more than one thousand burials in various parts of the ruins. It proved that, contrary to former assertions, the upper strata of the temple complex did not belong to the Babylonian period proper, but represented a huge Parthian fortress lying on the top of it. It definitely located the famous temple library of Nippur, from which thousands of tablets had been previously obtained, and in addition to many other inscribed objects, like the votive table of Naram-Sin, a large dolerite vase of Gudea, etc., it excavated about twenty-three thousand tablets and fragments, mostly of a literary character. Above all it endeavored to determine the extent of the pre-Sargonic settlement, discovered a very large ancient wall below the level of the desert in the southwestern half of the ruins, exposed nearly the whole eastern city wall, ascertaining the different periods of its construction and uncovering the earliest remains of its principal gate deeply hidden in the soil of the desert. It traced the ancient southeast wall of the inner temple enclosure, found its original chief entrance in a tolerably good state of preservation, ascertained the precise character of Bel's famous sanctuary, and demonstrated by indisputable facts that the *ziggurrat,* the characteristic part of every prominent Babylonian temple, does not go back to Ur-Gur of Ur, about 2700 B. c., but was a creation of the earliest Sumerian population.

It is evident from a mere glance at this summary of the total results obtained that they cannot be fully comprehended if treated exclusively under the head of each single campaign. On the other hand, it cannot be denied that a certain feeling of justice towards the various members of the expedition, who worked under different conditions and served at different times, render a separate treatment of the origin and history of every campaign almost imperative. We therefore propose first to relate the history and progress of the four campaigns in their natural order, and afterwards to sketch their principal results — due as much to the extraordinary efforts of the subscribers and the careful watchfulness and directions of the committee at home as to the faithful services and self-denying spirit of those in the field — in their mutual relation to each other, and chiefly from a topographical point of view.

A. ORIGIN AND HISTORY OF THE EXPEDITION.

First Campaign, fSSS-Sp. The meeting at which Dr. Peters submitted his plans to the public was held at the house of Provost Pepper on November 30, 1887. About thirty persons were present, including Dr. Ward, the previous leader of the Wolfe Expedition, and Professor Hilprecht, as the official representative of Assyriology in the University of Pennsylvania. Both had been invited by the chairman to express their respective views with regard to the contemplated undertaking. In the course of the discussion it became more and more apparent that the enthusiastic originator of the new scheme and the present writer differed essentially from each other on fundamental questions. On the basis of Dr. Ward's recommendation, the former declared in favor of a large promising site, like Anbar, Nuffar, El-Birs, etc. , as most suitable for the Philadelphia excavations. He proposed that the staff of the expedition should consist of four persons, a director, a well-known Assyriologist, formerly connected with the British Museum, and the photographer and the interpreter of the Wolfe Expedition; and he estimated the total expense for a campaign of three consecutive years, as previously stated by him, at 11 5,000. The present writer, on the other side, pointed out that while he fully agreed with Dr. Peters as to the importance of either of the proposed mounds for archaeological research, especially of Nuffar, so frequently and prominently mentioned in the earliest cuneiform inscriptions, he nevertheless felt it his duty to affirm that none of these extensive mounds could be excavated in the least adequately within the period stated, and that, moreover, according to his own calculations, even a small expedition of only four members and a corresponding number of servants and workmen would necessarily cost more in the first year than the whole sum required for three years. He furthermore called attention to the fact that the national honor and the scientific character of this first great American enterprise in Babylonia would seem to require the addition of an American Assyriologist and architect, and, if possible, even of a surveyor and a naturalist, to the proposed staff of the expedition. If, however, in view of a very natural desire on the part of the director and his financial supporters, the principal stress was to be laid on the rapid acquisition of important museum objects and inscribed tablets rather than on the methodical and complete examination of an entire large ruin, it would be by far wiser to select from among the different sites visited by Dr. Ward one which was somewhat smaller in size and considerably less superimposed with the remains and rubbish of the post-Babylonian period than any of the ruins submitted for consideration. The results showed only too plainly that the view maintained by the present writer was correct, and that his objections, raised for the sole purpose of preventing unpleasant complications and later disappointments with regard to " the white elephant," as the expedition was soon to be styled, were based upon a careful discrimination between uncertain hopes and sober facts. Notwithstanding all that has been said against Anbar (Persian, "magazine, granary") as a Babylonian site, I still hold with Dr. Ward, on the ground of my own personal examination of the immense ruins and of the topography of that whole neighborhood, that long before the foundation of Peroz Shapur a Babylonian city of considerable importance must have existed there. Traces of it would doubtless be revealed in the lower strata of its principal mounds. The mere facts that here the Euphrates entered Babylonia proper, that here the first great canal — on the protection of which the fertility and prosperity of an important section of the country depended — branches off, and that here a military station is required to complete the northern fortification line of the empire, — indicated by Tell Mohammed between the Tigris and the Diyala (covering the remains of a palace of Hammurabi, comp. p. 158, above), and 'Aqarquf between the Tigris and the Euphrates (the ancient Dur-Kurigalzu, comp. pp. 38, *seq.*, above), —forces us to look for the ruins of a Babylonian city on the site of Anbar, which represents the most important point on the whole northern boundary. At Dr. Pepper's request, I handed my own views to him in writing as to the composition, task, expenses, etc., of a Babylonian expedition on the morning following this meeting. This paper was returned to the writer shortly before Dr. Pepper's untimely death. The probable expenses of such an expedition with a staff of five or six persons was estimated for the first year at $19,200.

The same evening " The Babylonian Exploration Fund" was called into existence, about half of the sum requested (£15,000) subscribed, and an expedition with Dr. Peters as director recommended. On March 17, 1888, the organization of the new corporation was completed by the election of Provost Pepper as president, Mr. K. W. Clark as treasurer, and Professor Hilprecht as secretary. Dr. Peters was confirmed as director, but the general plan previously outlined by him was somewhat modified in accordance with the writer's suggestions. Upon the director's recommendation, Dr. Robert Francis Harper, then instructor in Yale University, was appointed Assyriologist, Mr. Perez Hastings Field, of New York, architect and surveyor, Mr. Haynes photographer and business manager, and Mr. Noorian interpreter and director of the workmen, while Mr. J. D. Prince, just graduating from Columbia College and offering to accompany the expedition at his own

expense, was attached as the director's secretary. But having fallen seriously ill on the way down the Euphrates valley, he left the expedition at Baghdad, and returned to America by way of India and China.

I had in mind a ruin of the type of Fara (recently recommended by me to the German Orient Society for similar consideration, comp. *Mittheilungfn,* no. 10, p. 2), where the pre-Sargonic stratum reaches to the very surface of the mound. -The whole Executive Committee consisted of fifteen members, including the three officers mentioned and the director of the expedition. The other members were Messrs. C. H. Clark (chairman of the Publication Committee), W. W. Frazier, C. C. Harrison (the present provost), Joseph D. Potts (t), Maxwell Sommerville, H. Clay Trumbull, Talcott Williams, Richard Wood, Stuart Wood, of Philadelphia; Professor Langley, of the Smithsonian Institute, Washington; and Professor Marquand, of Princeton University.

On April 4, I received an urgent note from Provost Pepper requesting me to see him at once and stating that it was his especial desire that I should serve on this expedition as the University of Pennsylvania's Assyriologist, all the necessary expenses to be paid by himself and Rev. Dr. H. Clay Trumbull, editor of" The Sunday School Times." I consented to go without a salary, as Harper and Field had done before. In the course ot the summer the members of the expedition lett at intervals for the East, finally meeting at Aleppo on December 10. Peters and Prince had spent three months in Constantinople to obtain a firman for successive excavations at El-Birs and NufTar; Harper, Field, and Havnes had visited the Hittite districts of Senjirli, Mar'ash and Jerabis (Carchemish);' while the present writer had worked on the cuneiform inscriptions of the Nahr el-Kelb and Wadi Berisa," at the same time searching the whole Lebanon region for new material. After an uneventful trip down "the great river" and a fortnight's stay at Baghdad, largely devoted to the examination and

purchase of antiquities, the partv proceeded bv way of Hilla to Nuffar, the scene of its future activity. For after a visit to the high-towering mound of El-Birs and the adjoining site of Tell Ibrahim el-Khalil, which together constitute the remains of ancient Borsippa, it had been decided unanimously not to commence operations here, but to move further on to the second place granted by the firman, which practically represented an entirely fresh site only superficially scratched before by Layard. Peters, *l. c.,* p. 9, adds: "At the time it was understood that Professor Hilprecht's health was too delicate to permit him to serve in the field. Later the physicians decided that he could go." Where and how this it was understood " originated, I do not know. There is an apparent misunderstanding on the part of Dr. Peters concerning the whole matter which I do not care to discuss within the pages of this book. Yet nevertheless I desire to state briefly as a matter of fact, 1. That I never had been asked to go to Babylonia before April 4, 1888. 2. That I never consulted any physician with regard to mv accompanying that first Babylonian expedition. 3. That consequently I never received medical advice or ' decision" from any physician in reply to such a question. Dr. Peters's two volumes (" Nippur," New York, 1897) unfortunately contain many other erroneous statements (comp. Ward's review in "The Independent," July 29, 1897, p. 18, and Harper's in "The Biblical World," October, 1897). In order not to appear through my silence to approve of them in this first coherent sketch of the history of the whole expedition, I am unfortunately frequently obliged to take notice of them. Personal attacks, however, have been ignored entirely; other misstatements, as a rule, have been changed quietly; only fundamental differences with regard to important technical and scientific questions have been stated expressly in the interest of the cause itself.

Comp. Harper in "The Old and New Testament Student," vol. viii (1889), pp. 183, *seq.* ("A Visit to Zinjirii ") and vol. ix (1889), pp. 308, *seq.* (" A Visit to Carchemish "). Comp. Hilprecht in "The Sunday School Times," vol. xxxi. (1889), p. 163 ("The Mouth of the Nahr el-Kelb"), pp. 547, *seq.* ("The Inscriptions of Nebuchadrezzar in Wadi Brissa "), and vol. xxxii *(%()o),* pp. 147, *seq.* ("The Shaykh of Zeta "); also *Die Inschriften NebukaJnezar's im Wadi Brissa,* in Luthardt's *Zeitschrift fir kirchliche Wissenschaft und kirchliches Leben,* vol. ix (1889), pp. 491, *seqq.* Comp. Harper in "The Old and New Testament Student," vol. x (1890), pp. 55, *seqq.,* Il8, *seq.,* 367, *seq.* (" Down the Euphrates Valley," i-iii); and */. c,* vol. xiv (1892), pp. 160, *seqq.,* 213, *seqq.,* and vol. xv (1892), pp. I 2, *seqq.* ("The Expedition of the Babylonian Exploration Fund," A-C). In the course of the first expedition there were purchased through different members of the staff five distinct collections of Babylonian antiquities, containing about 1 800 specimens (tablets, seals, jewelry), namely, Colls. Kh(abaza), KM, Sh(emtob), Mrs. H. V. H(ilprecht), D. J. P(rince), besides a collection of Cappadocian tablets and other antiquities, and a set of plaster casts of Assyrian and Babylonian monuments from the British Museum. Apart from Mrs. Hilprecht's and Mr. Prince's contributions, which did not pass through the treasurer's hands, Messrs. C. H. and E. W. Clark, W. W. Frazier, C. C. Harrison, Wm. Pepper, and Stuart Wood spent 56500 extra for the purchase of these collections, including a number of Palmyrene busts obtained by Dr. Peters in the following year, and the valuable plaster reproductions of the ruins of NufFar, which were afterwards prepared under Field's supervision in Paris. As to the Khabaza and Shemtob collections, comp. Harper in *Hckraica,* vol. v, pp. 74, *scqq.;* vol. vi, pp. 225, *seq.* (vol. viii, pp. 103, *seq.).*

The next military station from NufFar is Diwaniye, situated on both sides of the Euphrates and (according to the season and the extent of the inundations) about six to nine hours to the southwest of it. At the time of our first campaign it was a miserable and fast decreasing town consisting chiefly of mud houses, and governed by a *qaimmaqam* under whose immediate jurisdiction we were to be. But since the water supply of the lower Euphrates has been regulated through the construction of the Hindiye dam above Babylon, it has rapidly changed its aspect and become a neat and flourishing town. At the expense of Hilla it has been raised to the seat of a *mutesarrif* and received a considerable increase of soldiers, including even artillery, in order to check the predatory incursions of the roaming Bedouins of the desert, and to control the refractory 'Afej tribes around NufFar, which until recently acknowledged only a nominal allegiance to the Ottoman government, Comp. pp. 159, *ieqq.,* above.

regarding themselves as perfectly safe in the midst of their swamps and mud castles, the so-called *meftit/s.* Peters, Harper, and Bedry Bey, our Turkish commissioner, took this circuitous route by way of Diwaniye, to pay their respects to the local governor there and to make the necessary arrangements for the prompt despatch and receipt of our mail.

The rest of us, accompanied by thirty-two trained workmen from Jumjuma and another village near Kl-Birs, a crowd of women and children attached to them, and a large number qf animals carrying our whole outfit, provisions, and the implements for excavations, struck directly for Nuffar. The frequent rumors which we had heard at Baghdad and Hilla concerning the unsettled and unsafe condition of this section of the country, inhabited as it was said to be by the most unruly and turbulent tribes of the whole vilayet, were in an entire accord with Layard's reports, and only too soon to be confirmed by our own experience. The 'Afej and the powerful Shammar, who sometimes descend as far down as the Shatt el-Ha'i, were fighting for the pasture lands, driving each other's camels and sheep away, and two of the principal subdivisions of the 'Afej had a blood-feud with each other. On the second day of our march, while temporarily separated from our caravan, we were suddenly surprised by a *ghazu* (razzia) and with difficulty escaped the hands of the marauding Arabs. The nearer we came to the goal of our journey, the more disturbed was the population. Finally on the third morning Bint el-Amir, majestically towering above the wide stretched mounds of Nuffar, rose clear on the horizon. More than 2000 years ago the huge terraces and walls of the most renowned Babylonian sanctuary had crumbled to a formless mass. But even in their utter desolation they still seemed to testify to the lofty aspirations of a bygone race, and to reecho the ancient hymn once chanted in their shadow: — Comp. p. 287, note 2, above, and the illust. facing p. 349, below.

Comp. Layard, Nineveh and Babylon," London, 1853, p. 565: "The most wild and ignorant Arabs that can be found in this part of Asia." "O great mountain of Bel, Imgarsag,
Whose summit rivals the heavens,
Whose foundations are laid in the bright abysmal sea,
Resting in the land as a mighty steer,
Whose horns are gleaming like the radiant sun,
As the stars of heaven are filled with lustre.''

Even at a distance I began to realize that not twenty, not fifty years would suffice to excavate this important site thoroughly. What would our committee at home have said at the sight of this enormous ruin, resembling more a picturesque mountain range than the last impressive remains of human constructions! But there was not much time for these and similar reflections; our attention was fully absorbed by the exciting scenes around us. The progress of the motley crowd along the edge of the cheerless swamps was slow enough. The marshy ground which we had to traverse was cut up by numerous old canals, and offered endless difficulties to the advance of our stumbling beasts. Besides, the whole neighborhood was inflamed by war. Gesticulating groups of armed men watched our approach with fear and suspicion. Whenever we passed a village, the signal of alarm was given. A piece of black cloth fluttered in an instant from the *meftul,* dogs began to bark savagely, shepherds ran their flocks into shelter, and the cries of terrified women and children sounded shrill over the flat and treeless plain. Greeted by the wild dance and the rhvthmical yells of some, fifty 'Afej warriors, who had followed our movements from a peak of the weather-torn ruins, we took possession of the inheritance of Bel.

Immediately after our arrival we began to pitch our tents Comp. iv R., 27, no. 2, 15-24.

on the highest point of the southwestern half of the ruins, where we could enjoy an unlimited view over the swamps and the desert, and which at the same time seemed best protected against malaria and possible attacks from the

Plan of the Ruins of Nuffar /. *Ziggurrat and Temple of Be/, buried under a huge Parthian fortress. IT. North-east city wall. III. Great north-east (pre-Sargonic city gate. If. Temple library, covered by txtenuvt ruins of a later period. P. Dry bed of an ancient canal (Shatt en-Nil. fl Pre-Sargonic ivall buried under sixty feet cf rubbish with archives of later periods, 'fll. »,... Parisian palace, resting on Cassite archives. fill. Business house of Ulurashu Sons iL'i'h more ancient ruins beU'W.*

Arabs. With the aid of Berdi, shaikh of the Warish (a subdivision of the Hamza),who was ready to assist us, a number of native huts, so-called *sari/as,* made of bunches of reed arched together and covered with palm-leaf mats, were placed in a square around us. They served for stables, store-rooms, servants' quarters, workshop, dining-room, kitchen and other purposes, and also protected us against the sand storms and the thievish inclinations of the children of the desert. Before this primitive camp was established, Field began surveying the mounds, as a preliminary map had to be submitted to the wall of Baghdad, in order to secure his formal approval of our excavations. In the mean while the director and the two Assyriologists used every spare moment to acquaint themselves with the topography of the ruins and to search for indications on the surface which might enable them to ascertain the prob-

able character and contents of the more prominent single mounds.

In connection with repeated walks over the whole field I prepared a rough sketch of the principal ruins for my own use, gathered numerous pieces of bricks, stone and pottery, and immediately reached the following general conclusions: I. Certain portions of the ruins are remarkably free from blue and green enamelled pottery, always characteristic of late settlements on Babylonian sites, and show no trace of an extensive use of glass on the part of its inhabitants. As the latter is never mentioned with certainty in the cuneiform inscriptions (then at our disposal), and as the Assyrian excavations at Khorsabad, Nebi Yunus, and Nimriid had yielded but a few glass vessels, these parts of ancient Nippur must have been destroyed and abandoned at a comparatively early date. 2. In accordance with such personal observations and inferences and in view of Layard's discoveries in the upper strata of Nuffar, it became evident that the southwest half of the ruins, which on an average is also considerably higher than the corresponding other one, was much longer inhabited and to a larger extent used as a graveyard in the post-Christian period than the northeast section. 3. As Bint el-Amir, the most conspicuous mound of the whole ruins, no doubt represents the ancient *ziggurrat* or stage-tower, as generally asserted, it follows as a matter of course, that the temple of Bel, of which it formed part, must also have been situated in the northeast section, and therefore is hidden under the mounds immediately adjoining it towards the east. 4. The question arose, what buildings are covered by the two remaining groups of mounds to the northwest and southeast of the temple complex. The important role which from the earliest times the cult of Bel must have played in the life and historv of the Babylonian people, as testified bv the enormous mass of ruins and numerous passages in the cuneiform literature, pointed unmistakably to the employment of a large number of priests and temple officers, and to the existence ot a flourishing school

and a well equipped temple library in the ancient city of Nippur. Which of the two mounds under consideration most probably represented the residences of the priests with their administrative offices and educational quarters? 5. The large open court to the northwest of the temple, enclosed as it was on two sides by the visible remains of ancient walls, on the third by the *ziggurrat,* and on the fourth by the Shaft enNil, suggested at once that the undetermined northwest group flanking this court served more practical purposes and contained outhouses, stables, store-rooms, magazines, sheds, servants' quarters, etc., which were not required in the immediate neighborhood and in front of the temple. 6. It was therefore extremely probable that the houses of the priests, their offices, school, and library must be looked for in the large triangular southeast mound (IV), separated by a branch of the Shaft en-Nil from the temple proper. Situated on the bank of two canals, in close proximity to the sanctuary of Bel, open on all sides to the fresh breezes in the summer, and vet well protected against the rough north winds, which swept down from the snow-capped mountains of Persia during the winter, this section of the ruins seemed to fulfil all the conditions required, and from the very beginning was therefore pointed out by the present writer as the most important mound for our work next to the temple ruin proper. Comp. the brief description of the ruins on pp. 160, *sej.,* above, under La yard. Comp. pp. 161, *seqq.,* above.

It will always remain a source of deep regret that Dr. Peters did not rely more upon the judgment and scientific advice of his Assyriologists in deciding strictly technical questions, but that in his anxious but useless efforts to arrange all the essential details of this first expedition in person, he allowed himself frequently to be led by accidents and secondary considerations rather than by a clearly definite plan of methodical operations. The first trenches were opened on February 6 by the thirty-two workmen hired in Hilla. The circumstance that some of the Arabs, while gathering bricks for certain constructions in our camp, had accidentally struck a large tomb in a small gully near us influenced the director to begin the excavations at this point (VII), which soon led to the discovery of a construction of columns made of baked bricks and of such a mass of slipper-shaped coffins, funeral urns, bones, ashes, and other remains of the dead, that at first we were inclined to regard the whole southwestern half of NufFar as a vast graveyard or a regular " city of the dead," similar to those explored by Moritz and Koldewey at Surghul and El-Hibba. The next point attacked by him was an extremely insignificant out-of-the-way mound at the northwestern end of the Shatt en-Nil, selected chiefly because it was small enough to be excavated completely within a few weeks. Several days later, when a sufficient number of workmen had been obtained from the neighboring tribes, the systematic exploration of Bint el-Amir was undertaken in accordance with a plan prepared by the Assyriologists and the architect. The first task which we had set for ourselves was to determine the corners and walls of the stage-tower, and to search for barrel cylinders and other documents which might have been deposited in this ancient structure by the different monarchs who restored it. It ever they existed, — and certain discoveries made later in the rubbish around its base proved that they actually did, — these building records must have been destroyed at the time of the Parthian invasion, when the whole temple complex was remodelled for military purposes.

Apart from a stray cuneiform tablet of the period of Sargon I. — the first of its kind ever discovered, — three small fragments of inscribed stone picked up by the Arabs, a few Hebrew bowls, and a number of bricks bearing short legends of the kings Ur-Gur, Bur-Sin I. , Ur-Ninib,and Ishme-Dagan, all of the third pre-Christian millennium, no inscribed documents had been unearthed during the first ten days of our stay at Nuffar. No wonder that Dr. Peters, who began to realize that his funds of $15,00x3 were nearly exhausted, grew

uneasy as to the tangible results of the expedition, the future of which depended largely upon quick and important discoveries. I seized this opportunity to submit once more for his consideration my views, given above, concerning the topography of the northeast half of the ruins, pointing out that in all probability tablets would be found in that large isolated hill, which I believed to contain the residences of the priests and the temple library (IV), and requested him to let me have about twenty men for a few days to furnish the inscribed material so eagerly sought after. This was a somewhat daring proposition, which scarcely would have been made with this self-imposed restriction of time had I not been convinced of the general correctness of my theory. After some hesitation the director was generous enough to place two gangs of workmen at my disposal for a whole week in order to enable me to furnish the necessary proof for my subjective conviction. On February 11 two trenches were opened at the western edge of IV on a level with the present bed of the ancient canal. Before noon the first six cuneiform tablets were in our possession, and at the close of the same day more than twenty tablets and fragments had been recovered. Thus far the beginning was very encouraging, and far surpassed my boldest expectations. But it remained to be seen whether we had struck only one of those small nests of clay tablets as they occasionally occur in all Babylonian ruins, or whether they would continue to come forth in the same manner during the following weeks and even increase gradually in number. At the end of February several hundred tablets and fragments had been obtained from the same source, and six weeks later, when our first campaign was brought to a sudden end, mound IV had yielded more than two thousand cuneiform inscriptions from its seemingly inexhaustible mines. For the greater part they were unbaked, broken, and otherwise damaged. With regard to their age, two periods could be clearly distinguished. The large mass was written in old Babylonian characters not later than the first dynasty of

Babylon (about 2OOOB. c.), but less than one hundred tablets gathered in the upper strata were so-called neo-Babylonian contracts generally well preserved and dated in the reigns of Ashurbanapal, Nabopolassar, Nebuchadrezzar, Kvil-Merodach (2 Kgs. 25: 27; Jer. 52:31), Nabonidos, Cyrus, Cambyses, Darius, and Xerxes. Three of them were of unusual historical interest. Being dated in the second and fourth year of Ashuretililani, "king of Assyria," they proved conclusively that Nabopolassar's rebellion against the Assyrian supremacy (626 B. c.) was originally confined to the capital and its immediate environment, and that, contrary to the prevalent view, long after Babylon itself had regained and maintained its independence, important cities and whole districts of the Southern empire still paid homage to Ashurbanapal's successor on the throne of Assyria.

But the earlier inscriptions, though as a rule very fragmentary, were of even greater significance. None of them was evidently found in situ, except ten large tablets in a most excellent state of preservation taken from a kiln, where they had been in the process of baking when one of the terrible catastrophes by which the city was repeatedlv visited overtook ancient Nippur. They consisted of business documents referring to the registry of tithes and to the administration of the temple property, and of tablets of a decided literary character, comprising some very fine syllabaries and lists of synonyms, letters, mathematical, astronomical, medical and religious texts, besides a few specimens of drawing and a considerable number of mostly round tablets which must be classified as school exercises. Those which were dated bore the names of Hammurabi, Samsuiluna, Abeshum, Ammisatana, and Ammisadugga. As about four fifths of all the tablets were literary, there could no longer be anv doubt that we were not far from the famous temple library, unless indeed we already were working in its very ruins. In order to arrive at more definite results, it would have been necessary to continue the two large trenches which

I had started, through the centre to the eastern edge of the mound. In the course of the second half of March five extra gangs were put on "the tablet hill," as it was henceforth styled, to carry out this plan. But time and money were soon lacking, and circumstances arose which forced us to evacuate Nuffar before many weeks were over. Otherwise we could not have failed to discover, in 1889, those tabletfilled rooms which were unearthed eleven years later, when the present writer personally was held responsible for the preparation of the plans and the scientific management of the expedition.

Comp. Hilprecht, in *Zeitichrift fur Assyriologie,* vol. iv, pp. 164, *seqq.*

The work at the temple complex, where finally more than one hundred men were employed, proceeded but slowly, owing to the enormous amount of rubbish accumulated here and to the tenacity of the unbaked bricks which had to be cut through. Small and graceful terra-cotta cones similar to those discovered by Loftus at Warka, but generally broken, were excavated in large number along the base of the northwest wall of the *ziggurrat*. Evidently they had fallen from the top of the tower, and once belonged to a shrine contemporaneous with the inscribed bricks of Ashurbanapai, the last known restorer of the temple of Bel, near whose material they were lying. The remains of the lowest story of the huge building began to rise gradually out of the midst of the encumbering ruins. But they offered problems so complicated in themselves and with regard to other constructions discovered all around the *ziggurrat* at a much higher level, that it was well-nigh impossible to form a satisfactory idea of the character and extent of the temple, before the whole neighborhood had been subjected to a critical examination. For very apparent reasons there were only a few and very late tombs unearthed in this part of the city, while again they occurred more frequently in the lower mounds to the southwest of the temple. Among the various antiquities which came from the trenches of the sanctuary itself may be mentioned especially

about a dozen vase fragments inscribed with very archaic characters, two of them exhibiting the name of Lugalzaggisi, an otherwise unknown king of Erech whose precise period could then not be determined; a well preserved brick stamp of Naram-Sin (about 3750 B. c.), the first document of this half-mythical monarch which reached the shores of Europe; a fine marble tablet containing a list of garments presented to the temple; and a door-socket of the Cassite ruler Kurigalzu.

In the course of time our workmen had been gradually increased to about 250, so that experimental trenches could also be cut in the extreme western and southern wings of the ruins. A number of contract tablets of the time of the Chaldean and Persian dynasties were excavated in the upper strata of the last mentioned section. The fragment of a Comp. pp. 148, *iff.*, above.

barrel cylinder of Sargon, king of Assyria, which came from the same neighborhood, indicated that a large public building must have occupied this site previously, a supposition subsequently strengthened by the discovery of two more fragments which belonged to duplicates of the same cylinder. Stray cuneiform tablets and seal cylinders; a considerable number of terra-cotta figurines, mostly bearded gods with weapons and other instruments in their hands, or naked goddesses holding their breasts or suckling a babe; and a few clay reliefs, among which an exquisitely modelled lioness excited our admiration, were discovered in various other parts of the ruins. They belonged to the Babylonian period, in which naturally our interest centred. But, as was to be expected, most of the trenches yielded antiquities which illustrated the life and customs of the early post-Christian inhabitants of the country rather than those of the ancient Babylonians. Especially in the ruins of the Parthian building, with its interesting brick columns, which in the first week the Arabs had disclosed to the east of our camp, we uncovered hundreds of slipper-shaped coffins and funeral urns, numerous vases and dishes, and small peculiar

tripods, so-called stilts, which were used in connection with the burning of pottery in exactly the same way as they are employed in china-manufactories to-day. Terra-cotta toys, such as horses, riders, elephants, rams, monkeys, dogs, birds, eggs, marbles, and baby rattles in the shape of chickens, dolls and drums, spear-heads and daggers, metal instruments and polishing stones, Parthian coins, weights and whorls, jewelry in gold, silver, copper, bone, and stone, especially necklaces, bracelets, ear and finger rings, fibulae and hair-pins, together with about thirty bowls inscribed with Hebrew, Mandean and Arabic legends, and frequently also covered with horrible demons supposed to molest the human habitations and to disturb the peace of the dead, completed our collections.

Soon after we had reached NufFar, Dr. Peters had made us acquainted with the low ebb in the finances of the expedition. It was, therefore, decided to close the excavations of the first campaign at the beginning of May. But the working season was brought to a conclusion more quickly than could have been anticipated. The trouble started with the Arabs. The methodical exploration of the ruins had proceefled satisfactorily for about nine weeks till the middle of April, tablets being found abundantly, and the topography of ancient Nippur becoming more lucid everyday. Notwithstanding those countless difficulties which, more or less, every expedition working in the interior of Babylonia far away from civilization has to meet at nearly every turn, we began to enjoy the life in the desert and to get accustomed to the manners of the fickle Arabs, whose principal "virtues" seemed to consist in lying, stealing, murdering, and lasciviousness. And the 'Afej, on the other hand, had gradually abandoned their original distrust, after they had satisfied themselves that the Americans had no intention of erecting a new military station out of the bricks of the old walls for the purpose of collecting arrears of government taxes. But there existed certain conditions in our camp and around us which, sooner or later, had to lead to serious complications. Hajji Tarfa, the supreme shaikh of all the 'Afej tribes, a man of great diplomatic skill, liberal views and far-reaching influence, was unfortunately absent in the Shamiyewhen we commenced operations at Nuffar. His eldest son, Mukota, who meanwhile took the place of his father, was a sneaking Arab of the lowest type, little respected by his followers, begging for everything that came under his eyes, turbulent, treacherous, and a coward, and brooding mischief all the while. Two of the principal 'Afej tribes, the Hamza and the Behahtha, both of which laid claim to the mounds we had occupied, and insisted on furnishing workmen for our excavations, were at war with each other. At the slightest provocation and frequently without any apparent reason they threw their scrapers and baskets away and commenced the war-dance, brandishing their spears or guns in the air and chanting some defiant sentence especially made up for the occasion, as, *e. g.*, " We are the slaves of Berdi," "The last day has come," "Down with the Christians," " Matches in his beard who contradicts us," etc. The Turkish commissioner and the *zabtiye* (irregular soldiers), — whose number had been considerably increased by the *qaimmaqam* of Diwaniye, much against our own will, — picked frequent quarrels with the natives and irritated them by their overbearing manners. The Arabs, on the other hand, were not slow in showing their absolute independence by wandering unmolested around the camp, entering our private tents and examining our goods, like a crowd of naughty boys; or by squatting with their guns and clubs near the trenches and hurling taunting and offensive expressions at the Ottoman government.

It was also a mistake that we had pitched our tents on the top of the ruins. For as the mounds of Nuffar had no recognized owner and yet were claimed by the Turks, the Bedouins, and the Ma'dan tribes at the same time, we were practically under nobody's protection, while by our very conspicuous position we not only suffered exceedingly from hot winds and suffocating sand storms, but invited plundering by every loiterer and marauder in the neighborhood. Moreover, unacquainted as we all were then with the peculiar customs of Central Babylonia, we had not provided a *mudhif* or lodging-house, a spacious and airy *sari/a*, which in every large village of the country is set apart for the reception of travellers and guests. What wonder that the simple-minded children of the desert and the half-naked peasants of the marshes, who noticed our strange mode of living and saw so many unknown things with us for which they had no need themselves, shook their heads in amazement. On the one hand they observed how we spent large sums of money for uncovering old walls and gathering broken pottery, and on the other they found us eating the wild boar of the jungles, ignoring Arab etiquette, and violating the sacred and universal law of hospitality in the most flagrant way, — reasons enough to regard us either as pitiable idiots whom they could easily fleece or as unclean and uncouth barbarians to whom a pious Shiite was infinitely the superior.

Repeated threats to burn us out had been heard, and various attempts had been made to get at our rifles and guns. One night our bread-oven was destroyed, and a hole was cut in the reed-hut which served as our stable. Soon afterwards four sheep belonging to some of our workmen were stolen. The thief, a young lad from the Sa'id, asmall tribe of bad repute, half Bedouin and half Ma'dan, encouraged by his previous success, began to boast, as Berdi told me later, that he would steal even the horses of the Franks without being detected. Though he might have suspected us to be on the alert, he and a few comrades undertook to execute the long-cherished plan in the night of the fourteenth of April. Our sentinels, who had previously been ordered to occupy the approaches to the camp night and day, frustrated the attempt and opened fire at the intruders. In an instant the whole camp was aroused, and one of the thieves was shot through the heart. This was a most unfortunate occurrence, and sure to result in further trouble. No time was therefore lost to inform the 'Afej chiefs, to despatch a messenger to the next militarystation, and to prepare ourselves for any case of emergency. "Then followed a period of anxious suspense. Soon the death wail sounded from a village close beneath us," indicating that the body of the dead Arab had been carried off to the nearest encampment. "Then a signal fire was kindled. This was answered by another and another, until the whole plain was clothed with little lights, while through the still night came the sounds of bustle and preparation for the attack." On the next morning we decided to avoid the consequences of the severe laws of Arab blood revenge by paying an adequate indemnity to the family of the fallen man. But our offer was proudly rejected by the hostile tribe, and an old Sa'id workman, employed as a go-between, returned with torn garments and other evidences of a beating. The American party was equally prompt in refusing to give up the " murderer." The days and nights which followed were full of exciting scenes. Mukota, Berdi, and other 'Afej shaikhs, who professed to come to our assistance, had occupied the spurs around us. Thirty irregular soldiers, with six hundred rounds of cartridges, were sent from Diwaniye and Hilla, and others were expected to arrive in the near future. There were constant alarms of an attack by the Sa'id. The 'Afej, not concealing their displeasure at seeing so large a number of *zabtlye* in their territory, were evidently at heart in sympathy with the enemy. Besieged as we practically were, we were finally forced to withdraw our laborers from the trenches and make arrangements for quitting Nuffar altogether. On Thursday, April 18, long before the sun rose, the whole expedition was in readiness to vacate the mounds and to force their way to Hilla, when upon the treacherous order of Mukota, an Arab secretly set fire to our huts of reeds and mats and laid the whole camp in ashes in the short space of five minutes. For a while the utmost confusion prevailed, the *zabtive* got demoralized, and occupied a neighboring hill; and while we were trying to save our effects, many of the Arabs commenced plundering. Half the horses perished in the flames, firearms and saddle-bags and $1000 in gold fell into the hands of the marauders, but all the antiquities were saved. Under the war-dance and yells of the frantic Arabs the expedition finally withdrew in two divisions, one on horseback, past Suq el-'Afej and Diwaniye, the other on two boats across the swamps to Daghara, and back to Hilla, where soon afterwards the governor-general of the province arrived, anxious about our welfare and determined, if necessary, to come to our rescue with a military force.

On the way to Baghdad Harper handed in his resignation, Field gave his own a day later, Haynes, who, on the recommendation of the Philadelphia Committee, had been appointed United States Consul at Baghdad, prepared to settle in the city of Harun ar-Rashid, and with Noorian to await further developments, Peters was recalled by cable to America, and the present writer was requested to remain in charge of the expedition in Mesopotamia. But circumstances beyond his control made it impossible for him to accept this trust at once, and necessitated his immediate return to Kurope. Our first year at Babylonia had ended in a serious disaster. Dr. Peters, to quote his own words, "had failed to win the confidence of his comrades," and more than $20,000 had been expended merely to scratch the surface of one of the most enormous ancient sites in all Western Asia. How would the Ottoman government view the unexpected turn in our work among the turbulent Arabs? Would they allow the expedition to return in the fall? And if no obstacle was raised in Constantinople, would the Philadelphia Committee, after so many disappointments, be willing to resume the exploration of Nuffar, which had proved to be a task by far more expensive and wearisome than most of the contributors could have expected?

In the fall of 1888, when I departed from Germany for the East, my wife was so ill that her recovery was doubtful. Upon her own special request, however, I left her to meet my obligations in Asia. Soon after my return from Nuffar to Baghdad, April, 1889, I was informed that meanwhile she had been operated upon unsuccessfully, and that a second operation, for which my immediate return was required, was necessary. Twelve years later, when I was in the Orient again upon an important mission in connection with this expedition, she actually sacrificed herself for the cause of science, by concealing her serious illness in order not to interfere with my work, and by writing cheerful and encouraging letters to me, while she was sinking fast, and knew that she would not recover. When I finally returned to Germany in perfect ignorance of her condition, she was already beyond human aid and died soon afterwards (March, 1902), using the last hours of her unselfish life to execute a noble deed in the interest of Assyriology. Comp. Peters, "Nippur," New York, 1897, vol. i, p. 288. Besides this volume, which gives a subjectively colored and not always very reliable account of the origin and history of the first campaign, comp. Hilprecht in *Kolnische Zeitung,* June 30, 1889, Sunday edition, second paper, and Harper in "The Biblical World," vol. i, pp. 57-62. *Second Campaign, issq-isQO.* It is to the great credit of the small number of enthusiastic gentlemen who had previously furnished the funds, that far from being discouraged by what had occurred, they were rather " favorably impressed with the results accomplished by the first year's campaign," and decided to continue the excavations at Nuffar for another year under Dr. Peters, provided that the Turkish authorities at Constantinople would approve of their plan. The wali of Baghdad, who was principally held responsible for the safety of the party in a section of his province over which he had little control, most naturallyopposed the return of the expedition with all his power. But thanks to the lively interest and the energetic support of Hamdy Bey, the Grand Vizier viewed the whole matter very calmly

and in a different light from what it had been represented to him by the local officials. Accordingly he authorized the University of Pennsylvania's expedition to resume its interrupted labors in Babylonia in the same year. On October 10, Dr. Peters was able to leave the Turkish capital for Beirut, and from there, by way of Damascus and Palmyra, to travel to Baghdad, which he reached about the middle of December.

Important changes had meanwhile taken place in 'Iraq el-'Arabi. Soon after our departure, in May, 1889, a fearful cholera epidemic had broken out in lower Babylonia, and, following the courses of the two rivers, had spread rapidly to the northern districts. With the exception of Hit, Nejef, and some other remarkably favored places, it had devastated the entire country, with special fury raging in the marshy districts between Nuffar and the Shatt el-Hai, where our old enemy, Mukota, was carried off as one of its first victims, and in certain notoriously unclean and densely populated quarters of Baghdad, which for several weeks in the summer were almost completely deserted by the frightened population. In view of the lingering presence of the dreaded scourge in the valleys of the Euphrates and the Tigris, and the possibility of a renewed outbreak of the same plague in the spring, the director deemed it necessary to engage the services of a native physician of Syria, Dr. Selim Aftimus, who at the same time was expected to make those botanical and zoological collections for which the present writer had earnestly pleaded, before the first expedition was organized. Haynes and Noorian were again induced to associate themselves with the practical management of the undertaking on the road and in the field, and to serve in the same capacities in which they had been employed the previous year. But, at the special desire of Dr. Peters, this time an American scientific staff was entirely dispensed with, though Field and Hilprecht would have been willing to accompany the expedition again, without a salary but with increased responsibility. This was a most unfortunate decision on the part of the director. It is true, a solid scientific basis of operations had been established in the first campaign, and consequently there was no immediate need of an architect and Assyriologist at the beginning of the new excavations; and yet it was impossible to excavate properly for any length of time without the constant advice of either of them. If, nevertheless, this expedition, sent out to investigate the history of one of the largest, most ancient, and, at the same time, most ruined and complicated sites in the country, attempted to solve its difficult problem without the trained eyes and scientific knowledge of technically prepared men, it necessarily had to be at the expense of a strictly methodical exploration and at the sacrifice of half of the possible results, of which it deprived itself in consequence of its inability to follow up every indication on the ground, and to determine most of the perplexing archaeological questions in the trenches.

But while in the interest of scientific research we cannot approve of Dr. Peters' fatal course, to a certain degree we can explain it. He was anxious to save expenses in connection with an undertaking the original estimate of which he had considerably underrated; and not fully aware of the fact that he damaged his own cause, for which he was working with such an admirable patience, energy, and courage, he desired a greater freedom in his movements and decisions from the influence of specialists, who formerly had caused him great trouble, as they frequently differed with him in regard to the most fundamental questions. His mind being firmly fixed upon tangible results which by their mere number and character would appeal to the public, he naturally took great pains to obtain them at the least possible outlay of time and money, according to the manner of Rassam and other earlier explorers, rather than to examine these immense ruins systematically according to the principles laid down by the modern school of archaeologists. We must bear this circumstance in mind, in order to understand and judge his work leniently and to appreci-

ate his results, which, though one-sided and largely misunderstood by him, proved ultimately to be of great importance for our knowledge of the Cassite and Parthian periods of Babylonian history, and furnished welcome material for our restoration of the chronology of the second millennium.

On the last day of 1889 the caravan left Baghdad. After repeated unsuccessful attempts by the local governors of Hilla and Diwaniye at preventing the expedition's return to the ruins, the excavations were resumed on January 14, with about two hundred workmen from Hilla, who, in consequence of the ravages of cholera, lack of rain, and failing crops, had been reduced to the utmost poverty, and now looked eagerly for employment in the trenches of Nuffar. They continued this time for nearly four months, and terminated peacefully on May 3, 1890. In accordance with the advice of the natives, and profiting from our last year's experience, Dr. Peters and his comrades pitched their somewhat improved camp in the plain to the south of the western half of the ruins, and placed themselves under the protection of but a single chief, Hamid el-Birjud, shaikh of the Nozair, one of the six tribes which constitute the Hamza, a subdivision of the 'Afej.

There could be little doubt that the Arabs of the whole neighborhood were glad to see the expedition once more established among them. All the preceding troubles seemed to be forgotten entirely. The Sa'id themselves had conducted Haynes and his workmen to the mounds in the natural expectation of receiving some kind of recognition for their friendly attitude, doubly remarkable, as the old blood-feud existing between them and the expedition had not yet been settled. An excellent opportunity was thus given to remove the only cause for much annoyance and anxiety on the part of the Americans, and to make friends and valuable supporters out of deadly enemies, by recognizing the general law of the desert and paying a small sum of money to the family of the man who had been killed in the act of robbery. Only ten Turkish liras (=

$44) were demanded. But unfortunately, Dr. Peters, who otherwise entered into the life and feelings of the people most successfully, mistook the acknowledgment and prompt arrangement of the whole affair for a sign of weakness, and refused to listen to any proposal, thereby creating a feeling of constant uneasiness and unsafety on the part of Haynes, which was not at all unreasonable, and as a matter of course at times interfered seriously with the work of the expedition.

Like the Sa'id, who vainly endeavored to obtain a certain share in our work, the 'Afej could not always be trusted. They all wanted to guard the rare "goose that laid the golden egg," and soon became jealous of the Nozair chief, who had pledged himself for the security of the party. "Fabulous stories of our immense wealth were in circulation. Everything was supposed to contain money, even our boxes of provisions." "The Arabs believed that we were digging out great treasures, and it was confidently asserted that we had secured the golden boat, or *turrada*, which from time immemorial had been supposed to be contained in these mounds. " The mere sight of a gold crown on one of Peters' teeth, which was eagerly pointed out by those who had discovered it to every friend and newcomer, seemed to strengthen their conviction and excite their lust. The comparative ease with which in the previous year so much spoil had been carried off through Mukota's treacherous behavior, aroused the cupidity of all the Arabs and their ardent desire to repeat his example. The presence of two hundred workmen from Hilla and Jumjuma, who could not always be managed to keep peace with one another, was regarded by the 'Afej shaikhs as an affront intended to diminish their personal income, since they were entitled to one sixth of the wages recieved by their own tribesmen. Besides, murderers and other desperadoes, who had fled from various parts of the country to the safer districts of the Khor el-Afej, were never lacking, and were always ready to join in a conspiracy which would lead to stealing and burning, and thus raise their importance in the eyes of the people. In spite of the friendly assurances from the Arabs, there prevailed a general sense of insecurity all the while around Nuffar, which, indeed, is the atmosphere more or less characteristic of all modern Babylonia.

Fortunately, however, there was one circumstance which proved of priceless value to the members of the expedition. The notion was spread among the 'Afej and their neighboring tribes that the foreigners were armed with great magical power, and that, in punishment of the firing and plundering of their camp, they had brought upon their enemies the cholera, which was not quite extinct even in the year following. Several successful treatments of light ailments, and exceedingly bitter concoctions wisely administered to various healthy chiefs, who were curious to see and to taste the truth of all that was constantly reported, served only to assure and confirm this belief; and Peters, on his part, seized every opportunity to encourage and to develop such sentiment among the credulous 'Afej. He intimated to them that nothing was hidden from his knowledge, and that the accursed money which had been stolen would find its way back to him; he made mysterious threats of sore affliction and loss by death which would cause consternation among them; and to demonstrate his superior power and to indicate some of the terrible things which might happen at any moment, he finally gave them a drastic exhibition of his cunning art, which had a tremendous effect upon all who saw it. We will quote the story in his own language: "Just before sunset, when the men were all in camp and at leisure, so that I was sure they would notice what we did, Noorian and I ascended a high point of the mound near by, he solemnly bearing a compass before me on an improvised black cushion. There, by the side of an old trench, we went through a complicated hocus-pocus with the compass, a Turkish dictionary, a spring tape-measure, and a pair of field glasses, the whole camp watching us in puzzled wonder. Imme-

diately after our dinner, while most of the men were still busy eating, we stole up the hill, having left to Haynes the duty of preventing any one from leaving the camp. Our fireworks were somewhat primitive and slightly dangerous, so that the trench which we had chosen for our operations proved rather close quarters. The first rocket had scarcely gone off when we could hear a buzz of excited voices below us. When the second and third followed, the cry arose that we were making the stars fall from heaven. The women screamed and hid themselves in the huts, and the more timid among the men followed suit. As Roman candles and Bengal lights followed, the excitement grew more intense. At last we came to our *piece de resistance,* the tomatocan firework. At first this fizzled and bade fair to ruin our whole performance. Then, just as we despaired of success, it exploded with a great noise, knocking us over backward in the trench, behind a wall in which we were hidden, and filling the air with fiery serpents hissing and sputtering in every direction. The effect was indescribably diabolical, and every man, woman, and child, guards included, fled screaming, to seek for hiding-places, overcome with terror." Comp. Layard, "Nineveh and Babylon," London, 1853, p. 557.

Great as the immediate impression of the fearful spectacle was upon the minds of the naive children of the desert, who firmly believed in the uncanny powers of demons or *jinna,* this successful coup did not stop future quarrels, pilfering, and murderous attempts altogether, nor did it secure for the camp a much needed immunity from illness and the embarrassing consequences of the great drought which at the outset was upon the waters of Babylon, or of the subsequent deluge, which turned the whole country into one huge puddle and the semi-subterranean storehouses, kitchens, and stables of the camp into as many cisterns. Poor Dr. Aftimus, on whose technical knowledge the fondest hopes had been built, was himself taken down with typhoid fever the very day the party arrived at

N'uffar. Without having treated a single Arab he had to be sent back to Baghdad while in a state of delirium, but fortunately he recovered slowly in the course of the winter. After this rather discouraging first experience of medical assistance in connection with our archaeological explorations, we have never had courage to repeat the experiment. With a simple diet, some personal care, and a strict observation of the ordinary sanitary laws, the expedition as a whole escaped or overcame the peculiar dangers of the Babylonian climate during the following campaigns.

In spite of all the disappointments and hardships, which were scarcely less in the second year than they had been in the first, the great purpose of the expedition was not for a moment lost sight of. Our past excavations had been scattered over the entire surface of the mounds. Trial trenches had been cut in many places, to ascertain the general character and contents of the ruins, until work finally concentrated at three conspicuous points, — the temple (I), the so-called tablet hill (IV), and the more recent building with its fine court of columns near our old camp (VII) and the long ridge to the southeast of it. By means of written documents, the first expedition had adduced conclusive evidence that the ruins of Nuffar contained monuments of the time of Naram-Sin (about 3750 B. c.) and even of a period considerably antedating it. It had discovered numerous remains of the third pre-Christian millennium, and clearly demonstrated that thousands of tablets and fragments of the ancient temple library still existed in the large triangular mound to the south of the temple complex, thereby almost determining the very site of this famous library. It furthermore had traced the history of Nippur by a few inscriptions through the second millennium down to the time of the Persian kings, and lastly shown, in connection with Parthian coins and constructions, Sassanian seals, Hebrew and Mandean bowls, Kufic coins of the 'Abbaside caliphs, and other antiquities, that parts of the ruined city were inhabited as late as the ninth century of our own era. In other words, it had submitted material enough to prove that at least five thousand years of ancient history were represented by this enormous site. It remained for the second and the following expeditions to fill this vast period with the necessary details, and, if possible, even to extend its limits by concentrated methodical excavations at the principal elevations.

Among the various mounds and ridges which constitute the ruins of Nuffar, there was none more important than the conical hill of Bint el-Amir with its irregular plateau of *debris* (I), containing the stage-tower and temple of Bel. "This great mass of earth covered a surface of more than eight acres," the careful examination of which was an ambitious problem in itself, especially as none of the large Babylonian temples had yet been excavated completely. At the outset the expedition had therefore decided to investigate this complex methodically, to determine its characteristic architectural features, and to trace its development through all the periods of Babylonian history down to its final decay. But owing to the large accumulations of rubbish and the very limited time in the first year at our disposal, we had not been able to do much more than to fix the corners of the ancient *ziggurrat* and to run trenches along its peculiar lateral additions. As the latter were constructed of large crude bricks and surrounded by extensive remains of rooms built of the same material, and as numerous antiquities of the Hellenistic period and coins of the Arsacide kings (about 250 B. c-226 A. D.) were unearthed in connection with them, I had "reached the conclusion that the ruins we had found were those of a Parthian fortress built on the site of the ancient temple; and the majority of the members of the expedition inclined to this opinion." But soon afterwards Peters changed his conviction and put forth his own theory, according to which we "had found the ancient temple of Bel" itself. For the following years it was impossible for me to test his statements by a personal examination of the trenches; and as Haynes simply adopted his predecessor's theory

and failed to throw any new light on this fundamental question, there remained nothing but either to acquiesce in Peters' view, which, however, ignored essential facts brought to light by the previous excavations, and was contrarv to certain established laws of Babylonian architecture, or to regard the famous sanctuary of Bel as a hopeless mass of crumbling walls, fragmentary platforms, broken drains, and numerous wells, reported by Haynes to exist at widely separated levels, often in very strange places and without any apparent connection with each other.

Comp. Peters, "Nippur," vol. ii, p. 118, where he reproduces my view correctly, except that he substitutes Sassanian for Parthian, owing to his frequently indiscriminate use of these two words (comp. p. 129 of the same work).

What were the new features developed at this " perplexing mound" in the course of the second campaign? By engaging a maximum force of four hundred Arab laborers, half from Hilla and Jumjuma, half from the 'Afej tribes around Nuffar, and by placing the greater part of his men at the temple mounds, the director was able to attack the problem more vigorously and to remove such an enormous mass of rubbish that at the end of his work he could boast "that in cubic feet of earth excavated, and size and depth of trenches," his excavations " far surpassed any others ever undertaken in Babylonia," and that De Sarzec's work of several seasons at Tello " was probably not even the tenth part as large as our work of as many months." But this difference was due to various causes, and not the least to the difference of methods pursued bv the two explorers, quite aside from the fact that the amount of rubbish extracted from a ruin can never be used as a standard by which the success or failure of an archaeological mission is to be judged. Peters himself characterizes his manner of excavating as follows: "We sank small well-shafts or deep narrow trenches, in many cases to the depth of fifty feet or more, and pierced innumerable small tunnels (one of them 120 feet in length) after the native method." In

other words, he examined the mounds pretty much as the Arab peasants did at Babylon, F.l-Birs, and other places, only on Comp. Peters, /. c, vol. ii, pp. Ill, *scq.* a larger scale, — either by deep perpendicular holes or by "innumerable" horizontal mines, instead of peeling off the single layers successively and carefully. Was this scientific research? The results, as indicated above, were naturally commensurate with the method employed. Peters did not procure a satisfactory plan nor the necessary details of the originally well-preserved vast complex of buildings which occupied the site of the temple of Bel " at the time of its last great construction;" he failed to ascertain its character and purpose, and to define its precise relation to the *ziggurrat;* he was unable to determine its age, or even to fix the two extreme limits of the three successive periods of its occupation; and he did not recognize that the line of booths situated outside of the southeast fortified enclosure and yielding him a fine collection of inscribed Cassite monuments belonged to the same general epoch as the mass of crude brickwork covering the temple. As far as possible, his assertions have either been verified or corrected by the present writer's later investigations on the ruins. But, unfortunately, much of the precious material had been removed in the course of the second and third campaigns, or was subsequently destroyed by rain and other causes, so that it could no longer be used for the study and reconstruction of the history of the venerable sanctuary of Nippur.

The following is Peters' own view in a nutshell: There are about sixteen feet of ruins below a surface layer of three feet, which represent the last important restoration of the ancient temple by a monarch " not far removed from Nebuchadrezzar in time," and living about 500 B. c. This ruler consequently can have been only one of the Persian kings, notably Darius I, or perhaps Xerxes. The sacred precincts were no longer " consecrated to the worship of Bel," but stood in the service of "a new religion. " The old form of the *ziggurrat* was changed by " huge buttress-like wings added on each of the four sides," which gave the structure "a cruciform shape unlike that of any other *ziggurrat* yet discovered." The sanctuary continued to exist in the new form for about three hundred to three hundred and fifty years, until after the Seleucidan period, somewhere about or before 150 B. c., when men ceased to make additions or repairs, and the ancient temple of Bel fell gradually into ruins.

It is unnecessary to disprove this fantastic theory in detail. Peters' own excavations and our previous and later discoveries make it entirely impossible. But while we cannot accept his inferences, which are contrary to all the evidence produced, we recognize that he brought to light a number of facts and antiquities, which enable us to establish at least some of the more general features of this latest reconstruction. He showed that a considerable area around the *ziggurrat* was enclosed by two gigantic walls protected by towers. He ascertained their dimensions, followed their courses, and described the extraordinary size of their bricks. He excavated fourteen chambers on the top of one of the outer walls, and found the entire space between the inner wall and the *ziggurrat* occupied completely by similar rooms. He arrived at the conclusion that the various constructions belonged together and formed an organic whole. A long, narrow street, however, which ran parallel with the southeastern line of fortifications, divided the houses in the interior into two distinct sections. Several of the chambers in the southern part were filled with "great masses of water-jars piled together." They doubtless had served as storerooms; others were kitchens, as indicated "by the fireplaces and other arrangements;" while in some of the rooms "were curious closets with thin clay partitions." The rubbish of most of the chambers yielded numerous fragments of pottery of the Hellenistic and Roman periods, remarkable among them a fine brown enamelled lamp (head of Medusa), and many terra-cotta figurines, especially heads of women frequently wearing a peculiar high head-dress, children, and groups of lovers. 11 is a characteristic feature of these late Babylonian terra-cottas that they are generally hollow in the interior, while their outside is often covered with a chalk paste by which the artist endeavored to work out the delicate facial lines, the curled hair, the graceful foldings of the garments, and other details, with greater accuracy, and thus to produce a better effect of the whole figure, which sometimes also was colored. Teeth of wild boars repeatedly found in this stratum indicate that the occupants of those later constructions were fond of hunting the characteristic animal of the swamps around Nippur.

From the extraordinary amount of dirt and debris accumulated during the period of occupancy of the rooms, and from the different styles of art exhibited by the antiquities discovered in them, it became evident that these latest constructions must have been inhabited for several hundred years. A similar result was obtained by an examination of the stage-tower. It was observed that the *ziggurrat* of the cruciform shape above referred to, which consisted only of two stages, had two or three distinct additions, and that the unbaked material employed in them was identical with that found in the rooms around it.

Lamp in Brown Enamelled Terra-cotta *From a room of the latctt itmplc construction* Comp. *f. g.,* the central head of the illustration facing p. 128 of Peters' second volume, and Nos. 31 and 32 of Hilprecht, "The Babylonian Expedition of the University of Pennsylvania," series A, vol. ix, plates xiv and xv, Nos. 3 l and 32.

In his endeavor to reach the older remains before the more recent strata had been investigated in the least adequately, Peters broke through the outer casing of the *ziggurrat* built of "immense blocks of adobe," in a cavity of which he discovered a well-preserved goose egg, and perceived that there was an older stage-tower of quite a different form and much smaller dimensions enclosed within the other. By means of a diagonal trench cut through its centre, he ascertained its height and characteristic features down to the level of Ur-Gur, and came to the conclusion (which, however, did not prove correct) that the *ziggurrat* of this ancient monarch was the earliest erected at Nippur. "Wells and similar shafts were sunk at other points of the temple," especially at the northern and western corners, where he reached original constructions of Ashurbanapal (668-626 B. c.) and Ur-Gur (about 2700 B. c), and discovered scattered bricks with the names of Esarhaddon (681-668 B. c.), Ramman-shumusur (about iioo B.c.), Kadashman-Turgu (about 1250 B. c.), Kurigalzu (about 1300 B. c.), Bur-Sin of Nisin (about 2500 B. c.), in addition to those previously found, "showing that many kings of many ages had honored the temple of Bel at Nippur." At a place near the western corner of the *ziggurrat,* on the northwestern side, he descended through a tunnel some six feet below the plain level, striking a terra-cotta drain with a platform at its mouth and a wall of plano-convex bricks similar to those preceding the time of Ur-Nina at Tello, in which he unearthed also a beautiful, highly polished jade axe-head and an inscribed pre-Sargonic clay tablet..

Immediately in front of the southeastern face of the stagetower, Peters conducted a larger trench with a view of ascertaining the successive strata of the whole temple plateau. Below the level of the Parthian castle he disclosed " a mass of rubble and debris containing no walls, but great quantities of bricks, some of them with green glazed surfaces, and many bearing inscriptions of Ashurbanapal." In penetrating a few feet farther, he came upon fragments of pavements and soon afterwards upon the crude brick terrace of Ur-Gur. As he saw that the walls and towers of the Parthian fortress, which required a more solid foundation, descended to this deep level, he unhesitatingly pronounced them to have been in existence 2500 years before they were built, and "thought it not impossible" that at that ancient time two of these formidable fortification towers "were columns of the same general significance as the Jachin and Boaz which stood before the Temple of Yahweh Jehovah at

Jerusalem "! While excavating in the stratum immediately above Ur-Gur's platform, he came accidentally upon the first three door-sockets and a brick stamp of Shargani-shar-ali, soon afterwards identified by me as Sargon I, the famous king of Agade, who according to Nabonidos lived about 3800 B. c., but who until then had been regarded generally as a half-mythical person. In the same layer there were found about eighty fragments of stone vases and other antiquities inscribed with the names of Manishtusu and Urumush (Alusharshid), two kings of Kish little known, who lived about the same time; Lugalzaggisi and Lugalkigubnidudu, two even earlier rulers of Erech, and Kntemena, *patesi* of Lagash, familiar to us from De Sarzec's excavations. In spite of Haynes" very emphatic statement to the contrary, Peters claims to have reached the real level of Sargon and his predecessors at two points within the court of the *ziggurrat*, in one case descending almost sixteen feet below the present plain. Be this as it may, the building remains, which he had hitherto disclosed, were examined by him far too poorly and unsystematically to convey to us even a tolerably clear idea of the revered sanctuary of Bel; and the inscriptions gathered were so small or fragmentary that they furnished us little more than the names and titles of ancient kings and *patesis*. But the material obtained sufficed to show that there were considerable ancient Babylonian ruins, and numerous though generally broken cuneiform inscriptions, including even antiquities contemporaneous with the earliest monuments of Tello, contained in the temple hill of Nuffar.

It is characteristic of Peters' work in the second year that it was not carried on with the purpose of excavating one or two layers at one or more of the principal mounds of the enormous site methodically, but with the intention of "sounding" as many places as possible, and of discovering inscribed objects. Consequently he dug a little here and a little there and disturbed many strata at the same time. No wonder that he opened trenches also in the southern and

southeastern ridges of the *ziggurrat.* Nothing of importance came to light in the former, but his labors were crowned with a remarkable success in the latter. Examining the plan of the ruins of Nuffar on p. 305, it will be observed that the temple mound (I) is separated from mound IV, which I regarded as the probable site of the library, by a deep depression doubtless representing an old branch of the Shatt en-Nil. On the northeastern edge of this gully there is a low wall-like elevation, which rises only about thirteen feet above the plain. It was in this narrow ridge that Peters excavated more than twenty rooms resting on a terrace of earth and built of precisely the same material — " unbaked bricks of large, almost square blocks," as characterizes the late construction on the top of the temple of Bel. Under ordinary circumstances he probably would have drawn the obvious inference that both belong to the same period. But the discovery in one of these rooms of a large number of Cassite votive objects — the first great collection of antiquities of this dynasty ever found — induced him to ascribe this whole row of booths to a time a thousand years earlier than it actuallv was. He formulated a new fantastic theory, according to which these cameos of agate and thin round tablets of lapis lazuli, with their brief votive inscriptions, were sold as charms to pilgrims, some of them being " a sort of masses said for the repose of the soul of such and such a king." The true facts are the following. All these interesting Cassite relics in agate, magnesite, feldspar, ivory, turquoise, malachite, lapis lazuli, and an imitation of the last-mentioned three stones in glass, "together with gold, amethyst, porphyry and other material not vet worked," were originally contained in a wooden box, traces of which (carbonized fragments and copper nails) were lying around them. Most, if not indeed the whole, of this unique collection had been presented by a number of Cassite kings to various shrines of the temple of Bel somewhere between 1400 and 1200 B. c. A thousand years later, when the temple was in ruins, an inhabitant of

Nippur, and himself a dealer in precious stones, searched in the neighborhood of his booth for raw material, and discovered them, or purchased them from other diggers. He was about to manufacture beads for necklaces and bracelets, rings, charms, and the like out of them, when another catastrophe befel Nippur. Several other "jeweller's shops" of the Parthian period excavated by our expedition at different sections of the ruins established the correctness of this interpretation beyond any doubt. And when in May, 1900, I spent a few days with the expedition at Babylon, Koldewey had found a similar shop in the mound of 'O(A)mran ibn 'AH, which, besides purely Parthian antiquities, contained several more ancient objects from various Babylonian ruins, and for this reason proved particularly instructive. No sooner had the German explorer submitted the inscribed objects of this shop to me for examination, than 1 recognized and pointed out to him a number of Cassite objects, which, according to their material, forms, and inscriptions belonged originally to the temple at Nippur, illustrating in an excellent way how the trade in "useful" antiquities flourished in Babylonia even two thousand years before our own time.

A votive cylinder of Kurigalzu in agate had been cut into three beads without regard to its legend; a votive inscription had been erased insufficiently from an axe-head in lapis lazuli; a small block of the same material showed a deep incision beneath the inscribed portion, just about to be cut off, while several other blocks in lapis lazuli and magnesite had been reduced considerably from their original weight, as could easily be established. Comp. Hilprecht, "The Babylonian Expedition of the University of Pennsylvania," series A, vol. i, part 1, nos. 28, 50, 74, and plate xi, nos. 25 and 28; part 2, no. 140, and *Zeituhrift fur Asssriologic,* pp. 190, seqq., where, misled by Peters' reports, I gave an erroneous interpretation of the facts treated above.

An even more far-reaching discovery, the real significance of which lies in its bearing upon the topography of ancient

Nippur, but again unfortunately not recognized by Peters, was made a little to the northwest of these booths. This was a shrine of Bur-Sin I, the walls of which were built of baked brick laid in bitumen, and were still seven to fourteen courses high. Consisting of two rooms, it stood upon a platform of the same material and faced inward toward the entrance to the court of the *ziggurrat*. According to the legends inscribed on the bricks and on two doorsockets found *in situ*, it had been dedicated to Bel himself about 2600 B. c. A pair of clasped hands from a dolerite statue similar to those excavated at Tello, a number of inscribed fragments of bas-reliefs, and an archaic mortar dec As Thureau-Dangin has recently shown that there was only one dynasty of Ur in the third pre-Christian millennium, Bur-Sin of Nisin, hitherto classified as Bur-Sin I, must henceforth be called Bur-Sin II, while Bur-Sin of Ur takes the first place.

orated with an eagle and a snake evidently fighting with each other were taken from the debris around it, bearing witness to the elaborate manner in which the ancient Babylonians embellished their temples. As we shall have to say a few words about the relation of this shrine to the *ziggurrat* later, when we give a summary of the principal results of the Philadelphia expedition, we continue at present to sketch Dr. Peters' explorations on the other mounds of Nuffar.

To the east of our first camp we had previously discovered the remains of tapering brick columns, symmetrically arranged around an open square court (VII). It was natural to suppose that this peculiar structure belonged to a more pretentious building with interesting architectural features, as the mere presence of columns indicated sufficiently. Though the present writer had assigned it without hesitation to the Seleucido-Parthian period (about 250 B. c.), it was desirable and necessary to excavate it completely, before the more important Babylonian strata beneath it should be examined. In order to execute this task, Peters began to remove the Jewish and early Arabic houses representing the

latest traces of human settlements everywhere in the precincts of ancient Nippur, and the numerous Parthian and Sassanian coffins, sepulchral urns, and pottery drains immediately below them. The former were characterized by Kufic coins, Hebrew, Arabic, and Mandean incantation bowls, and other articles of domestic use, which were generally found in low and narrow rooms made of mud-bricks. We had frequently noticed the outlines of their walls in the preceding year, as we walked over the hills in the early morning, when the rapidly evaporating humidity of the ground drew the saltpetre contained in the clay to the surface. The tombs, on the other hand, occurred in an indescribable confusion in all possible positions and at nearly Comp. p. 283, above. every depth in the layer of rubbish which filled the space between the uppermost settlement and the floor of the building just mentioned to the height of six to ten feet. In no instance, however, were they discovered below the level of the court of columns, while repeatedly the burial-shafts were cut through the walls of the rooms grouped around it. Hence it follows that these interments must have taken place at a time when the imposing building was already in ruins, — in other words, at a period commencing shortly before our own era, and terminating about the sixth or seventh century A. D. , if the palace in question was really of Seleucido-Parthian origin. This, however, was contested by Peters, who believed to have found evidence that the structure was a thousand years earlier. His work in and around this building may be sketched briefly as follows:—

The open court flanked by columns having been excavated completely in 1889, Peters undertook next to search for the rooms to which it probably gave light and access. As, in consequence of the slope of the hill, a considerable part of the ancient building had been washed away in the northeast and southeast directions, he concentrated his efforts upon an examination of the highest section of the mound, exploring especially the ruined mass southwest of the colonnade. He was soon able to show that,

contrary to our previous theory, certain pieces of charred wood and small heaps of ashes discovered along the edge of the court did not belong to subsequent burials, but were remains of palm beams which originally rested on the columns and stretched across a narrow space to the walls of chambers surrounding the former on all four sides. We should expect that Peters, once having established this interesting fact, would have spared no pains to examine a building systematically, which, as late as 1897, he described as "the most interesting and ambitious structure excavated at Nippur next to the temple." But judging, as he did, the success of his expedition mainly "by the discovery of inscribed objects or failure to discover them," ' and nervously endeavoring to secure them at all hazards, he unfortunately adopted the injurious and antiquated methods of Layard and Rassam, which I have characterized above, also for the exploration of the west section of the ruins. Instead of removing layer after layer of all the superincumbent rubbish, he excavated only portions of seven rooms with their adjoining corridors by digging along their walls and leaving the central mass untouched. And when even this process proved too slow and tedious, he drove tunnels into the mound above and below the floor of the building, which afterwards caved in, ruined part of the construction, and caused infinite trouble to himself and his successors. At the same time the excavated earth was not carried to a previously explored place at a safe distance, but was dumped on the same mound, and in part on an unexplored section of the very ruins which he was desirous to examine, and whence the present writer had to remove it ten years later. We cannot, therefore, be surprised that the results finally obtained were correspondingly meagre and unsatisfactory. Peters ascertained that a building of considerable extent and importance, constructed "of unbaked brick in large blocks," was buried there; he determined its west corner, traced its southwestern boundary wall for 164 feet, found several uninscribed door-sockets *in situ*, and inferred from the numerous remains of charred wood, burned barley, and large red spots seen everywhere on the walls, doubtless due to the effects of intense heat, that the whole complex must have been destroyed by fire. Thus far we can follow him without difficulty. But though nothing but late antiquities' had been discovered within this enclosure, he arrived at the startling conclusion that the large structure was a Cassite palace, "erected somewhere between 1450 and 1250 B. c." How was this possible? These are his arguments: On the one hand, he unearthed a nest of about three hundred fine clay tablets and many fragments dated in the reigns of Kurigalzu, Kadashman-Turgu and Nazi-Maruttash, lying in the loose earth outside the southwest wall of the building in question, several yards away from it, and slightly below its level. On the other hand, he saw a building with similar columns on the top of a mound otherwise unknown, called Abu Adhem, a little to the south ofjokha. As antiquities of a period preceding 2000 B. c. had been picked up by various travellers at Jokha and other neighboring hills, which are situated "in the sphere of influence ofTello," he concluded — strange to say—that the building at Abu Adhem "belonged to the middle of the third millennium B. c." I confess my inability to follow this kind of reasoning or to appreciate his "evidence of the surrounding mounds." If, indeed, the colonnade of Abu Adhem were as ancient as Dr. Peters supposes it to be, and On p. 202 of his "Nippur," vol. ii, Peters makes the committee in Philadelphia responsible fur his methods of exploration. As I was secretary of that committee, I should know of "the constant demand of the home committee" for inscribed objects. But there is no such "demand" contained anywhere in our minutes, nor do I remember any such order ever having been sent through me to Dr. Peters. The true attitude of the committee is illustrated by the fact that it was "favorably impressed with the results accomplished by the first year's campaign" (comp. Peters, /. c, vol. ii, p. 5), and that ten years later it sup-

ported me energetically in my efforts to change the obnoxious methods of excavation inaugurated by Peters and adopted by Haynes.
Comp. pp. 103, seq., 194, seq., 321, seq. , 328, seq. Comp. Peters, /. c, vol. ii, pp. 179, seq., and the plan facing p. 178. Except the fragment of a statue in dolerite (a woman holding a lamb, comp. Peters, /. c., vol. ii, p. 184), which belonged to the third preChristian millennium. Being out of its original place, it was discovered in a Jewish house on the top of the hill. A ruin which, by the way, also has its Seleucido-Parthian palace lying on the top of the temple mound. As to Peters's naive arguments, comp. his "Nippur," vol. ii, pp. I 86, seqq. not, rather, Parthian, as everything indicates, why did he not make the columns of Nippur, which are " precisely like them," precisely as old? Apparently because the discovery of Cassite tablets outside the large complex did not allow this. But are we on their account justified in claiming the structure as Cassite? Certainly not. On the contrary, they prove that the Cassite houses once occupying this site must have been in ruins at the time when the palace was erected, and that consequently the latter and its brick terrace, for the construction of which the older stratum had to be disturbed and levelled, cannot be contemporaneous with the Cassite rulers mentioned above, but must be of a considerably more recent date.
The exploration of the large and important building remains grouped around the ziggurraf and "the court of columns" had formed one of Peters' principal tasks during his second campaign. But his hope of discovering many inscribed Babylonian tablets while excavating these ruins was not to be realized. To find these eagerly-sought treasures somewhere in the vast mounds he had conducted extensive excavations from the beginning in several other parts of the ruins. Above all, he most naturally had directed his attention to the triangular mound (IV) to the south of the temple, which had yielded almost all the tablets obtained by the first expedition. He now "riddled it with trenches every-

where" and without difficulty secured about 2000 tablets more of the same general type as those discovered previously — business documents, school exercises, and numerous tablets of a strictly scientific or literary character, especially astronomical, mathematical, and medical. As, however, Peters did not possess the necessary Assyriological knowledge to determine their age and contents, and as, moreover, these tablets were never deposited in any large number together, but "seemed to lie loose in the earth" or "confused among buildings with which they did not belong,"' he came to the conclusion that this hill with its two principal strata, which 1 had declared to be the probable site of the temple library, was " the home of well-to-do citizens, rather than the site of the great public building of the city," and abandoned it towards the middle of March, "because he had ceased to find tablets in paying quantities." Comp. the plan of the ruins on p. 305, above. Comp. Peters, I.e., vol. ii, p. 199.
It was about the same time that the southeastern wing of the mounds on the other side of the canal (VI, and the ridge immediately to the northwest of it) began to yield tablets " in an extraordinary manner." The prospect of a more rapid increase of the coveted inscriptions being thus given, all the "tablet diggers" were transferred at once to this new promising locality. Before many weeks had elapsed, more than 5,000 tablets and fragments had been gathered, so that with regard to the mere number of clay documents recovered, Peters might well be pleased with the success which he had scored. Without troubling himself about the methical examination and removal of the highest strata, which in the previous year had yielded contracts of the late Babylonian and Persian periods, he cut "soundingtrenches at various points in the interior, where the water had washed out deep gullies." In every instance he came upon rooms of mud brick containing "quantities of tablets," mixed with earth and grotesque clay figures of Bel and his consort. There was in particular one chamber,

thirtytwo feet long by sixteen feet wide, which was literally filled with them. So numerous were the tablets there "that it took thirty or forty men four days to dig them out and bring them into camp. " For the most part they were unbaked, and lay in fragments on the floor. But as the ashes observed in connection with them clearly indicated, they originally "had been placed around the walls of the Comp. *ibidem,* pp. 200-203.

room on wooden shelves," which broke or were burned, when the house was destroyed and the roof fell in. All the tablets discovered in these rooms and in this ridge in general are so-called private contracts and official records, such as receipts, tax-lists, statements of income and expense written in behalf of the government and of the temple, and, as a rule, are dated according to the reigns of the last kings of Ur (about 2600 B. C.), the first dynasty of Babylon (about 2300-2000 B. C), Rim-Sin of Larsa (a contemporary of Hammurabi), and especially several kings of the Cassite dynasty (about 1400-1 200 B. C). The older documents are valuable chiefly for their closing lines containing brief references to the principal historical events, after which the single years of the monarchs were called and counted. The tax-lists from the latter half of the second millennium are of importance because of their bearing upon the chronology of the Cassite kings, and because they give us a first insight into the civil administration of Central Babylonia under those foreign conquerors of whom previously we knew little more than their names, and these often enough only very imperfectly.

Peters confesses frankly: "My trenches here were dug principally for tablets." Little attention, therefore, could be paid to the fundamental question, whether at the different period»of its occupation this ridge was covered with "ordinary houses" only, or whether the single rooms formed an organic whole, an annex of the temple, a large government Peters' statement, /. c, vol. ii, p. 212, is one-sided and incorrect.

There are only about fifty to one hundred tablets among them which are dat-

ed in the reigns of Assyrian, neo-Babylonian, and Persian kings. They were taken from the upper stratum. /.. c, vol. ii, p. 212. Peters' statement "In no case did we find structures of any importance" (p. 211) is of little value. His comparison of the "ordinary houses" discovered in this ridge with those unearthed in mound IV illustrates his curious conception of the character of Babylonian public buildings. building with registering offices, a kind of bazaar, or both, as seems to result with great probability from a study of the tablets and from later discoveries made in this neighborhood by the present writer. Indeed, it was a dark day when Peters decided to excavate the ruins of Nuffar without the aid of a specialist, whether Assyriologist or architect. Fortunately Pognon, then French consul at Baghdad, occasionally lent a helping hand in determining the age and contents of some of the better preserved inscriptions from squeezes and photographs submitted to him, and Peters could congratulate himself that at the time of his greatest need a Hungarian engineer, in the employ of the Ottoman government, Coleman d'Emey, appeared suddenly in the camp to hunt in the Babylonian swamps. He was easily induced to devote part of his time to a renewed survey of the principal ruins and to the preparation of plans of the excavated walls and rooms of the two Parthian palaces. It is true, according to the director's own statement, the real merits of his dVawings are to be judged leniently, but in connection with Peters' scanty notes they enabled us at least to form a general idea of the character and disposition of the latest constructions on the temple mound.

On the third day of May the excavations of the second campaign came to a more peaceful ending than those in the previous year. Before the trenches were abandoned, Peters very wisely decided to send part of his material out of the country, "to insure the preservation of something in case of disaster." For in consequence of his stubborn refusal to pay the often demanded blood-money to the Sa'id, the disappointed tribe very

naturally sought to indemnify itself in another way. A first boat-load of antiquities had left Nuffar safely towards the end of April. At the same time Haynes, who not without reason feared being waylaid and plundered by a *g/iazu,* "stole away in the night," and "pressed through to Hilla in hot haste." To prevent an attack planned by the enemy upon his camp for the night preceding the final departure of the expedition, Peters "resorted once more to stratagem, and gave a second exhibition of fireworks," which again had the desired effect. The Sa'id then hoped to intercept him as he left the territory of the 'Afej, and try to extort blackmail. But the American slipped out of their hands before they realized that he had gone. As soon as all the workmen from Jumjuma had been sent in detachments through the marshes and everything was packed upon the last boats, including the Turkish commissioner and the *zabtiye,* Peters and Noorian, accompanied by some trusted Arab laborers and a personal servant, turned to the village of Hajji Tarfa to examine the more prominent mounds in the south. With a door-socket of GimilSin of Ur (about 2550 B. c.) picked up at Muqayyar, and with another of the same monarch and a whole box of fine tablets, through a fortunate accident discovered at Jokha after a little scratching of the surface, they returned to the north by way of Samawa, Nejef, and Kerbela, reaching Baghdad on the yth of June, 1890. About a week later Peters was on his way to the Mediterranean coast, returning to America in November, while Haynes and Noorian left the country separately by different routes and at different times in the course of the same year.

Comp. Peters, /. c,, vol. ii, pp. 51 and 280. Comp. Peters, /. c., vol. ii, pp. 90, *seqq. Third Campaign, 181)3-181)6.* In view of the large number of inscribed objects unearthed by him, Peters felt greatly encouraged as to future explorations at Nuffar, and looked upon his method of excavating in a somewhat different light from that in which it has been viewed by others. He was so much pleased with the tangible results which he had to show that before leaving the ruins he wrote to the committee urging early resumption of the work under Haynes alone according to the principles laid down by him. As the two men were in entire accord as to the feasibility of such a plan, and as two members of the committee "warmly advocated it,"" promising to work towards its realization if the Ottoman government should apportion a sufficient number of antiquities to the University of Pennsylvania, Dr. Peters' methods of exploring soon had another chance of being tested with regard to their actual merits. For upon the recommendation of Hamdy Bey, who had not forgotten the extraordinary difficulties and losses of our first expedition and the praiseworthy energy and perseverance displayed by the second, the Sultan presented to the American university all those tablets and archaeological objects not required to complete the collections of the Imperial Museum. As soon as the present writer had sufficiently recovered from a long and severe illness contracted at Nuffar, which had made him an invalid for almost a year, he commenced the study of the newly acquired cuneiform material and reported on its great interest and value. In the spring of 1892 the committee decided upon another expedition, the details of which were arranged "at a meeting in Newport between Dr. Pepper, Mr. K. W. Clark, Mr. Haynes, and Dr. Peters."

The last-mentioned gentleman "drew up with Haynes the plan of work, and drafted general instructions for the conduct of the excavations,"-while it was left to Professor Hilprecht to prepare a list of all the known Babylonian kings and *patesis* in cuneiform writing with an accurate reproduction of the pala?ographical peculiarities of the Nuffar inscriptions, and to write down such additional hints as might enable Haynes to find and to identify the names of the principal rulers on the different monuments.

About the same time a committee on publications was formed with Mr. C. H. Clark as chairman, and H. V. Hilprecht as secretary and editor-in-chief.

On the basis of a detailed plan submitted by the latter, the results of the expeditions were authorized to be published in four distinct series. With the aid of the American Philosophical Society the first volume of Series A appeared in 1893, and a second part in 1896, while two years later (1898), through the deep interest of a public-spirited citizen of Philadelphia, Mr. Eckley Coxe, Jr., the University of Pennsylvania was enabled to issue a third volume under its own name. As the most important antiquities had remained in Constantinople, it soon became necessary for the committee to despatch its editor to the Turkish capital for the examination of those antiquities. While engaged in this work, in 1893, he was approached by the administration of the Imperial Ottoman Museum with the proposition to reorganize its Babylonian section during his summer vacations in the course of the following years. He accepted the honorable task," but in declining the liberal remuneration offered, asked for the favor of this opportunity to show his personal appreciation of the energetic support which the Ottoman government had granted to the Philadelphia expeditions. With especial gratitude I testify here also to the extraordinary help which our subsequent scientific missions have received from the same government. Thanks to the gracious personal protection which His Majesty the Sultan henceforth extended to our various labors in his domain, and to the lively and cordial interest with which his ministers and the two directors of the Imperial Museum accompanied the progress of the work in Constantinople and at Nuffar, our ways were smoothed everywhere in the Ottoman empire. As often as I needed a firman, it was readily granted, while besides, His Majesty, desiring to give special proof of his personal satisfaction with the confidence thus established and with the services rendered, most generously and repeatedly bestowed magnificent gifts of antiquities upon the present writer, which subsequently were presented to the University of Pennsylvania, making the scientific value of its Babylonian collections not only equal

but in many respects superior to those of the British Museum. stay at the ruins. The two principal shaikhs of the Hamza, 'Abud el-Hamid and Hamid el-Birjud, in whose territory the mounds of Nuffar are situated, were summoned to the guest-chamber (mudhif of the ruler of all the 'Afej. But having carefully laid their own scheme, through which they hoped to squeeze the largest possible revenues out of the pockets of their old friends from beyond " the great upper sea in the West," they did not respond very eagerly to the call of the messenger. When finally they appeared in the course of the following day, both declared that it was utterly impossible to guarantee the safety of the expedition without a permanent guard of forty men from their own tribes. After much haggling the two interested parties agreed upon ten Arabs as a sufficient number to insure the welfare of Haynes and his party. Two hours later the explorer arrived with his boats at Berdi's old village, then governed temporarily by the latter's younger brother, 'Asi, with whom he pitched his tents for a few days until he had selected a suitable site for his own camp at Nuffar.

Comp. Peters' own story, /. (., vol. ii, pp. 342, *seq.* Comp. Peters, /. c., vol. ii, pp. 369, *seqq.* Comp. Peters, /. c., vol. ii, p. 371. "The Babylonian Expedition of the University of Pennsylvania, edited by H. V. Hilprccht, Series A: Cuneiform Texts." The volumes thus far published are vol. i, "Old Babylonian Inscriptions, chiefly from Nippur," by the editor, part I, 1893, part 2, 1896; and vol. ix, "Business Documents of Murashu Sons of Nippur," by H. V. Hilprecht and A. T. Clay, 1898. Several other volumes are in the course of preparation. A more rapid publication was hitherto impossible, owing to the extraordinary difficulties connected with the deciphering and restoration of the fragmentary inscriptions (comp. vol. i, part 2, plates 36-49) and the faithful reproduction of all their palzeographical peculiarities bv hand, and no less to the unusually heavy duties of the editor, who until 1899 was without an assistant in his manifold labors as academical teacher and curator of two museums, not to mention the fact that since 1893 he had to work almost every year in three different parts of the world, spending part of his time in America, part in Constantinople, and pan in the interior of Asia Minor. In 1899 Dr. Clay was called as his assistant, and at the end of 1901 further steps were taken by the Board of Trustees and the Committee of the Expedition to relieve him and to secure his principal time for the scientific study and publication of the results obtained at Nuffar. Comp. pp. 69 and below, under " Turkish Gleanings at Abu Habba."

On August 28, 1892, Haynes left America, spending the rest of the year in F. urope. In the first week of January, 1893, he landed at Alexandretta and travelled the ordinary route down the Euphrates valley to Baghdad. Towards the middle of March we find him at Hilla. In order to avoid the territory of the Sa'id and to pay a brief visit to the *qaimmaqam* of Diwaniye, he hired three large native boats *(meshhufs)* and sailed, accompanied by thirty-five skilled laborers and six *zabtiye,* who were to remain with him, through the Daghara canal to Suq el-'Afej. Cordially received by Hajji Tarfa, to whom he presented a gold watch from the committee in recognition of his past services, he appealed again to him for protection during his subsequent

After an absence of nearly three years he walked, on March 20, for the first time again to the ruins, a mile and a half from 'Asi's tower and reed huts. As the third expedition was expected to remain considerably longer in the field than either of the two previous ones, it became necessary to erect a more solid structure than mere tents and *sarifas,* a building which should afford coolness in the summer, shelter during the rainstorms, and protection against fire and the thievish inclinations of the Arabs. In the plain to the south of the ruins, not very far from Peters' last enclosure, Haynes marked out a spot, seventy feet long and fifty feet wide, on which, with the aid of his men from Hilla, he constructed a *meftul* or mud house with

sloping walls and without external windows. By the middle of April the primitive but comfortable quarters were finished, combining "the features of a castle, a store-house and a dwelling for the members of the party." And it was " with a perfect delight " that they all spent the first night within real walls, "free from the prying crowds of curious and covetous idlers " who looked upon every box of provisions as being filled with marvellous treasures of gold and silver.

About the same time (April 11) the excavations were started in the enormous ridge which stretches along the southwest bank of the Shatt en-Nil (VI-VIII on the plan of the ruins, p. 305), not only because it was nearest to the house, but because a large number of tablets had been discovered there by the second expedition. In accordance with instructions received from Philadelphia, this time Haynes employed only a maximum force of fifty to sixty laborers whom he could control without difficulty. Under these circumstances the work proceeded naturally much more slowly than under Peters. Nevertheless before fifteen weeks were over he had collected nearly eight thousand tablets and fragments from his various shafts, tunnels, and trenches. But toward the end of August the inscribed documents began to flow less abundantly, so that he regarded it best to transfer all his men to the temple mound, which he explored till April 4, 1894, without any serious interruption. As we prefer to consider later and coherently the whole archaeological work of the three consecutive years which Haynes spent in Babylonia, we confine ourselves at present to a brief statement of the general course of the expedition and of the principal events which affected the life and efficiency of the party during its long sojourn among the 'Afej.

At the beginning of 1894 it seemed for a while uncertain whether the home committee could secure the necessary financial support to authorize the continuation of the Babylonian mission for another year. A special effort was therefore made by several of its members, in-

cluding the present writer, to raise new funds which should enable the expedition to remain in the field until a certain task had been accom

I

I

DURING 19TU CENTURY: ASSYRIA AND BABYLONIA 351 plished. But the telegraph wires between Constantinople and Mosul being broken for almost two weeks, Havnes had left the mounds with about fifty large cases of antiquities (half of them containing slipper-shaped coffins and bricks), before the news of the fortunate turn which things had taken in Philadelphia could reach him. On June 4 he was back again in his trenches at Nuffar. During the few intervening weeks which he spent at Baghdad he had met a young American, Joseph A. Meyer, a graduate student in the department of architecture at the Massachusetts Institute of Technology, Boston, who held a travelling fellowship for two years and was on his way from India to the Mediterranean coast. Beginning to realize by this time that it would be impossible for him to excavate the temple complex, with its many complicated problems, without the constant assistance of a trained architect, Haynes readilv induced Meyer to change his plans and to accompany him without a salary for a year to the ruins of Nuffar.

A second time Providence itself, unwilling to see the most renowned sanctuary of all Babylonia cut up and gradually ruined by tunnels and perpendicular shafts, provided the much needed specialist, who through Peters' unfortunate recommendation had been withheld so long from the expedition. Indeed, the voting architect seemed eminently qualified for the peculiar duties required of him. He was deeply interested in the historical branch of his science; he had gathered considerable practical experience through his study of the ancient monuments in Kurope, Egypt, Turkey and India; he was an accurate draughtsman and enthusiastically devoted to his subject; and, further than this, he proved a genial and faithful companion to Havnes, who after his last year's isolation from all educated men naturally longed for a personal exchange of thoughts and the uplifting association with a sympathetic countryman, to whom he could speak in his own language. The influence of Meyer's active mind' and technical knowledge upon the work at Nuffar was felt immediately. Haynes' reports, previously and afterwards often lacking in clearness and conciseness and devoted more to the description of threatening dangers, illness of the servants, and other interesting though secondary questions than to the exposition of archaeological facts, aimed now at setting forth the characteristic features of the work in which he was engaged and at illustrating the weekly progress of the excavations by accompanying measurements, diagrams, and drawings. In order to derive the greatest benefit for the expedition from Meyer's presence, the exploration of the temple mound was made the principal object of their united efforts, and with the exception of a few weeks in September, all the laborers were concentrated around the *ziggurrat*. The trenches grew deeper every day, and Ashurbanapal's lofty terraces rose gradually out of the encumbering mass of later additions. The hot and trying Babylonian summer, more uncomfortable and inconvenient than dangerous to health, passed by without any noteworthy incident. But when the cooler nights indicated the approaching fall and brought with them the usual colds and chills frequently complicated by dysentery and malarial poisoning of the human system, Meyer's weakened body proved unequal to the demands made upon it.

At the end of September his physical powers of endurance gradually gave way. For seven weeks more he endeavored hard to overcome the effects of the malignant disease and remained faithfully at his post. By the end of November his condition had become so critical that notwithstanding the extraordinary hardships of the journey, it became necessary to convey him by boat to Hilla and from there in a covered litter to Baghdad. But his case was beyond human aid long before he left Nuffar. On December 20, 1894, he died in the house of Dr. Sundberg, Haynes' successor as United States consul at Baghdad, like George Smith having fallen a brave soldier in the cause of science. He was buried in the little European cemetery of the city on the banks of the Tigris. In the course of time the sandstorms of 'Iraq may efface his solitary grave. But what matters it? His bones rest in classic soil, where the cradle of the race once stood, and the history of the resurrection of ancient Babylonia will not omit his name from its pages.

The reaction of this sudden and serious loss upon the mind and activity of Haynes was soon apparent. He was alone once more on the vast ruins of an inhospitable region, directing his workmen in the trenches by day and developing negatives or packing antiquities at his " castle " in the evening. Feeling his inability to continue the exploration of the temple mound without technical advice and assistance, he wisely transferred his entire force to the southeastern extremity of the previously mentioned ridge on the other side of the canal (VI) and undertook to unearth a sufficient quantity of tablets to meet Peters' growing demands for inscribed material. He was successful again beyond expectation. At the beginning of January, 1895, he had gathered several thousand tablets and fragments and had obtained a fair collection of pottery, seal cylinders, domestic implements, and personal ornaments mostly found in the loose earth or taken from graves in which the upper twenty feet of rubbish abound everywhere at Nuffar. But unfortunately his methods of excavating and his weekly reports began to show the same deficiencies which characterized them before Meyer's timely arrival. We learn from them little beyond the fact that a larger or smaller " lot of tablets," enough to fill so and so many " cases of the usual size," had been discovered. Here and there an especially interesting antiquity or the number of tombs opened and the coffins prepared for transport are mentioned. Occasionally we even meet with some such statement as: "In nearly all of the trenches crude bricks, eleven inches square and four inches thick, occur. They are finely modelled bricks, and are firm and solid, as they are taken from their walls. They are the prettiest crude bricks I have anywhere seen." But we look in vain for an attempt to describe these remarkable walls, to trace their course, to measure their dimensions, to draw their ground plan, or to ascertain the prominent features and original purpose of the rooms and houses which he was clearing all the while of their contents.

It was the depressive and enervating effect of the solitude of the Babylonian desert and marshes which began seriously to tell upon Haynes. The rapidly growing fear of constant danger from "greedy " and revengeful Arabs, which was the natural outcome of the former, took hold of him in an alarming manner. "The great strain of maintaining security of life and property is a weariness to the flesh." "The atmosphere is thickening with danger, and I have been compelled to appeal to the governor general of Baghdad for protection." "I am getting worn out with the very intensity of the increasing strain and struggle." "I have never seen the time at Nuffar when the danger was so great as it is in these wearisome days of intrigue and fanaticism, of murder and robbing." These are only a few of the sentences which I quote from as many different letters written in February and March, 1895. Three years later Haynes viewed the conditions around Nuffar more calmly and in a more objective light, for he did not hesitate for a moment to take his wife among the same Arabs. And it is a remarkable fact, deserving special notice, that in all the ten years during which the expedition has owned its house *(meftui)* at the edge of the Babylonian swamps, no attempt has ever been made to open its door, to cut a hole into its walls, or to steal its furniture and stores, whether the building was occupied or left to the care of the neighboring tribes.

There can be no doubt that excavations carried on in the territory of the warlike 'Afej or in other remote districts of 'Iraq el-'Arabi are even to-day beset with certain dangers, for the greater part unknown to explorers of ruins like Babylon, Abu Habba, Tello, and others which are situated near the caravan road or larger towns protected by a strong garrison. The experience gathered by the first two Philadelphia expeditions, and the stories told by different travellers who visited Nuftar prove it sufficiently. But conditions have considerably changed from what they previously were, and every year the feeling of the Arabs has grown more friendly towards us. In 1894 Haynes could state with great satisfaction that the entire community from shaikh to the humblest individual openly rejoiced over his speedy return, ascribing the copious rains, the abundant crops, and all other blessings to his presence among them. Besides Hajji Tarfa himself, the powerful and renowned chief of all the 'Afej, had guaranteed the safety of the new expedition. And further than this, the two principal shaikhs of the Hamza had furnished the necessary guards, while the Ottoman government had stationed six *zabtlye* at the mounds, ready to increase their number at any time. The only real cause for anxiety was our blood-feud with the Sa'id, but a pair of boots and a bright-colored garment which soon after his arrival in 1893 Haynes had sent as a present to their shaikh Sigab (generally pronounced Sugub), had been favorably received by him, and seem to have reconciled his tribesmen temporarily, for the explorer was never molested by them during his long stay at Nuftar.

And yet in further explanation of Haynes' extraordinary state of nervousness, it must not be forgotten that the peculiar climate and the frequent unforeseen disturbances of the country where conditions and persons sometimes change kaleidoscopically, require the full attention of every foreigner at all times, especially when he is alone, as Haynes generally was during the third campaign. In the first summer of his long stay hewas greatly hampered in his movements through the repeated illness of his servants, while at the same time cholera was reported to be advancing from Nasriye and Hilla. It really never

reached the camp, but the mere anticipation of a possible outbreak of the dreaded disease weighed heavily upon him. Moreover, the Arabs were frequently on the war path. Sometimes the whole region around Daghara and Suq el-'Afej was in a state of great unrest and excitement, no less than fifteen or sixteen petty wars being carried on between the various tribes within one year. One day the 'Afej quarrelled with the Elbuder, who lived to the south of the swamps, about disputed lands. Another time the Hamza were at loggerheads with Hajji Tarfa over revenues from certain rice fields. Then again the former fought with the Behahtha on some other matter. And at the beginning of December, 1893, when the capital of the *sanjak* was transferred from Hilla to Diwaniye, to protect the newly acquired crown property of the Sultan near Daghara and Suq el-'Afej, and to reduce the rebellious 'Afej to submission, an unusually hot battle took place between the latter and the Behahtha, in which seventy-one warriors were slain. Though the sound of firing could often be heard in the trenches of Nuffar, these turmoils never threatened the safety of the expedition in a serious way, and they affected its efficiency directly only in so far as it became sometimes difficult to find a neutral messenger to carry the weekly mail through the infested territory, or to obtain suitable substitutes for native basket men, who in obedience to the summons of their shaikhs would suddenly throw down their peaceful implements, seize their clubs and antiquated matchlocks, improvise a war-song, and with loud yells run away to the assistance of their fighting comrades.

It unfortunately happened also that in the years 1894 and 1895 the 'Afej swamps, always a favorite place of refuge, a regular land of Nod (Gen. 4: 16), for dissatisfied elements and the doubtful characters of modern Babylonia, harbored a famous Kurdish outlaw and bold robber, Captain *Kyiis-bashi)* Ahmed Bey, a deserter from the Turkish army, who during eighteen months terrorized all travellers between Hilla and

Baghdad and extended his unlawful excursions even to the districts of Kud(t) el-'Amara on the banks of the Tigris, until after many futile efforts on the part of the government he was finally captured and killed by an Arab. In order to prevent anv combined action against himself by the consuls, he had been verv careful never to attack anv foreigner. It is therefore reasonably certain to assume that he would not have dared to molest an American who, moreover, was the especial *protege* and guest of the same tribes with whom he generally hid himself and his plunder. But troubled in mind as Havnes was in those days by the weight of responsibility and by numerous other causes, the temporary presence of the Kurd in the neighborhood of Nuffar increased his nervous condition and sleeplessness to such a degree that he smelled danger and complots against his life everywhere, and, to quote his own words, looked upon "every bush as concealing a waiting robber." What wonder that under these circumstances the daily petty annoyances from the good-natured and hard-working but undisplined laborers, who frequently behaved more like a crowd of frolicsome and naughty children than like real men, began to worry him beyond measure; that their occasional small pilferings of seal cylinders; a short-lived and almost ridiculous strike of the native basketmen misled by a disloyal overseer from Jumjuma; the broken leg of a foreman injured by falling bricks, or the more serious sudden cavein of a deep undermined trench and the subsequent death of another workman —occurrences familiar to him from the previous expeditions — should in his mind assume an importance entirely out of proportion to their real significance.

The committee at home was not slow in recognizing the real cause of this growing melancholy on the part of its delegate at NuffFar, and the detrimental influence which it began to exercise upon the work of the archaeological mission entrusted to him. At first favorably impressed with the contents of the reports and the character of the drawings received during the six months of Haynes' and Meyer's common activity on the ruins, it had authorized the two explorers to continue their excavations till February, 1896, a decision which was in entire accord with the former's frequently expressed personal desire. But at the end of March, 1895, when it became fully aware of all the details which threatened to undermine the health of its representative, it advised him by cable to return at once to America for rest, and to resume his work later. However, the encouragement drawn from the committee's sympathetic letters, the brief visit of an Englishman returning from India to London by way of NufFar, and the approaching spring with its new life and tonic air seem to have revived Haynes' depressed spirits so completely that he now viewed the danger as practically over, and immediately asked permission to remain a year longer among the 'Afej, at the same time earnestly pleading for a postponement of the announced despatch of an architect until another expedition should be organized. This last-mentioned recommendation, well meant as it doubtless was, could not be received favorably in Philadelphia, where every member of the board of the expedition by that time understood the need of having specialists in the field to assist Haynes. Mr. E. W. Clark began to take matters into his own hands, and a subcommittee consisting of himself and the present writer, later increased by the addition of the treasurer, Mr. John Sparhawk, Jr., was appointed to engage the services of an experienced architect, and to devise such other means as should lead to more efficient and scientific exploration of the ruins and to the complete success of the expedition. This committee has been in session at stated times until the present day.

In the meanwhile Haynes continued to deepen his trenches and to extend his tunnels in the long ridge on the west side of the ancient canal as fast as he could, endeavoring to exhaust the supply of tablets in this section sufficiently to create the general impression at the time of his departure that no more tablets were to be found at Nuffar. For the constant rumors of whole donkey loads of tablets passing through Suq el-'Afej on their way from Tello, and the great eagerness with which, in many places, Arabs had abandoned their flocks and cultivation for the more profitable secret diggings at De Sarzec's inexhaustible ruin, where the business archives of the temple had been found almost intact, foreshadowed the fate of every other Babylonian ruin upon which the antiquity dealers of Hilla and Baghdad might cast their covetous eyes. By the middle of July the proper moment seemed to have come to withdraw all the workmen from those attractive mounds which had been Haynes' great tablet mine in the past, yielding him nearly nineteen thousand inscriptions in the course of the third expedition. About the sixth part of these documents represents complete tablets, while the other fifteen thousand are more or less damaged and mutilated, including many fragments of very small size.

The last half year of the period set apart for the exploration of NufFar commenced. It was devoted almost exclusively to an examination of the southeastern part of Bint elAmir (I). Only for a fortnight in the middle of the summer Haynes transferred his entire force in the morning hours regularly to the narrow ridge of mounds (II-III) which confine the large open space to the northwest of the ziggurrat, in order to determine the foundations of the great wall wherein he and Meyer in the previous year had discovered crude bricks with the name of Naram-Sin. Owing to the relative height of the stage-tower and the enormous mass of Parthian ruins grouped around it, and no less owing to Haynes' peculiar method of excavating the lowest strata of the open court beneath them, it became more and more wearisome for the basketmen to climb the rude steps and steep roads leading from the interior of the hollowed mound to the dumping places on the top of the neighboring ruins. The photographs of the indefatigable explorer illustrated his remarkable progress in clearing the lower temple court of more than sixty thousand cubic feet of earth, but they also revealed the alarming growth of important unexplored sections of the adjoining mounds. These were high enough in themselves, but they were raised fifty to eighty feet higher by the rubbish deposited on them, so that their future excavation threatened to become a serious problem (comp. the frontispiece).

Before the Arabs understood the full value of these treasures, they sold them at ridiculously low prices to the dealers, who sometimes made 5,000 per cent., and even considerably more, on them. According to exaggerated rumors, a woman was doing the marketing for her tribesmen, selling the tablets at the uniform rate of a qufa (a round boat) full for one Persian kran, then worth about two and a half Turkish piastres, or eleven cents in United States currency. This clandestine business continued at TcllS, until at Hamdy Bey's representation the government ordered the "tablet mine" to be closed, and even placed a temporary guard over it.

After many fruitless endeavors the committee had succeeded in despatching two young Englishmen to Babylonia at the beginning of October. They had served for a little while under Flinders Petrie in Egypt, and seemed to be fairly well prepared for the more difficult labors awaiting them at NufFar. They had received instructions to work several weeks under Haynes, until they were generally acquainted with the mounds, the history of our past excavations, the country and the manners of the Arabs, upon whose good will the success of the expedition largely depended. At the same time our representative at the ruins was requested to initiate his assistants properly into their various duties, and then to leave them in charge of the field, and to return for a vacation to America, until the time should have come for his resumption of the work in company with the two Englishmen and such other assistants as the committee might deem necessary to send out with him. In consequence of quarantine and other delays, the two substitutes unfortunately did not arrive at Nuffar before February,

1896, about the same time when he whom they were expected to relieve had planned to depart from the country. Much to our astonishment and regret, Haynes did not find it advisable to execute the instructions of his committee, but induced the two young men, after they had spent a few days at the ruins, to return with him to Europe, as he regarded it "both unwise and emphatically unsafe to commit the property and work to the care of any young man who has not had a long experience in this place, and with this self-same defiant, covetous, treacherous, and bloody throng about us."

In examining Haynes' three years' labors with regard to his methods, discoveries and views on the latter, as they are laid down in his weekly reports to the committee and illustrated by numerous photographs and Meyer's drawings, we must not forget that, like Peters, he was no expert in architecture, Assyriology, or archaeology, and, therefore, could furnish only raw material for the use of the specialist. He will always deserve great credit for having demonstrated for the first time, by his own example, that it is possible to excavate a Babylonian ruin even during the hottest part of the year without any serious danger to the life of the explorer. With an interruption of but two months, and most of the time alone, he spent three consecutive years " near the insect-breeding and pestiferous 'Afej swamps, where the temperature in perfect shade rises to the enormous height of 120 Fahrenheit, and the stifling sand-storms from the desert often parch the human skin with the heat of a furnace, while the ever-present insects bite and sting and buzz through day and night." Surrounded by turbulent tribes and fugitive criminals, he worked steadfastly and patiently towards a noble aim; he even clung to his post with remarkable tenacity and great self-denial when his lonely life and a morbid fear of real and imagined dangers threatened to impair his health and obscured his judgment. But on the other hand, he also illustrated anew by his example that even the most enthusiastic explorer, cautious in his

course of proceeding, accustomed to climate, and familiar with the life and manners of the natives, as he may be, is plainly unable to excavate a Babylonian ruin satisfactorily without the necessary technical knowledge and the constant advice of an architect and Assyriologist. Haynes' principal mistake lies in the fact that, in accordance with Peters' unfortunate proposition, he consented to imitate the latter's example with regard to the methods of excavation, and to dwell and to dig at Nuffar alone without educated technical assistance; and furthermore that when the committee as a whole, realizing the impossibility of such an undertaking, called him home or proposed to send him assistance, he preferred to remain in the field and declined the latter.

According to the manner of Rassam and Peters, Haynes gathered an exceedingly large number of valuable antiquities, he removed an enormous mass of rubbish, he made us acquainted with a great many details of the interior of the mounds, he worked diligently in exposing walls, following drains and uncovering platforms. But these discoveries remained isolated and incoherent. It was frequently impossible to combine them and to obtain even a moderately accurate picture of the temple of Bel by means of his reports in the form in which they were written. Often unable to At the time these reports were received, it was naturally understood that they were only preliminary letters written under peculiarly trying circum distinguish between essentials and secondary matters, or failing to recognize the significance of certain small traces occurring in the loose debris or represented by fragmentary walls which are of paramount importance to the archaeologist, he would remove them without attempting to give their accurate location and description, and occasionally allow his imagination to become an inadequate substitute for sober facts and simple measurements by feet and inches. In consequence of these peculiarities his reports frequently enough present almost as many puzzles as Nuffar itself, and require their own excavation,

through which the original details furnished by the trenches scarcely improve. What with Meyer's aid he submitted concerning the *ziggurrat* of Ashurbanapal, its dimensions, conduits, etc., was on the whole correct and in many ways excellent. It showed what Haynes might have accomplished in addition to the unearthing of the numerous tablets, sarcophagi, drains, and walls which we owe to his untiring efforts, had he been assisted properly. We must keep this in mind in order to explain, and to a certain degree excuse his methods and subsequent one-sided results, but also to understand, in part at least, why the picture of the temple of Bel, which I drew in 1896 on the basis of his reports, is inaccurate and differs considerably from what I have to present below after my personal visit to the ruins in 1900, when I had an opportunity to study the architectural remains as far as they were still preserved, and to submit all the tunnels and trenches of my predecessors to a critical examination.

nances, and that all the scientific details required to complete them would be found in the books of entry, exhaustive diaries and many other note-books, as they are usually kept by every expedition. It became apparent, however, in 1900, that no such books existed, and that these weekly or fortnightly letters represented all the written information which Haynes had to give on his long work of three years. I am still inclined to explain this strange fact to a certain degree by his mental depression referred to above, though, to my sincere regret, the words of praise as to the character of his work, so liberally expressed in my introduction to " The Bab. Exp. of the Univ. of Pa.," series A, vol. i, *pan z* (Philadelphia, 1896), pp. 16, *itqq.*, wilV have to be modified considerably. Not of Ur-Gur, as on the basis of Haynes' reports was stated in my fint tentative sketch of the *ziggurrat, "*The Bab. Exp. of the Univ. of Pa.," series A, vol. i, part 2, pp. 16, *itqq.*

As indicated above, Haynes excavated chiefly at two places during his long stav at Nuftar, devoting about eighteen months to Bint el-Amir (I), which represents the ancient *ziggurrat,* and twelve to the long furrowed ridge situated on the southwest side of the canal and defined bv the numbers VI and VIII respectively on the plan of the ruins (comp. p. 305), while two to three months were allowed for the exploration of several other sections, including a search for the original bed of the Shatt enNil. In order to enable the reader to follow his work on the stage-tower with greater facility, I shall classify and consider it in the following order: *a,* His examination of a part of the latest constructions; *b,* his clearing of the stage-tower of Ashurbanapal; *c,* his excavation of three sections on the southeast court of the *ziggurrat* down to the water level.

a. In continuing Peters' work on the temple mound, Haynes committed the same grave error, to start with, as the first director of the expedition. He descended to the successive Babylonian strata by means of deep shafts, and cleared important sections even down to the virgin soil, before the uppermost imposing structure had been excavated completely and methodicallv. This is the more remarkable as Havnes, like his predecessor, regarded this gigantic settlement around the remodelled *ziggurrat* not as an entirely new Parthian creation, as the present writer did, but as the latest historical development of the famous sanctuary of Bel at the time of "the second Babylonian empire," or about the period 600-550 B. C, — reason enough to treat it with special reverence and to examine it with the greatest care. In consequence of his strange procedure he could not help destroying essential details of all the different strata which later were missing, and at the same time to report other discoveries inaccurately and incoherently. It became, therefore, exceedingly difficult, and in many cases impossible, for me to determine and to arrange the defective results of all these perpendicular cuttings, with their eight to ten different strata, in a satisfactory manner, the more so as they often had been obtained at long intervals, and as a rule were unaccompanied by even the poorest kind of sketch or ground plan, while the portable antiq-

uities had never been numbered to allow of their identification with certainty afterwards.

In spite of the plainly un-Babylonian character of the large crude bricks which constitute the bulk of the latest fortified walls around the *ziggurrat,* Haynes regarded them with Peters as the work of Ur-Gur, differing, however, from him in one important point, by declaring at least a large part of the southeast enclosing wall as the work "of the first rebuilder of the *ziggurrat* in cruciform style about *600* B. c.." He removed a number of rooms in the east corner of this settlement, and as Meyer fortunately was on the ground a few months later, we have a well executed plan of these chambers in addition to a few sketches and a general description of their principal features and contents by Haynes. The two explorers came to the interesting conclusion, confirmed later by my inspection of the few remains of their trenches, that three different periods are clearly to be distinguished with regard to their occupancy. They also make us acquainted with the exact dimensions of these rooms and their mutual relation to each other, with the average thickness and height of their ruined walls, with certain important details of their doors, with their drainage and ventilation and several fireplaces discovered in them. Apart from a few stray Babylonian antiquities which later may have been used again, all the typical objects gathered in these rooms are decidedly later than 300 B. C, as I convinced myself by a careful investigation. Among the objects betraying an undoubtedly Greek influence I only mention several fragments of a cornice in limestone representing the vine-branch, well known from the so-called sarcophagus of Alexander the Great, and the stamped handle of a Rhodian amphora bearing the inscription EΠI BEAIAHTOT BATPOMIOT, *i. e.,* "this amphora was made or gauged under the eponymous magistrate Theaidetos in the month of Badromios." According to Professor Furtwangler of Munich, to whom I submitted a photograph of the last mentioned antiquity, this magistrate is

known from other similar handles found on the isle of Rhodes itself," and must have lived in the second or first century preceding our era. The same scholar confirmed my conclusions with regard to the age of the characteristic terra-cotta figurines previously described (comp. pp. 330, *seq.),* which I had unhesitatingly assigned to the Parthian, *i. e.,* the Hellenistic and Roman periods.

The removal of the enormous mass of crude bricks with which the builders of this latest settlement had covered, changed, and enlarged the old stage-tower of Bel was a slow and tedious task. But it was not without interesting results. Babvlonian antiquities of the Cassite, and even much earlier times, were repeatedly discovered inside these bricks. Their comparatively fine state of preservation, their frequent occurrence, and, in a few cases, their large size, proved sufficiently that they had not gotten accidentaily into these walls, while the long period of about two thousand years represented by them, their character and their inscriptions, indicated in some manner how and where they had been obtained. Most of them came from the temple complex, where they had been found when the ground was levelled and important early structures destroyed to furnish welcome building material for the later descendants of the ancient population. All the objects unearthed had been gathered scrupulously, for they were no less valued in those days than they are to-day by the modern inhabitants of the country. They were either sold as raw material to engravers and jewellers (comp. p. 335), or worn as personal ornaments, or converted into useful household implements, or used as talismans which protected the living and the dead alike against the evil influence of demons. We found inscribed tablets, seal cylinders, and other Babylonian antiquities of the most different periods very commonly in and around the Parthian and Sassanian urns, coffins and tombs of Nuffar. These discoveries ofttimes led Peters and Haynes astray in their efforts to prove the Babylonian character of these burials and to support their startling theories concerning the age and the different types of ancient potten'. But they also occur in platforms, under thresholds, in the foundations of houses, inside numerous bricks, as stated above, and for very simple reasons, especially frequently in the mortar uniting the latter. No wonder that Haynes discovered them in considerable quantities in the clay mortar of the fortified palace which rests on the ruins of the ancient temple, thereby unconsciously establishing an exact parallel to De Sarzec's results in the upper strata of the temple mound at Tello (comp. pp. 226, Jyy., particularly pp. 232, *sec.* , and at the same time providing further evidence against his own personal view of the signification of these antiquities. In addition to their talismanic character many of the objects deposited seem to have carried with them the idea of a sacrifice or an act of devotion on the part of their donors to secure greater stability for this public building, to express gratitude for an unknown successful transaction, or to obtain the favor of the gods for the fulfilment of a certain desire. In the light of such votive offerings I view a collection of antiquities discovered together in the foundation of the latest southeast enclosing wall and comprising a Persian seal, a Babylonian seal cylinder, a pair of silver earrings, eleven pieces of corroded silver, about forty silver beads and three hundred odd stone beads, which apparently represent the gift of a woman; or the goose-egg with its undeveloped germ of life to be sacrificed (comp. p. JJ2), and, above all, a surprising find which was made on the northwestern side of the *ziggurrat.* Imbedded in the mortar of clay and straw that filled a large space between Ashurbanapal's stage-tower and its later addition Haynes uncovered three human skulls placed on the same level at nearly equal distances from each other. There can be no doubt that we here have an authentic example of the practice of bloody sacrifices offered in connection with the construction of important new buildings, — a practice widely existing in the ancient world and prevailing even to-day in several parts of the Orient. The T in the name of the

month as offered by the inscription is a mistake of the scribe, as Furtwangler informs me.
Comp. Hiller de Gaertringen, *Inscriptiines Grttcainsularum Rhodi,* etc., 1895, No. 1135. *b.* The labor that would have been required to clear the original Babylonian stage-tower entirely of the later additions will be easily understood by considering that more than one hundred thousand cubic feet of tenacious *lib(e)n,* or mud bricks, and other accumulated rubbish had to be removed before only one of the four huge arms which proceeded from the centres of the four sides of the ancient *ziggurrat* far into the court had disappeared, — a fact sufficiently illustrating the remarkable power and energy of these Peters, failing to recognize the meaning of this class of antiquities, comes to the remarkable conclusion *(I. c.,* vol. ii., p. 123), that "some humorous or mischievous workman had walled it in two thousand years or so ago." Comp. H. Clay Trumbull, " The Blood Covenant," zd edition, Philadelphia, 1893, and "The Threshold Covenant," New York, 1896.
Nurtbwe\$tern Facade of the Ziggurrat as restored by Ashurbanapal about 650 B. c.
Parthian rulers, who were able to erect similar castles on the top of most of the large temple ruins in the country. In view of the great difficulties in his way, Haynes confined himself to a complete removal of the southeastern wing, cutting away only so much of the other three arms as was absolutely necessary to disengage the earlier building from its surrounding brickwork by means of narrow perpendicular trenches. Applied to the huge massive lateral arms alone, this method was doubtless correct, as it saved considerable time and expense, and did not deprive us of any essential knowledge for the time being. But as soon as it was carried further than this it became incompatible with a systematic investigation of the entire mound. These dimly lighted narrow corridors prevented the photographing of important details of the lowest story of the stage-tower, while at the same time they gave cause for Haynes' further descent into

the depth, before the rest of the sacred enclosure had received proper attention. Consequently it was impossible until very recently to determine the precise relation of the *ziggurrat* to the temple with which it formed an organic whole, or even to find out what the entire court around the former looked like at any given period of its long and varied history. As a matter of fact, the following picture presented itself to me upon my arrival at NurTar in 1900. The crumbling remains of the *ziggurrat* had been exposed to the level of the period of Kadashman-Turgu, large sections in its neighborhood were explored only to the level of the Parthian fortress, others had not been touched at all, again others were cleared to the platform of L'r-Gur, still others down to the upper Pre-Sargonic remains, while by far the greater part of the large place in front of the stage-tower, which contained a number of brick pavements, serving as an excellent means for dating the different strata of the whole enclosure, had been excavated down to the virgin soil (comp. frontispiece). At one time Haynes himself very keenly felt the unsatisfactory manner in which he was proceeding. For in one of his reports of 1894, written during Meyer's presence at the ruins, we read the significant passage: "I should like to see systematic excavations undertaken on this temple enclosure, not to be excavated section by section, but carried down as a whole, to distinguish the different epochs of its history, each well defined level to be thoroughly explored, sketched, photographed, and described, before the excavation of any part should be carried to a lower level. This method would be more satisfactory and less likely to lead to confusion of strata and levels." We naturally ask in amazement: Though knowing the better method, why did he never adopt it at a time when he was in complete charge of the expedition in the field, and the committee at home readv to support him with all the necessary technical assistance? In tracing the upper stages of the *ziggurrat,* Haynes discovered the fragment of a barrel cylinder inscribed with the cuneiform signs characteristic of the period of the last great Assyrian kings (722-626 B. C). It belonged to Sargon or Ashurbanapal, both of whom took part in restoring the temple of Bel. Small as it was, it proved that documents of this kind once existed at Nuffar, as they did in other Babylonian stage-towers. But in order to determine the number and size of the upper stories, which no longer had facing walls of baked brick, the explorer had to proceed from the better-preserved lowest one. For the later occupants of the temple mound, while utilizing all the other baked material of the older building for their own purposes, had evidently been obliged to leave the panelled walls of baked bricks in the lowest story standing in order to prevent the gradual collapse of the heavy mass above it. More than this, they had trimmed its corners and repaired other defective places, as could easily be recognized from the bricks there employed and their use of clay mortar instead of bitumen, the common binding material of all the baked bricks of the *ziggurrat* found still *in situ.* This circumstance explains why even the lowest stage of the tower yielded us no building records, though Haynes continued to search for them.

Most of the stamped bricks taken from this story bore the Old Babylonian inscription: "To Bel, the king of the lands, his king, Ashurbanapal, his favorite shepherd, the powerful king, king of the four quarters of the earth, built Ekur, his beloved temple, with baked bricks." Intermingled with them were bricks of Kadashman-Turgu (about 1300 B. c.) and Ur-Gur (about 2700 B. c.), the latter's name occurring in the lowest courses frequently to the exclusion of all others. It was therefore clear that each subsequent restorer of the tower had made extensive use of the material of his predecessors, thereby enabling us to fix at least the principal periods of this monumental structure. But some of the royal builders had not been satisfied with a mere repairing of cracks and replacing of walls; they at the same time had enlarged the original size of the tower. This fact was disclosed by a

trench cut into the northeast face of the *ziggurrat,* where Haynes discovered the fragmentary remains of Ur-Gur's casing wall six feet behind the outside of Ashurbanapal's. The southeast fa$ade alone seems to have remained unchanged for more than two thousand years; for all the inscribed bricks removed from this neighborhood exhibited the name of the ancient king of Ur on their lower faces, a sure indication that they were still in their original position. What is the reason for the unique preservation of this particular side during such a long period? Two almost parallel walls, constructed by the same monarch and running at right angles from the southeast face of the *ziggurrat* into the large open court, acted as a kind of buttress and prevented an uneven settling of the ponderous mass behind and above it. But this was not their original and chief purpose. Certain projections of the second stage over this so-called causeway, which are absent from the other three sides of the pyramid, prove conclusively that here we have the last remains of the ancient approach to the top of the *ziggurrat.* A door-socket in dolerite inscribed with the ordinary votive legend of Ur-Gur was found at the foot of this stairway, while a strav soapstone tablet of the same king came from a room of the Parthian fortress considerably above it.

The excavation of the southwest and northeast facades were no less important for our knowledge of the architectural details of the *ziggurrat.* Both contained deep and wellbuilt conduits in their centres, designed to carry the profuse water of the Babylonian autumn and winter rains from the higher stories over the foundations of the lowest encasement walls into a gutter which surrounded all but the front sides of the high-towering building. Loftus' so-called "buttresses" of the Buweriye at Warka, " erected on the centre of each side for the purpose of supporting the main edifice " (comp. p. 146, above), are evidently nothing but such water conduits, misunderstood by him, and the remains of an entrance to the top of the tower. If we can rely upon Haynes'

examination, the southwest conduit was the exclusive work of Ur-Gur, except at the bottom, where it had repeatedly been filled and paved to discharge the water at a higher level in accordance with the gradual rising of the court below. The northeast conduit, on the other hand, goes back only to Ashurbanapal, who repaired the conduit of Kadashman-Turgu, placed over the older one of UrGur.

Havnes did not recognize the significance of these projections for the whole question of the original ascent, but, substituting his lively fantasy again for an accurate description, imagines that " a sacred shrine or altar may have stood at the far end of the causeway," or " that the officiating priest may at times have harangued the people in the great court below him from that height." What a conception of a Babylonian temple!

It is Haynes' view, as reproduced by me in 1896, that, with the exception of the lowest front face and the two conduits, Ur-Gur's *ziggurrat* was built entirely of crude bricks, and that even at the time of the Cassite and Assyrian occupations the upper stories had no casing walls of baked bricks. This theory seems to me untenable. For there are many indications which necessarily lead to the conclusion that the whole pyramid, from the time of Ur-Gur down to Ashurbanapal, was properly protected. I cannot go into details here. To mention only one circumstance, it would be impossible to explain the presence of so many stamped bricks of Ur-Gur, found out of their original position everywhere in the ruins of Nuffar, except on the assumption of a casing wall for every stage of the *ziggurrat.* It was only natural that the bricks of the earlier builders should be removed by the later monarchs before they repaired and enlarged the temple. But the very fact that the material of Ashurbanapal's casing walls of the lowest story consists largely of bricks of Ur-Gur and Kadashman-Turgu, and that the construction of the Seleucido-Parthian rulers contained a great number of stamped and unstamped bricks of all the three Babylonian kings mentioned, is alone sufficient evidence to demonstrate that the entire outside of the *ziggurrat* must have been built of baked bricks.

While working towards the second stage from the upper edge of the lowest story, Haynes discovered the opening of a large well in the centre of its northeast facade and partly overlapping the ancient conduit. It was built of baked bricks, and descended through the crude mass of the stage-tower down to the water level. Though unable to determine its age and special purpose at this remarkable place, Haynes was inclined to ascribe it to Ashurbanapal. But this is impossible. In connection with my subsequent visit to the ruins, I could prove conclusively that this well did not belong to the *ziggurrat* proper, but was constructed of Kadashman-Turgu's and Ashurbanapal's material by the Seleucido-Parthian princes, who selected this peculiar place in order to obtain the coolest water possible and to secure its supply for the highest part of their castle, even in case the lower palace should have been taken by an enemy.

A word remains to be said about the interior and the upper stages of the *ziggurrat*. The large body of the hightowering building consisted of crude bricks nine by six by three inches in size. They represent the standard dimension of Ur-Gur's material, but they were already in use before his time. For bricks of the same size and form, but different in color (the latter being yellowish, the former gray), were discovered in the lower courses of the interior of the *ziggurrat*

Apart from the unusually large adobes employed by the Parthian builders and completely covering and embedding the ancient stage-tower, there is only one other kind of crude bricks traceable in its upper part, which may belong to one of the Cassite rulers or to Ashurbanapal. This fact will scarcely surprise us, since little is left of the higher stages of the *ziggurrat*. We can state with certainty only that Haynes found considerable remains of a sloping second terrace, largely ruined in the centre of its southwest and northeast facades, where apparently water conduits, similar to those of the first story,

previously existed, and that he believes himself to have discovered faint traces of a third story. The amount of rubbish accumulated on the top of the second stage is comparatively small. But this circumstance does not constitute an argument against the assumption of more than three stages. It only testifies to the rapid disintegration of crude bricks after they had been exposed to the combined action of heavy rains and extraordinary heat, and to the remarkable changes which the *ziggurrat* under Comp. what is said below, p. 390, in connection with the two treasury vaults opening into the pavements of Ur-Gur and Naram-Sin. went at the hands of the occupants of the latest castle, who practically turned the Babylonian ruin into a huge cruciform terrace with an additional central elevation or watch-tower. *c.* The excavation of the southeast court of the *ziggurrat* forms the most interesting though the most pernicious part of Haynes' work on the temple of Bel. He accomplished it in his own manner during the last half year of his stay at the ruins by dividing the whole space into four sections and clearing three of them by as many large perpendicular shafts from the walls of the Parthian rooms down to the virgin soil. The fourth had been excavated only to the brick pavement of Ashurbanapal, when he departed from Nuffar on February 19, 1896. Whatever seemed important enough at the different altitudes, he left standing, supporting the uncovered remains of the past by solid pillars of earth, or by artificial arches cut out of the rubbish below them. In consequence of this unique method of operation, the southeast section of the temple court, as seen in the frontispiece, looks as picturesque and attractive as possible, while in reality it presents a picture of utter confusion and devastation to the archaeologist. In sketching Haynes' work, therefore, I can only attempt to set forth certain striking features of the different strata which I have been able to develop out of his incoherent and frequently contradictory reports, and to give a brief description of some of the more important antiquities discovered by him. For

the sake of greater clearness we take a pavement of Sargon and Naram-Sin, which extends through a considerable part of the mound, as a dividing line, and examine the ruins which lie above it first, and afterwards those which were hidden below it. i. *Post-Sargonic Ruins*. The rubbish which filled the court between the platform just mentioned and the bottom of the stratum of well-packed earth, prepared by the Seleucido-Parthian princes as a foundation for their fortified palace, was about sixteen to seventeen feet high, or a little less than the remains of buildings above the latter, which represent the post-Babylonian history of Nippur. This mass of debris accumulated within a period of more than three thousand years (3800-350 B. c.), was graduated to a certain degree, if I may use this graphic expression. For a number of pavements, running almost parallel with that of Naram-Sin, divided it into as many horizontal layers of different depth and importance. At the time of excavation none of these pavements were complete, for the very simple reason that every king who levelled the court with its ruined constructions and laid a new pavement, saved as many of his predecessor's bricks as he could extract from the rubbish without difficulty. The fact that from the time of Ur-Gur practically the same mould (eleven to twelve inches square), was adopted for the ordinary baked bricks by all the Babylonian monarchs who repaired the renowned sanctuary at Nippur, encouraged their liberal employment of the old material, the more so as proper fuel was always scarce and expensive in the valleys of the lower Euphrates and Tigris.

The topmost of these pavements extended from the "causeway" of the *ziggurrat,* a distance of sixty-three feet towards the southeast, and was covered with debris one foot to one and a half high. Though none of its bricks was stamped, I have no doubt that it goes back to Ashurbanapal, whose inscribed bricks, sometimes green (originally blue) enamelled on the edges, were repeatedly found near its upper surface. As Haynes reports to have seen no trace of buildings of any sort resting upon the pavement, this section of the court seems to have been a large open place at the time of the last great Assyrian king (seventh century B. C).

Several photographs clearly show that originally there was another pavement about two feet to two and a half below the first. If ever it covered the entire court, only fractional parts of it had been preserved, so that the illustration facing this page does not even indicate its former existence. The layer of earth enclosed between the upper and the lower pavements was "so firmly stratified that it seemed to have been formed gradually by the agency of water," which was incessantly washing away the unprotected parts of the ziggurrat. But Haynes' observation is not quite accurate; for a band of "mingled bitumen, charcoal, and wood ashes, varying in thickness from two to four inches," and running nearly through the middle of this stratum, indicates sufficiently that some kind of light structures must have existed on this part of the court at some time during the second millennium, to which I ascribe the second pavement. In all probability it was laid by a Cassite ruler, presumably Kadashman-Turgu, who not only restored but enlarged the ziggurrat and provided it with new casing walls. If I interpret correctly Haynes' somewhat confused reports of the different sections of the court excavated by him, and adjust his results properly with one another, this pavement must be regarded as a continuation of the lower course of a border pavement, which surrounded the four sides of Kadashman-Turgu's stage-tower, being ten feet wide in front of the latter and somewhat narrower on its other three sides, where it terminated in a gutter. This border pavement consisted of two courses of bricks laid in bitumen, and served as a basis for a sloping bed of bitumen designed to protect the foundations of the pyramid from falling rain. None of the bricks were inscribed except one, which contained the name of Ur-Ninib on its upper face, thereby indicating that it was out of its original position and belonged to much

older material used again. An interesting discovery made at the same level, on the back side of the ziggurrat near its west corner, confirms my theory expressed above that the whole court around it was studded with smaller buildings at the time of the Cassite dominion. For while clearing the northwest face of the stage-tower Haynes came upon a room resting on the brick pavement now under consideration, and containing six whole cuneiform tablets, a little over a hundred small fragments of others, and an unpolished marble weight in the shape of a duck, which was nearly a foot long.

It seems as if the pavement of baked bricks was confined to the immediate environments of the ziggurrat and continued by a pavement of crude bricks (11 J by 11 J by yf, inches), repeatedly referred to by Haynes at about the same level.

At an average depth of a foot and a half below the second pavement was a third, much better preserved. It was laid by Ur-Ninib, one of the kings of the dynasty of (N)isin, which occupied the throne of Babylonia about the middle of the third pre-Christian millenium. Out of a section of 143 bricks, taken up by Haynes, 135 bore the inscription: "Ur-Ninib, the glorious shepherd of Nippur, the shepherd of Ur, he who delivers the commands of Eridu, the gracious lord of Erech, king of (N)isin, king of Shumer and Akkad, the beloved consort of Ishtar." One was stamped with Ur-Gur's well-known legend, and six were uninscribed. From the reports before us we receive no information as to any walls or noteworthy antiquities having been discovered in the layer of rubbish once covering the pavement.

The most important of all the strata above the level of Naram-Sin is that which lies between the pavement of UrNinib and the next one below. As the former was not always exactly parallel to the latter, it is in some places almost three feet deep, though its average thickness is scarcely more than two. It rests upon a "platform" of clay and unbaked bricks, which, in size, color, and texture are identical with the mass of

crude bricks forming the body of the ziggurrats of Nuffar and Warka, and therefore may be safely ascribed to Ur-Gur, king of Ur (about 2700 B. c.). The layer of rubbish and earth which covered the pavement deserves our special attention, as it yielded more inscribed' antiquities than any other part of the temple enclosure hitherto examined. Over six hundred fragments of vases, statues, slabs, brick-stamps, and a number of doorsoclcets were gathered by the different expeditions in this remarkable stratum, doubly remarkable as most of the objects obtained from it did not belong to Ur-Gur and his successors, as at first might be expected, but to kings and high officials whom, on the basis of strong palaeographic evidence and for various other reasons, I was forced to ascribe to the earliest phase of Babylonian history antedating Sargon I (about 3800 B. c.) by several centuries. As practically nothing but heavy door-sockets in dolerite and some shapeless blocks of veined marble (technically known as calcite stalagmite) were found whole; as most of the fragments were extraordinarily small in size, and as, moreover, portions of the same vases repeatedly were discovered at places widely distant from each other, we cannot avoid the conclusion that these precious antiquities had been broken and scattered on purpose; in other words, that these numerous inscribed vases and more than fifty brickstamps with the names of Sargon and Naram-Sin upon them, which had been scrupulously preserved and handed down from generation to generation, must have been stored somewhere within the precincts of the court of the ziggurrat, until they were rudely destroyed by somebody who lived between the reigns of Ur-Gur of Ur, and Ur-Ninib of (N)isin. Apart from a brick of Ur-Ninib, the latest inscribed monument recovered from this well-defined stratum is a door-socket of Bur-Sin of Ur, or rather an inscribed block of dolerite, presented to Bel by Lugalkigubnidudu, a very ancient king of Ur and Erech, and afterwards turned into a door-socket and rededicated to the temple of Nippur by Bur-Sin. Hence it follows that the last-mentioned monarch must have lived before Ur-Ninib, and is more closely connected with Ur-Gur than has generally been asserted, a fact fully corroborated by the recent investigations of Thureau-Dangin, who has shown that there was only one dynasty of Ur in the third pre-Christian millennium. But we draw another important conclusion. It is entirely impossible to assume that a native Babylonian usurper of the throne, however ill-disposed toward an ancient cult and however unscrupulous in the means taken to suppress it, should have committed such an outrage against the sacred property of the great national sanctuary of the country. The breaking and scattering of the vases not only indicates a period of great political disturbance in Babylonia, but points unmistakably to a foreign invasion. Whence did it come?

We know on the one hand, from the chronological lists of dates and the last lines of thousands of business tablets of the third millennium, that the powerful kings of Ur had led their armies victoriously to Elam, conquered even Susa, and established a Babylonian hegemony over the subdued cities and districts of their ancient enemies. And we know on the other hand, from numerous references in Babylonian and Assyrian inscriptions, remarkably confirmed by De Morgan's excavations in Susa, that towards 2300 B. C. the Elamites were for a while in the complete possession of the lower country of the Euphrates and Tigris, even establishing an Elamitic dynasty at Larsa after they had devastated and ransacked all the renowned temples of Shumer and Akkad. Between these two historical events, which reversed the political relations between Babylonia and Elam completely, we must place the native dynasties of (N)isin and Larsa, preceded by a first Elamitic invasion, which occurred about two hundred years before the second one. It was this first Elamitic invasion which caused the destruction of the temple property at Nippur, brought about the downfall of the dynasty of Ur, and apparently led to the rise of the dynasty of (N)isin, to which UrNinib be-

longs, whose pavement covered the layer of debris with the numerous broken vases. If the text of a votive inscription of Enannatuma, son of Ishme-Dagan, king of (N)isin, king of Shumer and Akkad, published many years ago by Rawlinson, is entirely correct, the last representative of the dynasty of Ur would have been Gungunu, since he no longer has the proud title of his immediate predecessors, "king of the four quarters of the earth," nor the less significant one borne by his first two ancestors, but is styled only "king of Ur." In this case IshmeDagan should have been the founder of the new dynasty, who allowed Gungunu to lead the life of the shadow of a king until his death, under the control of one of his own sons, whom he invested with the highest religious office in the temple of Sin at Ur. If, however, Gungunu, "king of Ur," mentioned in Enannatuma's inscription should prove to be a mistake for Gungunu, " king of Larsa," a ruler whose existence was recently communicated to me by Thureau-Dangin, Ishme-Dagan would be the last and Ishbigirra (succeeded by Ur-Ninib?) probably the first representative of the dynasty of (N)isin. In this case Gungunu must have been the founder of the native dynasty of Larsa, which would have followed immediately upon that of (N)isin, continuing to reign (Nur-Ramman and Sin-idinnam), until it was overthrown in connection with the second Eiamiric invasion, about 2300 B. c. However this may be, whether we have to distinguish two kings by the name of Gungunu — the one king of Ur, the other king of Larsa (as we have two rulers, Bur-Sin, the one king of Ur, the other king of (N)isin),— or whether there was only one Gungunu, namely, the king of Larsa, this much can be regarded as certain, that the dynasties of Ur, (N)isin and Larsa succeeded each other in the order just quoted, and that for at least one hundred and fifty to two hundred years the city of (N)isin appeared as the champion of Babylonian independence, until its leading position was contested by Babylon under Sin-muballit in the North. But how important a role to the

very last (N)isin must have played in resisting the imperialistic ideas of the Elamitic invaders, whose ultimate aim was the establishing of a kingdom of Shumer and Akkad under the sceptre of an Elamitic prince, becomes evident from the mere fact, that Rim-Sin, son of KudurMabuk, who supplanted the native kings of Larsa and realized the Elamitic dream for about twenty-five to thirty years, introduced a new era by dating the single years of his government after the fall of (N)isin.

Comp. i R. z, no. vi, I, and 36, no. 2. Bur-Sin I, Gimil-Sin, Ine-Sin. Ur-Gur and Dungi. The latter was the first to adopt the more comprehensive title in connection with his successful wars some time between the $x + 21$ st and $x + 29$th years of his long government. Comp. ThureauDangin in Comptes Rendus, 1902, pp. 84, seqq. Comp. the date of a tablet mentioned by Scheil in Maspero's Recutil, vol. xxi (1899), p. 125: mu Gu-un-gu-nu ba-til, "the year when G. died." If the former view, set forth above, be correct, this tablet would belong to the government of Ishme-Dagan or his successor, and its peculiar date would thus find an easy explanation. In the other case the date would appear somewhat strange, as it was not customary to call a year after the death of an actual ruler, but rather after his successor's accession to the throne. There exist a few other tablets which are dated according to the reigns of kings of the dynasty of (N)isin. Among the results of the third Philadelphia expedition I remember distinctly to have seen one dated in the reign of UrNinib, and Scheil (in Rccucil, vol. xxiii, 1901, pp. 93, irq.) mentions another from Sippara which bears the name of King Damiq-ilishu, a second member of the same dynasty (comp. next page below), whom Scheil, however, wrongly identified with his namesake of the second dynasty of Babylon. In a personal letter of July 29, 1902, in which, on the basis of a new brick fragment recently acquired by the Louvre, Thureau-Dangin is inclined to doubt the existence of a Gungunu, king of Ur. The fact that in both of his inscriptions Enannatuma has the title *shag Uruma,* which (along with *u-a Uruma*) the Babylonian kings of Larsa place at the head of their titles, speaks decidedly in favor of an identity of Gungunu of Ur with Gungunu of Larsa. For evidently the rise of the dynasty of Larsa was connected as closely with the possession of the sanctuary of Sin at Ur as the rise of the dynasty of (N)isin with that of the temple of Bel at Nippur (comp. the fact that all the members of this dynasty place *iik (u-a* or *sag-uih) Nippur* before all their other titles). It comprised at least seven kings, Ishbigirra, Ur-Ninib, Libit-Ishtar, Bur-Sin II, Damiq-ilishu, Idin-Dagan, and Ishme-Dagan, all but the first and the sixth kings being represented by inscriptions from Nippur. The question arises now, whether kings like Bel-bani, Rim-Anum, etc., generally classified with the kings of the first dynasty of Babylon, must not be regarded rather as members of the dynasty of (N)isin.

As remarked above, with but few exceptions all the objects rescued by Haynes from the stratum beneath UrNinib's platform were in a most lamentable condition. Yet, after infinite toil, I succeeded in dividing them in groups according to certain palaeographic peculiarities exhibited by them, and ultimately restored a number of inscriptions almost completely, notably the famous text of Lugalzaggisi, "king of Erech, king of the world," with its 132 lines of writing obtained from eighty-eight often exasperatingly small fragments of sixty-four different vases. The new material proved of fundamental importance for our knowledge of the early history of Babylonia in the fifth and fourth preChristian millenniums. In connection with the inscriptions from Tello these texts enabled us to follow the general trend of the political and religious development of the country. We see how a number of petty states, sometimes consisting of nothing more than a walled city grouped around a well-known sanctuary, are constantly quarrelling with one another about the hegemony, victorious to-day, defeated to-morrow. The more prominent princes present votive offerings to Bel of Nip-

pur, which stands out as the great religious centre of Babylonia at the earliest period of its history. For the first time we meet with the names of Utug, *patesi,* and Urzag(?)uddu and En-Bildar, kings of Kish, Enshagkushanna, " lord of Kengi, king of the world," Lugalkigubnidudu and Lugalkisalsi, kings of Erech and Ur, Urumush, " king of Kish," and others, or we gather further details concerning monarchs previously known, as, *e. g.,* Entemena of Lagash, Manishtusu of Kish, Sargon and Naram-Sin of Agade. Above all, we get acquainted with the great "hero," Lugalzaggisi, "who was favorably looked upon by the faithful eye of Bel,... to whom intelligence was given by Ea..., and who was nourished with the milk of life by the goddess Ningarsag." Indeed a great conqueror he must have been, one of the mightiest monarchs of the ancient East thus far known, a king who, long before Sargon I was born, could boast of an empire extending from the Persian Gulf to the shores of the Mediterranean Sea.

In addition to the many broken vases with their interesting forms and inscriptions equally important for archaeology, history, and palaeography, this unique stratum also yielded a few fragments of statues, reliefs, and other antiquities similar to those of Tello. They illustrate again that the Babylonian artist was as ready to glorify Bel of Nippur as he was to place his talents in the service of Ningirsu and Bau of Lagash. And they indicate at the same time that in all probability great surprises will await the future explorer of NufFar who will turn his attention from the *ziggurrat* to the temple proper, which to the present day has scarcely been touched, as both Peters and Haynes regarded the temple of Bel and its stage-tower practically as the same thing, and, unconscious of what they were doing, covered the neighboring ruins with fifty to seventy feet of rubbish, excavated by them in the court of the *ziggurrat.* Among the objects of art from beneath the pavement of Ur-Ninib which claim our special attention, I only mention a straight nose in basalt originally belonging to

a statue in life size; the tolerably well-preserved shaved head of a small white marble statue of the period of Ur-Nina; and the torso of a large The second sign is doubtful. Possibly my former reading Ur-Dun (Shul) pauddu is correct.

The name means "Bildar (a well-known star-god) is lord." This reading of Hommel is preferable to Thureau-Dangin's *Enbi-lshtar* or my former provisional reading *Enne-Ugun.*

Torso of an Inscribed Statue in Dolerite, about 2700 B. c.

Original rwo-tkirdi of life uxe

statue in polished dolerite, about two-thirds of life size. The material and certain details of the statue remind us of the famous sculptures of Gudea (comp. p. 237, above). The attitude of the whole body, the peculiar position of the arms with the clasped hands, the swelling of the muscles of the right arm, the delicately carved nails of the fingers, and the fine shawl with its graceful folds passing over the right breast and loosely thrown over the left arm are equally characteristic or" the statue of Nippur and of those from Tello. But on the other hand the torso under consideration presents distinctive features of its own. It has a long and flowing beard already curled and twisted in that conventional style with which we are familiar from the Assyrian monuments of Nineveh and Khorsabad. A richly embroidered band, one inch and a third wide, passes over the left shoulder, and seems to be fastened to the shawl, which it holds in place. Each wrist is encircled with a bracelet of precious stones, and the neck is adorned with a necklace of large beads strung on a skein of finely spun wool, and in its whole appearance not unlike the *ugal* with which the modern Arab shaikhs of Babylonia fasten their silken headdress *(keffiye).* A short legend with the names of Bel and the donor of the monument was originally engraved on the back of the statue between its two shoulders. But the barbarous and revengeful Elamites who broke so many fine votive gifts of the temple at Nippur cut the inscription away with the exception of the last line, " he made it." In all probability the statue was erected by one of the kings of the dynasty of Ur (between 2700 and 2600 B. C).

The storage room where all the antiquities referred to had originally been kept was discovered by Haynes in his excavations along the southeast wall of the fortified enclosure. It was a well-planned cellar, 36 feet long, li4 feet wide, and 82 feet deep, built entirely into this wall, evidently bv Ur-Gur himself. Descending as far down as the level of the pavement of Naram-Sin, it had, some two and a half feet above the floor of stamped earth, a ledge of crude bricks 1 / feet wide, which was capped by a layer of baked bricks arvd extended completely around the four walls of the room. A discovery made in connection with the next pavement below proved that it had served as a shelf for the safe keeping of treasures, sacrificial gifts, and documents. A construction of baked bricks, which we notice in the illustration facing P-377 (No. 3), seems also to have been built first by one of the kings of the dynasty of Ur, possibly by Ur-Gur himself. But as Haynes did not extend his excavations of the third campaign to the northeast section of the court, we leave it for the present out of consideration.

Comp. the terra-cotta head from Nippur published by me in "The Bab. Exp. of the U. of Pa.," series A, vol. ix, pi. xii, no. 22. Comp. my treatment of the whole question in "The Bab. Exp. of the U. of Pa.," vol. i, series A, part 1, pp. 28, seqq.

A word must be said about Peters' and Haynes' socalled "platform of Ur-Gur," which was covered with the layer of debris containing the precious vase fragments and the door-sockets of Sargon I. Some portions were made of crude bricks, but by far the greater part of it consisted of large lumps of kneaded clay, which "in a moist condition, had been laid up en masse in two thick layers," each one about four feet thick. This " platform," however, did not constitute a large terrace, raised to support the ziggurat itself, and consequently did not run through the whole mound, as I formerly assumed in accordance with the

erroneous views of my predecessors; but, like all the pavements lying above it, it was only an especially thick pavement laid by Ur-Gur as a solid floor for his open court around the stage-tower, and naturally also bore the weight of his additions to the latter. As soon as Haynes commenced to remove it, he made an interesting discovery, which illustrates the great antiquity of a custom previously observed in connection with the Parthian fortress (comp. pp. 366, se-qq.). At different places between its layers of clay he found a number of valuable antiquities. These evidently had been, taken from the rubbish below at the time when Ur-Gur levelled the court, to be placed as talismans in the new foundation. Among the objects thus obtained, we Comp. pp. 247, seqq. , above.

mention several well-formed copper nails and fragments of copper vessels, a fine brick stamp of Sargon I., the fragment of a pre-Sargonic mace-head, two slightly concave seal cylinders in white shell and stone, about twenty well-preserved unbaked clay tablets antedating the period of Sargon, a great quantity of large but badly broken fragments of similar tablets, and, above all, an important stone tablet 7 inches long, 52 inches wide, and a little over 1 inches thick, completely covered on all its six faces with the most archaic cuneiform writing known from the monuments of NufTar and Tello.

Ur-Gur's clay pavement was separated from the next one below, i. e., the fifth one from the top, by a layer of earth generally onlv a few inches deep, — a circumstance that cannot surprise us, as that ruler very evidently removed a considerable mass of debris in order to secure a solid basis for his own unusually thick pavement. Having cut through this thin layer, Havnes, in truth, could exclaim with King Nabonidos: What for ages no king among the kings had seen, the old foundation of Naram-Sin, son of Sargon, that saw I. More than this, he saw the inscribed bricks of both of these ancient rulers, whose very existence until then had been seriously doubted by different scholars. The extraordinary

value of this pavement f[...] archaeology lies in the fa[...] plied the first irrefutable [...] historical character of this ancient Semitic kingdom, that it enabled us more clearly to comprehend the chronological order of the rulers of Tello and Sargon I, and that it enabled us to establish new and indubitable criteria to distinguish between pre-Sargonic and post-Sargonic constructions and antiquities. It is, therefore, a matter of the utmost regret that Haynes, not fully realizing the unique importance of what he had been so fortunate to discover, removed this precious pavement almost completely. It consisted of two courses of baked bricks. The upper one was composed of enormous bricks of uniform size and mould, 15 to 16 inches square and 3 inches thick. Several of them were stamped with the brief legend: "Shargani-shar-ali (the original fuller name of Sargon '), king of Agade, builder of (at) the temple of Bel;" others bore the words: "Naram-Sin, builder of (at) the temple of Bel," while still others were without any inscription. The bricks of Naram-Sin were more numerous than those of his father, the ratio between them being about three to one. Haynes adds the interesting observation that some of these bricks were colored red when he found them, but that their color faded slowly whenever they were exposed to the air and the sunlight. The lower course contained only imperfect bricks of both Sargon and his son and many plano-convex bricks with a thumb-mark on their upper (convex) side. It became evident at once that these peculiar plano-convex bricks, 11 by 7 by 2 inches in size, represent an earlier (pre-Sargonic) period, and that the pavement itself was originally laid by Sargon and relaid by Naram-Sin, both of them utilizing older material in connection with their own bricks.

The same intermingling of earlier bricks with those of the Sargon dynasty was noticed in connection with several fragments of narrow watercourses, which Haynes found at the level of Naram-Sin's pavement, but, as it seems, disconnected with it. His notes at our disposal are very meagre, and refer only to one of these conduits, which came from the middle of the open court and very perceptibly sloped down towards the angle formed by the front face of the *ziggurrat* and the two parallel walls representing part of its entrance. This meandering section, which was traced for twenty-five feet, consisted of nine joints of troughshaped tiles, 15 feet in aggregate length, with an average depth of *i* inches and an average breadth of 3 /£ inches, and continued on either side by peculiarly arranged bricks laid in a clay cement (comp. frontispiece).

Comp. my discussion on this question in "The Bah. Exp. of the U. ot Pa.," series A, vol. i, part I (i893),pp. 16, *seqq,,* and part 2 (1896), pp. 19, *iff.*

As Ur-Gur's pavement rested in some places almost directly upon that of his predecessor, no remains of other buildings were noticed by Haynes in the thin layer between them. However, beneath the storeroom referred to above, but separated from its floor by two feet of rubbish, was found an earlier cellar of the same form, yet slightly smaller in its dimensions. It was also provided with a ledge, upon which a circular tablet, two small rectangular ones, and the fragments of five others were still lying. Four brick stamps of Sargon, with broken handles, which, together with the tablets just mentioned, seem to have been left intentionally or by mistake when Ur-Gur removed the contents of this earlier vault into his own cellar, were recovered from the debris which filled it, while a fifth one was found immediately underneath its eastern corner. The partly ruined walls of this lower structure were only 3 feet high, but originally they must have measured between 5 and 6 feet. About one foot below their top was a deep bowl of yellow pottery, decorated with a rope-pattern ornament on its outside, and set in a rim of thumb-marked bricks. Its use could no longer be determined. The building material of both storerooms was identical in form and size, though somewhat different in color and texture. It follows, therefore, that the small mould employed by UrGur for his crude flat

bricks originated at a much earlier period, a result which is in entire accord with what we learned from our study of the interior mass of the *ziggurrat* (p. 374, above). The important new fact derived from an examination of this lower cellar is that these small crude bricks (9 by 6 by 3 inches) can be traced to about the It was 32 feet long by 7 feet wide. time of Sargon and Naram-Sin, who in all probability were the original builders of the southeast enclosing wall. 2. *Pre-Sargonic Ruins.* According to the date furnished by Nabonidos (comp. p. 273), from which we have no reason to deviate, the pavement of Sargon and Naram-Sin marks the period of about 3800-3750 B. c. in the history of Bel's sanctuary at Nippur. As we saw previously, the accumulation of debris above this pavement during the subsequent 3500 years amounted to 16 or 17 feet, including the clay pavement of Ur-Gur — which alone was 8 feet thick — or 8 to 9 feet, disregarding the latter. This is comparatively little for such a long period, considering the rapidity with which ordinary mud buildings, such as doubtless occupied the temple court at different times, generally crumble and collapse. However, we must not forget that every ruler who laid a new pavement razed the ruined buildings of his predecessors and levelled the ground for his own constructions. But a real surprise was to await us in the lowest strata. In descending into the pre-Sargonic period below Naram-Sin's pavement, which itself lies six to eight feet above the present level of the desert, Haynes penetrated through more than thirty feet of ruins before he reached the virgin soil, or thirty-five feet before he was at the water level.

What do these ruins contain? To what period of human history do they lead us? How was this great accumulation beneath the level of the desert possible? What geological changes have taken place since to explain this remarkable phenomenon? Such and other similar questions may have come to many thoughtful students when they first read these extraordinary facts. Naturally enough, they also occupied the mind of

the present writer seriously for the last six or seven years. I will try to give an answer later in connection with our fourth campaign, when I had the much desired opportunity to study personally the few remains left by my predecessors in the southeast court of the *ziggurrat,* and to compare them with the results of my own excavations in the same temple complex. With the mere reports of Peters and Haynes to guide us, I am afraid we would never have suspected the real nature of these pre-Sargonic ruins. For though the numerous brick and pipe constructions laid bare in the lower strata belonged to the most characteristic and best preserved antiquities unearthed by the Philadelphia expeditions, the work of the two explorers in the debris around them is, perhaps, the least satisfactory part of all their excavations at Nuffar. In consequence of their destructive methods and their superficial work in the upper strata, not being sufficiently prepared for the much more difficult task in the lower ones, they found themselves, with their untrained eyes, suddenly surrounded by the little known remains of Babylonia's earliest civilization,—small bits of mud walls crushed and half dissolved, indistinct beds of ashes, and thousands and thousands of fragments of terra-cotta vases generally not only broken, but forced out of their original shape and position by the enormous weight of earth lying above them. What wonder that they were unable to recognize the essential features of this *tohii wabbhii* themselves, or to communicate what they saw in such a manner as to make it intelligible to others who might feel inclined to trv to untangle the problem for them. These measurements are quoted from the results of an accurate survey of the remains at the southeast court of the *ziggurrat* by Gcere and Fisher in 1900, when I was personally in charge of the excavations.

Haynes' task in the lower strata of the temple court was as clearly defined as that in the upper strata. He had to determine *(A* the earliest form of Bel's sanctuary beneath the *ziggurrat,* as far as this could safely be done by means of tunnels and without a complete removal of the whole ponderous mass above it; *(B)* the character and contents of the court adjoining the latter on the southeast. The proper way to proceed would have been to descend gradually and equally on the whole section to be excavated. But Haynes, repeating his former mistake, attempted to carry out the two parts of his task consecutively, thereby lessening our chances of comprehending the sanctuary as a whole and depriving us of an opportunity of controlling and checking his results at every step. He accordingly descended first by two shafts along the southeast face of the *ziggurrat,* and excavated what was left of the court afterwards. Much against my will, I am obliged to observe his arrangement and to present his work in the manner in which he executed it. He again made several interesting and important discoveries, but he totally failed to ascertain the character of the sanctuary and the real contents of its surroundings, and was often unsuccessful in understanding the single antiquities excavated and their mutual relation to each other.

What after hard work and with an unbiassed mind I could put together from Haynes' reports was published in "The Bab. Exp. of the Univ. *of* Pa.," series A, vol. i, part *z,* pp. 23, *seqq.* It is natural that the picture had to be defective, as the premises communicated on which it was draw» turned out to be largely incorrect. *A.* Haynes was doubtless most eager to find out what was lying beneath the *ziggurrat.* In the course of his excavations he disclosed four constructions either beneath the tower or in its immediate neighborhood, which deserve our special attention. They stood apparently in direct connection with the earliest sanctuary, or even formed part of it.

I. About three and a half feet below Naram-Sin's pavement he came upon the top of a narrow strip of burned brickwork (No. 6). It was about twelve feet distant from the front face of the stage-tower, with which it ran roughly parallel, continuing its course equally to the southwest under the entrance walls of Ur-Gur and to the northeast of the court-yard, in the rubbish of which it

disappeared. This peculiar curb seemed to define an earlier sanctuary towards the southeast. It was 18 inches high, and consisted of seven courses of plano-convex bricks (8 by 5 by 2 Comp. the illustration facing p. 453, which enables the reader to understand the method by which Haynes proceeded.

South-Eastern Section of the Ziggurrat. Designed by H. V. Hilprccht, drawn by C. S. Fisher.
/. Southeast facade built by Ur-Gur. 2. Remains of the entrance ivalli built by the tame. 3. Northeast conduit built by Ur-Gur , repaired by Kadashman-Turgu and Ashurbanapal. 4. Pavement of Ur-Gur. j. Pavement of Naram-Sin. 6. Pre-Sargonic curb. f. The L-shafe d structure. 8. The sc-calleil altar, q. Drain iufth arch. inches and evidently forming the basis for Ur-Gur's standard size of flat bricks). They were curiously creased lengthwise, and their convex surface, without exception, was placed upward in the wall. 2. Inside this enclosure, directly below the pavement (No. 4) of Ur-Gur's *ziggurrat* (No. i) and practically leaning against the latter, if we imagine its front face continued farther down, stood another interesting structure (No. 8). Its top was three feet below Naram-Sin's pavement, and accordingly two feet higher than the base of the curb, from which it was distant about four feet. It was 13 feet long, 8 feet wide, and constructed of unbaked bricks laid in bitumen. The upper hollowed surface of this massive concern was surrounded by a rim of bitumen, 7 inches high, and was covered with a layer of white ashes 2 inches in depth, which contained evident remains of bones. To the southwest of it Haynes discovered a kind of bin also built of crude bricks and likewise filled with (black and white) ashes about a foot deep. He arrived at the conclusion, therefore, that this was an altar, " the ancient place where the sacrificial victims were burned." This explanation is possible, but not probable. In fact, the enormous size of the structure and the rim of bitumen, which necessarily would have been consumed at every large sacrifice, speak decidedly against his theory. Be-

sides, an OldBabylonian altar has an entirely different form on the numerous seal cylinders where it is depicted. My own explanation of this structure will be found in connection with the results of the fourth expedition. 3. Directly below the east corner of Ur-Gur's *ziggurrat,* and parallel with its northeast and southeast faces, was another building, exhibiting the peculiar ground-plot of an L (No. 7), but with regard to its original purpose even more puzzling than either of the two structures just described. Its top was on a level with Naram-Sin's pavement, while its foundation was laid eleven feet below it. This solid tower-like edifice, disconnected with any other structure in its neighborhood, "had an equal outside length and breadth of 23 feet" (northeast and southeast sides), and was about 12 feet thick. "Its splendid walls, which show no trace of a door or opening of any kind, were built of large crude bricks" (on an average 16 inches square and 3/ inches thick), made of " tenacious clay thoroughly mixed with finely cut straw and well kneaded. " They are "of good mould, and in proportions, size, and texture closely resemble the stamped crude bricks of Naram-Sin." Though Haynes devoted much time to their identification, he could determine neither the design of the building nor " the era of its construction." Yet he felt sure that it was " the lowest and most ancient edifice" thus far discovered in the temple enclosure of Nippur, and that its bricks are "the prototype of those of Naram-Sin, which they doubtless preceded by at least several centuries." To my regret, I must differ again with these conclusions after having studied the history of the *ziggurrat* in connection with a second personal visit to the ruins in 1900.

While examining the surroundings of this interesting edifice, Haynes came first upon the same gray or black ashes as are found everywhere in the court of the *ziggurrat* immediately below Naram-Sin's pavement, next upon "lumps of kneaded clay," then upon several stray bits of lime mortar. All these traces of human activity were imbedded in the debris characteristic of the lower strata, which largely consist of earth, ashes, and innumerable potsherds. When he had reached a depth of nine feet from the top of the solid structure, — in other words, had descended about four feet below the bottom of the ancient curb on the southeast l g' side of the stage-tower, — he found a large quantity' of fragments of terra-cotta water pipes of the form here shown. Though the reports before me offer no satisfactory clue as to their precise use, there can be little doubt that they belong to the real pre-Sargonic period. I will try to explain their purpose later, Haynes' interpretation being better passed over in silence.

"Several hundred of these objects were found within a radius of five feet." 4. The explorer's curiosity was aroused at once, and having sunk his shaft a few feet deeper at the spot where the greatest number of these terra-cotta pipes were lying, he made one of the most far-reaching single discoveries in the lower strata of Nippur. After a brief search he came upon a very remarkable drain (No. 9), reminding us of the advanced system of canalization, as *e. g.* we find it in Paris at the present time. It ran obliquely under the rectangular building described above, starting, as I believe, at a corner of the early sanctuary, but evidently having fallen into disuse long before the L-shaped building was erected. It could still be traced for about six feet into the interior of the ruins underlying the *ziggurrat.* But its principal remains were disclosed in the open court, into which it extended double that length, so that its tolerably preserved mouth lay directly below the ancient curb, — a fact of the utmost importance. For it constitutes a new argument in favor of the theory previously expressed that this curb marked the line of the earliest southeast enclosure of the *ziggurrat,* or whatever formerly may have taken the place of the latter. But it also follows that a gutter of some kind, which carried the water to a safe distance, must have existed in this neighborhood outside the curb.

No sooner had Haynes commenced removing the debris from the ruined aqueduct than he found, to his great astonishment, that it terminated in a vaulted section 3 feet long and was built in the form of a true elliptical arch, — the oldest one thus far discovered. The often ventilated question as to the place and time of origin of the arch was thereby decided in favor of ancient Babylonia. The bottom of this reliable witness of pre-Sargonic civilization lies fifteen feet below Naram-Sin's pavement, or ten feet below the base of the curb, which it probably antedates by a century or two. We may safely assign it, therefore, to the end of the fifth pre-Christian millennium. It presented a number of interesting peculiarities. Being 2 feet i inch high (inside measurement), and having a span of i foot 8 inches and a rise of i foot i inch, it was constructed of well baked plano-convex bricks laid on the principle of radiating *voussoirs.* These bricks measured 12 by 6 by 2/ inches, were light yellow in color, and bore certain marks on their upper or convex surface, which had been made either by pressing the thumb and index finger deeply into the clay in the middle of the brick, or by drawing one or more fingers lengthwise over it. Primitive as they doubtless are, they do not (as Haynes inferred) "represent the earliest type of bricks found at Nippur or elsewhere in Babylonia," — which are rather smaller and sometimes a little thicker,— though for a considerable while both kinds were used alongside each other and often in the same building. The curve of the arch was effected "by wedge-shaped joints of the simple clay mortar used to cement the bricks." "On the top of its crown was a crushed terra-cotta pipe about 3 or 3/£ inches in diameter," the meaning of which Haynes declares unknown. I cannot help thinking that it served a purpose similar to the holes provided at regular intervals in our modern casing walls of terraces, etc.; in other words, that the pipe was intended to give exit to the rain water A similar arch, though not quite as old, was soon afterwards unearthed in Tello. Comp. pp. 251, *ieq.,* above.

Thus, *e. g.,* in a drain discovered by the fourth expedition in the east section of the temple court at the lowest level of any of the baked brick constructions hitherto excavated at Nuffar. It contained bricks of the size i 2 by 5 7 a by *z/* inches, and others measuring only 85/g by 48 by 2 inches, while at the foundation of the northeast city gate of Nippur the two kinds of bricks marked two pre-Sargonic periods succeeding each other precisely as in the two lowest buildings of Mound B at Tello (comp. p. 241, above). Comp. also p. 251, above. He who built the drain in part doubtless used older material.

The Earliest Babylonian Arch known. About 4000 ». c.

Seen from the inside of a vaulted tunnel. Observe the T-shaped brick construction at its opening, and a portion of the tivo clay pipes imbedded in its bottom. percolating the soil behind and above it, and in this way to prevent the softening of the clay cement between the bricks of the arch, and the caving-in of the whole vault which would result from it. This explanation being accepted, it necessarily follows that the floor of the court surrounding the earliest sanctuary was not paved with burned bricks, an inference entirely confirmed by the excavations.

There is much to be said in favor of the theory that this skilfully planned tunnel was arched over originally along its entire length. Like its vault, the lower part of the aqueduct presented several most surprising features. "Just beneath the level of the pavement and in the middle of the water channel were two parallel terra-cotta tiles, 8 inches in diameter, with a 6-inch flanged mouth." Haynes, regarding this tunnel as a drain rather than the protecting structure for a drain, was at a loss to explain their presence and significance. They were laid in clay mortar and consisted of single joints or sections, each 2 feet long, cemented together by the same material. We may raise the question: Why are there two small pipes instead of one large one? Evidently because they carried the water from two different directions to a point inside the sacred enclosure, where they met and passed through the arched tunnel together.

They surely testify to a most highly developed system of drainage in the very earliest period of Babylonian history. I have, therefore, no doubt that the so-called "watercocks" previously mentioned served some purpose in connection with this complicated system of canalization, and that in all probability they are to be regarded as specially prepared joints intended to unite terra-cotta pipes meeting each other at a right angle.

The mouth of the tunnel was provided with a T-shaped construction of plano-convex bricks, which Havnes is inclined to consider as " the means employed for centring the arch," or as "a device to exclude domestic animals, like sheep, from seeking shelter within it against the pitiless sun's rays in midsummer," while the present writer rather sees in it a strengthening pillar erected to protect the most exposed part of the tunnel at the point where the arching proper begins and the side walls are most liable to yield to the unequal pressure from the surrounding mass of earth. That the last-mentioned view is the more plausible and the explanation of the single pipe placed over the arch as given above is reasonable, follows from what happened in the course of the excavations. A few months after Haynes had removed the brick structure with its two arms, he reported suddenly that the arch had been "forced out of its shape, probably from the unequal pressure of the settling mass above it, which had been drenched with rain water." Truly the original purpose of these simple means, which had secured the preservation of the arch for six thousand years, could not have been demonstrated more forcibly. At the same time, Haynes, who never thought of this occurrence as having any bearing upon the whole question, could not have paid a higher compliment to the inventive genius and the extraordinary forethought of the ancient Babylonian architects.

Like all other parts, the long side walls of this unique tunnel were built with remarkable care. They consisted of eleven courses of bricks laid in clay mortar — a sure indication that the tunnel itself was not intended to carry water. The six lowest courses, the eighth, the tenth, and eleventh, were placed flatwise with their long edge presented to view, while the seventh and ninth courses were arranged on their long edges like books on a shelf with their small edge visible. Considering all the details of this excellent system of canalization in the fifth pre-Christian millennium, which not long ago was regarded as a prehistoric period, we may be pardoned for asking the question: Wherein lies the often proclaimed progress in draining the capitals of Europe and America in the twentieth century of our own era? It would rather seem as if the methods of to-day are little different from what they were in ancient Nippur or Calneh, one of the four cities of the kingdom of "Nimrod, the mighty hunter before the Lord " (Gen. 10:9, seq.),a.t the so-called "dawn of civilization," — a somewhat humiliating discovery for the fast advancing spirit of the modern age! How many uncounted centuries of human development may lie beyond that marvell o u s age represented by the vaulted tunnel with the two terra-cotta pipes imbedded in cement at its bottom, four feet below the former plain level of "the land of Shinar "!

In the earliest days of Babylonian architecture, bitumen is the regular cement used for important baked brick walls constantly washed by water. Comp. p. 252, above. Small gutters and similar conduits carrying water over open places, etc., show clay mortar occasionally.

B. The results obtained by Haynes in excavating the space between the ancient curb and the later enclosing wall of the *ziggurrat* cannot be considered separately, as they are not only less conspicuous than those just described, but have been reported in such a manner as to defy all efforts to comprehend them from any point of view. At different levels and apparently belonging to different epochs, he found perpendicular drains almost everywhere in the court. They were constructed of single terra-cotta rings, sometimes with perforations in their sides, placed above each other, and occasionally provided with a bell-shaped top-piece, in one case' even bounded by a terra-cotta floor, with a rim around it and made in four sections. The level at which the opening of the lowest perpendicular drain seems to occur lies ten and a quarter to eleven feet below Naram-Sin's pavement, according to mv own measurements of the remains of Haynes' excavated antiquities. It is about identical with that which I ascertained from later researches at the ruins as the original plain level. Here and there Haynes struck a small piece of pavement, which he explained as a fireplace, because of the ashes seen near and upon it. At some places he unearthed fragments of gently sloping water conduits, at others wells built of plano-convex bricks laid in herring-bone fashion, at still others low walls, remains of rooms, too nearly ruined, according to his statements, to allow of a restoration of their ground plan. But above all, he discovered many large terra-cotta jars in various forms and sizes, and without any order, standing in the rubbish around and below them. Wherever he dug he came upon "a multitude of potsherds scattered profusely through the vast accumulation of debris, earth, decomposed refuse matter and ashes." The lowest vase of this large type found whole by him stood about twenty feet below Naram-Sin's pavement. Haynes' idea is that all these vases — and he excavated no less than fifteen at one place within a comparatively small radius — served "for the ablutions of the pilgrims," while some of the drains he regards as urinals and the like. To what inferences are we driven by his reports! The entire sacred precinct of the earliest *ziggurrat* of Bel one huge lavatory and water-closet situated from nine to twenty feet below the ancient level of the plain!

Pre-Sargonic Drain in Terra-Cotta *About 4300 B. C.* This special drain, shown in the illustration on p. 401, descended six and a half feet and had an average diameter of 2 3/£ feet.

Comp. the illustration below ("Section of a Pre-Sargonic Well, Brick laid in Herring-bone Fashion") in the chapter

"On the Topography of Ancient Nippur."

A few additional facts which I have been able to gather after much toil from his reports and descriptions of photographs may follow as an attempt on my part to complete the strange picture of these lowest excavations. They have been arranged according to the levels given by Haynes. Yet be it understood expressly that the present writer cannot always be held responsible for the correctness of the recorded observations. A little below the pavement of Naram-Sin there seems to have been "a very large bed of black and gray ashes of unknown extent, varying in depth from i to i *y* feet." The next objects below this which attracted Haynes' attention are "a fragment of unbaked clay bearing the impression of a large seal cylinder, and a large vase, *i* feet 8 inches in height, which contained the skeleton of a child, several animal bones, and small vases." The importance of this unique find as the first sure example of a pre-Sargonic burial is

Pre-Sargonic Clay Tablet apparent. We therefore look naturally for further details. But our search is unsuccessful. The notes before us contain nothing beyond what I have stated and the remark that "the skeleton is by no means complete; even parts of the skull have decayed."

At about the same level (" two feet below the pavement" mentioned), but evidently at another locality, Haynes reached another "bed of mingled light gray ashes and earth not less than 9 feet in diameter and perhaps 8 inches in extreme depth." It contained two seal cylinders, one gold bead, one badly corroded silver bead, two hundred stone beads, " chiefly of a dull gray slate color, quite in contrast to the more highly colored beads of agate, jasper, etc., generally found in these mounds," and six finger-rings made of several silver wires each about 's of an inch in diameter.

Our interest is roused again by a label accompanying a photograph. It reads: "A large covered jar set in a dais of brick-work. Its top is four feet below the

level of Naram-Sin's pavement." We ask at once: Was there anything in it to show its purpose — ashes, earth, deposits of some kind? The veil drops; we hear nothing more about it. From the same stratum we have "a perfect and well wrought copper nail, i3 inches long," and the fragment of a copper knife or sword?, 4 inches long and i5/ inches wide. "Five archaic tablets" are also reported to have been found "not less than four feet below the level of the same pavement." They are "rudelv fashioned, and appear to be inscribed with numbers oniy represented by straight and curved lines in groups of two, three, nine, and ten. In one instance a column of nine curved marks made by the thumb nail is flanked on either side by a column of ten straight lines, made by the use of some other instrument than the stylus. One tablet has a single group of nine marks on one side of the tablet, and on the opposite side are two groups of two lines or marks each." This description of the first pre-Sargonic cuneiform tablets found *in situ* at Nippur is brief and lacks essential details, but for the time being it sufficed, as the present writer was expected to examine the originals later in Constantinople, and therefore had an opportunity to verify and supplement the reports sent from the field. He found them to be the school exercises of a Babylonian child living in the fifth pre-Christian millennium. But the case unfortunately was different with regard to the many large pre-Sargonic vases unearthed in the lower strata of the court of the *ziggurrat*. Precious as these witnesses of a hoary antiquity appear to us as welcome links in the history of archeology, they do not seem to have been viewed by Haynes in the same light. He took photographs of a few of the jars and caldrons, but he saved none of the originals, though quite a number of them were discovered whole or only slightly broken, and others, which were dug out in fragments, could have been restored without difficulty. If, indeed, any was packed and forwarded with the other excavated antiquities, it surely was not accompanied by a label, and consequently

has not been identified.

One in bone. "It is deeply and rather rudely engraved with two large birds standing upright with outstretched wings." "Between the birds is an unknown animal form."

Exercise Tablet of a Child *From the pre-Sargnrtic Fire Ntcropolil*

The lack of accurate information is especially felt in connection with the following two specimens of early Babylonian pottery which are reported to have been found in a room the walls of which were 11 feet high and lay entirely below Naram-Sin's pavement. How large this room was, whether it had any door, and other necessary details are not stated. It contained two open vases about fourteen feet distant from each other. They stood in their original positions at two different levels, the one being placed about two and a half feet higher than the other. We notice remarkable differences also with regard to their forms and sizes. One was bell-shaped, and had a flat bottom about twice as large in diameter as its mouth. The other was a little over two feet high, measured one foot nine inches across the top, and was decorated with a rope pattern.

In descending a little farther and reaching a level of fifteen feet below the often mentioned pavement, Haynes picked up "a fragment of red lacquered pottery " so much superior in quality to "anything unearthed in the strata subsequent to the time of Ur-Gur," that heat first doubted whether it really belonged to that ancient period. But soon afterwards he obtained another red piece twenty-three feet below the line of demarcation given above, and a small fragment of a black cup of the same-high degree of workmanship three feet below that. It is a well known fact today that similar vases occur also in the lowest strata of Susa in Persia and in the earliest Egyptian ruins.

We cannot close this brief resume of Haynes' activity in the lowest strata of the temple mound without mentioning briefly that he found " a fragment of black clay bearing several human forms in relief upon its curved surface," also twenty-three feet below Naram-Sin's pavement, and another According to my estimate, the accuracy of which I cannot guarantee.

Comp., also, the illustration published in Hilprecht, "The Bab. Exp. of the U. of Pa.," series A, vol. i, part 2, plate xxvii. It appears to have been found in a fine state of preservation according to the photograph, but according to Haynes' report it was "too much broken to be removed." This seems to have been blackened by fire. larger piece two feet deeper; and furthermore, that he took a small gray terra-cotta vase, which he fortunately saved, from the layer between these two objects and described by him as being "literally filled with potsherds of small size, and generally brick red in color." He concludes his observations by stating that

"the lowest strata show a large proportion of black ashes and fine charcoal mingled with the earth," but contain "potsherds in only moderate quantities;' and that "the very earliest traces of civilization at Nippur" — thirty feet below Naram-Sin's pavement! — " are ashes where fires were built on the level plain. "

But Havnes' "level plain" lies rather eighteen to nineteen feet below where it actually was. He will, therefore, pardon us for looking for a more reasonable explanation of these remarkable ashes and potsherds discovered — as the Babylonian scribes would say — in "the breast of the earth," around the sanctuary of Bel, instead of accepting his own, according to which "they mark the level of the alluvial plain where the first inhabitants grazed their flocks and made their primitive abodes."

In view of the prominent position which the temple of Bel, as the oldest and most renowned sanctuary of all Babylonia,

Earliest Vase from Nippur

Pre-Sargonic Cup occupied in the political and civil life of its population, it has been necessary to lay before the reader all the principal facts which I could extricate from the often obscure reports at my disposal, in order to enable him to comprehend the condition and characteristic features of the ruins and to acquaint himself with the history and methods of their exploration. My review of Haynes' work on the western side of the Shatt en-Nil will have to be briefer, as he, like Peters, never attempted to explore those mounds systematically, but, on the whole, was satisfied with recovering all the tablets and other antiquities from the numerous unbaked brick buildings which they contained. Most of the twenty thousand cuneiform records and fragments excavated between 1893 and 1896 in the long ridge limited by the numbers VI and VIII on the plan of the ruins (p. 305) are lists (and a few contracts) dated in the reigns of Cassite rulers (about 1500-1250 B. C), several of which show exceedingly interesting and peculiar seal impressions. Some two or three thousand belong to the third pre-Christian millennium. They include many so-called contracts (and receipts) from the time of the kings of the dynasties of Ur, (N)isin, Larsa, and Babylon. There are a few letters and literary tablets among them, which may originally have formed part of the temple library situated on the opposite bank (IV) of the canal. The neo-Assyrian, Chaldean and Persian dynasties are represented by about twelve hundred contract tablets.

More than seven hundred of these are of especial importance. At the end of May, 1893, they were discovered in one of the rooms of a ruined building at a depth of twenty feet below the surface (VIII on the plan of the ruins, p. 305). The great care with which they had been made, the exceptionally pure and soft clay chosen, and the large number of fine seal impressions exhibited by many of them attracted my attention at once. Upon closer examination they proved to belong to the business archives of a great Babylonian firm, Murashu Sons, bankers and brokers at Nippur, who lived in the time of Artaxerxes I. (464-424 B. c.) and Darius II. (423-405 B.C.), in whose reigns the documents are dated. According to a system better known I remember, c. g., a tablet dated in the government of Ur-Ninib of (N)isin, about five hundred to eight hundred dated according to Rim-Sin's new era (fall of (N)isin), several dated in the reign of a king Bel-bani, and a few dated in the reigns of other kings previously not known. Comp. p. 38.

Clay Tablet with Seal Impressions from the Archives of Murashu Sons from the later Roman Empire, this banking-house acted also as an agent for the Persian kings, from whom it had rented the taxes levied upon their Babylonian subjects at Nippur and neighboring districts. The contents of these 730 tablets accordingly had an unusual interest. The active life and motion which pulsated in the streets of the famous " city of Bel," in the fore-courts of its temple, and in the fields on the palm and corn-laden banks of " the great canal " at the time when Ezra and Nehemiah led the descendants of Nebuchadrezzar's exiled Jews from these very plains to Palestine, were unfolded vividly before our eyes. We were enabled to confirm and supplement what the Greeks tell us about the large number of Persians settled in the various provinces of the vast empire. We became acquainted with the names and titles of the different officers — among them the *databari*, known from Daniel 3: 2, *seq.* — who were stationed all over the fertile country between the lower Euphrates and Tigris, to look after the interests of their government.

From early days Babylonia was a land of many tongues, but at no other period of its varied history are we so impressed with the great proportion of the foreign element in this rich alluvial plain as during the centuries following the fall of Babylon, 538 B. c. The population of Babylonia at the time of Artaxerxes J and Darius II appears about as thoroughly mixed as that of the United States in our own time. And as the emigrants from Europe and Asia brought their customs and religions, their languages and the local and personal names of their native lands to their new settlements in the New World, so Persians and Medians, Arameans and Sabeans, Judeans and Edomites, etc., transplanted those of their former abodes, from which they often had been carried away by the vicissitudes of war, to ancient Babylonia. Very numerous are Persian and Aramean personal proper names in these documents. Unusually large is the number of Jewish names known from the Old Testament, especially from the books of Ezra and Nehemiah. There can be no doubt that a considerable number of the Jewish prisoners carried away by Nebuchadrezzar were settled in Nippur and its neighborhood, where many of their descendants continued to live as long as the city existed (about 900 A. n.), to judge from the many inscribed Hebrew bowls excavated everywhere in the upper strata of its ruins. The Talmudic tradition which identifies Nippur with the Biblical Calneh gains new force in the light of these facts, strengthened by the argument that the earliest and most important Babylonian city, which occupies the first place in the Sumerian story of the creation, could not well have been omitted by the writer of Genesis 10: 10. And we feel we tread on sacred ground, considering that even Ezekiel himself, while among the captives of his people at Tel-Abib, while admonishing and comforting the scattered inhabitants of Judah's depopulated cities, and while seeing his famous visions of the cherubims on the banks of " the river Chebar in the land of the Chaldeans " (Kzek. 1:1,3; 3:15510:15), stood in the veVy shadow of Babylonia's national sanctuary, the crumbling walls of the great temple of Bel. For soon after the business archives of Murashu Sons had been cleaned and catalogued by the present writer, he was fortunate enough to discover the river Chebar, for which hitherto we had searched the cuneiform literature in vain, in the *nar Kabari,* one of the three or four large navigable canals of ancient Nippur.

Since the publication of Tiele, *Baby/.- Assyr. Geschichle,* p. 427, the modern commentators have begun to change the Hebrew 2'2S bn (*TelAb'ib,* "Mound of" the ear of corn ") with good reason into the Babylonian 212S b»"li *Til-Abub,* "Mound of the storm-flood," a name by which the Babylonians used to denote

the large sand-hills scattered over their plain even in those early days. Comp. espccially the 'ate Richard Kraetzschmar's *Das Buck Eztchiel,* Gottingen, 1900, pp. 5, *sea.,* 34. To-day such enormous sand-hills are found in several districts of 'Iraq, notably in the neighborhood of Jokha, Warka (comp. pp. 144 and 152, above), Tell-Ibrahim (= Cuthah, comp. p. 277, above), and Nuffar. Those of Nuffar are very extensive, but not very high. They rise about ten to thirty feet above the desert, three to four miles to the north of the ruins. I regard them as identical with the 777*Abi(i)b* of Ezekiel chiefly for the following four considerations: 1. The archives of Murashu Sons proved that many Jewish exiles actually must have been settled in the districts around Nippur. 2. All these Babylonian sandhills, while constantly changing their aspect within the area covered by them owing to certain whirlwinds, and gradually extending even farther into the fertile plain, on the whole have remained stationary, as we can infer from a comparison of the reports of early travellers with our own observations. 3. The remarkably large number of Hebrew bowls found everywhere in the smaller mounds within a radius of five to ten miles to the east and north of Nuffar testify to a great Jewish settlement in these regions as late as the seventh century of our own era. 4. The extensive sand-hill, or *til-abub,* of Nuffar lies about a mile or more to the cast of the ancient bed of the Shatt en-Nil, a fact which agrees most remarkably with a statement in Ezek. 3:15, according to which the prophet went from the Chebar to Tel-abi(u)b, so that this Jewish colony cannot have been situated in the immediate fertile neighborhood of " the great canal."

The question arose at once, which one of these canals still to be traced without difficulty by their lofty embankment walls represents " the river" under consideration. It seemed natural to identify "the Chebar," or *nar Kabari,* meaning literally "the great canal," with the now dry bed of the Shatt en-Nil, which passes through the ruined city. But while having even so expressed myself in my

lectures, I preferred to withhold this theory from my introduction to vol. ix of our official publication until I could examine the topography of the entire region once more personally and search the inscriptions for additional material. I am now prepared to furnish the required proof and to state the results of my later investigations briefly as follows: I. The largest of all the canals once watering the fields of Nippur is often written ideographically as "the Euphrates of Nippur," a name occurring even in the old-Babylonian inscription of the third millennium. It is evident that only the canal on which Nippur itself was situated, *l. e.,* the Shatt en-Nil of the Arabs, which divides the mounds into two approximately even halves, could have been designated in this manner. 2. An examination of all the inscriptions at my disposal revealed the fact that *nar Kabari* is the phonetic pronunciation of the ideographic writing "The Euphrates of Nippur," and therefore also the former Babylonian name of the Shatt en-Nil. Hence it follows that " the river Chebar in the land of the Chaldeans" was the greatest canal of Babylonia proper, " the great canal " *par excellence,* which branched off from the Euphrates somewhere above Babylon and ran through almost the whole interior of the country from north to south. It was the great artery which brought life and fertility to the otherwise barren alluvial plain enclosed by the Euphrates and the Tigris and turned the whole interior into one luxuriant garden. The *nar Kabari* had the same significance for Nippur, the most ancient and renowned city of the country, as the Euphrates for Sippara and Babylon, or the Nile for Egypt, and therefore was called most appropriately "the Euphrates of Nippur" by the Sumerians, " the great canal" by the Semitic Babylonians, and the "river Nile" by the Arabic population of later times. In some parts of Southern Babylonia the bed of the canal was wider than that of the present Euphrates below Hilla, while its average depth at Nippur measured from fifteen to twenty feet.

For the present comp. the passages

quoted by me in " The Bab. Exp. of the U. of Pa.," series A, vol. ix, p. 76, and the cone inscription ot Samsu-iluna translated below (Fourth Campaign). Wherever Haynes drove his tunnels into the real Babylonian strata of the long ridge on the west bank of the Shatt en-Nil, he came upon extensive remains ot mud buildings, broken tablets, scattered weights and seal cylinders. My examination of all the portable antiquities excavated there led in every case to the same result, that this long-stretched mound represents the business quarter of ancient Nippur, and conceals the large mercantile houses, the shops of handicraftsmen, — the bazaars of the citv, which occupied this site at least from the time of Ur-Gur, and probably even from the days of Sargon I. The contents of the archives of the firm ot Murashu Sons; the strictly businesslike character of all the neo-Babylonian tablets obtained from there; the eighteen thousand administrative lists and books of entry ot the Cassite period; the thousands of case tablets of the third pre-Christian millennium; the large number of trian gular clay labels — and more espe cially fifty-six of ellipsoidal form found together in one room — all of which bear a short legend or a seal impression, or both at the same time, and without exception are provided with holes for the thread by which they were tied to sacks, baskets, boxes, merchandise ot every description; the many oblong" and in stone, one

Triangular Label (" One Lamb, the Shepherd Uzi-ilu") duck-shaped weights (fragmentary) even sculptured in the form ot a resting lamb inscribed with seven lines of early Babylonian writing, and the much more numerous ones in clay, sometimes evidently belonging to a series; the exceptionally large number of seal cylinders, as a rule cracked, broken, badly effaced or otherwise damaged by fire, which for the greater part were gathered in the accumulated debris of the ravines or in the loose earth

Label with Seal Impression
Abnui 2200 B. C.
Haynes regarded them as amulets or charms, a pardonable mistake, as he could not read their inscriptions.

Among them the fine inscribed hematite weight with the inscription, "ten shekels, gold standard, the *Jumkar,"* published in Hilprecht, "The Bab. Exp. of the U. of Pa.," series A, vol. i, part *z,* no. 132. on the slopes of the mounds, — these and many other facts and considerations which cannot be set forth here in detail afford positive proof for the correctness of my theory.

Some of the houses seem to have covered a considerable area. Haynes calls them palace-like buildings. It is, therefore, the more to be regretted that the unscientific method of excavating introduced by Peters and continued by Haynes especially in this section, where confessedly they endeavored to secure the largest possible amount of inscribed material at the least possible outlay of time and money, has thus far deprived me of the possibility of restoring the ground plan and describing the inner arrangement of even a single real Babylonian business house. In several instances "the archives were found in the very position in which they had been left when the building was destroyed." The tablets were "placed on their edges reclining against each other like a shelf of leaning books in an ill-kept library of to-day." As a rule, however, they lay broken and in great confusion on the ground, or they were buried between the layers of rubbish which covered the floor. Some of the tablets, particularly those of the Cassite period, must have been of an enormous size. Restored on the basis of excavated fragments, the largest unbaked tablet was loby 14 by 3 inches and the largest baked, 16 by 12 by 3 2 inches. As most of the tablets discovered were unbaked or baked insufficiently, they not only are badly broken and chipped off everywhere, but they have suffered exceedingly from the humidity of the soil in which they lay. In many cases the salts of nitre contained in the clay had crystallized and caused the gradual disintegration of complete documents, or at least, the flaking off of the

Ellipsoidal Label.

King

Dated in the Reign of inscribed surfaces. Frequently they crumbled to dust immediately after their discovery or soon afterwards, on their way from Nuffar to Constantinople. The often advised baking of such tablets was not only useless, but proved repeatedly even most damaging, as it accelerated the process of dissolution and hardened the dirt, filling the cuneiform characters to such a degree that it could not be removed later. Thus far, none of the means generally recommended has proved an effective preservative for tablets doomed to destruction long before they are discovered. While the large mass of documents obtained from this ridge (VII—VII) has to do with transactions of private individuals, there are others which evidently have reference to government affairs and to the business administration of the temple. This is especially the case with a number of tablets excavated in the southeast section (VI), situated opposite the priests' quarters and the temple library (IV). It seems, therefore, not unlikely that the temple owned some property on the west side of the canal also, and that a large government building once occupied part of this mound. The fragments of several barrel cylinders of Sargon of Assyria (722-705 B. C.) discovered at VI by the first (comp. pp. 3 12, *seq.,* above) and third expeditions point in this direction. It cannot be denied, on the other hand, that a number of the objects coming from these hills most assuredly were out of their original places, and very probably were carried at different times from the temple quarters to the west part of the city. I count among these antiquities a terracotta dog with a brief neo-Babylonian legend; several stray lapis lazuli discs from the upper strata with votive inscriptions of Kurigalzu, Nazi-Maruttash and

Cassite Account Tablet. About 1400 B. c.
Votive Tablet *of* Ur-Enlil. About 4000 B. C. *Upper Section: Ur-Enlil offering a libation to Enlii (Bel).*
Lotcer Section: A pastoral scene goat, sheep, herdsmen).

Kadashman-Turgu (about 1400 B. c.); a fine inscribed terra-cotta vase, about 3 inches high, of the third preChristian millennium, originally filled " with the choicest oil" and presented as "a bridal gift" to some deity, the flat round ends of two inscribed terra-cotta cones found in 1893 and 1895 respectively, at places and levels widely apart from each other, and containing identical inscriptions of Damiqilishu, a little-known " powerful king, king of (N)isin, King of Shumer and Akkad," who " restored the great wall of (N)isin and called its name *Damiqi/is/iu-migirNinib"* (" D. is the favorite of the god Ninib"); three inscribed unbaked clay prisms of the same period; a soapstone tablet of Dungi of Ur recording his constructing a temple to the goddess Damgalnunna in Nippur; the very ancient exquisite stele of Ur-Enlil, a high officer in the service of Bel, and several other valuable votive objects, sculptured and inscribed. Most of them were gathered in the loose earth, or in the rubbish which had accumulated at the foot of the mounds and along the ancient bed of the Shatt en-Nil. Haynes discovered even a brick stamp of Naram-Sin and fragments of others, and one redcolored stamped brick of the same great ruler, of which he speaks himself as not having been found *in situ*.

From the material before us it becomes certain that this whole ridge must have been occupied from the earliest times to the Christian period. The numerous slippershaped coffins with their ordinary contents, a good many Kufic and Arsacide coins, Hebrew bowls, the fragments of an egg-shell inscribed with Hebrew letters in black ink, and other antiquities taken by Haynes from rooms just beneath the crest of the long-stretched hill belonged to the latest inhabitants of Nippur in the first millennium of our era. The last three thousand years of Babylonian history are represented by dated business documents found in crude brick structures lying one above another. The age of these houses can frequently be determined also from the different sizes of bricks employed in them, which are familiar to us from the study of the successive strata in the southeast court of the *ztggur-rat*. The deepest trenches and tunnels cut by Haynes into different parts of this ridge revealed abundant plano-convex bricks, crude and baked, with the well-known ringer impressions which characterize the pre-Sargonic settlements everywhere in Babylonian ruins. Comp. p. 382, note *2.* -Comp. Hilprccht, *l. c.,* vol. i, part *2,* no. 123. Comp. the illustration on tle previous page (417).

In connection with the last statement it is interesting and important to know that not far from the place which indicates the business house of Murashu Sons on our plan of the ruins (p. 305, above), Haynes sank a shaft, 4 ? feet square, through nearly ninety-eight feet of debris, the last eighteen or nineteen feet of which lie below the present level of the desert. Only the lowest thirty feet of these ancient remains of human civilization thus examined deserve our attention, as the shaft was bv far too narrow to determine details and differences in the higher strata which could claim a scientific value. Here, as at the temple mound, the lowest thirty feet consist principally of ashes, potsherds, and lumps of clay worked by the hand. "Numerous traces of fire abound everywhere."..." The fire or ash-pits are still clearly shown."... "The ashes are often three or more inches in depth."..." Occasionally a decayed bone is met with. "..." Bits of charcoal and unconsumed brands charred" are mixed with ashes and earth. In view of Haynes' theory concerning the lowest strata of the court of the *ziggurrat,* it cannot surprise us to find that he connects all these traces with the daily life of the earliest inhabitants, and interprets them as " marking the places where the evening camp-fires were built by the first semi-migratory dwellers on this spot."

The lowest real brick structure observed by the excavator was about thirtv feet above the undisturbed soil; in other words, at about the level of Naram-Sin's pavement in the temple mound. We are led to this period also by an examination of the crude bricks, which measured 17 inches square and about 4 inches thick. What was the nature of this ancient structure? "It was a long, narrow cell, 5 feet 9 inches long, 1 foot 7 inches wide, and 1 foot 1 inch high, — a grave covered by a gable roof made of similar bricks, which rested on the sides of the low wall and met in an imaginary ridge-pole like the letter A." The tomb contained nothing but the crumbling remains "of a medium-sized adult and a broken vessel of coarse potterv."

A corbelled arch of crude bricks and "a vaulted cellar of burned bricks," the latter about 12 by 8 feet in length and breadth, were discovered somewhere at " a low level " in the same mounds. From general indications, I should ascribe them to about 2500 B. C. They give evidence to the fact that arches and vaults were by no means uncommon in ancient Nippur, but as accurate details have not been given bv the excavator, we must be satisfied with this simple statement.

In August, 1893, Haynes began a search for the original bed and embankment of the Chebar. He accordingly cut a long trench into the narrowest part of the depression marked V on the plan of the ruins (p. 305), and directed it from the middle of this open area to its northeast boundary and along the latter. At a depth of twenty and a half feet below the surface, which is somewhat higher than the present level of the desert, he reports to have found the ancient bed "in the middle of the stream." The northeastern embankment of the canal proved to be "a sloping bank of reddish clay," so that the natural inference would be "that there was no well-built quay at this point" of the watercourse. While excavating the rubbish accumulated in the bed of the canal, Haynes unearthed three large fragments of a round terra-cotta fountain originally from I 2 to 2 feet in diameter, and on its outer face showing a group of birds in high relief coarsely executed.

Corbelled Arch of Crude Bricks *About 2300 B. C.*

Early Babylonian Terra-Cotta Fountain from the Bed of the Chebar

One of the fragments exhibits a richly dressed person standing on the backs of two of these creatures, through the open mouths of which the water passed. The antiquity belongs to a period prior to 2000 B. c.

It is unnecessary to follow Haynes through all the trial trenches which at various times he opened in the mounds around the temple complex. Among the Parthian and Sassanian graves in which the upper strata abound everywhere, I mention particularly one containing "a very

Three Jars found at the Head of a Parthian Coffin. About 200 B. C. high bath-tub coffin" and three jars placed around the head. The latter were filled with as many beautiful small alabaster bottles, a large number of decayed pearls, precious stones, necklaces, ear-rings, nose-rings, finger-rings, one in-scribed seal cylinder in red jasper still retaining its bronze mounting, and six-teen uninscribed ones, several scarabaei, a pair of iron tweezers, and remains of linen and woolen stuffs showing the structure and fibre of the fabrics, and the white and dark-brown colors of the threads. Havnes opened al-together six hundred graves in the dif-ferent parts of Nuffar, some of them very elaborate, most of them, however, being slipper-and bath-tub-shaped coffins in terra-cotta. Others were crude brick boxes; many consisted only of one or two urns greatly varying in size and form; a few were made of wood, which generally had crumbled to dust. Nearly fifty representative urns and coffins were saved and sent to Constantinople. One gray slippershaped coffin was dec-orated with "a male figure with sword and short tunic over a long shirt, four times repeated in as many panels." Another richly ornamented and blue enamelled but fragmentary sarcophagus of the same type showed "six human-headed bulls in two long, narrow panels. " By far the greatest number of the enamelled slipper-shaped

Blue Enamelled Slippcr-Shapcd Cof-fin with Conventional Female Figures coffins were decorated with a conven-tional female figure, a pattern seeming-ly reserved for the burial of women.

The northwest mound of the eastern half of the ruins yielded a few unbaked tablets of the neo-Babylonian and Assyrian periods, a stray stamped brick of Dungi, and the largest uninscribed baked brick hitherto discovered at Nuf-far, measuring no less than 20 inches square. In the upper strata of the low mounds which lie about midway be-tween the temple of Bel and the Shaft en-Nil, Haynes unearthed a peculiar building originally covered with a dome, " in the style of the ziarets or holy tombs of India, Persia, and Turkey." Its ruined walls, which formed a square 32 feet long, were constructed of specially made soft yellow baked bricks (123 inches square by 3 inches thick) laid in lime mortar. They were 6 feet 9 inch-es thick, and still stood 7 feet 8 inches high. In the sides, which run parallel with the four faces of the *ziggurrat*, were openings 7 feet 10 inches wide. The one towards the southeast was part-ly occupied by an altar, which stood up-on a raised platform and consisted of three receding stages. Within the build-ing and exactly in front of the altar was a raised block of crude bricks " smooth-ly plastered with lime mortar," like the sides of the latter and the walls of the edifice. "Upon and around the altar to a considerable distance from it were wood ashes 6 inches in depth, an accu-mulation that could not have been ac-counted for by an occasional fire." It doubtless represents a sanctuary of the late Parthian period.

The most important discovery report-ed from the trenches in the western sec-tion of the same mounds, where they slope gradually towards the Shatt en-Nil, is the quadrangular terracotta lid of a coffin ornamented with the rude bas-relief of a lion. It belongs to the same age as the building just mentioned. For a few days excavations were carried on also in the great elevation to the east of the temple. They revealed the existence of unbaked cuneiform tablets of a very large size in a part of the ruins scarce-ly yet touched by the expedition. The large triangular mound to the south of the temple (in 1889 designated by the present writer as the probable site of the temple library) was not examined by the explorer during the three years which he passed almost without interruption at Nuffar.

It was stated above (p. 360) that in the summer of 1895 Haynes spent the morning hours of two weeks at the long, narrow ridge (II-III) to the north of the temple, in order to ascertain the foun-dations and dimensions of the ancient city wall, where in 1894 he and Meyer had discovered stamped crude bricks of Naram-Sin immediately below

Ur-Gur's material. He unearthed great numbers of terracotta cones, sometimes colored red or black at their round bases, and fragments of water spouts "in the debris that had gathered at the bottom of the wall." The former were either small and solid or large and hollow, and evidently had been used for decorating its parapet; the latter had served for draining the upper surface of the structure. As Haynes accidentally had laid his trench diagonally through a bastion of the wall, as was determined by the architects of the fourth expedi-tion, his measurements obtained at that time proved by far too great, and conse-quently may be disregarded at present, while his theory connected with the oc-cupation of" the spacious and airy sum-mit" of the wall by rooms for the pil-grims is based upon the plan of modern *khans* or caravansaries rather than upon a correct conception of an early Baby-lonian temple, and therefore has no real merit. We close this sketch of his work at the city wall by mentioning that he reports to have discovered " a bubbling spring" — he probably means an open well — on the northeastern side of the great open court confined by this ram-part, and "the brick platforms and curbs where the water-pots rested " on either side of the "spring." The bricks were those in use at the time of Naram-Sin and his immediate successors.

Fourth Campaign, iSaS-igoo. The first three American expeditions to NurTar had been sent out by the trustees ot the Babylonian Exploration Fund of Philadelphia in affiliation with the University of Pennsylvania; the fourth stood under the direct control of the University of Pennsylvania. A large new museum building had been erected principally by private subscriptions, and a reorganization of the Archaeological Department of the University had taken place under Provost Harrison. The late Dr. Pepper, who had worked so energetically for the development of archaeological interests in his city, became its first president. The property of the Exploration Fund was transferred to the university, and the expedition committee henceforth discharged its duties in immediate connection with and as one of the most effective bodies of the new department. The beginning of actual American excavations in Babylonia will forever remain connected inseparably with the name of E. W. Clark, of Philadelphia, who was faithfully assisted by Mr. W. W. Frazier. It was at the initiative of the former's brother, Mr. C. H. Clark, the well-deserving chairman of the Babylonian Publication Committee, that the fourth expedition was called into existence. A small but distinguished group of generous Philadelphia citizens, whose names have become regular household words in the archaeological circles of the United States, was ready again to support the scientific undertaking. In May, 1898, the present writer left New York, in order to secure the necessary firman for the new expedition. As His Majesty the Sultan continued his gracious attitude towards the University's representative, and as the Ottoman government and the directors of the Imperial Museum facilitated his work in every way, the important document was granted so speedily that a fortnight after his arrival in Constantinople he was enabled to cable the welcome news to Philadelphia and to advise the formal appointment of the new expedition staff, the details of which had been arranged previously. Soon afterwards Dr. Pepper died suddenly in California, from heart-failure. His loss was seriously felt; but Mr. E. W. Clark, as chairman of the Expedition Committee, assisted by Mr. John Sparhawk, Jr., as treasurer, carried on the great work with unabated energy. The Babylonian Committee of the Department of Archaeology, considering the serious disadvantages which

had accrued to science from the unsatisfactory equipment and the one-sided methods of exploration pursued by the second and third expeditions at Nuffar, was determined to profit from its past experience, and to relieve Haynes, who had offered his services again to the University of Pennsylvania, of that extraordinary nervous stress under which he had been laboring most of the time during the previous years. It was decided to imitate the example set by the British Museum at the first period of Assyrian exploration, when the responsibility of the work in the field was divided successfully between Sir Henry Rawlinson, as scientific director of all the English excavations carried on in Assyria, Babylonia, and Susiana, and Hormuzd Rassam, as chief practical excavator (comp. pp. 128, seq.). The present writer accordingly was appointed Scientific Director, and Haynes, as Field Director, was entrusted with the practical management of the work at the ruins. H. Valentine Geere, of Southampton, England, one of the two gentlemen who had been sent in 1895 to the assistance of Haynes (comp. pp. 360, seq.), and Clarence S. Kisher of the Department of Architecture at the University of Pennsylvania — the latter going without a salary — were chosen as the two architects of the new expedition. At Haynes' special request his wife was allowed to accompany the party as a guest of the committee, which most generously defrayed all her travelling and living expenses. It should be stated at the very outset that the remarkable comfort which the members of the fourth expedition enjoyed, in comparison with the numerous deprivations experienced by the previous ones, was in no small measure due to Mrs. Haynes' active interest in their personal welfare. She not only assisted her husband as his private secretary in his manifold duties, but she took complete charge of the household of the expedition in such an admirable manner that the members of our camp at Nuffar breathed a true homelike atmosphere thoroughly appreciated by our several visitors from Susa, Babylon, Baghdad, and Basra. This

changed condition appeared so strange to the present writer, who had retained such a vivid recollection of the primitive style in which we lived in 1889, that, though our windows consisted only of spoiled photographic negatives, he at times could almost imagine himself transplanted to one of the watering-places of the Arab caliphs in the desert. Comp. p. 148, above. Comp. the zinctvpc of a section of this wall below (Fourth Campaign, Temple Mound, Section 6). As reproduced in Hilprecht, "The Bab. Exp. of the U. of Pa.," series A, vol. i, part 2, pp. 20, seq. The fine large pavilion erected for an exhibit of antiquities obtained chiefly from the temple of Bel was the magnificent gift of Mr. Daniel Baugh, of Philadelphia, whose name it very appropriately bears. On September 22, 1898, the formal contract was executed with Haynes, and the resumption of the excavations at Nuffar authorized for a period of two years, including the time consumed by travel, at an expense of £30,000, the work in the field to be carried on with an average force of 180 Arab laborers. Two days later Haynes left New York for England, where he was to meet his architects and to complete the necessary outfit, to which a number of prominent American firms most liberally had contributed general supplies, foods, and medicine.-Soon afterwards a final meeting was held by the present writer with the members of the expedition at the harbor of Southampton, in which the plans of operation and other details were discussed once more, whereupon the former returned to Philadelphia in the hope of joining the party at Nuffar in the course of the following year, as soon as the organization of the University Museum should have been completed. Mr. Haynes, with his wife and the two architects, proceeded to Marseilles, whence they sailed to Baghdad by way of Port Said, Aden, and Basra, arriving in the city of Harun ar-Raschid on December 18 in the same year. Comp. Alois Musil, *Łuseir 'Antra una andere Schlosser ostiieh von Moab*, part i, in *Sitzutigsberichtc der Wiener Akademie Jer Wistemchaften, phil.-hist. Cl.,* cxliv, vol. 7, pp. 1-51 (1902). In behalf of the committee and the members of the expedition, I take this opportunity to express the University's warm appreciation of the public spirit displayed by the representatives of these firms in the interest of science, and append their names in alphabetical order: The Adams & Westlake Co., Chicago, 111.; Z. & W. M. Crane, Dalton, Mass.; Erie Preserving Co., Buffalo, N. Y.; Genesee Pure Food Co., Leroy, N. Y.; H. J. Heinz & Co., Pittsburg, Pa.; C. I. Hood, Lowell, Mass.; Horlick Food Co., Racine, Wis.; Libby, McNeill & Libby, Chicago, Ill.; Richardson & Robbins, Dover, Del.; Rumford Chemical Works, Providence, R. I.; Edward G. Stevens, New York; Trommer Extract of Malt Co., Fremont, Ohio.

The sub-committee created in 1895 (comp. PP-358, *seq.*), and consisting of Messrs. E. W. Clark, John Sparhawk, Jr. , and the Scientific Director, acted again as an advisory board to those in the field. The plan which I had outlined as a basis for the work of the fourth campaign was, if possible, to determine the following points: 1. The precise character of the temple of Bel at the principal periods of its long history, and especially before the time of King Ur-Gur (about 2700 B. c), whom Haynes regarded as the probable monarch who at Nippur had introduced the stage-tower, the most important part of all the large Babylonian temples. 2. The general dimensions of pre-Sargonic Nippur; that is, to ascertain whether outside of the temple of Bel and the ashes and potsherds, etc., previously disclosed by Haynes' tunnels and shafts in the ridge to the west of the Shatt en-Nil, trails could be found which would allow us to draw more positive conclusions with regard to the size and nature of the earliest settlements. 3. The length and the course of the city walls, so far as they were not discernible above ground, and the location of one or more of the three or four large city gates of Nippur, so frequently mentioned in the later Babylonian inscriptions which had been unearthed by the first three expeditions. 4. The exact position, extent, and charac-

ter of the temple library, which, since mv first ride over the mounds of NufFar, I had consistently declared was buried in

Comp. Hilprecht, "The Bab. Exp. of the U. of Pa.," series A, vol. i, part 2, p. 17.

the most southern group of mounds on the eastern side of the Shatt en-Nil (IV). 5. The distinguishing features in the modes of burials practised at ancient Nippur, and the various types and forms of pottery once used, by means of well-defined strata, dated documents, and accurate labels, in order to obtain satisfactory rules for dating the numerous vases which, so far, we had been unable to assign to any period of Babylonian history with a reasonable degree of certainty. 6. To these important problems, at Mr. E. W. Clark's special request, was added the task of excavating completely the large building with its colonnade on the west side of the Shatt en-Nil (VII), which had been discovered and partly explored by the first expedition (comp. pp. 308, 313), and which received some attention also during the second campaign by Dr. Peters (comp. pp. 337, *seqq.* who assigned it to the Cassite period (about 1300 B. c.), while the present writer had declared it to be Parthian (about 250 B. c.).

In order not to influence Haynes unduly in his own judgment, and to secure for him a necessary amount of liberty of action in the field within the bounds of a clearly defined course, it was decided not to communicate to him the reasons for our plans nor the hopes we expected to realize by their proper execution. Accordingly we confined ourselves to positive instructions with regard to the use of photography, the manner in which his note-books were to be kept, the preserving and packing of the antiquities desired for transport, and impressed upon him the following rules as a basis for his operations: T. To devote only one third to one fourth of his force to the methodical exploration of the temple mound; to select the east section of the court of the *ziggurrat* and the enclosing wall of the latter as the object of his mission; and to pay greater at-

tention to the peculiarities of the different layers than had been the case in the past. 2. While recommending " the whole of the mounds" to his care, to concentrate his efforts principally upon two of the other mounds, namely, the so-called "Tablet Hill" (IV, the probable site of the temple library), which he had not touched at all during the third campaign, and which, above all, needed a methodical exploration; and the mound represented by the so-called " Court of Columns" (VII) at the north end of the ridge to the west of the Shatt en-Nil. 3. To make the settling of the numerous topographical questions one of the most essential tasks of this expedition, and to regard the location of one or more of the ancient city gates, particularly of the eastern and southern gates, in all probability represented by the *abullu rabu* (" the large gate "), and the *abulia S/iibi*

The Daghara Canal and a Freight-Boat *(Mcshhuf)* of the Expedition *Uruku* of the inscriptions, as "one of the necessary points to be determined during this campaign." The critical examination of the exposed structures and antiquities, the determination of their age, character, or contents, and their topographical and historical bearing upon our knowledge of ancient Nippur, and the acquiring of all such other details as should enable us to carry the plan, as outlined above, to a successful issue, had naturally to constitute the Scientific Director's principal share in the work of the fourth expedition.

How far did the proceedings of the party in the field justify the committee's hopes and expectations? Towards the end of January, 1899, the expedition left Baghdad, accompanied by a caravan of sixty-two camels and several mules, which carried its equipment and stores to Hilla. Here they were transferred to six large native sailing-boats, used also for conveying the stafFand the Ottoman commissioner, half-a-dozen servants, about 150 of our former workmen from the vicinity of Babylon with their families and supplies, and six *zabtiye* furnished by the government as a guard, down the Euphrates, through the Daghara canal and the Khor el-'Afej to

Nuffar. Unfortunately by that time the active staff had been reduced temporarily to Haynes alone. A few weeks after the expedition's arrival at Baghdad, Geere fell violently ill with pneumonia and dysentery, which gradually developed into typhoid fever and excluded him for a long while from the field. And scarcely had he recovered sufficiently from the two maladies when he was attacked by six date-boils at the same time. Truly this beginning was anything but encouraging; and to make matters worse, the English physician was then absent from the city, and an "intelligent English-speaking trained nurse" could not be had, so that Fisher's very natural proposal, to remain with his sick comrade until together they could join the party in the field, was accepted by Haynes.

On February 4, the six boats reached Nuffar. Welcomed by a special messenger from Hajji Tarfa and by a large crowd of the Hamza, who did not conceal their pleasure at seeing the expedition again among them, well knowing that the presence of the foreigners "meant to them a season of prosperity," the party established itself at once in its old quarters. The seals attached to the *meftul* were found unbroken, and the three Arab guards, to whom the property

Headquarters or' the University or Pennsylvania's Fourth Expedition at Nuffar *Meftul turrounded by gardens and reed-huts at the south foot of the ruins. The 'Afitj sivamps in the background.* had been entrusted, had remained "faithful to their charge under very great discouragement," waiting year after year patiently for Haynes' return and for the expected reward of their doubtless conspicuous services. They had lived near the house, and also watered the garden regularly, so that many date trees had sprung up spontaneously from the stones which our former workmen had thrown awav thoughtlessly. The little plants, scarcely visible when Haynes departed from the ruins in 1896, had become waving palm trees. Some of them even bore fruit after a growth of only three and four years, thus vivid-

ly illustrating the proverbial fertility of ancient Babylonia, and through their flourishing state demonstrating more forcibly than many arguments could do, what might be made again of the treeless desert and pasture grounds of modern 'Iraq through well-directed human labor and proper irrigation.

The ordinary time required for a date-palm to bear fruit is five years at Basra, and eight years in the less tropical gardens of' Baghdad, according to the information which I received directly from the Arab gardeners at both places. The first task for Haynes was to put the wells in order, as the procuring of suitable drinking-water had gradually become a vital question for the expedition. During the first and second campaigns, which lasted only a *few* months, we had troubled ourselves very little about the qualitv of the water. We drank it as the Arab women brought it from the marshes, without boiling it and with an occasional joke as to the animal life which we observed in our jars and cups. But in 1893, when Haynes went to Nuffar with the understanding that he was to remain there through summer and winter for several years, he had to take greater care of his health and to face the problem, how to obtain the necessary supply of water during the hottest months of the year, when the marshes usually recede from the ruins. At first he had adopted the Arab method, and conducted the water to his "castle" by digging a small but sufficiently deep canal to one of the principal streams in the midst of the *Khbr.* But after the neighboring tribes, for the sake of gain, repeatedly had closed his canal, he decided in 1894 to make his camp independent of the interferences of the Arabs bv digging wells around his house. This experiment led to a very unique result. The water obtained from three of them, dug at a distance of only forty to fortyfive feet from each other, was as different as it possibly could be. That of the first well was "very bitter," that of the second " absolutely undrinkable for men and animals," that of the third, which subsequently was lined with bricks and provided with a pump, was "drinkable,

slightly impregnated with various salts, and yet scarcely rendered unpalatable thereby." In the latter part of the fourth campaign a still purer and, in fact, most excellent water, was procured from a new fourth well, which afterwards was vaulted over entirely to prevent its pollution by the Arabs, while the precious liquid was conducted by subterranean pipes into the court of the *meftu/,* so that in case of a siege we should never suffer from lack of water.

For almost three years the building of the expedition had remained unoccupied and had been exposed to the heavy rains of the winter and the equally damaging effect of the hot rays of the sun. But though consisting only of clay laid up *en masse,* it was found in better condition than could reasonably have been anticipated. As the fast days of Ramadhan were drawing to their close, Haynes, in true Arab style, had it announced by heralds in the camps and villages of the 'Afej that no native workman would be engaged before the approaching festival of Bairam was over. At the same time he divided his large body of Hilla men into three groups, ordering the one section to prepare the tools for work in the trenches and to re-open the excavations; the second to dig roots and gather thorn bushes as fuel for the kitchen; the third to build reed huts for the families of the laborers and to repair the "castle." In consequence of the increased staff of the expedition, the *ineftul* proved by far too small. Arrangements had, therefore, to be made at once to accommodate the larger party by adding another story to the old structure. As a number of Arabs, well versed in the art of primitive house-building, were at Haynes' disposal, the difficulty was soon removed, and all his time could be devoted to the principal task of the expedition.

A word remains to be said about the attitude of the 'Afej, Hamza, Sa'id and other neighboring tribes. Without exception, they remained friendly towards us during the whole campaign. Hajji Tarfa proved the same staunch supporter of our plans as he always had been. Though less elastic in his movements than when we met him the first time, and slightly bent by the burden of years, the " Moltke of the 'Afej," as he was styled very appropriately by the wali of Baghdad, had understood how to retain and even to increase his influence among his shiftless but refractory subjects, and hold the younger shaikhs in discipline, who often were eager to win their own laurels and to strengthen their position at the expense of the venerable patriarch. The Turkish government, realizing how valuable his services were in controlling the most troublesome province of the whole vilayet, was ready to assist him in his efforts to keep peace, and repeatedly gave him visible proofs of the high esteem in which he was held throughout the country. At his earliest opportunity Haynes hurried over to the great chieftain's *meftul,* about six miles distant, to pay him an official visit. In the presence of his warriors he put around his neck a long chain of gold (for the watch previously given to him), and threw over his shoulder a fine cloak *('ala),* woven with silver thread, presents from the committee, to which, a year later, the present writer added a Whitman saddle, for which Hajji Tarfa had expressed a genuine admiration.

The care for the safety of the expedition through proper guards was entrusted by the shaikh of all the 'Afej to the same two Hamza leaders who in former years had been responsible to him. They kept their pledges honorably to the end of the campaign. All the tribes inhabiting the borders of the marshes intermingled freely with our men and looked upon us with a certain feeling of pride, almost as upon members of their own clans, who from time to time appeared on their territory, for a while sharing their pasture grounds and leaving behind them untold blessings when they departed. A great change had taken place on these barren plains since I had seen them last. It was the natural result of the transfer of the capital to Diwaniye, and in no small measure due to the tactful but energetic treatment of the 'Afej tribes on the part of the Ottoman government. A sacred calm lay

in the air, — not the calm preceding a disastrous storm, but that divine calm which announces a new era of happiness to the people. Every flower and reed, every shepherd and bird seemed to be conscious of it and to realize that Isaiah's and Jeremiah's curse of two thousand years was about to lift from the country. The dry bones of Babylonia's vast graveyard began to rise and to be clad again with sinews and flesh under Jehovah's life-breathing spirit that blew softly through the land of Bel (Ezek. 37). There can be no doubt that Babylonia stands at the dawn of a general resurrection. Unmistakable signs of a new and more peaceful development of the many natural resources of Shumer and Akkad are visible everywhere. A great movement and expectation has taken possession of the tribes of the interior, partly brought about in consequence of the acquisition and cultivation of large tracts of land along the canals for the Sultan, and partly inspired by the various scientific missions from Europe and America. Through their continued exploration of the ruins these foreign excavators have introduced new ideas into the country, made the people acquainted with important inventions, and, above all, taught them the value of time and work, thus preparing the way for the planned German railroad, of which even the 'Afej speak with great anticipation, and which surely will play the chief missionary role throughout the country.

When, after a long absence, I stood again on the airy top of Bint el-Amir, as far as my eye could scan the horizon I saw nothing but immense flocks of sheep and goats, donkeys and cows and buffaloes pastured by cheerful boys and men, Arab villages and encampments scattered over the plain, and small green patches of cultivated ground on the edges of the inundated districts; the camel herds and black tents of the Sa'id in the distance, and far away beyond the Tigris towards the east, only now and then visible, the snowcapped mountains of Luristan. At my first meeting with the Hamza shaikhs and their retinues, they were somewhat disappointed because they did not recognize me. In

order to establish my identity, they submitted me to a cross-examination, inquiring whether I remembered the burning of our camp. But scarcely had I begun to recount the details of the disaster, the destruction of my fine horse, Marduk, and the fortunate escape of another, *Abu khams ("* father of five," namely, Turkish liras), as I had named it, with due regard to its low price — a joke thoroughly appreciated by the Arabs, — and to refer to the principal persons connected with the catastrophe, asking on my part for the ill-fated The Assyrian word for "east" is *shadu,* "mountain," as the Hebrew one for " west " is *yam, "*ocean."

Mukota's little son and Berdi's tall brother, who restored my saddle-bags, when their eyes sparkled with excitement. They exclaimed, " *Wallah* by God, he is *Abti dhaq(a)n* father (*/. e.,* owner) of a beard," the name by which I used to be known among them; and drawing closer upon me, they lighted their cigarettes, drank their coffee, rehearsed old jokes, chatted like children, and asked hundreds of questions about Harper and Field, the new railroad, the speed of its trains, their prospect of exporting sheep and butter and rice, etc. "Oh, *Abti dhaq(a)n,* how times have changed. Once we wanted to rob you, and now you are our brother, whom may Allah bless." Of course the petty quarrels did not cease altogether among the various tribes; and murderers and other desperadoes took refuge in the Khor el-'Afej then, as they did before, but they never molested us. The most exciting scene that occurred while we were at Nuffar, was the settling of a very old case of bloodfeud, under the very walls of our *meftiil,* and the cowardly and atrocious manner in which, on this occasion, the life of a perfectly innocent Arab was taken.

Excavations were commenced at the extreme southeastern end of the west ridge (VI) on February 6, 1899, with all the available workmen from Hilla. In order to strike any possible remains of the ancient city wall, if ever it should have existed in this section of Nippur, Haynes opened a trench at a little distance from the ruins and descended gradually below the level of the plain in the direction of the mounds. But, strange to say, still convinced that his chief task consisted in a "successful tablet-hunting" rather than in a strictly scientific exploration of Nuffar, as had been impressed so emphatically upon him, he also set to work at once to clean a large old trench abandoned three years before, and endeavored "to push the excavations forward into the mounds towards the points where great quantities of tablets had been found " previously.

Three days after the resumption of the work he came upon "a wall of burned bricks crossing the line of the first mentioned trench transversely, but lying at a lower level." Our expectations were raised exceedingly when this report reached Philadelphia. But three weeks later, long before the first weekly letter was in our hands, Haynes abandoned it on his own responsibility, having followed its course for 489 feet "without finding either end of it" or discovering "any trace of door or window" in it. We were disappointed. Spring and summer were spent in a well-meant, nervous search for tablets and other portable antiquities by carrying a trench 155 feet wide with an extreme depth of 36 feet a distance of 75 feet into the mound, and by opening smaller trenches and tunnels at other points in the same general locality. In this manner about five thousand cuneiform tablets, mostly fragmentary contracts and lists of the third pre-Christian millennium, about thirty seal cylinders, as a rule much worn off or otherwise damaged, about a dozen interesting clay reliefs, and a few other antiquities were gathered from the lower levels of the ridge in the course of the first six months. An arch of baked bricks and the fragment of a watercourse similar to those discovered in the lower section of the temple mound were also briefly referred to. The upper strata and the slopes of the mounds yielded about 450 late coffins of various types with their usual contents, a number of bronze bowls, several thin blue glass bottles of the post-Christian period, a jar containing miscellaneous coins, articles of jewelry and junk, — the store of a Parthian jeweller!—about thirty Hebrew and Mandean bowls, among them two containing an inscribed skull in pieces, besides other minor antiquities.

The reports became more meagre every day, furnishing practically no information about the excavations beyond a simple statement as to how many tablets, seal cylinders and other more striking objects had been discovered during the week, and how many coffins had been opened. Neither photograph nor sketch accompanied the letters. Haynes doubtless worked very seriously with his 208 Arabs. But notwithstanding his honest efforts, it was naturally impossible for him to control such a large body of men. The results would have been more satisfactory to himself and to the committee, if he had retained only fifty workmen in the trenches as long as he was alone, and devoted a part of his time to a technical description of his excavations, to photographing and other necessary details upon which the success of an expedition largely depends. As matters stood, it became next to impossible for the committee to form any adequate idea as to what actually was going on at Nuffar. Besides, letters required five to seven weeks before they reached Philadelphia. Something had to be done quickly, if the plans we had formulated were ever to be realized. To complicate matters even more, misunderstandings arose between the two architects at Baghdad on the one hand and the managing director in the field on the other. This led to Fisher's resignation in April and his immediate return to England, and for a second time threatened to bring about Geere's separation from the work of the Philadelphia expedition. At the beginning of June we were in the possession of all the facts necessary to meet, to act, and to decide as to the future course of the expedition. The results of this important meeting became soon apparent. Fisher returned to Baghdad in the early fall, and soon afterwards, together with Geere, who by that time had fully recovered his usual health, departed for Nuffar, arriving there on October 20, 1899. Upon the unanimous decision of the committee the scientific director was to follow and to take charge of the excavations at the ruins in person as soon as the organization of the University Museum should have been completed. Haynes at the same Comp. pp. 360, *jtq.,* above. time received more positive instructions as to the manner in which he was to proceed to carry the work of the expedition to a satisfactory issue. In accordance with the desires of the committee he henceforth directed his attention principally to the exploration of the eastern half of the court of the temple, to the search for the northeast city gate, and to the excavation of the probable site of the temple library, the so-called "Tablet Hill" (IV), so that his Arabs were not scattered over too large a surface, and with the subsequent assistance of the two architects could be controlled without difficulty.

Owing to Haynes' praiseworthy energy and characteristic devotion to his duties, he soon could report conspicuous tangible results, and illustrate them by his own photographs and by sketches drawn by his assistants. He evidently worked hard according to the best of his ability. But unfortunately our positive knowledge as to the topography of the ruins was advanced but little thereby. The statements were too vague to enable us to draw any conclusions. On October 28 he wrote with regard to the northeast city gate: "Up to the present moment, we have found no certain clue beyond a mere fragment of very archaic wall, to indicate the existence at that point of a gate or other structure." The whole important subject was never mentioned afterwards except in the brief title of a photograph despatched three months later, which, however, reached Philadelphia only after my arrival at Nuffar. By the middle of December tablets began to be found in such large quantities in the northeastern part of the " Tablet Hill," that even Haynes was forced to admit that this collection of tablets looked very much as if " constituting a distinct library by itself." But whether it was merely another of these collections of contract tablets so frequently found in the west half of the ruins and always styled by him "libraries," or whether it was *the* library for which I was looking so eagerly, the temple library, could not be determined, as proper descriptions were lacking and no attempt was made to reproduce a few lines of some of the better-preserved documents.

It was very evident that, above all, the assistance of an experienced archaeologist and Assyriologist was required at Nuffar to decipher tablets, to determine the characteristic features of strata, to fix the approximate age of walls and other antiquities, to ascertain their probable purpose and use, to lay trenches for other reasons than to find tablets, and to gather all the loose threads together and to endeavor to reconstruct some kind of a picture of the ancient city on the basis of his examination and studies. The architects did their very best to assist Haynes and to promote the cause of the expedition. But entirely unfamiliar with Babylonian archaeology as they then were, and for the first time confronted with the complicated problems of a Babylonian ruin, they needed technical advice as to how to overcome the difficulties. Being left entirely to their own resources, they decided to undertake what they were able to do under the circumstances. They sketched drains, tombs, vases and various other antiquities to illustrate Haynes' weekly reports; they tried to make themselves acquainted with the remains of the *ziggurrat* previously drawn by Meyer, and to survey and plot the constructions occupying the eastern corner of the temple court prior to their removal. But they also facilitated my later work on the ruins in one essential point. As we saw above (pp. 371, *seq.),* in the course of the third campaign, Haynes had discovered the remains of the original approach to the *ziggurrat,* indicated by two almost parallel walls, extending nearly at a right angle far into the court from the southeastern face of the stage-tower. It had appeared, therefore, most natural to the present writer to assume that the principal gate or entrance to the temple court

must lie in the enclosing wall somewhere opposite that approach. In 1897, when I first had occasion to examine all of Haynes' negatives thoroughly, I was surprised to find that he had exposed a number of stepped recesses precisely at the place where the gate should have existed, and that he had actually discovered the entrance without knowing and reporting it, as unfortunately he had cut one half of the gate completely away by one of his wretched perpendicular shafts which proved so disastrous to the temple court. The architects were not slow in recognizing the importance of these stepped recesses, and asked at once for permission to remove the large round tower of the latest fortification, lying directly on the top of them — the same which Peters had compared with the pillar of Jachin or Boaz at the temple of Jerusalem (comp. p. 333, above).

Haynes gave it reluctantly, as he thought the expense of time and labor involved in this work too great in comparison with the probable results expected by him, and left the architects in complete charge of this excavation. They solved their first independent task very satisfactorily, uncovered the remaining part of the gate, found a door-socket *in situ,* and disclosed the existence of an important tomb near the south corner of the latest enclosing wall, on which we shall have to say a few words later.

By the middle of November, 1899, the scientific director had finished the organization of the Semitic section of the University Museum, so that he could leave for the East to join the other members of the expedition. But in consequence of considerable delays caused to the boats by storms in the Atlantic, by the discharge of a heavy cargo at the Somali coast, by quarantine in the Shaft el-'Arab for having touched at the plague-, cholera-, and small-pox-stricken harbor of Maskat, and finally by the sudden rise of the Tigris, he did not reach Nuffar before March i, 190x5. Having gone out "as the representative of the committee and with the full powers of the committee," he naturally was held responsible for the proper execution of the

plans as outlined above. After a careful examination of all the trenches and a full discussion of the whole situation with Haynes, I found it necessary to change entirely the methods hitherto employed. Accordingly all the excavations carried on for the mere purpose of finding tablets and other antiquities were suspended, especially as I had ascertained through a study of representative tablets, an inspection of the rooms in which they had been discovered, and a brief continuation of the work in the trenches, that the "Tablet Hill" actually represented the site of the temple library, as I had maintained for so many years. I regarded the further exploration of this library as by far less important than the solving of some of the many other complicated topographical problems which in the past had received so little attention, before the exposed building remains should have crumbled beyond recognition. Originally it had been my intention also to excavate the largely untouched southwest section of the temple court methodically, in order to supplement and to correct the one-sided information received previously and to study personally layer after layer, pavement after pavement, with a view of providing new material for settling the question as to whether important buildings had occupied the temple court at the different periods of its history. But when I found that enormous dump-heaps had been raised there by my predecessors I had to give up this plan, as the examination could not begin properly before the latter had been removed to a safe distance — a task alone requiring more time and labor than was at my disposal for the various tasks together.

Considering all the circumstances, there was nothing to be done but to accept the situation as it presented itself, and to make the best of it. In the interest of science I therefore decided to leave the unexplored sections of the court of the *ziggurrat* and the temple library to a subsequent fifth expedition, as both doubtless were safer when covered with earth than if inadequately examined and exposed to the fury of the elements. This expedition was sent out to endeavor to understand Nuffar as a whole, not to remove large mounds of debris merely for the sake of finding portable antiquities and tablets by the bushel and to count their market value in dollars and cents. I was personally despatched to solve scientific problems and to interpret the ruins. The more essential topographical questions once having been settled, it would be a comparatively easy task for the committee to have the single mounds excavated one after another by somebody else, if necessity arose, who was less familiar with the ruins and the history of their exploration than the present writer, who had been connected with this undertaking from its very beginning. Kvery trench cut henceforth — and there were a great many — was cut for the sole purpose of excavating structures systematically and of gathering necessary *data* for the history and topography of ancient Nippur. If these trenches yielded tangible museum results at the same time, so much the better; if they did not, I was not troubled by their absence and felt just as well satisfied as if I had packed several thousand tablets, or perhaps even more so. But in order to state this expressly here, antiquities were found so abundantly in the pursuit of the plan described, that the principle was established anew that a strictly scientific method of excavating is at the same time the most profitable.

The number of workmen was increased and maintained until the middle of April, when many of the native Arabs began to quit the trenches to harvest their barley and to look after their agricultural interests. Haynes retained full charge of the men in the field under my general supervision. Fisher and Geere were instructed to make a complete survey of all the remaining walls, buildings, drains, pavements, etc., excavated by the second, third, and fourth expeditions, and to prepare special plans of all those structures which I was able to assign to certain periods and to bring into closer relation with each other. As far as it served to facilitate their task and to introduce them into the archaeological work proper, both were placed in charge

of their own gangs under Haynes' immediate control, while I reserved to myself the right of advising them and of modifying or changing the courses of all the trenches whenever new developments in them should require it. The entire length of the northeast city wall was traced and studied, and a number of interesting structures and antiquities found in connection with them. All the explored rooms of the temple library and of the later buildings lying over them were surveyed and drawn. The long brick wall reported to have been found and abandoned by Haynes at the southeast edge of the west half of the ruins (p. 440, above), was explored successfully and its real nature and purpose determined. In accordance wjth Mr. K. W. Clark's request, the so-called "Court of Columns "(VII on the plan of the ruins) received very considerable attention. After its complete excavation I could only confirm my view formulated in 1889, that this fine little palace belongs to the Hellenistic period, in other words, is of Parthian, not of Cassite origin. The upper strata covering this building afforded me an excellent opportunity to examine into the manner in which the inscribed incantation bowls had been used by the Jewish inhabitants of Calneh in the eighth and ninth centuries of our era. For the present it may suffice to state that most of the one hundred bowls excavated while I was on the scene were found upside down in the ground, as will be seen from the illustration on page 448. It is very evident that they had been placed thus intentionally, in order to prevent the demons adjured by the spiral inscription on the inner face of most of the vases, from doing any harm to the Comp. p. 337 with p. 340.

people living in that neighborhood. Sometimes two bowls facing one another had been cemented together with bitumen. In one case an inscribed hen's egg was concealed Hebrew Incantation Bowls in their Original Position

Seven placed upside doivn one ivitk the inscribed face upnuard

under the bowl. This egg;, like the inscribed skulls previously reported

(comp. p. 440), is probablv to be regarded as a sacrifice to those demons to appease their wrath and check their evil influence.

The excavation of those upper strata also enabled me to studv the numerous late burials contained therein, which almost exclusively belonged to the post-Christian period. In order to obtain more definite results concerning the dates of other tombs, not so favorably situated, we examined a section of the ruins to the northwest of the temple, which was literally filled with graves, and compared their forms and contents with the other ones. As it is impossible to present here the results of a studv of more than 2,500 tombs excavated by all the four expeditions at Nuffar, including over 1,100 examined during the fourth campaign, I confine myself to stating in this connection that with but few exceptions all those excavated tombs belong to the post-Babylonian period. But it was also ascertained that prior to the time of Sargon I (about 3800 B. c), as we shall see presently, Nippur was one of the sacred burial-grounds of the earliest inhabitants of the country, who cremated their dead there, as thev did at Surghul and El-Hibba. Comp. the skulls and egg discovered in the mortar of the Parthian palace lying on the top of the ruins of Bel's sanctuary, p. 368, above, and Pognon, *Inscriptions Mandaites des Coups dc Khouabir,* Paris, 1 898, pp. *2, seq.*

The most difficult problem confronting me was the explanation of the ruins at Bint el-Amir and its environments, owing to the previous removal and frequent involuntary destruction of much valuable material on the part of my predecessors. Some of the results which I obtained this time were incorporated in my above sketch of the second and third campaigns. The other more important ones will be treated briefly below. They may be summarized as follows: 1. A stage-tower of smaller dimensions existed at Nippur before Sargon I (about 3800 B. c). 2. In pre-Sargonic times the ground around the sacred enclosure was a vast graveyard, a regular fire necropolis. 3. One

of the names of the stage-tower of Nippur suggested the idea of tomb to the
early inhabitants of the country. In the
course of time certain *ziggurrats* were
directly designated by the Babylonians
as tombs of the gods. 4. The stage-tower
of Bel did not occupy the centre of the
enclosed platform, but the southwest
section of it, while the northeast part
was reserved for "the house of Bel," his
principal sanctuary, which stood at the
side of the stage-tower. 5. The temple
of Bel consisted of two large Comp. pp.
283, *seqq.,* above.

courts adjoining each other, the northwest court with the *ziggurrat* and "the
house of Bel" representing the most
holy place or the inner court, while the
southeast (outer) court seems to have
been studded with the shrines of all the
different gods and goddesses worshipped at Nippur, including one for Bel
himself. 6. *Imgur-Marduk* and *Nit-
nitMarduk,* mentioned in the cuneiform
inscriptions as the two walls of Nippur
(duru and *shalkhu),* cannot have surrounded the whole city-According to
the results of the excavations conducted
under my own supervision, only the
temple was enclosed by a double wall,
while in all probability the city itself remained unprotected. 7. The large complex of buildings covering the top of
Bint el-Amir has nothing to do with the
ancient temple below, but represents a
huge fortified Parthian palace grouped
around and upon the remains of the
stage-tower then visible. In order to understand the temple correctly, this
fortress has to be eliminated completely
from the ruins, as was demanded by the
present writer as early as 1889.
A thorough treatment of the whole important question will be found in a special work entitled " Ekur, the Temple of
Bel at Nippur," which will be fully illustrated and accompanied by large plans
and diagrams prepared by the architects
of the expedition according to my re-
constructions and their own survey of
the actual remains still existing. For the
present I must confine myself to a brief
sketch of the principal results as obtained by the combined efforts of all the
members of the staff" during the latter

part of the fourth campaign and interpreted by the present writer.
1. An examination of the inscriptions
from Tello," the fact Comp. p. 327,
above, and Peters' "Nippur," vol. ii, p.
118: "One of our Assyriologists reached
the conclusion that the ruins we had
found were those of a fortress... built on
the site of the ancient temple." Comp. p.
232, note 2, above, and Hommel, *Auf-
satz und AbhanJlungen,* part iii, 1 (Munich, 1901), pp. 389, *seqq.* that all the
Babylonian temples and stage-towers
have Sumerian names, and other considerations had convinced me that the
origin of the *ziggurrat* at Nippur must
lie far beyond the time of Ur-Gur. The
mere circumstances that the pavement
of Sargon and Naram-Sin covered about
the same space between the inner wall
and the *later ziggurrat* as those of the
following rulers; that nowhere in the excavated large section of the temple court
it extended beneath the tower; that the
store-room or cellar found within the
southeast enclosing wall by the third expedition (pp. 386, 390, above), occupied exactly the same place at the time
of Sargon as in the days of Ur-Gur, —
indicated sufficiently that the temple
enclosure showed practically the same
characteristic features at 3800 B. c. as at
2800 B. c.
The massive L-shaped structure (p. 395,
above) underlying the east corner of Ur-
Gur's *ziggurrat,* and constructed of the
same unusually large bricks as those
which thus far at Nippur have been connected exclusively with the names of
Sargon and Naram-Sin, evidently was
the work of a member of that powerful
ancient dynasty. As it descended eleven
feet below Naram-Sin's pavement, it is
also clear that this structure, which puzzled Haynes so much, must have served
a similar purpose as UrGur's crude
brick pavement, which was eight feet
deep and extended all around and beneath the edges of the stagetower in
support of the latter. In other words, it
was the foundation for the east corner
of Naram-Sin's *ziggurrat.* Similar foundations may be found at the three other
corners, but it is more probable to assume that it occurs only at this particu-

lar point, where the necessity of an extraordinary foundation can be explained
without difficulty. We saw above (p.
397), that Haynes discovered a ruined
vaulted aqueduct, about 3 feet high, beneath it. With the exception of a small
section near the orifice (directly below
the ancient curb and supported by the T-
shaped structure) the whole upper part
of the vault had collapsed without leaving extensive traces of the baked material of which it originally consisted. On
the other hand, large numbers of pre-
Sargonic bricks were found in the lower
row of Naram-Sin's pavement. It seems
therefore reasonable to connect the two
facts and to explain the situation as follows. About the time of NaramSin, perhaps even in consequence of his enlarging the heavy mass of the *ziggurrat,* the
ancient aqueduct below had caved in.
In order to secure a more solid foundation for the east corner, it became necessary to ascertain the cause of the subsequent depression of the surface. Naram-
Sin therefore descended about twelve
feet, removed the rubbish, saved all the
good bricks for his pavement, and built
the peculiarly shaped massive structure
eleven feet high directly over it, in order
to prevent the formation of crevices in
his structure by the uneven settling of
the disturbed ground below it.

This much is sure, that the mere existence of this solid foundation at the
eastern corner of the *ziggurrat* at the
time of Naram-Sin necessarily leads us
to the conclusion that also a large building which it was intended to support,
a stagetower, must have existed at that
ancient period in Nippur. This conclusion is.fully corroborated by the fact
that below Ur-Gur's gray-colored
bricks in the centre of the *ziggurrat,*
other similar bricks were found, which
in texture, color and size are identical
with those of Naram-Sin's store-room
or cellar, in the southeast enclosing
wall. The southeast face of this early
ziggurrat was actually discovered by
means of a tunnel following a pre-Sargonic water-course which ran into the
strata below Ur-Gur's stage-tower. It
lay four feet behind Ur-Gur's facing
wall, and was carefully built of the same

crude bricks just mentioned, which form the kernel of the *ziggurrat*

Since the water-course thus traced continued its way under i Comp. the zinctype " Section of the Stage-Tower and the Adjoining Southeast Court," in the chapter on the topography of Nippur, below.

Naram-Sin's tower, and sloped gently from a point near and within the pre-Sargonic curb towards the former, it was evident that if a pre-Sargonic *ziggurrat* existed at Nippur it must have been considerably smaller than that of NaramSin and lay entirely within and largely below it. In order to ascertain all the desirable details both of Naram-Sin's and of this possibly earlier structure, it would have been necessary to remove Bel's *ziggurrat* completely by peeling off layer after layer. This method is the only one by which the precise nature and history of this important part of the venerable sanctuary can be determined satisfactorily, but it involves much time, labor and expense, and the destruction of one of the earliest landmarks of the country.

All that the Philadelphia expedition could do under the circumstances was to operate with a few carefully made tunnels — a somewhat dangerous proceeding in view of the ponderous mass of crude bricks above, but one already successfully begun by Haynes in previous years, and without any serious accident also continued by our ablest workmen during the fourth campaign. It seems, however, absolutely essential, in view of the important problem before us, that a complete vertical section, about a fourth of the whole mass, should be cut out of the *ziggurrat* at one of its four corners by a future fifth expedition. The smooth and plastered surface of the southeast side of a pre-Sargonic *ziggurrat* built of crude bricks was discovered at two places about forty feet distant from each other. It lay nearly fourteen feet within the outer edge of. Ur-Gur's facing wall, and was traced for about six to ten feet in its descent to the ancient level of the plain. Whether and how far it went below that point could not be ascertained without exposing the work-

men and the explorers to the risk of being entombed and suffocated suddenly within the sacred precinct of Bel.

Two similar but sloping tunnels were carried into the mass beneath the northeast side of the *ziggurrat.* But as the clay was too wet, the light too poor and the trenches perhaps too short, they did not reveal positive traces of the earlier building. We were, however, rewarded by another discovery made in the most northern trench. At a point several feet below the level of Naram-Sin's pavement and still outside of the *ziggurrat,* we came upon a well-defined small bed of black and gray ashes 3 to 4 inches high. Several rude blocks of stone lay around it, and the fragments of a bronze sword or dagger were found among the ashes. What did these few ancient remains from below the Sargon level in the neighborhood of the *ziggurrat* indicate? Hay nes had found such beds of ashes mixed with fragments of pottery and occasionally accompanied by objects in copper and bronze (nails, knives, battle axes, portions of vessels) or beads in stone, silver, and even gold, rings and other jewelry, seal cylinders, etc., everywhere in the lower strata to the southeast of the stage-tower (comp. pp. 401, *seqq.).* My curiosity was aroused, and I was determined to make an effort to ascertain the meaning of these remarkable relics.

1. Unfortunately the greater part of the southeast section of the temple enclosure had been removed before my arrival. But Havnes' perpendicular cuts enabled me at least to obtain an excellent side view of all the single strata of the remaining unexplored portions from the Sargon level down to the virgin soil. As soon as I began to examine them one after another, I was struck with the enormous mass of larger and smaller fragments of pottery intermingled with ashes which peeped out of the ground wherever my eye glanced. I set to work to extricate these pieces carefully with a large knife, in order to secure the necessary information with regard to the original sizes, forms and structures of these broken terra-cotta vessels. Without exception they belonged to large, thick

urns of various shapes, or small pointed vases, peculiarly formed cups, dishes and similar household vessels. In descending gradually from the pavement of Naram-Sin, I suddenly came, three feet below it, upon a group of potsherds lying in such a manner as to suggest at once to the observer the original form of a large vase, to which they belonged. In which antimony took the place of tin. The analysis of one of the fragments by the late Dr. Helm of Danzig showed 96. 38 parts of copper, 1.73 parts of antimony, 0.24 part of iron, 0.22 part of nickel, 1.43 parts of oxygen and loss, traces of lead. Comp. Helm and Hilprecht in the proceedings of the *Berliner anthropohgiichen Gesellschaft,* session of February 16, 1901, p. 159.

It was a large oblong-ovate jar over 2 feet long and nearly 1/ feet at its largest diameter. The heavy weight of the debris of six thousand years lying on the top of it had crushed the vessel, which was placed almost horizontally in the ground, into hundreds of small pieces. It contained gray ashes mixed with small bits of charred wood and earth, and two long but thin streaks of yellowish ashes. Without difficulty I could determine that the gray ashes represented the remains of bones and wood consumed by fire, and the yellowish ashes those of two large bones which had decayed gradually, but apparently had belonged to the same human body-There were four or five fragmentary small cups and dishes in the urn. They were in a much better condition than the large jar which enclosed them. Two of them, which accidentally had stood almost upright and consequently offered much less resistance to the pressure from above than those which lay on their sides, were nearly whole, and had retained even the forms of decayed dates and fishbones in the fine earth that filled them. Without knowing it, Haynes had cut through the remains of this jar lengthwise, leaving only half of it for my examination. There could be no doubt, we had here a true pre-Sargonic burial. The human body contained in it had been subjected to cremation without, however, being destroyed completely by this process.

Both the ashes and the bones had afterwards been gathered, and with food and drink placed in this jar were buried in the sacred ground around the *ziggurrat*. The ash-bed unearthed at the northeast side of the stage-tower represented the place where another body had been cremated, apparently that of a man, perhaps a warrior, as the fragments of a sword found in the ashes suggested.

In the light of this discovery and Haynes' previously reported pre-Sargonic burial (pp. 403 *seq.*), of all the ashbeds and their characteristic objects, so often mentioned but completely misunderstood by him, it was a comparatively' easy task for me to trace the outlines of a number of other urns, though even more injured. I also secured a good many tolerably well-preserved cups and dishes, or large fragments of the same, from the debris that filled the whole ground from the undisturbed soil deep below the ancient plain level to the pavement of Naram-Sin, far above the latter. In short, I gathered sufficient evidence to show that all these ash-beds occurring in a stratum twenty-five to thirty feet deep on all the four sides of the *ziggurrat* are to be regarded as places where human bodies had been cremated. The thousands of urns discovered above and below them, and as a rule badly crushed, but in some cases well preserved, are funeral vases, in which the ashes and bones left by the cremation, together with objects once dear to the person, besides food and drink, were placed and buried. The fragments of unbaked walls and rooms repeatedly met with in these lowest strata, and always containing whole or broken urns, are remains of tombs, so-called funeral chambers. The large number of terra-cotta pipes composed of several (often perforated) rings, and descending eight, ten, and even more feet from the surface of the ancient plain and from higher levels, without, however, reaching the water level, are drains which protected the single tombs and the gradually rising mound as a whole. The less frequent wells, always constructed of plano-convex bricks, were to provide the dead with that "clear but I fear in

this case often brackish! water," which the departed pious souls were believed to drink in the lower regions. Comp. pp. 402, *seqq.,* 419 above.

In two instances the rooms had been vaulted, and were constructed ot" baked plano-convex bricks.

Koldewey has described the fire necropoles of Surghul and Kl-Hibba (comp. pp. 283, *seqq.*, above), so intelligently that it is unnecessary to repeat all the details of my own investigations in the pre-Sargonic cemeterv of ancient Nippur, which confirm the German scholar's results in all essential details and at the same time prove conclusively that his view concerning the great age of these two South Babylonian ruins is perfectly correct. Suffice it to state, that here as there "ash-graves" and "body-graves" occur alongside each other in the upper layers, while the former, as the older burials, appear exclusively in the lower strata. In all the three ruins we observe the same peculiar forms and positions of urns and vases, the same kinds of sacrifices offered in connection with the cremation and the final burial, the same customs of depositing weapons, instruments, seals, jewelry, toys, etc., both with the body to be cremated and with the remains interred, the same praxis of building drains, wells and houses for the dead, the same characteristic deep red color of so many potsherds (pointing to their long exposure to an open fire), and, above all, the same scattering ot ashes, charred pieces of wood, fragments of vases and other remains of human burials which is so appalling to the senses and yet was the natural result of the combined action of man and the elements.

Apart from other cuneiform passages, comp. the closing words of several recently published terra-cotta cones from Babylonian tombs: If a person finds a coffin and treats it with due respect, "his manes may drink clear water below!" Comp. Thureau-Dangin in *Orient. Litteratur-Zeitung,* Jan. 15, 1901, pp. 5, *seqq.,* and Delitzsch in *Mitteilungen der Deutsche Orient-Gesellschaft,* no. 11, pp. 5, *seq.*

It will now be clear why I was unable to accept Haynes' view as stated above (p. 395), with regard to the large solid structure within the ancient curb, which he interpreted as an immense altar. The white ash-bed found on its hollowed surface, its rim of bitumen, *i. ?.,* a material liberally used in connection with the cremations, its extraordinary size (14 feet long and 8 feet wide), the ash-bin discovered near its base, and the peculiar surroundings suggest the idea that it rather represents one of the crematoriums on which the bodies of the dead were reduced to ashes. As it stood within the sacred enclosure we involuntarily connect the cremation and burying of the bodies of all these thousands of ancient Babylonians, who found their last resting-place around the sanctuary of their god, with the *ziggurrat* of Bel itself, remembering that at fc'.l-Hibba Koldewey also excavated a two-staged *ziggurrat,* or, according to his theory, " the substructure of an especially important tomb,"' around the base of which, exactly as at Nippur, nothing but "ash-graves" occurred. But we then naturally ask: What was the original significance of a Babylonian *ziggurrat*? Were these stage-towers, like the step pyramids of Medum and Saqqara in t.gypt, in certain cases at least, only "especially important tombs"? Did the Sumerian population of the country after all somehow connect the idea of death or tomb with Bel's high-towering terrace at Nippur? The stage-tower of El-Hibba was round, consisted of two stages, and was provided with a water-conduit like that of Nippur. Comp. pp. 286, *seq.,* above, and *Zeitschrift fur Assyrio/ogie,* vol. ii, pp. 422, *seq.* It appears almost strange at present, that the German explorer discovered and excavated one of the earliest Babylonian *ziggurrats* thus so far known, without realizing it. In view of the existence of a stage-tower at El-Hibba, I am convinced that both Surghul and El-Hibba cannot have been cemeteries exclusively. The German excavations carried on at the two places were by fir too brief and limited compared with the enormous extent of those ruins to settle this question. All the pre-Sargonic ruins of Babylonia, as far as I have had an opportunity to examine them, consist largely of tombs. They occur in great numbers also at NufFar, Fara, Abu Hatab, and other mounds, but it would be utterly wrong to pronounce them for this reason nothing but " firenecropoles." The pre-Sargonic monuments of art and the very ancient cuneiform tablets coming from all those mounds enable us to speak more positively on this question. 3. It is generally known that Strabo (16:5), in speaking of Babylon, mentions " the sepulchre of Bel " (6 *Tov Bijkov* Tcuos), evidently referring to *Etemenanki,* the famous stagetower of the metropolis on the Euphrates, which he seems to regard as a sepulchral monument erected in honor of Marduk or Merodach, " the Bel of Babel " or " the Bel of the gods." In a similar manner Diodorus (ii, 7) informs us, that Semiramis built a tower in Nineveh as a tomb for her husband Ninos, a story apparently based upon the conception that the *ziggurrat* of Nineveh likewise was a tomb. This view of classical writers concerning two of the most prominent stage-towers of Babylonia and Assyria has never been taken very seriously by scholars, as nothing in the cuneiform inscriptions seemed to justify it. But we may well ask: Are there really no passages in the Babylonian literature which would indicate that the early inhabitants of Shumer and Akkad themselves associated the idea of "tomb" with their stage-towers? Comp. the illustrations of the two pyramids, under "Excavations in Egypt," below. Comp. Ktesias, 29, 21, *teq.,* Aelian, *far. hist.,* xiii, 3. Merodach of Babylon is thus styled as the citv's supreme god who became heir to the rank and titles of Bel of Nippur, the " father" and *"* king of the gods." While reading the last proofs of this book, I received Professor Zimmern's important contribution to the history of Babylonian religion incorporated with Schrader's *Die Keilinschriften und das Alte Testament,* 3d edition, Berlin, 1902, part 2. Comp. pp. 355, *seq.,* 373, *seq.,* of this work.

'Interpreted by Hommel as *Nin-ib,* by

the present writer as the Sumerian *Nin* (meaning ' lord" and " lady *")* -(-the Greek ending 05.

Apart from Rawlinson and other earlier explorers, who actually searched for the two above-mentioned tombs, it was Hommel who first expressed it as his conviction that " the Babylonian stage-towers originally were sepulchral monuments," and that Ningirsu's temple at Tello was a combination of a sanctuary for the god and of a mausoleum for Gudea, his *patesi.* Though the former statement is too general and comprehensive according to the scanty materia! at our disposal, and the latter incorrect, since, according to the context, Gudea clearly erected not his own, but his god's "sepulchral chapel" in the temple of Ningirsu, Hommel deserves credit for having recognized an important fact in connection with Babylonian stage-towers and for having endeavored to find proofs for his theory in the inscriptions, before he could have known of the results of a series of investigations carried on by the present writer at NufTar in March and April, 1900.

It does not lie within the scope of this book to treat all the cuneiform passages which directly or indirectly bear upon the important question under consideration. I shall therefore confine myself to a single text from the latest excavations at Nuffar which will throw some light on the way in which the Babylonians viewed the *ziggurrat* of Bel at Nippur, and to a few passages of published inscriptions referring to other *ziggurrats.*

Among the antiquities found in the debris that covered the pavement of Ashurbanapal near the east corner of the court of the stage-tower at Nippur, there were three inscribed fragments of baked clay which seemed to belong to a barrel cylinder. When trying to fit them together, 1 found that they constituted the greater part of a truncated cone of an interesting shape similar to that of the recently published cones from Babylonian tombs. The curious form of the document attracted my immediate attention. On closer examination, it proved to be a building record of twentyfive lines of neo-Babylonian cuneiform charac-

ters inscribed Comp. Hommel, *Aufihtxe und Abhandlungen,* part iii, 1 (Munich, 1901), pp. 389, *seqq.,* especially p. 393. Comp. p. 457, above, note. The same peculiar form is known from

Truncated Cone containing Ashurbinapal's Account of his Restoration of the Stage-Tower of Nippur. lengthwise by " Ashurbanapal, king of Assyria." Only lines 15—19 of the mutilated legend are of importance for the sub

Nabopolassjir's fine cylinder, now *m* Philadelphia, and containing his building record of *Etemenanki,* "the tower of Babe!" (comp. Hilprecht, "The Bab. Exp. of the U. of Pa.," series A, vol. i, part 1, pi. xiii). A "cylinder" from Nuffar containing Samsu-iluna's account of his restoration of the *dim* (inner wall) of the temple of Bel, and a cone in the Louvre of Paris, containing Hammurabi's record of his construction "of the wall and canal of Sippara" (according to information received by letter from Thureau-Dangin), also show the same form. It doubtless represents the prototype of the later barrel-cylinder. Nevertheless, it remains a most remarkable fact that cylinders of this peculiar form were deposited both in the *ziggurrati* and their enclosing walls, and also in the ancient tombs which, as we now know, originally surrounded the former. ject under consideration. I quote them in the king's own language: "*E-gigunu,* the *ziggurrat* of Nippur, the foundation of which is placed in the breast of the ocean, the walls of which had grown old, and which had fallen into decay — I built that house with baked bricks and bitumen, and completed its construction. With the art of the god of the bricks I restored it and made it bright as the day. I raised its head like a mountain and caused its splendor to shine."

This inscription furnishes us a new name of the *ziggurrat* of Nippur, *E-gigunu?* " House of the tomb," the other two names of the same building, with which we were familiar before, being *Imgarsag, "*Mountain of the wind" or " Mt. Airy," and *E-sagash,* " House of the decision." *E-gigunu,* however, was not altogether unknown to us. There are several cuneiform passages in which it appears in parallelism with *Ekur,* " House of the mountain," the well-known temple of Bel and Beltis at Nippur. A fourth name, to state this distinctly here, occurs in another unpublished text inscribed on a large vase of Gudea also belonging to the results of our latest excavations at Nuffar, namely, *Dur-an-ki,* " Link of heaven and earth." How was it possible that the *ziggurrat* of Nippur, which constitutes the most prominent part of the whole temple complex, this high towering terrace, which "connects heaven and earth," could appear to the Babylonians as " the house of the tomb" at the same time?

Most of the names of Babylonian temples express a cosmic idea. According to the old Babylonian conception of the gods and their relation to the world's edifice, En-lil or Bel of Nippur is "the king of heaven and earth," or "the father" and "king of the gods" and " the king of the lands," /'. *e.,* the earth. Bel's sphere of influence, therefore, is what we generally style " the world." It extends from the upper or heavenly ocean (the seat of Anu) to the lower or terrestrial ocean (the seat of Ea), which was regarded as the continuation of the former around and below the earth. In other words, Bel rules an empire which includes the whole world with the exclusion of the upper and lower oceans, or an empire confined on the one hand by the starry firmament which keeps back the waters of the upper ocean (Gen. I: 6-8) and is called heaven *(an),* and on the other hand by that lower "firmament " which keeps the waters of the lower ocean in their place (Gen. i: 9, 10) and is called earth *(ki).* But his empire not only lies between these two boundaries, it practically includes them. The *ziggurrat* of Bel is "the link of heaven and earth" which connects the two extreme parts of his empire; that is, it is the local representation of the great mythological "mountain of the world," *'Kharsagkurkura,* a structure "the summit of which reaches unto heaven, and the foundation of which is laid in the clear *apsu,"* i. ?., in the clear waters of the subterranean ocean,— epithets af-

terwards applied to other Babylonian *ziggurrats,* some of which bear even the same, or at least a similar, name. Thus, *e. g.,* the *ziggurrat* of Shamash, both at Sippara ' and at Larsa, was called *E-Duranki,* " House of the link of heaven and earth," or abbreviated *E-Duranna,* "House of the link of heaven," and the *ziggurrat* of Marduk at Babylon, *Ete-menanki,* " House of the foundation of heaven and earth." A fifth (unknown) name seems to have stood in the mutilated passage, ii R. 50, if the present sign of line 4, a, was copied correctly from the original.

Comp. Jensen, *Die Kosmologie dcr Babylonier,* Strasburg, 1890, pp. 1 86, *seq.* On the Babylonian conception of the world's edifice, comp. especially Jensen, *Die Kosmologie der Babylenier,* Strasburg, 1890; Hommel, *Das babylonische U'fltbi/d* in *Aufshtze und Abhandlungen,* part iii, I, Munich, 1901, pp. 344-349; and a monograph received immediately before the issue of this book. It is written by one of my pupils, Dr. Hugo Radau, and bears the title, "The Creation-Storv of Genesis 1, a Sumerian Theogony and Cosmogonv " (Chicago, London, 1902), — a very useful and commendable treatise, which, however, might have been improved considerably, if the author had written in a more becoming manner about one of his teachers, Professor Hommel, to whose lectures and extraordinary personal efforts in his behalf at Munich he owes some of his best knowledge. Much valuable material is also found in several writings of A. Jeremias, Winckler, and Zimmern. Comp. the poetical passage quoted above, p. 304, from a hymn addressed to Bel and his consort. Bel therefore is designated (ii R. 54, 4, a) ideographically also as the god of *Dur-an* (abbreviation for *Dur-an-hi)* or even ' the great mountain" itself *shadu rabu).*
Bel, "the lord " par excellence, who took the place of the Sumerian *En-lil* in the Semitic pantheon, is, as we have seen, the king of this "middle empire." His manifestation is " the wind " *(HI),* and his name designates him therefore as "the lord *(en)* of the wind (//'/) "

or" storm," and of all those other phenomena which frequently accompany it, "thunder," "lightning," etc. The hundreds of terra-cotta images of Bel or En-lil discovered at Nippur accordingly represent him generally as an old man (a real " father of the gods ") with a long flowing beard, and a thunderbolt or some other weapon in his hand. He and his consort Beltis reside in a house on the top of the great "mountain of the world," which reaches unto heaven (Gen. 11:4). There the gods were born, and from thence " the king of heaven and earth " hurls down his thunderbolts. This house is localized in *Ekur* (" House of the mountain "), Bel's famous temple at Nippur. Though this name generally designates the whole temple complex in the inscriptions, originally, as the etymology of the word indicates, it can have been applied only to the most important part of it, /. *e.,* the shrine which stood on the top of the *ziggurrai.* This high-towering terrace being regarded as the "link which connects heaven and earth," that divine palace resting on it was a heavenly and terrestrial residence at the same time. This stage-tower, however, also penetrates far into the earth, its foundation being laid in the waters of the lower ocean. On the one hand it rises from the earth, inhabited by man, unto heaven, the realm of the gods; on the other, it descends to " the great city " *(urugal)* of the dead, the realm of the departed souls. For, according to Babylonian conception, " the nether world " *(Aralu* the abode of the dead, lies directly below and within the earth, or, more exactly, in the hollow space formed by the lower part *(kigal)* of the earth (which resembles an upset round boat, a socalled y«/rt),and by the lower ocean, which at the same time encircles this " land without return." The mountain of the world, therefore, is also called " the mountain of the nether world" *(shad Aralu)* in the cuneiform inscriptions. As *gigutiUy* "grave," "tomb," is used metonymically as a synonym of *Aralu,* "the nether world," it follows that the *ziggurrat* of Nippur, which is the local representation of the great mountain of the world, also could be called "the house of the tomb" (E-giguau) or "the house of 'the nether world.'' It is the edifice that rises over the Hades, quasi forming the roof beneath which the departed souls reside. It was therefore only natural that the earliest inhabitants should bury their dead around the base of the ziggurrat of Nippur to a depth of thirty to forty feet, so that the latter appears to us almost like a huge sepulchral monument erected over the tombs of the ancient Sumerians who rest in its shadow. Rising out of the midst of tombs, as it did, the stage-tower of Bel even literally may be called a " house of the tomb(s)." In view of what has just been stated in the briefest way possible, it will not surprise us that in the cuneiform literature Ekur sometimes is used as a synonym of " heaven," ' and sometimes stands in parallelism with Gigunu and Aralu' I infer this from the fact that an ancient king of Sippara, known from a text of the library of Ashurbanapal, has the name Enme-Duranki, concerning whom comp. Zimmern, in the third edition of Schrader's Keilimchriften sad das Alte Testament, vol. i, part 2 (Leipzig, 1902), pp. 532, seqq. Comp. also Jensen, /. -., p. 485.

For the present comp. the illustration facing p. 342, above. Sargon, " Khorsabad," I 55, scq.: " The gods Ea, Sin, Shamash, Nebo, Adad, Ninib, and their sublime consorts, who are born legitimately tn the house of situated on the top of the great mountain of the world, the mountain of ' the nether world.'" Sargon, Khorsabad, 155, seq. Comp. Jensen,/. f., pp. 203, 231, ttqq. Comp. A. Jeremias, Die Baby Ioniseh-Assyrischen ontfllungea vom Lebtn nach Jem ToJe, Leipzig, 1887, pp. 61, The tower of Bel at Nippur appears to us as a place of residence for the gods, as a place of worship for man, and as a place of rest for the dead — a grand conception for a sanctuary in the earliest historical period of Babylonia, which has continued even to the present time. For the hundreds and thousands of Christian churches, which contain tombs within their confines or are surrounded by a graveyard, practically express the same idea. As to a certain degree most of the other Babylonian temples were modelled more or less after the great national sanctuary of Bel at Nippur, we must expect, a priori, that excavations at FJ-Hibba, Fara, Larsa, Muqayyar, and other pre-Sargonic ruins, will likewise disclose extensive cemeteries around their ziggurrats. But it is interesting to observe how certain religious ideas of the Semitic conquerors, possibly in connection with considerations similar to those which led to a transfer of the cemeteries from the environments of the churches to districts outside the cities in our own days, seem finally to have brought about a radical change of the ancient burial customs in Babylonia. With regard to Nippur, this change can be traced to about the period of Sargon I, after whose government no more burials occur in the sacred precinct of Ekur. As remarked above, there are comparatively few among the 2500 postSargonic tombs thus far examined at Nuffar that can be with certainty assigned to the long interval between Sargon I and the Seleucidan occupation. Nearly all those reported by Peters and Haynes as being true Babylonian are Parthian, Sassanian, and Arabic. In fact we do not know yet how the Semitic inhabitants of ancient Nippur generally disposed of their dead. Comp. ii R. 54, no. 4. Comp. iv R. 24, 3-8; 2", 26, 27 a. Comp. pp. 154, stq., 233, note 3, above.

From the difficult passage' preceding Gudea's account of his restoration of Ningirsu's temple at Lagash, I am inclined to infer that originally a vast fire-necropolis surrounded the sanctuary of Tello also, and that Gudea did the same for Shir-pur-la as Sargon I (or some other monarch of that general period) had done for Nippur. He stopped cremating and burying the dead in the environments of the temple of Ningirsu, and levelled the ground of the ancient cemetery around it, with due regard to the numerous burial urns and coffins previously deposited there. In other words, "he cleaned the city " and " made the temple of Ningirsu a pure place like F.ridu," the sacred city of F.a, where, apparently, in the earliest davs, burials were not allowed. From the same inscription we learn another important fact. Gudea states expressly, that " he restored Eninnu-imgig(gu)barbara Ningirsu's temple and constructed his i. e. the god's beloved tomb (gigunu) of cedar wood in it." It cannot be ascertained precisely where the god's funeral chapel was, in the extensive household provided for him by Gudea. From another passage (Gudea, Statue D, ii, 7-iii, 1), however, it would seem that it formed part of the temple proper, which stood at the side of the ziggurrat, while the room on the summit of the stage-tower (called Epa) was the one chamber above all others in which Ningirsu and his consort, Bau, were supposed to reside, and where, accordingly, "the wedding presents of Bau" were deposited. Here, then, for the first time, we meet with the idea that a Babylonian god has his tomb. Startling as this statement may seem at first, it is in entire accord with the character of the principal god of Lagash, as a god of vegetation and as a sungod. For Ningirsu, "the powerful champion" and "the beloved son" of Enlil of Nippur, originally the god of agriculture, was later identified with Ninib, "the son of Ekur," the god of the rising sun, "who holds the link of heaven and earth and governs everything. " According to the Babylonian conception, he suffers death in the same way as Tammuz (Ez. 8: 14), the god of the spring vegetation and of the lower regions, with whom Ningirsu is practically identical; or as Shamash, the sun-god himself, who descends into the apsu, the terrestrial and subterranean ocean, every evening, and rises out of it again in the morning; who in the spring of every year commences his course with vouthful vigor, but gradually grows weaker and weaker until he dies during the winter. The sun dwelling in "the nether world " for half a year, the sun-god himself naturally is considered as dead during this period,' and Shamash consequently has his tomb in Larsa, and Ai, his wife, at Sippara, as Ningirsu in Lagash. More than this, the ziggurrat of Larsa itself is Shamash's tomb. For on a barrel cylinder from the temple of Shamash and Ai at Larsa, Nabonidos unmistakably calls the god's stage-tower " his lofty tomb."' Statue B, iii, 12-v, 1 1.

Comp. Gudea, Statue B, v, 15-19; Statue D, ii, 7-iii, I. Comp. Thureau-Dangin's translation and brief treatment of Gudea's two large cylinders (A and B) in *Comptes Ren Jus,* 1901, pp. I 12 *seqq. (Le songt ae Gudea,* Cyl. A), *Revue a"histoire et de literature rcligieuses,* vol. vi (1901), no. 6, pp. 481, *seqq. (La famif/e et /a (our d'un dieu chaldeen,* Cyl. B.), and *Zcitschrift fur Asiyriologie,* vol. xvi (1902), pp. 344, *seqq. (Le cylindre A de Gudea).* Comp. pp. 469, *seqq.,* below. Comp. Gudea, Cyl. A, ii, 12, where it is even said that "Ningirsu is lord or prince *(nirgal)* at Nippur." See i *R.* 29, 3, *seq., markas shame u irsiti,* the Assyrian translation of the Sumerian *Duranki,* which, as we saw above, was the name of the *ziggurrat* of *Ekur.* Comp. Jensen, *Kosmokgie,* Index. Who dies in the month sacred to him. Comp. Jensen, */. e.,* pp. 197, *seqq.* Comp. Winckler, *Arabisch-Semitisch-Orientaliseh* in *Mitteilungen der Vorderasiatischen Gesellse ha ft,,JSerWn,* 1901, no. 5, pp. 93, *seqq.* Comp. Scheil, *Code Jes Lois de Hammurabi* (D. Morgan's *Memoires,* vol. iv) Paris, 1902, col. ii, 26-28, —a passage which 1 owe to Hommel, I not yet having seen the book recently published.

From what has been said, it follows (i) that the Babylonians themselves associated the idea of " tomb " closely with their *ziggurrats,* and (2) that the inscriptions not only know of tombs of certain deities (of light) in general, but in one case at least directly call the *ziggurrat* of a god "his sepulchre." As Marduk, the supreme god of Babylon, likewise is a sun-god, namely, the god of the early sun of the day (morning) and of the year (spring), we have no reason to doubt any longer that the conception of the classical writers concerning *Etemenanki,* the stage-tower of Marduk, as "the sepulchre of Bel," is correct, and goes back to trustworthy original sources. 4. The excavations conducted along the southeast enclosing wall of the *ziggur-*

rat established the important fact that the stage-tower did not occupy the central part of the temple court, and that the ascent to the high-towering terrace and the entrance gate of the enclosing wall did not lie opposite each other. Upon entering the sacred precincts one was compelled to turn westward in order to reach the former. It became, therefore, very probable that the remains of a second important structure were hidden below the rubbish accumulated at the northeast side of the *ziggurrat.* In order to ascertain this, we proceeded with our excavations from the east corner of the temple court A passage generally misunderstood by the translators. The text waj published and first translated by Bezold in the " Proceedings of the Society of Biblical Archeology," 1889. Comp. col. ii, 16: *zi-ku-ra-ti gi-gu-na-aihu si-i-ri.* Comp. Jensen, *Kosmotogie,* pp. 87, *iffy.* A somewhat different view of the same scholar is found in Schrader's *K. £.,* vol. vi, p. 562.

Comp. Lehmann in *Wodienschrift fur klassische Philologie,* 1900, p. 962, note 1, and *Beitrage zur alien Guchichte,* vol. i, p. 276, note i. Also Zimmern, *K. A. T.,* p. 371. Ground plan of Ekur, Temple of Bel at Nippur *Restored and designed by Hilprceht, drawn by Fisher A. Inner Court: /. Ziggurrat. 2. House of Bel. j. Front and rear gates. f and c. Storage 'vaults, b and 7. fVater conduits draining the z-iggurrat. S. Shallow basin forming the junction of the watercourses at the rear. B. Outer Court: I. Small Temple of Bel. 2 and j. Excavated portions of the enclosing avails. excavated restored ivalls.* northward, until we came upon a wall of baked bricks which ran parallel to the southeast enclosing wall. We followed it for a considerable distance towards the southwest, when suddenly it turned off at a right angle in a northwest direction, continuing its course tor 157 feet, nearly parallel with the northeast facade of the *ziggufrat,* and at a distance of nearly sixteen feet from it. When we had reached a point a little beyond the north corner of the stage-tower, it again turned off at a right angle to the east.

We traced it for seventy-one feet in this direction by means of a tunnel, without, however, being able to follow it to the end.

The excavated portions sufficed to determine that the wall enclosed a space 152 feet long and about 115 feet wide, 1. e., an area of 17,480 square feet. The prominent position which the structure occupied at the side of the stage-tower, the fact that it was built of burned bricks (laid in clay mortar), and the circumstance that, with the exception of the entire southeast side and the adjoining part of the southwest face, the wall was panelled in the same way as the corresponding sides of the *ziggurrat,* indicated clearly that it was not a mere enclosing wall, but the facing of a large house. As it had served as a quarry for later generations, it was unfortunately reduced considerably in height. At some places not more than one or two courses of bricks had been left, while at others there were as many as a score. With the limited time then at my disposal it was impossible to examine and to remove the mass of debris covering the building as carefully as it ought to be done. I therefore decided not to ruin this important section of the temple area by adopting the methods of mv predecessors, but to leave its interior as far as possible untouched, and to confine myself to an exploration of its exposed edges. We were thus enabled to gather the following details, *a.* The facing wall varied in thickness from a little over 3 to about 5 % feet. *b.* A number of unbaked brick walls ran at right angles to the facing wall, and with it constituted a number of larger and smaller rooms, *c.* The building had two entrances in its longer southwest side. The one near the south corner, being the principal one, was io feet wide, while that near the north corner measured only about half that width. *d.* As the visible part of this large house seemed to rest on the same level as the pavement of Kadashman-Turgu and was completely covered by the pavement of Ashurbanapal, naturally I assumed that it had been restored for the last time by a member of the Cassite dynasty. The correctness of this theory was proved by an inscription taken from its walls. Among the various bricks examined, one of them (discovered *in situ)* bore a brief legend on one of its edges, from which we learned that "Shagarak-ti-Shuriash (about 1350 B. c), king of Babylon, prefect *(sag-ush)* of the house of Bel," was one of the rulers who devoted his time and interest to this remarkable building, *e.* Immediately beneath the southwest wall of the Cassite edifice are fragments of an earlier wall which ran somewhat nearer to the northeast face of the *ziggurrat.*

What was the original purpose of this extensive structure? To judge from its mere size and conspicuous position in connection with the characteristic inscription just mentioned, there can be no doubt that it represents the "house of Bel" itself, the palace in which the household of the god and his consort was established, where sacrifices were offered and the most valuable votive offerings of the greatest Babylonian monarchs deposited. In other words, it was the famous temple of Bel, which, together with the stage-tower, formed an organic whole enclosed by a common wall, and was generally known under the name of *Ekur,* "House of the Mountain." This divine palace stood "at the side of the *ziggurrat"* of Nippur, precisely where, on the basis of Rassam's excavations at Borsippa and Sippara, and according to numerous indications in the building inscriptions of Babylonian temples, I had expected to find it.

My conclusions with regard to the importance and nature of this structure were fully confirmed by the discoveries made in its immediate neighborhood. Apart from numerous fragments of stone vases, as a rule inscribed with the names of pre-Sargonic kings familiar to us from the results of the former campaigns, we unearthed several interesting antiquities in a far better state of preservation than the average relic previously excavated in the court of the temple. Their number increased as we began to approach the large edifice described. Among the objects of art thus obtained I mention the leg of a large black statue from the level of Ur-Gur, the head of

a small marble statue covered with a turban, like those of the time of Gudea found at Tello, and two small headless statues of the same material but considerably older. Each of the latter bore a brief votive inscription of four lines. They came from the same stratum that produced the large mass of broken antiquities gathered by the second and third expeditions. Immediately below it was the section of a pavement which consisted of stones and pieces of baked brick mixed and laid in bitumen. When examined more closely it was found to contain three fragments of a large inscribed slab in limestone once presented to the temple of Bel by a "king of Shumer and Akkad." Not far from this pavement there was a large heavy vase in dolerite. It stood upright, was over 2 feet high, had a diameter of nearly i *y* feet, and bore the following inscription: "To Bel, the king of the gods, for the house *(es/i)* of Nippur and, or namely *Duranki,* Gudea, *patesi* of Lagash, has presented the long boat (*/'. e.,* a *tur-rada)* of *Ekur* for the preservation of his life." i For the present comp. Nabonidos" barrel cylinder from Larsa (published by Bezold in the "Proceedings of the Society of Biblical Archirology," London, 1889), vol. iii, 13, *itq.: pa-pa-khi shu-ba-at i-lu-ti-shu-un tirtim iha i-tt-e zi-qu-ra-tim ri-tu-u te-mt-en-shu.*

It soon became evident that the house of Bel at the side of the *ziggurrat* must have existed as early as the time of Sargon I and Naram-Sin. A few brick stamps of the latter, and a door-socket and many brick stamps of the former were discovered slightly above their well-known pavement. Soon afterwards the workmen unearthed a small piece of spirited sculpture (exhibiting the larger part of an incised quadruped), which doubtless belongs to the fourth millennium, and a round marble slab over *i* feet in diameter and nearly 3 inches thick, which contained the name of "Naram-Sin, king of Agade, king of the four regions of the world," accompanied by the somewhat effaced name of a contemporaneous "priest of Bel, thy servant."

Even the pre-Sargonic period was represented by several fairly well preserved objects. We refer briefly to the fragment of a perforated votive tablet in limestone showing a sacrificial scene with Nin-lil, or Beltis, in the centre. The goddess, accompanied by a bird, apparently sacred to her,-' is seated on a low chair and holds a pointed cup in her right hand. A burning altar (which became the regular ideogram for "fire" in Assyrian) and a lighted candlestick stand in front of Beltis, while behind her a priest, remarkable for the long hair of his beard and the back of his head, leads a shaved worshipper, carrying a young goat on his right arm, before the goddess. Among the other antiquities found in the immediate neighborhood of Bel's house, I mention a small carving in mother-of-pearl (a warrior with drawn bow); a piece of lapis lazuli with a human head in low relief; another round stone slab dedicated to En-lil by King Lugalkigubnidudu; a model in limestone for making plano-convex bricks; about forty fragments of clay bearing impressions of archaic seal cylinders; and more than one hundred inscribed clay tablets taken from below the level of Naram-Sin. With regard to several other antiquities found in the strata immediately beneath If it were Bel, he would be represented with a beard, according to the general custom observed. The garment and the peculiar hair-dress of the deity likewise favor my interpretation.

Comp. the raven of Ningirsu (p. 230, note I, above), the raven of Woden, the eagle of Jupiter, the peacock of Juno, the owl of Athene, etc.

Pre-Sargonic Votive Tablet in Limestone, Sacrificial Scene it — as, *e.g.,* a quantity of large beads in crystal (quartz), a hollow cone of silver, a vase of jewelry containing rings and a well preserved chain in the same metal, several excellently fashioned nails, scrapers, knives, a saw, and many fragments of vessels, all in copper — it must remain doubtful whether they belonged to "the house of Bel" or, as seems more probable to the present writer, in part at least were originally deposited in the numerous ash-graves which begin to appear directly below the pavement of the Sargon dynasty.

Several fragments of small pavements were discovered slightly above that of Naram-Sin in the east section of the temple court immediately before the sanctuary of Bel. They had been laid by unknown persons prior to the time of Ur-Gur. One of these sections contained many inscribed bricks with the short legend: "Lugalsurzu, *patesi* of Nippur, priest of Bel." A shallow rectangular basin built of burned bricks and coated with bitumen on its floor and sides, an open conduit leading from it to a neighboring vertical drain, and the above-mentioned stone vase of Gudea indicate that it was probably reserved for the ablutions of the priests, for cleansing the sacred vessels, and other functions of the temple service for which water was required. It is possible also that the sheep, goats and other sacrifices to be offered were killed there. From an inscribed door-socket of Bur-Sin of Ur previously unearthed in the eastern half of the temple court, it can also be inferred that a store-room called "the house for honey, cream and wine, a place for his Bel's sacrifices,"' must have existed somewhere within the temple enclosure not very far from "the house of Bel."

The large number of inscribed and sculptured objects gathered in the lower strata of the court of the *ziggurrat* by the American explorers and in its upper ruins centuries ago by the later inhabitants of ancient Nippur, to a certain degree enable us to form an idea of the elaborate manner in which the temple of Bel was equipped and embellished in early days. But the ruinous state of its walls and the very fragmentary condition in which all the statues and most of the reliefs and vases thus far have been discovered, indicate what in all probability will await us in the interior of the sanctuary itself. A methodical exploration of the large building at the side of the *ziggurrat* will doubtless result in the unearthing of other fragmentary inscriptions and important objects of art, but its principal object will have to be the

restoration of the ground-plan of Babylonia's great national sanctuary at the middle of the second pre-Christian millennium.

Comp. Hilprecht, "The Bab. Exp. of the U. of Pa.," series A, vol. i, part I, no. 21. On the use and significance of wine, cream and honey in the Babylonian cults, comp. Zimmern, *K. A. T.,* p. 526. *E. g.,* all the fine votive objects originally deposited by the Cassite kings in the temple of Bel, but found by Peters in the box of a jeweller of the Parthian period (pp. 35, *icq.,* above), outside of the temple proper. 5. Much has been written on the analogies existing between Babylonian and Hebrew temples, and, strange to say, even an attempt has been made to trace the architectural features of the temple of Solomon to Babylonian sources, though as a matter of fact not one of the large Babylonian temples has as yet been excavated thoroughly enough to enable us to recognize its disposition and necessary details. The little Parthian palace of Nippur on the west side of the Chebar, plainly betraying Greek influence, was quoted as a pattern "of the architecture of Babylonia,' and the Parthian fortress lying on the top of the ruined temple of Bel was interpreted as "affording us for the first time a general view of a sacred quarter in an ancient Babylonian city." There remains little of Peters' theories concerning the topography of ancient Nippur and the age of its excavated ruins that will stand criticism. We can therefore readily imagine to what incongruities any comparison resting on his so-called interpretations of the ruins must lead us. It will be wise to refrain for the present entirely from such untimely speculations until the characteristic features of at least one of Babylonia's most prominent sanctuaries have been established satisfactorily by pick and spade.

In my previous sketch I have endeavored to show, on the basis of my own excavations and researches at NuflFar, that *Ekur,* the temple of Bel, consisted of two principal buildings, the *ziggurrat,* and "the house of Bel" at the side of it. Both were surrounded by a com-

mon wall called *Imgur-Marduk* in the cuneiform inscriptions. It may reasonably be doubted whether the average pilgrim visiting Nippur was ever allowed to enter this most holy enclosure. The question then arises: Was there no other place of worship, a kind of outer court, to which every pious Babylonian who desired to pay homage to " the father of the gods," had free access?

In 1890 Peters fortunately came upon the remains of a building in the lower mounds situated to the southeast of Bint el-Amir. He found that most of its bricks were stamped upon their edges, one to three times, with a brief legend, and discovered two door-sockets *in situ,* from which we learned that the little edifice of two rooms was a temple called *Kishaggulla-Bur-Sin,* " House of the delight of Bur-Sin,"' erected in honor of Bel by Bur-Sin of Ur, who reigned about 2550 B. C. (comp. pp. 336, *set. ,* above). Fragments of sculptures scattered in the debris around it testified to the great esteem in which the chapel had been held by the ancient worshippers. From the mere fact that it stood in the shadow of *Ekur,* directly opposite the ascent of the stage-tower, towards which it faced, I arrived at the conclusion that it must have been included in the precincts of the temple, and that future excavations carried on in its neighborhood would show that the complex of the great national sanctuarv in all probability extended much farther to the south than, on the basis of Peters' statements, we were entitled to assume. When therefore, in 1899, I went a second time to the ruins, I was in hope of finding some clue as to the precise relation in which this shrine stood to the principal enclosure. As the enormous dump-heaps raised on that important mound by my predecessors again interfered seriously with the work of the expedition, there remained nothing else to be done but to try to solve the problem in connection with our excavations along the southeast enclosing wall of the court of the *ziggurrat* as far as this was possible. The attempt was crowned with a fair amount of success bevond that which could have been anticipated (comp. the zinctype, p. 470).

Comp. Hilprecht, "The Bab. Exp. of the U. of Pa.," series A. vol. i, part i, no. zo, 11. 15, *seq.* The two signs *shag-'gul* (heart + joy, *Herxensfrcude*), must be an ideogram with a meaning like "delight, cheerfulness. ''

While tracing the panelled outer face of the last-mentioned wall, our workmen were suddenly stopped in their progress both at the eastern and southern ends of the long and deep trench by a cross-wall joining the former at a right angle. In order to ascertain the course and nature of these two walls they were ordered to follow them for a certain distance by means of tunnels cut along their inner faces at about the level of Naram-Sin's pavement. These tunnels revealed the existence of numerous ash-graves in the lower strata, and enabled us to determine that the two walls were constructed of the same unbaked material and adorned with the same kind of panels as the southeast wall of the temple enclosure. The northeast wall was traced forty-eight feet without reaching its end, when the excavations were suspended in order not to destroy valuable remains of constructions which might have been built against it. For the same reason the southwest tunnel was cut less deep, especially as the evidence gained from it sufficed to confirm the results obtained from the other tunnel. It could no longer be doubted that a second, somewhat smaller court, in which Bur-Sin's sanctuary stood, adjoined the court of the *ziggurrat* on the side of its principal entrance. This outer court seems to have extended to the edge of the depression which represents the ancient bed of a branch of the Shatt en-Nil. An opening in the low narrow ridge running along its northern embankment, and evidently marking the remains of an ancient wall later occupied bv Parthian houses, indicates the site of the gate which once gave access to it.

These are all the positive facts that could be gathered. At least two years will be required to remove the dumpheaps completely and to excavate the whole mound systematically. From a tablet found in the upper strata of the

temple library, I learned that besides Bel, at least twenty-four other deities had their own "houses " in the sacred precincts of Nippur. Where have we to look for them? The absence of any considerable building remains in the inner court, apart from those described above, the existence of a small temple of Bel in the outer court, and several other considerations, lead me to the assumption that in all probability they were grouped around Bel's chapel in the enclosed space between the southeast wall of the *ziggurrat* and the eastern branch of the Shatt en-Nil, — in other words, are to be sought for in the outer court of *Ekur.* 6. One of the principal tasks of the latest Philadelphia expedition was to search for the gates and to determine the probable course and extent of the walls of the ancient citv. According to the inscriptions, Nippur had two walls, called *Imgur-Marduk* (" Merodach was favorable ") and *NimitMarduk* ("Stronghold of Merodach"). The former was the inner wall *(dilru)*, the latter the outer wall or rampart *shalkhu)*. The mere fact that both names contain as an element Marduk, the supreme god of Babylon, who, in connection with the rise of the first dynasty of Babylon (about 2300 B. c.) gradually took the place of Bel of Nippur, indicates that they cannot represent the earliest designations of the two walls. This inference is fully confirmed by a discovery made in the debris near the eastern corner of the court of the *ziggurrat*. In clearing that section the workmen found a small and much-effaced terracotta cone of the same form as that of Ashurbanapal described above (p. 461), which originally must have been deposited in the upper part of the temple wall. The docu Literally " Foundation, establishment of Merodach." ment, inscribed with two columns of old-Babylonian writing (twenty-five lines each), and in the Semitic dialect of the country, conveys to us the information that Samsu-iluna, son and successor of Hammurabi, restored the inner wall of Nippur *(diiru)*. We thereby obtain new evidence that the kings of the first dyn-'s'-v did noi '"ct Bel's sanctuary, though their ap-

parent reason tor lortitying the temple was less religious than political. Their interest in the wall of Nippur seems to be closely connected with their operations against the city of (N)isin, which was situated not far from the latter, and which subsequently became the stronghold of Rim-Sin of Larsa.

As the greater part of the inscription is intelligible and of importance for our question, I give it in an English translation. "Samsu-iluna, the powerful king, king of Babylon, king of the four quarters of the world. When Bel had granted him to rule the four quarters of the world and placed their reins into his hand, Samsu-iluna, the shepherd who gladdens the heart of Marduk, in the sublime power which the great gods had given him, in the wisdom of Ea... he raised the wall *(duru)* of Bel, which structure his grandfather Sinmuballit had made higher than before, like a great mountain, surrounded it with marshv ground *(npparam)*, dug 'the Euphrates of Nippur' *i. e.,* cleaned and deepened the river Chebar; comp. pp. 412 *seq.,* and erected the dam of ' the Euphrates of Nippur' along it. He called the name of that wall ' Link of the lands ' *(Markas-matatim)?* caused the population of Shumer and Aklcad to dwell in a peaceful habitation... and made the name of Sinmuballit, his grandfather, famous in the world." Sinmuballit's repairing of the wall of Nippur, which we also learn from Samsu-iluna's cone, was probably mentioned in the mutilated passage of the list of dates (" Bu. 91, 5-9, 284 "), following his conquest of (N)isin. Accordingly it would have taken place in one of his last three years, immediately before he lost (N)isin and Nippur again to Rim-Sin of Larsa. Comp. Scheil, *Code des Lois de Hammurabi:* Nippur, *Dur-an* (p. 463, above), *Ekur. I. r.,* the wall which unites all the lands (the whole world). It was thus called, because the title *shar kibrat arba'im, "* king of the four quarters of the world," was closely connected with the sanctuary of Nippur, in which Bel, as "the king of the world," appointed his human representative on earth and bestowed the significant title upon him.

Comp. Hilprecht, "The Bab. Exp. of the U. of Pa.," series A, vol. i, part *z*, pp. 56, *seq.* (and part I, pp. 24, *seq.).*

From the place where the cone was discovered, from the designation of the wall as *dur Bel,* and from the description of the king's work following, it may be inferred with certainty that Samsu-iluna has reference to the temple wall. This result agrees with the fact that our excavations have furnished evidence to the effect that the city proper on the west side of the Shatt en-Nil was never fortified by a wall, to say nothing of two walls. On the other hand, the double wall which surrounded and protected the sanctuary from the earliest days can still be traced without difficulty, notwithstanding the radical changes which took place at the temple complex in post-Babylonian times. The *Markasmatati* of Samsu-iluna and the *Imgur-Marduk* of the later period must therefore designate the same inner wall enclosing the two courts of the sanctuary and separating them from the other buildings of the vast complex which constituted the sacred precincts of Nippur. The general course of this wall was indicated through the boundary line of the Parthian fortress lying directly over it, and besides has been fixed definitely at several points by our excavations. We exposed nearly the whole southeast wall of the inner court, disclosed part of its northwest wall, and traced the two sidewalls of the outer court far enough to enable us to reconstruct the general outlines of the temple enclosure.

Aside from the depression in the unexcavated southeast ridge marking the boundary of the outer court, which doubtless represents the principal entrance of the latter, two gates have been found in connection with our explorations around the stage-tower, the large southeast one, which connects the two courts, and another smaller one, which leads from the rear of the *ziggurrat* into the large open space to the northwest of the temple. The axis of the rear gate, which is nearly seventeen feet distant from the lower face of *Im'garsag,* is in line with the front gate. Though only one corner of the former has as yet been

uncovered, it suffices to show that its construction was similar to the one in front of the *ziggurrat.* Comp. the plan ot the ruins on p. 305.

The southeast wall, which contained the principal gate of the temple, exhibits the same general characteristic features as the fragment of wall from the time of Gudea, which De Sarzec discovered beneath the Seleucidan palace at Tello, with the exception that the wall around *Ekur* was constructed entirely of unbaked material, while the much less imposing one of the temple of Ningirsu consisted of baked bricks. To judge from the excavated southeast section, the interior face of the wall at Nippur, into which a number of store-rooms were built, was plain and without any ornamentation, while the monotony of the long exterior surface was relieved by a series of panels. On an average these panels measured about 16 feet in width, and were separated from each other by shallow buttresses projecting one foot from the wall, and 9 to 10 feet wide. The gate, which occupied nearly the centre of this wall, was a very elaborate affair, considering that its plan and general disposition, similar to that of the city gates of the Assyrian kings discovered at Khorsabad and Nineveh, go back to the time of Sargon of Agade." It was 52 feet long and nearly as wide, and was flanked on each side by a pair of tower-like bastions, still preserved to a considerable height. They projected sixteen feet towards the northwest and about nine feet towards the southeast. Like the wall itself, which was 26 feet thick, including the storage vaults of the inner court, the front faces of these towers were panelled. A kind of vestibule marked the entrance of the gate on both sides. By means of three stepped recesses projecting from each tower these vestibules (14 feet wide) narrowed into the passageway proper, which measured only 6 feet in width. In the middle of the gate this passage opened into a long gallery, probably serving as a guardroom. The door of the gate which closed the opening towards the outer court swung in the direction of the eastern section of this gallery, as a socket in

dolerite imbedded in baked bricks allowed us to infer. This stone, though inscribed with the common legend of Ur-Gur, did not seem to lie in its original position, but apparently had been used over and over, the last time by Ashurbanapal, at the level of whose pavement it was found. The remains of *Imgur-Marduk* were deeply hidden below the ruins of later constructions. As regards *Nimit-Marduk,* the outer wall of the temple, we find the case somewhat different. To a considerable extent the course of the ancient rampart could still be recognized and traced through a series of low ridges lying on the northwest and northeast (II) limits of NufFar. Seen from the top of Bint el-Amir, they formed two almost straight lines (more or less interrupted by gaps) which originally must have met at an obtuse angle in the north (comp. the plan of the ruins, p. 305). In the course of the third expedition Haynes had driven two tunfloor of the gate was raised by the gradually accumulating dirt and debris, the doorsocket was carried higher and higher, so that Ashurbanapal's entrance lies about six feet above that of Ur-Gur, a fact in entire accord with the difference of altitude observed between the pavements of the two monarch within the temple enclosure.

Comp. the zinctype, p. 470, above, and " Ekur, the Temple of Bel" (restored) below. Traces of a crude brick pavement of the period prior to Ur-Gur were discovered at the bottom of the gate walls. In the same proportion as the nels through the northeastern ridge (near III), thereby ascertaining that both Naram-Sin and Ur-Gur, whose bricks at some places lie directly upon each other, had done work on the outer wall. His deductions, however, with regard to its original size and construction, turned out to be erroneous, as accidentally he had struck a kind of large buttress, through which his tunnels ran obliquely. At the committee's request, he had resumed his excavation there in the fall of 1 899, in order to search for the northeast city gate, the original position of which seemed to be indicated by an especially large gap near the middle of the ridge.

Soon after my arrival at the ruins in 1900, I placed a large force, divided into a number of small gangs, along the whole line, with the intention of tracing the course of the entire wall. The examination of the northern section was completed within seven weeks; that of the eastern will require considerably more time and work to obtain a full insight into the meaning of the many fragmentary walls which sometimes run alongside and sometimes above, and sometimes overlap each other. Owing to the heavy mass of ruins, particularly of the Parthian period, under which these remains are buried, they cannot be exposed and understood fully without subjecting to a critical examination the whole group of mounds adjoining them in the direction of the temple. It may be safely asserted that extensive excavations in this section of the ruins will yield important results. For, aside from very large tablets which trial trenches brought to light, we have reason to believe that the buildings which occupied this site stood in a closer relation to the sanctuary, in all probability representing the palace of the *patesis of* Nippur and the houses of the higher class of priests and temple officers serving immediately under them.

The excavations conducted along the outer face of *Nimit-Marduk* yielded several interesting objects. At the base of the pre-Sargonic and Sargonic walls we gathered a large quantity of baked terracotta balls, about t J to i /£ inches in diameter, and a few small stone eggs. Both balls and eggs had previously been classified under the general title of playthings, but in view of the peculiar place where they mostly occurred, this explanation can no longer be maintained. There is little doubt in my mind but that they are to be regarded as missiles thrown by the slingers of hostile armies attacking the city. As stones could not be obtained in the alluvial soil of Babylonia, clay was turned into war material as it served many other purposes. The marble eggs may have originally belonged to foreign invaders, notably the Rlamites, who brought them from their mountainous districts, or they were thrown by certain Babylonian warriors

of one of the petty states near the Arabian desert who could afford this luxury. The other weapons employed in the battles around the walls of the temple, according to our discoveries, were arrows, spears, axes and clubs, the heads of the first-mentioned three weapons being made of copper; those of the clubs of stone, especially porphyry and granite. In one case we came upon the twisted remains of a quiver. The wooden parts of the receptacle had decayed long ago, but its copper fastenings, consisting of a round, thin plate with two corroded arrowheads attached to it, a narrow copper strap and a nail of the same metal, were still preserved. The excavations tracing the base of *Nimit-Marduk* revealed also some of the means to which the besieged inhabitants sometimes resorted in order to protect themselves against attacks from without. In case of necessity they seized any heavy object upon which they could lay their hands, and hurled it down upon the heads of the storming enemies, as was shown by the stone weights, mortars in dolerite, broken statues and reliefs, stone pestles, etc., unearthed along the outer face of the wall. We here found some of the oldest fragments of sculptures discovered at Nuffar, *e. g.,* several Comp. p. 242, above.

portions of a large stele in limestone, adorned with human figures, similar in design to those which are depicted on a small bas-relief from Tello representing the meeting of the two chiefs. It was natural that in the debris which had Pre-Sargonic Cis-Relief in Limestone accumulated on both sides of the rampart we should find many broken terracotta figurines of gods and goddesses. And it was entirely in accord with what we observed in other parts of the mounds that here and there in the slopes of the ruined wall late Arabic tombs were met with. But it was entirely unexpected to find that the pre-Sargonic burials (ash-beds, urns and drains), which at low levels we had previously traced outside of the inner wall of the post-Sargonic period, extended even slightlv bevond *Nimit-Marduk* in the neighborhood of the temple.

As the northeast section of the outer wall confined a large open court, there was no difficulty in carefully examining the whole structure by means of two long trenches following its course on either side. We soon found that originally a series of small rooms was built against the inner face of the rampart. Three of them opened into a long corridor which ran along the wall (No. n). Two, exhibiting no entrance at all, seemed to have served as store-rooms, accessible only from above. Some could be identified onlv from insignificant traces, while still others had disappeared so completely that their former existence could only be inferred from certain indications in the soil. To the northwest of the five preserved chambers was a peculiar receptacle in the shape of a jar made of three different materials (No. 10). A round terra-cotta plate, thickly covered with bitumen, represented the bottom. The lower part of its side consisted of bitumen, while the upper part was unbaked clay coated inside and outside with a thin layer of bitumen. Evidentlv this receptacle had been a kind of a safe inserted in the floor of a room, the walls of which had decayed long ago. The man who devised this unique specimen of a small "cistern" had probably intended to construct it entirely of bitumen on a foundation of terra-cotta, but finding that his material was not sufficient, he substituted clay, and used only as much bitumen as was absolutely necessary to exclude the humidity from the interior of the vessel. The relative age and purpose of this vase could be determined by the aid of seven fragments of cuneiform tablets lying within it, and also of a few others picked up at about the same level in the loose earth of the neighborhood. A shopkeeper of some sort, who lived at the time of the dynasty of Ur (about 2600 B. a), had kept his account books in this jar. Similar tablet jars were repeatedly found in other parts of the ruins. Comp. p. 250, above.

Comp. the zinctype illustrating the " Northwestern Section of the Northeastern City Wall," p. 498, below. The numbers placed in parenthesis above refer to it. Comp. my remarks in connection with the temple library below.

Our excavations along the northwest section of *NlmitMarduk* had shown that in the first half of the third millennium a row of magazines, booths, and closets occupied the space along the inner face of the long wall. In one case a room had been built even into the latter. Our continued explorations in that neighborhood confirmed this result in all particulars. Near the northern extremity of the large enclosure we uncovered a small fireplace with ashes on its top and around its base (No. 9). It was a very simple affair, being merely a hard clay platform surrounded by a row of burned bricks set on edge. A much more elaborate concern (No. 8) was discovered a little to the north of it. Our Arabs identified it at once as a large oven or the same tvpe as is used to-day in the large native restaurants of Baghdad, Hilla, and other places of the lower Euphrates and Tigris valleys, or employed in connection with the burning of pottery. This is another striking illustration of the tenacity with which ancient Babylonian customs are preserved even by the present population of'Iraq el-'Arabi.

This peculiar brick structure, which combined the characteristic features of a kiln and of a kitchen furnace, was about 13 feet long, a little over 7 feet wide, and nearly 4 feet high.

Section of a Babylonian Baking Furnace in Use (Time of Abraham

It was built against Ur-Gur's wall, and consisted of crude bricks, which, in consequence of their constant exposure to the intense heat, had completely turned red. As the interesting fireplace stood on a somewhat higher level than the curious tablet jar described above (p. 488), it probably is not quite as ancient, and must be ascribed to the time ot the kings of (N)isin or to the first dynasty of Babylon, — in round numbers, to about 2400 or 2300 B. C. Its upper surface showed a kind of panelled work, while there was an arched opening at one of its two shorter sides, that towards the northwest. The outside appearance of the whole structure was not unlike a large box such as is used everywhere at

the present day to ship birds and other living animals.

Upon closer examination, the furnace was found to be composed of a series of seven (originally nine) arches rising parallel to a southeast solid wall which terminated the whole structure, and alternately joined to one another by fragments of bricks in order to keep the single arches intact. The vertical flues thereby formed descended into the vaulted fire-box, which was about *i* feet wide, nearly as high, and ran lengthwise through the whole kiln. But they also communicated with a horizontal flue of the same length near the top of the structure close to the rampart. The accompanying cross-section of the restored building, drawn by Fisher, will convey a tolerably clear idea of the manner in which the building was heated, the necessary draft obtained, and the smoke discharged from the interior. The draft was regulated by means of tiles placed over the longitudinal flue, or removed from the same.

The upper surface of this oven now appears worn oft" at the edges and otherwise damaged, but originally it was entirely level. The pots containing the food to be cooked were put over the open spaces between the single arches. Whenever they did not cover the entire space the remaining openings were closed by bricks, several of which were found *in situ*. In case pottery was to be burned, all the available space was filled with different kinds of earthen vessels. Low dishes were piled on the top of each other, their sticking together being prevented by small terra-cotta stilts of precisely the same form as those used in the china manufactories of Kurope and America to-day. They were gathered in large quantities at . 7 . various parts and levels of the ruins.

Many enamelled dishes of the Parthian period were brought Comp. p. 313, above.

Stilt used in Modern China Manufactories *From Tinier:, N. j.* to light which exhibit those stilt-marks very plainly inside and outside. In order to save fuel, to concentrate the heat, and to secure an even burning of the pottery, the struc-

ture doubtless was roofed over.

After this brief review of the principal discoveries made in connection with our tracing the inner face of the great enclosing wall, we turn our attention to the construc '«

The long narrow ridge (II-III, on the plan of the ruins, p. 305), which conceals the remains of the frequently repaired rampart to the north of the temple, varies considerably in height. At some places it stands only a few feet above the plain, while at others it rises to more than twenty feet above the same. Its average height may be regarded as about twelve to fifteen feet. The comparative steepness of the ridge, the absence of extensive traces of later (post-Babylonian) settlements on its top, and the noteworthy fact that the excavations at the highest points of the ruined structure did not disclose the remains of specially fortified bastions or high towers at these places would indicate that at the time of its latest restoration *Nimit-Marduk* cannot have been less than twenty-five feet high, and possibly was somewhat higher.

The question arises at once, why is it that certain parts of the ancient rampart are preserved almost in their original height, while others have been reduced considerably, and still other large sections of the northwest, northeast and southeast walls have disappeared completely. It is not difficult to give a correct answer. A careful examination of the large adobes which characterize all the true Parthian buildings at Nippur revealed the fact that they were made of clay previously worked. *It* is generally known among the present inhabitants of'Iraq el-'Arabi that the clay of old mud houses refashioned into bricks furnishes a much more tenacious and lasting building material than the clay taken directly from the soil. We have ample evidence to show that the early Babylonian builders had acquired the same knowledge by experience. There can be no doubt, therefore, that the enormous mass of clay required for the construction of the huge fortress erected on the temple mound, and for the extensive

Parthian settlements on the site of the library, on the mounds to the east of the temple, and on the west side of the Chebar, was principally obtained from the abandoned outer walls of the ancient city. This theory was fully corroborated by our excavations in the wide gap of the northeast wall, marked III on the plan of the ruins (p. 305). While searching there for the possible remains of one of the former city gates, we came upon a very large hollow or depression in the ground filled with mud washings and drift sand from the desert. It proved to be one of the clay beds worked by the brick-makers of the post-Babylonian period, who, after having torn down a section of about 360 feet from the old rampart, penetrated to a considerable depth into the soil below and around it.

In descending somewhat deeper into the ground than the Parthian clay diggers before us had done, we disclosed the ruins of a pre-Sargonic gate, or more exactly, part of its substructure and stepped ascent. It lay four to eight feet below the present level of the plain, which at this point is considerably higher than elsewhere in the vicinity of Nuffar. The structure, as it now stands, is entirely isolated. But while excavating we observed a mass of worked clay, largely disintegrated adobes, and a number of bricks of Naram-Sin scattered through the loose earth in its immediate neighborhood. These, with certain inferences to be drawn from a fragment of the same king's wall about 175 feet to the northwest of it, and several other considerations, lead us to the conclusion that at all the different periods of Nippur's varied history the northeast gate of the city must have been situated at about the same place. Hence it follows that *Nimit-Marduk* ran in the form of a great bastion or bulwark around the gate, giving to it additional strength and architectural prominence.

From the illustration facing this page we can recognize without difficulty that the original gate consisted of three divisions, a central roadway (1) for the use of beasts and vehicles, and two elevated passageways *(2* and 3) for the people. There have remained only insignificant traces of the main division and of the left sidewalk — practically nothing beyond a few courses of burned bricks sufficient to determine the general plan and disposition of the gate, while the right or northwest passageway was found in a tolerably fair state of preservation. The central road was about 12 feet wide, or nearly three times as wide as each sidewalk. The pavements, steps, and supporting walls were built of that primitive type of bricks which constitutes one of the most characteristic features of the pre-Sargonic age. These bricks, however, exhibiting, as they do, two distinct moulds, represent two different periods. This becomes evident from the fact that they occur separately in the two constructions of the right passageway (5 and 6) which lie above each other, and most assuredly were built with a considerable interval of time between them. The older bricks are more rudely fashioned than the later ones, and only occasionally show a thumb impression. At the same time they are somewhat less in length and width and more emphatically convex than the more modern bricks. The average dimensions or the earlier bricks are 8l£ by j by 2-j inches, those of the later ones 11 by 7 *y,* by 2 inches.

The foundation of this once doubtless imposing structure was laid five to six feet below the foot of the central division. It consisted of stamped earth mixed with potsherds and fragments of bricks. In order to prevent the waters of the moat, which ran parallel to the northeast wall of the city, from gradually washing the earth away, the outer edge of this road-bed (4) was cased with large rude blocks of gypsum laid in bitumen to a height of more than two feet. The main road leading over this foundation from the bridge of the moat to the temple enclosure sloped gradually but perceptibly upward while passing through the gate. It was paved with the later kind of pre-Sargonic bricks, likewise laid in bitumen. They were arranged in a peculiar manner, somewhat similar to those which formed the walls of the arched tunnel in the lower strata of the *ziggurrat* (comp. p. 400).

The two sidewalks were provided with low balustrades, about one foot high. They were elevated above the central path and reached by a flight of eight steps, the topmost of which lay six feet higher than the road reserved for animals. This difference in altitude naturally grew less as the three passageways approached the end of the gate, where possibly they entered the sacred precincts at the same level. It is interesting to observe that the preserved right staircase already exhibits the same stepped recesses which are characteristic of later Babylonian gates. In consequence of this peculiarity the horizontal passageway starting at the head of the stair is about half a foot narrower than the lowest step. Another remarkable feature of this pre-Sargonic ascent is to be seen in the tapering of the steps with regard to their depth, every higher step being smaller in width of tread than the next one below. Apart from the peculiar casing of the foundation of the road, which otherwise cannot be explained satisfactorilv, the former existence of a moat follows with certainty from another fact. We discovered a number of drains in our excavations along the wall, which emerged from the rubbish around the temple, passed beneath the city wall, and continued their sloping course a little outside the latter until they suddenly terminated abruptly in the open plain. It is very evident that they must have discharged their contents into an open watercourse or ditch, which probably branched off from the Chebar near the beginning of the northwest wall, followed the entire course of *NimitMarJui,* and ran back into the great canal somewhere to the south of the sanctuary.

Apart from certain necessary repairs made by later hands along the top of the dwarf walls on either side of the right passageway and at the edge of the lower steps, the entire body of this elevated sidewalk was built exclusively of the smaller kind of pre-Sargonic bricks. Its inner face adjoining the central road had a very distinct batter or slope (easily to be recognized in the illustration opposite page 494), while its outer face was perfectly vertical. It would seem reasonable to assume that the cause of this difference in construction is due to the fact that the inner face was exposed to view, while the outer face was built against the mud bricks of the city wall. As the present length of the sidewalk, which on the whole is identical with what it originally was, is a little over 35 feet, the great bastion of the city wall through which the road passed must have had approximately the same thickness.

The three divisions of the earliest gate ran in a straight line from the moat to the enclosure. But at a subsequent, though still pre-Sargonic period, a remarkable change took place, doubtless in connection with a rebuilding of the walls, and a slight altering of their course. As we shall see later, this assertion can be proved positively with regard to NaramSin's line of fortifications, which ran nearly perpendicular to the axis of the upper flight of stairs. This second staircase lies directly over a section of the earlier sidewalk, which it crossed at a slight angle. It started at a distance of nearly fourteen feet from the upper edge of the lower stair, leading in eight or nine steps to another corridor. As previously remarked, this later structure was composed solely of the larger kind of pre-Sargonic bricks. The time which elapsed between the erection ot the two staircases is unknown. However, the period cannot have been very short; it probably embraced several hundred years, for the second elevated path lies three and a half feet above the former. Doubtless it was built because the debris accumulated at the base of the wall and in the open court behind it had grown to such a height as to necessitate a change in the level of the road. At the time of Naram-Sin the roadbed again must have been raised considerably; for the lowest traces of his ruined wall are four and a half feet above the upper pre-Sargonic sidewalk, while those of Ur-Gur's rampart, which followed a slightly different course from that of Naram-Sin, lie even six feet higher. From this circumstance alone it follows that Ur-Gurand Naram-Sin cannot have lived in close proximity to one another, as was asserted by Lehmann and others, who endeavored to reduce the 3200 years quoted by Nabonidos to 2 200 years..

i I took the following measurements of the width of tread of the different steps constituting the lower stair. The lowest step measured 39 cm., the second 33 cm., the third and fourth 29 cm., the fifth 25 cm., the sixth 23 cm.; the seventh, again being deeper, measured 37. 5 cm. A similar observation was made with regard to the upper stair. The lowest step measured 37 cm., the second 35 cm., the third 33 cm., the fourth 29 cm. , the fifth and sixth 23 cm., the seventh 22 cm.

A thorough examination of the long ridge to the northwest of the pre-Sargonic gate (No. 6, p. 498) enabled us to form a tolerably clear idea of the original size and character of *Nimit-Marduk*. As only the lower parts of the wall are preserved, the details which we ascertained apply exclusively to the structures of Naram-Sin (No. 3) and Ur-Gur (No. i). Neither earlier nor later remains could be determined with certainty. The general trend of the ridge is from northwest The base of an excellently preserved perpendicular water-conduit draining the wall of Naram-Sin.

l to southeast, and fairly represents the direction of Ur-Gur's rampart. Apart from their fragmentary height, the excavated portions are in almost perfect condition. Though uninscribed, the crude bricks of which they are composed in size, color, and texture are identical with those in the centre of the *ziggurrat*, and therefore may safely be ascribed to the great royal builder from Ur (about 2700 B. c.). The exposed northwest section is a little over 750 feet long and 25 feet thick. Its exterior is effectively broken up by eighteen ' buttresses, which average in width eleven feet,' and project two feet from the face of the wall. The spaces or panels between them, as a rule, measure almost thirty feet. The inside surface of the structure is not nearly so well preserved as the exterior, but there is evidence that buttresses were also used to some extent, similar to those on the outside. Both faces of the wall were covered with a thin plaster of clay which protected the sloping sides against storm and rain. The highest part of Ur-Gur's ruined structure measured nine feet, and was covered with a mass of disintegrated adobes. Its base rested on a foundation of clay laid up *en masse* (No. 12), which extended seven feet beyond the outer face of the wall and was nearly six feet high, with practically the same slope as the latter.

Northwestern Section of the Northeastern City Wall /v *Fiskrr* We found only seventeen, but the eighteenth can be restored with certainty. It stood in the deep cut (marked No. 2 in the zinctype), through which the latest inhabitants passed out *of* the ruined enclosure into the open plain.

The second from the pre-Sargonic gate is an exceptionally wide buttress, which measures 132-3 feet in width. The slope or batter of the wall was in the proportion of I to 3.

The remains of Naram-Sin's wall (about 3750 B. C.) are very insignificant compared with those of Ur-Gur's. The reason is very apparent. A glance upon Fisher's accompanying sketch shows that Naram-Sin's wall (No. 3) met Ur-Gur's in an angle of 10 30'. The last-mentioned king therefore, in modifying the plan of the earlier ruler, was forced to raze the old wall in order to prevent the enemy from using it as a base of operation against his new rampart. Consequently Naram-Sin's structure is preserved only where it lies beneath the wall of Ur-Gur, who, as far as possible, utilized it as a foundation for his own bulwark. From the fact that the axis of the upper sidewalk of the pre-Sargonic gate (No. 6), previously described, is perpendicular to the line of Naram-Sin's fortification restored, we infer that Sargon's famous son built his wall according to the plan of one of his predecessors. The course of this wall, however, differed essentially from that of the earliest rampart and from that of the time of Ur-Gur, both of which practically followed the same general trend. All attempts on the part of the architects to fix the inner face of Naram-Sin's enclosing wall have been unsuccessful, so that, Haynes' previous assertions to the contrary, we still are in absolute ignorance of its original thickness. From the excavations carried on ar the extreme southeast end of the ridge, it seems to follow that some parts, possibly representing bastions, must have been at least 40 feet thick.

It descended, therefore, to the level of the present plain, which lies somewhat above that of Ur-Gur's time. This indicates that the ground on which the foundation was laid had previously been raised. It is very probable that an earlier wall, afterwards partly covered by Ur-Gur's foundation, once occupied the same site. Which must have been perpendicular to the axis of the lower sidewalk of the pre-Sargonic gate. Reproduced in Hilprecht, "The Bab. Exp. of the U. of Pa.," series A, vol. i, part 2, pp. 20, seq.

The fragment of wall laid bare (No. 3) is nearly 300 feet long. Its building material was enormous crude bricks made of well-worked clay mixed with chopped straw. These adobes are exceedingly tough in texture, regular in form, and measure 19 inches square by 3 inches. Many of them are stamped with Naram-Sin's well-known legend upon their lower faces. Our excavations did not reveal any traces of buttresses and panels on the outer face of the wall. The sole attempt at relieving the monotony of the structure seems to have consisted in the use of heavy return angles (Nos. 4 and 5 in the above sketch), similar to those which characterize the long pre-Sargonic wall disclosed by the fourth expedition on the west side of the Shatt en-Nil. In one of these angles (No. 5) is a fine water-conduit of baked bricks laid in bitumen and still rising to a height of 53 feet. It is in such an excellent state of preservation that we scarcely can realize that it was constructed nearly six thousand years ago. The lower part of this drain is a solid base, a little over 6 feet wide, 8 feet deep, and 2 feet high, covered on its top with a heavy layer of bitumen. The only evidence of a former batter of the wall is found in the two sides of the conduit (which is 4 feet 8 inches deep), each course of brick receding slightly from that below

it. In 1895 Haynes unearthed a large number of terra-cotta cones and water spouts at the base of the small section of wall examined by him. None, however, were discovered five years later when we subjected the whole ridge to a most careful examination. The reason for this seemingly strange circumstance can only be that Haynes accidentally had struck an architecturally prominent part of the wall (No. 7), a bastion well drained and ornamented with parapets, which flanked the great northeast gate of the city.

1 Comp. p. 388. Most measurements given and certain architectural details stated in my sketch above were obtained from Fisher's report on the outer wall. Comp. pp. 424, seq., above. 7. Two theories had been advanced with regard to the extensive building remains discovered in the upper strata of Bint el-Amir. Peters regarded them as the ruins of the temple of Bel according to its latest reconstruction by a Persian king living about 500 B. C, and dedicating the sacred enclosure to a new religion (p. 329, seq.). The present writer from the very beginning interpreted the vast structure as an entirely new creation of an even later period, which stood in no historical relation to the Babylonian sanctuary beneath it. He believed that it was a fortified Parthian palace built around the ziggurrat as a citadel on the site of the ancient temple (pp. 327, 364, 373, seq.). The former was convinced that the huge enclosing walls and the two round towers protecting them originated with Ur-Gur (about 2700 B. c.). The writer declared them to form an inseparable part of the Parthian construction built 2500 years later than the time assigned to them by Peters.

In sketching the work of the four Philadelphia expeditions at Nuffar, I repeatedly took occasion to indicate that it is impossible to reconcile Peters' view with all the facts brought to light by our various excavations. The crude bricks characterizing the latest edifice are different from those which we meet in the Babylonian and Persian strata. And with but few exceptions, the antiquities gathered in its rooms point unmistakably to

the Hellenistic and Roman periods as the real time of their construction and occupancy. I refer briefly to the numerous coins of the Arsacide kings (about 250 B. c. to 226 A. D.) found in the debris filling those chambers, in the bricks of their walls, and in the mortar which united them (p. 327). Or I mention the peculiar class of terra-cotta figurines and the fine enamelled lamp with the head of Medusa, described above (pp. 330, seq.), the graceful small flasks, vases, and other vessels in glass, the exceedingly thin and fragile bowls in terra-cotta (p. 288), the fragments of cornices in limestone with their Greek and Roman designs (comp. p. 366), the Rhodian jar handle with the Greek inscription (p. 366), and many other equally instructive antiquities which cannot be considered in this connection. The evidence already submitted is conclusive, and shows that the building under consideration belongs to that period which we generally call Parthian, — a period characterized by the welding together of classical and Oriental elements and the subsequent rising of a short-lived new civilization and art. This period lasted about four to five hundred years, and represents the last flaring and flashing of a great light, once illuminating the whole world, before its final extinction.

Comp. Peters' " Nippur," vol. ii, pp. 148, stqq., esp. pp. 157, seq. Stray antiquities belonging to different periods of Babylonian history which occur occasionally in the upper strata of all the mounds of Nuffar. Comp. pp. 340, note I, 366, seq., 372.

Two new important proofs were adduced in connection with the work of our latest expedition to substantiate and to supplement those general conclusions at which I practically had arrived in the course of our first campaign. The complete removal of the large fortification tower opposite the entrance of the ziggurrat (p. 444) revealed the interesting fact that it stood directly over the ruined gate of the Babylonian temple (p. 483). More than this, a stray cuneiform tablet of the firm of Murashu Sons, dated in the reign of Darius II (423-405

B. C), was discovered in its foundation. It had evidently been placed there as a talisman" by those who erected the first fortified palace on the site of the ancient temple. Consequently the banking-house of Murashu Sons, situated on the western side of the Chebar, must have been in ruins for some time previous to the building of that palace. Hence it follows that the latter cannot be older than the second half of the fourth century, when cuneiform writing no longer was understood by the mass of the people, and under the influence of a foreign power that new civilization, to which I referred above, began to be grafted upon the native Babylonian. This leads us to the period of the Seleucidan rulers as the earliest possible time when the first fortress was constructed on the temple mound of Nuffar. To this period must be ascribed all the remains marked I on the plan of the " Parthian Palace built over the Ruins of the Temple of Bel," which appears below. They are comparatively insignificant, consisting only of a few rooms and two round towers, one of which was incorporated with the second fortress. But, as the two architects observed correctly, they can easily be distinguished from the other buildings by the size and quality of their bricks, the greater depth of their level, and the direction of their walls, the later walls crossing the earlier ones at an angle of 8 10'. "A line drawn through the centres of the two earlier towers is parallel to the walls of the various groups of rooms of that period; and similarly a line through the centres of the two larger towers forming part of the inner wall is parallel to the rooms of the second palace," and —we may add — also to the principal facades of the ancient *ziggurrat.* No satisfactory reason has as yet been found to explain why the builders of the earlier fortress deviated from the direction fixed thousands of years before by the architects of the Babylonian temple. The difference of bricks used in the two fortresses can very distinctly be seen in the illustration facing p. 444. The other principal results obtained in the course of our fourth campaign with regard to the large complex covering the

temple mound are incorporated in a subsequent chapter, " On the Topography of Ancient Nippur." In this place it may suffice to state a second important reason for assigning its construction to the Parthian rulers of the country. Comp. Peters' "Nippur," vol. ii, p. 118, with the passages quoted on the preceding page. Comp. pp. 154, *seq.,* 168, 233, *scq.,* 367. In the chapter " On the Topography of Ancient Nippur." The earlier bricks measure 12 *4* by 12 '/. by 6 inches, and contain less potsherds than the later bricks, which are almost cubical, measuring *124 by* 11 V£ by 9 inches. The remains of the older fortress lie six to eight feet below the rooms of the later palace. Quoted from Gccre's report.

Toward the end of November, 1899, an unusually interesting tomb was disclosed in the ruins to the south of Bint el-Amir (comp. p. 444). It was situated beneath the mud floor of one of the rooms built into the top of the outer enclosing wall of the fortress, and consisted of burned bricks generally placed on their edges. This funeral chamber was reached by a flight of steps of irregular height and tread, constructed of the same material. Both the tomb proper and the stairway leading to it were arched over. When discovered, the entrance way was closed with bricks loosely laid on the steps and some pieces of a large slab, which seem to have belonged together originally and formed the cover stone for the whole stairway. The walls and the poorly constructed ceiling were laid in clay mortar coated with bitumen and plastered with a stucco of mud. The floor of the tomb was paved with two layers of baked bricks, so that dampness was effectively excluded from the room.
Marked No. 3 on the plan of the *"* Parthian Palace, built over the Ruins of the Temple of Bel," p. 559, below. - Comp. the illustration, p. 512, below, which represents two similar arched tombs of the same period excavated in the southeastern slope of the library mound. As the writer was not present when the tomb was opened, he gathered the facts from the reports of Haynes and

Geere. The latter remarks: «« It is to be supposed that in raising this slab on some later occasion — probably when the second burial took place — it was broken, whereupon the tomb w as closed with its fragments and bricks in the manner indicated."
This vaulted funeral chamber was ten feet long, eight feet wide, and a little over five feet high, while the room above it measured almost twelve feet square. "Entering the cell a gruesome sight was before us. Side by side upon the floor lay two adult skeletons of more than average size." Both were considerably injured by pieces of plaster which had fallen from the roof. The one farthest from the door (II, p. 506), had suffered most. The skull was completely broken, and many of the larger bones had been pressed out of their original position and lay buried in dust and debris. The better preserved (I) had been placed in a wooden coffin, which, with the exception of a few half-decomposed fragments, had long since " crumbled away and mingled its reddish brown ashes with the gray ashes of the grave-clothes and the decayed tissues of the body." By means of these relics and a number of iron and bronze nails, which evidently had held the boards together, it was comparatively easy to trace the outlines of the entire coffin. Two iron bands (i), slightly projecting beyond the long sides of the coffin, at either end of it, had been fastened as a support to the bottom of the box. To the ends of these bars silver rings (2), now badly corroded, had been attached as handles for the purpose of lifting and carrying the coffin.

Fortunately this tomb had not been rifled in ancient times, like so many others of the same general period in various parts of the ruins. We therefore found all the less perishable objects deposited with the two bodies, as far as they had not been damaged and displaced by the falling stucco, exactly where they originally had been laid. Evidently the men buried there had been persons of high rank in the service of the Parthian princes who ruled the country.. Near each skull lay a square sheet of beaten gold (3) "almost large enough to cover the exposed portion of the face," and a scalloped band of the same metal (3), which once encircled the brow. Two barrel-shaped gold beads (4), possibly used in connection with cords ending in tassels to hold the garment in place, were found near the Indicated by dotted lines in the accompanying zinctype. - Geere writes, "Judging by the clothes, bones and skulls, I should say that there can be no doubt that the bodies were those ot" males."

Plan of Tomb of Two High Officers from the Parthian Palace. First Century A. a. waist of each body. Around the ankles (5) of the betterpreserved skeleton, and at intervals along the legs, lay fortyeight small gold buttons provided with ears, and twelve larger rosettes, which apparently had served as ornaments of the outer garment. Two heavy gold buckles with thick wedge-shaped gold latchets, taken from the floor at the feet, were the gems of the collection. They doubtless represented some sort of sandal fastenings. Each buckle was adorned with a well-executed head of a lion in high relief, richly enamelled with turquoise and set with rubies. A small gold ring, the use of which is unknown, and a beautiful gold coin (lying near the head) completed this remarkable collection.

Each band is about twelve to thirteen inches long, and over an inch

"The body lay at full length in a natural position on its back," with the head turned toward the southeast. From remaining traces of clothing, Geere was inclined to infer " that the man had worn a cotton shirt and what looked like a leather over-shirt, reaching as far as the knees." In accordance with the general custom, food and drink were deposited with the two corpses. The former was originally contained in four terra-cotta dishes (7) placed on a small brick shelf (6) and on the floor in the north corner of the chamber.-The latter was provided for in two large jars (8). They stood near the eastern corner, and were partly damaged by the fallen plaster.

Every object contained in this unique Parthian tomb, which may serve as a representative example of many similar graves, is most instructive. But our chief interest centres in the gold coin, which enables us to date this burial with greater accuracy than usual. It shows the head of a Roman emperor, surrounded bv the Latin inscription TI(BERIUS) CESAR DIVI AUG(USTI) F(ILIUS) AUGUSTUS, by which it is proved conclusively that the two high officers buried there cannot have died before Emperor Tiberius (14-37 A. D.); that consequently the palace must have been inhabited at least as late as the first century of our own era. Other antiquities discovered in the debris of the palace make it very probable that the fortress was kept in repair even in the century following.

Resembling a heavy earring more than anything else. Similar rings, generally occurring in pairs, were found repeatedly in Parthian.coffins containing bodies of women. When discovered, nothing but "some light grayish powder" indicated the former contents of the dishes.

After this brief review of the principal results obtained by the fourth'expedition in connection with its work on the temple mound, we occupy ourselves for a few minutes with the large triangular hill to the south of the latter. As previously stated (p. 445), the exploration of this much neglected part of the ruins, strongly urged by the present writer, led to a unique result, which not without reason has been pronounced one of the most far-reaching Assyriological discoveries of the whole last century — the locating and partial excavating of the famous temple library and priest school of Nippur.'

The excavation of this vast site (IV on the plan of the ruins, p. 305) began at its northwest extremity, where the depression separating it from the temple complex proper is covered by a series of low elevations. It was about the middle of October, 1899, when Haynes dug a trench at this place to water level. As it yielded nothing but late graves and a few stray cuneiform tablets, the workmen were soon afterwards withdrawn, to be replaced bv a larger force a month

later. Trenches were now opened at different places along the three sides of the mound. Bv the middle of December fragmentary tablets were discovered in large quantities, and at the beginning of January, 1900, complete specimens came forth abundantly. For about two months and a half more the search was continued, until on March 19, for reasons given above (pp. 445, seq.), I suspended the excavations in this part of the ruins entirely, in order to devote all mv time and attention to the many purely scientific problems of the expedition, for which the assistance of the architects was constantly required.

Comp. my first communication to Professor Kittel of Leipzig, published in *Literarisches Centralblatt*, 1900, nos. 19, zo; and " The Sunday School Times," Philadelphia, May 5, 1900, pp. 275, *teq.*

Haynes unfortunately seems to have taken no particular interest in the extensive building remains prior to my arrival, or in the precious documents buried within them, beyond saving and counting them as they were gathered day after day. He did not ask Fisher and Geere, who then stood under his direct control as field director, to superintend the excavations in the temple library, nor did he order the different walls and rooms exposed by him to be measured and surveyed. Consequently our knowledge as to how and precisely where the tablets were found is extremely limited. As I must depend almost exclusively on Haynes' official entries and records for this important question, I deem it necessary to submit a specimen of my only written source of information for the time prior to my arrival when most of the tablets were taken out of the ground. I quote literally from his diary.

"*Jan. 16, 1900:* 30 sound tablets of promise from a low level in' Tablet Hill.'-Many large fine fragments of tablets, i pentagonal prism, y3 inches long; its five sides from i to 2 inches wide. An hour after dark last evening one of our workmen's huts burned down so quickly that nothing was saved and the occupants barely escaped with their lives. By vigorous efforts the neighboring houses were saved.

"*Jan. 77, 1900:* 28 sound tablets from low level from Tablet Hill.' Very many large and fine fragments of tablets, *2* prisms and half a prism also from a low level. The tablets are covered with 18, 20, and 24 feet of debris, so that it requires a good deal of time to secure them, quite unlike Tel-Loh, where the accumulations are slight.

Except one day in February, when Fisher was requested to show a visitor how tablets were excavated. To this fortunate circumstance I owe my knowledge as to tablets lying on the shelves of the library. I cannot even find out in which section of the large mound he unearthed these particular tablets. Nor is the slightest indication given by him as to whether he worked in a room, or found the tablets in the loose earth, or in both. "*Jan. 18, /poo:* 23 sound tablets from a low level on 'Tablet Hill.' A multitude of imperfect tablets on 'Tablet Hill.' Three most beautiful days! And the nights with full moon are days in shadow, the air soft and balmy. "*Jan. /g, igoo:* 49 sound tablets all from low level 'Tablet Hill.' Many fine fragments of tablets."

After an inspection of all the unearthed buildings and an examination of a sufficient number of representative tablets and fragments, I could declare positively at the beginning of March that we had discovered the temple library of ancient Nippur, and the most important of all the earlier Babylonian schools, where about the time of Abraham the younger generations were instructed in the art of tablet writing and in the wisdom of the god Nabu. Upon the basis of Haynes' scanty notes; Geere's drawings and reports on the buildings; my own investigations and brief excavations, and an examination of the more intelligent Arab foremen who previously supervised the laborers in the trenches, I present the following general picture.

The mound containing the remains of the educational quarter of the city rises to an average height of twenty to twenty-six feet above the level of the present plain, and covers an area of about thirteen acres. In other words, it occupies about the sixth part of the entire site included in the vast temple complex of Bel on the northeast side of the Chebar. Only about the twelfth part of this library-mound has thus far been satisfactorily examined with regard to the ruins lying above the plain level. The upper layer is easily distinguished from those below by the extensive remains of Parthian buildings constructed of the same kind of large unbaked brick which characterizes the two excavated palaces on the temple ruins and on the west bank of the Shaft en-Nil. No important traces of Jewish and early Arabic settlements were disclosed in this particular mound. Parthian and Sassanian graves abound in the slopes of the entire hill. They were not unfrequently found even in the central part of the ruins, where. they are sometimes accompanied by terra-cotta drains and wells' descending far into the lower strata.

Altogether about four hundred tombs, coffins and burial urns of different sizes and shapes were opened in the course of the sixteen weeks during which excavations were carried on in "Tablet Hill. " The two vaulted brick tombs seen in the illustration facing this page evidently represented family vaults, for the one contained six, the other two skeletons. Unfortunately both were rifled in ancient times, since they could easily be reached by robbers, situated, as they were, directly on a public street, whence a narrow inclined paved way led to the door of each tomb.

More than four thousand cuneiform tablets had been discovered in the upper twenty feet of accumulated debris at Mound IV during our excavations of 1889 and iSpo. They included several hundred contract tablets and temple lists written at the time of the Assyrian, Chaldean, and Persian rulers (about 700-400 B. c.), a few fragments of neoBabylonian hymns, letters and syllabaries, a considerable number of business documents, dated in the reigns of the kings of the first dynasty of Babylon (about 2300-2100 B. c.),and more than twenty-five hundred literary fragments of the third pre-Christian millennium

generally half effaced or otherwise damaged. I consequently had reached the conclusion that either there were two distinct libraries buried in "Tablet Hill," — an earlier more important, and a later comparatively insignificant one lying on the top of the former,— or the mound concealed the remains of but one library continuously occupied and repeatedly restored, which contained documents of many periods in the same rooms. For apart from other considerations, the lists of Cassite names and words known from the Qoyunjuk collection, which Ashurbanapal's scribes doubtless had copied at Nippur, proved sufficiently that occasional additions were made to the tablets of the earlier library in the long interval of fifteen or sixteen hundred years which elapsed between the reign of Hammurabi and that of the last great Assyrian monarch. The fact that by far more ancient documents were unearthed than tablets written in the neo-Babylonian script was in entire accord with what we know of the two great periods to be distinguished in the history of Nippur.

Comp. nos. 4 and 5 on the plan of the " Northeast Portion of the Temple Library at Nippur," on p. 523, and the illustration facing p. 362, above. Comp. pp. 309, *itqq.,* and 341, *itf.*

In the earlier days, when the sanctuary of Bel formed the great religious centre of the country, the library and school of the city naturally flourished and received greater attention than in the centuries following the government of Hammurabi, when Marduk of Babylon and his cult were extolled at the expense of the venerable temple of " the father of the gods" on the banks of the Chebar. While Bel of Nippur decreased, " the Bel of Babylon " increased in power and influence upon the religious life of the united country. Even the brief renaissance of the older cult under the Cassite sway did not change very essentially those new conditions which had been the natural result of great historical events in the valleys of the Euphrates and the Tigris. It was but an artificial and short-lived revival of a fast disappearing worship, ceasing again when the national uprising under the native house of Pashe in the twelfth century led to the overthrow of that foreign dynasty which had been its strongest advocate and principal supporter.

When, in 1899, the excavations were resumed in "Tablet Hill," two large sections were excavated in the eastern and western parts of the mound respectively. Both yielded large quantities of exclusively ancient tablets at practically the same low level, and only single tablets or small nests of old-Babylonian and neo-Babylonian documents mixed in the upper strata. From this general result it became evident that the library doubtless continued to exist in some form or another at the old site through the last two thousand years of Babylonian history, but it also followed that the large mass of tablets was already covered under rubbish at the close of the third millennium. The period in which the older library fell into disuse could be fixed even more accurately. A small jar of baked case tablets dated in the reigns of members of the first dynasty of Babylon was unearthed at a higher level than the body of those ancient "clay books." This seemed to indicate that the tabletfilled rooms and corridors beneath it were in ruins before Hammurabi ascended the throne of Babylon, and, more than this, that there must have been a sudden break in the continuity of the history of the temple library of Nippur. How can this apparently natural inference be substantiated by other facts? Comp. p. 459, note 3, above.

It is impossible to assume that the burying of those thousands of tablets was the result of an ordinary though specially disastrous conflagration. The peculiar condition in which the larger part of the contents of the library was found speaks decidedly against it. The tablets occurred in a stratum from one foot to four feet thick at an average depth of twenty to twenty-four feet below the surface. They frequently were badly mutilated and chipped *off,* and lay in all possible positions on the floor of the ruined chambers, upon low fragmentary clay ledges extending along the walls, and in the rubbish that filled the corridors and open courts of the vast building. In some of the rooms which produced especially large numbers of tablets, they were found in clusters, " interlacing, overlapping, lying flatwise, edgewise, endwise, two, three, four deep,"' so that it was very apparent that they had been stored upon wooden shelves, whence they were precipitated when the roof collapsed and the walls cracked and fell.

This is the only statement in Haynes diary which attempts to throwany light upon the position in which the tablets were found "in one of the rooms '' (Feb. 16, 1900).

If the destruction of the library had been due to an unfortunate accident, by far more tablets would have been discovered on the clay ledges, where they occurred only sporadically, and the corridors and courts would have been comparatively free from them. Moreover, the priests doubtless would have searched the rooms and extracted the most valuable and complete texts from the debris as soon as the heat would allow, preparatory to rebuilding the entire complex. The mere fact that the library unmistakably was allowed to lie in ruins for a considerable length of time points to a great national calamity from which the entire city and the country as a whole likewise suffered for years. We are thus led to a conclusion similar to that at which we arrived when we examined the results of our excavations at the temple mound. The breaking and scattering of so many thousands of priceless documents of the past was an act of gross vandalism on the part of the Elamitic warriors, who invaded and devastated the Babylonian plain about the middle of the third millennium and played such terrible havoc with the archives and works of art in the court of the *ziggurrat.*

It is not generally known that at the time just mentioned legal documents and important income and expense lists of the temple, in whatever ruins they have been found, were commonly burnt into terra-cotta, while the contemporaneous scientific productions, as a rule, were inscribed upon unbaked clay. The reason for this scarcely accidental peculiarity is easily understood by considering that in case of litigation, everything depended upon the careful preservation of the original and unaltered legal document. It was different with the other class of tablets. Compared with the price of fuel necessary to bake the "manuscript," the time and labor required for re-writing a damaged tablet was an insignificant matter to every scribe, since clay was to be had abundantly throughout the country. As nearly the whole of the excavated material from the ancient library is literary and scientific in its character, the tablets, with but few exceptions, are unbaked. Thev consequently have suffered not only from the hands of the Elamites, but also from the humidity of the soil to which they were exposed for more than four thousand years; from the varying atmospheric conditions after their ultimate rescue; and from the unavoidable effects of long transportation bv land and sea. The difficulties of the decipherer are thereby increased enormously, and it will require more than ordinary patience to overcome them and to force those halfeffaced crumbling tablets to surrender their long-guarded secrets to our own generation.

Comp. pp. 342, *seq., above.* Comp. pp. 380, *itqq., above.*

There is, however, one circumstance which to a certain degree will reconcile us to the ruthless procedure of those revengeful mountaineers into whose quiet valleys and villages the Babylonian rulers so often had carried death and destruction in the name and "in the strength of the god Bel." Mutilated and damaged as these tablets are, when fully deciphered and interpreted they will afford us a first accurate estimate of the remarkable height of Babylonian civilization, and of the religious conception and scientific accomplishments of a great nation at a period prior to the time when Abraham left his ancestral home in Ur of the Chaldees. They will impart to us knowledge of a fixed early period which the better-preserved copies of the royal library of Nineveh did not convey, and which probably for a long time to come we should have been unable to obtain, had the temple library of Nippur not been destroyed by the Elamite hordes. For those fragile " clay books," as often as injured or broken in the library and schoolrooms of Nippur, would have been re-copied by the scribes in the developed form of the script of a later period, and in the case of Sumerian texts frequently translated into the Semitic dialect of the country, which would have made it difficult and often impossible for us to determine with any degree of certainty whether the contents of those copies were already-known in the third millennium, or to what period of Babylonian history they actually belonged.

The question may be raised, How did those earlier tablets which we found in the rooms and rubbish of the upper strata come to form part of the later library? After the expulsion of the Elamites, when normal conditions began to prevail again in Shumer and Akkad, the priests of Nippur returned to their former quarters and rebuilt their schools and libraries at the place previously occupied. In levelling the ground they necessarily came upon many of the texts of the ruined library. Other earlier tablets, however, must have been added at a much later period as the result of regular excavations, as is shown by the following instance.

Soon after my arrival at NufFar in 1900, an important jar in terra-cotta was unearthed in the upper strata of the southwestern wing of the library. It contained about twenty inscribed objects, mostly clay tablets, which constituted a veritable small Babylonian museum, the earliest of its kind known to us. These antiquities, already more or less fragmentary when deposited in the jar, are equally remarkable for the long period which they cover and the great variety of the contents of their inscriptions. They had apparently been collected by a neo-Babylonian priest or some other person connected with the temple library. For there is evidence at our disposal to show that at the time of Nabonidos (556-539 B.c.), whom we may style the royal archaeologist on the

throne of Shumer and Akkad, wider circles among his subjects began to interest themselves in archaeological work. There were persons who not only followed the king's excavations of half-forgotten sites with great attention in general, but who were eager to profit by them, and even to imitate the example of their ruler. To illustrate by a new example this remarkable spirit of scientific investigation fostered especially in the Babylonian priest-schools, I refer briefly to a fine object in half-baked clay, several years ago acquired by me for the University of Pennsylvania. On the front it bears an old-Babylonian legend in raised characters reading backwards, while a label in neoBabvlonian writing is inscribed on the other side. To mv astonishment, the antiquity proved to be nothing less than an excellent squeeze or impression of an inscription of Sargon of Agade prepared by ascribe whose name is identical with that of several scribes occurring on contract tablets of the British Museum dated in the reign of Nabonidos. The label informs us that the object is a "squeeze " or " mould" (z'tpu) of an inscribed stone, " which Nabuzerlishir, the scribe, saw in the palace of King NaramSin at Agade."

But to return to the interesting jar from the library mound of Nuffar: the owner, or curator, of the little museum of Babylonian originals must have obtained his specimens by purchase or through personal excavations carried on in the ruined buildings of Bel's city. He doubtless lived in the sixth century, about the time of King Nabonidos, and was a man well versed in the ancient literature of his nation and deeply interested in the past history of Nippur. This follows from the fact that his vase was found in the neo-Babylonian stratum of "Tablet Hill," and from the It consists of five lines, reading (I) Shargani-shar-ali (2) the powerful (3) king (4) of the subjects (5) of Bel. This inscription is identical with lines 1, 3, 4, 7, 8 of the same ruler's legend from Nippur, published in Hilprecht, "The Bab. Exp. of the U. of Pa.," series A, vol. i, part 1, no. 2.

Squeeae of an Inscription *of* Sargon I. (3800 . c.) *Taken by a Babylonian scribe of the sixth century B. C.*

Large Fragment or'a Clay Tablet containing the Plan or" Nippur and its Environments circumstance that the latest antiquity of his collection is dated in the government of Sinsharishkun, the last representative of the Assyrian dynasty (about 615 B. C).

Every object contained in this vase is a choice specimen, and evidentlv was appreciated as such by the collector himself, who had spared no pains to secure as many representative pieces as possible. The first antiquity of mv

Babylonian colleague which I examined was the fragment of a large tablet with the plan of houses, canals, roads, gardens, etc. I could well realize the delight he must have felt in acquiring this specimen. For even before having cleaned it, I recognized that it represented a section of the ground plan of the environments of Nippur, — a subjective view soon afterwards confirmed by discovering that the ideogram of " the city of Bel," *En-lil-ki, i. e.,* Nippur, was written in the middle of the fragment. The next piece I picked up was a somewhat damaged brick stamp of Bur-Sin of Ur (about 2600 B. c.), the only one of this ruler thus far excavated at Nuffar. The third was a well preserved black stone tablet (about 2700 B. c.) with the Sumerian inscription: "To Bel, the king of the lands, his king, Ur-Gur, the powerful champion, king of Ur, king of Shumer and Akkad, has built the wall of Nippur." The fourth was a tablet containing most welcome information as to the number of temples and shrines once existing at Nippur, and the names of the gods and goddesses worshipped in them. The fifth bore the name and titles of Sargon of Agade (3800 B. c.), at whose time it had been inscribed. The next two antiquities represent the first contract tablets dated according to the reigns of members of the Pashe Dynasty, the one being a tablet dated "in the fifth year of Marduk-na-di-in-akh-khi, king of the world *(shar kishshatf)"* a contemporary of Tiglathpileser I. (about 1100 B. c.), the other being dated

" in the tenth year of Adad-apal-iddina, the king" (about 1060 B. c.), father-in-law of the Assyrian king Ashurbelkala. The eighth and ninth tablets are of chronological importance for the final period of the Assyrian empire, as both of them mention certain years of " Ashuretililani, king of Assyria," and Sinsharishkun in connection with loans and payments of interest. The tenth contains an interesting astronomical observation concerning Virgo and Scorpion, closing with the words, " thus the calculation " *(ki-a-am ne-fi-shu)*, etc., etc.
Written (without the determinative for man) 'MM-TUR-USH-SE-tfd. It was previously known that this monarch built at Nippur.

This remarkable collection of mostly fragmentary tablets illustrates the high esteem in which those ancient texts, as historical sources, were held by the learned priests, and the methodical manner in which they were gathered and preserved in the latest temple library of Nippur; while at the same time it serves as a good example of the variety of subjects treated in the "clay books" of the Babylonian archives.

According to the results already obtained, there can be no doubt that the whole area occupied by the large triangular mound was included in the temple library and school of the city. The real Babylonian buildings, as far as excavated, may naturally be divided into a northeast and a southwest section. An enormous barrier of unexplored debris, "pierced only by one large tunnel and a few branch tunnels," ' lies at present between the two quarters. The ground plan of the entire complex can therefore not yet be determined. Both wings consist of a number of chambers, corridors, fragmentary walls, streets, etc., found at the same low level as stated above (p. 512). Both were constructed of crude bricks of the same size, and otherwise present the same general characteristics. For reasons previously set forth (p. 513), they must be ascribed to the third pre-Christian millennium. Apart from other considerations, we know from the remains of burnt brick structures lying immediately above the earlier rooms,

and at least in part following their lines, that the library was rebuilt after its destruction by the Elamites, and probably continuously occupied during all the subsequent periods of Babylonian history.

Mv present sketch of architectural details deals exclusively with the lowest building remains. As it is extremely difficult to distinguish wet crude bricks laid in mud mortar from the earth and rubbish around them, the Arab workmen could not always avoid injuring them or cutting them away entirely. Consequently it often was impossible to ascertain the original thickness and direction of the walls with any degree of certainty. In accordance with what is generally known as a characteristic feature of Babylonian architecture, we observed that "the walls of chambers are frequently not made at right angles to one another." In some cases, especially in the southwest section, extremely narrow openings are to be seen. Being too narrow, and otherwise unsuitable for passageways, and sometimes terminating abruptly, they may have been used as recesses for storing tablets and other objects.
Words and sentences placed in quotation marks on this and the following pages are extracts from Geere's report on the architectural features of the temple library.
The excavated part of the southwest wing of the large complex comprises forty-four rooms and galleries, more or less connected with each other; the northeast section about forty. The various chambers differ greatly as to their dimensions, varying, as they do, from 33 by 9 feet to 14 by 25 feet. The average thickness of the walls being only 2 to 3 feet, it is safe to assume that the houses had but one story. We nowhere discovered traces to indicate how the rooms were originally lighted, nor how they were roofed. "The roofing probably was by means of wooden beams which supported flat roofs of matting and mud, similar to those constructed in the country at the present day." If ever there were windows in the rooms, they must have been very small and high up

near the ceiling. The explored sections are not large enough to show whether the halls and chambers were grouped around open courts and constituted one enormous building, or, as seems more probable, belonged to separate houses which formed one organic whole, but were divided into single quarters by narrow streets and covered passageways. In not a single case was any trace *of* pavement observed. We must therefore presume that the rooms consisted only of earth, well trodden, covered with reed or palm mats over which rugs were doubtless often spread. In a like manner the walls were kept entirely bare, no attempt being made at relieving their dull faces with any kind of decoration. "We saw no sign of paint and no remains of plastering, not even of mud plaster."

These early Babylonians, who excelled all other ancient nations of the same period in their lofty religious conceptions, in the depth of their sentiment and in the scientific character of their investigations, did not suffer anything in their schoolrooms that would tend to distract the minds of the pupils and to interfere with their proper occupation. The temple library of ancient Nippur was eminently a place of study and a seat of learning, where the attention of all those who assembled for work was concentrated upon but one subject, — the infusing or acquiring of knowledge. In accordance with an ancient Oriental custom even now universally prevailing in the East — in the great Mohammedan university of Cairo as well as in the small village schools of Asia Minor — we should imagine the Babylonian students of the time of Abraham being seated on the floor with crossed legs, respectfully listening to the discourses of the priests, asking questions, practising writing and calculating on clay tablets, or committing to memory the contents of representative cuneiform texts by repeating them in a moderately loud voice.

The "books" required for instruction, reference and general reading as a rule were unbaked clay tablets stored on shelves, or sometimes deposited in jars. The shelves were made either of wood,

— as ordinarily was the case also in the business houses on the western side of the Chebar, — or of clay, for which rooms Nos. 1-3 on the accompanying plan of the "Northeast Portion of the Temple Library" offer appropriate examples. These clay ledges were built up in crude bricks to a height of nearly twenty inches from the apparent floor level, and on an average were about one and a half feet wide. Two of the rooms (Nos. i and 3), yielded tablets and fragments by the thousands, and are among the largest thus far excavated in " Tablet Hill." To preserve the fragile "books" from dampness, the clay shelves were probably covered with matting or with a coating of bitumen. According to the report of the architects, traces of the last-mentioned material seem to have been disclosed on the ledge of the large hall (No. I).

To judge from the contents of more than twenty-four thousand tablets hurriedly examined, it is almost certain that the vast complex of houses buried under the triangular mound was used by the Babylonians for at least two distinct purposes. Though literary tablets in small numbers occurred almost everywhere in the hill, the large mass of them was found within a comparatively small radius in and around the central rooms of the northeast portion. On the other hand, there was not a single business document unearthed in that general neighborhood, while more than one thousand dated contracts, account lists, and letters came from the southwest rooms of the mound. It would therefore seem natural to conclude that in view of the doubtless large traffic carried on by boats on the Chebar, the business and administrative department of the temple was established on the bank of " the great canal," and the educational department — the school and the technical library — in the rooms nearest to the temple. Tablets were doubtless frequently taken out of the one section and placed temporarily in the other, while certain works of reference seem to have been deposited in both.

The character of the northeast wing as a combined library and school was

determined immediately after an examination of the contents of the unearthed tablets and fragments. There is a large number of rudely fashioned specimens inscribed in such a naive and clumsy manner with old-Babylonian characters, that it seems impossible to regard them as anything else but the first awkward attempts at writing by unskilled hands, — so-called school exercises. Those who attended a class evidently had to bring their writing material with them, receiving instruction not only in inscribing and reading cuneiform tablets, but also in shaping them properly, for not a few of the round and rectangular tablets were uninscribed. The contents of these interesting "scraps " of clay from a Babylonian " waste basket" are as unique and manifold as their forms are peculiar. They enable us to study the methods of writing and reading, and the way in which a foreign language (Sumerian) was taught at Nippur in the third pre-Christian millennium.

The very first lesson in writing that the children received is brought vividly before us. I refer to several large tablets comparatively neatly inscribed. They contain the three simple elements of which cuneiform signs are generally composed, in the order here given and repeated again and again over three columns. Or I mention a much smaller table showing nothing but the last given wedge dozens of times inscribed in horizontal lines upon the clay. When the first difficulties had been mastered by the student, he had to put those three elements together and make real cuneiform signs. As we do in our Assyrian and Babylonian classes to-day, the easiest and most simple characters were selected first. The pupil was then told to group them together in different ways, generally without regard to their meaning, simply for the sake of fixing them firmly in mind. There are a good many specimens preserved which illustrate this "second step" in the study of Babylonian writing. We have, *e. g.*, a large fragment with two identical columns, in which every line begins with the sign *ba*: i. *ba-a*, i. *ba-mu*, 3. *ba-ba-mu*, 4. *ba-ni*, 5. *ba-ni-ni*, 6. *ba-ni-a*, j. *ba-ni-*

mu, etc. Another fragment deals with more difficult characters placed alongside each other in a similar manner: I. *za-an-tur*, i. *za-an-tur-tur*, 3. *za-an-ka*, 4. *za-an-ka-ka*, 5. *za-an-ka-a*, 6. *za-an-ka-mu*. A fragment of the easier sort of exercises offers, i. *an-ni-si*, 1. *an-ni-su*, 3. *an-ni-mu,* etc. A fourth one is of additional value, because it contains no less than four mistakes in a comparatively small space. Let me correct the exercises of this young Babylonian who lived prior to Abraham and transliterate what he has to say: i. *shi-ni*, 2. *shini-mu*, 2-*shi-ni-da-a*, 4. *shi-tur*, 5. *shi-tur-tur.* It would be interesting to know how such apparent carelessness or stupidity was dealt with by the professors in the great Bel college and university of Calneh.

But it is impossible for me to go through the whole prescribed " college " course, which possibly even at those early times lasted three years, as it did in the days of Daniel (Dan. 1: 4, 5). After the student had been well drilled in writing and reading the simple and more complicated cuneiform signs, he began to write words and proper names. At the same time lists were placed before him from which to study all the difficult ideographic values which the Sumerians associated with their numerous characters. These syllabaries and lexicographical lists are of the utmost importance for our own scientific investigations, and will greatly help us in extending and deepening our knowledge of the Sumerian language. I remember having seen hundreds of them among the tablets which I cleaned and examined in Nuffar and Constantinople. Even in their outside appearance, as a rule they are easily distinguished from tablets dealing with other subjects. They generally are long but very narrow, rounded on the left edge and also at the upper or lower end, or both at the same time. The right side, on the contrary, is always flat, as if cut off a large tablet, which while wet was divided into several pieces.

There are also grammatical exercises, exhibiting how the student was instructed in analyzing Sumerian verbal forms, in joining the personal pronouns to different substantives, in forming entire sentences, in translating from the Sumerian into the Semitic dialect of Babylonia and *vice versa*. His preparations look pretty much like those of the modern student who excerpts all the words unknown to him from Caesar's "Gallic Wars" or Xenophon's *Anabasis* for his work in the class room.

Owing to their long delay in reaching Philadelphia, those tablets which were presented by His Majesty the Sultan to the writer have not as yet been unpacked. Comp. two similar specimens from Jokha, published in Hilprecht, ' The Bab. Exp. of the U. of Pa.," series A, vol. i, part 1, pi. viii, nos. 18 and 19. Special attention was paid to counting and calculating, as will be illustrated below by a few examples. Even instruction in drawing, and surveying lessons were offered. There are a few tablets which contain exercises in drawing horizontal and inclined parallel lines, zigzag lines, lines arranged in squares, lozenge forms, latticework and other geometrical figures.

The course in art led gradually up to free-hand drawing from nature, and probably included also lessons in clay modelling and in glyptics and sculpture (seal cylinders, bas-reliefs and statues). Several fragments of unbaked tablets exhibited portions of animals and trees more or less skilfully incised in clay. One bird was executed very poorly. A lioness, two harnessed horses and a chariot—the latter two pieces doubtless from the upper strata — showed decided talents on the part of those who drew them. Ground plans of fields, gardens, canals, houses, etc., were found more commonly. As according to my knowledge the horse appears in Babylonia first shortly before the middle of the second millennium, without hesitation we can fix the date of the drawing of those harnessed horses as being about a thousand years later than the school exercises previously treated. That art in general was greatly esteemed and cultivated by the priests of Nippur may be inferred from the considerable number of clay figurines, terra-cotta reliefs and even fragments of sculpture (the head

of a negro, etc.) discovered in the ruins of the temple library. Apart from several new mythological representations of the earlier time which need a fuller discussion in another place, I refer briefly to two fine identical reliefs of the later period made from different moulds and exhibiting a hog, the animal sacred to the god Ninib/ son of Bel; or to an exquisitely modelled buffalo walking slowly and heavily, and holding his mouth and nose upward in a manner characteristic of these animals. There is another well executed basrelief which shows Beltis adorned with a long robe. In her left hand the goddess has the same symbol which we often see with Bel, while with her right hand she leads a richly dressed worshipper to

Beltis leading a Worshipper . ' her shrine. Lastly I mention a much earlier terra-cotta relief depicting a somewhat poetical pastoral scene. A shepherd playing the lute has attracted the attention of his dog, who is evidently accompanying his master's music by his melodious howlings, and another unknown animal (sheep?) is likewise listening attentively. (See opposite page.) The whole scene reminds us of certain favorite subjects of the classical artists.

The general character and wide scope of the temple library of Nippur has been illustrated to a certain degree by the tablets contained in the jar mentioned above (pp. 518, *seqq.)* and by my remarks on the work in the Babylonian classroom. The technical " books" on the shelves gave all the necessary information on the subjects treated in the school.

Comp. Hilprecht, /. *c,* vol. ix, pi. xiii, no. 28. Comp. Zimmern in *K. A. T.,* p. 410. Comp. Hilprecht, /. *c,* vol. ix, pi. xiii, no. 27. Preserved in two or three copies made from different moulds. Comp. Hilprecht, /. *c,* vol. ix, pi. xii, no. 25.

Luranist surrounded by Animals

But they also included more scientific works, tablets for religious edification, and "books " of reference. To the firstmentioned class belong the many mathematical, astronomical, medical, historical and linguistic tablets recov-

ered; to the second the hymns and prayers, omens and incantations, mythological and astrological texts. Among the books of reference I classify the lists of dates giving the names of kings and the principal event for every year, the multiplication tables, the lists of the different measures of length and capacity, the lists of synonyms, geographical lists of mountains and countries, stones, plants, objects made of wood, etc. It must be borne in mind that thus far only about the twelfth part of the entire library complex has been excavated, and, though it would be useless to speculate as to the exact number of tablets once contained in the temple library, it is certain that whole classes of texts, only sporadically represented among our present collections, must still lie buried somewhere in the large triangular mound to the south of the temple. During our latest campaign we struck principally the rooms in which the mathematical, astronomical (see p. 530), astrological, linguistic, grammatical and certain religious texts had been stored. This fact alone proves that the library was arranged according to subjects and classified according to scientific principles.

In consequence of the unscrupulous proceedings of the barbarous Klamites we can say very little as to the manner in which the single tablets were arranged on the shelves. But there is hope that we may find some better-preserved rooms in the course of our next expedition. From the catchlines and colophons frequently occurring at the end of tablets we can infer with safety that there were works which consisted of several " volumes," sometimes even of a whole series of tablets. They doubtless were kept together on the same shelf.

Hundreds of very large crumbling tablets, mostly religious and mythological in character, have not yet been

Astronomical Tablet from the Temple Library deciphered. They need careful repairing before they can be handled with safety. From a mere glance at Bezold's "Catalogue of Cuneiform Tablets in the Kouyunjik Collection of the British Museum "' (five volumes), we learn that Ashurbanapal's scribes copied chiefly religious, astronomical and astrological texts for the royal library in Nineveh from the originals at Nippur. Representative tablets of the classes mentioned must therefore have existed at Bel's temple even in those later days, though the large body of the earlier library had been buried in the ruins beneath their feet for more than fifteen hundred years. With the limited Comp. , *t. g.,* K. 7787, K. 8668, K. 10826; Sm. 1117; 80-7-19, 64; Bu. 88-5-12, 11, etc. space here at my disposal it is impossible to give examples even of those branches of Babylonian literature which are written on tablets already examined.

In order to illustrate by one example the important role which arithmetic played, I call attention to the fact that about 2300 B. c. the temple library owned a complete set of multiplication tables from 1 to at least 1350. The mere circumstance that they existed, sometimes in several copies, speaks volumes for the height of that ancient civilization. They doubtless were used constantly in connection with astronomical calculations, somewhat according to the manner of our logarithmic tables. Among the texts of this class which attracted my attention are the multiplication tables 2x1,3x1,4x1,5x1 (two copies), 6x1,8x1,9x1,12x1 (two copies), 24x1, 25x1, 40xi, 60x1, 90x1, 45ox 1, 75ox 1, Iooox 1, 1350X 1. As a rule thev contain the multiplications of all the consecutive numbers from 1 to 19, followed by those of the tens from 20 to 50. At the end of most of the tablets we find a catch-line. Thus, *e. g.,* the multiplication table 750 x 1 has the catchline "720x1=720," thereby indicating that all the multiplication tablets from 720 to 750 (probably even to 780) were classified in the library as one series, known under the name " Series 720 xi."'

There are three different ways in which these tables are written. The following abbreviated specimens may serve as examples: —

Multiplication Tabic / X 6 = 6
Concerning the character of the busi-

ness and administrative department established in the "library," where contracts were executed, orders given out, income and expense lists kept, etc., I have to add little to what has been previously stated (p. 524). A number of letters were found intact. The envelopes sealed and addressed more than four thousand years ago, immediately before the city was conquered and looted, were still unbroken. While writing these lines one of those ancient epistles of the time of Amraphel (Gen. 14) lies unopened before me. It is 3 inches long, 2/£ inches wide, and i3/£ inches thick. One and the same seal cylinder had been rolled eleven times over the six sides of the clay envelope before it was baked with the document within. It bears the simple address, "To Lushtamar." Though sometimes curious to know the contents of the letter, I do not care to break the fine envelope and to intrude upon Mr. Lushtamar's personal affairs and secrets, as long as the thousands of mutilated literary tablets from the library require all my attention.

At the beginning of our fourth campaign a long peculiar wall had been disclosed below the level of the desert on the west side of the Shatt en-Nil (pp. 440, 447). It ran roughly parallel to the south slope of the ridge marked VI on the plan of the ruins (p. 305). Haynes traced it for 489 feet, but having found no opening in the wall, abandoned it after a few weeks without being able to fix its age and purpose. After my arrival at the ruins in March, 1900, we resumed the excavations at this place, and having followed the wall its entire length, I succeeded in ascertaining its real nature. Geere surveyed the entire structure, and prepared the accompanying diagram, which may help to illustrate the principal features of the explored section.

Adu, literally meaning "time," is the common expression also for "times" in this class of tablets.
Kxcept at one point where a complete gap 22 feet wide occurs (between Nos. 2 and 3), the original direction of the wall could be traced without difficulty for about 590 feet, though sometimes

only by means of a few courses of bricks still lying *in situ.* Towards the east it ran almost as far as the bed of the Chebar. Towards the west it cannot have extended much farther than is indicated on the diagram, because the boundary of the mound, which doubtless stood in a certain relation to the wall, turns northward at the point where the latter practically ceases. The original height of the structure must remain unknown. In its present ruinous state it varies from two courses of bricks to thirty-nine, or from six and a half inches to eleven feet four inches. In a like manner the thickness of the wall is not uniform. This peculiarity, however, is not the result of subsequent causes, but goes back to the original builders of the wall, who planned and executed it in such a manner as to have the central part the strongest, and the sections flanking it on both sides successively decreasing in thickness.

'Words and sentences in quotation marks are extracts from Gcere's report on this wall.
Facing W
Pre-Sargonic
all of *i*
Cemetery
Another characteristic feature of this structure is the remarkable fact "that the various sections of the wall are not built in a straight line or from a uniform level." The lowest course of bricks in some places lies about six feet below the average level of the present plain, in others five and a half, in still others only four and a half. In other words, there is a decided difference of from six to eighteen inches between the levels of the lowest courses of bricks. It is very evident, therefore, that the builder of the wall did not dig or level a special foundation for it, but placed his bricks directly on the undulating surface of the ancient plain.

What was the purpose of this wall? We remember that everywhere in the lowest thirty feet of the ruins, even on the west side of the canal, Haynes had discovered nothing but ashes, bits of charcoal, an occasional decayed bone, lumps of clay worked by the hand, crude and baked planoconvex bricks, etc., mixed with earth and sand, and a complete tomb of the general period of Naram-Sin (comp. pp. 419, *seq.*). Our excavations immediately behind and before the wall led to a similar result. We did not excavate enough to reveal an intact burial vase, but we found sufficient evidence to show that the western half of Nippur, like the eastern section grouped around the *ziggurrat* (pp. 434, *seqq.*), consisted largely of pre-Sargonic burials. Everywhere we came upon traces of cremation, such as ashes and earth mixed, small pieces of charred wood, potsherds, fragmentary walls and pavements of funeral chambers. The portable results accordingly were but few, consisting chiefly of three fragments of pre-Sargonic cuneiform tablets, a clay impression or an early type of seal cylinder, a fragmentary cylinder in soapstone from the interior of a mud brick, a few terra-cotta figurines (toys), the fragment of a large alabaster bead, two copper tubes partly filled with an unknown white substance (handles?), two fragments of a copper arm ring, an entire pre-Sargonic terracotta cup, and a few pieces of stone vessels of the same early period.

The places marked Nos. 2 in the diagram represent pavements of baked bricks. Remains of" cross-walls meeting the long wall at right angles are seen near the two ends of the latter.

In continuing our search for possible building remains at both ends of the long wall, we unearthed the fragment of a crude brick wall, 18 *4* feet thick (No. 3), near the west bank of the Shatt en-Nil and the remains of a burned brick pavement coated with bitumen close by. Under the latter were a bell-shaped drain (No. 4) and fragments of a second smaller one to the west of it. At the opposite (west) end of the wall we discovered a pre-Sargonic well built of brick, laid in herring-bone fashion. In accordance with the ordinary form of the earliest Babylonian wells, it was considerably narrower at the top than near the bottom. We commenced clearing it of the rubbish with which it was choked up, when at a depth of over eight feet we were stopped in our progress bv the wa-

ter of the spring rains. 'The top of the well itself was almost upon a level with the bottom of the drain at the east end of the wall," — a circumstance sufficiently explaining why the baked bricks of the drain pavement are of somewhat more recent date than those of the well at the west end.

There can be no doubt that the long wall was a regular facing or boundary wall, — a huge buttress of the same kind as repeatedly excavated by Koldewey at the edges of the vast cemeteries of Surghul and El-Hibba (pp. 285, *seq.*). It supported the light masses of ashes and dust of the fire necropolis of Nippur, which otherwise would have been blown into the plain or washed away by the rains of the winter. In view of the characteristic form and size of its yellow bricks, which are similar to those found in the lowest strata of a section of *Nimit-Marduk,* to the east of the temple, we can state positively that this buttress belongs to a period immediately preceding Sargon I. When the cemetery rose higher and higher, its facing wall did not prove strong enough to bear the additional pressure. "The burned bricks. were therefore overlaid by large crude bricks," completely imbedding the old wall and extending considerably beyond the exterior face of the latter, into the plain, as indicated by the cross-lines in the diagram above. In many cases it was extremely difficult and often impossible to ascertain the thickness of this additional wall, as the material of which it consisted had "been subjected to a process of infiltration and compression for so many centuries that the debris at the foot of the mound was practically a homogeneous mass." This much, however, was learned with certainty, that the bottom course of the outer crude brick wall was laid at a higher level than the upper courses of the remaining inner burned brick wall, thus illus The bricks being slightlv smaller in size than those of Sargon I., and Naram-Sin, indicate a period of construction not very far remote from the governments of the two rulers.

These doubtless pre-Sargonic bricks are of a peculiar type. Averaging 11)£ by

75g by 33 inches in size, they are nearly flat on the top, but have a slight furrow along the one long edge. Three feet one inch internal and nearly six feet external diameter. The average size of the wellbaked bricks from the cemetery wall was *3/i i4* inches square by 31 inches thick, while the corresponding bricks from the lower strata of *Nimit-MarJuk* measured only 1 1 'A inches square by 2/j inches thick. The latter evidently were somewhat older than the former. Apart from their color we noticed another characteristic feature of both classes of bricks. They were not entirely flat, but slightly raised at their longer edges. Outside the central section of the burned brick wall, which required strengthening most, the crude brick wall was from 22 to 28 feet thick, while at its east end it was not quite 19 feet. trating that the constant mud washings from the mound and the burials gradually taking place along the base of the wall, had changed the contour of the ground to such an extent that they threatened to efface the boundary line between the necropolis and the plain entirely.

There are several other interesting features to be observed in connection with this burned brick wall, which attract our attention. I refer briefly to the fact that at its thickest part the remains of a staircase, by which the cemetery could be ascended from the south, seem to have been discovered; furthermore that patchings and repairings of the wall could be traced at several points without difficulty; or that an opening (No. i) to give exit to the percolating rain water was found in the eastern section of the wall six and a half feet above the level of the brick pavement (No. 2). But it is beyond the scope of this book to discuss strictly technical questions which are of value chiefly to the architect.

On May 11, 1900, the most successful campaign thus far conducted at Nuffar terminated. Fxcavations having been suspended, the *meftul* was sealed, Arab guards were appointed, shaikhs and workmen rewarded, and the antiquities transported to six large boats moored in the swamps. Accompanied by the workmen from Hilla, their wives and children, and blessed by thronging crowds of Afej, who had assembled to bid us farewell, eagerly inquiring as to the time of our next return, we departed with a strange feeling of sadness and pleasure from the crumbling walls of *Duranki*, "the link of heaven and earth," which Ninib's doleful birds, croaking and dashing about, still seem to guard against every profane intruder.

As far as time and work would permit, we always made it a rule to explore and survey the neighboring ruins, with a view of placing the information thus obtained at the disposal of some other American or European expedition. During the Kaster week I decided to extend our excursions considerably farther to the south and to examine especially the low mounds of *Abu Hatab* and *f'ara,* where, since the days of Loftus, antiquities had constantly been excavated and sold by the Arabs. No trustworthy account of either of these ruins was yet at our disposal. In fact, there was not one modern map which indicated even their general situation, because they lie outside the ordinary track taken by Babylonian explorers. It is true some travellers had been in that neighborhood before, two of them even paying a hurried visit to the low site of Kara, but nobody thus far had been able to ascertain anything definite with regard to their age and importance. Having previously gathered all the necessary information from several members of the tribes camping along the Shatt el-Kar, the present writer, accompanied by Haynes, Geere, and half-a-dozen trusted Arabs, left NufFar one day in April shortly after sunset to examine that whole district. We crossed the Khor el-'Afej in two long narrow boats *(turradas),* and entered the great canal on the opposite side of the swamps, descending the latter in our primitive means of conveyance. The white blossoms of the caper shrub (Babyl. *sikhltt)?* growing abundantly along the embankments of the Shatt el-Kar and the smaller canals, filled the air with their strong aroma. Nothing but the occasional cry of an unknown water-bird, disturbed in his rest by our swiftly gliding boats, interrupted

the impressive stillness of that beautiful Babylonian night. At a place nearly opposite the two ruins we halted. Stretched on the ground or in the bottom of our boats we awaited the first rays of the sun that we might proceed with our archaeological mission.

An opening 33 inches wide and 16 inches high. Jo The only attempt made by the earlier travellers at locating Fara is found on Loftus' map. The proof for this identification will be found in Hilprecht, " The Bab. Exp. of the U. of Pa. ," series A, vol. x, Introduction.

As the results of this exploration tour will be published in another place, I confine myself to a general statement. Both ruins were well worth the pains we had taken in examining and surveying them. Abu Hatab, considerably smaller than Kara, is also the less remarkable of the two. Several half-effaced bricks and a little excavating in one of the rooms, easily to be traced in the early morning hours, convinced me that the site was occupied as late as the third preChristian millennium. Kara, a few miles to the south of it, is a very extensive but low ruin of the utmost importance. F. very where the characteristic pre-Sargonic bricks, wells, and drains peep out of the ground and excite the curiosity of the explorer. The higher elevation of the mounds is at the southern end, but some of our most valuable antiquities obtained from there were discovered two feet below the surface in a depression near the centre of the ruin. Like Nuffar and all such other pre-Sargonic ruins of the country with which I am personally acquainted, it contains thousands of burial urns, funeral chambers, pieces of charred wood, masses of potsherds, clearly indicating that a very extensive fire necropolis was connected with the ancient city buried there, which doubtless played an important role in the religious lite and the early history of the Sumerian people. If vigorously attacked with the spade and subjected to a strictly methodical examination, which, however, should not cease before the end of five to ten consecutive years, it probably will yield as important results as Nuffar and Tello. The accompanying

exquisite head of a Markhur goat (p. 540) of about the time of Ur-Nina (4000 B. C) and an even better-preserved larger head of the same animal (two thirds life size), were excavated at Kara, together with a pre-Sargonic sword in copper, a fine marble lamp in the shape of a bird, several complete stone vases, a very archaic seal cylinder, a number of pre-Sargonic clay tablets, and about sixty incised plates of mother-of-pearl, representing warriors, animals, handicraftsmen, pastoral and mythological scenes, rosettes, etc., in the style of the earliest monuments of Nuffar and Tello. These antiquities prove that considerable treasures of art must lie concealed in those low and insignificant-looking mounds which date back to a time when Sargon I. was not vet born.

Comp. Helm and Hilprecht in *Verhandlungen der Berliner anthropologischen Gaelhch,ift,* Feb. 16, 1901, pp. 157, *seqq.*

B. ON THE TOPOGRAPHY OF ANCIENT NIPPUR.

In the previous pages an attempt was made to sketch historicallv the archaeological work carried on by the University of Pennsylvania in Babylonia since 1889. In order to complete the picture and to obtain a clearer conception of Comp. pp. z $2, *seq.,* 474, *seq.* the contents of the ruins of Nuffar as far as explored, it will only be necessary to summarize the principal results obtained by the four expeditions, to place them in their mutual relations, and to consider them in a coherent manner from a topographical point of view. To avoid undesirable repetitions, constant references will be made to what has been submitted before. The chapter necessarily must be brief, especially as the new facts, which by their very nature were excluded from the previous history, will be easilv understood in the light of my former expositions.

The ruins of ancient Nippur (comp. pp. 160, *seq.,* 305, *seqq.*) are divided by the dry bed of the Shatt en-Nil (Chebar) into an eastern and western section. Both are nearly equal in size, each covering an area of about ninety acres of land (p. 305). The western half represents the remains of the citv proper, the eastern half the large complex of the temple of Bel, generally known by the name of *Ekur* (pp. 464, *seq.)*-Twenty-one different strata can be distinguished in the mass of debris which constitutes the present site of Nuffar. It should be understood, however, that these twenty-one layers, marking as many different phases in the history of Bel's renowned city, by no means occur in every section of the ruins. In some places the remains of the second millennium rest immediately on the top of pre-Sargonic Nippur, in others the two are separated by ten to fifteen feet of rubbish, in still others the earliest remains appear almost on the surface. At first sight, therefore, it would seem evident that certain parts of Nippur must have been in ruins for centuries, while others were occupied by houses continually. To a certain degree this view is doubtless correct. But we must not forget that our knowledge on this question will always remain more or less defective. For on the other hand we know positively that earlier building remains were frequently razed to the ground by later generations, often enough for no other reason than to obtain building material, worked clay (pp. 493, *seq.,* as well as baked bricks (pp. 373, *seq.,* 376, *seq.,* 389), for their own constructions in the easiest and cheapest manner possible.

Apart from Bint el-Amir, which is considerably higher than the rest of the ruins (pp. 160, *seq.),* the mounds of Nuffar on an average rise thirty to seventy feet above the present plain and the ruins descend from one to twenty feet below it. The twenty-one strata or historical periods represented by these ruins may naturally be grouped together under three different headings briefly designated in the following sketch as the Sumerian period, the Semitic Babylonian period and the post-Babylonian period.

a. In the earliest (Sumerian) stratum we recognize six phases of historical development by means of the different kinds of bricks employed. The first is characterized by the entire absence of baked bricks, and the exclusive use ot adobes.

The other five are easily distinguished according to the different forms and siz.es of baked bricks subsequently adopted. The earliest bricks are very small, flat on the lower

Pre-Sargonic Bricks in their Historical Development and strongly rounded on the upper side, which generally also bears a thumb-mark. They look more like rubble or quarry stones, in imitation of which they were made (Gen. 11:3) than the artificial products of man (p. 251). Gradually they grow larger in size and flatter at the same time. The thumb-mark ' begins to disappear, and one, two or more longitudinal streaks made with the index finger or bv drawing a reed leaf over the clav-come into use, first with a thumb-mark Icomp.

the third brick in the above illustration), later without the same. None of all the pre-Sargonic bricks thus far excavated at Nuffar bears an inscription. Wells and drains are the earliest constructions for which these baked bricks were required. According to the results furnished by our excavations, the bricks are generally laid in a peculiar manner in those ancient wells. The architects call it herringbone fashion. Theupper and lower three rows of bricks seen in the accompanying cut are especially indicative of the principle followed by the first builders in "the land of Shinar." It is interesting to observe that the sign used in Babylonian writing for "brick" originally represents a section of such a well in which the bricks are laid in herring-bone fashion. The Sumerian stratum extending from the virgin soil to a point about five to ten feet above the ancient plain level is Sometimes two and even four such marks occur. The fibre and form of the leaf are clear! v recognized on a number of bricks now in the archaeological museum of the U. of Pa. The case is somewhat different at Tello; comp. p. 251.

Section or a Hre-Sargonic Writ. Bricks Lid in

Herring-bone Fashion

twenty to thirty-five feet high in the temple mound, where the pavement of Sargon and Naram-Sin forms an important boundary line. It is characterized

by scattered ashes mixed with earth or well-defined ash-beds greatly varying in size, bits of charcoal, an occasional bone, innumerable potsherds often colored red or blackened from exposure to fire, manv cracked jars found in different positions, a few of them in a tolerable, some even in a fine state of preservation, thousands of thick fragments of small vases, dishes and pointed cups, broken weapons, damaged seal cylinders, personal ornaments in stone, shell, copper and silver, frequent drains, wells, and abundant remains of ruined chambers built of adobes, exceptionallv also of plano-convex baked bricks (comp. especially p. 456, note 2). In other words, wherever we reached this lowest stratum at Nuffar we came upon extensive traces of pre-Sargonic burials, so that we cannot avoid the conclusion that the sacred ground around the temple or Knlil and certain districts even on the west side of the Chebar were largely used as a cemetery, or, more exactly, as a fire necropolis (pp. 456, *seq.),* by the earliest population of the country. Apart from the court and general neighborhood of the temple, we excavated funeral vases and other remains illustrating the praxis of cremating the dead in various other parts of the ruins, especially in the mounds to the south and east of Bint el-Amir (p. 479), along the foot of the outer wall (p. 487J, and in the long ridge marked by the numbers VI and VIII on the plan of the ruins (p. 305; comp. pp. 419, *seq.)*

A small *ziggurrat* (p. 453), the foundation of the northeast citv gate (pp. 493, *seqq.),* and partly explored building remains in the mounds to the east and west of the temple proper are the onlv witnesses of a pre-Sargonic "city ot the living" so far discovered in our excavations at Nippur. In view of the enormous amount of rubbish covering the earliest strata this result will not surprise us. Small as the unearthed remains are, they suffice to show that in pre-Sargonic times the city had nearly the same extent as in the days of Ur-Gur (about 2700 B. C.) or Kadashman-Turgu (about 1350 B. c). But how much of the ground was reserved for the dead and how much for the living cannot be ascertained for many years to come. The numerous single pre-Sargonic bricks, the remains ot walls and other early constructions already excavated, together with several hundred inscribed clav tablets (pp. j88, 403, *seqq.*), objects of art (pp. 383, *seq.*, 474, *seq.*) and other antiquities (*e.g.,* pp. 485, *seqq.*) of the same ancient period, and the frequent references to Nippur in the earliest inscriptions from other ruins, allow us to infer that the earliest city must already have had a comparatively large population.

The period of transition from the earliest chapter of Babylonian history to the age of Sargon and Naram-Sin, the so-called sixth pre-Sargonic period, is closely connected at Nuffar with the appearance of the first square bricks made in a rectangular mould. In general it probably coincides with the time of Entemena of Lagash (p. 251). Bricks of this period have been found *in situ* in large numbers at low levels on both sides of the Shatt en-Nil (p. 535). Though still uninscribed, they are readily distinguished from other later bricks by their yellow color and the circumstance that the edge of the upper surface is somewhat higher than its central portion.

b. The line ot demarcation between the Sumerian and Semitic periods in the historv of Babylonia cannot be drawn very sharply. Doubtless centuries of commercial intercourse and peaceful intermingling between the early inhabitants of the country and the neighboring Semitic tribes preceded the final conquest of the Sumerians and the subsequent amalgamation of the two races. Kven after the former had lost their political independence, in many regards no perceptible change seems at first to have taken place in the life of the people. The foreign invaders remained in the fertile plain and became the docile pupils of the subdued nation. They learned how to cultivate the soil and to dig new canals, how to fortity cities and to erect lofty temples. They adopted and further developed the system of writing which they found in the country, and

they made themselves acquainted with the literary and artistic products, and the religious and cosmological ideas of their new subjects. At the time of Sargon and Naram-Sin, the Semitic element is firmlv established throughout the land and in complete possession of the ancient Sumerian civilization, which was successfully directed into new channels, and thus stagnation was prevented. The votive objects and seal cylinders from the period of the Sargon dynasty represent the best epoch and the highest development of ancient Babylonian art, while the inscribed tablets and monuments "are characterized by an exquisite style of writing."

In the western portion of the ruins of Nippur the change from the old *regime* to the new one is scarcely visible. Burials were made there for some time afterwards (pp. 419, *seq.*), as they had been before. But in the course of time, thev ceased altogether, and the site of the ancient cemetery was occupied by great business houses and the bazaars of the city (pp. 413, *seqq.*). The 30,000 contracts and account lists excavated from numerous houses along the bank of the Chebar enable us to trace one settlement above another from the fourth millennium down to the time of Artaxerxes and Darius, at the end of the fifth century.

A more abrupt and radical change took place in the eastern half of the citv. The burial ground around the *ziggurrat* was levelled, the sacred enclosure extended, and the whole temple court provided with a solid pavement and surrounded with high walls. No cremation was henceforth permitted and no funeral urn deposited anywhere within the precincts of Bel's sanctuary at Nippur. The city became "a pure place like Eridu " (p. 467), and the temple an exclusive place of worship for the living. It preserved this character for over 3000 years, until Babylonia's independence was lost, and another people with another religion, which did not know of the ancient gods of the country, established itself for a few centuries on the ruined site of Bel's venerable city.

Notwithstanding the almost continuous occupation of the city during this

long period of Babylonian history, nine strata can be distinguished more or less accurately in the temple court. Six of these do not offer any difficulty at all, as they are separated from each other by brick pavements (pp. 376, *seqq.*, 475, *seq.*). The other three overlap the next lower ones to a certain degree in the excavated southeast section of the sacred enclosure, but are recognized more clearly in other parts of the ruins. The debris representing these different strata, with their nearly 3500 years of historv (from about 3800 to 350 B. C), and including the pavement of Naram-Sin, measures only 17 to 19 feet in the temple court. As we saw above (p. 391), this comparatively small accumulation of rubbish within such a long period finds its natural explanation in the double fact that a considerable part of the court in front of the stage-tower and temple must always have been unoccupied (p. 376), and that everv ruler who laid a new pavement necessarily razed the crumbling buildings of his predecessors around the *ziggurrat,* in order to secure an even surface (p. 388) and a solid foundation for his own constructions.

The six periods easily determined by fragmentary pavements of baked or unbaked brick in the temple court are the following: 1. Sargon and Naram-Sin, about 3750 B. c. (pp. 388, *seqq.*, 497, *seqq.*); 2. Lugalsurzu, about 3500 B. c. (p. 475, *seq.*); 3. Ur-Gur and his dynasty, about 2700 B.C. (pp. 378, *seqq.* , 383, *seqq.*); 4. Ur-Ninib of(N)isin, about 2500 B.c. (pp. 378, 380, *seq.*); 5. KadashmanTurgu of the Cassite dynasty, about 1350 B. C. (pp. 376, *seqq.*); 6. Ashurbanapal, king of Assyria, 668—626 B. C. (p. 376). Besides the names here mentioned, other members of the same dynasties have left us traces of their activity in Nippur through fragmentary walls, wells and houses containing their inscribed bricks, or in the shape of votive offerings bearing their names and titles. In the zinctvpe facing this page I confine myself to indicating onlv those five pavements which could be traced more or less through the whole excavated temple court, or at least through the larger part of it.

The three periods referred to above as being less clearly defined are, 1. the first dynasty of Babylon, about 2200 B. c. (comp. pp. 480, *seqq.)*; 2. the dynasty of Pashe, about 1100 B. c, and 3. the neo-Babylonian and Persian period. They are represented by ruined buildings or inscribed documents found in limited numbers in their respective strata.

According to the evidence furnished by the trenches, the temple complex as a whole presented very much the same picture during all the different periods of its long and interesting history. Of course the stage tower gradually grew larger, and the temple at its side, consequently (p. 4721 somewhat smaller in the latter half of the second millennium. The number of chapels, shrines and other houses connected with the cult of Bel and his large retinue of minor gods doubtless also varied at different times, since Nippur, as the seat of " the kingdom of the four regions of the world," more than any other city in the country reflected the politi Including Rim-Sin of Larsa, whose inscriptions occur in the same general stratum. For the present, comp. p. 408, and Hilprecht, " The Bab. Exp. of the U. of Pa.," series A, vol. 1, part 2, no. 128.

Represented by several fragmentary boundary stones only in part published (comp. Hilprecht, *l. c,* part 1, pi. 27, no. 80, and pi. *XII,* nos. 32, *seq.),* a fine unpublished boundary stone of Nebuchadrezzar I. with six columns of writing, and a few dated documents (p. 519).

Section of the Stage-Tower and the Adjoining Southeast Court
Restored and designed by Hdprccht draivn by Fisher
A-B-P-L. Ashurbanapal. N-S. Naram-Sin. U-G. Vr-Gur. P. Pavement, tm. Baked Brick. =. Pavement of tzvo layers of bricks. Measurements given in feet.
cal ups and downs ot Babylonia. We know even now on the basis of our latest excavations that the outer wall of the temple constructed by Naram-Sin followed a slightly different course from that of Ur-Gur and all the subsequent rulers (pp. 497, *seqq.).* And it is likewise certain that the temple library of

the period antedating the Elamitic invasion was more important and probably also of greater extent than that of the time of Ashurbanapal (pp. 511, *seqq.).* But notwithstanding these and other distinctive features which the temple presented in different centuries, and which easilv could be multiplied, the general plan and disposition of the sanctuary changed but little. In accordance with the conservative character of the Babylonian religion, the space enclosed by the walls *Imgur-Marduk* and *Nimit-Marduk,* or whatever their former names may have been, remained nearly stationary, and the principal buildings erected upon it practicallv occupied the same position at the time of Sargon I. and in the days of Artaxerxes I. and Darius II.

Roughlv speaking, the entire area covered with the ruins of the temple complex (comp. the plan on page 305) forms a trapezoid, the longest side of which runs parallel with the northeast bank of the Chebar. By disregarding the triangular library mound in the south, which never seems to have been included in the walled territory, we obtain a parallelogram with nearly equal sides, each measuring about 2700 feet. Except on the southwest side, where the waters of the great canal, probably lined by a dam or quay, afforded a sufficient protection, this large space was enclosed by a huge wall 25 to 40 feet thick (pp. 498, *seqq.),* and at least 25 feet high (p. 492). Since the government of Ur-Gur this so-called outer wall of the city was adorned with buttresses (p. 498), while at all times, as far as we can determine at present, it was strengthened bv a number of well-drained bastions (pp. 494, 496, 503), and by a deep moat which ran along its entire base (p. 495), forming a regular navigable canal on the southeast side, where the principal entrance of the temple must be looked for. A large gate was discovered also in the middle of the northeast wall, through which the main road from the east passed behind the *ziggurrat,* leading to a bridge over the Chebar into the city proper (pp. 493, *seqq.).*

The northwest half of this fortified

enclosure consisted of a large open court, along the northeast edge of which tradesmen and handicraftsmen had their shops (pp. 488, *seq.),* and of a group of substantial buildings near the canal which probably represent the outhouses, servants' quarters and magazines of the temple. The mounds between the *ziggurrat* and the Chebar, and between the temple and the northeast wall, have not yet been examined sufficiently to enable us to ascertain their contents with any degree of certainty. A plausible theory with regard to the possible character of the doubtless imposing building which lies buried under the enormous mass of debris in the east corner of the outer wall was formulated on p. 485, above.

The accompanying zinctype, prepared by Mr. Fisher on the basis of my interpretation of the excavated ruins (p. 552), may serve as a supplement to my previous discussion (pp. 368, *seqq.,* 469, *seqq.,* 477, *seqq..* Viewed in the light of a first attempt on our part to restore the principal features of the most renowned sanctuary of Babylonia in accordance with real facts, this sketch will help the reader to gain a clearer conception of the general plan and disposition of the temple of Bel during the last three thousand years of its remarkable history. A complete list of measurements of all the examined building remains, photographs and accurate drawings illustrating the necessary architectural details, my reasons for assuming a *ziggurrat* of five stages, and a full treatment of all such other questions as by their technical nature had to be excluded from the present pages, will be found in a special monograph entitled " Kkur, the Temple of Bel at Nippur." For the present it may suffice to repeat that the

Ekur, the Temple of Bel at Nippur
First attempt at a restoration by Hilprccht and Fisher I. Slage-toiver ivith shrine on the top. 2. The temple proper, j. ' House for ktnry cream and wine." 4. "Place of the delight of Bur-Sin." j. Inner ivall (/eyer Mardui). 6. Outer wall (Nimit-Mardui). temple proper consisted of two courts (pp. 478, *sec/.)* and to

emphasize that the exact size of the inner court containing the stage-tower and the house of Bel at its side cannot be given, before the Parthian fortress covering the Babylonian ruins has been removed completely. As the latter construction, however, on the whole followed the outline of the older enclosure pretty accurately, the measurements quoted in connection with the Parthian fortress can be used in a general way also to restore the dimensions of the inner court of the ancient temple beneath it. The *ziggurrat,* the most conspicuous part of the whole complex, rose highest and was largest at the time of Ashurbanapal. It then covered an area forming a rectangular parallelogram, the two sides of which measured 190 and 128 feet respectively. The outer temple court, probably studded with the chapels of all the different gods worshipped at Nippur (p. 480), appears to have been nearly square, each side being about 260 feet long.

c. Babylonia's independence was lost forever when the Persian ruler removed the golden image of Marduk from his famous sanctuary on the Euphrates. At the end of the fourth century it seemed for a little while as if the ancient cult would be revived with even greater magnificence than at the time of Hammurabi and Nebuchadrezzar. The ruined stages of *Etemenanki,* which the destroyer of Jerusalem " had raised like a mountain" in honor of Bel, were torn down by foreign soldiers to secure a solid foundation for the more sumptuous structure of their own king. Alexander the Great had returned from India to Babylon, with the intention of residing in this city, as the metropolis of his vast empire. Inspired with new and ambitious plans, the execution of which should establish the glory of his name among the nations forever, he was about to rebuild " the tower of Babel " and "to cause its summit to rival the heavens" again, when suddenly he was carried away by an untimely death in the vigor of his manhood. One involuntarily thinks of Gen. 11:5 (and 8): "And the Lord came down to see the city and the tower which the children of men

builded." Proclaimed as a god in Egypt, Alexander shared the fate of the supreme god of his capital on the Euphrates. Not far from "the sepulchral mound of Bel" (pp. 459, *seqq.),* which his soldiers had razed to the ground, the unconquered hero succumbed to the Babylonian fever in the palace of Nebuchadrezzar. In consequence of this historical fact travellers and explorers have hitherto searched in vain for the remains of the " tower of Babel." Nothing but the lowest foundations of the famous structure will ever be discovered. For modern Arab brick-diggers completed the work of demolition which Alexander's soldiers had begun zooo years ago. In connection with their pernicious digging they discovered the building records of Nabopolassar and Nebuchadrezzar in their original niches. A fine bomb-shaped clay cone of the first-mentioned monarch and fragments of three duplicate cylinders of his son were obtained from them more than twelve years ago for the Archaeological Museum of the U. of Pa. The place where the stage-tower once stood can he recognized even now with absolute certainty from the peculiar form of the depression which the extracted bricks have left in the soil. The Arabs call it *es-suhan,* " the bowl." Unlike the stage-tower of Nippur the ground-plan of *Etemenanki* seems to have formed a square. A curious depression extending from the centre of its southeast side marks the entrance of the ancient tower of Babvlon, in the same way as that of Nippur is indicated in the light-shaded centre of the ground-plan of the " Parthian Palace built over the Ruins of the Temple of Bel" (p. 559, below). The peculiar depression marking the ancient site of the " tower of Babel" is reproduced accurately in the topographical map of "Tell Amran," published by the German Orient Society. Comp. also Bruno Meissner, *Von Babylon nach den Ruinen* r«r *Hira und Huarnaq,* Leipzig, 1 go 1, p. l.

The enormous empire which the great Macedonian had founded was divided among his principal generals. Seleucia on the Tigris took the place of Babylon

under the new dynasty. Insignificant traces of this period have been discovered also at Nippur. But the rich province was soon lost by Alexander's heirs to more powerful invaders. About a hundred years after the great king's death we find the Parthians in possession of the entire country, erecting their castles and palaces with ancient material on all the important ruins of Shumer and Akkad (pp. 159, 226, *seqq.,* 368, *seq.).* The stage-tower of Nippur was remodelled for military purposes (pp. 501, *seq.),* and a strongly fortified palace arose on the site of the temple of Bel (see p. 555).

For the last time a certain prosperity pervades the country, and all the mounds of Nippur are covered with flourishing Parthian settlements (pp. 309, 313, 327, *seqq.,* 334, *seqq. ,2,66,seqq.ySeqq.).* But compared with the ancient civilization and wealth of the people, the period of the Parthian rule is a period of deterioration and decay. The resting places of the dead begin to occur side by side with the residences of the living. The city of Bel rapidlv becomes again what it had been at the beginning of its long and varied history — a vast cemetery.

With the rise of the Sassanian dynasty (a. D. 226-643) the importance of the city is gone. The magnificent palace grouped around the *ziggurrat* as a citadel lies in ruins; no imposing new building is henceforth erected within the

Section through the Parthian Foruess covering the Temple of B-l, looking southwest *Restored and draivn hy Fisner* precincts of ancient Nippur. Of course small mud houses and insignificant shops continue to occupy the most prominent parts of the high-towering ruins for centuries longer. A great number of Hebrew, Mandean and Syriac bowls (pp. 326, 337, 447, *seq.),* the wooden box of a Jewish scribe containing his pen-holder and inkstand and a little scrap of crumbling parchment inscribed with a few Hebrew characters, large quantities of late pottery and several rotten bags filled with Kufic silver and copper coins were gathered bv our different expeditions in the upper stratum of NufFar. All these antiquities show that the city existed in some form or other even as late as the early Arabic period, and that the Jewish element was strongly represented among its inhabitants. About A. D. iooo or soon afterwards the site must have been abandoned definitely. Arabic historians occasionally refer to it. But the latest inscribed antiquities thus far excavated are thin silver coins of Mervan ibn Mohammed, the last 'Omayyade caliph (744-749), and others of the first 'Abbaside caliphs of Baghdad, among them Harun ar-Rashid (786-809 A. D.), the well-known contemporary of Charlemagne, and several of his less famous successors in the ninth century. We excavated hundreds of tombs from the four hundred years when the Arsacide dynasty held sway over Babylonia (about 250 B. C. to A. D. 226) in the slopes of the mounds and under the floors of the houses of the later inhabitants.

In examining the post-Babylonian ruins of Nuffar, which represent about twelve hundred years of strange historv, we distinguished six different periods. Two of them, however, can be recognized with certainty only in the large temple area. Beginning at the surface of the mounds, we first come upon the extensive remains of the early Arabic period, easily determined by low mud houses containing vessels and potsherds, Hebrew Mandean and Syriac incantation bowls, Kufic coins, shallow graves, etc. (pp. 313, 337). Next we reach the numerous Sassanian burials, characterized by certain forms of coffins and different kinds of pottery drains which often descend far into the real Babylonian strata below, by rude seals badly engraved with human figures, animals, plants and the like (p. 326), and by many minor antiquities. The layers then following are filled with the typical objects of the Hellenistic and Roman age (pp. 330, seq.), including a number of vaulted tombs and other graves. They represent three different periods of occupancy during the Parthian rule (pp. 331, seq., 365, seq.). A huge Parthian fortress covers

the ruins of the temple of Bel. The doors of the excavated houses and corridors had been walled up from below once or twice, as can still be recognized from the central column of the debris seen in the frontispiece and the illustration facing p. 453. "All of the doors, as we found them, were at least five to six feet and a half above the proper level of the floors." The later inhabitants of Nippur very evidently experienced something similar to that which Nebuchadrezzar describes in connection with his palace and the street of procession at Babylon. The streets and passageways, which originally were on a level with the floors of the rooms, " filled up with debris and mud washed down from the walls and rooms of the houses." It consequently became necessary for the inhabitants " to descend from the street level to the house doors by steps," which still exist in the case of two of the doors directly in front of the *ziggurrat.* This circumstance doubtless rendered the rooms comparatively cool during the summer. But during the rainy season these *serdabs* often enough must have looked more like cisterns than human habitations. Those who occupied them were therefore forced from time to " time to fill up the houses within to the level of the street, block up the old doorways and cut new ones, build an addition on the walls, and raise the roofs " correspondingly." According to information from Halil Bey, Director of the Imperial Ottoman Museum, who at my request kindly examined all our excavated Arabic coins, as far as thev had then been cleaned.

Some six to eight feet below the rooms of the last Parthian palace were remains of an earlier post-Babylonian fortress, which probably belonged to the Seleucidan period (about 320-250 A. ix). As previously stated (pp. 503, s«j.), apart from the greater depth of their level, these ruins can be distinguished easily from those lying above them by the different quality and the smaller size of their bricks and by the direction of their walls. Arsacide coins, commonly found in the upper layers (p. 327), are wholly absent from

these lower rooms.
Comp. p. 225, above. "Comp. Peters, « Nippur," pp. 155, *seq.*

It will have become apparent from our brief sketch of the post-Babvlonian history of Nippur that the only building remains deserving our special attention in this connection are those of the Parthian period. They occur practically on all the prominent mounds of the ancient city, and many years more of methodical excavation are therefore required in the upper strata of Nuffar before we shall be able to understand the topography of this last important settlement in the least adequately. All that we can do at present is to illustrate the general character of the larger buildings of this period by the example of the two Parthian palaces already excavated. Their plan and disposition were ascertained chiefly through the labors of the fourth expedition.

The more imposing of the two structures occupies the central part of the temple area. A glance at the plan opposite this page will convince us that the Parthian fortress, like the Babylonian temple beneath it, consisted of two courts. They did not communicate with one another, except perhaps by means of a large staircase, the remains of which seem to have perished. The southeast court not beintj explored yet, we confine ourselves to setting forth the principal features of the great palace grouped around the remodelled *ziggurrat.* The huge building comprised an area no doubt intended to be rectangular. The entire space was surrounded by a double wall of colossal proportions. It varied considerably in thickness, and was about 560 feet long on its southeast side. The north corner of this vast enclosure has not yet been determined, while its west corner was found to be washed away by the action of rain water Indicated by the number I in cut on opposite page.

Parthian Palace built over the Ruins of the Temple of Bel
Restored by Hilprecht, surveyed and draivn by Fisher and Geerc
I. Remain! of an earlier, probably Se/eucidan building, about joo B. C. The re-

it represent! tie remaim of a Parthian palace, grouped around the ziggurral at a citadel (about 2yO B. C. to 200 A. D.). A. Public reception rooms and private apartment! for the prince and his officer! (partly unexcavated). B. Harem (largely unexcavated). C. Domeitic juarteri, store-rooms, barracks, etc. J (on the ziggurrat). The only tvell of the palace. 2. Street separating the palace proper from the domestic fuartert. 7. Room icith a tomb beneath. cutting a deep gulley into the ruins. The bricks generally used in all the constructions of the fortress are large, almost square blocks of adobe (pp. 334, 365, 503).

The southeast side has been examined more carefully than the rest of the building. The ruined outer wall, when excavated, still rose to the height of over sixty feet and was more than thirty feet thick at its top, and almost forty feet at its base, which besides was cased with baked bricks taken from various earlier ruins. This wall was strengthened by two huge buttresses at the corners, and by two smaller ones erected at equal distances between the former. Along the summit of three of the outer walls was a series of rooms at uneven distances and of different sizes. Most of them, entered by doors from the enclosed yard below, apparently served as barracks for the soldiers. Others were accessible only from above, and must have been used as prisons or magazines. The outer northeast wall in reality consisted of two separate walls, the space between them being filled in with mud and debris.

Along the inner face of the southeast wall ran a corridor or passageway over twenty-four feet wide. Beyond it was an inner wall relieved by two buttresses and (probably) three solid round towers, each of which was about thirty feet in diameter and crowned with a parapet. The large open space thus strongly fortified was occupied with a great many rooms and corridors, more or less connected with each other and evidently forming an organic whole. They were generally stuccoed with a plaster, and frequently tinted in green, pink, and yellow colors. Several of them had a win-dow or ventilator of baked bricks high up in one of the walls, while drainage was often effected by an opening under the threshold of the door or through the solid wall of the house. In one case a large perforated vase was sunk below the floor of stamped earth in the north corner of the room.

The north section of the vast complex was set apart for a number of fine large rooms. Two of them, surrounded on all sides by spacious corridors, were composed of double walls with an air space between them, scarcely wide enough to admit of the passage of an adult. Similar passageways ran around a few other rooms in the southeast wall of the fortress. The size of these chambers and the greater care with which the whole quarter evidently had been planned and constructed suggested their use as public reception halls adjoined by the private chambers of the prince or governor and his officers. As practically only a narrow room or corridor connected this wing of the palace with the west section, which to a large extent is still unexplored, we may assume with a reasonable degree of probability that the latter was reserved for the harem. No regular gate having been found in the south and east parts of the enclosure, it follows almost with certainty that the principal entrance of the castle must exist somewhere near the unexcavated north corner of the large structure.

From many characteristic objects discovered (pp. 330, 365) we know that the kitchens, storerooms, servants' quarters, etc., were located in the southeast section of the building. A narrow street running parallel with the principal facade of the stage-tower separated them from the palace proper. In the middle of this unpaved street was a well-made gutter of burned bricks, into which the drains of the adjoining rooms discharged their contents.

Out of the midst of all these chambers and corridors rose the stage-tower as an almost impregnable bulwark. It served as a citadel, on the top of which the garrison and inhabitants of the palace would find refuge even after the lower parts of the fortress had fallen into the hands of the enemy. The infinite toil with which the only well of the whole enclosure must have been cut through the core of the *ziggur.rat* to the water level, and the great care manifested in enlarging and strengthening the Babylonian stage-tower bv four irregular buttresses, projecting like so many gigantic wings from the centres of the four sides, indicated sufficiently what strategic importance the Parthian rulers attached to this part of their palace. The peculiar cruciform shape of the massive building was originally suggested bv the ancient entrance or causeway of the tower (on its southeast side). The first buttress-like additions to the *ziggurrat* accordingly were not much wider than the latter. As they were built of the same kind of bricks which characterizes the remains of the earlier castle, thev must belong to the Seleucidan period. Under the Parthian rulers these arms, like the rest of the structure, were broadened considerably. At the same time the ruined stages were trimmed and overbuilt with large crude bricks, thus making an immense platform rising no less than twenty-five to thirty feet above the rest of the fortress. A second stage rose like a huge watch-tower from the centre of the first. To judge from the height of Bint el-Amir as we first saw it, this cannot have been lower than twenty feet. Both stages were naturally surrounded by a parapet to afford the besieged garrison sufficient protection against the weapons ot its enemies. In times of peace this elevated gallery, with its superb view over the endless plains, must have been a favorite place of rest for the residents of the palace, where they enjoyed a fresh breeze and doubtless spent their nights during the hottest months of the year.

They measure 28 by 41 and 21 by 22 feet respectively. Indicated in the cut, p. 559. Comp. p. 246.

The fortified palace with which we have occupied ourselves cannot be considered as typical for the architecture of the Parthian period; for the size and general plan of the vast structure were largely determined by the ruined tower and walls of the Babylonian temple beneath.

It was different with regard to the much smaller palace on the west Marked / in the cut, p. 559.

They were from 45 to 63 feet wide, and projected 30 to 50 feet into the court from the Babylonian tower.

Section through the Stiu'.l Parthian I'.il icr on West Side of the Chebar, looking Northeast *Restored and draivn by Fiihcr* side of the Chebar, which belongs to the third or second century preceding our era. The material of which it consists is mostly crude brick, of size, shape and texture similar to that forming the core of the fortress on the opposite bank of the canal. To speak more exactly, the adobes of the west palace are in size between the bricks of the earlier and those of the later fortress, their average dimensions being 12 by 12 by 7 '.j. inches. Like the latter they are made of clay obtained from the breaking up of older material. That the smaller building cannot be older than the date just assigned to it, and possibly is somewhat younger, follows with necessity from a small thick copper coin discovered in one of the bricks. Much corroded as it was, it could be assigned with a reasonable degree of certainty to one of the rulers of the Arsacide dynasty. A number of stone seals engraved with animals — among them an agate ring showing a fish,— which were taken from the floor level in different parts of the building, afforded additional proof to my theory as to the late origin of the structure.

The absolutely un-Babylqnian character of the palace becomes evident also from an examination of its groundplan and a study of its architectural details. The clear and regular division of the entire building, the methodical grouping of its rooms around two open courts, the liberal employment of columns as a decorative element, a certain refinement and beauty with regard to proportion, the verv apparent aiming at unity, with due consideration of convenience, are characteristic features of the ancient Greek houses on Delos rather than of those known from ancient Babylonia. The building was intended to be square, each side measuring about 170 feet. Its foundation was laid upon the ruins of

the early city more than forty-two feet above the level of the plain. In accordance with a well-known Babylonian custom, its four corners pointed approximately to the four cardinal points. As the house stood upon the outskirts of a mound bordering the Shatt en-Nil, the east corner of the structure is almost completely washed awav.

There can be little doubt that the building had but one entrance, which was situated nearly in the centre of the northwest facade. It consisted of an elaborately finished doorway and porch, reached by two steps from the street. As there is undeniable evidence that the southwest and southeast sides of the palace were originally broken up bv a system of shallow buttresses, we may assume that the exterior surface of the badlv damaged northwest wall was decorated with similar panels or recessings. The northeast side, however, which faced the river, seems to have been left without any ornamentation. "The pilasters on either side of the doorway and the columns of the courtyards were stuccoed," while the rest of the building was covered with a mud plaster.

More exactly the northwest side measured 174, the northeast 1683, the southwest 170, the southeast 1723 feet. Comp. the plan of the ruins on p. 305. The quotations in this and the following lines are from Fisher's and Geere's report on the building.

The walls of the house varied in thickness from three feet to eight feet and a half. From fragments of pavements found in some of the rooms we may infer that the floors of the principal apartments at least were of baked brick. In the construction of steps, pillars, thresholds, fireplaces, beds and the like the same material was used, while the open courtyards were paved with unbaked bricks. The floor of the bathroom was covered with bitumen. As the many charred pieces of wood indicated sufficiently, the roof of the building consisted of palm logs, matting and earth. "We may safely assert that there was no second story to the building." The doors were made of mulberry or tamarisk wood and swung on door-sockets of

stone, baked brick, or cement. In the case of quite a number of the rooms, rugs or curtains seem to have taken the place of doors. Owing to the destruction of the house by fire and its farther devastation bv rain and later inhabitants who used the ruins of the once imposing structure as a quarry and graveyard, we know little or nothing " as to the methods of decoration adopted by the builders for the interior of the palace." It was probably plastered and painted according to the manner of the more ambitious structure on the other side of the Chebar.

A word remains to be said about the courts and columns. The larger courtyard (4)' measured nearly 64 by 70 feet, the smaller (21) was about 28 feet square. "The central part of the former was probably open to the sky, to give light and fresh air to the rooms, while columns, placed at nearly even distances from one another, served to support a roof over the adjoining gallerv or colonnade which surrounded it." There were four round columns on each side of the principal courtyard and a square one at each angle. They were built of baked bricks especially made for the purpose, and must have been at least fifty courses, or 12 '£ feet, high. Comp. the cut, p. 567.

The lower parts of twelve of them were still standing (comp. the illustration facing p. 340). The circular columns were 2 feet 9 inches in diameter at the base, and 2 feet I inch at the fiftieth course of bricks. From the first to the seventeenth course, /'. e., during the first third of the entire height, the diameter remained nearly constant; after that it gradually diminished. Certain fragments of curiously moulded bricks found near the courtyard proved that these tapering brick columns also had capitals. As Babylonian imitations of Doric columns, they naturally had no regular base, but rested upon burnt brick foundations eleven courses deep, which were completely hidden in the soil. "Between these square foundations ran an edging, or curbing, of the same material, but only two courses deep."

All the other characteristic features

of the interesting building can be studied best in connection with the accompanying plan. We observe that the little palace is divided into two almost equal parts, the northeast half reserved for the public functions of the men, and the southwest half for the family life proper. From the entrance lobby (i) two doors open off, the one towards the west leading through a small anteroom (8) and a long corridor (9) to the servants' quarters (10-15) and harem (16, *segq.*)', the other towards the east through a similar anteroom (2), the main vestibule (3), and the colonnade into the large courtyard (4), flanked by a number of rooms. It will be noticed that the vestibule is not situated exactly in the middle with reference to the courtyard. In leaving the latter and continuing our way towards the southeast, we first pass an altar on our left (5), and next enter the two largest halls of the whole building (6 and 7). They are connected with one another by a large doorway which generally was closed by a double door, as two sockets found *in situ* on either side of the entrance and fragments of iron hinges and nails plainly indicated. One step edged with burned bricks leads from the colonnade to the *atrium* (6), and three steps from the latter into the assembly hall proper (7).

The harem could be reached from the colonnade directly

Plan of a Small Parthian Palace at Nippur, about 250 B. C.

Discovered in iSSq, andexcavatedcompletely in /goo. About thirty-six rooms and halls grouped around open courts. Entrance on the north-ivcst side. Surveyed by Fisher and Geere draivn by the former. by a narrow passageway (17), either end of which was closed by a door. A kind of anteroom (16) formed a connecting link between the men's quarters, the servants' rooms and the section reserved for the women. Thus the private apartments of the family were securely shut off from the rest of the building. The general plan and arrangement of this section do not require special interpretation, as they are similar to those of the northeast half of the palace. The elevated constructions

built against the southeast wall in rooms 19 and 22 probably are places for reclining and rest (so-called beds). The floor of the bathroom (18) was paved with bitumen, with a border of brickwork coated with the same material, and laid in such a way as to drain perfecdv towards the opening shown in the plan. The kitchen and storerooms were naturally situated in the servants' quarters. The former (11) was easily identified by its hearth; the latter were characterized by large jars, abundant ashes, and quantities of charred barley and other seeds. 1 This was ascertained from two doorsockets found *in situ.* TURKISH GLEANINGS AT ABU HABBA, UNDER SCHEIL AND BEDRY BEV.

The recent awakening of archaeological interest in Turkey, and the gradual appreciation of the literary and artistic monuments of the past on the part of the Mohammedan population, are closely connected with the period of reform and progress inaugurated by Sultan 'Abdul Hamid in different departments of the public administration. For not only was the army reorganized after European patterns, large tracts of fallow land acquired by the crown and rapidly changed into flourishing estates (the so-called *arazi-i-seniye),* railroads constructed and the many natural resources of the country opened and developed, but the public schools were increased, technical colleges and a university established, daily papers appeared and — something formerly entirely unknown in the Ottoman empire — illustrated journals were published, and even a great national museum was founded. The man called upon to carry out the ideas of his sovereign in the field of archaeology was Hamdy Bev, son of Edhem Pasha, a former Grand Vizier. Richly endowed with natural gifts and liberally educated in the congenial atmosphere of France, where his pronounced personal inclinations found ample nourishment in the *Eco/e des Beaux Arts* and in the studios of great painters, he had subsequently entered the service of his own government and gathered considerable experience in prominent positions. Appointed director

of foreign affairs in the vilayet of Baghdad under the famous Midhat Pasha, he had afterwards won the favor of 'Abdul 'Aziz and become introducer of ambassadors, and for a short while even governor of Pera, the European quarter of Constantinople. He had participated in the expedition against the refractory 'Afej tribes of Babylonia and had seen active military life in the Turkish war against Russia. Hamdy Bey being well versed in the general questions of archaeology and not unfamiliar with the most prominent ruins of Western Asia, and widely known for his deep sense of honor and his frank and chivalrous manners, at the same time possessing firmness of character and a rare understanding for the tasks of his mission, it would have been difficult to find a better equipped man as director-general of the Imperial Museum in the whole Ottoman empire.

The beginnings of the Turkish archaeological museum go back to the middle of the last century. Fethi Ahmed Pasha, grand-master of the artillery, then gathered a number of stray antiquities in a room and in the court of the ancient church of St. Irene. Twenty-five years later, when Dr. Dethier was in charge of these modest collections, they were transferred by an imperial *irade* to the quaint little palace of Tshinili Kiosk, one of the best types of early Turkish architecture and faience work in existence. But the subsequent rapid development and phenomenal growth of this embryonic museum into a great archaeological storehouse of international reputation is almost entirely due to the energetic measures and wise administration of Hamdy Bey, who has been its real soul and characteristic central figure. No sooner was he entrusted with the management of the archaeological affairs of his country (1881), than the antiquated and detrimental laws of excavations, under which a national Ottoman museum could not prosper, were radically changed and remodelled. The spacious subterranean vaults of Tshinili Kiosk were carefully searched and long-forgotten monuments rediscovered. System and order began soon to prevail, where formerly nothing was accessible to science. Small as the annual sum proved to be which was placed at Hamdy Bey's disposal for meeting the current expenses and for realizing the many new projects constantly cherished by his active mind, the lofty terrace of the old seraglio with its superb view on the Golden Horn presented an entirely different picture at the close of the nineteenth century. Out of the midst of luxuriant gardens and pleasing alleys adorned with Greek and Roman statues, bas-reliefs, pillars, and tombstones, there rise three magnificent fire-proof buildings filled with rich archaeological treasures open for public inspection, while close by the museum we notice the School of Fine Arts, with its three sections of architecture, sculpture and painting, created to propagate knowledge and love of art and archeology among younger generations.

One cannot but admire the courage and determination of this single man, who,in the face of numerous obstacles thrown in his way by his own countrymen, by dissatisfied explorers and foreign diplomats, was able to accomplish this gigantic task within the short period of twenty years, — a fact even more remarkable when we consider that the inner consolidation of the whole department kept pace with the external growth and development. New sections were created, more officers appointed, a well-equipped library was added, and Compare above. A translation of the present Turkish law on Archaeological Excavations is given in Appendix D of John P. Peters' "Nippur, or Explorations and Adventures on the Euphrates," New York, 1897, vol. i, pp. 303-309. Recently, however, there have again been made certain changes with regard to the relations between the government and private landowners.

Unfortunately the monument known as " Sennacherib Constantinople" was not among these antiquities. Comp. Hilprecht, *Sanherib Constantintpel,* in *Zeitschrift fur Anyrhlogie,* vol. xiii, pp. 322-325, and p. 211,

The Imperial Ottoman Museum at Constantinople *This building contains a representative collection of ancient sarcophagi, and the Babylonian, Assyrian, Egyptian, and early Turkish antiquities.* competent specialists were invited to classify and catalogue the various collections. In order to protect the more exposed monuments carved in the rocks of mountain passes, built in modern bridges and houses, or accidentally found in the ground by the natives, special regulations were drafted, and orders were issued to the officials in the provinces to report new antiquities and to look after their preservation. There is scarcely a branch of archaeology which did not profit in some way by these and similar measures which originated in the brain of Hamdy Bey. The inscribed basrelief of Naram-Sin discovered in 1892, near Diarbekr, the fine alabaster slab of Bel-Harran-bel-usur from Tell Abta (1894), and the important stele of Nabonidos unearthed by the brick-diggers of Babil (1895) indicate some of the more prominent monuments which hereby were saved for Assyriology.

Among them the two brothers of Hamdy Bey, the late Ghalib Bey and Halil Bey, Director of the Imperial Ottoman Museum, for Oriental coins and Moslem antiquities; Prof. Andre Joubin, of Paris, for classical and Byzantine antiquities; Prof. V. Scheil, of Paris, for the Egyptian monuments; Consul J. H. Mordtmann for South-Arabian and Palmyrene antiquities; and Prof. Hilprecht, of the University of Pennsylvania, for the Assyrian and Babylonian collections.

Apart from the numerous antiquities received as gifts, purchased from dealers, and obtained through the personal interest and watchfulness of local governors, the Ottoman Museum drew its principal collections from its own excavations and from the trenches of European and American expeditions in Western Asia. The first tentative Turkish diggings at Nebi Yunus, undertaken more to satisfy curiosity and to secure hidden treasures than to serve the cause of archaeology, were soon followed by the serious exploration of the temple of Hecate at Legina, by Hamdy Bey's and Osgan Effendi's scientific mission to the snowy summit of Nimrud Dagh, by the former's famous discovery in the royal necropolis of Sidon, by Scheil's and Bedry Bey's gleanings at Abu Habba, and by Makridi Bey's recent researches at Bostan esh-Shaikh.-The new spirit of progress and enlightenment which emanated from the palace and which found an eloquent herald in the halls of the Imperial Museum is best characterized by the unique fact that several years ago a young officer of the Turkish army submitted an essay on the Sumerian question to the present writer for criticism. Though leniently to be judged as to its real merits, this manuscript speaks volumes for the far-reaching influence which the cuneiform collections at Stambul exercised as an educational factor upon the minds of intelligent Moslems. No wonder that it was the Sultan himself who became the originator of the first Turkish archaeological expedition to Babylonia. Deeply interested in the epochmaking results of the French and American explorers by which the Imperial Museum had been greatly enriched, His Majesty placed a special sum of money out of his private purse at the disposal of Hamdy Bey for methodical excavations at a Babylonian ruin.

At the request of Hamdy Bey the present writer was commissioned to report to the Ottoman Minister of Public Instruction as to the best manner of protecting the Babylonian and Assyrian relics and mounds. The report was submitted in 1894, and action was soon afterwards taken in accordance with the recommendations. Comp. pp. 68, *seq.;* and Hilprecht, *Turkisctu Bestrebungen auf dem Gebiete der Asssriologie,* in *Kolnische Zeitung,* second supplement of the Sunday edition, March 8, 1896; also Hilprecht, " Recent Researches in Bible Lands," Philadelphia, 1896, pp. 81—93. Comp. p. 211, above. Comp. Hamdy Bey and Osgan Effendi, *Le Tumulus de Ntmrottd-Dagk,* Constantinople, 1883.

Immediately after Rassam's departure from Baghdad in 1882, Arab diggers, encouraged by unscrupulous landowners and antiquity dealers, had commenced their clandestine operations at most of the places where their former employer had successfully excavated. For several years Abu Habba and Der, Kl-Birs and Babylon, thus became the principal sources from which European and American museums were supplied with archaeological contraband. Only a few of these monuments were confiscated and reached the Ottoman Museum. Abu Habba, as was well known to the authorities in Constantinople, proved an especially rich and almost inexhaustible mine for the illegal traffic. It was therefore decided to apply the imperial fund to a renewed examination of the ruins of Sippar, especially as brief but successful excavations had been conducted there previously (1889) by the Civil Cabinet under the control of the governor of Baghdad. The carrying out of this scientific project was entrusted to Father Scheil, a young and energetic French Assyriologist, who had rendered valuable services to the Stambul museum in connection with the organization of the Egyptian and Babylonian sections, and to Bedry Bev, a well-known Turkish commissioner, who had gained no small experience in the trenches of Tello and Nuffar. In the beginning of 1894 this Ottoman commission reached the place of its destination. Strongly supported by the officials of the vilayet, and confining their work chiefly to a search for inscribed monuments, the two men were able to execute their task satisfactorily in the brief space of two months, at the end of which their limited means were exhausted. No complete report of these excavations having yet appeared, we can only sketch the principal results obtained on the basis of Scheil's notes published in Maspero's journal, and in accordance with my own personal knowledge of the collections of the Imperial Museum.

Comp. Hamdy Bey and Th. Reinach, *Une Ketropole rotate a SiJtn, Ftiuillfs de Hamdy Bey,* Paris, 1896. A few miles from Saida (Sidon). Comp. Hilprecht, in "The SundaySchool Times," vol. 43, p. 621 (Sept. 28, 1901), and in *Deutsche Literaturztitung,Nov.* 30, 1901, pp.

3030, *seq.,* and in " Sunday School Times," Dec. 21, 1901, p. 857. Most of the antiquities discovered were lost to the museum in Constantinople. Among the few which were sent are the interesting archaic stone fragment published in Hilprecht, "Old Babylonian Inscriptions, chiefly from Nippur," part I, Philadelphia, 1893, plates vi-viii (comp. also, Scheil in *Recueil de Travaux relatifs a la Philologie et a /' Archeologie egyptiennei et assyriennes,* vol. xxii (1900), pp. 29, *seqq.),* and the brick from a well constructed by Nebuchadrezzar, published *ibidem,* part 2, Philadelphia, 1896, pi. 70. Comp. *Recueil de Travaux relatif a la Philologie et a /' Archeologie egjptiennes et assyriennes,* vol. xvi (1894), pp. 90-9Z, 184, *seqq.,* vol. xvii (1895), pp. 184, *seqq.,* and the following numbers of the same journal. According to a communication from Prof. Scheil, a book on his work at Abu Habba will appear in the course of 1892 in Cairo, under the title *line saissn it fouilles a Sifpar* (with plates, numerous vignettes and a plan of the ruins), and forming vol. I of *Memoires tie /' Institut fratifaii d' Archealogit orientale Ju Cairf.*

Among the objects of mere archaeological interest a number of rude clay animals sitting on their hind legs, and on an average about one foot high, attract our attention. There is, *e.g.,* one which represents a monkey, another a dog, a third a bear, while others are modelled so poorly that it is difficult to say what animals are intended by them. Apparently they belong to the earlier period of Babylonian history and must be regarded as votive offerings, like a neo-Babylonian dog in the same material and from the same ruins, which bears a dedication of two lines of cuneiform inscription to the goddess Gula. Small terra-cotta figurines and bas-reliefs, including images of Shamash and his consort, and the mask of an ugly demon, several utensils and weapons in bronze, the common beads, seal cylinders, stone weights, and other minor antiquities as they are generally found in Babylonian ruins, complete the collection. There are also a few bricks of King Bur-Sin II.

, Kurigalzu, Shamash-shum-ukin and Nebuchadrezzar II. But the most important part of the recovered antiquities are nearly seven hundred clay tablets, complete or fragmentary, most of them letters and contracts dated in the reigns of rulers of the first Babylonian dynasty, especially Samsu-iluna, the son and successor of Hammurabi. Some of the inscriptions are of a literary character and belonged originally to the famous temple library of Sippara. We notice several syllabaries and lists of cuneiform signs, school exercises on round tablets, proverbs, incantations, hymns and two fragments of historical interest. The one reveals to us the name of a new member of the third dynasty of Ur, Idin-Dagan (about 250x5 B. c.), the other contains in chronological order a number of dates from the time of Hammurabi and Samsuiluna, by means of which the single years of their governments were officially designated and known to the people.

Unfortunately, most of the letters discovered contain, according to Scheil, only accounts. But nevertheless there are many among them which bring before our eyes scenes from the daily lives of the ancient Babylonians in such a realistic manner that human conditions and circumstances may seem to have changed but little during the past four thousand years. For example, an official, stationed in a small village, Dur-Sin, complains to his father that it is impossible to procure anything fit to eat, and begs him, therefore, to buy with the accompanying piece of money some food, and send it to him. But let the writer of this epistle speak for himself: "To my father from Zimri-eramma. May the gods Shamash and Marduk keep thee alive forever. May all go well with thee. I write thee to inquire after thy health. Please let me know how it goes with thee. I am stationed in Dur-Sin, on the canal Bitimsikirim. Where I live there is no food which I am able to eat. Here is the third part of a shekel, which I have sealed up, and forward unto thee. Send me for this money fresh fish and other food to eat."

Another letter, addressed to a female

by the name of Bibeya, reads as follows: "To Bibeya from Gimil-Marduk: May Shamash and Marduk grant thee, for my sake, to live forever. I write this in order to inquire after thy health. Let me know how it goes with thee. I am now settled in Babylon, but I am in great anxiety, because I have not seen thee. Send news when thou wilt come, that I may rejoice at it. Come at the month of Arakhsamna NovemberDecember. Mayest thou, for my sake, live forever." It is clear that this letter was not written to a mother, sister, daughter, or any other relative, because, according to Babylonian custom, relationship is generally indicated by a word placed in apposition after the name of the person to whom the letter is addressed. Therefore we can scarcely be wrong in regarding this clay tablet as a specimen of an ancient Babylonian love-letter of the time of Abraham.

Recently published by Scheil in *Textes tlamites-Semitiques* (forming vol. ii. of De Morgan's *Delegation en Perse, Memoires)*, series l, Paris, 1900, p. 83, note 1; and by Lindl in *Beitrage zur Assyriologic,* vol. iv, part 3 (Leipzig, 1901), pp. 341, *seqq.*

Finally, there may be mentioned a small round tablet of the same period, and from the same ruins, which contains, in the Babylonian style, a parallel passage to Daniel 12:3: "They that be wise shall shine as the brightness of the firmament." It has but three lines of inscription written in Sumerian, the old sacred language of that country: — 1 *Sha muntila 1 ki namdupsara-ka* 3 *ugim gena-e* That is, "Whoever distinguishes himself at the place of tablet-writing in other words, at the school or university of the Babylonians shall shine as the day." Semirism for Sumerian *galu.* For the above sketch comp. Hilprecht, "Recent Researches in Bible Lands," Philadelphia, 1896, pp. 81-86.

RESEARCHES IN PALESTINE RESEARCHES IN PALESTINE RESEARCHES IN PALESTINE BY LIC. DR. J. BENZINGER

Palestine became the object of most general interest earlier than any other Oriental country. It was known to Christendom from its earliest days as the "Holy Land," being regarded as the land where God frequently had revealed himself and where sacred history had been enacted. Nevertheless Palestine research is but a child of the century just closed, die systematic exploration of the land in all its aspects beginning, properly speaking, with the foundation of the Knglish Palestine Lxploration Fund in the vear 1865. This late awakening of scientific interest in Palestine is quite in accordance with its associations and with the character of the land, as being a " holy" one.

The so-called Tomb of Absalom

From the time that Christians began to make pilgrimages to Palestine until our own century, the causes that impelled them to do so have been religious. To pray in sacred places was thought particularly meritorious, and extensive indulgences were secured through a visit to them. The interest of the pilgrims was excited, however, only by those places which were pointed out to them as the scenes of sacred events. The knowledge of Palestine which they brought home with them consisted substantially in an enumeration and description of the places that were held in special veneration. Concerning these they wrote for the edification of other Christians and the guidance of future travellers. All this is to-day of inestimable value to those of us who endeavor-to trace accurately the history of the individual sacred places, but it was no scientific exploration of the land.

Besides, during the first centuries of Christendom such a veneration of sacred places was not yet known, — a fact which renders the value of the traditions handed down by the pilgrims practically almost *nil.* To know Christ "after the flesh" seemed to a Paul almost worthless (2 Cor. 5: 16); and the gaze of the first Christians was fixed not backwards but forwards, upon the glorious future; the Jerusalem for which they were looking lay not in Palestine. It was only after the great persecutions during which the Christians had learned to esteem as holy the martyrs and their burial-places, that they also thought of the greatest of martyrs. Only after Christianity had, under Constantine, become the state religion could the Christian Church look upon Palestine as its own possession; and only after Mary came to be quite generally regarded as the mother of God could the cult of the saints and of sacred places blossom forth in all its vigor. It is necessary to keep this in mind in order to understand how tradition — even the oldest and best — is separated from the time of Christ and the Apostles by a gap of well-nigh three hundred years, a striking fact, and one that in the interest of Palestine research is in many ways deeply to be deplored.

How supremely indifferent that early period was towards such historical spots, and how completely their exact location was forgotten, is best illustrated by the history of the chief sacred place of Christianity, the Sepulchre of Christ. In his letter to Makarius, the emperor Constantine regards the discovery of the cross and sepulchre of Christ as a miracle; and according to still later accounts the empress Helena needed a divine inspiration in order to find the holy sepulchre. Not even the situation of this spot could therefore be given with certainty at that time; much less, then, were men still able to point out other less important places. Jerusalem had become a new city; the old one lay deep under ruins. And yet, in spite of this, tradition thrived, and became the most prolific source of legends. From century to century the number of sacred places increased, while the more important ones were gradually surrounded by a web of tradition so dense as almost to defy disentanglement. We cannot blame the monks of the Middle Ages who, often in good faith, were constantly finding new sacred places. The pilgrims compelled them so to do, and did not cease compelling them until they were shown the precise spot for everything imaginable. This sort of tradition was in a certain sense terminated in the sixteenth century, when the scholar Francesco Quaresmio collected and reduced the existing material to writing in his great work *Elucidatio Terr Sanct.* That tradition has, however, not become entirely torpid, but that it still possesses enough vitality to send forth new shoots, has been strikingly demonstrated in the last few years. Scarcely had the German Kmperor presented to the German Catholics a piece of land on Zion, where tradition locates the so-called *Dormitio, i. e.* the place of Mary's demise, when it was loudly proclaimed that the place of the *Ccenaculum,* where Christ celebrated the Last Supper with his disciples, is to be sought there.

These historical antecedents of Palestine research must be kept in view in order to understand the peculiar development of our knowledge of Palestine as a science in our century. This development had to begin with a struggle against these overpowering traditions, and this struggle above all made manifest the need of undertaking a reliable geographical and scientific exploration of the land, the results of which would for all time to come put an end to the making of fables. Even the excavations in Jerusalem were performed in the interests of topography, having for their object the determining of the course of the walls and other important points; and in the case of not a few questions the contention in regard to the authenticity of sacred places has been the starting-point and goal of the discussions. Over against these the excavations undertaken purely in the interests of archaeology were accorded only a secondary place, although the finds, few in number, were so much the more weighty in significance.

It does not lie within the scope of this sketch to refer to all the self-sacrificing and enthusiastic men who have given their strength to the exploration of the Holy Land; nor is it even possible in a brief treatise to make mention of all the important results, or to describe the methods by which these have been reached. We shall therefore limit ourselves to an enumeration of only those very important results in the fields of labor mentioned which will serve best at the same time to show what is the task of the future; and to the presentation here and there of an illustration typical of the manner in which the investigators worked.

TOPOGRAPHY

In the year 1841 there appeared, in three volumes, the work entitled " Biblical Researches," in which an American, Edward Robinson, professor of theology in New York, gave the results of his travels in Palestine during the year 1838. The book was looked upon, by the few who at that time made a careful study of Palestine, as the turning point in the whole matter of Palestine research. No one felt this more keenly than Titus Tobler, the father of German Palestinian research. He was at first somewhat depressed bv the thought that the problem to the solution of which he had for years applied all his energies now seemed to be almost entirely solved by another man. But Tobler after all still found a rich field in which to work, and to this day Palestinian research has never been embarrassed for lack of problems to solve. Nevertheless it is quite true that Robinson's work marked the beginning of a new era in our knowledge of Palestine.

What was it that made the man and his book so important and placed them at the beginning of a new departure in the development of this branch of science?

Robinson himself found that in all former descriptions by travellers two defects were inherent. In the first place, travellers simply followed the footsteps of the monks. It made little difference whether thev were Catholics or Protestants. Almost all, *e. g.,* in Jerusalem, were entertained in the monasteries. The monks served as their guides; and from the great storehouse of the monasteries they obtained their information. The majority of them were also rather credulous as regards the things that were told them. Thus it comes that their accounts are substantially alike. Even when one had his doubts as to the trustworthiness of a tradition, he was unable to furnish anything better than the questionable tales from the monasteries. Robinson, on the contrary, from the first took the position that only such ecclesiastical tradition is to be regarded of value as is authenticated by the testimony of the Holy Scriptures; or in other

words, only that which is traceable to contemporaries and which has been constant from the beginning.

The other mistake was that travellers were ignorant of the Arabic language and could hold intercourse with the people only through interpreters; accordingly thev never stepped off from the well-beaten paths which all their predecessors had trodden. In this way the valuable traditions, which still continued to live among the people, escaped them. Robinson found such sound traditions preserved especially in the names of places. The Semitic names have maintained themselves with remarkable tenacity among the Semitic population of Palestine, even where the Romans endeavored to replace them with new names. Lvdda, Kmmaus, Accho, Bethshean, and many other places for a time bore Roman names (Diospolis, Nikopolis, Ptolemais, Skvthopolis), but with the downfall of the Roman government these names almost entirely disappeared. Only the towns Shechem and Samaria form an exception, their Roman names Neapolis and Sebaste still remaining in an Arabicized form (Nablus and Sebastiye). Robinson could appreciate the value of these traditions and understood how to make them render service. His companion at that time was F.li Smith, an American missionary in Beirut, well versed in linguistic knowledge. For years he had industriously gathered proper names, from every available source, in order that when the opportunity came on his journeys he might test them on the spot. His trained ear kept him from hearing out of the mouths of the Arabs the frightful monstrosities which had hitherto been paraded before the reader in almost all works on Palestine.

Viewing their task from this standpoint, both of them travelled over the entire Holy Land. The first journey was from Egypt to Sinai, thence by way of Akabah and Hebron to Jerusalem, where they remained for a time. After making a complete tour of Judea, they continued their journey by way of Nazareth and Tiberias to Beirut. A second journey followed fourteen years later

(1852), which took the investigators especially through Galilee and Samaria, upon the Lebanon range, and to Damascus.

Neither of these two journeys consumed quite four months, yet an amazingly large amount of new and hitherto unknown material was collected; for bv preference the explorers travelled over unfrequented ways, which lay apart from the great highways of the pilgrims. With ceaseless industry they worked, always accurately measuring the distances, and describing the route, even to the smallest details, so minutely that with their book as a guide one imagines he could here and there find his way without the aid of chart or compass. Wherever possible they took angle-measurements of the more important localities; their measuring rod was constantly in their hand; and, whether they examined the walls of Jerusalem, or inspected a house, or saw a pool or wll, everything was measured in the most exact manner. They were the first to crawl through the Siloam conduit (see below), which they did with great difficulty, part of the way sliding on their stomachs in the water. More important still than the number of new observations is the circumstance that everything which was observed and described had been thoroughly and reliably investigated. Thus was laid the foundation upon which, without fear or doubt, the further researches could rest.

As an historical topographer Titus Tobler perhaps accomplished still more than Robinson. He made his first journey to Palestine in his early years merely as an amateur, and soon after he had begun the practice of medicine in the mountains of the Canton of Appenzell. But this pleasure trip, while it served to excite his interest and to afford him instruction, did not satisfy his thoroughgoing spirit of investigation. Hence when he had reached home he at once began the study of Palestinian literature, at the same time unceasingly and indefatigably collecting, reading, and excerpting whatever accounts of pilgrimages and travels he was able to obtain. In a manner hitherto unattained, he mas-

tered the literature that in his day dealt with the sphere which he had chosen for himself. This sphere had in course of time become somewhat restricted. After studying Robinson's epoch-making work, he concentrated his labor mainly upon Judea; for he soon recognized that here even after Robinson's researches, as far as the history and topography of sacred places were concerned, there remained still enough to be done.

In the autumn of 1845 started on his second journey, and remained in Jerusalem for twenty weeks. The results thereof he recorded in seven volumes, numbering altogether 3753 Pg-Supported by his very extensive reading, Tobler sought to give the most complete historical proofs for all his observations; and consequently his works contain the history of all places and monuments investigated by him, so far as this is possible. To this very day, he who desires to concern himself with the history of these places must begin with Tobler's investigations. Moreover, his historical presentations excite special interest because they enable us to trace the rise and growth of legends, in the frequently peculiar yet at the same time so significant variations of tradition that mark the development of the history of civilization. Besides this Tobler mercilessly exposes the credulity and lively imagination of so many modern travellers, and their pious or poetic phrases. He allows nothing to pass but a clear, sober, precise description of what actually exists, just as he himself takes pains to give a purely objective and trustworthy account of the condition of things as he found them.

Accordingly we owe to him the first thorough and clear description of the Church of the Sepulchre and of the sacred places surrounding it, a description which makes clear to us the sepulchre's confused construction and its still more complicated conditions of ownership. In order to come to an independent judgment regarding the Holy Sepulchre, he undertook an extensive investigation of the ancient Jewish tombs surrounding the city, and thus was the first to disclose to science these most remarkable and most genuine monuments of an an-

cient period. To him we are also indebted for the first correct map of the network of streets in Jerusalem with their native names.

A third journey, in the year 1857, was devoted above all to the exploration of Judea. It showed how little was hitherto really known of this section of the land, how scarcely a single one of the characteristic, deep-cut valleys was correctly indicated on the maps, and how the whole traditionaJ view of a " barren and desolate " Judea was entirely erroneous.

On his last journey, in the year 1865, Tobler, then nearly sixty years of age, intended to explore Nazareth in the same thorough manner, but cholera interfered with his journey to that place. Nevertheless he succeeded, by means of numerous inquiries, in informing himself so extensively that his book on Nazareth is not inferior to his other works.

Besides what he observed and found in the land itself, we must not forget what he accomplished at home in investigating the old descriptions of travels. One of his favorite wishes was to publish all descriptions of travels from the third to the fifteenth century in the most carefully edited form possible. This project he could, however, carry out only in a fragmentary way, and mostly at his own expense. His excellent annotations made a number of the old writings for the first time really serviceable. To him belongs the honor of being to this day unsurpassed, so far as knowledge of the Palestine of the Middle Ages and modern times is concerned.

If, after reading the great mass of early Palestinian literature, one turns to the works of Robinson and Tobler, he gets the impression that these two men had really been the first to discover the land. As remarked above, onlv a very small part of the many hundred names of places was previously known. Through these investigators it was also first discovered that something was to be seen and learned in the Holy Land besides the sacred places which the monks pointed out to pilgrims; that in addition to the Christian Church and the monasteries it was also worth while to concern oneself about the customs and manners of the people, the nature of the soil and climate, and many other things. How much Palestine itself could still contribute to a better understanding of the Bible is clearly shown in their books. But these also made it evident that Palestine was still to a great extent an unknown land, waiting to be explored according to the principles and with the thoroughness of these two pioneers.

II THE GEOGRAPHICAL SURVEY OF THE LAND

The land that first felt the new impulse was England. Here it was first realized that only now the real beginning of the systematic exploration of Palestine was to be made, that such a task was beyond the power of individual travellers, and that in general such isolated research, devoid of system and unity, had no great value.

In the year 1865 a number of friends of Palestine met in London and organized a society known as the Palestine Exploration Fund. Its object was to be the complete systematic and scientific exploration of the Holy Land, and thus above all to aid in elucidating the Scriptures. Nevertheless the society did not profess to be a religious society, and proposed to do its work along strictly scientific lines. The idea was taken up with great enthusiasm. Within the first three years the munificent sum of. £8,000 (about $40,000) was voluntarily contributed, and with great expectations the first expedition, under Captain Wilson, proceeded to the Holy Land. They hoped to be able in a few years to solve all problems and to bring to an end the thorough exploration of Palestine, — an error indeed, but a pardonable one. Only as the exploration progressed was it discovered how many questions remained to be answered.

The standard work that the Palestine Exploration Fund accomplished was the geographical survey of the land. Such a survey had become a pressing necessity. To what extent former maps, even the best of Robinson, Van de Velde and others, were unreliable was made very evident by a comparison with the results of this first survey. Scarcely a place was

altogether correctly located, not a line of hills was accurately marked, no valley course was properly placed, and not one indicated distance was reliable. It could not be otherwise; for leaving the coast surveys of the admiralty out of consideration, there were lacking everywhere thoroughly trustworthy astronomical determinations of the location of places. The distances were estimated and indicated according to the time consumed by the individual travellers on their way. In addition, only a small fraction, about one sixth of all the names, were marked at all on the two above-mentioned maps. The English expedition was on the field from the year 1872 until the summer of 1875, again from 1877 till 1878, under the leadership of Captain Conder and Lieutenant (now Lord) Kitchener. The whole country west of the Jordan was carefully surveyed. Not only was every place, every little valley, and every hill indicated, but also every road and every spring. All wells and cisterns of any significance were recorded; and all the old structures and graves which were found were measured and sketched. The ground was literally searched foot after foot, and more recent explorers have scarcely succeeded in making anv important additions. Numberless plans and sketches bear witness to the industry and carefulness of the workers.

The results are put on record in the great map of the country west of the Jordan and in the memoirs which fill four stately volumes. A few figures will help to show the value of the work. Over 10,000 names are entered upon the map, while the Index General of Robinson contains onlv 1712. Before the expedition was sent out, it was believed The same who is at present *(* 1 go 1) commander in chief of the English troops in South Africa. — The Editor.

that about *6a r,f* ok -arches enabled him to brinl foTM "-fijoas, so that would Low *"TM* TMB.bhca places. As *TM* " o-thirds of the regards the proposed identifications there

W of course mh chaff ie with e wheat, many of '" not having stood the test in the *ght of* sober sci - may forced be

said that in TM aspect our knowledge of the topography of the 'v Land has not yet advanced much 'ond its begin'gs- The names h'ch can be identified with comnlere . ""ipiete-nirum, near Tyre certaintv *lac* A- numLyXn possible, are n. 'hese.dentifications attempted S' "' greater value that historical*Z* FT " undat,o,, in this exact surfevTu ? «ou,,d TM vve have a trustworthy and ev " ' ole district as it is to-day *of T* ation of the names, of the old *rutlsTTM* ' » Pnngs and *dJfc* of commerce, systeat,c treatment of Biblik," t " P« correct dec.s.on regarding the situation of a place is conditioned not merely by a knowledge of its name and of the site of its supposed ruins, but to an equal extent by the consideration of the roads and of the general contour of the ground. According to the statement of distances given in the " Peutingerian Tables" and others, the ancient Capitolias, an important city of the East-Jordanic country, should be looked for on the road from Gadara to Adraha, /. ?., to the east or northeast of Gadara. An accurate survey of the ground by Schumacher within the last few years has shown, however, that this road never could have run due east, but that deepcut ravines with almost perpendicular sides lying between both cities, compelled the road to make a considerable circuit to the south. Consequently we find the city looked for to the southeast of Gadara, in the ruins of the present Bet Ras, the important remains of which leave no doubt that here at one time a great and flourishing city existed.

The survey of the country west of the Jordan was to be followed by that of the country east of the river, and in 1881 Captain Conder set out once more. It was hoped that the old firman of the Ottoman government would still hold good. This was however not the case. After a few weeks, work Conder received peremptory orders from the governor of Es-Salt to suspend work. By means of somewhat protracted negotiations Conder succeeded in gaining a little time; and when he was finally obliged to return he took home with him abundant material. Five hundred English square miles had been surveyed, and hundreds of plans, sketches and photographs had been made, so that a stately volume of memoirs could be published. The surveyed region lies in the southern part of the land, the old Moabite cities Heshbon, Elealeh, and Medeba, and Mount Nebo, forming the central point.

What the English, in this way, did not succeed in doing, the German Palestine Society took up in the last decade, with better success. This society was likewise founded (in the year 1878) for the purpose of making a strictly scientific exploration of the Holy Land. For the geographical surveys of the land itself it acquired a valuable expert in the person of Dr. Schumacher in Haifa. In the year 1884 he undertook the survey of the Jolan, a stretch of country extending to the east of the lakes of Tiberias and Hule as far as the plain of Bashan. In the following year this survey was pursued still farther towards the south (south of the Yarmuk). The publication in 1886 of the map of the Jolan, with a detailed description of this district, was followed in 1897 by the map of Southern Bashan, which includes the land towards the east as far as the mountains of I l.iur.m, so difficult of access. Since the year 1889 we have been in possession of the first map of the latter prepared by the hand of a specialist.)r. Stiibel, the geologist, visited the region in the year 1882. On the basis of his surveys, and by utilizing all other Accessible material, the German Palestine Society was enabled to have a map prepared which, diverging widely from fcrmeV representations, for the first time offered a true picture of-this region. The numerous lava fields of varying size and iform, the broad and flat top of the mountain range in great measure volcanic, and the long level valleys *of* old Bashan are the characteristic features of this region so extraordinarily interesting as regards geography and especially geology.

These regions in the northern part of the East-Jordanic territory indeed form but to a small c:xtent part of the land of Israel proper, but they are often mentioned in the Old Testament. The Hau-

ran range is mentioned in Psalm 68: 14, under its old name of Salmon, preserved among the Greeks in the form Asalmanos; and in the same psalm (verse 15) it is designated as a "gable-range," an appellation which strikingly characterizes the form of the range as we now know it. Mention is also frequently made of Bashan, the fertile pasture-district with its magnificent oxen; of the strong cities of King Og, As(h)taroth and Kdrei; and of other places, like Golan, Salchah, Kenath, etc. A large portion of the region between the Yarmuk and Jabbok is already surveyed, and the map is in preparation. Here again a single glance at the new maps will serve to show in how many respects our previous conception regarding this region was altogether faulty. The lists of names, containing new and entirely unknown material to a far greater extent than those of the country west of the Jordan, offer rich subject-matter for historical geographers to work upon.

The English Version renders the Hebrew *har gabhnvmnm* inaccurately by "an high hill (mountain)." —The Editor. The great significance of an accurate knowledge of ancient Gilead for the understanding of the Bible does not need to be specially emphasized With the same painstaking care observed by the English in the country west of the Jordan, Dr. Schumacher L.re collected all manner of antiquities that came under his vnotce. It is to be hoped that the further labors of the Geri Palestine Societv on this territory will be attended wit ,h the uame successful results, and that within a few years jwe shall i act description of the whole of Palesti,. j,ot', 'des of the Jordan, from Lebanon down to tle southern en of the Dead Sea.

r j in r JERUSALEM

That to a certain extent Jerusalem has always been looked upon as tjne centre of Palestinian research is not strange. For thfe correct understanding of h' city, like few o thers, imposes upon us the ny *of* acquiring an accurate knowledge of its topog'Py- this city Jiopographieal research also meets v' " *J* mous difficulties as are found nowhere else.

These grow out of the city's history. More frequently than any other city has Jerusalem been conquered, and destroyed, and almost levelled to the ground; and upon the ruins of the old a new city always rose again. In many places the debris that conceals the old city from our sight is over 100 feet deep. Laborious and expensive excavations are therefore everywhere necessary in order to arrive at any degree of certitude regarding the form of the ancient city. In many

Herod's Temple, 30 B. c., according to the Model by Dr. Schick places these are impossible, inasmuch as upon the debris the new houses of the modern city have been built, underneath which digging cannot be done.

Owing to the fanaticism of the populace which compelled the government to withhold its permission, no excavations could be made during the first half of the nineteenth century. Good luck, however, led to many discoveries. The building of a new house, the walling up of a cistern and like operations afforded opportunities for seeing something of the ground beneath Jerusalem, and thus many interesting facts came to light. The indefatigable German architect Dr. Schick, like a faithful watchman, kept an eye on all such opportunities and improved them to the utmost. He has now resided in Jerusalem for over fifty years, and is still with youthful ardor observing everything that is likely to throw light on ancient Jerusalem. He has neglected nothing worth seeing, and has carefully surveyed, sketched, and recorded everything that came under his notice. Thus in the course of years an abundance of material has been gathered. During the last decades the work has also been facilitated by the willingness of the government to permit excavations, a privilege of which the English and the German Palestine societies availed themselves, so far as their means allowed.

It is due to all these circumstances that in the last few years our knowledge of ancient Jerusalem has made sufficient progress to enable us to come to a substantial agreement regarding a number of points of fundamental importance. It is now no longer disputed that the Temple of Solomon stood on the east hill, about where the present "Dome of the Rock " *(Qubbat es-Sak/ ira),* also called the Mosque of'Omar, stands, or that the site of the Church of the Holy Sepulchre corresponds with that of the old Basilica of the Resurrection. Only twenty years ago Fergusson still maintained that the Sepulchre of Christ was under the Mosque of'Omar, and that the Temple stood on the southwest corner of the present Haram.

In order to come to a clear understanding of the chief points in dispute, let us picture to ourselves the city's site. Jerusalem is situated on a calcareous plateau, waterless and unfertile, a tongue of land, as it were, nearly 900 acres in size. It is surrounded on three sides by deep-cut ravines. The valley of the Kidron runs on the east and northeast sides, separating the plateau of Jerusalem, first from the so-called Scopus, and secondly from the Mount of Olives. In its upper course, to the north of the city, it is broad and flat, but at the northeast angle of the city begins to become an increasingly deep and narrow ravine, with tolerably precipitous sides. The valley of Hinnom starts in a flat depression to the west of the city, runs at first parallel with the west wall of the city towards the south, and then — rapidly deepening — curves toward the east and unites with the valley of the Kidron at the so-called "Well of Job," the old Fount of the Fuller (En-rogel, Joshua 15: 7). At this point the valleys have already fallen 348 feet below the level of the Temple area.

The site of the ancient city lying between these two valleys has undergone important changes in its configuration by reason of the vast accumulations of debris. As a matter of fact the tongue of land above mentioned began to split north from the present city wall, and a considerable depression, running from north to south, divided the whole limestone mass into two parts. The westerly and wider part, the traditional Zion,is 108 feet higher than the easterly part, the traditional Moriah, which declines

very precipitously to the east and west. This valley is not mentioned in the Old Testament; in the works of Josephus it is called Tyropoeon. To-day it is almost entirely filled up with rubbish, only a slight trough still revealing its course. Excavations at the southwest corner of the present Haram have shown that the ancient watercourse lies 42 to 46 feet under the level of the ground as it is to-day. It is chiefly due to the excavations of Warren that the course of this vallev, which is of fundamental importance in establishing the topography of Jerusalem, has been made known to us. Robinson and Tobler, for instance, in the preparation of their otherwise fundamental works on the topography of Jerusalem, did not have an exact idea like this of the original configuration of the ground.

Further down, the two ridges just mentioned were again split by cross valleys into separate spurs, the west ridge being divided by a small side valley of the Tyropoeon, coming from the west, into a northerly half connecting with the high land, and into a southerly isolated half. The east ridge broke into three spurs. The northerly one, also connected with the Plateau in the north, was separated from the south by a depression which, running through under the northeast corner of the present Temple place, opened into the Kidron valley; the second or middle spur, the Temple hill proper, was separated from the third southerly spur by a small ravine. The former existence of the latter depression was first disclosed through the excavations of the German Palestine Society.

A word must be said with regard to the ancient names of these hills. It is a fact acknowledged lately, even on the Catholic side, that the name Zion belongs to the east hill of Jerusalem and not to the west hill. Through a misunderstanding of the Biblical references, tradition has with great persistency applied the name Moriah to the lower but more precipitous east hill, and the name Zion to the higher and flatter west hill. These two names, however, designate one and the same hill, the mount on which the Temple stood, on which also

the palace of David and Solomon and the City of David are to be sought. The results of the excavations and the examination of the ground have made it possible, with still greater accuracy, to determine the location of the palaces of David and Solomon, though not a trace of these buildings has been found.

The ancient east hill, whose original form as it now lies buried under debris has been ascertained with reasonable accuracy by means of excavations, is an extraordinarily narrow arm of the high plateau. Of its three spurs or» elevations only the middle one, on which the present Haram stands, has a fairly level surface of any considerable extent, or that could be readily made so. This is about 330 feet long and 130 to 165 feet wide. In situation this area corresponds with the middle of the present Haram. It was a place adapted by nature for a great complex of buildings. Everywhere else on the east hill, even in the most favorable case, gigantic substructures would have been necessary, in order to provide only a small level surface. Of such, on a large scale, we cannot think. It was Herod who, according to the accounts of Josephus, first built the large substructures which are still in existence. We must rather assume that the entire plan of construction accommodated itself as much as possible to the exigencies of the ground. This being so, the palace of Solomon with its various buildings can have been situated only to the southeast of the Temple, in the direction of the ridge. From the northwest corner, the place of the ancient Antonia, the surface of the rock steadily and very considerably declines to the southeast. Consequently the palace buildings lay somewhat lower than the Temple. A person went up from the palace to the Temple (compare Jeremiah 26:10 and many other passages.) On the other hand, it is said that Solomon brought the ark up from the old City of David to the new sanctuary, and that Pharaoh's daughter came up to the new women's house; therefore Solomon's palace lay higher up than the City of David. The latter, identical with the ancient Jebus *(i* Sam. 5:6 among other passages), therefore lay still further to the southeast on the most southerly of the three spurs or elevations of Zion. Here also was an entirely suitable place for a mighty fortress. Although somewhat higher and wider, the western hill was readily accessible from the northwest, and the slopes to the south and east were by no means particularly steep. On the contrary, the statement that " the blind and lame were able to keep an enemy at a distance" (2 Sam. 5:6) fits the almost perpendicularly precipitous rock sides of the eastern hill very well. The question of the water supply must also have had decisive influence in establishing the ancient stronghold of the Jebusites and the City of David at this particular place. While the western hill is over a large area entirely waterless and without a spring of any kind, there gushes forth at the eastern base of the eastern hill the copious perennial St. Mary's Well, as it is now called, which doubtless corresponds to the ancient Gihon (i Kings i:*33)*.

The two great problems of the topography of Jerusalem, with which all other important questions are really more or less connected, are the questions in regard to the course of the city wall and the genuineness of the Church of the Sepulchre. These are themselves again closely connected with each other, for the answering of the latter question depends to a certain degree on the determination of the course of the wall. The excavations of the English and German Palestine societies in the last two decades have primarily had for their object this fixing of the course of the wall. Neither problem has yet been solved, but on some important points certainty has nevertheless been reached by the past excavations.

The city, as Josephus tells us, was protected by three walls. To speak more accurately, the wall on the southern half was single, the steep slopes of the hills and the deepcut ravines forming a natural defence for the city. It was different in the north, where the plateau of the city connects with the remaining highland; here there was always unobstructed access, on account of which the city

on that side required especially strong fortifications. With the growth of the city there arose here in the course of time three lines of wall.

The first wall is the one that ran around the city at the most remote period. As Nehemiah in rebuilding the wall kept to the old line, the wall of the pre-exilic city corresponds to his wall. Through the various excavations the course of this wall on the southern half has now been completely established. According to Josephus, it started on the west from the place of the later Hippicus, the present David's Tower, at the citadel near the Jaffa Gate. While Bishop Gobat's school was being built on the southwestern part of the west ridge, remains of a wall were found, which Tobler correctly assigned to the oldest wall. A little to the south of this, Maudslay, in 1874, found the artificially cut off" scarp of rock which here supported the wall. In making his excavations in the southeast of the Haram area on the socalled hill of Ophel, Warren likewise found a considerable portion of the wall. Farther south from the latter, also on the east side of the eastern hill, Guthe discovered various portions of it. But most important of all is the fact that the latest excavations of the English Palestine Exploration Fund under the direction of Bliss, in the year 1897, restored the connection between these points in the southwest corner as well as the southeast.

Accordingly the old city wall ran around the southern edge of the western hill, and then crossed the Tyropicon valley running eastward in a tolerably straight line, the southeast corner of the wall being close by the old pool of Siloam, which lay within the city wall. Thence the wall ran up on the east side of the eastern hill to the southeast corner of the present Haram and apparently outside this area, to the Golden Gate at the east side of the Haram wall. The course of the wall on the north, though not similarly established by excavations, is nevertheless in the main indicated by the condition of the ground. It could follow only the above-mentioned side valley of the Tyropoeon at the edge

of the hill, and then cross the valley where it was somewhat level, so as to join the west wall of the Temple. This part of the first wall was not restored by Nehemiah, but his wall here rather followed the course of the so-called second wall.

The second wall, built by Hezekiah, had its starting-point on the west at the Gate of Gennat close to the Tower of Phasael, which, somewhat to the east of the Hippicus, protected the Palace of Herod. Here traces of the wall still exist. It has likewise been definitely ascertained that its terminus is near the present Antonia in the northwest corner of the temple area. Regarding the portion of the wall between, the discussion is, however, still very animated. The question is whether the wall ran from the Tower of Phasael in a narrow curve south and east of the present Church of the Sepulchre, or with a greater curve north of the church, corresponding in part to the modern city wall. On this question depends also another concerning the genuineness of the Church of the Sepulchre, in so far as every possibility of its genuineness is excluded from the start, if the Church of the Sepulchre is situated within this wall. For according to the express testimony of the Bible Golgotha must have been situated outside the city wall (comp. John 19:17, Heb. 13: 12, and elsewhere).

In spite of the claims made by those who advocate the genuineness of the Church of the Sepulchre and who contend for the southward course of the second wall, the question must nevertheless be looked upon as still entirely undecided. Schick rests his theory, that the wall ran south and east of the Church of the Sepulchre, substantially upon

Russian Exploration near the Holy Sepulchre the new discoveries which were made bv the Russian Palestine Society in connection with the excavations for the Hospice east of the Church of the Sepulchre. These are parts of an ancient ditch hewn out of the natural rock, together with the remains of walls. Schick regards these as remains of the second wall and of the city moat. His explanation, however, is not convincing in it-self, and there stand opposed to it im-portant considerations of a general na-ture. The elevation of the modern Gol-gotha and, more important still, the dominating hill at the northwest corner *of* the present city wall, are thus left lying outside the second wall, which would have run pretty far down along the slope of the excluded northern el-evation of the west hill. And had this been the course of the wall, Jerusalem could in no wise have accommodated its great population at the time of Christ, even if we place the number much low-er than Josephus, who in one place speaks of 2,700,000 people celebrating the Passover festival. For this very rea-son Robinson first maintained that this second wall ran farther north, a consid-erable part corresponding with the pre-sent city wall, in which various remains of ancient walls have likewise been dis-covered.

These latter are explained by the cham-pions of the genuineness of the Holy Sepulchre as belonging to the third wall. This wall, which branched *off* near the Hippicus, was built by Agrippa I. in or-der to include the northern suburb with-in the city limits. It was constructed of huge square stones, and is said to have had ninety towers. The strongest of these was the so-called Psephinus, at the northwest corner, at the highest point of the city, apparently still preserved in the so-called castle of Goliath, at least in the substructures. The wall was not completed, the emperor forbidding its continuation. Those that would extend the second wall on the north up to the present city wall must allow the third wall to extend farther to the north, where Robinson discovered, at an av-erage distance of 440-550 yards from the present wall, great blocks of stone which he explained as remains of a wall. The whole question can be decid-ed only through renewed excavations. In the interest of an exact topography of Jerusalem it would be a great pity if the investigations in this region should be prematurely concluded and the question at issue considered definitely solved.
The strictly archaeological material that

the excavations have thus far brought to light cannot of course be compared with the rich discoveries that have been made in Egypt and Babylonia. This in part is due to the fact that the excavations were mostly pursued with the fixed pur-pose of determining the topography of Jerusalem. Royal tombs as in Egypt, or such vast buildings and ostentatious in-scriptions as in Egypt and in Babylo-nia, have not yet been brought to light, as can be readily understood. To a cer-tain degree they will never be found in Palestine, inasmuch as the Jews were and are a people without art. One cannot escape a feeling of envy when he con-trasts with the poverty of the Palestinian monuments the new discoveries which are, for instance, continually made in Egypt, and which gradually give an un-broken picture of the whole develop-ment of the mental life of the people. It can be confidently asserted, however, that the soil of Palestine also still con-tains within its bosom much that is valu-able. If the Moabite king Mesha perpet-uated his great exploits on stone, a Jer-oboam II. or a Hezekiah may have done the same thing. The places in which such inscriptions must be supposed to exist, *e. g.,* Samaria, are as yet quite unexplored. Just as Tell el-Hesy, one of the few mounds so far excavated, at once yielded an unexpected result, so many others in the land may hide de-stroyed cities under the surface.

In the spring of 1890 Flinders Petrie, who had become famous through the magnificent results of his excavations in Egypt, was sent to Palestine by the Eng-lish Palestine Exploration Fund, in or-der to search for the site of the ancient Lachish, which was supposed to be rep-resented by

Umm Lakis. Petrie soon saw that nothing was to be found there and ac-cordingly commenced work on a mound in the neighborhood, called Tell el-Hesy, which seemed to him to promise particularly good results. He was not disappointed. Though he found neither splendid buildings nor inscrip-tions, he nevertheless succeeded in bringing to view the successive periods of the history of Lachish in the layers of

debris which lay one upon the other. At the top, almost on the surface, he came upon remains of Greek times of about 450 B. c. Deep underneath, forty-five feet below ground, he uncovered ruins of the time of the eighteenth Egyptian dynasty, *i. e.,* about 1400 B. c. In the middle, twenty feet under the surface, the potsherds he discovered proved to be Old-Phenician, belonging to about the ninth century. The fact here strik-ingly brought out, that in each century the height of the debris increased on an average five feet, was likewise con-firmed wherever Petrie took the depth as an index for the age. The picture of the city so often destroyed and rebuilt, rose anew before the eves of the ex-plorer. The ramparts of the oldest pe-riod, behind which the inhabitants per-haps sought protection against the Egyptian invasions, are no less dis-cernible than the walls of a higher stra-tum, which may be the fortifications of Rehoboam mentioned in the Bible (2 Chron. 11:9). New walls again arose on the top of these, till finally Ne-buchadrezzar besieged and no doubt al-so destroyed the city, about 590 B. c. (Jer. 34: 7). After that the city was left without walls. The discoveries show that it was still populated as an open city after the return of the Jews in the second half of the fifth century, but only to be-come desolate again in a short time. The settlement, it appears, was soon trans-ferred from here to another place.

After the excavations in tracing the course of the wall at Jerusalem (comp. above, pp. *bo2,seqq.*) were completed, the English Palestine Exploration Fund in 1899 and 1900 continued the explora-tion of the numerous mounds by making excavations at Tell Zakariya and Tell es-Safi, in the socalled Schephelah, on the western slope of the mountains of Judea, toward the sea. The first-named place is usually supposed to be the Azekah of the Old Testament, a forti-fication of Judah, built by Rehoboam (2 Chron. 11:9), and besieged by Ne-buchadrezzar (Jer. 34: 7). Here the ex-cavations again revealed many interest-ing and important facts regarding the history of the place. Even in pre-Israelitish times it was inhabited; in the time of Israel it was twice fortified, and also for a short time occupied by the Romans.

The other mount, Tell es-Safi, is by many scholars believed to mark a still more celebrated spot of the ancient world, namely, the old Philistian city of Gath. Unfortunately the excavations have disclosed no inscriptions nor anything similar to substantiate this theory. In fact no inscriptions were found; yet even here, the deposits of the debris, and the earthen vessels imbedded in the different layers, go to show that the place was uninterruptedly inhabited from the earliest pre-exilic time until the late Greek period, and that in Israelitic times it must have been an important fortification. Insignificant as the relics found at these places may seem, consisting, as they do, only of clay vessels, potsherds, small images, etc., they nevertheless demonstrate in a most interesting way that Mycenean art at one time extended its influence even into these regions of Southern Palestine.

The most recent excavations of the Palestine Exploration Fund were again in charge of Dr. Bliss, assisted by Mr. Stewart Macalister. In the course of 1900 they were carried on at Tell ej-Judaida and Tell Sandahanna. In connection with the former, the recovery of thirty-seven jar-handles with royal stamps showing the names of four different towns (one of which is otherwise unknown) must be regarded as the most important find. It was unfortunate that the English Exploration Fund, after a successful examination of but a small portion of the whole area of this interesting ruin, abandoned Tell ej-Judaida again, without having been able to identify the name of the ancient town which occupied this place at the time of the Hebrew kings.

Short as the excavations at Sandahanna (so-called from the neighboring ruined church of St. Anne) were, they have furnished a complete picture of the appearance of a Jewish town of the Seleucidan times, with its gates, streets, open places and houses. It also became evident, from a clearing of an area of fifty

feet by thirty feet carried down to the rock, that an earlier Jewish town going back to about 800 B. c. previously occupied this site. Of especial importance is the discovery of fifty tablets of soft limestone, inscribed in Greek and Hebrew (four of them), and sixteen small figures in lead representing chained men and women. Not without reason Bliss is inclined to identify the excavated site with the ruins of Mareshah (Josh. 15: 44), which seems to have had a continuous history from pre-Israelitish times until the first century of our era.

No less do the other discoveries which have been made give grounds for high hopes. In the year 1868 a German minister, the Rev. F. Klein, discovered at Diban, the ruins of the ancient Dibon (Daibon), royal city of Moab, a large stone with an inscription of King Mesha of Moab. He succeeded in purchasing the stone for the Berlin Museum. Through French interference, however, the stone never came into the possession of the purchasers. Before it reached any Kuropean country, the Bedouins, on whose territory it stood, demolished it in the hope of finding treasures hidden in it. The fragments of the stone, so far as they were still to be obtained, are now in the Louvre at Paris. A squeeze fortunately taken before the stone was shattered made it possible at least to read the whole inscription in its connection. In external form the stone resembles that of the Assyrian royal steles of Esarhaddon in the British Museum or ofSargon in the Berlin Museum. The Mesha stone, however, has no picture of the king, but merely an inscription of thirty-four lines. As the earliest monument of the Hebrew language and writing, this inscription has a unique importance, not only for Hebrew grammar but especially also for palaeography. We have here the earliest Semitic alphabet accessible to us, and on this account the monument, with its frequently new forms, also bears upon the evolution of Greek. writing.

The brief synopsis of the excavations at Tell ej-(udaida and Tell Sandahanna was added by the editor. For a more detailed account of the English excava-

tions at Tell Zakariya, Tell es-Safi, Tell cj-Judaida and Tell Sandahanna, compare my articles in the "Sunday-School Times," Sept. 9, 1899; Oct. 14, 1899; Dec. 23, 1899; Oct. 6, 1900; Jan. 26, 1901. — The Editor.

Its contents are a valuable complement of the Biblical narrative in *i* Kings 3. Mesha is a contemporary of Ahaziah and Jehoram, kings of Israel, and Jehoshaphat, king of Judah. The Bible relates how Jehoram and Jehoshaphat made a combined attempt to subjugate again the kingdom of Moab which had revolted. Mesha on his stone recounts the events that led up to this war, and relates how Omri, king of Israel, and his son Ahab oppressed Moab and took possession of the land of Medeba. By the grace of Chemosh, god of the Moabites, Mesha recovered the land. He took from the Israelites the fortified towns of Ataroth, Nebo and others; and in honor of Chemosh put the garrison of Ataroth to death. He also rebuilt a number of other Israelitish cities which apparently had been abandoned by their inhabitants.

Victory Stele of King Mesha of Moab

Another monument, that in point of time is not so very far removed from this monument, is the Siloam inscription. This was found in 1880 by some boys (while bathing) in the conduit which connects St. Mary's Well with the Pool of Siloam, not far from its outlet into the latter. The German Palestine Society immediately had it more closely examined. In order to make the inscription, which lay partly in water, entirely accessible, the water in the conduit had to be lowered by cleaning the bottom. Then Shick and Guthe made several copies and squeezes of the inscription. Guthe also succeeded in preparing a plaster cast of it. On account of the peculiar conditions, these were all very difficult operations, and in consequence of the foul air in the conduit Dr. Shick was taken ill.

It is due to the labors of these men that the text of the Siloam inscription has in the main been ascertained, though later it met with a fate similar to that of the Mesha stone. A certain unscrupulous person, with an eye to business, undertook to steal the inscription, by breaking it out of the rock; and, as may be imagined, it was seriously damaged. Fortunately the Ottoman government succeeded in capturing the thief and his plunder, and the fragments of the inscription are now in Constantinople.

The inscription mentions no king, but appears to be merely a private production, so to speak; in other words, not an order of the sovereign, but the impulse of the workmen led to its being cut. Its contents refer to the digging of the conduit, the completion of which it evidently celebrates. It describes how at the piercing of the conduit the sharp picks of the diggers, who had begun at the opposite ends and worked towards each other, suddenly met; how when three cubits still remained to be pierced, the workmen heard one another's voices; and how after the completion of the work, the water poured into the pool a distance of 1200 cubits. The spot where the diggers met was 100 cubits beneath the surface of the rock.

Together with a cleverly made forgery, though no exact copy of the same inscription, which is now also exhibited at the Imperial Ottoman Museum in Constantinople. — The Editor.

The construction of the conduit and hence the date of the inscription can with all confidence be put in the time of Hezekiah. To insure for the city, in case of its siege, a

The Siloam Inscription supply of the excellent water from the spring Gihon, situated outside its walls, must at an early period have occupied the thought of the kings. A conduit discovered by Dr. Shick in 1890, which conveyed the water to the Pool of Siloam overground, was probably the first attempt in this direction. This latter may be referred to in Is. 8: 6, where, as early as the time of Ahaz, the " waters that go softly" are mentioned. Naturally this conduit would not have answered in time of war, inasmuch as it lay almost entirely outside the wall and exposed to the enemy. Hence the later attempt to reach the reservoir of the spring from the inside

of the city by the construction of a subterranean passage, completely protected from the enemy.

A last endeavor was to put the spring itself and its water out of the reach of a besieging enemy, so that the latter in turn might suffer from want of water. The Siloam conduit in which the inscription was found served just this purpose. It conveyed the water entirely underground to the Pool of Siloam, which lay farther below in the Kidron Valley, but inside the city wall. The conduit is cut through the rock in a rather crude manner; here and there even a rift in the rock appears to have been utilized. The length of the conduit is about 583 yards. The 1200 cubits (about 689 yards) mentioned in the inscription is probably only an estimate. In a straight line the termini are only 366 yards apart, the difference being due to the very tortuous course of the conduit. The statement in the inscription that the conduit was begun from both ends inward is borne out by the fact that the strokes of the chisel in the southern half go in an opposite direction from those in the northern half. This also accounts most readily for the winding course of the conduit. The place where the workmen met may likewise still be recognized. We can also clearly see how the men, before they succeeded, and depending on the sound of their picks, made repeated but futile attempts to meet. The blind passages to be found, which are in reality abandoned galleries, also show that even long before they met, they more than once abandoned the course they were following and took another. That they should nevertheless finally come together in this subterranean passage is a performance worthy of all recognition. We can explain it only on the theory that the one or the other of the upward shafts, which are still in existence, served also for giving the workmen the direction.

The discoveries in Sidon bring us to a later period. The unimportant little town of Saida was to all intents completely unknown until the year 1855, when the attention of all Orientalists was drawn to it by the discovery of the sarcophagus

of King Kshmunazar. To the east of the town there is a large necropolis. Hewn into the lower ridges of the calcareous mountain-chain that juts out from the shore are a great mass of tombs. In one of these was found a remarkable sarcophagus of black basalt bearing a long inscription of 990 words. It is written in Phenician characters, is very well engraved and in an excellent state of preservation. Along with the Mesha stone and the Siloam inscription it is the most important of all the Semitic inscriptions found in Syria.

It narrates that Eshmunazar, son of Tabnith, King of Sidon, built his tomb himself. He adjures the entire kingdom " that no man open this bed of rest and no one seek for trinkets,—for no trinket is to be found,— and that no one remove the stone of my bed of rest." A heavy curse is laid upon him who nevertheless disturbs the rest of the dead: " May he not have a bed of rest with the dead, and may he not be interred in a tomb, and may he not have a son in his stead." As an interesting historical fact we learn that Eshmunazar extended the boundaries of Sidon by the conquest of Dor and Joppa, " the magnificent lands of Dagon, that are in the plain of Sharon." Because of this service every one is once more adjured to honor the rest of the dead, " lest the offender and his seed be cut off forever." It is to be noticed how these expressions are identical with the Biblical manner of expression. No less do these forms of cursing remind one of the inscriptions on the Nabatean tombs or of those that are often found in the tombs of Egyptian notables. The ideas that we here meet are extraordinarily significant for the Phenician religion. The greatest punishment with which the transgressor is threatened is that he should rest in no tomb and have no son. These views are quite the same as those found among the ancient Israelites. Eshmunazar probably lived in the first half of the fourth century before Christ.

Induced by these discoveries, the French expedition which under Renan in i860 to 1861 investigated the Phenician coast, among other things, devoted itself especially to the necropolis of Sidon. Renan carefully examined the tombs which he found and discovered numerous other beautiful sarcophagi. Most of them, and in many respects even the arrangement of the tombs, remind one of Egyptian cemeteries. This is another proof of the great influence exercised by Egypt on the development of Phenician civilization. The Egyptians furnished the originals, the Phenicians imitated them.

The other discoveries of the expedition were no less valuable for the investigation of the whole mental life of the Phenicians, above all of their religion and art. As regards the latter, attention is directed to but a single point, which will clearly show how much the civilization of the Israelites was dependent upon the art of the Phenicians. The conclusion drawn from the results of his investigations of Phenician buildings Renan gives in the following characterization of Phenician architecture: "The principle of architecture is the hewn rock, not as in Greece the pillar. The wall supplies the place of the hewn rock without entirely losing this character." This description applies also word for word to Hebrew structures. They also have no pillars; when such are found (as they are reported to have been in Solomon's so-called " house of the forest of Lebanon," i Ki. 7: i) they are explained by the influence of North Syrian architecture. Old Hebrew architecture, like the Phenician, had a predilection for massive squared stone structures; the more massive the squared stones, the more closely the wall resembles a natural precipice.

The treasures of the necropolis of ancient Sidon were not all recovered by the French Expedition. Many a tomb, whose entrance lay concealed beneath the ground, escaped Renan's searching eye. So much the more carefully did the inhabitants of that region dig for hidden treasures in their fields and gardens; and the results obtained prompted the Ottoman government to send Hamdy Bey, Director General of the Imperial Archaeological Museum at Constantinople, to Sidon in order to make fresh investigations at the place. These again brought to light magnificent sarcophagi, among them that of Tabnith, the father of the above-mentioned Eshmunazar, an inscription upon which agreed in part verbatim with the inscription on Eshmunazar's coffin. In connection with this sarcophagus it is interesting to note that no effort had even been made to remove the old hieroglyphic inscription and design. In this latter inscription the sarcophagus is said originally to have been the tomb of an Egyptian general. The Phenician inscription was simply placed beneath the Egyptian. When the coffin was found it still contained the well preserved body of Tabnith lying in an unknown fluid.

The so-called Alexander sarcophagus, however, surpasses all the other great and rich discoveries made by Hamdy Bey. It is a masterpiece of art from the best period of the Diadochs. It certainly is not the coffin of Alexander the Great himself, as has been supposed, for Alexander lies buried in Alexandria, and his mausoleum was repeatedly visited by Roman emperors; but it is the coffin of one that stood near him, of one of his great generals. Above all, it is a work of art of the first rank, and fills every one that sees it with admiration.

Of quite another sort is the most recent archaeological find made on the soil of Palestine. In the fall of 1896, in Madaba, as the Greeks were building a new church on the ruins of an old basilica, a portion of the mosaic floor of the old church came to light. This mosaic was found to represent nothing less than a map of Syria, Palestine and Egypt. The greater part of it is unfortunately destroyed. Only remnants of the map of Palestine and Egypt are preserved, amounting to about forty-nine square yards in extent, being in part of admirable execution. The difference between plain and highland is strikingly expressed by the. artist. The valley of the Jordan, the plain of Sharon, and the wilderness of Mount Sinai are distinguished from the dark mountains of Judea by being colored light. A deep green indicates the Dead Sea, while white and light blue fishes sport in the Jordan and Nile. The map accurately shows the location of mountains and hills, of wilderness and forests, of cold and hot springs, of pools and lakes, of palm trees and wells, and represents these in their natural colors. Each city may be recognized by its distinguishing features. The obelisks of Ashkelon; the great street of Gaza which leads to a basilica; the oval place in Lydda: all these are anything but accidental things. To be recognized at the first glance, Kerak is seen enthroned on a high rock. How carefully the artist did his work, even to the minutest detail, is illustrated by the Church of the Sepulchre in Jerusalem. From its representation we can definitely conclude that Constantine did not build three different sanctuaries to mark the sacred places of the Lord's death, and resurrection, and the finding of the cross, but only one large church; that the three entrance doors and also the *atrium* were situated on the east side, etc.

The map was probably made between 350 and 450 A. o. Next to the " Peutingerian Tables" this is the oldest map of Palestine. The importance of this new discovery cannot be too highly estimated. By reason of its great mass of details, its exact representation of the form, size and plan of towns and the style and outline of buildings, its references to several hitherto unknown places, its indication of the then current traditions regarding certain sacred places and their location, etc., the map proves to be of inestimable value in the study of Hebrew and Christian archaeology and in determining the geography and the historical conditions of the period to which it belongs. An accurate edition, especially in the colors of the original, is still wanting.

This, however, may soon be expected from the German Palestine Society, and then for the first time a fruitful study of the map and a conclusive judgment will be possible.

After all these valuable discoveries on the soil of Palestine, one of the most important still remains to be mentioned, namely, the Tell el-'Amarna tablets, found in Egypt in the year 1887. These consist of several hundred letters in cuneiform writing and almost entirely in the Assyrian language. They acquire a unique importance in the study of Palestinian archaeology from the fact that very many of them were written in Phenicia and in Palestine itself, by the petty vassal kings there, and sent to their liege lords Amenophis III. and IV., about 1400 B. C. Our knowledge of Palestine at this period had hitherto practically amounted to nothing, but the general political situation seems to have been this:

Egyptian suzerainty still has official existence in Palestine, but everywhere shows signs of decay. On the north the Hittites are pushing farther and farther to the south, and many of the princes of Palestine clandestinely conspire with them, while others accuse the disloyal ones before the king. The latter then make amends, etc., and thus is unfolded an interesting picture of the mutual intrigues of small courts. In the south the Khabiri people cause trouble to the loyal vassals of Egypt. The name of this people has not without reason been associated with that of the Hebrews. Here in the south Abdi-Kheba of Urusalim (Jerusalem) remains especially loyal to the Egyptians. How very interesting these ancient letters from Jerusalem are need hardly be said. If the Khabiri really were the Hebrews, the fight of the Israelites with Adoni-Bezek, recounted in Judg. 1, would appear in quite a new light.

But even more important than such historical details is the view these letters enable us to get of the civilization of the period. The mere fact that about 1400 B. C. a ruler at Jerusalem writes a letter on a clay tablet, in Babylonian cuneiform characters and in the Assyrian language, to his sovereign in Egypt, already speaks volumes! Who would have believed this to be possible, even twenty years ago? A stronger proof for the prevalence of Babylonian and Assyrian civilization in the whole of Western Asia Minor is not conceivable! What inferences may and must be drawn from this regarding the existence of many other evidences of Babylonian civiliza-

tion and conceptions in ancient Canaan and therefore also among the ancient Israelites, cannot yet be fully conceived. These letters also have a philological value. Along with and instead of Assyrian words are sometimes found Canaanite words and forms, more familiar to

Letter of Abdi-Kheba or Jerusalem, 1400 B. c.
the writer. These Canaanite glosses demonstrate — what was previously suspected but could not be proved — that the language of the Canaanites was essentially identical with Hebrew. Our geographical knowledge is likewise enriched by the mention of numerous cities, in part heretofore unknown, while the proper names lead to important inferences in regard to the religion of the Canaanites.

If such discoveries were made in Egypt, may we not hope that the soil of Palestine still conceals treasures just as precious? The above-mentioned excavations in Tell el-Hesy have also brought to light an epistolary tablet which in form and contents belongs to this correspondence. It can therefore confidently be affirmed that we stand not at the end but only at the beginning of discoveries on the soil of Palestine.

With lively satisfaction the friends of the Holy Land must therefore have heard of the recent inauguration of two new and extensive movements in the interest of Palestinian research. The American Institute of Archaeology and a number of other scientific organizations of North America (universities, colleges, theological seminaries) have provided the means for establishing a " School" at Jerusalem, which during the first year (1900-01) was under the direction of Professor Torrey, of Yale University. A somewhat older project, but likewise not yet fully carried out, is that of the United Evangelical Churches of Germany to found an Institute of Archaeology in Jerusalem. Abundant means have been provided for this, and it is to begin its operations in the autumn of 1901.

These institutions will supply a long-felt need. Their primary purpose is to introduce young scholars into different

branches of investigation, and to encourage them to undertake researches of their own. At the same time they will serve as a local centre for all the operations. Well provided with libraries and collections, they will in the future place the necessary scientific apparatus at the disposal of every scholar. Finally, so far as their means will allow, they will themselves engage in making researches, arrange for excavations, study the country and its characteristics, the people and their customs, etc. The favorable attitude which the Sultan of Turkey and the Ottoman government have in the last years generally exhibited towards such endeavors, affords good reason to believe that by these combined efforts Oriental study will be greatly promoted, and diligent search be rewarded by corresponding discoveries.

EXCAVATIONS IN EGYPT EXCAVATIONS IN EGYPT BV PROF. GEORGE STEINDORFF, PH. D.

During the nineteenth century, Kgypt has gradually gained a prominent place in the science of archaeology, so that it can justly lay claim to be considered as the general storehouse for every science.

The valley of the Nile gives up to the spade of the explorer its almost inexhaustible supply of monumental treasures, — treasures which, thanks to the dryness of the climate, are in a most remarkably fine state of preservation. Not a single year passes by but that we are surprised by some new discovery. The monuments and texts which are brought to light are naturally of the utmost importance for the study of the history and civilization of Kgypt. By means of them we are enabled to follow the past life of the country almost without interruption into the fourth millennium before the Christian era. From that period forward, we are in a position to trace the development of the Egyptian language and literature, so that we have gained an insight into the civilization and art, religion and science, and even the administration of the country. There is hardly a branch of daily life in which we are not instructed by the monuments.

Great Pyramid of Cheops at Gize

But not only has the science of Egyptology gained bv the discoveries made in Egypt, but nearly every department of learning has reaped some material advantage. In order to give only one or two of the best known examples, the field of classical archaeology may be cited as having gained considerably by these discoveries, inasmuch as we now c.in fix the date of the earliest Greek, the so-called Mycenean civilization, by means of the vases found in Naukratis and other Greek colonies. We have in this way been able to add to our knowledge of a branch of this most important art. The numerous Greek portraits which have been discovered in the later Egyptian tombs have greatly increased our knowledge in the large sphere of pictorial art, about which up to the present we have known very little.

None the less important have been the additions to classical philology which we have derived from Egypt. The great papyrus finds of the last decade have furnished us with literary works previously known only by name or at the best in fragments. Among these may be prominently mentioned, Aristotle's "Constitution of Athens," the Poems of Bachylides, the " Mimiambi " of Herondas and others. Manv manuscripts of the known works of classic literature have come to light in Egypt, the importance of which cannot be overrated, since by their copious vocabulary thev have tended either to verify previous readings or to improve those already' in use.

In the same way as the classical so has also the earlv Christian literature received extremely valuable additions, which for the knowledge of the earliest history of Christianity and the writers of the first centuries are of the greatest importance. We would only mention here the numerous gnostic works in Coptic, the fragments of the *Logia 'lesou* (Sayings of our Lord), the Coptic Apocalypse of Elias and Saphonias, and the Acts of St. Paul, which have been brought to light from the libraries attached to the monasteries, from the ancient tombs, and even from among rubbish heaps. Besides these branches, cuneiform research, ancient

Papyrus containing Portion of Aristotle's Constitution of Athens

Oriental history, Grasco-Roman history, jurisprudence, and even medicine are indebted to Egypt for new material.

Above all, the history of the Old Testament and the history of the people of Israel have had fresh light thrown upon them by means of the Egyptian monuments. It is true that up to the present we have no monuments which give direct evidence of the sojourn of the Hebrews in Egypt. For the lack of such monuments, however, we are amply compensated by the records discovered in Egypt, more than in Babylonia or Assyria, which enrich our knowledge of the most ancient history and civilization of Syria and Palestine preceding the entrance of the Hebrews into the promised land.

Most of these important discoveries which have been made on Egyptian ground, apart from those which have been thrown in our way by chance, are due to the systematic archaeological examinations carried on by the leading civilized nations since the close of the previous century.

HISTORY OF THE EXCAVATIONS

To the military expedition of Napoleon Bonaparte to Egypt, conducted in the summer of 1798, belongs the honor of having first turned the attention of the West towards the Egyptian monuments and of having brought them within the reach of science. The expedition was accompanied by devotees of every science as well as artists, who amidst the clamor of war studied the hoary remains of antiquity and the modern conditions of the conquered country. As proof of the great diligence which was brought to bear upon the subject by the French Academy we have only to mention the masterly work entitled "Description of Egypt," ' which appeared from 1809-1813 in twelve volumes of plates and twenty-four of text. It was through this magnificent publication that Europe first became acquainted with the treasure of mighty monuments preserved in Egypt from a remote past, and we were astonished at the wonderful remains of a vanished civilization and art which was

far superior to that of classic antiquity.

Among the antiquities thus collected by the French The French title of this work is: *Description de l' Egtyte ou RectitU Jt-: observation ct dcs recherches qui ont ete faites en £gypt(pendant lexpedition de l'ttrmee frartfiiise.* expedition, which, according to an arrangement made between the French and English commanders, had passed into British possession and are now deposited in the British Museum in London, was a large slab of black granite covered with inscriptions. It was discovered by a French artillery officer in August, 1799, at Fort St. Julien near Rosetta, a few miles to the east of Alexandria, while excavating for fortifications. At once it attracted the attention of the scholars attached to the expedition. No less than three different inscriptions were inscribed on this "Rosetta Stone:" one in the long known but undeciphered hieroglyphic or picture writing, the other in a shorter or cursive script, which was also unintelligible, and a third in Greek. From the last mentioned it was noticed that we had to do with a decree in honor of Ptolemy V. Epiphanes (205-181 B. c). In order that this decree might be intelligible to all inhabitants of the country, Egyptians as well as Greeks, it had to be in sacred letters, in " common " script and in the Greek alphabet. Thus it was evident that the different inscriptions all dealt with the same subject, and that the contents of the Greek text was the same as the other two. Here, then, was furnished the key to the decipherment of the Egyptian writing.

As earlv as the year 1802, the attempt was made by the eminent French Orientalist, Silvestre de Sacy, and the Swedish scholar, Akerblad, to decipher the cursive text of the Rosetta stone, and thev were in so far successful as to fix the values of some of the characters. The real honor of having solved the mystery of the hieroglyphics and having found the key to the understanding of the Egyptian writing and language belongs to the Frenchman Francois Champollion, who in a treatise published in 1822 ' fixed a portion of the Egyptian alphabet with the help of the Rosetta stone. With enormous perseverance and wonderful acumen he pursued his discoveries, and at last brought it so far in the domain of hieroglyphic study that at the time ot his early death in 1832 he was able to leave behind him in manuscript a complete Egyptian grammar and vocabulary.

Letlrt a M. Devrier relative a V'alphabet des Aieroglyphes phonetiques employe par les Egyptian pour inscrire sur les monuments les litres, les noms et Its surnoms des souverains grecs et romains.

Through this discovery of Champollion, the interest in ancient Egypt in all learned circles grew considerably. In order, therefore, to gain a closer acquaintance with the monuments, it was necessary to bring together considerable and trustworthy material in the shape of sculptures and inscriptions, much more, in fact, than was brought by the members of the French expedition of 1798, who were ignorant of the hieroglyphic script.

In 1828 an expedition was sent out by the Tuscan government, provided with a number of scholars, and supported by Charles X. of France. At the head were Champollion and the Italian Ippolito Rosellini, professor in Pisa. The most important ruins were examined, and the pictures and inscriptions in the tombs and temples were copied. Also the ruins of the temples of Nubia, which shortly before had been explored by the German architect Gau, were more thoroughly examined. Owing to the outbreak of the revolution, Champollion was unfortunately compelled to return to France, where very soon afterward he died from exhaustion consequent upon the wear and tear of travel, which affected his weak constitution. The task of continuing the work fell to the lot of Rosellini. In spite of this misfortune the results of the Franco-Tuscan expedition were very great, being published in two large works, which have remained to this day the most important storehouse of Egyptological science. This Italian publication, the work of Rosellini, arranges the collected monuments according to subjects. One volume shows

us the historical side, another gives us insight into the private life of the people, while others present to us monuments referring to religious history. Eight volumes of text accompany the plates, giving the necessary descriptions. The French publication was only brought out after the death of Champollion, and was arranged in geographical order, according to the plan adopted in the work of the Napoleonic expedition. Far more valuable than these volumes of plates are the notes which Champollion collected and put together during his travels. He not only described the monuments which had been seen, but also furnished a quantity of valuable archaeological material. It is astonishing to see the amount of Egyptological knowledge Champollion was enabled to get together during the short time that he worked, and which he laid before us in this publication,—the ripest work of his genius.

During the decade following Champollion's death Europe was busy deciphering the hieroglyphs, and great pains were taken to lift the veil covering Egypt's antiquity. In Egypt itself the explorations were continued not by expeditions, but by individuals. The most important of these was carried on in the cemetery of Memphis in 1837 by two Englishmen, the engineer F. E. Herring and Colonel Howard Vyse. A large number of pyramids, foremost those of Gize, were examined, accurate measurements taken, and their architecture studied. In this way a foundation was laid for the study of an important branch of the Egyptian history of architecture.

In the mean time the interest of Germany was aroused in the decipherment of the hieroglyphs, and especially by such men as Alexander von Humboldt and Karl Josias von Bunsen. These were they who moved Friedrich Wilhelm IV. , King of Prussia, who ascended the throne in 1840, to follow the example set by the French and Italians, and also to send an expedition to Egypt. In accordance with their wish, the young scholar Karl Richard Lepsius was intrusted with the mission, and a staff of eminent co-workers accompanied him, among others the architect Erbkam and

the draughtsmen Karl and Ernst Weidenbach. The expedition under Champollion in the main had been a voyage of discovery, concerned only with those monuments which chance happened to throw in his way. Lepsius, on the other hand, armed with greater knowledge of the localities to be examined, could attempt to supply the gaps which his predecessor had left.

Above all things, he had set about to bring historical order into the arrangement of the monuments, to devote a certain amount of time to each monument, and later to place Egyptian history, art, and civilization on a permanent basis. That this methodical system was followed by the best results is well known to-day.

The Prussian expedition began its explorations on the pyramid field of Memphis, the importance of which did not seem to have struck Champollion and consequently had been left by him almost untouched. Lepsius, and especially Erbkam, undertook the investigation of the pyramids which had been begun by Perring and Vvse, and attempted to find the history of the building of these greatest of royal tombs of the world. They came to the conclusion that the Egyptian kings did not raise up these structures to their enormous height at one time. Every king began building his pyramid as soon as he ascended the throne, beginning on very small lines in order to be sure of his tomb even if he occupied the throne only for a short time. As his reign increased in years, so the pyramid increased in size by means of laying on outside casings. These monuments of the dead were therefore alwavs commensurate with the lives of their builders. For if a king died while his pyramid was in the course of construction, it was finished with an outside mantle or casing, the pyramid thus corresponding in size to the length of the king's life. This theory, which was propounded by Lepsius, has often been attacked; but on closer examination it turns out to be in the main correct, needing modification only in one or two important points.

Along with the pyramids a large

number of private tombs were examined for the first time. These tombs were situated in the necropolis of Memphis, and yielded an unparalleled harvest. Over one hundred and thirty tombs were discovered, nearly all of which belonged to the same period as the pyramids, and furnished us with enormous material for the study of the history, civilization, and art of the period, which, following the example of Lepsius, has been called the period of " the Old Empire." Erbkam photographed the graves, the draughtsmen copied texts and sculptures from the walls, and numerous objects were collected during the excavations for the Berlin Museum. Then the Fayum was visited, and inquiries were instituted concerning the position of Lake Moeris and the Labyrinth, which were connected with the country. In Upper Egypt they not only visited the well known ruins, but discovered a large number of others, until then unknown. Special attention was paid to the tombs dating from about the end of the Old Empire and the Middle Empire, which yielded valuable material for the study of the earlier periods of Egyptian history. The curious ruined sites of El-'Amarna, with its rock-tombs dating from the time of Amenophis IV., were also visited.

Besides the exploration of ancient Egyptian sites, the expedition had from the first set itself another not less important task, namely, that of examining the ancient Egyptian and Ethiopian monuments which were to be found on the Upper Nile, and which had only been superficially examined by Champollion, Rosellini, and previously by Gau, as far as the second cataract. Through Lepsius the whole Ethiopian civilization was opened up to us, which showed that it was closely connected with that of Egypt, remains of which were discovered in the two principal towns of the Ethiopian kingdom, at Napata on the Gebel Berkel, and in Meroi, the present Begerauie.

The Prussian expedition pressed forward deep into the Soudan, past Khartum on the Blue Nile, with very great success. On the return journey the Peninsula of Sinai was visited, from Cairo; and the copper mines, which according to the inscriptions and representations cut in the rocks at Wadi Magara were worked as early as the beginning of the Old Empire, were examined for the first time. At the same time the problem of the probable route of the Exodus, which at that time caused much discussion, was seriously taken up. Lepsius advanced the opinion that the mountain called by the monks Gebel Musa was not the Sinai of the Bible, but that the mountain of God, Horeb or Sinai, corresponded more probably with the one situated a few days' journey to the north of Gebel Musa, which is called Serbal.

The "Monuments from Egypt and Ethiopia" which were discovered by the Prussian expedition were published by Lepsius in twelve volumes. They were not arranged according to geographical order, nor according to the subjects they contained, but they were put together in historical order. This historical arrangement was the principal outcome of the undertaking, securing for Lepsius and Erbkam a permanent place of honor in the history of their science.

A new period of Egyptian excavation opened when in the year 1850 the French savant Augustus Mariette went to Egypt. His name stands connected with the epoch-making discoveries on Egyptian soil from 1850 to 1880. The greatest and most important, which placed Mariette foremost in the science of Egyptology, was his discovery of the Serapeum, the burying-place of the sacred Apis bulls in Memphis. As far back as the time of the Emperor Augustus, when the Greek geographer Strabo travelled in the Nile valley, this ancient sanctuary was covered with the sands of the desert, and only the Sphinx, together with part of the road leading up to it, could be seen in the sands. Mariette began his excavations by the avenue of the sphinxes, and following it was led to the entrance of the Serapeum. In the night of the thirteenth of November he forced his way into the subterranean passages and was amply rewarded for his trouble. Sixty-four Apis tombs, which dated from the Eighteenth Dynasty down to the latest periods in the time of Cleopatra, were discovered, together with funereal figures, amulets, and ornaments. Above all, thousands of memorial stones, which pious pilgrims had erected, were recovered from a longforgotten past, and were sent by the fortunate discoverer to enrich the collection at the Louvre. Great was the value of the inscriptions found from an archaeological standpoint, yet still greater because of their historical interest, for nearly all the stones and coffins were dated in the reigns of different Icings, and thereby supplied most important material for the chronology of Egyptian history.

This first excavation was followed by a second at the great Sphinx at Gize, which led to the discovery of a large temple built of blocks of granite and alabaster, in which Mariette soon recognized the sanctuary of the God Sokaris Osiris of Ro-setew, so often mentioned in the inscriptions.

In the year 1857 Mariette was appointed director of the newly established museum in Cairo, the collection of which was temporarily stored in the port of Bulaq, and is even now awaiting the completion of a new building in the castle of the viceroy at Gize. At that time Mariette received from his patron Said-Pasha full permission to excavate in any part of Egypt in order to gain monuments for the new museum. The result was that in the following years Mariette used his spade in no less than thirty-seven places, and although he was not always so richly rewarded for his trouble, nevertheless fortune seems to have favored him. It must be said, however, that in these researches there was not always the necessary care bestowed upon the objects discovered, and in the search for treasures by common workmen and unlearned overseers — for Mariette could not be always present—many important remains of antiquity were destroyed. Mariette has often, and not without cause, been blamed for not having published the results of his discoveries, except here and there in an unfinished manner and many of them not at all, so that, for instance, to-day after a lapse of fifty years a comprehensive work on the Serapeum excavations is still badly needed. Concerning such matters, however, we will not judge the dead, but tender him our thanks for his untiring activity in all branches of Egyptian archaeology.

While in the Delta the excavations at Sais, Bubastis, and other places remained almost without results, there were unearthed in the temple of ancient Tanis, besides statues of the Middle Empire, those curious human-headed sphinxes in which Mariette thought to recognize a likeness of the Hyksos kings, but which on the basis of recent discoveries more probably represent kings of the Twelfth Dynasty. In the necropolis of Memphis, near Gize, and especially at Saqqara, Mariette continued the work which Lepsius had begun. More than three hundred new tombs, or as they are now called "mastabas," were discovered, and in addition to the valuable inscriptions and sculptures which covered the walls of these stone structures, there were a number of statues brought to light. Among the latter are some of the best works of the Egyptian artists, such as the famous seated statue of the scribe in the Louvre and the "Village Chief" *(Shaikh el-heled)* in the Cairo museum.

Among the excavations carried on by Mariette in Upper Egypt those conducted on the site of the ancient sacred city of Abydos must take the first rank. There he laid bare the temple of Seti I., of the Nineteenth Dynasty, with its beautifully executed wall sculptures, which scarcely have their equals, and also the famous and most valuable " List of the Kings " of Abydos, sculptured in relief, representing how Seti I. with his son Rameses II. offered incense to seventy-six of his ancestors seated on their royal thrones, accompanied by their names and titles. See the illustration on page 679. —The Editor. Statue of the so-called Village Chief

Further may be mentioned a rather mutilated temple of Rameses II., a smaller chapel founded by the same ruler in the town, as well as the large temple of the god Osiris. Enormous finds were made in the different bury-ing-places in the neighborhood of the town, dating from the earliest to the latest times. Over fifteen thousand monuments are reported to have been discovered, and the catalogue alone published by Mariette shows over eight hundred tombstones, most of which belong to the Middle Empire and bear important inscriptions. At Dendera, the Greek Tentyra, the great sanctuary of the goddess of love, Hathor, built under the last Ptolemies, was in the main cleared of rubbish, and numerous other temples and chapels in the neighborhood were laid open. The numerous inscriptions and sculptures found covering the temple were copied and afterwards published in large volumes.

On the ground of ancient Thebes there was hardly a known monument which was not examined. On the east bank of the Nile, in the royal temple of Karnak, extensive excavations were undertaken, which were productive of numerous finds of inscriptions and other monuments. The discovery of the oldest part of the temple, which dates from the Middle Empire, being also a success, Mariette was in a position to fix the architectural history of these temple buildings from their foundation in the time of the Ptolemies down to the latest periods. On the west bank of the Nile, at Thebes, there were laid open in the south the temple buildings of Medinet Habu, and partly cleared of rubbish. In the north, near Drah Abu'l-Nagga, the tombs belonging to the Middle Empire were examined, and the matchless terrace temple of Der el-Bahri was partly uncovered. In connection with the latter, on the middle terrace the interesting relief sculptures representing an expedition in ships to the incense country of Punt were discovered.

In Edfu, the ancient Apollonopolis Magna, Mariette had one of his greatest successes. Here the temple of the Sun-god Horus, constructed during the time of the Ptolemies, was found to be completely covered with rubbish, and on the roof of the sanctuary a whole Arab village had settled itself. Mariette's first work there was to have the modern houses cleared away and the village re-moved into the plain. Then the court-yard and the chambers of the temple were cleaned, and little by little there arose the magnificent sanctuary with its columns, reliefs, and inscriptions almost intact. It is now one of the finest temples in the Nile valley.

As long as Mariette lived, he guarded almost jealously his privilege to excavate. It is true that he permitted travelling scholars to study the monuments which had been discovered by him or even any of those which had been previously brought to light, but to no one was given the permission to excavate on his own account, not even to his greatest friend, the German scholar Heinrich Brugsch. Conditions were not changed until after the death of Mariette. Nevertheless the principal management of the Kgyptian antiquities and the state excavations remained in the hands of the French, and Mariette's successors, G. Maspero, K. Grebaut, J. de Morgan, and Victor Loret, continued in this capacity the work of their genial predecessor. But besides these, other nations and other French savants were allowed to take part in the excavations, and in this way early in the eighties a thorough examination of the different ruined sites was set on foot, which has borne rich fruits for science and has furthermore developed the methods of excavation in this scientific contest, which had been largely neglected by Mariette, who was mostly concerned in obtaining fine specimens for the Museum.

The sites chosen for the official excavations of the Egyptian government under French authority were especially the wide pyramid fields of Memphis, where also Mariette had worked, and the great temples of the old capital Thebes, where the ancient sanctuaries of Luxor and Medinet Habu were cleared of their rubbish, and the beautiful Ptolemaic temple of Kom Ombo (Ombos), which has been, so to speak, conjured up from the ground in a fine state of preservation. To these must be added a large number of minor, but yet important excavations on other sites of ancient Egypt, especially those by Loret in the " Valley of the Kings," near

Temple of Kom Ombo

Thebes, which led to the discovery of the tombs of the kings of the New Empire.

Side by side with the authorities above mentioned, there has been working since 1883 with the permission of the Egyptian government a society of excavators known as the "kgypt Exploration Fund." This is a private undertaking supported by small contributions from its members scattered in different countries, who study the Egyptian language, or at least are interested in Egypt's past history. This society has done very creditable work by publishing quickly and in useful form the results of its discoveries. The men who have worked under the orders of the Egypt Exploration Fund are principally E. Gardner, F. L. Griffith, Ed. Naville, and W. M. Flinders Petrie. The first sites taken in hand by the Exploration Fund were the much neglected ruins in the Delta. The most important finds made there were the Biblical Pithom and the famous Greek Naukratis. Since 1891 this Fund has made Upper Egypt the scene of its operations, and has had the temple of Der el-Bahri, one of the jewels of Egyptian architecture, cleared of its rubbish. Also Petrie, after giving up his connection with the Egypt Exploration Fund, exchanged his field of work in the Delta for that of the Nile valley, and supported by two private persons, Jesse Haworth and Martyn Kennard, began excavations on his own account. In the Favum, the position of the Labyrinth and Lake Moeris was established; the pyramids of Hawara and El-Lahun were examined, and in the neighborhood of the former an extensive Roman cemetery was discovered; and finally a whole town, dating from the second half of the Middle Empire, was brought to light. These magnificent archaeological works Petrie followed up by exploring the pyramids of Medum, and the famous ruins of Tell el-'Amarna, which have come so prominently to the front through the discovery of the clay tablets of Amenophis IV. In 1894 the temple remains of ancient Coptos were dug out. The excavations

carried on in 1895 on the west bank of the Nile near Naqada and Ballas led to the discovery of Ombos, mentioned by Juvenal, and manv remains of the earliest Egyptian civilization. After working once more on his own responsibility near Thebes in 1896, Petrie again entered the service of the Egypt Exploration Fund, where he had earned his first laurels, and in whose interests he has since been carrying on excavations in the necropolis of Deshashe (1897), Dendera (1898), and Hou (1899).

In order to give young Egyptologists a chance to excavate on their own account, a new excavation society was founded by Petrie called the " Egyptian Research Account," whose members, similar to those of the Egypt Exploration Fund, contribute yearly towards the cost of the excavations. Already in 1896, under the supervision of Quibell, one of the best of Petrie's pupils, work was commenced at the Rameseum, which was very successful, and continued in the following years at El-Kab, the site of Eileithyaspolis, and at the ruins of ancient Hierakonpolis near Kom elAhmar.

Other scholars became rivals of these masters of archaeology and the excavation societies. Two young Swiss Egyptologists, F. G. Gautier and G. Jequier, undertook in the winter of 1894-95 the exploration of the group of pyramids of Lisht, south of Dahshur, and discovered that the pyramid lying to the north was the tomb of Amenophis I., and that to the south was the monument of Usertesen I., both belonging to the Twelfth Dynasty. In the last named were discovered limestone statues of the king more than life size, which are masterpieces of the plastic arts of the Middle Empire. Since 1896 the Frenchman Amelineau has continued the excavation in the ruins of Abydos, which Mariette had begun. Although totally inexperienced in the art of excavating, he has managed to lay bare a number of very old royal tombs and has discovered the famous tomb of Osiris. Further, the excavations on the island of Philae remain to be considered. They were undertaken with the purpose of examining the buildings and

monuments on the islands on the south frontier of Egypt with a view to ascertain how far they would suffer by the construction of the great dam, and if possible to guard them against injuries. At that time not only was the well-known great temple cleared of rubbish by the English engineer Captain Lyons and the German Egyptologist Borchardt, but a large number of smaller sanctuaries and chapels, as well as the remains of Christian churches were brought to light.

In recent times Germany, which had not undertaken any excavation since the expedition of Lepsius, has come again to the front. By order of the Berlin Museum, the Berlin Egyptologist H. Schafer has excavated a pyramidal ruin near Abusir, and found in it a sanctuary dedicated by King N-user-Re of the Fifth Dynasty to the Sun-god. At the same time Spiegelberg of Strassburg, in conjunction with the English Egyptologist Newberry, has been working with good result at Drah Abu'l-Nagga on the west bank of the river near Thebes, and has discovered besides important tombs and temples also the ruins of a palace of Queen Hatshepsowet. So we see that nearly all nations have taken part in recovering the remains of Egyptian antiquity.

When I now in the following make an attempt to give a brief account of the results which these excavations have had for Egyptian history as well as for archaeology in general, I must sav at the outset that I cannot go into all particulars of the greater discoveries. I will therefore restrict mvself to those excavations which either have tended to solve old and oft discussed problems or which are of paramount importance in certain branches of Egyptian, Biblical, or classical archaeology.

THE RESULTS OF THE EXCAVATIONS

I THE DELTA

Of the flourishing cities, temple gardens, and extensive cemeteries which once in antiquity existed in Lower Egypt, comparatively few remain, fewer than in the Nile valley itself. In the Delta, the dry, almost rainless climate and the sandy desert which have proved so beneficial for the preservation of antiquities in Upper Egypt are missing. The rain and moisture have had a destructive effect, and besides these the salts which exist in the ground have played havoc with the work of human hands. Topographical changes have also been partly responsible; for the ruins of many ancient towns which stood in the midst of fruitbearing countries are now wholly or partly covered with water, and places which were once quite dry have now been turned into swamps. Moreover, that which had escaped destruction through the agency of nature has been demolished by human hands. Lower Egypt is poor in stones, and the ruins of the ancient towns and temples lent themselves to the inhabitants for excellent stone quarries, from which they could with little trouble get material for millstones or buildings, and which could even be burnt to produce lime. The result has been that for centuries these ruins have been plundered for this purpose, and from the sanctuaries of Tanis and Bubastis all the limestone blocks have been carted off, only the heavy useless granite and sandstone being allowed to remain. Under these circumstances we cannot wonder that most of the large towns of ancient times like Buto, Sebennytus, Sais, etc., have vanished from the face of the earth, while others exist only in part.

Tanis, the Biblical Zoan, in the eastern part of the Delta, is the only one which can show anything like the remains of a city, and has therefore from the first attracted the especial attention of the explorers. As far back as 1860, Mariette had begun excavations at this site, and discovered those curious statues and sphinxes in granite which he himself, and afterwards many others, attributed to the Hyksos kings, but which by recent discoveries have shown themselves to be more probably kings of the Twelfth Dynasty (Amenemhat III.). Later, in 1866, Lepsius examined the temple ruins and discovered a trilingual inscription, a decree of the Egyptian priests in honor of Ptolemy III., Euergetes, which is not only of great historical interest, but also proves the accuracy of the decipherment of the hieroglyphs. As large portions of the ruin remained unexamined, it was considered wise that Petrie should in 1884 begin excavations there, under the auspices of the Kgypt Exploration Fund. The whole temple district was laid bare, and many valuable

Ruins of Tanis, the Biblical Zoan pieces discovered were described. Only by these means could an idea of the size of this sanctuary and its surroundings be obtained. Its records reach back to the earliest times of Egyptian history; for not only Pepi of the Sixth Dynasty but also the great Pharaohs of the Twelfth added their works to it, and furnished the temple, dedicated to the god Set, with obelisks, pillars, statues, and sphinxes. Like many of the old temples, this also fell into decay during the troublous times of the Hyksos rule. Rameses II., the great builder among the Pharaohs, restored its ancient splendor by using the still remaining materials of the older structure. He created a building of the first order, having a length of one thousand feet — an edifice which could stand side by side with the great sanctuaries of the city of Thebes in Upper Egypt.

No less imposing must have been the temples of the town of Bast, the Greek Bubastis, the ruins of which lie near the town of Zaqaziq, and the name of which Tell Basta) reminds us of the ancient city. The ruins have suffered considerably in the course of time, and the city must have been destroyed by an earthquake. Nevertheless, the excavations carried on bv Naville in 1887-89, by order of the English society, have been productive of much valuable material for the study of the history and surroundings of the sanctuary. Especially the pyramid builders Cheops and Chefren were active there, and also the kings of the Middle Empire who have erected halls. In later times Rameses II. rebuilt a great part of it, until at last it received, prior to its final catastrophe, its present form under the kings of the Twenty-second Dynasty and Nechterehbet (Nektanebes I.). At that time it consisted of four large halls, which together had a length of six hundred English feet, and according to Herodotus was entered through a pvlon ornamented with reliefs, which had a height of ten fathoms. Above all, Naville's excavations have brought to light remains of the Middle Empire, especially columns of different styles (of *sistrum* or palm leaf), which illustrated the fact that about the third millennium before Christ Egyptian architects were well acquainted with those principles of art which show us a development that until Naville's discoveries was thought to be known only in later times.

Among the smaller ruins of the Eastern Delta situated on or near the great caravan road to Syria and Palestine, two which were excavated by Petrie for the Egypt Exploration Fund deserve to be mentioned. The one which is now called Tell Nebeshe comprises what was called by the Egyptians *Erment*, the capital of the nineteenth district *nomas)* of Lower Egypt, and is possibly Buto, mentioned by Herodotus (2:75) as lying on the Arabian frontier. Far more important than the two little sanctuaries, one of which was built by Rameses II., the other by King Amasis, is the great cemetery, in which tombs of the New Empire and of the Saitic times have been discovered. Among the latter were found besides pure Egyptian burials also some Greek tombs, which were full of Cypriote vases and weapons. Petrie has assumed, and probably quite rightlv, that they belong to the Greek mercenaries, who entered the Egyptian service in large numbers about the sixth century before Christ, and who were stationed by Amasis on the eastern borders of his kingdom.

Tell Defne, which is situated to the east of the Pelusic branch of the Nile, takes us back to about the same period. Here were discovered the remains of a fortress surrounded by a large strong wall, which was built by Psemtek I., and remains of buildings in which were found quantities of Greek potsherds and weapons. Probably we have here to do with the camp which, according to Herodotus, was occupied by

Sphinx from Pithon

Ionian soldiers under the first Psemtek, who were afterwards transferred to Memphis. On the other hand, it is hardly possible that this Greek town can be the Daphnae mentioned in other places, or even be considered as identical with the Biblical Tahpanhes, to which, according to Jeremiah and

Ezekiel, the Jews went after the fall of Jerusalem, in order to found a new home. Although the search for the town mentioned in the Bible has been fruitless, the excavations of recent times have thrown much light on other points of Bible study, namely, on the position of Pithom and Goshen, the country which Pharaoh gave to the children of Israel.

To the east of the modern town of Zaqaziq, the Bubastis above referred to, there extends towards the Suez canal a narrow valley watered by a canal which branches off at Cairo and flows towards Suez. This valley is known as the Wadi Tumilat, and the canal, which is called Isma'iliya canal, was constructed in the years 1858-63, in order to supply the workmen engaged in the building operations at Suez with drinking water. In ancient times a canal ran here which connected the Nile with the Red Sea, turning the valley into fertile ground. On the south side of this watercourse, about twelve English miles from the modern Isma'iliya, is situated an abandoned settlement, Tell el-Maskhuta, "Mound of the Statue." At the time of the French expedition a group of statues was discovered here which represented Rameses II. between the gods Atum and Re. Also a large number of sandstone and granite blocks were

Tell el-Maskhuta, the Biblical Pithom brought to light, which were covered with hieroglyphs such as usually mark the sites of ancient ruins in the Delta. Since many of these blocks bore the name of Rameses II., it was at first supposed that the Biblical Rameses, on the building of which the Israelites labored according to Exodus (chapters i and 2), was represented by this Tell el-Maskhuta, as it is thought to have existed in the eastern part of the Delta. New finds, and especially Naville's ex-

cavations, have proved this opinion to be erroneous. On the other hand, there is good reason for believing that here was situated the Biblical Pithom, which was called in Egyptian *Per-A turn*, " House of the god Atum," and which also bore the profane name of *Seku*. The temple was surrounded by a wall, inside of which was the little sanctuary built by Rameses II. to the god of the city, Atom. Not far from the temple, granaries were discovered, which took the shape of deep rectangular compartments without doors, into which the grain was poured from the top. To judge from the bricks of which they are built, they belong to the time of Rameses II., and it is therefore possible that they may be the store cities built by the Israelites at the command of Pharaoh. Naville's excavations have further proved that Tell el-Maskhuta contains the remains of the ancient Kro or Heroonpolis, at which, according to the Greek translation of the Scriptures, the meeting took place between Joseph and his father, and which in a Coptic translation is regarded as identical with Pithom.

As the real seat of the Hebrews we find in the Old Testament the land of Goshen, the *ge Gesem 'Arabias* of the Septuagint. This *Gesem* (in Egyptian also Gesem) has been rediscovered by Naville in the ruins called to-day Saft elHenne, to the east of Zaqaziq. It was the capital of a particular district called *'Arabias nomos,* and was known by the profane name of *Per-Sopt,* " House of the god Sopt." The Egyptian name of the god has survived in the modern Arabic name of the god. The land of Goshen must therefore be looked for in the neighborhood of Saft el-Henne. In that district to the east of the Bubastic branch of the Nile, perhaps in the triangle formed by the cities Zaqaziq, Belbes and Abu Ham mad, the Septuagint has placed the traditional sojourn of the Israelites, and it is highly probable that the old (Jehovistic) narrator meant by the "Land of Goshen" this district in the eastern part of the Delta.

Many other ruins were examined in this eastern part of the Delta, but most of them are not of very great interes-

tThere may, however, be mentioned Tell el-Yehudiya, situated near Shibin el-Qanatir, the ancient city of Onias, where Rameses II. once built a temple with glazed bricks in the mosaic style. In later times the Jewish high priest Onias, with the support of King Ptolemy Philomotor I., built a temple according to the plan of the temple of Solomon for those Jews who had been driven out of Jerusalem. This temple, however, has disappeared without leaving a trace behind; but many tombstones bearing Hebrew inscriptions have been discovered, pointing to a large Jewish cemetery.

We now leave the eastern Delta and continue our travels towards the west, tarrying a little at one of the most important sites excavated by Petrie for the Egypt Exploration Fund, the Greek city Naukratis. It was by chance that Petrie's attention was drawn to this mound of remains near Xebire, situated on the west side of the road leading from Tanta to Damanhur, known as Kom Ga'if. In the year 1884 he began to look for this site. He found a long low hill, doubtless containing the remains of a town, and exhibiting a large number of Greek potsherds of archaic character. Up to that time nothing Greek had been discovered on Egyptian soil older than the time of Alexander the Great and his successors, the Ptolemies. Here for the first time were older fragments, showing plainly the high antiquity of the town. In the year 1885, when Petrie began his excavations here, at the outset he came upon an inscription which proved that the workmen with their spades were digging in the Greek commercial city Naukratis, founded by Amasis.

The town was not very large, extending from north to south a distance of over 2600 feet by an average width of about 13CX) feet. This would represent the extent of a middle-class Greek town. Of the many Greek temples which according to the Greek writers existed in Naukratis, Petrie discovered the sanctuary of the Milesian Apollo, the temple of Hera built by the Samians, and the great Hellenium, that famous sanctuary to the building of which the different

Greek colonies from the Ionian towns Chios, Teos, Phocea, Clazomenae, the Dorians from Rhodes, Knidos, Halicarnassus, and the Lycian Phaselis, and the iEolians from Mytilene leagued themselves together. Besides these sites, which are proved by tradition, the ruined city contained also the remains of a temple of the Dioscuri and a sanctuary of Aphrodite, the foundation of which is supposed to date back to 600 B. c. Petrie was able to trace the close network of streets, but owing to the great destruction the outlines of the houses could no longer be followed. All sorts of domestic appliances were brought to light, especially tools and an enormous quantity of vases and fragments of vases, many of which had dedicatory inscriptions, which are all the more important as they furnish us with samples of the earliest Greek script. Also a great scarab manufactory was found in the town, in which the scarabaei were made of a white and blue material and cast in earthenware moulds, and which supplied the whole of Greece and the colonies with these articles as amulets. Thus the discovery of Naukratis is not only a very important find for ancient history and geography, but also for archaeology and palaeography.

With Naukratis we will quit the Delta and turn to those ruins which are situated in the Nile valley proper, and which through the recent excavations have gained in importance.

II THE PYRAMIDS OF MEMPHIS

On the western bank of the Nile, opposite Cairo, on the edge of the Libyan high plateau, there rise the gigantic pyramid buildings. From the north above Abu Ruash past Gize and Saqqara as far as Medum, which is situated at the entrance to the Fayum, they divide themselves into seven large groups. That the three larger pyramids had been built by the old kings Cheops, Chefren and Mvkerinos was already known to the Greek classic writers. Thev knew also that they were to serve no other purpose than to be burving-places of the kings. This valuable knowledge had been lost for centuries; and the pyramids came to be regarded

as water reservoirs or granaries or astronomical observatories. Onlv through the careful architectural examination of Vyse and Perring, 1837-38, has the real purpose of the pyramids been scientifically proved. The Knglish discoveries have shown that it is more than probable that the group of pyramids at Abusir, situated farther to the south of Gize, belong to the Fifth Dynasty, which followed on the throne after the dynasty of Cheops.

The pyramids which join those on the south at Abusir and cluster around the curious brick pyramid at Saqqara remained unopened and unexplored. Even at the time when Mariette was in charge of the excavations in Egypt, nothing was done to solve the question as to who were the builders of these pyramids. Mariette's whole energy seems to have been concentrated on reclaiming valuable antiquities or large inscriptions from the desert sands; and as former examinations seem to have taught him that neither gold treasures nor statues nor hieroglyphic inscriptions were to be found in the pyramids, he never attempted to open those at Saqqara. He always avoided also the demands of scholars to examine them. They were — as he firmly believed — of only minor importance in comparison with the gigantic structures at Gize. And moreover in all probability they had been plundered, if not by the Egyptians themselves in ancient times, certainly at a later period by the early Christians or the Arabs under the caliphs. And, lastly, he was convinced that the sepulchral chambers inside would show no inscriptions, so that for all the trouble the explorer would not even be rewarded by finding the name of the builder. This view of the famous and successful archaeologist was not accepted by his colleagues in Egyptology. When therefore in 1880 Maspero gained the upper hand in Egyptian excavations, it was his first thought to insist on the opening of the pyramids at Saqqara. His endeavors were realized in the years 1880-81, when it was shown that the five small pyramids were built by the last king of the Fifth and the first four rulers of the

Sixth Dynasty, namely, the Pharaohs Onnos, Othoes, Phiops I., Methusuphis, and Phiops II. But this first result was superseded by one of much greater importance; for the pyramids were not, as Mariette had thought, "silent," but they spoke by means of thousands of signs. The chambers within were completely covered with inscriptions. These texts, represented by over 4000 lines, are the oldest Egyptian literary monuments which we possess. Although they may not reach back to prehistoric times, that is, before the foundation of the Egyptian state, as Maspero in his first enthusiasm wrote, they nevertheless date back to the earliest historical period, to the beginning of Egyptian history, /. e., the time of King Menes.

The contents of the pyramid texts are all religious. They contain hymns and prayers, magical formulae and magical incantations, which were intended to secure life eternal in the next world and to accompany the dead to the realms beyond. The Egyptian believed in a life after death, but he also believed that the deceased needed to eat and drink in the next world the same as in this. These necessaries of life were obtained for him by means of various formulae. The deceased, in one passage, is addressed thus: "Receive thy bread which does not dry up, and thy beer which does not turn sour, for thee the corn is cut and barley is harvested." Hunger and thirst are the conditions mostly feared by men, as they bring not only earthly but also eternal death. Against these dangerous enemies, therefore, many of these incantations are directed. In one of them we read: "Hunger, go not to King Pepi, hurry instead into the celestial waters." Pepi is satisfied; he has no hunger because of the bread of Horus, which he has eaten, and which his eldest daughter has prepared for him in order that he might satisfy himself thereon. Then four demons, which protect the human body, are called to "drive away the hunger in the body of Pepi and the thirst upon his lips." While the liberated image of the man, his other "Self," his " Psyche," remains in the grave upon earth eating and drinking, his soul in the form of a bird flies to heaven or sails with the Sun-god by day in his bark or shines as a star on the firmament.

Nearly all these texts, which reflect the manifold popular ideas of life after death, are permeated with the notion that after man has done with this temporary existence, he shall become one with Osiris, and that he must suffer the same fate as once Osiris suffered. As Osiris, the son of the Earthgod Keb and of the goddess of heaven Newt, was killed by his brother Set, so also must man suffer death. And as Horus takes revenge against the accusers and murderer of his father Osiris, he will do the same for man. A hymn to the dead says: " Hear, hear, what Horus has done for thee, he has slain those who slew thee, he has bound those who bound thee. Ended is the lamentation in the hall of the gods, thou goest out to heaven, thy son Horus leads thee to heaven; to thee the heavens are given; to thee the earth is given; to thee are given the fields of the Blessed."

Most of the sayings contained in the pyramid texts are composed in poetical language, practically the same which runs through the poetry of the Hebrews and which is known as parallelism. It is made up by allowing one sentence to be followed by one or more which in contents and form are equal to the first. In other respects the correct understanding of these texts is extremely difficult, as they mostly contain a play on traditions, legends or myths which have been lost or with which we are not acquainted. At the same time there is some consolation in knowing that many of these texts were not understood even at the time when they were inscribed in the pyramids of the kings of the Fifth and Sixth Dynasties. The several chapters show blunders of the most pronounced type, which can only be explained by the fact that the scribes themselves did not understand their meanings.

The discovery and publication of these pyramid texts is not only of value for the history of the Egyptian religion, but it is also of epoch-making importance for Egyptian philology. For these texts show us the oldest known forms of the Egyptian language. Through them we have become acquainted more particularly with the vocalization of the ancient Egyptian; they have given us for the first time an insight into the oldest construction and inflexion of the verbs; in short, nearly every branch of grammar has been most unexpectedly enriched with the numerous examples which these newly discovered sayings offer. But it will take decades in order to raise the whole linguistic treasure which they contain, and to put it to use. The value which these pyramid texts have for Kgyptology will perhaps be better understood if we compare them with the Vedas, the oldest literary monuments of India, with which in their contents they are closely related. Imagine what would be the state of the science of Indogermanic Philology and Indogermanic Archaeology without a knowledge of these oldest literary productions of India! In this way we can appreciate the treasure which has been handed down to the science of Egyptology, and in fact to history in general, by the unlocking of the pyramids of Saqqara.

The good fortune which accompanied Maspero in his opening of the Onnos pyramid and its neighbors caused him to attack four others lying in the cemetery of Saqqara, but without result. They contained no inscriptions. Besides the excavations of the pyramids the examination of the private tombs, the so-called mastabas, was continued, which had been begun by Lepsius and Mariette. Near Saqqara a large number of well preserved tombs of the Old and Middle Kmpires was discovered by Maspero, while De Morgan had the good fortune to lay open the greatest of the known mastabas near the pyramid of Othoes. It belonged to a certain Mereruka, who lived under the first kings of the Sixth Dynasty, and consists of not less than thirty-one chambers and passages, most of which were furnished with fine reliefs and inscriptions.

The group of pyramids of Dahshur which joins those of Saqqara on the south, and which consists of three pyramids of limestone and two of Nile mud bricks, had up to that time defied all attempts to explore their interior or to discover the name of their builder. In the spring of 1894, however, De Morgan attacked the northern and southern brick pyramids anew. Having first examined the private tombs, which were situated around about the northern pyramid, he discovered that the material of which the pyramid consists corresponded to that of the tombs to the north or the pyramid, and that as the tombs, according to their inscriptions, belong to the period of the Middle Empire (about 2200-1800 B. c), the pyramid must have been built at the same period. As, moreover, the entrance to the burial chamber of these sepulchres was not in the sepulchral building itself as in the more ancient periods, but outside ot it, De Morgan came to the conclusion that the entrance to the pyramid must be looked for between its base and the surrounding wall. Following this idea, he discovered in the ground to the north of the monument a shaft leading to a number of underground chambers which were all situated in one passage. Further systematic examination led to the discovery of a second gallery. The subterranean tomb chambers were half filled with rubbish and ruins. The coffins had been opened and ransacked by thieves in ancient times. The remains of the skeletons were strewn about upon the floor amid broken alabaster and terra-cotta vases.

De Morgan gave orders to remove the rubbish and dust of the rooms and to lay bare the naked rock. Through these troublesome labors it was possible to discover two hollows in the floor of one of the galleries in which a treasure of gold and jewels was found, the finest which the art of the Egyptian goldworkers could produce. These valuables had been originally deposited in a wooden box, inlaid with gold. The box was destroyed, as the wood was rotten, and the treasure lay in the sands. Breastplates of gold and precious stones, golden necklaces, bracelets, shells made of gold, which were strung on chains, were mixed with scarabari of amethyst, lapis lazuli or enamel, which were set in golden rings, together with silver mirrors and beautiful vases. All these articles show great skill in workmanship, and give the most laudable proof of the art and taste of the Egyptian goldsmiths. The jewels themselves probably ornamented the persons of two princesses, Hathor Set and Merit, whose tombs are situated near the spot where they were found. They belonged. to the families of the Twelfth Dynasty and were related in a manner at present unknown to the kings Usertesen II., Usertesen III. and Amenemhat III. One of these Pharaohs was probably buried under one of these brick pyramids, although his sepulchral chamber has as yet not been discovered. As we shall see later on that the kings Usertesen III. and Amenemhat III. were buried in the pyramids of El-Lahun and Hawara, it is probable that the northern brick pyramid of Dahshur was built by Usertesen II.

No less glorious were the results which De Morgan gained at the second southern brick pyramid ot Dahshur. Within the walls which inclosed the pyramid territory he found many subterranean tombs, one of which belonged to King Hor hitherto unknown, and another lying close by to the princess Nebhotep. Although the first had been visited in ancient times, nevertheless the mummy of the monarch lay unmolested in its ebony coffin, ornamented with a golden inscription. A gold mask set with crystal eyes covered its head; breastplates and other ornaments of value decorated the mortal remains of the ruler. A wonderful statue of the protecting deity of the king, nearly four feet high and here and there ornamented with gold plates, was also discovered in a wooden box which had the form of a shrine.

Breastplate of King Amenemhat III.

The sepulchral chamber of the princess was quite undisturbed. All the objects were in the same place as when deposited at the time of the funeral 4000 years ago. The corpse lay peacefully in its coffin of acacia wood, which was ornamented with gold stripes. A silver diadem.encircled her head, and a rich necklace of gold and carnelian beads, the ends of which ended in the heads of hawks, surrounded her neck. A pretty

little dagger stuck in her belt. Arms and legs were ornamented with circlets of beads of gold, carnelian and emeralds. On her brow shone the royal insignia,— a golden eagle's head and the head of the Uraeus serpent, which were inlaid with emeralds and carnelian. Near her, besides a club, were also deposited other signs of royalty, a sceptre and a whip, both of very artistic workmanship. Although we cannot with certainty fix the historical position of King Hor and Princess Nebhotep, yet we may assume from the style of the objects found in the tomb that they also belong to the period of the Middle Empire. The brick pyramid under which they were discovered must accordingly be placed in the same period.

In the following year, 1895, the stone pyramid situated between the two brick pyramids was examined by De Morgan. It had been badly disturbed and almost carried away. By this excavation it was proved that it was the tomb of Amenemhat II. of the Twelfth Dynasty, and therefore belonged to the same period as the other two pyramids. Within the surrounding wall of this pyramid also other smaller tombs were laid out for members of the royal family. Two of them, in which two princesses had been buried, had fortunately escaped the hands of the ancient grave robbers. They were close by two large blocks of limestone, and the coffins, as well as the chambers in which sepulchral offerings were offered, had remained intact, and were found in the same condition in which they were the day when the two princesses were buried in them. Here were also found a number of valuable ornaments, veritable masterpieces of the goldsmith's art, among which a dagger with inlaid hilt and two fillets of gold inlaid with stones and enamels, made in the shape of wreaths, excelled all others in beauty and fineness of workmanship.

As it is very probable that the second large pyramid at Dahshur, which is the largest of all pyramids next to those of Gize, was built by the predecessor of Cheops, Pharaoh Snofru, there only remains to be determined the age and the builder's name of the so-called "Blunt-

ed Pyramid," which it is hoped will soon be ascertained.

The two stone pyramids lying to the south of Dahshur at Lisht have for centuries been used as stone quarries, so that they look more like two hills rising from the edge of the desert than the works of man. These have also been recently examined, first by Maspero in 1883-86 and later by Gautier and Jecquier in 1894-95. Through their excavations it was discovered that they likewise belong to the period of the Middle Empire, and that the southern one is the tomb of Usertesen I., while the northern in all probability is that of Amenemhat I., the founder of the Twelfth Dynasty. Up to the present it has been found impossible to enter the sepulchral chambers, because through infiltration the chambers have been completely filled with water. Nevertheless Gautier and Jecquier were able to lay open many tombs and other monuments near the southern pyramid, above all a kind of " hall," in which were deposited for some unexplained reason ten life-size sitting figures of Usertesen I. marvellously wrought in limestone.

Usually the pyramid field in the south ends with the pyramid of Medum, like the pyramid of Zoser at Saqqara, a step pyramid, which originally consisted of seven towers, of which only three remain, one rising above the other. In the year 1882 these towers were examined by Maspero, who gained an entrance, and through a long passage reached the sepulchral chamber of the pyramid. This he found had been plundered, and its coffin was missing. Twelve years

The Step Pyramid of Medum later, Petrie continued the excavations here, being successful in discovering a small temple, which was erected on the east side of the pyramid and intended for the worship of the king who was buried there. It is a plain sanctuary built of limestone, consisting of only two chambers and ending at the foot of the pyramid in a court, in which stood an altar for offerings between two limestone tablets, rounded at the top. Neither inscriptions nor reliefs are found on the walls. Everything is plain and in the simplest form, and we should not have known to whom this little temple was dedicated, and who was buried in the pyramid, had not at a later time some visitors scribbled their names and the purposes of their visit. From these writings we learn that the pyramid of Medum belonged to the very ancient king Snofru, the predecessor of Cheops, and that in the sanctuary offerings were made to the manes of this Pharaoh. Consequently we have to regard the latter as the oldest known Egyptian temple. Thus we are now acquainted with the two pyramids of King Snofru, the one at Dahshur and the other at Medum. This fact agrees with what is stated in the inscriptions, in which two pyramids, one in the south and another one, are mentioned. In which of these the ruler was buried, and why he had built two such enormous tombs, remains an open question.

Together with the pyramids at Medum we can fix the date of the large number of private tombs which are situated to the north and south of it. By order of Mariette they were examined, and a large number of interesting wall sculptures and fine statues were discovered in them. There can be no doubt that they were built about the same time as the pyramids, that is, at the beginning of the Old Empire. The sanctuary by the Medum pyramid is the only well preserved mortuary temple of all those which were built near the pyramid tombs.

A kind of temple of the Old Empire was made known to us through the excavations carried on by the Berlin Museum from the winter of 1898 to 1900. From inscriptions it was previously known that the rulers of the Fifth Dynasty were particularly devoted to the worship of the Sun-god, Re, regarding themselves as his descendants. Each of these Pharaohs built a sanctuary to Re, consisting of a stone foundation with sloping walls, upon which an obelisk was erected. Through the excavations at Abusir such a monument has actually been brought to light. Unfortunately this sanctuary has suffered more than any other temple from the ravages of time,

chiefly through having been used as a quarry for many years by the fellaheen. It was constructed by King N-user-Re, and called Seshep-eb-Re (" Pleasing the heart of the Sun-god ").

The temple was built exactly from east to west, rising upon an artificial platform. A street led up to it from the town which was situated in the plain. Through a magnificent gate one entered an open court, at the end of which the imposing structure of the obelisk presented itself to the eye. Before the obelisk there stood a large altar measuring not less than twenty by eighteen and one third feet, entirely preserved. It consists of a flat and a round middle piece surrounded by four huge slabs, which have the form of the Egyptian hieroglyph for *hotep* (" sacrifice "). To the right of the entrance gate, in the open air, nine alabaster basins had been placed in the court. They are still standing at the spot where they were discovered. Part of the court had been set apart for the killing of the victims, as is proved by the small furrows still extant through which the blood flowed. The entire courtyard seems to have been surrounded by covered galleries, which in part were adorned with beautiful reliefs. Although even these are terribly mutilated, yet enough can be recognized to ascertain that they represent a festival celebrated under the Pharaoh. Still finer are the reliefs with which several mortuary chambers on the southern base of the obelisk were adorned, belonging to the best specimens of Egyptian relief art known to us. Especially vivid are the scenes which represent life in ancient Egypt during the three seasons of the year. Above all things these reliefs prove that the houses of the gods of the Old Empire were fitted out just the same as those of later times, and did not, as was for a long time believed, show only bare walls devoid of every kind of ornament.

Concerning the old town of Memphis, situated near the modern villages of Bidrashen and Mitrahena, only little is known. The enormous mound which marks its site has been little, if at all, explored; and of the great sanctuary of

Ptah which adorned the town, little more is left than the t;.vo colossal statues of Rameses II., which once stood at its entrance, one of which was discovered by Caviglia and Soane in 1820, and the other in more recent times.

We will now leave the ancient metropolis and turn to another district, which has for a long time been neglected by archaeologists, but which during the last decade has yielded us rich treasures, namely, the Fayum.

ill THE FAYUM

The Favum is a depression in the desert plain, situated on the western edge of the Nile vallev, which even in ancient times had been turned into most fertile land by a branch of the Nile. The ancient capital of this district was Shedet. The Greeks of older times called it Crocodilopolis, because the crocodiles, sacred to the local deity Suchos, were held in veneration there. Under the Ptolemies its name was changed to Arsinoe.

Up to the middle of the seventies important finds of monuments had not been made in it. But in the year 1878 were offered for sale large and small papyrus fragments, some of which were covered with Greek, Coptic or Arabic characters; others with Latin, Persian and Hebrew, comprising literarv fragments and letters of various kinds. Arab peasants had hit upon the archives and dust bins of the old provincial town and had brought these manuscripts to the market at Cairo, whence they found their way into different European museums, for the most part those of Vienna and Berlin. This sensational find was followed by a second, which was also made in the nome of Crocodilopolis. I mean those wonderful and masterly Hellenistic portraits, which were placed on the faces of the mummies, and which passed into the possession of the Viennese carpet dealer Th. Graf.

These discoveries at once attracted the attention of scholars to the Fayum, which up to that time had been somewhat neglected. This was probably the reason why Petrie began working on its different sites.

Two important questions have long

been asked in connection with the Fayum: first, as to the site of Lake Maeris, and second, as to the site of the Labyrinth. Herodotus savs that an ancient Egyptian king named Mceris ordered a large lake to be dug out in the neighborhood of Crocodilopolis, the circumference of which was 3600 stadia, and which was 300 feet deep in its deepest part. In the middle of this lake stood two pyramids, the total height of which was 600 feet, 300 feet over the ground and 300 feet below the ground. On top of each pyramid was a colossal stone statue seated upon a throne. The water of the lake did not come from a spring, but from the Nile by means of a canal: six months it flowed into the lake and six months it flowed back into the Nile.

Who sold many of them to museums and art amateurs in Europe and America. Two of them are in the Egyptian Section of the Archaeological Museum of the University of Pennsylvania. The portrait here given b ooe of the latter. — The Editor.

Portrait painted in Wax (*From the Fayum*)

While in olden times it was generally assumed that Birket-Qarun, situated in the northwest of the Fayum, was identical with Lake Moeris, Linant Bey, a French engineer in the Egyptian service, ventured in 1840 to express himself as being opposed to this view because of certain difficulties arising from the differences in the level. He therefore placed it in the southeast of the province; but even this had its difficulties, because then the Lake Moeris of Linant would not have the same dimensions as that of Herodotus. In spite of this, however, the hypothesis put forward by the French engineer was the only one accepted for a long time, and Lepsius seems to have agreed with it. Recently other localities have been proposed: for instance, one by the Englishman Cope Whitehouse, — Wadi Rayan, situated in the southwest of the Fayum.

In the year 1888 Petrie carefully examined the pyramids of Biahmu, situated a little over three miles north of Arsinoe, and thereby gave quite another aspect to the question concerning the site of Lake Mceris. It appeared that the "pyramids " were not pyramids at all, but supporting walls for two colossal sitting figures. But of these figures made of sandstone only a few fragments were discovered: the nose of one, parts of a throne, and fragments of inscriptions which bore the name of King Amenemhat I. Yet these small pieces were sufficient to enable Petrie to calculate the original size of these two monuments. According to him the statues were about thirty-five feet high, which would make the total height, including the masonry of the base, sixty feet. If we now remember Herodotus' description of the two pyramids in Lake Mceris, it is not improbable that the two colossal statues discovered bv Petrie at Biahmu are those pyramids with the colossi which are said to have stood in Lake Mceris. The Greek traveller or his informant had possibly visited the neighborhood of the "Lake" at the time of the Nile inundation; from a distance he saw the curious monuments standing out of the water, and was thereby deceived as to their true condition.

With this discovery we should have gained a startingpoint from which to fix the true site of the ancient Lake Mceris. It must, according to this theory, be sought neither in the southeast nor in the southwest of the Favum, but to the northwest of Arsinoe. We would therefore come back to the district of Birket-Qarun, and in this case the old conception would again claim precedence, namelv, that this is covered by Lake Mceris or at least is a part of it. Then, however, Herodotus does not seem to be right in saying that the lake was an artificial work constructed bv King Mceris, for Birket-Qarun is not of human creation, but a natural lake dating from the remotest times. Nevertheless the statement of Herodotus stands out as unique. The "pyramid texts," the compilation of which goes back to the remotest antiquity, mention the Fayum under the name of" Sea-country." They recognize, therefore, a lake as the characteristic feature of this district, which can be no other than Lake Mceris. For we cannot reasonably suppose that the country had two lakes, one the Birket-Qarun, and the other the artificial Lake Mceris, which was constructed later, nor is this anywhere mentioned. Strabo, likewise, who is a most reliable informant, does not mention "Lake Mceris" as an artificial lake, but looks upon it as a natural inland sea, which "was as large as an ocean and had the color of the ocean," and the banks of which looked like the beach of the ocean. We must also take into account the fact that the supposed constructor " Moeris" is a pure fiction. The name Moeris is Egyptian, and means nothing more or less than "great sea." By this designation the lake situated in the Fayum was known to the people. As has often happened, the Greeks transferred this name which the lake bore to some supposed originator, whence arose a King Moeris.

We have therefore good ground for assuming that Lake Moeris was a natural lake corresponding to the Birket(,)arun. Only the sluices were artificial which regulated the influx of water from the Nile at the entrance to the Fayum near El-Lahun, and the dikes and dams which enclosed the lake, and which were to protect the country thus reclaimed from being submerged by the inundation.

Next to Lake Mcrris the traveller was told of a sight which baffled all description, also situated in the Fayum, namely, the Labyrinth. Herodotus, who saw it, speaks of it with the highest admiration, and places it not only above all Greek buildings in magnificence, but also above the pyramids, at which he was so much astounded. According to his description it was a great construction like a temple, with twelve courts and three thousand rooms, of which one half were above and the other half under ground. At one end was a pyramid. As builders of the Labyrinth Herodotus mentions the Dodekarchy, that is, those native minor princes, who before the reign of Psemtek, 663 B. c., had divided the country among them under the suzerainty of the Assyrian or Ethiopian kings. Manetho, however, who was well versed in Egypt's past history, ascribes the erection of this building to Lachares, a king of the Twelfth Dynasty, who would correspond to Amenemhat III.

The site of the Labyrinth has been debated no less than that of Lake Mirris. Lepsius assumed that it could only have existed near the pyramids of Hawara, in the southeast corner of the Kayum, and accordingly took the ruins of some brick buildings at that place to be the remains of this giant structure. His hypothesis has often been doubted, inasmuch as it turned out that the remains of buildings which he had taken to be the Labyrinth did not belong to it, but that they were the houses of a Roman village, which stood there in later times.

Now through Petrie's excavations Lepsius' hypothesis has been proved correct, with the exception of the Roman houses. Under the remains of these walls is a stratum of broken stone six feet thick, under which again the mortar in the foundation of a building can be distinctly traced. This field of ruins is, according to Petrie, large enough to include not only the precincts of the temple of Karnak and Luxor, but quite a number of other temples besides. This extent precisely agrees with that of the Labyrinth, as we could imagine it from the descriptions of Herodotus and Strabo. Its position also agrees with what Strabo says, namely, that it was thirty to forty stadia (about four to five English miles) from the entrance to the Fayum canal. And lastly it agrees also with the fact that according to the excavations of Petrie the pyramid at Hawara, which joins this field of ruins, was the tomb of Amenemhat III., probably the same that Manetho calls King Lachares, the builder of the Labyrinth.

Unfortunately an architectural plan can no longer be obtained from the ruins which remain. It may be reasonably assumed that the building was a temple. Its complete destruction must probably be attributed to the fact that, as Pliny says, this giant structure was used as a stone quarry for centuries, and entirely cleared *off* from the face of the earth excepting those small stones which could serve no possible purpose. So we see that the vexed question of the site of the Labyrinth cannot be definitely settled any more than that of Lake Moeris. As important as are the solutions of these problems for science, they are overshadowed by three other discoveries, which Petrie also fortunately made in the "Sea-country" of the Fayum.

To the north of the pyramid of Hawara, a large cemetery extends in which the inhabitants of Shedet (Crocodilopolis = Arsinoe), from the times of the Egyptian Middle Ages (2000 B. c.), had buried their dead. The graves of the earlier generations have been destroyed, while those of the GrascoRoman epoch, which were built under the Ptolemaic kings and Roman emperors, are in a remarkably fine state of preservation. Many bodies have been brought to light in them, including over sixty, which bore the portrait of the deceased painted on thin cedar wood in wax colors, placed over their faces. These mummy pictures from Hawara agree in style and workmanship with the Graf portraits, which came from Ruba'at, and some of them compare in beauty and execution very favorably with the latter. Besides those bodies, which were ornamented with portraits, also a large number of others have been found, furnished in the pure Egyptian style, which, like the former, date from the second or third century before our era.

Quite different is the picture of a second ruined site in the Fayum, which is situated only about six miles to the southeast of Hawara. There, near the present El-Lahun, on the borders of the desert, King Usertesen JI. of the Twelfth Dynasty built a residence, in which he lived, together with all his court. Near this town, which received the name *Hetep-Usertesen* ("Satisfied is Usertesen "), he built also his pyramidal tomb, in which he wished to find his last resting-place. Soon after the death of the king this place — now called Kahun — was abandoned and deserted by its inhabitants, so that it was not inhabited for more than a century. This city ruin Petrie also discovered and excavated, succeeding even in making a ground plan of it.

A first glance at the arrangement of the town shows that it is not the result of a gradual growth, but that it arose at once as a whole. It was square shaped, and was surrounded by a wall, which measured a little over 1312 feet on each side, so that the area of the town was 193,360 square yards. A thick wall divided the town into two parts, a greater, which contained the houses of the better class of people, higher officials and courtiers, and a smaller for the common people, workmen and shopkeepers. Each of the two parts of the city was intersected by a principal street,

Pyramid of El-Lahun, Fayum from which the other streets branched off. The houses of the working classes were simple enough. A small courtyard, in the middle of which stood a receptacle for corn, near which were two or three living-rooms and perhaps also a stable or shed for cattle, was about all they contained.

Larger houses were very rarely found. In these, likewise, the principal portion of the premises was the court, where, as in modern Egypt, the inhabitants spent the greater parr of the dav. A colonnade on one side of the court shaded the whole space, furnishing ample shelter against the rays of an African sun. From the courtyard one entered the women's apartments, the " harem," the principal room of which was an open court surrounded with colonnades. Towards another side a door led from the courtyard to the diningrooms, and farther, into the sleeping-apartments of the owner and his grown-up sons. Behind these were the spacious kitchens and stables. Servants' rooms, larder and a granary, which was filled through a door reached by a ladder, completed the arrangements of such an Egyptian house. In the buildings there were discovered all sorts of remains of the ancient inhabitants: pots and bowls, plates and little lamps of earthenware, sewing needles in bronze, flint knives, balls of wool, fishing nets, toys and simple ornaments.

Rich bootv was obtained from the rubbish heaps, upon which at one time potsherds and old paper had been thrown. Especially the fragments of papyri discovered in this way are the most important for us, as up to the present only very few documents of the profane literature of this period have come down to us. Their contents are various: to the literary pieces, such as parts of a papyrus on medicine, like the famous one of Ebers, or a book on veterinary medicine, must be added all sorts of private letters, official documents, bills and such like. And so by means of these we gain an interesting insight into the life of a small Egyptian town, an insight which cannot be gained from the tomb inscriptions and the sepulchral objects deposited with the dead.

Similar are the results obtained by the excavation of a second town in the Fayum, the ruins of which are called today Gurob. This town is about four or five hundred years later than Kahun, above described. Its existence was likewise of only short duration. It joined a temple founded by Thothmes III. in the first half of the fifteenth century before Christ, and was deserted, after many struggles, under the successor of Rameses II., King Merenptah, 1300 B. C.

To the same period as Gurob belongs a third city, which, however, was not a mere provincial town, but as a royal residence played an important part in the political and religious development of the Pharaonic kingdom, — the city of El'Amarna. It is situated on the right bank of the Nile about halfway between Thebes and Memphis, and owes its foundation to that religious revolutionist and fanatic Amenophis IV. This ruler had made the bold attempt to reform the Egyptian religion and to put in the place of the numerous old gods, concerning whom distorted ideas had grown up, the worship of the planetary system of the sun. Whether the old capital Thebes, in which his forefathers resided, reminded him too much of the god Ammon, whom he persecuted, and who had a large temple there, or whether his revolutionary ideas found strong resistance on the part of the orthodox priests, is not yet known to us. Certain it is that Echenaten (" Spirit of the Sun ") — the name he had taken in place of

Amenophis, in which the hated name of "Ammon" occurs — broke up the court at Thebes and built a new residence at El-'Amarna in the plain, whither he removed with all his court. The town grew rapidly. Temples and palaces arose. Near the royal castle stood the houses of the aristocracy in the midst of well attended gardens. But this glory was of short duration. Soon after the death of the king a reaction set in and finally prevailed; the court was once more removed to Thebes, and the newly founded city decayed rapidly.

After Lepsius had made accurate plans of the city ruins, together with the outlines of the streets and private buildings, the royal palace and the temple of the Sun, and also of many of the rock tombs in the neighboring mountains, where Amenophis IV.'s contemporaries rested, systematic excavations were not undertaken for many decades. In the winter of 1887-1888 some Arab peasants found on this site some cuneiform tablets which contained the diplomatic correspondence of the monarchs of Western Asia and of the governors of Palestine with Pharaoh Amenophis IV. and his father Amenophis III. They have for the greater part gone to the museums of Berlin and London, a smaller portion to the museum at Gize (Cairo), while some others are in the hands of private persons. By the discovery of these writings all previous ideas of the affairs of nations and international relations in antiquity have been changed.

The finding of these clay tablets was soon followed by the discovery of the tomb of the heretic king himself, which some French scholars discovered in a side valley of the mountain. In the winter of 1891—92 the untiring energy of Flinders Petrie led him to this place, where he commenced new excavations in the ruins of the town, especially in the royal palace.

Apart from important architectural remains, such as hitherto unknown varieties of columns, floors of stucco with animal designs, which had been produced in a form remarkably true to nature, showing indifference to the usual

conventional style; apart also from remains of beautiful statues of the king's family and large inscriptions, these excavations have yielded a rich assortment of smaller antiquities, corresponding to those pieces discovered at Gurob, and both in material and workmanship belonging to the same period. All the rings and different amulets of pearls and faience show that the end of the Eighteenth Dynasty, about 1400 B. c., was the best period of Egyptian art, especially in the manufacture of glass and faience articles. Never again was such a fine glaze, such a fresh blend of colors, reached as in the pieces of that period.

In still other respects these discoveries are of great importance. Even in earlier times vases had come from Egypt of the same style as those found at Mycenae and other sites of the same period of civilization. But just as little was known of the place where they had been found, or of the age to which they belonged, as was the case with similar Greek pieces. Now there have been found at Gurob as well as at El-'Amarna quantities of Mycenean earthenware, the amount of which far exceeds any of this class whigh have hitherto come from Egypt. As the date of this site can be accurately determined, we can also fix the date for the flourishing period of Mycenean art. We must place it at about 1400-1250 B. c., a date corresponding exactly with that which has been assigned to the Egyptian scarabaei and potsherds discovered in Mycenean tombs.

THE TOMBS OF THE KINGS OF ABYDOS AND NAQADA AND THE OLDEST EGYPTIAN CEMETERIES

Until recently the earliest history and civilization of Egypt was, so to speak, *terra incognita.* For the period prior to the Fourth Dynasty we were dependent, to a great extent, on the information of Manetho, with a large mixture of mythical elements, on the royal lists of kings, taken from older sources, and on occasional passages in Egyptian texts of the Old Empire and of later times. From these, however, we learnt little more than the names and probable order of the kings who ruled from Menes down to Snofru (Sephuris), the predecessor of

Cheops. Of the monuments of this period only the tomb pyramid of Zoser and a few remains of mastabas of the Third Dynasty were known. In consequence of this paucity of information, it has often happened that serious scholars have considered the kings of this earliest period of Egyptian history as mythical personages, or at least have come to the opinion that the lists of the kings were nothing but artificial compilations.

Little by little we are gaining more light upon this dark period. The honor of having opened up this field of research belongs again to the untiring Flinders Petrie. In the beginning of the year 1895, with the assistance of his pupil Quibell, he discovered many cemeteries on the western bank of the Nile, between the districts of Naqada and Ballas, the contents of which differed considerably from those of other graves in Egypt, and which he therefore regarded not as Egyptian, but as belonging probably to a Libyan race. While the bodies in the Egyptian tombs — with only few exceptions—are generally found lying on their backs or on their sides at full length, these bodies were found doubled up, the knees drawn up, the hands before the face, and lying on the left side. In some graves, which had not been ransacked, some members of the body were found broken from the trunk, or else the whole body mutilated.

The funereal objects were also peculiar. Among the many pots placed with the dead, most conspicuous are some red painted polished vases with a black rim, light brown pots with wavy handles, pots with red-brown paintings (boats, goats, ostriches, spirals, and undulating lines) on a light brown ground; black bowls with ornamentation scratched on them and filled in with white. Besides these better specimens there were found also some quite rough, which, like the majority of the others, had been made not on the wheel, but by free hand.

Especially numerous are stone vessels of various materials (such as breccia, alabaster, and diorite), wrought with wonderful skill, and polished. The same perfection in the artistic shaping of stone shows itself also in the flint weapons which have been discovered in these graves, and which surpass everything that is known up to the present in works of this kind. A characteristic feature of these graves is the stone plates of green slate, mostly in the shape of animals or ornamented with the heads of birds, some of which were used in the preparation of colors for dyeing the eyelashes, while others were worn as amulets. No less remarkable are the hairpins and combs made of bone, which were ornamented in a similar manner. Metal objects were comparatively rarely discovered.

Cemeteries like those here described were examined in 1896 and 1897 either bv De Morgan himself, or some one under his authority, in different places in Upper F.gypt; the most southerly being Gebel Silsile (according to Petrie there exists one still farther south at Kom Ombo) and the most northerly near Kawamil (to the west of Menshive). As onlv few objects of copper or bronze have come to light from these, they have been called by De Morgan "neolithic" and ascribed to prehistoric times. All these tombs are furnished plainly and belong to private persons. Aside from the marks on pots, no inscriptions have been discovered in them.

Kven more important was the discoverv made bv the French Egyptologist Amelineau in the winters 1895—96 and 1896-97. He succeeded in finding five large roval tombs, from which he took many short hieroglyphic inscriptions. These tombs are situated in the rubbish mounds known as Umm el-Ga'ab, near the ancient sacred city of Abydos, where since the days of Mariette no systematic excavations had been made. According to the gravestones discovered there and the seal inscriptions from the covers of beer jars, they belonged to the kings Ze, Ke-'a ("high armed"), 'Kbsed ("variegated tailed"), Kha'-sekhmui (?) and Den. They are built of sun-dried bricks in a rectangular form. In the tombs of the two lastnamed kings steps led down, just the same as in many of the better graves of private persons which Petrie had excavated at Tukh. The tombs of the kings Ze and Kha'sekhmui (?) showed complicated arrangements. There were situated around the middle hall, in which probably the body of the ruler rested, a large number of smaller Since the winter of 1899 these excavations have been continued for the Egypt Exploration Fund by Flinders Petrie, who not only found a large number of antiquities in the royal tombs already examined, but also discovered several new roval tombs.

The Temple of Srti I. at Abydot chambers, which, judging from the gravestones found in them, were used for burying the earthly companions of the king, his wives, dwarfs, and favorite dogs, or for depositing the sepulchral offerings.

Besides the objects already mentioned, which were placed in the tomb of the dead, such as gravestones and clay stoppers of earthen jars, there were also numerous large and small fragments of stone vessels, fine ivory carvings, flint weapons of the best workmanship, copper utensils, etc. In execution all these pieces are so much like the deposits found in the cemeteries of Tukh and elsewhere that there can be no doubt that the tombs of the kings of Abydos, as well as those of Tukh and other places in Upper Kgypt, belong to the same period of civilization. The tombs of the kings at Abydos, however, being purely Egyptian (as the inscriptions found in them prove), it naturally follows that the civilization brought to light through these tombs is also Egyptian, and does not belong to another people, as Petrie at first assumed.

It was, however, not so easy to fix their date. It is true that the names of many kings were discovered (to those mentioned above must be added many others), but these names, by which the ruler is designated as the god Horus, are not the same as the birth names of the monarchs given by Manetho and the Egyptian tablet of kings. Fortunately, three kings are mentioned by their birth names on two stone fragments found at Abydos, and in these we recognize the kings Usaphais, Miebis, and Lememses, mentioned in the native lists, as well as by Manetho. All three belong to the First Dynasty, that is, to the period before the builders of the great pyramids, which therefore is also about the time when the tombs of Abydos were built and the period to which belong the other similar cemeteries of Upper Egypt, a date which has been otherwise confirmed.

In the spring of 1897 De Morgan discovered a sixth royal tomb in the neighborhood of Naqada, which belonged to no one less than Menes, whom Egyptian tradition and the Greek writers placed at the head of all the Egyptian kings. In contrast to the royal tombs at Abydos, the tomb of Menes was a separate building constructed entirely of perforated bricks, a great mastaba, which was ornamented on the outside with niches in regular order. The tomb contained five chambers, in the central one of which the body of the king was laid, while the remaining four were intended to receive the funereal deposits. Among the latter were discovered ivory carvings, stone vessels, flint weapons, earthen beer jugs with stamped lids, etc., which are in every respect similar in style to those found in Abydos, so that even by these the correctness of the theory has been again confirmed, that all these tombs belong to the same period. After this oldest Egyptian civilization — the civilization

Royal Cemetery at Abydos before the erection of the pyramids — had once been discovered, traces of it have come to light in other parts of Upper Egypt, for instance, through the excavations at Kl-Kab and Hierakonpolis. At the last-named place Ouibell discovered two slate palettes, covered with archaic reliefs which differ essentially from those of the Old Empire. Palettes similar to these had been found at Abydos and classed by SteindorfFas belonging to the earliest Egyptian art.

The more we know of this oldest civilization, its arts and works, the more plainly we see that it could not have ended with the beginning of the Old Empire, — in other words, with the

Fourth Dynasty. As is most natural, in the province the method of burial remained the same, even afterwards, when at the capital and in the cemeteries of Memphis new forms had been adopted; and in the same manner in Upper Egypt during the Old Empire, and even far into the Middle Empire, the old forms of vessels and other objects were still in use at a time when in other places in the Nile valley new and more modern ideas had supplanted them.

VI THEBES

While only a few traces remain of the temples of Memphis, the northern capital of the Egyptian empire, most of the great sanctuaries of the southern residence, the hundred-gated Thebes, are in a remarkably fine state of preservation, namely, on the east bank the temples of Luxor and Karnak, on the west bank the temple group of Medinet Habu, the small Ptolemaic temple of Der el-Medine, and the terrace temple of Der el-Bahri. And even where great damage has been done, as at the temple of Mut in Karnak, the Rameseum or the sanctuary of Sethos in Qurna, still there remains enough to enable us to form an idea of their past magnificence, and to restore with ease what has disappeared.

Many of the temples were partly covered with rubbish. In the courts of the temple of Luxor even modern houses had been erected. To clear away this debris was one of the tasks which the authorities in charge of the Egyptian antiquities had to perform. The temple of Luxor was cleared in the years 1885-93, with the exception of a small portion, which is occupied by an Arab mosque, against the moving of which there were strong religious scruples. Then followed the unearthing of the great temple of Medinet Habu, already begun by Mariette, and at the order of De Morgan completed by Daressy in the years 1894-96. Since 1896 the reconstruction of the great temple of the empire at Karnak has been taken in hand. The small temple of Rameses III. has already been opened up, and the imposing

General View of the Temple of Luxor hypostyle, the columns of which threatened to fall, has been restored; but it

will certainly take many years before this greatest of all Egyptian temples is thoroughly cleared of rubbish and secured from further destruction. The great service which the Egypt Exploration Fund has done through its agent Professor Naville, in clearing and securing the temples of Der el-Bahri, has already been mentioned.

Besides these more or less entirely preserved sanctuaries, for the preservation of which much has been done in recent times, there were a number of other Theban temples which, with the exception of unimportant remains, have vanished from the face of the earth. These are the greater and smaller memorial temples erected on the west bank between Medinet Habu and Qurna, the centre of which was formed by the comparatively well preserved Rameseum. There lay in the neighborhood of Medinet Habu, the sanctuary of Amenophis III., the mighty doorkeepers of which, the so-called colossi of Memnon, are still standing, while all other portions of the building have fallen into ruins. Then we have, going from south to north, the sanctuaries of Menephtah, in which the famous Israel stele was discovered; of Queen Tewosret (the wife of the ephemerical king Si-Ptah); of Thothmes IV.; of Prince Wezmose; of Amenophis II.; of King Si-Ptah, and of Thothmes III. All these were thoroughly examined, and some for the first time discovered by Petrie during his excavations in 1896. Spiegelberg also recognized here, though existing only in unimportant remains, a sepulchral temple of Amenophis I.

The royal tombs of the Eleventh, Thirteenth, and Seventeenth Dynasties, which consisted of massive brick pyramids, and which stood on the desert to the north of Qurna, are quite destroyed, and with few exceptions have disappeared without even leaving a trace. Most of these pyramids had already in ancient time been broken into and robbed of their valuable contents, as, e.g., the tombs of kings Kemose and Amosis as well as that of Queen Ahhotep. Yet their treasures were curiously preserved for us by accident. In the year 1860 some fellaheen discovered the coffin of Ahhotep hidden in the sand, in which lay not only the mummy of the queen but a great quantity of valuable weapons and ornaments, which, according to the inscriptions on them, belonged to the Pharaoh mentioned and to Queen Ahhotep, and doubtless came from their tombs. How this coffin together with its treasures came to be in the place where it was discovered remains a mystery. It is possible that some thieves had broken into the royal tombs, and then secreted their booty until such time as they could carry it away at their leisure. But before this happened, they were probably discovered, and executed; and with them was buried the secret of its hiding-place until it was recently discovered. Mariette seized the objects and had them sent to the Cairo Museum, where they have become one of the interesting exhibits.

A systematic excavation of the cemeteries of Qurna and Drah Abu'l-Nagga, in which besides the pyramids of the kings are also a number of tombs of private people erected since the close of the Old Empire, has up to the present not been undertaken. So much the more, however, they have been ransacked by treasure-seekers supplying the various European museums with valuables. Champollion paid considerable attention to the rock tombs of Shaikh 'Abd el-Qurna, and published their inscriptions and wall sculptures. Since then they have often been examined, recently by Newberry, who opened many new tombs; but the valuable texts and sculptures contained in them have in no way yet been exhausted. For the history of the politics and civilization of the New Empire, especially that of the Eighteenth Dynasty, they are of the same importance as the mastabas in the cemeteries of Memphis are for the times of the pyramids.

Not far from the mounds of Shaikh 'Abd el-Qurna, between these and the temple of Der el-Bahri, lies also the rock pit in which the most famous of all finds was made, namely, the common graves of the kings of the Eighteenth to the Twenty-first Dynasties. As

early as the year 1876 antiquities were offered for sale which showed clearly that they had been discovered in royal tombs, but all attempts to find out the whereabouts of these graves were frustrated by the craftiness and silence of the modern thieves. It was not until the summer of 1881 that Maspero and Emil Brugsch, the curator of the Cairo Museum, succeeded in discovering the secret of their hiding-place and in bringing the contents to the light of day. By means of a well nearly 38 feet deep a subterranean . passage was reached, extending about 25 feet in a westerly direction, and then continuing for nearly 200 feet toward the north, and finally ending in a large chamber.

These underground ///j% U rooms were filled with coffins and mummies and all sorts of deposits. There were found the coffins and mummies of the famous kings of the Seventeenth and Eighteenth Dynasties: Sekenyen-Re, who drove out the Hyksos, and Amosis, Queen Ahmes Nefertari, the mother of the princes of the New Empire, and her son Amenophis I., Thothmes 1., II., and III. The Nineteenth Dynasty was represented by Sethos and the famous Rameses II. and Rameses III. Besides, many princes and princesses of the Eighteenth Dynasty were found. To these must be added the coffins and mummies of the Theban high priests, the Pinotems, and others who under the last Ramesides had gained great power in the state, and finally seized the Egyptian throne themselves.

Here then was discovered a cemetery such as has never been found elsewhere; here the most famous kings of Egyptian history, who had been known to us only through their inscriptions, arose and stood before us. But how did all these bodies come into one common grave? That this had not been their original tomb was very evident. Under the Twentieth Dynasty, when the power of the state began to fail, it was not possible to protect the resting-places of the dead from thieves. In the different cemeteries the tombs were plundered, and the graves of the kings, which afforded rich spoil, were much sought af-

ter by the thieves. As it was found impossible to overcome this state of affairs, it was thought advisable to carry the bodies of the kings to a place of safety. So we learn, for instance, from an inscription that the body of Rameses II. was removed from its original tomb to the safer one of Seti I., and when this also was pronounced unsafe, it was transferred to the tomb of Amenophis I. Finally, at the beginning of the Twenty-second Dynasty, it was decided to bury them together in a rock cave which had been artificially constructed at Der el-Bahri, and in this way to protect them against further molestation. Also the bodies of the kings and royal relatives of the Twentyfirst Dynasty were buried here. Thus all the great kings rested in peace, until they were discovered by the fellaheen. Now they have been placed together with their coffins and treasures in the Museum at Cairo. But it is doubtful whether it will be possible to preserve from destruction the

Head from the Sarcophagus of King Rameses II.

valuable remains which were unrolled at the wish of the Khedive in 1875, and to keep them for posterity.

Here must also be mentioned another common grave which was found by Grebaut in 1881, close to the lowest terrace of the temple at Der el-Bahri, and from which nearly one hundred and fifty mummies were brought to light. Most of these were found lying in double coffins, the lids of which were in the form of a mummy. They all belonged to the priests of Ammon of Thebes and their relatives, and were buried here in the time of the Twenty-second Dynast'. The coffins are for the most part older, but through changing the names written upon them they were used for new bodies. Here also were found numerous deposits such as sepulchral figures, earthen jars, papyri, etc., a perfect mass ot material for information concerning the burial customs and the history and art of the Twenty-second Dynasty.

The tombs of the Pharaohs of the Eighteenth and Twentieth Dynasties are known to exist in two lonely ravines, that branch off from a valley of the

Libyan mountains to the north of Drah Abu'l-Nagga. Strabo knew of forty royal tombs " worth seeing " which were cut out ot the rock. The scholars attached to the French expedition mentioned eleven, to which at the beginning of the first decade of the last century fourteen others were added by different travellers, so that up to recent times twenty-five were known. The oldest of these was that of Amenophis III., which lies in the western valley; the latest belongs to Rameses XII., the last of the Ramesides, and is situated in the eastern valley. All these tombs, as has already been stated, were broken into and plundered in ancient times, and nowhere is there found the mummy of a Pharaoh in its coffin. Of the forty tombs mentioned by Strabo fifteen remained unknown, and all attempts to discover them had been fruitless.

In the year 1 898 the director-general of Egyptian antiquities began again to examine " the Valley of the Kings," and after a few days a workman had the good fortune to discover a new rock tomb, which proved to be that of Thothmes III., the great Egyptian conqueror. A long slanting pit led over a well down to a hall supported by two pillars, from which there was a descent by a stairway into a large hall which measured nearly fifty by thirty feet, the roof of which was also supported by two pillars. Here stood the sandstone sarcophagus, painted red, its lid lying sideways on the floor. The mummy had been taken out of it thousands of years ago, and, as we shall see later, buried at another place. Both halls were entirely covered with sculptures and inscriptions of a religious nature, representing subjects the knowledge of which according to Egyptian belief was necessary for the dead in the next world.

Shortly after this important discovery Loret found the tomb of the successor of Thothmes III., Amenophis II. Its arrangements are similar to those of the tomb just described. Here also, through a slanting passage, a small hall was reached, from which a stairway led to a larger one supported by six columns, at the back of which was a small crypt.

Here stood the sandstone sarcophagus, also painted red, and without a lid, which contained the mummy of Amenophis II., covered with flowers, the first royal mummy discovered in this rock valley which had not been displaced. But this was not the greatest surprise which this tomb offered its fortunate discoverer. To the right and left of the great hall of columns were two chambers, in both of which all sorts of sacrificial offerings were piled up, jugs, embalmed pieces of meat, and bundles of cloth. In the room to the right were also found, besides a number of sepulchral figures, which had been taken out of their wooden coffins, a woman, a boy of about fifteen years, and a man. The other chamber, which was enclosed by a wall, contained quite a storehouse of royal mummies. Here rested, mostly in coffins not their own, the mortal remains of Thothmes IV., Amenophis III., Merenptah, the son of Rameses II., Set: II., Si-Ptah, and Rameses V., as well as three other monarchs, whose names cannot be ascertained. It is plain that this was a hiding-place, similar to that at Der el-Bahri, in which the royal mummies had been placed in order to protect them against violation by thieves.

In the year 1899 Loret discovered two more rock tombs in the "Valley of the Kings," so that altogether twenty-nine royal tombs are now known. One of them belongs to Thothmes I., the founder of the Eighteenth Dynasty, and is only of very small dimensions, being together with its two chambers the smallest of the rock tombs there situated. But it is the oldest of the tombs built in this locality.

Amenophis I., predecessor of Thothmes I., had his pyramidal tomb built on the border of the desert, but the new Pharaoh was the first to choose the quiet valley in the desert as his resting-place, and other Pharaohs followed his example for centuries. In the second of the tombs, discovered in 1899, no king had been buried, but a dignitary, a certain Meiherp-Re, the fan-bearer probably of one of the princes of the Twentieth Dynasty. This grave is of particular interest owing to the rich and peculiar

funereal deposits found in it, among other things a bier, the like of which has never been found in any other tomb. It consists of a quadrangular wooden frame overspread with a thick rush mat, over which were stretched three layers of linen with a life-size figure of the god of death, Osiris, drawn upon the outer layer.

Only the most important discoveries in Egypt have been treated in this sketch. Many points have only been superficially touched upon, and others have been passed over entirely. More, considerably more, still remains hidden, waiting for the fortunate discoverer; and the day is still far remote when the cry of " nothing new from Africa " will be heard bv the civilized world.

EXPLORATIONS IN ARABIA EXPLORATIONS IN ARABIA BY PROFESSOR FRITZ HOMMEL, PH. D.

I

We can form a true idea of the size of the Arabian peninsula only by comparing it with other lands. The small country of Palestine contains about 10,000 square miles, and covers an area as large as the states of New Jersey and Delaware combined; Belgium nearly 10,500 square miles; while Arabia contains over 800,000, and is three times as large as the state of Texas, or over one fourth the size of the United States of America with Pennsylvania added. In other words, it is nearly as large as British India (excluding Burma); or about as large as the European countries of France, Belgium, Holland, Germany, Switzerland, Italy, Austria-Hungary, Servia, Roumania, and Bulgaria, all combined.

Considering the inadequate facilities for transportation, which are the same in Arabia to-day as in ancient times, we can fully understand, in view of such enormous extent of territory, the statements of the ancient classic writers, that the caravans of the ancient Mineans, bearing frankincense and other merchandise, required fully seventy days Native of S.W. Arabia for the journey from South Arabia to the Gulf of Akabah, while they spent forty days on the way from Hadhramot (or the Frankincense Country) to Gerrha, opposite Samak or Dilmun — one of the Bahrain Islands.

Presupposing a general knowledge of the geographical position of Arabia I may in reference to its physical features confine myself to a few brief remarks. In no other country on the earth are found such contrasts as here in Arabia. One half of its vast territory is composed of sandy deserts, — not, of course, entirely destitute of vegetation,— affording, especially after the spring rains, the roving Bedouins a meagre subsistence for their camels, but which has always proved unfit for any permanent settlement. Then again, of greater or less extent, we find smiling oases studded with palms, extensive fertile highlands and pastures, above all the famous horse-breeding country of Nejd (the" Highland" proper), tropical districts on the coast of the Red Sea, the Indian Ocean, and the Persian Gulf; and finally the wildly picturesque mountain regions with their lone ranges of peaks, which in the mountains of 'Oman (Jebel Akhdhar, more than 10,000 feet high) and especially in the Alpine region of Yemen are of truly imposing height, extent, and beauty. Here, and still more in the central part of South Arabia, the ancient Hadhramot, not far from the coast were the Frankincense Terraces; and not far from them the land of the myrrh and of various spices and perfumes; while at the present day, in the western part of Yemen, especially in the district of Yafi'a, east of Yemen proper, the delicious Mocha coffee is produced, so that the name Arabia Felix, or " Arabia the Happy," is still, to a certain extent, justified.

We may speak even of a river system in this sun-parched land, properly embracing the region of the so-called wadis, or river beds, which in midsummer are entirely dry. Not to mention the Euphrates, which always contains water, and which forms the northeast boundary of the peninsula, there are several large clearly recognizable wadis in Arabia. Of these two in particular traverse almost the entire width of the land, which are more or less traceable

to the Euphrates and the Persian Gulf, while during and shortly after the rainy season through some parts of their channels real rivers flow. Where, farther on, they are lost in the sand of the For fuller information see the map of Arabia at the end of the book.

Desert Landscape in South Arabia desert, a comparatively luxuriant vegetation still marks their existence almost to the points where they formerly emptied into the Euphrates and the sea. We may safely assume that in ancient times they carried more water than they do at the present day. Of the two most noted ones the Wadi er-Rumma starts in the vicinity of Khaibar, making a wide circuit around the mountain group of Shammar (Aja and Selma), while farther to the east toward the Euphrates it is lost in the sand. The Wadi ed-Dawasir (plural of *Dosar),* rising south of Mecca, also runs eastward, then, encircling the rich mining region of Yemama, turns in the direction of Bahrain, the ancient "Sea-country" of the Babylonians. Besides these two large wadis of Central Arabia, there are several smaller ones, such as the Jof (meaning" valley ") in North Arabia, also called the Wadi Sirhan, which rises east of the Jordan, first taking a southeasterly, then an easterly

The Oasis or'Jof" in Northern Arabia direction. It is probable that it likewise formerly emptied into the Euphrates. There is also in South Arabia (in the ancient country of the Mineans) a Jof, or the Wadi Kharid, which perhaps (its eastern course being still unexplored! is continued in the great wadi of Hadhramot, the latter emptying into the Indian Ocean. We mention finally the Wadi Hamdh in Northwest Arabia, which was more definitely located by the Englishman Doughty.

Only a few stretches of coast, and in the southwest only the country as far as San'a belong to the Turks, while the whole of the interior is the stamping ground of the Bedouin tribes, as of old almost constantly fighting among themselves. This is the reason why Arabia is mostly unexplored, and why, moreover, the question of excavating the sites of

castles, towns, and temples, once of political and religious importance, has never as yet been raised, although the ruins upon the site of Marib, the ancient capital of Saba (Sheba), for instance, would doubtless yield just as rich results as any in Southern Babylonia. The mere possibility of undertaking such excavations has hitherto been precluded by the conditions prevailing in that country, which unfortunately will remain the same for an indefinite period of time to come. But the various exploring expeditions since the end of the eighteenth century, conducted mostly by individual men of courage and energy, not only produced rich geographical results, but also from time to time were the means of discovering, above ground, very important inscriptions, often copied at great risk. These proved especially interesting and valuable for the interpretation of the Old Testament. Truly Arabia is one of the so-called " Bible lands," among which it occupies at present even a far more important position than we ventured to imagine a decade ago.

A complete and exhaustive account of the exploration of the " Brown Continent," /'. e., Arabia, belongs more to the province of geography and ethnology, particularly of descriptive geography. In the following pages, we will consider foremost those travels that made us more familiar with ancient Arabia, and furnished new material for its reconstruction and for the understanding of its most interesting history, as well as its peculiar conditions with reference to religion and civilization. These materials consist of inscriptions and monuments, of which especially South Arabia has thus far yielded many. But modern Arabia too, the country and people of the present day, is of real importance for the history of the Semitic race, though perhaps overestimated by

HeaU from Minean Tombstone some scholars. In no other country have old manners and customs been so firmly retained as among the Semites in Western Asia, and here again most of all in Arabia; so that a more exact knowledge of those customs often furnishes an instructive commentary upon the life of past ages, as we see it in the Bible and in other ancient records. Of course work in this field requires such a faculty of keen observation as not every traveler possesses; still books of travel like those of Burckhardt and Doughty prove that, even without the results gained from inscriptions, a tour into Central Arabia may be exceedingly instructive and profitable to the Orientalist, and most of all to the student of the Bible. But yet these works only furnish information of a more general character, however valuable it may be, often giving only interesting analogies sometimes leading to wrong conclusions (e.g., those of Robertson Smith concerning gyna;ocracy among the Semites). Such evidence is not to be compared with that which comes directly from an antiquity contemporaneous with the Bible, like the evidence gained from inscriptions or statuettes, votive tablets, small works of art, old utensils, etc., or even from the ruins of whole castles and temples. A single line of an inscription often sheds more light on an expression in the Old Testament than descriptions, however numerous and exact, of conditions existing at the present day.

As for the exploring expeditions to Arabia undertaken by Europeans since the year 1763, all that was done in that field up to 1846 was presented with great care and, considering the time, with admirable discrimination in Karl Ritter's colossal work, "Geography of Asia."' Ritter has also incorporated the statements of the ancient classic writers (Agatharchides, Kratosthenes, Strabo, Pliny, the author of *Periplus Maris Erythraei,* and Ptolemy) and of the Arabian geographers, so far as they were accessible to him. Since Hamdani's "Arabian Peninsula," Bekri's and Yaqut's geographical dictionaries, and other such works are accessible in good editions; since also the extremely valuable data found in the Assyrian royal inscriptions, which at the same time enable us to understand the Biblical references more fully than was before possible, and since the South Arabian inscriptions have been added to these, of course such a work as Ritter's would at the pre-

sent day have an entirely different aspect, regardless of all the cartographical achievements of the expeditions made since i 847. Nevertheless Ritter's "Arabia" is even now an indispensable work, a shining memorial of the diligence of German scholars in those decades and especially of the as yet unequalled Karl Ritter, who found a rival and successor worthy of himself only in the late Heinrich Kiepert, the indefatigable cartographer and learned author of the "Compendium of Ancient Geography. "

In his excellent work " Arabia and the Arabs for a Century, a Geographical and Historical Sketch," Albrecht Zehme, purposely excluding the ancient records, has in a clear and attractive style reedited what Ritter had gathered, and has continued to record the researches to the year 1874. For a good and concise account of the most important results of explorations from the time of Carsten Niebuhr, 1763, to that of Halevy's and Heinrich von Maltzan's travels, we most heartily recommend the first 318 pages' of Zehme's work, which proceeds, however, upon a geographical rather than upon a chronological basis.

Die Erdkunde von Asicn, comp. the eighth double volume, treating of Arabia, or vols. xii. and xiii. of his collected works.

'*Lehrbuch der alttn Geographic,* Berlin, 1878.

Arnbien und die Araber seit hundert Jahren, eine geographiuhe und geichichtliche Siizze, octavo, 407 pp., Halle, 1875.

In the following let us proceed to give briefly our own account of the work done during the same period, differing, however, from Zehme's in being arranged in chronological order and with special reference to that which throws light upon the Old Testament.

The scientific exploration of Arabia began with the expedition,in 1761-64, of the famous scholar Carsten Niebuhr, which was undertaken according to the desire and at the cost of the Danish government. With a number of followers, among them the botanist ForskSl, all of whom, however, died on the way,

Niebuhr travelled especially in South Arabia (Feb. to Aug., 1763). In two publications he gave the first remarkably exact and scientific account of the country. His work is not yet obsolete; even at present it is a real pleasure to read it, and the accompanying map of all the southwest territory of Yemen as far inland as San'a was prepared with such extraordinary care that it has been hardly improved by the later travels of others. We should also mention especially his travels along the coast of Hijaz and of South Arabia as far as the Sakhalitic Gulf, where he gathered interesting information about Hadhramot, or the "Frankincense Country" mentioned in the table of nations (Gen. chap, io). Pp. 319 to end give a resume of the political history of Arabia from the rise of Wahhabism (about 1750) to 1874. Unfortunately the book has no index, so that much time is wasted in finding the proper names.

Reisebeschreibung nach Arabien, 2 vols., and *Beschrribung von Arable,* 1 vol., the latter published also in French. The large bay between Ras Fartak and Mirbat (comp. the accompanying map). —The Editor. In this connection we ought to remark that the name Sakhalitic Gulf can hardly be derived from such a general term as the Arabic *sahil,* "coast"

Next in the order of time comes the English agent Reinaud, who in 1799 made a tour from Qatif on the eastern coast to Der'iya, in the interior of Yemama, then the capital of the newly established dominion of the Wahhabites. A very brief report of this journey, undertaken bv order of the Hast India Company, and which was therefore merely for commercial purposes, was given bv Seetzen (see below) in 1805. Reinaud, while fifteen days on the way to Der'iya, remained there only eight days. Though contributing nothing to science through this journey, he was the first to visit that interesting region, and was also the only European who saw the kingdom of the Wahhabites at its height, and (whence *sawahil,* "inhabitants of the coast," the name of the Suaheli in Northeast Africa), but rather from the old word for "frankincense," Hebrew *shekheleth* (Exod. 30: 34), Ethiopic *sehhin*. Probably also *Shihr (Shehr)*, the name for the coast of the "Frankincense Country," is but a variant of this word for " frankincense." In Zach's *Monatliche Correspondent*. the famous ruler 'Abd ul-'Aziz, who was then sixty' years old.

Near the end of the first decade of the nineteenth century the Russian college assessor Ulrich Jasper Seetzen, a native of Oldenburg, in the guise of a dervish visited Mecca and the district called Hijaz. Soon afterward (1810—i 1), as the first and for a long time the only European traveller, he made the interesting overland journey from Aden to San'i, at which time he copied the first South Arabian inscriptions, in Tzafar, the ancient capital of Himyar, three hours south of Yerim. Niebuhr had already heard of such inscriptions, but his efforts to find them had been unsuccessful. Seetzen's copies were published at once, but failed to attract the attention of the Orientalists; moreover, with a single exception, the copies were so poor that without other materials nothing could have been done with them. Soon afterward Seetzen disappeared. Probably he suffered a premature death in Yemen either by murder or from the treacherous tropical fever; but the fragments of his diary, which had been sent to Europe before his death, were published nearly half a century later, 1854-59. Unfortunately this diary does not contain his visit to Mecca nor his travels in Yemen.

We now come to one of the most distinguished explorers of Arabia, Johann Ludwig Burckhardt, a Swiss, who in 1814-16, under English auspices, went out to the coast of Hijaz. Though visiting only Jidda and Yambo', yet he was the first who, in the guise of a pilgrim, completed the pilgrimage to Mecca and Medina, of which he gave a minute account in his classic works, published after his death, "Travels in Arabia" (2 vols., London, 1829) and " Notes on the Bedouins and Wahabys" (2 vols., London, 1831).

Apparently a mistake. 'Abd ul-'Aziz was born in 172 I, and was murdered October 14, 1803. In 1799 he was therefore 78 years old. Comp. Euting, *Tagebuch einer Reise in Inner-Arabien*, i., pp. 159, *see*.—The Editor. Not to be confounded with the Tzafar in the coast region of Hadhramot (Sapphar of Ptolemy), which incorrectly has been regarded as identical with Sephar, a mountain mentioned in Gen. 10: 30. In the second volume of the *Fundgruben des Orients*, Vienna, 181 1. *Rtisen durch Syrien, Palistina, Phonizien, die Transjordan-Lindtr, Arabia Petrtta and Unter-Agypten*, 4 vols., edited by Kruse, Hinrichs, Miiller, and Fleischer.

In 1819 another expedition was made to Eastern and Central Arabia by the Englishman Captain Sadlier, who travelled from Qatif (Katif) to Medina, whence he proceeded to Yambo (Yanbo) on the western coast. Following in the footsteps of Ibrahim Pasha, the conqueror of the Wahhabites, he made the journey hastily and without any considerable scientific results. His diary, " Account of a Journey from Katif to Yambo," was published in the Transactions of the Literary Society of Bombay, vol. iii.

As a worthy successor of Niebuhr and Burckhardt we mention the Englishman Captain T. R. Wellsted, who in 1834-35, travelling in the service of the English Coast Survey of Arabia, found opportunity to make various interesting excursions into the interior, the most important being to 'Oman and to Wadi Maifa'at (Mefa'at) in Hadhramot. His " Travels in Arabia" appeared in two volumes (London, 1838), and in an excellent German translation (Halle, 1842) revised by the Orientalist Rodiger, who added an excursus "On the Himyaritic inscriptions made known by Lieut. Wellsted."

Charles J. Cruttenden, who had travelled with Wellsted in South Arabia, made in 1838 an independent tour from Mokha (Mocha) to San'a, in the course of which he succeeded in copying five more South Arabian inscriptions in San'a. The previous year (1837) he had already made a journey of three days from Mirbat on the coast of the Frankincense Country through the district of

Tzafar. To complete this series we should add Wellsted's important "Report on the Island of Socotra " in iSjf. The travels of Wellsted and Cruttenden form an epoch in the history of South Arabian inscriptions, to be discussed hereafter in Part II. in connection with Rodiger's and Gesenius' fundamental essays on their decipherment.

Comp. Reinaud's travel above. Comp. , also, Ryan, "Captain Sadlier's Diary," Bombay, 1866. *I.e.*, the two inscriptions from Hisn el-Ghurab (Raven Castle ") on the coast and Naqb el-Hajar in Wadi Maifa'at, equally important linguistically and historically. 'Comp. the German translation, vol. ii., pp. 3 5 2-41 I.

A most remarkable journey was made in 1843 by the German Adolf von Wrede, the details of which, however, were not made public until nearly thirty years later, when his diary was published by Heinrich von Maltzan. This bold traveller's narrative, which in all chief points was confirmed later by information gained from natives, reads like a romance, giving for the first time a more vivid picture of the principal valleys of this wonderful land, especially of the rich and fertile Wadi Do'an. Von Wrede had the good fortune also to discover and copy an important inscription, of five long lines, in Hadhramot at 'Obne, a place situated in a valley branching off from the Wadi Maifa.

In the same year, 1843, the French pharmacist Thomas Joseph Arnaud made an equally bold, though much shorter journey from San'a to Marib, which up to the present time has been visited by only three Europeans (Arnaud, Halevy, and Glaser). Marib is in the midst of a rich mining region and was the capital of the ancient kingdom of Saba (Sheba). The report of this trip and of the five days' sojourn in Marib was published in 1845 by the Parisian Orientalist Mohl in the *Journal Asiatique*. The chief result of this journey are the description of the remains of the famous dam of Marib, and a collection of fifty-six mostly very short inscriptions, of which numbers 4-11 were from Sirwah, His reports of this tour are to be found in the Journal of the Royal Geographical Society of London, vol. viii. , pp. 276—289, and in the Proceedings of the Bombay Geographical Society, 1838, pp. 39—55.

Comp. the Proceedings of the Bombay Branch of the RoyaJ Asiaric Society, 1837. Comp. the Journal of the Asiatic Society of Bengal, vol. iv., pp. I 38—166. *Adolf von Wrede's Reise in Hadhramaut,* Braunschweig, 1870.

See below, especially Van den Berg's *Hadhramout.*

Requiring about five days' travel.

Sandstorm in the Widi Er-Rajel a ruined place west of Marib, the remainder, 12-56, from Marib itself.

We are now taken to entirely different parts of Arabia by the two following explorers. First in order of time is to be mentioned the Swede Georg Wallin, who in 1845 travelled to Havil and from there to Medina, while in 1848 he went from Muelih on the Red Sea to Tabuk, Taima, and Hayil, whence he proceeded by the old northern caravan route to the Kuphrates. This was the first time that North Arabia had been traversed from west to east. Wallin's report, which was a model of accuracy, appeared in the Journal of the Royal Geographical Society of London, vols. xx. and xxiv. A number of modern Bedouin songs, of great linguistic value, from Central Arabia, which he had collected in Hayil (Jebel Shammar) and in the Jof, were published in the Journal of the German Orient Society.

In 1853 the famous Englishman Richard Burton, to whom we owe the first complete translation of the "Arabian Nights," undertook a pilgrimage to Mecca and Medina, like Burckhardt disguised as a Mussulman. Hisvork, " Personal Narrative of a Pilgrimage to el-Medinah and Mecca" (3 vols., London, 1856), may be regarded as an importan: supplement to Burckhardt's. Here we may in advance mention the fact that Burton (well known also as an African explorer) in 1877 and '78 again explored Arabia. This time we find him in the northwest portion, known from the Bible as the Land of Midian. His two expeditions to that quarter, made in close succession, were described in the

attractive style peculiar to him in the two works, " The Goldmines of Midian and the Ruined Midianite Cities" (London, 1878) and "The Land of Midian Revisited" (2 vols., London, 1879).

Toward the end of 1861, Jacob Saphir, a Jew from Jerusalem, made an interesting tour to Yemen, travelling from Hodaida to San'a, then via Shibam to Kaukaban and 'Amran, and finally via San'a to Aden. The account of this journey published in Hebrew was not mentioned by Zehme, D. H. Miiller being the first to call attention to it. Evidently this trip of Saphir served as a guide for Halevv, since he learned from it about the existence of Jewish communities in Yemen, and therefore resolved that he also would travel as a Jerusalemitic Jew; although from San'a following routes entirely different from those followed by Saphir. D. H. Miiller in his above-mentioned treatise gave German translations of several extracts from Saphir's memoir, which is generally inaccessible to European and American readers.

Zeitschrift der Deutschen Morgenlandischen Geselhchaft, vols. v. and vi. *Eben Saphir,* vol. i., Lyck, 1866. Comp. his *Burgen und Schlosser Sudarabicns* (published by the Academy of Vienna), pp. 6, *sea.* See below.

The memorable second tour across the Arabian peninsula was made in 1862-3 by the Englishman Win. Clifford Palgrave, a Jesuit father who t r a v e l le d from the Dead Sea to Qatif, whence he went by sea to 'Oman. Zehme has well said in his summary of these achi evemen t s: while Wallin " revealed to us the great northwest territory between the Sinaitic penins u l a, the E uphrates, Jebel Shammar (Hayil), and Medina, thus conducting us to the very portals of Nejd proper (the highlands of Central Arabia), Palgrave for the first time opened these portals, traversed the whole of Central Arabia, — practically unknown before his day,— reaching again the ocean billows on the shores of the Persian Gulf." The haste with which Palgrave was dragged through the country by his guide (many parts being traversed only by night) often cut short his

observations. So much the more interesting are those he made at the places where he remained longer. His description ofYemama and his information concerning the remarkable Wadi ed-Dawasir are the most important results of what was an epoch-making tour, notwithstanding many opinions to the contrary.

See his book, "A Narrative of a Year's Journey through Central and Eastern Arabia," 2 vols., London, 1862-63.

South ol Azab

Many of his statements have since been verified by the Italian traveller Guarmani, Palgrave's next successor, who went from Jerusalem by way of Taima to Hayil and thence southward as far as 'Onaiza, while the Austrian traveller Glaser afterward in San'a met the very Arab who had been Palgrave's guide to Yemama, and through him established the fact that the former Jesuit father Palgrave had really visited all the places where he himself declared that he had been.

After Wallin's tour from Jebel Shammar to the Euphrates and that of Palgrave from Nejd to the Persian Gulf, the only thing really necessary to make our knowledge of Central Arabia in the main complete was to fill the gap between these two. This was done in 1865 by the English "Resident " in Bushire, Colonel Pelly, who journeyed from Quwait (Koweit) at the northwest point of the Persian Gulf, due south to Riyadh, in the district called Nejd. Just before reaching Riyadh he made a short detour to Sedus, while on the return trip he travelled due east via Hofhuf to the Gulf, by a somewhat more northerly route than that taken by Palgrave. Although in important discoveries his tour cannot compare with those of Wallin and Palgrave, still with scientific precision he located Riyadh, Hofhuf, and other places, and determined the physical character of the whole region between Riyadh and the Gulf. Here we should mention the fact that between Yemama, with its capital Riyadh, and the coast region of Bahrain — the ancient "Sea-country " of the Babylonian inscriptions — lies a sandy desert (the so-called Dehna) about eight days' journey in width, which Pelly and before him Palgrave had to cross on their way. See above, pp. 695, *ley.* Comp. Guarmani's report *Neged septentrional* in the *Bulletin lie la Ssfirtf de Geographic,* Paris, 1865, later published in book form under the title *11 NegeJ Settentrionale,* Jerusalem, 1866. It might interest the reader to learn that this remarkable man, whose work reads like a charming romance, first served as a Jesuit missionary in Beyrout, where he had a great reputation on account of his sermons delivered in Arabic. On the above-mentioned journey, besides the Arab guide referred to, he was accompanied by a certain Jeraijiri, the present Grxco-Melchitic patriarch of Damascus, who went with Palgrave as far as Qatif on the Persian Gulf, whence he returned via Baghdad to Beyrout. After his expdition Palgrave went to Paderborn, then left the Jesuit order and went to Berlin. He died in 1891, while serving as English minister resident at Montevideo.

In the same year, 1865, Wetzstein, at that time Prussian consul at Damascus, published the important information which he had gained from different Arabs concerning the principal highways of Central and Northern Arabia.

The names coming next in order, those of the Jewish Orientalist Joseph Halevy of Paris, and Heinrich von Maltzan, bring us back to South Arabia. The former took advantage of the fact that in Yemen there are a number of Hebrew communities, tolerated by Islam. Near the end of the year 1869, in the guise of a poor Jew from Jerusalem, he undertook important explorations in South Arabia, the land of the Queen of Sheba, around whose name so manv legends cluster. The character which Halevy had assumed exposed him often to unfair treatment, but he also was thereby free from too close a surveillance, which might incidentally have become dangerous. Of course the role which he had to play quite often interfered with his exact topographical survey of the region and copying the inscriptions. But notwithstanding this difficulty, he brought back with him nearly 700 inscriptions (about 50 of medium length, the remainder consisting of only a few words or a few lines) as the rich fruit of his memorable travels. He was the first and is as yet the only European to advance northward as far as Wadi Nejran and to traverse the so-called South Arabian Jof, the ancient land of the Mineans. He was also in Marib and Sirwah (see under Arnaud, above), where he could stay, however, only a few hours, thus failing to gain substantial results. On account of Halevy's tour, the year 1870 marks a new epoch in the study of the ancient history of South Arabia. The report of his travels appeared in 1872. In geography his achievements were less important, because at each place the distinguished explorer was allowed to stay only a short time. But his collection of inscriptions, published also in 1872, proved the more valuable on account of Halevy's critical notes, which laid the first real foundations of Sabean philology.

See Pelly's own report, "A Visit to the Wahabee Capital," in the Journal of the Royal Geographical Society of London, vol. xxxv. Under the title *Nordarabien unci die syrische Wiste nach den Angaben der Eingeborenen* in the *Berliner Zeitichrift fur allgemeine Erdkunde,* vol. xviii.

In 1870-71 Heinrich von Maltzan made a few short trips from Aden along the coast. The value of the book in which he describes them is much increased by the great variety of information that he gathered in Aden from the natives of Eastern Yemen and of Hadhramot, — information now largely, if not altogether, antiquated in view of the much more thorough investigations of Count Landberg in the country between Yemen proper and Hadhramot. Yet Maltzan undoubtedly has the credit of having created an interest in Arabian geography and ethnology in wide circles and of having himself given much new, though not always accurate, information on these subjects. It was really a new world that Maltzan by his accounts of Dathina, Yafi'a, Baihan, etc., revealed to the western world, though then *Rapport sur une mission archeologique dans le Ye-men,* in *Journal Asiaiique,* series 6, vol. xix. For a fuller report see *Bulletin Je la Seeirte Je Geographie,* 1873 1877 *Voyage au Nedjran).* His book on A. von Wrede's travels, published in 1870, was mentioned above in connection with the year 1843.

Reise nach Sudarabien, Braunschweig, 1873 (with maps). Comp. his *Arabica,* parts 4 and 5, Leiden, 1896 and 1898. South Arabian Princes *(Seai cf tke Sultan of Lakij-jink nun limits J*

only seen as through a glass darkly. It was first proved by Glaser's explorations that these districts made up most of the ancient kingdom of Qataban, which along with Ma'in, Saba (Sheba), and Hadhramot flourished nearly a thousand years, ending shortly before the birth of Christ. In his book Maltzan was able also to utilize the report of a tour made in 1870 by Captain Miles and Werner Munzinger, who explored the Wadi Maifa'at as far as Habban. Comp. Journal of the Royal Geographical Society of London, vol. xli.

In 1873 Charles Millinger travelled from Hodaida to San'a, the present Turkish capital of Yemen. The report of this journey, which contained little that was new, is given as the last of Zehme's extracts in his book " Arabia and the Arabs," above mentioned. Zehme continued his valuable reports only to the year 1879, in the geographical journal *Globus.* His lamented death occurred April 29, 1880, at his home in Frankfort on the Oder.

We here mention briefly and in chronological order the exploring expeditions to Arabia from 1876 to 1900: —

In 1876-78 Charles M. Doughty made his memorable tour to Medain Salih (where he discovered Nabatean, Lihyanian or Tamudian, Minean and so-called Proto-Arabic inscriptions), to Jebel Shammar (especially Hayil), to the Harra (Volcanic Region) of 'Owairidh, Taima, Khaibar, Boraida, 'Onaiza, and Tayif, to mention here only the principal stopping places during these travels, which lasted for two years. The great importance of Doughty's narrative was well set forth by Wellhausen, — Aloys Sprenger, the famous biographer of Mohammed, having already previously enlarged ' upon the geographical significance of Doughty's work for our knowledge of the region between 'Onaiza and Tayif. Doughty had lived nearly two years in the tents of the Arabs — not in the lordly style warranted by his means, but as one of their equals, sharing their privations and hardships; so that his narrative is a rare source of knowledge upon the present manners and customs among the Bedouins of Central Arabia. And owing to the con This is the wadi in which in 1898 the expedition of the Academy of Vienna, conducted by Count Landberg, proceeded as far as 'Azzan. This valley is not to be confounded with the Wadi Maifa, which lies farther to the east.

See Journal or the Royal Geographical Society of London, vol. xliv. 1874. Under the title *Aus und uber Arabien,* 1-8, 1876-1879; nos. 5 and 8 containing fuller accounts of Manzoni's first two excursions in Yemen, no. 7 of Burton's exploration of Midian; while the other articles give information of a more general character. See his " Travels in Arabia Deserta," 2 vols., Cambridge, 1888. The work contains I 300 closely printed pages. *Zeiti thrift tier Dcutschen Morgcnlandischen Geselisthaft,* vol. xlv.,1891, pp. 172-80. servative character of the Arabs, it is also a valuable objective commentary upon numerous passages of the Old Testament. The most important geographical information in Doughtv's work is that concerning the Wadi el-Hamdh (running from Medina northwest and then west to the Red Sea), which he and Burton to a certain extent discovered anew, and that concerning the beginning and course of Wadi er-Rumma, identical with the river of Eden called Gihon. *Zeitschrift der Deutichen Morgenlandiichen Geselhchaft,* vol. xlii., 1888, pp. 321-34C.

In 1877-80 Renzo Manzoni, grandson of the famous writer of the *Promessi Sposi,* made three excursions, the goal and chief point of interest of each being San'a, the Turkish capital of Yemen, a place still rarely visited by Europeans.

Manzoni's work, which contains two excellent maps of the entire region between Aden, San'a, and Hodaida, is also the first of the illustrated books on travel in Arabia. The woodcuts, copied from photographs, certainly give a far more vivid impression of the nature of Arabia — still in many respects so strange to us — than the best verbal descriptions. Through Manzoni's description and cuts we obtain an especially' good idea of San'a (nearly 6600 ft. above the sea), particularly as an accurate plan of the city is added, the first of its kind ever published.

Burton's two works on Midian have already been mentioned above in connection with his pilgrimage to Mecca (see p. 706). An important geographical supplement, which appeared in 1879, mav here briefly be referred to.

Lord Byron's granddaughter Lady Anne Blunt wrote an interesting account of a tour made by her in company with her husband, Sir Wilfred Scawen Blunt, lasting from December, 1878, to the end of February, 1879, and extending from Damascus through the North Arabian Jof and through the Nefud desert to Hayil, then along the pilgrim road *El Yemen, Trc Anni nell' Arabia Felice, Escursioni fatte da I Stt. 18 J J nl Marzo 18S0.* Rome, I 880. (First tour, Sept., 1877, to u»e, 1878: Aden to San'a and back; second tour, Apr., 1878, to Jan., 1879: Mocha, Ta'izz, Zebid, Hodaida, San'a, Aden; third, Jan., 1879, March, 1880: Aden to N. E. Africa, then Ta'izz, Ibb, Yerim, San'a, Hodaida. Manzoni always writes Tez inaccurately for Ta'izz.) The tours described in these works were made partly in April, 1877, and continued from Dec, 1877, to April, 1878.

See Journal of the Royal Geographical Society, vol. xlix., pp. 1 — 1 jo. to Meshhed Ali and Baghdad. The value of the lively and entertaining narrative is enhanced by a number of fine woodcuts. Sir Wilfred and his wife had a better opportunity than their predecessors (excepting Doughty, whose work, however, was not published until eight years later) to survey and describe the region; especially their measurements o f alti-

tudes make a real addition to our geographical knowledge.

Only for the sake of completeness we here refer to the tour made from June to September, 1879, by Shapira, the Jewish antiquity dealer from Jerusalem, who gained a certain notoriety in connection with the well-known Moabite and other forgeries. He first travelled from Aden to San'a, whence he made a trip to 'Amran, about twelve hours northwest of San'a and 7700 feet above the sea, and from there over the pass of Kaukaban, 9200 feet (the highest peak being 10,000 feet), to Tawila, whence he returned to San'a. On his way home he went via Menakha to Hodaida. " A Pilgrimage to Nedjd, the Cradle of the Arab Race. A Visit to the Court of the Arab Emir and « Our Persian Campaign ' " (the latter being described only in vol. ii.,pp. 113—232), 2 vols., London, 1880 (2d edition,

Azab (*Halfway between Aden and San'a)*

In April and May, 1881, the island of Socotra, lying apart from the highway of the world's commerce, though famous in antiquity as the Isle of Incense, was visited by Riebeck's expedition in the interest of natural science, the English botanist Balfour having previously spent six weeks there in 1880. A graphic account of this visit, illustrated with interesting woodcuts, was written by the famous African explorer and botanist Georg Schvveinfurth, who was a member of that expedition. This visit, as well as an excursion made later by the same scholar Schweinfurth from Hodaida to Menakha, — /'. e., from the seacoast to the foothills of the Alpine region of South Arabia,— gave him the opportunity to establish that the sycamore and mimusops, the two sacred trees which played so important a role in the Old-Egyptian worship, were indigenous to South Arabia, which was also the real source of the incense early imported into Egypt through Nubia. Now, when archaeological discoveries make it more and more apparent that Egyptian civilization came from Babylonia, Schweinfurth's observations seem to prove that Arabia was the original connecting link between the two.

A tour not entirely without results in geography and epigraphy was that made between February 21 and March 26, 1882, by the Austrian Siegfried Langer, who travelled from Hodaida via Bet el-Faqih and Dhuran to San'a, but unfortunately was murdered in Mav of the same vear at a point northeast of Aden. See the short description of this tour from the pen of the distinguished geographer H. Kiepert, of Berlin, in *Globus*, vol. xxxviii., 1880, pp. 183-87. *Ein Besuch auf Socotra*, in Westermann's *llustrierte Monatshefte*, vol. xxxiv., 1891, pp. 603-626, and vol. xxxv., 1891, pp. 29-53. *Verhandlungen der Gcse Use haft fur Erdkunde zu Berlin*, vol. rvi, 1881, nos. 4, 5 and 7. See his report in *Auiland*, 1882, no. 39, and in the same periodical views of San'a and Dhuran from lunger's papers, published in Hommel's essay *Zur Geschichte und Geographic Sudarabiens (Auiland*, vol. hi. 1883, pp.

In the next place we should note the first of the four fruitful expeditions made between October, 1882, and March, 1884, by another Austrian scholar by the name of Eduard Glaser. For a whole year Glaser was detained in San'a by the Turkish authorities. This time he devoted to astronomical calculations and to inquiries of all kinds. Finally he was allowed to accompany the Turkish army invading the territory of Suda (northwest of San'a) from October 16 to November 15, also to' make two exploring expeditions to Shibam, Kaukaban, Tawila, 'Amran, Raida, etc., and to Khamr, Dhi Bin, and Na'at in the district of the wild Banu Hashid (end of November, 1883, to February, 1884). The numerous inscriptions found were published''' in the Parisian *Corpus Inscriptionum Semiticarum*, Himyaritic section, parts 1—3. In March, 1884, Glaser returned to Furope.

The joint expedition carried on from September, 1883, to the summer of 1884 by the Strassburg librarian and professor Julius Futing, with the Frenchman (orig. Alsatian) Charles Huber, brings us again to North Arabia. Huber, to whom we owe the discovery

of the interesting Aramaic inscription of Taima (sixth century before Christ), was murdered near Jidda, July 29, 1884; but his complete diary, illustrated by numerous drawings and maps, is now at hand in printed form, while of Futing's diary only the first volume has thus far appeared, this ending with November 16, 1883.

S'z-ST) The usual and direct route leads through Menakha.

See Glaser's narrative, *Meine Rcise durch Arhab und Hashid*, in Petermann's *Geographische Mittheiiungen*, vol. xxx., 1884, nos. 5 and 6. *Journal d un voyage en Arabic*, Paris, 1891. *Tagebuch einer Reise in Inner-Arabien*, i., Leiden, 1896.

The expedition went from Damascus via 'Orman and Kaf to the Wadi Sirhan or the North Arabian Jof, the H iddDekel ("wadi of palms") of the Bible storv of F.den, from there through the Nefud desert to Havil (Hail), the residence of the Wahhabite princes of Shammar, whence several excursions were made. From Havil the two ex plorers proceeded to Taima, Tabuk, and El-'Ola (El-Oelai, where Euting made squeezes of the important Minean (South Arabian) and Lihvanian (Tamudian) inscriptions, which in part had been previously copied by Doughty and Huber. On March 19 Euting and Huber separated. On March 25 Euting completed his epigraphical re The Ashur (English Version: Assyria) mentioned there is the Arabian Ashur; not until later was the name Hiddckel applied to the river Diklat or Tigris, on the Assyrian border.

Published by D. H. Miiller, *Epigraphisthe Denkmaler aus Ambit*, Vienna, 1889; later and fuller treatment of the Minean inscriptions by . H. Mordtmann, *Beitrage %ur minhischen Epigraphik*, Weimar, 1 8q6. searches in that region, while Huber returned to Hayil, whence he travelled via Jebel Nir to Jidda. A full treatment of the rich geographical results will not be possible until the completion of Euting's report, which is not only beautifully written but also illustrated by a number of fine drawings. But even now we cannot put an estimate

high enough upon the epoch-making discovery of South Arabian inscriptions in the southeastern part of the Land of Midian (in the above-mentioned Kl-'Ola). They belong to the flourishing period of the Minean kingdom (about 1200-800 B. C.), and mention priests and priestesses of Wadd, the Minean Moon-god.

A short excursion into the interior of 'Oman was made in 1884 by Colonel S. B. Miles, who but recently gave a personal account of the same. According to all descriptions, including the earlier ones, 'Oman must be a veritable paradise; and if ever there existed closer relations between ancient Arabia and India, the principal rendezvous must have been in this region, which as yet is far from being fully explored. Whether the civilization of South Arabia extended to 'Oman, we do not know, since unfortunately there has been no search yet for inscriptions in that quarter.

Proceeding in chronological order, from this remote corner of Arabia we must go to Mecca, the centre of Islam. There in 1884-85 the Dutch Arabist C. Snouck Hurgronje stayed for nearly a year, having embraced Mohammedanism for this special purpose. To this man, who was already distinguished for his knowledge of Islam, such a long sojourn gave the materials for his epoch-making work *Mekka?* Never before had been written such a scholarly and at the same time such a graphic description of the Holy City, of its inhabitants and pilgrims, and of the customs prevailing there, never such a history of the city. Thanks to the copious illustrations in the photograph atlas, the city, with its lofty houses, in the true South Arabian style, with the picturesque features of its environment, and with its various human types, stands out vividly before our eyes.

According to Burton, there is still in North Midian a well of Moses and a chapel of Moses (*muiallat Muni*, literally, the " praying-place of Moses "); especially the chapels *(sit/tvat)* play an important part in these Minean inscriptions. "Journal of an Excursion in Oman, in South-East Arabia," with map, in the "Geographical Journal," vol. vii., London, 1896, pp. 5 537. Concerning Miles' tour to Hadhramot see record for 1870, above.

The following works, with the sole exception of Nolde's, bring us again to that treasure house of antiquities and legends, Southern Arabia, which, by virtue of its ancient civilization, to the people of Northern and Central Arabia was invested with a halo of romance even at the first period of Islam.

On his second expedition to Yemen, April, 1885,10 February, 1886, Kduard Glaser made a topographical and archaeological survey of the country to the southeast and south of San'a as far as Aden, especially the country of Tzafar (southeast of Yerim), the ancient capital of Himyar. Such thorough investigations as those of Glaser, on all of his four expeditions, had never before been conducted by any one in South Arabia. Unfortunately he has thus far published only a partial report of his second expedition. However, a large number of inscribed stones, mostly Minean, which Glaser obtained during this expedition are now in the British Museum in London.

Two vols. written in German (The Hague, 1888), with picture atlas, a supplement to which appeared in 1889, *Bildcr aus Mtkka*. See especially the instructive little book by the Austrian Orientalist Baron Alfred von Kremer, *Die Sutiarabische Sage* (Leipzig), and the chapter on this subject in his larger work, *Kulturgnchichte ties Orients unter Jen Ckalifem. Von Hodeidah nach San'a*, in Petermann's *Mitthcilungen*, 1886, nos. I and *2*. In the accompanying map are shown also the regions northwest of San'a traversed by Glaser in 1 884. See edition of same by Derenbourg in "Babylonian and Oriental Record;``

In the year 1886 there appeared in Batavia the valuable work of the Dutch Arabist Van den Berg, *Le Hadhratnout*, in which accurate data, procured from native travellers to Dutch East India, are wrought into an interesting narrative containing description o f this portion of Arabia — hitherto so little known, despite the work of Wrede, Maltzan,

Hirsch, and Bent.

Merely for the

'Village of Aredoah, South ot Khorjibj purpose of studying botany the Frenchman A. Defters made an excursion to Yemen in 1887. Other botanical excursions from Aden to the north of the Turkish frontier, and eastward to Dathina, were made subsequently by the same explorer, who reported his results in the *Revue d'Egypte.*

F.duard Glaser's third expedition, October, 1887, to September, 1888, was still richer in epigraphical results than his first two—richer in fact than all former ones put together, including Halevy's. The time from the middle of March to the end of April, 1888, was spent in Marib, the ancient Sabean capital, he being the third European to visit that region. While there he copied nearly four hundred inscriptions, among them the " dam inscription " containing about 100 lines, and dating from the time shortly before Mohammed— published in Berlin in 1899. But the jewel of his collection is the large inscription from Sirwah, west of Marib, consisting of about 1000 words, and dating from the rise of the Sabean kingdom, about 550 B. c. An edition of this famous text by Glaser is in course of preparation. The inscribed stones obtained by Glaser on his third expedition are in the Berlin Museum. The only report as yet published by Glaser on his memorable expedition to Marib, which lies clearly outside of the Turkish sphere of influence, is contained in two articles published by Hommel; but a larger work, *Saba*, is in course of preparation.

D. A. Muller in the *Wiener Zeitichrift fir Kunde dts Morgenlandes*, and Hommel facsimiles of the larger of these inscriptions in his *Sudarabische Chrtit'jmathie*. Of 292 pages, large octavo, with map and illustrations.

Journal d'une excursion botaniqut, 246 pp., Paris, 1889. In *Mittheilungen der Vorderasiatischen Geselhchaft*, Berlin. It was only a pleasure trip that the English tourist Walter B. Harris made in January, 1892, from Aden to San'a; yet his publication is valuable on account of the numerous photographs of land-

scapes, which for the first time give a clear idea of the grandeur of the Alpine region in South Arabia.

Of Eduard Glaser's fourth expedition (from the beginning of 1892 to the spring of 1894) little more than brief notices have been as yet given to the public. Its results were confined to the field of epigraphy. Glaser, who remained most of the time in San'a, taught Bedouins to make squeezes, Published by Mordtmann, Berlin, 1893. *Beilage der Allgemeinen Zeitung*, 1888, nos. 293 and 294 (*EJitarJ Glaser's Reiie nach Marib*). A Journey through Yemen," in the " Illustrated London News," nos. from Aug. to Nov., 1892; afterward issued in book form, London, 1894. and trained them so admirably that these people brought to him, as precious trophies, excellent squeezes of all of Halevy's larger inscriptions from the Jof, also of about one hundred (atabanian texts from the country south of Marib, and of many other valuable inscriptions, the (atabanian inscriptions coming from a region in which no Kuropean had ever before set foot. This time also Glaser obtained a number of inscribed stones, which now adorn the CourtMuseum in Vienna, and which were recently published' by D. H. Muller.

To the same period belongs Baron Eduard Nolde's journey, of which he wrote a charming description, from Damascus to the North Arabian Jof, to Hayil, then to the camp of Ibn Rashid, Emir of Shammar, at that time halfway between Shaqra and Riyadh, and finally from there to Baghdad (January to March, 1893).

No less interesting is the tour of Leo Hirsch, of Berlin, to Hadhramot (January to August, 1893), he being the first European to reach the present capital Shibam and even Yerim. Not even A. von Wrede had reached these two places. But no one as yet has succeeded in visiting Shabwa (Sabota of the classic writers), the ancient capital of the kingdom of Hadhramot and so rich in inscriptions.

While Hirsch's visit to Mahraland, remarkable for its dialect, was limited to a short stay at the two coast towns of Sehut and Gishin (Keshin), in the beginning of the year 1895 Frankincense Country proper, or the district of Tzafar, lying east of these places and west of Mirbat, was visited by the late lamented explorer J. Theodore Bent (fi897) and his wife, who was his constant companion. Both spent the winter of 1893-94 in Hadhramot, where they travelled as far as Shibam. *Siidarabische Alterthumer im Kunst-historischcn Hofmuseum, mil 14 Lichtdrucktafeln,* Vienna, 1 899. Compare, also, Hommel, *Aufiatze ttuJ Abhandlungen,* ii. pp. 129-206 (with a glossary of those texts, pp. 168, Died by his own hand, March II, 1895, in London.

See his *Reise nach Innerarabien, Kurdistan and Armenien, 1892* (error for 1893), Braunschweig, 1895. Special attention is called to the two instructive chapters on the camel and the horse. *Reisen in Sudarabien, Mahraland and Hadhramut,* Leiden, 1897. Concerning the defects in the otherwise meritorious narrative of Hirsch see the competent opinion of Eduard Glaser in Petermann's *Mittheilungen,* 1897, no. 3, pp. 37-39 He published an account of his visit — " Exploration of the Frankincense Country, Southern Arabia " — with photographic illustrations, in the " Gcographical Journal," vol. vi., 1895, pp. 109—134. See, also, his recently published book "Southern Arabia," London, 1900, pp. 227-285. Several years before (in 1889) Bent had already made a trip to Bahrain, which is treated on pp. 1—43 of his but recently published book "Southern Arabia," London, 1900. In addition, however, to Bent's interesting discourse upon the Frankincense Country, the reader is hereby re

South Arabian Wadi and Castle ferred to Glaser's comments in his book on the Abessinians in Arabia and Africa."

In February, 1896, the distinguished Arabist Count Carlo Landberg, one of the best experts in the Arabic popular dialects, visited the " Raven Castle " (Hisn el-Ghurab) on the coast of South Arabia, whence he brought back squeezes and photographs of the inscription there, long known but not accurately copied. Of these and of his inquiries, in the winters of 1895-96 and 1896-97, among the natives in Aden concerning the regions of Dathina, 'Awaliq and Kl-Hadina comparatively still unknown, he has given a full report in his *Arabica,* no. 4 (Leiden, 1897). In no. 5, of the same publication, which appeared in the fall of 1898, he continues these inquiries, giving us new and most surprising information about the exact location of Baihan, Maryama, Raidan, Harib, Timna', the Wahidi land, and Shabwa, the ancient capital of Hadhramot.

See "Southern Arabia," pp. 71-225. *Die Abessinier in Arabien und Afrika,* Munich, 1895, pp. 182-189.

In December, 1898, the expedition of the Vienna Academy to Shabwa, conducted by Count Landberg and accompanied bv the Viennese Orientalist D. H. Miiller, departed from Bal-Haf. But it failed to get farther than 'Azzan in the Wadi Maifa'at, whence it had to return to the coast. Although unsuccessful in its attempt to reach Ansab and Shabwa, by the mediation of Count Landberg the Vienna expedition succeeded in securing a new squeeze of the inscription found near Naqb el-Hajar and in copying there two more inscriptions hitherto unknown. From these it was proved that the people in the Wadi Maifa'at in antiquity were devoted to the worship of the god 'Amm (/. e., the Moon as the divine "uncle" or protector) and were therefore probably mere subjects of the powerful kingdom of Qataban, which must have extended farther eastward than was formerly supposed. In Aden, in consequence of disagreements with Miiller, Count Landberg quit the expedition; while the former with some other scholars from Vienna, mostly naturalists, proceeded (February, 1899) *to* the island of Socotra, to study with Dr. Jahn the dialect ot the island, which is related to the Mahra language. Rich as it is in ruins and inscriptions, Shabwa is still unvisited bv Europeans, awaiting exploration in the twentieth century.

II

The great importance of Arabia in relation to the Old Testament and to Biblical study depends not upon its deserts and oases, not upon its palm trees and camels, nor even upon its famous products, gold, precious stones and perfumes (frankincense and myrrh), although the latter did also play an important part in the Hebrew worship, — but upon the inscriptions found by bold travellers east of the Land of Midian, and especially in Southern Arabia, and upon the valuable cuneiform records left to us by the Babylonians and Assyrians concerning the different divisions and tribes of Arabia, mostly the very ones that are mentioned in the Bible.

Beginning with the inscriptions found in Arabia itself, it is only for the sake of completeness that we mention at the outset the Nabatean inscriptions dating from the centuries nearest to the time of Christ. Such were found on the peninsula of Sinai, in Petra and also in Kl'Ola (Oela). The language of these inscriptions is Aramaic, though the names of their authors are mostly Arabic. The style of writing, from which the later Arabic writing was immediately derived, is a semi-cursive corruption of the so-called Old-Aramaic, which in turn represents a later offshoot of the Phenician. There are, however, some inscriptions from Taima, not later than the sixth century before Christ, which are written in the Old-Aramaic characters and in the Aramaic language; the largest of them was mentioned above in connection with Huber, 1883. The stele (*suwita* Assyr. *asumitu* on which it was engraved shows Assyrian influence, as do the names of gods mentioned in it (*Ma/iram, Shungalla* = Babyl.-Assyr. *Us/iumga//u, Ashira,* and *Selem* = *Salmtt*). In El-'Ola were found, along with Nabatean (socalled Proto-Arabic, usually containing only names of per See under Doughty, Huber, and Euting above.

sons) and Minean inscriptions, also Lihyanian inscriptions, written in a variety of the South Arabian alphabet and near in time to the Nabatean inscriptions (according to Glaser dating from a time no earlier than that between the Nabatean supremacy and Mohammed). They are, therefore, of no greater importance for Biblical antiquity than the Nabatean inscriptions, though it is to be observed that they contain proper names of such an archaic form as Talmai (comp. Judges i: 10 and *i* Sam. *3:3),* and that their language represents a North Arabian dialect showing many points of contact with the Hebrew, — *e. g.,* the article *han-, ha*(comp. Hebr. *ham-melek* from *han-melek,* Arabic *al-malik* from *han-malik).* The so-called Proto-Arabic inscriptions, or rather merely scribbled names, are also written in an alphabet very similar to that of South Arabia, and are often hard to decipher. This alphabet shows some striking points of similarity to the writing of the Abessinian inscriptions and seems to belong properly to the Frankincense Country.

However, most of the inscriptions found in Arabia belong, in style of writing as well as in language, to a family group embracing two dialects and to be regarded as native to South Arabia, although for various reasons it is most probable that it originated in East Arabia, — *i. e.,* the socalled "Sea-country " of the ancient Babylonians (Bahrain) and Yemama, or in short Magan (=Maan). These two dialects are the Minean and the Sabean.

In the older dialect, the so-called Minean, are written: — 1. The Minean royal inscriptions (about 1400-700 B. c), found in the South Arabian Jof (see, above, Halevy, under 1870) and in El-'Ola in Northwest Arabia (see, above, Euting, 1883), where the Mineans had colonies extending to the borders of Edom.
2. The Qatabanian royal inscriptions (see, above, Glaser, See D. H. Miiller's essay in the Transactions of the Oriental Congress at London, vol. ii., 1893, pp. 86-95. 1893), excepting one ' that a Greek trader sent to Europe, are still unedited. These were found chiefly in the country south of Marib, viz., Harib (Timna') and probably also Baihan and 'Awaliq, /. e., the whole territory between Yemen proper and Hadhramot. The kings of Qataban were contempo-

rary with those of Ma'an (later pronounced Ma'in, hence *Me'ivaloi, Mivaloi),* and with the Sabeans until about 200 B. c. 3. The inscriptions of Hadhramot, of which only two are as yet known, one from Shabwa, the ancient residence of the kings of Hadhramot, and the other from 'Obne, written in the later language of Hadhramot and discovered by A. von Wrede. The kingdom of Hadhramot was also contemporaneous with that of Ma'an, continuing, however, until the first or second century of our era. Also the Minean tomb inscription found in Egypt and dating from the age of the Ptolemies is probably of Hadhramotian origin.

All the other inscriptions are written in the Sabean dialect, the oldest dating from the time of the so-called priestkings *(makrub,* plural *makarib)* of Sheba and written mostly boustrophedon (beginning about 700 B. c); others from the time of the " Kings of Saba (Sheba) " (to about 115 B. c), then those from the time of the " Kings of Saba (Sheba) and Dhu-Raidan " (after Qataban lost its independence, to about 300 A. D.), and finally those from the time of the " Kings of Saba (Sheba), Dhu-Raidan, and Hadhramot" (to the middle of the sixth century of our era).

Perhaps also the inscription of Naqb el-Hajar (Wadi Maifa'at), though hitherto regarded as Hadhramotian, is of Qatabanian origin, considering the mention of 'Amm (as seen in Count Landberg's new squeeze), the chief god of the Qatabanians. See Hommel's edition in *Zeitschrift der Deutsche/! Morgenlandischen Geselhthaft,* vol. liii., 1899, part 1. Osiander, No. 29 = British Museum, No. 6. See Hommel in the " Proceedings of the Society of Biblical Archaeology," March, 1894.

The Mineo-Sabean writing was derived from the same alphabet as that of Canaan (the so-called Phenician, the oldest monument dating from about iooo B. C). Since according to native tradition the Phenicians (compare Herodotus) came from East Arabia, we have another reason for believing that this original alphabet of all the western

Semitic forms of writing (Phenician, Canaanean, and Aramaic on the one hand, the South Arabian on the other) originated in the country of Magan (= Ma'an), not later than in the first half of the second millennium before Christ. In palaeography the Minean roval inscriptions are most closely related to the oldest Sabean —as is quite natural, since the Minean kingdom, according to the Sirwah inscription (discovered by Glaser, but still unedited), was indeed finally conquered by the priest-kings of Saba (Sheba) not later than about 550 B. C. The inscriptions of the " kings" of Saba (Sheba) exhibit letters of a somewhat later form. Moreover, the alphabet of the Christian Abessinians (the so-called Ethiopians), the oldest forms of which are found in inscriptions of the fourth centurv of our era, is derived from the South Arabian, or rather from a variety of it, that must have been used in the southern and western parts ot Hadhramot. Its origin in this region, in which the so-called Mahra dialect is now spoken, is indicated by the linguistic relation of the Ethiopic in phonology and morphology as well as in vocabulary. From this quarter the ancestors ot the Semitic Abessinians, perhaps even before the time ot Christ, emigrated to Habesh.

The most important facts concerning the discovery of the South Arabian inscriptions have been given in Part I. (Exploring Expeditions). Arnaud, Halevy, Euting, and above all, Eduard Glaser, are the men who procured most of the inscriptions proving at the same time the most interesting. If Glaser had published all of his results, not only would his name head the list, but it would stand almost alone, since he, *e. g.* , has excellent squeezes even of Halevy's M inean inscriptions, which had in many cases been imperfectly copied. As for the interpretation, including the decipherment, all the main points had been settled by the two epoch-making essays of Gesenius and 1. Kodiger,'-' despite the meagre material then at their disposal. Next, coming before Halevy's 686 inscriptions, were Arnaud's 56 numbers (published by Fresnel in

1845).

Contributed only few inscriptions, but the more important because thei came from El-'Ola in Northwest Arabia. *Uber die Himjaritisehe Sprache tin J Schrift*, in the *Allgemeine LitemturZeitung*, July, 1 841. *Excurs uber die von Lieutenant Weltsted bckannt gemnchten himjuritischen Insehriften*, in Wellsted's " Travels in Arabia," German edition, Halle, 1842, vol. ii.,pp. 352-411.

Bronze Tablet with Sabran Inscription (*From 'Amran*)

The material treated by the two German scholars Gesenius and Rodiger having been increased bv Arnaud's fiftysix numbers and in 1863 by fourteen inscribed stones and twenty-eight bronze tablets from 'Amran acquired bv the British Museum, even before the publication of Halew's 686 new inscriptions, the decipherment of the South Arabian inscriptions — except in a few minor points — was actually completed by Osiander, whose interpretation of the British Museum texts just mentioned appeared in 1865, a year after his death, while his resume of all the results hitherto obtained was published in 1866.

The history of Sabean philology from 1866 to 1892 can best be followed in connection with the full bibliographical summary in Hommel's "South Arabian Chrestomathv." The most distinguished names in it are those of the scholars Joseph Halevy, Franz Prastorius, T. H. Mordtmann, D. H. Midler, and Kduard Glaser. As showing the progress of epigraphical research in the last decade, we must refer also to Part IV of the *Corpus Inscriptionum Semiticarum*, edited by Hartw. Derenbourg and published bv the Paris Academy, to Hommel's above-mentioned "South Arabian Chrestomathy," and to several publications by Mordtmann, Hommel, Hugo Winckler, and especially Glaser.

Most important are the religious features presented to us in the South Arabian inscriptions, which since the time of Osiander have in fact received no systematic treatment except in Baethgen's "Contributions to the History of Semitic Religion," ' and there only in brief and not based upon the original sources. It is almost incredible that, despite the abundance of new material at hand, C. P. Tide's " History of Ancient Religion," as well as Friedrich Jeremias' chapter on this subject in Chantepie de la Saussaye's "Handbook of the History of Religion," have entirely neglected the Mineo-Sabean mythology, which in many points is so closely related to the religion of the Babylonians, Canaanites, and Arameans. The fact alone that the South Arabian proper names consisting of two elements are formed in entire analogy with those belonging to the other Western Semites commands our attention. Died March 21, 1864, as minister *(diaconus)* at Goeppingen.

In *Zcitschrift der Deutschcn Morgenlandischen Gesellschaft*, vol. xuc., pp. 159-293, with 35 lithographic plates, under the title *Zur himjarisehei dlterthumskunde*, I. In the same journal, vol. xx., 1866, pp. 205-287: *Zur himjeritch(Alterthumskunde*, II., a. Writing and Language of the Inscriptions, b. Historical and Archaeological Significance of the Same. *Sudarabischc Chrotomathie* (Grammar, Bibliography, Minean Inscriptions with Glossary), Munich, 1893. Published in three sections, 1889, 1892, and 1899.

Whenever several gods are mentioned together in the inscriptions of any of the four chief nations of South Arabia (Mineans, Hadhramotians, Qatabanians, and Sabeo-Himyarites) the first name is usually that of the male deity *'Athtar*, probably a personification of the morning or evening star respectively. The second place is occupied by the national deity, differently named by all the four nations, but in each case to be recognized as the Moon-god: by the Mineans called *Wadd* (literally, "love," or rather "lover " = friend); by the inhabitants of Hadhramot, *Sin* (compare the Babylonian Sin =moon); by the Qatabanians, *'Amm* (literally, " father's brother," in the sense of fatherly friend or protector); by the Sabeans, *Almaquhu* (" his lights " or " stars "), his full name being *Haubas iva-almaqu-hu* (= "the moon and his shining attendants " — compare Jahveh Jehovah Zeba'oth. The third place in the Pantheon of the Mineans is always occupied by *An-Kurah* (" Hate," as opposed to Wadd), written *Nkrh*, the vowels being omitted in the writing of South Arabia, — the people of Hadhramot having in his place the god *Huwal* or *Hoi*, and the Qatabanians *Anbay* (probably = *Nabiyu*, Nebo of the Babylonians). The fourth place among all the four above-named nations is held by a number of sun deities, always represented as females and only locally distinguished according to their different temples *(e. g.,"* the mistress of Nashq " in the land of the Mineans, "the mistress of Ba'dan" and of other places in the land of the Sabeans). For, as differing from the Babylonians proper and the Canaanites influenced by the former (with both of whom *Ba'at* = " Sun " is the chief deity, while *'Ashtoreth* = "Moon-goddess" is his consort), the Arabs, and so originally the Arameans and Hebrews, regarded the moon as the chief deity and the sun as his female counterpart. In Babylonia the two principal sanctuaries of Shamash or the Sun-god were at Larsa and Sippar (the Moon-goddess, Ai or Gula, being his consort); while in the district of Ur, Chaldea proper, which from ancient times was under the influence of the Arabian "Sea-country" (later called *Bit-Takia)*, and also in the Aramean city Haran, the moon *(Ai, Ta, or Sin)* was the chief deity, being represented as male. That the ancient Babylonian god of the earth and sea in the Semitic-Babylonian texts got the surname Ya, while Sin was received in the pantheon as a deity distinct from Ya — these facts belong to the later' syncretism and are evidently due to West Semitic, Arabian influence.

Published in German, *Bcitrage zur Semitischen Religionsgeschichte*, Berlin, 1888. In Dutch *(Gachiedenis*, etc. , Amsterdam, 1893), and in German (*Genhichte der Religion im Altcrtum*, etc., i.,part z, *Vorderasien*, Gotha, 1896). *Lehrbuch der Religionsgeschichte*, 2d edition, Freiburg, 1897, i., pp. 163-zzi. See the treatment of this subject in Hommel's 'The Ancient Hebrew Tradition," New York and London, 1897. By means of" cuneiform inscriptions the proper names can now be traced back to the time of Abraham and Khammurabi (about zioo B. c.), in some cases even to the time of Sargon and Naram-Sin of Agade. And in Syria also, as is shown by the Nerab inscriptions found near Aleppo, the Moon-god (*Sahar*) and his consort *Nikkal* (Babylonian *Nimgal*) were the chief deities. Compare South Arabian *Wadd Shahran* (Glaser, no. 324, 3).

Besides the above-named deities, in the South Arabian inscriptions we occasionally find still others, most frequently the tutelary deity of Riyam (north of San'a, *Talab* (comp. the Arabic *talab*, "ibex;" hence perhaps *Capricornus* in the Zodiac), then a god called *Sami'* (= " the Hearer," *set/.* of prayers), a western and eastern *Nasr* (= the two eagles in the sky), a god called *Qatnan* (comp. Hebrew Q(K)ainor the Midianite tribe of Qenites; perhaps the patron of goldsmiths and musicians), another named *Ramman* in Shibam, northwest of San'a, identical of course with the Babylonian god Rammanu (by Syrians and Assyrians called Hadad) and with the Biblical Hadad-Rimmon. There was also a god named *Hagir* (/'. *e.,* "he who prevents, wards off"," *idl.* misfortune), another named *Dhii-Samwa* (Samwa being a sanctuary of the Band Amir in the district of Nejran), then a Qatabanian god named *Dhaw* (= Palmyranian Saw and Hebrew Saw, Hos. 5: 11), and still others.

As in the inscriptions of Senjirli (situated in the extreme northwestern part of the Semitic territory) immediately after Hadad, the Syrian Moon-god (originally Hodad, comp. Wadd and alongside the later Arabic Udd and Udad), there appears a god named Kl (" god " par excellence, but here by the side of others), so we find a god named // at two places in South Arabia, once in the originally Minean city Harim and again in the territory of Qataban. We have from Harim a number of inscriptions recording the consecration of virgins to the god *Motab-Natiyan,* probably a Midianite deity. One of the consecrators is there called " Priest of II and of Athtar."' We have every reason to

believe that here II is only the true name of Motab-Natiyan,'-as the special gods of Harim were rather Wadd and Yada'asumhu. And in a Qatabanian inscription are named in succession *'slthtar* — the Riser, *'A mm, Niswar* (or *Nasawir,* com p. *JVasr* above), and // *Fakhr* (or *Fukhr),* the last named to be translated perhaps as " God of the Universe," or else (according to North Arabian meaning *of fakhr)* " God of Fame." Though brought about before 2000 B. C. See Glaser, no. 119.

Translated wrongly " the commandment " or " command " in the English Version. —The Editor. Comp. Hommel, "The Ancient Hebrew Tradition," p. 320. Halevy, nos. 144 and 150.

Since, moreover, the language and religion of the inhabitants of Sam'al (Senjirli) show remarkable points of contact with those of Midian, the worship of El, as whose priest appears Jethro, the father-in-law of Moses, was probably brought from there to both Sam'al and Harim. Also the designation of God as " the Rock " *(Ziir)* is found anions the Midianites as well as in the proper names of the inscriptions from Sam'al and Harim, a fact of deep significance in its bearing upon the history of Old Testament religion and the fidelity of Old Testament tradition.

But before we turn from the South Arabian inscriptions to the Israelites and the Old Testament, let us mention three other sources for the geography and ethnology of ancient Arabia.

i. The statements of the ancient classic writers (Strabo, Pliny, the author of *Perip/us Maris Erythrai,* and Ptolemv) who lived shortly before and after the birth of Christ. 2. The numerous works of Arabian writers on the geography of Arabia, Hamdani's *Jezirat el- Arab,* edited bv D. H. Miiller, Bekri's and Yaqut's geographical dictionaries, edited by Wiistenfeld, the latter two dealing principally with the names of Arabian places, mountains, and rivers frequently mentioned in the Bedouin songs dating from the time shortly before and after Mohammed. All that pertains to this subject, especially the information given bv the classic writers, was system-

atically treated in A. Sprenger's work "The Ancient Geography of Arabia"' and in the second volume of Ed. Glaser's "Sketch of the History and Geography of Arabia," -of which the latter work is especially rich in new facts and new views. Supplements to the former work are to be found in Sprenger's essay on Hamdani's description of the Arabian Peninsula, and his other essay referred to above in connection with Doughty. This would correspond to a Hebrew *moshab han-nbtah,* " throne or him (/'. *t,* the god) who stretches forth the hand" or "who spreads out the heavens." Joannis Kallisperis, 1. 8, *seq.* Comp. Hommel, " Ancient Hebrew Tradition," p. 320, *seq.* 3. The third source, to which we are introduced by Glaser's work, are the Babylono-Assyrian cuneiform inscriptions. These supply more or less detailed information on several parts of Arabia from about 3000 B. C. The rich information contained in the royal inscriptions from Tiglath-Pileser III. to Ashurbanapal (8th and 7th centuries before Christ) had already been gathered by Friedrich Delitzsch. But the correct location of so many places and tribes mentioned in those inscriptions is due to the bold but accurate observations of Glaser, who proved that not all of them were to be sought for in the Syro-Arabian desert, but that many were found in Central Arabia. For the old Babylonian period the most important result is that for the first time Glaser properlv defined the geographical meanings of Magan and Melukh, proving Magan (according to Winckler and mvself = Ma'an) to be East Arabia, and Melukh Central and West Arabia as far as the Sinaitic Peninsula. In German: *Die alte Geographic Arabiens,* Bern, 1875. In German: *Skizze der Geschichte und Geographic Arabiens,* vol. ii. (*Geographic*), Berlin, 1890. *Versuch einer Kritik von Hamdani's Beschreibung der arabischen Halbinsel,* in the *Zeituhrif't der Deutschen Morgenlandischen Gcsellschaft,* vol. xlv., 1891, pp. 361-394. In his book *W0 lag das Paradies?* Since the appearance of Glaser's epoch-making work our knowledge of Arabia from ancient Babylonian sources has become more and more clear. Among the scientific contributions made in this line, may be numbered my own proofs of the crossing of Arabia referred to in the Nimrod Epic and of the Arabian origin of the so called Hammurabi dynasty ruling at the time of Abraham (about 2100 B. c.l. Of especial importance are the following facts: —

Even the very old Sumerian inscriptions of the kings and priest-kings *patesi)* of Sirgulla in South Babylonia know of Arabia, stating that from Magan (written *Ma-al,* but pronounced Magan) "all sorts of timber " were brought to Babylonia. Fuller information concerning Arabia is obtained from the inscriptions of the famous *patesi* Gudea (about 3000 B. c.), who procured copper from the "great ancestral gate" of the land of Ki-mash (probably Jebel Shammar in Central Arabia), *usliu* wood and iron from the mountains of Melukh (Northwest Arabia as far as the peninsula of Sinai), gold-dust from the mountains of *Khakhum* near Medina), gold-dust and dolerite from the mountains of Magan (written *Ma-gan).* Also Gubin, the mountains of the *khalub* trees, mentioned after the aforenamed countries, is to be sought for in Arabia. Furthermore, in the same inscriptions Magan, Melukh, Gubi, and the mountains of Nituk are mentioned together in one sentence as the source of all kinds of trees. Nituk, in Semitic Dilmun (by dissimilation from Dilmum, *urn* representing the Arabic nominative ending), is the larger of the Bahrain Islands — the ancient Tylos, the modern Samak. There, and also on the opposite coast of Arabia (Magan) from ancient times there must have been Sumerian sanctuaries, and Arabian and Sumerian influences must have intermingled. The goddess Zarpanit ot To be found in my book "Ancient Hebrew Tradition." - Generally transcribed by Assyriologists *Shir-pur-la.* — The Editor.
Other Assyriologists regard this reading as doubtful. — The Editor.
Nitulc was called Lakhamun (by dissimilation from Lakhamum), Erua, Zaggi-si, and Telam, while the god Nebo

was called En-zag (abbreviated for En-zag-gi-si, — i. e., " lord of the goddess Lakhamu"), Muat Izuzu, Dul-azagga (generally = Shamash, "Sun "), etc., names partly of Sumerian and partly of Arabian origin. In fact an inscription found on the island of Samak mentions the " Palace of Rimum, servant of the god Inzag." Furthermore we know that
Granite Range ot'Jcbcl Shammar Effect of Mirage) (*In the background the mountains Aa and Se/ma " the gate of ancestors " of the inscriptions of Gudea)*
Naram-Sin of Akkad (about,3700 B. C.) took from Magan, along with other booty, an alabaster vase, and that the kings of Ur (c. 2500 B. C.) had a great deal of intercourse with Ki-mash (see above) and Sabum (Seba of the Old Testament) in Central Arabia. As above stated, about 2200 B. c. an Arabian dynasty succeeded in gaining supremacy over Northern Babylonia. Later, under the sixth king of this dynasty, Khammurabi (or, more exactly, 'Ammu-rahi, the Biblical Amraphel), the contemporary of Abraham, their sway extended over the whole of Babylonia. In accordance with this is the fact that under this dynasty an " Isimanean " is mentioned (comp. the Arabic tribal name larSimani under Sargon of Assyria), and the importation of palms and cassia from the wooded mountains of Yadi'a-ab (comp. the land of Yada'u in the inscriptions of Esarhaddon) and from Guti is referred to.

Finally, in the Assyrian royal inscriptions of the 8th and 7th centuries Arabia is spoken of, and here far more in detail. For our present purpose it may suffice to give a verv brief synopsis of the more important points: —

Tiglathpileser III.: 738 B. C, tribute from Zabibi, queen of Aribi (Jof); 733 B. C, campaign against Samsi, queen of Aribi (the Biblical Jareb, Hos. 5:13; 10: 6); tribute from the Sab'eans (S2D, Seba), Mas'eans, Taimeans (Taima), Sab'eans (ndst, Saba = Sheba), Khayappeans ('Ephah of the Old Testament), Badaneans (comp. the modern Badan in Northern Midian), Khattieans, and Idiba'ileans (Adbe'el). To the latter is in-

trusted the protection of the northern boundary of the land of Midian (Musri, different from Musri = Egypt).

Sargon: 715 B. C, rebellion and defeat of the tribes Tamud, Ibadid, MarSimani (compare Isimanai above), and Khayappa. Tribute from King Pir'u of Musur (Midian), Queen Samsi of Aribi, and from It'i-amra (a name appearing as Yith'iamara in the South Arabian inscriptions, comp. Hebrew Yish'i) of Saba', namely, gold, frankincense, precious stones, ivory (pointing to commercial intercourse between Arabia and East Africa), different spices, and horses (the latter from Musur = Midian).

Esarhaddon (680-668 B. C): Khaza'ilu, King of Aribi (capital Adumu) dethroned, in his place a queen Tabu'aand Ya'ilu, son of Khaza'ilu (comp. the proper name Ya'u-ilu found in texts of the time of the Hammurabi dynasty). Campaign against the country of Bazu in Central Arabia (= Buz of the Old Testament), in connection with which the country of Khazu (= Khazo of the Old Testament), and the places Ilpiati (Ptolemy's Olaphia), Dikhran (the Dacharenians of Ptolemy), Qataba'a, Gauan (comp. Guti above), Ikhilu, Yadi'u (comp. above), and others — all situated in Yemama and neighborhood — are mentioned.

Ashurbanapal: Campaign against the Arab tribes Kedar (Qidrai) and Nebaioth (Nabayati)— which took "the great king" at least into the North Arabian Jof. The land of Mash there mentioned and also playing an important role in connection with Nimrod's journey across Arabia, extended beyond the Jof, a fact which was clearly demonstrated by Kd. Glaser in his sketch of the "Geography of Arabia" (pp. 309, *seqq.).* To Glaser also belongs the credit of first having recognized the true location of Bazu (= Buz).

Ill

The numerous data given in the Old Testament concerning the names of countries and tribes in Arabia are rather general; but the statements contained in the South Arabian and the Babylono-Assyrian inscriptions put those of the Old Testament in an entirelv new light.

Indeed from a study of the oldest West-Semitic proper names and the conceptions of God, it becomes now evident that even the origin of the children of Israel is much more closely connected with North Arabia than we have hitherto ventured to suppose, that therefore the knowledge of Arabia, as derived from inscriptions and from the archaeological exploration of the country, has a more direct and important bearing upon Biblical science than the knowledge of Fgypt and Assyria.

First, considering the genealogies as given in the tenth chapter of Genesis and similar passages (Gen. 22: 20, *itqq*and 25: i, *seq.* and 12, *seq.)*, it is remarkable to see what a close kinship between Hebrew and Arab is indicated b Hebrew tradition, — a kinship second only to that existing between the former and Amnion, Moab and the really half Arabian Edom. Edom, it is true, was regarded as the twin brother of Jacob, but Ishmael, the father of twelve Arab tribes (Gen. 25: 13-15), was at least the half brother of Isaac. And there are others, among them the Midianir.es (prominent in the stories of Joseph and Moses and in the Book of Judges), who are mentioned as half brothers of Isaac and Ishmael; even the Joktanides (Gen. 10: *i6 stag.)*, living farther away, are connected at least with F.ber, the pre-Abrahamic ancestor of the Hebrews. Besides the references to them in the inscriptions, numerous passages in the prophetic literature throw valuable light upon many of these names (see especially Is. 21; Ezek. 27, etc.).

Engl. Version: Hazo. For a full treatment of this subject see chap. iii. of my "Ancient Hebrew Tradition," pp. 56-117.

Further light upon the part played by Arabia in the Old Testament comes from the fact, now well established, that the oft-mentioned Rush, or rather Kosh, means Ethiopia only in 2 Kings 19: 9 (= Is. 37: 9) and perhaps in Is. 11: 11, Nah. 3: 9 and Jer. 46: 9, — while in all other passages, beginning with the story of Eden and the table of nations (Gen. 10), it means Arabia, especially the district around the Jebel Shammar (Hay-

il). Kosh, arisen from Kevosh, is identical with the Babylonian Kivash (written Kimash). The Gihon is a wadi of Arabia (Kosh), as Nimrod is a son of Arabia (see his above-mentioned journey through Arabia in the Babylonian epos), as Zerah (2 Chron. 14) is an Arab shaikh (comp. the camels mentioned in verse 14), and the wife of Moses, whether Zipporah (Ex. 2: 21) or perhaps another (Num. 12: 1), is an Arab woman. "The Sabeans in Central Arabia, men of stature " (Is. 45: 14) and " the nation tall and smooth " (Is. 18: 1, *seq.)* " be Hebrew text; in English version v. I J. — The Editor.

yond the rivers of Kush " (;'. *e.* the rivers of Eden), are one and the same; also in Is. 20 the reference is merely to Arabia as being in league with Musur= Midian. For there is no doubt that the present text of the Old Testament in the passages referring originally to *Musur (i. e.,* Ma'an = Musran of the South Arabian inscriptions) erroneously now offers rather *Misrayim* (-Egypt), *e. g.,* Is. 45: 14 and also Ps. 68: 31, etc.

Another name, hitherto mistaken, of a district in Arabia is Ashur (abbreviated Shur, hence the desert of Shur, north and east of the Sinaitic peninsula, and possibly also Geshur — *i. e.,* Ge-shur, "lowland of Shur "), in the South Arabian inscriptions A'shur (north of Midian), mentioned by the side of "'Ibr of the river," just as in the prophecy of Balaam (Num. 24: 24) Ashur is found with 'Eber, and probably also originally in Job 5:5," Ashur mows (the harvest), 'Eber eats it."" The most interesting of these passages is without doubt Gen. 2: 14, in which the third one of the rivers of Eden is named Khadd Deqel (Engl. Version Hiddekel) — /'. *e.,* the wadi of Diqlah (Gen. 10: 27), "which goeth in front of Ashur." The confusion with the Tigris (Dan. 10: 4) and Ashur (= Assyria) did not arise until later. For details see mv book " The Ancient Hebrew Tradition," pp. 235, *seqq.* and pp. 313, *seqq.*

The northeast part of Arabia (the modern Bahrain), bordering on Babylonia, was called by the Babylonians " Seacountrv" or *Kaldu* (Chaldea). In the

Assyrian period it was called *Bit-Yakin,* after the reigning dynasty to which Nebuchadrezzar belonged. Prom the southern part of this country, according to ancient tradition, the Phenicians had See my article "Assyria" in Hastings' "Dictionary of the Bible," written before Winckler treated the same subject.

Comp. Hommcl in the " Expository Times," x., p. 283. The first, Pishon, is the Wadi ed-Davasir; the second, Gihon, is the Wadi cr-Rumma, as Ed. Glaser has proved. i emigrated to Palestine; the northern part with its capital Ur, the ancient sacred city of the moon, was the home of the family of the patriarch Abraham, and therefore of the children of Israel, and of many Arab tribes. On the whole it appears that East Arabia was the original home of all the Western Semites, especially also of the Arameans. In Abraham's time the latter were still a part of the Arab race;

Inside of Harbor of Maskat with Castle at Entrance in fact even the patriarch Jacob, of Biblical tradition, was regarded simply as an Aramean (Deut. 26: 5).

This fact is directly confirmed by the complete uniformity in the formation of proper names consisting of two elements as found in the South Arabian inscriptions as well as in use among the Hebrews and Arameans. Those of the Babylonians, on the other side, are different, showing more polytheistic features. Between these two groups stand the proper names of the Canaanites (Phenicians included), which in consequence of Babylonian supremacy lasting for centuries (before and after 2000 B. C.) are interspersed with many Babylonian elements. Most of these names are compounded with *ilu,* "god; " *abu,* "father;" *'ammu, "* father's brother" (= protector, guardian); sometimes also with *Ai* or *Ya* (name of a god). Comp. Abi-melek, " my father is king;" 'Ammi-el, "my protector is god;" Kli-'ezer, " my god is helper;" Yishma'-el, "God hears;" Ai-kalab or Ya-kalab, " Ya is priest." In those names which are especially Canaanite we find also *ba'al,* "lord" (Babyl. *belu),* and *adbn,* " lord," pointing, however, already to Babylonian influence.

It has already been remarked, in Part II., that the genuine Babylonians preferred sun-worship, while among the primitive Arabs moon-worship prevailed, the sun (as wife of the Moon-god) being of minor importance. Especially in Ur the Moon-god was worshipped under a system almost monotheistic, as is shown bv the oft-translated hymn in "Inscriptions of Western Asia," vol. iv., plate 9. The moon was lord of the heavenlv hosts, — *i. e.,* of the stars,— the "father" *(abu)* and god par excellence; that he was also called *'ammu* is proved bv the name for the Moon-god among the Qatabanians' in South Arabia (see *'Amm* in Part II.). There is of course a very close connection between this and the use of *ilu, abu,* and *'ammu* in the old proper names among the Western Semites. Abraham's family itself was devoted to this moon-worship, as is shown even by Hebrew tradition (see Joshua 24: 2), although Abraham and the other patriarchs had doubtless already embraced a purer monotheism, so that probablv the orb of the moon shining at night was to them merely a symbol of the one true god, and not the real image of God himself. The name Ai or Ya, which was occasionally used alongside *of ilu* They arc even called *WaLid 'Amm, "* Sons of 'Amm," just as in the Old Testament the Ammonites are always called *Bene 'Ammin.* (comp. Ai-'ezer, Yo-chebed'), meant originally "moon." Moses first gave this ancient name a new significance by changing it, in the spirit of popular etymology, to Yahve, "he who exists," (by the way, another purely ArabicoAramaic formation, which in Hebrzeo-Canaanite would rather be Yi-hye), thus freeing it from every trace of polytheism. But not unfrequently the memory of the former Arabian moon-worship in the family of Terah was revived among the children of Israel, as is shown by the golden calf (comp. "young bull" as an appellation of the Moon-god), also by the name, purposely avoided in the Pentateuch, Yahve Zebaoth (Lord of the heavenly hosts), by the liturgical formula Hallelu-Yah (from *hila/=new* moon), etc. Even the

fact that Terah emigrated from Ur, one centre of the moon-worship, to Haran, the other centre of the same worship among the western Semites, is to be judged accordingly, likewise the other fact that the "mountain of the moon "(= Sinai) was the very place chosen by Moses for transmitting to the children of Israel the law revealed to him by God; from the earliest times this had been a holy mountain, a " mountain of God " (Kx. 3: i).

Finally, the holy " name " of the Moon-god, from fear often only hinted at without being pronounced, is signified in the numerous personal proper names beginning with *sumu-hu, "* his name." Such proper names occur among the inhabitants of South Arabia, especially the Mineans, as well as among the Arabians mentioned in the Babylonian contract tablets dating from the time of Abraham, — *f. g., Sumu-atar,* "His name is glorious" (South Arabian *Sumuhu-watar).* Compare Hebrew *Shemi-da'* (corresponding to *Sumuhu-jada')* and *Shemu-el?* There is an exact parallel to this in the holiness of the "name Yahve " among the Hebrews and of the name of the god Ya among the Babylonians, who adopted this adoration from the Arabians of Ur. It may now be regarded as certain that this surname for the god of the earth and sea, *viz.,* Ea, or rather Ya, is only secondary, originally meaning rather" moon." No less certain is it that in ancient times the Semitic moon-worship was universal in Arabia, and that this country was its real home. How vivid, especially in Edom and the country east of the Jordan, were the reminiscences of a former and far closer connection between the Arab tribes extending from the banks of the Euphrates through Central Arabia to the Jordan, is seen in the Book of Job, which in this respect is unique among the books of the Old Testament, and which Professor Sayce regards as really a Hebrew adaptation of a remnant of Edomite literature. Its historic background,at all events, is pictured with such remarkable fidelity as would have been impossible to invent in the later period of the Exile. Three kings (ac-

cording to the Septuagint) appear there as friends of the powerful Edomite chief Job of the land of ' Os: Eliphaz from Teman (between Edom and Midian), Bildad (Bir-Dadda) from Shukh (on the west bank of the Euphrates, north of the Kaldu district), and Zophar from Ma'an. There is present a fourth person, Elihu from Buz, for which country see above in connection with Esarhaddon, p. 740. The robbers invading 'Us are Sab3 (Sheba) and Chaldeans; the former, according to the South Arabian inscriptions, in the Minean period were still Bedouins, and with the Havileans attacked the Minean caravans, while the Chaldean robbers were from the vicinity of UrKasdim. Along with the rarely used name Yahve we commonly find Shaddai (from Shadu Ai); but the most common name for God is Eloah, whence, by analogy with Elonim, the Canaanite plural of majestv, the ordinary Hebrew form Elohim arose. As in the prophecv of Balaam, Ashur and 'Eber are mentioned as neighbors of Edom (Job 5: 5, see above, p. 743), and the robber caravans from Tenia, and Saba' (Sheba) we meet in Job 6:19. Star-worship (see especially 31: 26) is still universal in the region around Job's place; and the gold of Ophir (like Magan, designation of East Arabia) and the precious stones ot Arabia are often spoken of as familiar things. Especially interesting is the passage, Job 29: 18, where Khol, the incense-bearing messenger of the gods, appears in the familiar role of the Phoenix, being burned amid the smoke of incense and rising again from his ashes. Thus the Book of Job forms the chief source of evidence as to the authenticity (so strikingly confirmed by the inscriptions and proper names) of Hebrew tradition concerning the East Arabian origin of the children of Israel and concerning the otherwise close relationship between the Hebrews and Arabs. Not until the time of Joshua did the former exchange theirafter, owing to the excesses by the sons of Eli, the whole institution of women Levites was evidently abolished. That the Minean, or perhaps indeed more especially the Midianite word *law'i,* and the

Hebrew word *levl* (temple servant) were originally identical has without reason been doubted by Schwally and others.

In the English Version Jeezer or Iezer and Jochebed, comp. Num. 26: 30, 59. —The Editor. See my *Semitische ytilkcr und Sprachen,* vol. i., p. 487, annotation, and my *Gcschichte Babylaniem und Assyrians,* p. 215, annotation. See Hommel, " The Ancient Hebrew Tradition," p. 99. This subject is discussed by Hommel in "The Ancient Hebrew Tradition," pp. 65, *iff.* (Ea and Sin synonyms), and in "The Expository Times," Oct., 1898 ('Ea the same name as Ya, the basis for the Mosaic name Yahve). Comp. G. Margoliouth, "The Earliest Religion of the Ancient Hebrews: A New Theory," in "The Contemporary Review," Oct., 1898 (the names of Ea and Yahve identical, and the next significant step, Yahve also originally Moon-god); and finally the reader is referred to Hommel's article in "The Expository Times," Dec., 1898 ("Yahve, Ea, and Sin "), now supplemented and confirmed by the above statements. Comp. the name Ayah on one of the Tell cl-'Amarna tablets (Hommcl, "The Ancient Hebrew Tradition," p. 261). The Septuagint read Mivoio«. Comp. the variant *Havilim* to be inferred from the Septuagint. -This etymology seems rather doubtful. — The Editor. Comp. Apir situated opposite on the Persian coast, which Rawlinson hi already associated with Ophir. In the Hebrew Text. The English Version translates "the sand." There was a god of the same name in Hadhramot. Compare Part II.,

Indeed as regards the cult we find the most remarkable analogies between the inscriptions of Southern Arabia and the ancient Hebrew ceremonial laws, as is shown, *e. g.,* bv such words as *mabsal* (or *mubassil),* " the holy place " (literally, the place where the meat offered in sacrifice was boiled; comp. Ezek. 46: 23, fern, *mebashshelbth); khattaat, "* sinofFering," and *maslam,* "altar of incense" (literally, the place of the *shelem* or peace-offering, comp. Lev. 7:11, *seqq.,* etc.). The fact also that sexual defilement on the third day of the feast

was by the inhabitants of Harim considered an especially grievous offence finds an instructive parallel in Ex. 19: 15.

Even the Minean inscriptions abound in expressions for sacred vessels, etc., quite in harmony with the rich cult prescribed by Moses, and as he no doubt daily saw it with Jethro in Midian. A fine example is afforded by the word *makanat,* used to designate a kind of framework for supporting the lavers, ornamented with sphinxes and palms. The corresponding word in the Mosaic law is *ken,* but in describing the building of the temple, 1 Kings 7, the word *mekbnah* is used.

Finally, the proof recently furnished through Glaser's inscriptions of the existence of a Minean goddess named *Athirat,* the wife of the Moon-god Wadd, throws a significant light on the Canaanite goddess Asherah so often mentioned in the Old Testament.

Comp. Hommel, "The Ancient Hebrew Tradition," pp. 321, *seq.* Comp. Hommel, *Aufsatze und Abhandlungen,* ii., pp. 222-229. Comp. Homme, *Aufsatze und Abhandlungen,* ii., pp. 206-213 " 269, *seq.*

Another Arabian god known from proper names as early as 2000 years before Christ was called *Basht* (commonly pronounced *Besa).* Originally this was probably only a surname of the deified Gilgamesh-Nimrod; but what strikes us as most remarkable is the fact that the name is also found in Palestine during the time of the Judges, as a part of compound proper names, as, *e. g.,* in Ish-Bosheth (Chron., Ish-Ba'al, where Ba'al is substituted for the then unintelligible Bosheth), and others.

There are still many other obscure expressions in the Old Testament that new inscriptions and discoveries will yet serve to make plain. For the districts still unexplored in Arabia by European travellers are numerous, and systematic excavations in the ancient ruins have never yet been undertaken. It will require the united efforts of fearless and enthusiastic representatives of all the interested nations to secure those priceless inscriptions and antiquities of the

interior of South Arabia which for centuries have been known only to the roving and distrustful sons of the desert.

The queen of Sheba proved Solomon with hard questions, all of which in his wisdom he answered her. Now we who study the Old Testament, reversing the process, go to the wonderland of that queen with a multitude of inquiries, to many of which it has already given us a satisfactory reply. For the fact that we now have such comparatively clear views on all these points is due chiefly to the results of epigraphical researches in Arabia during the nineteenth century. Were it not for our knowledge of the proper names and of the different kinds of worship in South Arabia, and of the Minean kingdom extending as far as Midian and Edom, it is not likely that any light would ever have been shed upon the Arabian origin of the earliest Hebrew proper names and of the first dynasty of Babylon ruling at the time of Abraham. And our understanding of the worship of the Moon-god, in the family of Terah, so important for the history of Hebrew religion, could scarcely ever have become so exact as at present, were it not for the discovery of the many South Arabian inscriptions by the two intrepid and successful explorers Halevv and Glaser.

Comp. Hommel, *Aupatxe und Abhandlungen,* ii., p. 216. The English Version reads Eshbaal. THE SO-CALLED HITTITES AND THEIR INSCRIPTIONS THE SO-CALLED HITTITES AND THEIR INSCRIPTIONS BY PROFESSOR P. JENSEN, PH. D.

In Book II, 106, Herodotus, the father of history, tells us of two figures of the Egyptian king Sesostris which stand, one on the road from Sardis to Smyrna, the other on the road between Ephesus and Phocea, carved on the rocks and bearing an inscription running across the breast from shoulder to shoulder. This inscription means, he is further able to inform us, "With my shoulders did I win (acquire) this land." In 1839 what we may presume to be one of these was discovered by Renouard, while in 1856 Beddoe found another like it in the neighborhood, approximately on a straight line drawn from Smyrna to Sart

(Sardis), about twenty-five English miles east of Smyrna, south of Nimfi in the pass of Karabel. Upon the first named of these figures faint traces of an inscription are still to be recognized, though this, contrary to what Herodotus tells us, is certainly not Egyptian.

Before this time, in the year 1736, Otter had found at Ivriz, west of the Taurus, inscriptions in hieroglyphic characters, also non-Egyptian; in 1812, still further to the

Hittite Inscription from Hamath east, in Hamath in Syria, the Hama of to-day, Burckhardt found an inscription likewise hieroglyphic, which he took to be non-Egyptian; in 1834, in the northern part of Asia Minor, north of the lower course of the Halys or Kyzylirmak, at Boghazkoi, Texier found figures of gods accompanied by hieroglyphic inscriptions not of Egyptian type; while in 1851, as far to the east as Nineveh, Layard found seals which were stamped with non-E.gyptian hieroglyphs.

These discoveries could of course awaken no particular interest until some one who knew them all should bring them into relation with each other and conceive the idea that one and all belonged to the selfsame category. The great distance between the places of discovery gives a satisfactory explanation for the length of time which elapsed before this conclusion was reached. Who was there equally at home in Asia Minor, Syria, and Assyria?

In 1872 the situation was changed, for in that year Burton in his " Unexplored Syria " published a first though not very accurate copy of the Hamath inscription noticed above, along with others like it from the same neighborhood; and in the same year another Englishman, Dr. W. Wright, rendered the important service of securing all the Hamath inscriptions for the museum at Constantinople, thus making them accessible to scientific investigation.

Before long there came from many quarters, from Svria and Asia Minor, and in one case, and quite recently in another, from Babylon itself, tidings of similar inscriptions and sculptures of apparently the same origin having been found. To name the more important of them, I mention those in the pass of Karabel between Sart (Sardis) and Smyrna (referred to above) as belonging to the western part of Asia Minor; and those at Boghazkoi and Uyiik north of the lower course of the Halys as coming from the north; while between these two districts in the west and north we have examples from Beikoi (northeast of Afiun-Karahissar) and from Giaur-Kalesi (southwest of Angora). Besides there are others from Kolitolu and Iflatunbunar, northeast and east of the Beishehr Lake. West of the Taurus and AntiTaurus we notice inscriptions from the neighborhood of Bulgharmaden and Ivriz, from Bor and Andaval, from Fraktin and from Akrak, northeast of Kaisariye (Cssarea). In Syria we have those from Hama (Hamath) and Aleppo, from Iskanderun and (southeast of Hittite BowifiTM fcbyta.

In still another way Dr. Wright's name occupies a prominent position in the history of the young science ot" Hittitology." He was the first who gathered together all the Hittite inscriptions then known in his well-biow-n and much-used book " The Empire of the Hittites" (zd edition, London, 1886), at the same time discussing the numerous passages from Egyptian, Assyrian, Biblical, classical and other sources in which the Hittites or their monuments are mentioned. Even after the recent publication of Messcrschmidt's *Corpus Imcriptionum tiittiticarum* (Berlin, 1900), Wright's book has a certain value chiefly for its pictorial representations. — The Editor. the latter) from Kirtsh oghlu, and especially those from Jerabis on the Kuphrates, which lies in the territory, perhaps on the very site, of the ancient Karkemish. From the region between the Fuphrates and Anti-Taurus we have examples from Mar'ash and from Samsat on the Fuphrates, from Izgin (west of Albistan), from Palanga and from Giirun, from Ordasu near Malatya (the ancient Melitene), and lastly from Birejik (north of Jerabis) on the east bank of the Fuphrates. Of the inscriptions known to have been discovered in regions different from where they were originally cut, by far the most important are the above-mentioned inscription from the ruins of Babylon upon some sort of a bowl, and the recently discovered inscription from the same ruins engraved behind a figure of the Hittite Zeus, the god of the sky. To these latter is to be added the inscription upon the pommel of a king generally read Tarkondemos, which will be discussed later.

It was after the discovery of a number of these inscriptions that Sayce in particular, the versatile and active English scholar, pointed out an identity of kind existing between several of them, thereby rendering a service the importance of which is not to be underestimated. Thus there sprang into existence an historical people whose very existence up to that time seemed wholly unknown to us. To all appearance this people was possessed of a great past. It had extended or at least had marched victoriously over a considerable part of Asia Minor; it had reached the Euphrates, perhaps even crossed it, penetrating into the East, and had passed down into Syria. It boasted of an art derived, it is true, from Egvpt and the lands of the Tigris and Euphrates, but still it was independent and creative enough to work out its own method of writing. Even here, however, it is possible, or rather, as my investigations have placed the matter beyond doubt, it must be regarded as certain that it followed the model of the Egyptian hieroglyphic characters. Was this people reallv unknown to us or have we information respecting it from other sources?

Wright and Sayce, whose services in the matter of these inscriptions have been mentioned, thought they were able to answer this question in the affirmative. As we have seen above, some of the inscriptions were found in Syria and the district lying to the north of it. Here the pre-Indogermanic Armenians, the Assyrians and the Egyptians (as their inscriptions tell us), know of the land Khate. Its inhabitants are called in the Old Testament Khittim, *i. e.* Hittites, and consequently the above-mentioned investigators, followed by the bulk of scholars, and therefore of course by the world at large, have designated the inscrip

The Hittite God of the Sky (*Stele in dolente excavated by Dr. Koidtiucy in the palace of Nebuchadrezzar at Babylon tn tStg)* tions by the name Hittite. But such a designation appears at first sight to be inappropriate. For the name Hittite, derived as it is from the name of a country, could properly speaking only be employed if it was sure that all the inscriptions were found in the so-called land of Khate, which they were not; or that they were the product of a people belonging exclusively to Khate, something that could not be known. In the latter case they could tell us nothing at all as to the particular nationality of this people. But even supposing that the name Khittim (= Hittite), and its equivalents in the above mentioned inscriptions, applied to a single definite people (and no more) belonging to the country Khate, and that the Khate-folk of the Egyptians, Assyrians, and preIndogermanic Armenians were therefore all one stock, which is a mere hypothesis; and supposing futhermore that these Hittites from Khate had at a certain time been settled in Asia Minor, or had even enjoyed a supremacy there — the proof that they, and they alone, were the authors of the hieroglyphic inscriptions in Syria and Asia Minor is still lacking unless we are able definitely to assign the inscriptions in question to their period. Therefore in order to arrive at a positive knowledge, we must first of all determine the time when the inscriptions were written. This fundamental work having been omitted by Sayce and Wright, their hypothesis lacked the necessary confirmation.

The problem may be attacked from more than one side. It would be a great step in advance, if with some degree of certainty we could fix the relative chronology of the inscriptions, the relative order of their composition. It is a species of picture writing that we have to deal with, and in many of the inscriptions, though not in all, the constituent characters, to a considerable extent, may still be recognized as pictures. Thus in some instances we find an animal head with certain characteristic features; in others, however, we find corresponding to it what is recognized to be an animal head only by the help of the former. Or again we find a human head in relief with a tuft above and something looking like a handle or support underneath, while in other inscriptions this head, perhaps only the fore-part of it, is merely outlined in relief; in still others we find instead only a zigzag line produced. It is of course evident that the simplified and reduced symbols are of later date than the full hieroglyphs, since the former must have been developed from the latter. For this development the influence of a cursive writing, existing alongside the hieroglyphic writing used in connection with stone and monuments, was in the main responsible, for this cursive writing naturally tended to become more and more simple, thus gradually departing further from the hieroglyphic original. It is in particular one circumstance which brought this result about. Suppose one wished for business purposes to transfer this picture writing to an even surface, it would practically have been impossible to carve all the characters in relief, or engrave or depict them completely. It would have consumed by far too much time to do this. Accordingly, as also happened in the course of the development of cuneiform writing, the pictures were, for business purposes, drawn or scratched in outline only. But as a necessary consequence, this very cursive writing produced many an additional line, wanting in the original pictures. To such an extent this manner of writing in outline was imitated in inscriptions that we meet not only with inscriptions with incised characters in outline, but also characters partially outlined in relief. Thus we see the influence of cursive writing operating in two directions at once; the original hieroglyphs occurring, firstly, in simplified form, and secondly, amplified by additional strokes.

If now it is evident that the cursive writing is a development of the original full picture writing, it is no less clear that the more traces we find of the influence of the cursive writing, the later

in general the writing must be. Here, then, we have a criterion which will enable us to determine the relative date of the inscriptions themselves, with, upon the whole, a fair degree of certainty: inscriptions with simplified characters will in general be later than those where the corresponding pictures still occur in full. This is confirmed by a second consideration. In some of the inscriptions the writing, as has already been said, is in relief; in others it is engraved. In their sculpture work the people of the inscriptions knew only the relief; their pictures are cut out, not cut in. The relief writing will therefore be the original, and accordingly inscriptions where the writing is in relief must in general be assigned to an earlier date than those with engraved characters. On the other hand, we can observe that pictures which exist in both the simplified and non-simplified form, as a rule appear in the simplified form when the inscription is engraved. On the whole, therefore, our two criteria coincide and support each other.

Without fearing to fall into any very serious error we may now proceed to determine the relative chronology of the inscriptions, resting our various conclusions upon the form or shape of the characters and the method of their representation. Thus in any event the Hama (Hamath) inscriptions must be counted amongst the oldest; none of those from Jerabis can be regarded as so early; while for example the inscription on the bowl from Babylon mentioned above will be one of the latest.

But this gives us no absolute date. It remains still undetermined whether the inscriptions belong to the first, second, or even the third millennium before Christ. It will be possible, however, to fix the absolute chronology approximately, if in connection with the inscriptions or with the sculptures accompanying the former, we can find certain evidences or distinctive marks characteristic for a particular period. Thus — to quote some examples — at the time of Rameses II., of Kgypt (about 1300 B. c.) a certain king of Khate is represented by an Egyptian artist as wearing a pointed hat, while another king of the time of Rameses III. (about 1200 B. c.) wears a skull cap (or perhaps a bandeaul. Both head-dresses are found in connection with the kings of the people of our inscriptions. With them the pointed hat is the older fashion, as is proved by the fact that it is worn by the gods, even at a time when we find the kings wearing a skull cap or bandeau, as e. g., on the sculptures of Boghazkoi and Ivriz. Fashions, like other products of civilization, migrate freely from people to people, particularly from those who possess both a higher civilization and a greater political influence. From the dates of the abovementioned kings of Khate with some degree of certainty we may therefore argue for the approximate dates of those kings who on their sculptures appear'with a similar headdress, whether they are related to each other or not. Accordingly, such of the latter as wear a high pointed hat, e. g., the Pseudo-Sesostris in the pass of Karabel, will perhaps date from a time prior to Rameses III. (1200 B. c), while those who appear with a skull cap or bandeau, e. g., the kings on the monuments of Boghazkoi, must be regarded as later than Rameses II., i. e., later than 1300 B. C. Thus the inscription of the Pseudo-Sesostris in the pass of Karabel would be older than 1200, the inscriptions accompanying the Boghazkoi sculptures later than 1300 B. C.

Sculptures and Inscriptions near Ivri/

Without any doubt Jerabis on the Euphrates lies in the territory of the ancient Karkemish (Carchemish). In 717 B. c. Karkemish was absorbed by Assyria, and for this and other reasons we are forced to conclude that the numerous hieroglyphic inscriptions from Jerabis belong to a period prior to 717 B. c. Furthermore, in part they are of a very distinct style and character, and, as may here be premised without prejudice to our argument, belong to a number of different kings. We must distribute them accordingly over at least a couple of centuries, say the eighth and ninth centuries before Christ, the oldest known inscription from Jerabis thus being certainly not later than 900 B. c.

At Boghazkoi, which we have had occasion to mention more than once already, we find inscriptions with the winged disk of the sun at the top. This is the symbol of royalty, and is once borne by a genius after the fashion of the two who at Boghazkoi carry the lord of the gods upon their shoulders. In one instance at Boghazkoi the winged disk is represented as an eight-rayed star enclosed in a ring. Above it appears Venus, likewise represented as a star, and probably even as an eight-rayed star surrounded by a ring. In Assyrian sculptures the king has the same winged disk before or above him, and with it very often we find other symbols and characters, the moon and the Venus star being especially frequent. This winged solar disk is represented by Assyrian artists sometimes as a simple disk, sometimes as a disk surrounded by a ring, and lastly as a star enclosed in a ring. I know of only one example in Assyrian sculpture,— the black obelisk of Shalmaneser II., 860-825 » — where the king has before him only the sun and the Venus star, and in this single instance both appear as eightrayed stars within a ring. Again, only once in the sculptures of the people with which we are dealing, namely, in the case noted above, is the winged sun as emblem of royalty coupled with the Venus star, and in this single instance both appear as stars inclosed in a ring, the sun at least as an eight-rayed star. Now if Shalmaneser II. , as we may infer from the inscriptions hitherto published, was the very first Assyrian monarch who overran the country between the Taurus and the Euphrates as far as Melitene, making it really tributary to himself, it is not hard to draw the further conclusion that those two monuments which are identical in points so remarkable must date from approximately the same time. Shalmaneser's march on Melitene took place in the year 838 B. C, while his obelisk was erected in or after the year 830. The Boghazkoi sculpture therefore, with its accompanying inscription, will approximately date from the second half of the ninth century before Christ. Besides, the king to whom the

inscription refers wears a skull cap or a bandeau, and should therefore, according to what has been stated before, have flourished later than 1300 B. c, which harmonizes with our third conclusion.

In Jerabis, as mentioned above, we find a whole series of inscriptions exhibiting most various forms of characters, but in no instance are the latter engraved. We are therefore justified in concluding that before the incorporation of Karkemish in the Assyrian empire, in 717 B. C, engraved writing, in Karkemish at least, was not in vogue at all or else only to a very slight extent. Moreover, so far as we can see, complete identity of language can be easily proved for at least the greater number of our inscriptions, and similarly a certain development in the character of the writing,— a fact from which we may infer that between the authors of the different inscriptions very close relations existed, and that therefore the kind of writing in use at Karkemish was also in use in the other parts of the territory covered by these inscriptions and vice versa. Hence inscriptions in engraved characters are at the most not much older than 717 B. C, probably even later. This will apply to those from Bulgharmaden, Bor, Andaval, and Akrak, to the two found in Babylon, to one from Mar'ash, and so on. This agrees with the fact that the Old-Aramaic inscriptions from Senjirli in North Syria, found within the territory of our inscriptions, up to the second half of the eighth century are written in raised characters.

In connection with a further argument, this result helps us to extend our determination of the chronology. In the so-called Tarkondemos inscription the Assyrian marginal inscription is in Babylonian characters. This points to an origin at a time when the Babylonian and not the Assyrian influence was predominant in Western Asia, /'. e., to a period at least before about 1100 B. c. or after 606 B. c., when Nineveh fell, or else, as was formerly the opinion of Sayce, to the reign of Sargon (722-705 B. c.), whose inscriptions frequently exhibit a Babylonizing tendency in their cuneiform characters. Moreover, we find among the hieroglyphs of the Tarkondemos inscription one sign, that denoting *mi* and *me,* of quite a characteristic form. We find this elsewhere in only two or three inscriptions with engraved characters, and therefore, of relatively late date (say later than 700 B. c.), and besides in a relatively late inscription (say of about 750 B. c.), and a little amulet or seal inscription, with characters in relief, from Jerabis. From this fact we may conclude that the bilingual inscription of Tarkondemos belongs to about the eighth century. In any event it cannot be earlier than Itoo B. c., and we must accordingly place it either after 606 B. c., or, as the cuneiform writing of the Assyrio-Babylonian version represents rather Babyloni/ing than Babylonian characters, at the time of Sargon, 722—705 B. c., or thereabouts; a result which coincides with that drawn from the mere shape of the hieroglyphs. This determination of the age of the Tarkondemos inscription applies also to inscriptions where the writing resembles that of the Tarkondemos; and as the characteristic form for *mi* occurs also in two or three inscriptions with engraved characters, it will apply to these too and others like them. These inscriptions, therefore, written in the engraved character may be safely referred to Sargon's time or later (perhaps even later than 606 B. c.) — a conclusion at which we had already arrived for another reason discussed above. Finally, certain Hittite seal inscriptions found in the ruins of Nineveh cannot be of later origin than 606 B. C, because in this year Nineveh was destroyed.

From arguments of this nature it is plain that at all events the great mass of the inscriptions belongs to a period between 1000 and 600 B. C, allowing perhaps a little on either side. The approximate chronology thus arrived at for the series tallies well enough with that reached by the other methods indicated above, also with that fixed bv Puchstein for the accompanying sculptures. Our results may therefore be held to be approximately correct. These results will make, *e.g.,* the Hamath inscriptions, the character of which is of an earlier type

than that of any inscription from Jerabis, date from about 1000 B. C, or earlier, while according to them the inscription on the bowl from Babylon will date from about 600 B. C. An analysis of the inscriptions corroborates this view. Thus, an inscription from Ordasu (accompanying a lion hunt), where the characters exhibit a relatively late form but still are cut out in relief, must date from between 712-708 B. C, because it belongs to Mud(t)allu of Kommagene, who according to the cuneiform inscriptions during this period held Melitene. On the other side two inscriptions in engraved characters, including that on the bowl, seem to have been composed after 606 B. C. or not much earlier, because according to their contents Karkemish is apparently held no longer by an Assyrian king but bv a king of Cilicia.

At this point the further question may be put, how old this hieroglyphic system of ours really is. We may point to the fact that even in the inscriptions from Hama (Hamath), which, apart perhaps from that carved on the rock of the Pseudo-Sesostris, are undoubtedly the oldest of the series, we find no longer a pure picture-writing, but one

Hittitc Inscription on a Bowl from Bibylon already modified by the influence of the cursive. It follows from this that the system is of earlier date than the Hamath inscriptions, that is, earlier than about 1000 B. c. It is to be noted on the other hand that about 1400 the Assyrio-Babylonian cuneiform writing then in use in Western Asia was also employed in the royal despatches sent to the king of Kgypt by the various princes ruling in the southern section of the area covered by our hieroglyphic inscriptions and in that neighborhood. Hence about 1400 B. c. our hieroglyphic system does not yet seem to have been introduced, at least in Hamath, or Karkemish. It does not follow from this, of course, that it may not have been used in the region to the north and in Asia Minor at this period.

In some respects it follows the Egyptian model, just as certain types of Egyptian art are also found among the

people employing our hieroglyphs. It must therefore have been first introduced in a region lying close to the Egyptian sphere of influence and at a time when Egypt was there the predominant power, that is to say, proDably in Syria; at least sometime after 1400 B. c, when the Egyptian supremacy in that region gradually broke down; perhaps about 1300 B. c, when after a prolonged struggle Rameses II. became the friend and ally of Khate-sere, king of Khate; or may be not until about 1200 B. C, in the reign of Rameses III.

If, then, matters stand as I have shown at length above, that is, if we know of no inscription in Syria and to the north of it which is certainly much earlier than 1000 B. C, then there is absolutely no ground left for going back to the old kings of Khate mentioned in the Egyptian inscriptions of say 1300 B. c. and earlier, as the authors of our inscriptions. It rather follows from this chronologv that we must attribute those found in Khate to the pettv princes, or their predecessors and successors, whom we find in Svria and to the north of it during the time of the Assvrian supremacv, *i. e.,* after 900 B. C. My decipherments have confirmed this throughout. As far as is known at present, no king of Khate has left any inscription in Syria or north of it. At the same time my decipherments have shown that at least the large inscriptions from Asia Minor are of relatively late date, and that the great extent of ground thev cover gives not the slightest ground for postulating a great Hittite empire in ancient times extending as far as the shores of the jEgean Sea, as the " Hittitologists" have done. If, therefore, we understand by the name " Hittite," as is commonly done, both the Khate of the Egyptian kings and the later non-Semitic inhabitants of Syria, we have no right to call the authors of our inscriptions Hittites as long as a relationship between the two has not been proved. But if we are content to apply this name only to the non-Semitic population in Assyrian times inhabiting Syria and the district to the north,;'. *e.,* Khate, whosoever these inhabitants were and of whatever nationality, then we may apply it to the authors of the inscriptions found there, but only to these, not to the authors of those monuments found over a great part of Asia Minor, the conquest of which by "Hittites" from Khate has still to be proved. Out chronological investigations have shown that the use of the name " Hittites" for the people of our inscriptions is as yet most precarious, though justifiable under certain suppositions, which, however, are nothing more than suppositions.

Though it was comparatively easy to fix the chronology of the inscriptions approximately, insurmountable difficulties seemed to stand in the way of their decipherment. Writing, language, and content were equally unknown. In the year 1880, however, Sayce anew discovered the so-called Tarkondemos bilingual inscription, and with this there emerged the hope of at last extracting from the inscriptions their hidden meaning. Sayce made the attempt at attaining to the end desired, but it miscarried and had to miscarry. For the very peculiar character of the bilingual inscription made it impossible to reach a sure result by its aid. For, in the first place, the Assyrio-Babylonian version was to all appearances the work of an unskilful engraver, and many points of reading, even the very name of the king, were confessedly doubtful, while the arrangement of the hieroglyphic version was by no means self-evident or certain. Furthermore, of the six symbols which occur in the hieroglyphic version, only three, or at most four, have with certainty (in spite of Sayce's supposition to the contrary) been found in other inscriptions of this character. Without a doubt, in his reading of the Assyrio-Babylonian version Sayce in some points was more probably wrong; than right. He arranged the hieroglyphic version wrongly, and he found all six symbols in other inscriptions; some of them he recognized in characters which he regarded as mere variants, but which in reality were absolutely distinct forms. Accordingly, as the bilingual was essentially the foundation on which he built, it follows that his further " decipherin-

gs" in the main can have but little claim to this title. It should be noted, however, that his efforts have not been altogether in vain. Thus with the help of the bilingual he has by chance made out correctly, but not proved, the meaning of a sign for *me* and *mi,* also of a sign for "king" or its equivalent. Further, a symbol which according to mv reading stands for *dei* " lord," he has by chance translated approximately correctly as "king." Two other signs he takes, not without good reasons, to serve as case-endings, and another sign from the inscriptions which accompany the figures of gods at Boghazkoi he takes to be the determinative for " god," all of which are correct or at least approximately

Biiingual Inscription on the Silver Boss of Tarkondemos In the "Transactions of the Society of Biblical Archeology," vol. vii., pp. 274, *seqq.,* and 299, *seqq.,* also in Wright, "The Empire of the Hitrites," 2ded., pp. 166, *seqq.,* etc. so. Unfortunately for himself, he identified with the last another symbol with quite a different meaning,—the symbol for "country," — thus raising a barrier which made further advance impossible. Curiously enough, once before he had guessed the meaning of this same sign correctly, though it is true accidentally, and on quite untenable ground. Any further contributions of Sayce towards the deciphering of the inscriptions are quite arbitrary and without foundation.

No essential advance was made by Sayce's successors, namely Ball, Menant, Peiser, and Halevy. It should be mentioned, however, that Halevy is correct, though accidentally so, in taking (independently from my own researches) a symbol, which can apparently be added or left out at pleasure after that for *me,* to represent the vowel *e.* The rest we may pass over in silence. In the works of the above mentioned scholars a wild logic runs riot, and its extravagances call for no description.

Peiser took a direction quite different from that of the other decipherings, in the main confining himself to the seal-inscriptions found in Sennacherib's palace at Nineveh. These he arbitrarily

attributed to Hittite kings, and as Sennacherib in his cuneiform inscriptions had omitted to preserve us the names of such, he assigned them in the same arbitrary fashion to two kings belonging to the time of his predecessors, Tiglath-pileser III. and Sargon. Since these hypotheses which form the basis of his argument are absolutely groundless throughout, and the names of other couples of" Hittite " kings of the same period, according to Peiser's method of reasoning, would have suited the inscriptions equally well, and since, moreover, his further results rest upon a series of similar postulates, it is clear how exceedingly vague these "results" must be. Besides, he is directly wrong in his arrangement in connection with one of the inscriptions as in various of his other suppositions, a circumstance which makes it still more evident that all his conclusions with respect to the phonetic deciphering of the inscriptions are equally false. However, his efforts too have not been quite without result; his recognition of one symbol as a punctuation mark is approximately correct. Anything he may have done for the correct or approximately correct determination of the sound values he owes to chance; to the interpretation of the inscriptions he has not contributed an iota. So much for the labors of my predecessors and their results.

In the " Proceedings of the Society of Biblical Archeology," vol. x., pp. 437, *seqq. Memoires de T'Academic dcs Inscriptions,* vol. xxxiv., pp. 1, *seqq. Die Hettitischcn Inschriften. Revue Semitique,* vol. i., pp. 55, *seqq.,* and 126, *seqq.*

They have all failed sufficiently to remember that the decipherer has two tasks before him, — one being the determination of the contents, and the other the reading of the words — and that these two sections of the work, while often running parallel and frequently overlapping, still cannot be too strictly kept separate. We may be able to read an inscription without understanding it, and to tell the contents of another without being able to read it. Throughout mv decipherings, which I now proceed to describe, I have endeavored as far as possible to keep the two problems apart.

At the first sight one perceives that the inscriptions are written in the so-called boustrophedon manner, which Hayes Ward was the first to see as early as 1873. In the inscriptions there are no empty spaces separating the different word-groups from one another. Hence the first step was by comparing the inscriptions to delineate (/. e., to separate from each other) the various word-groups. In course of this process it became evident that different signs, an upright knife — Peiser's "Sintrenner" — and a similar sign served to keep the word-groups apart. These again made it possible to determine many other word-groups, which occurring perhaps only once and in unfamiliar connections could otherwise not have been recognized as such.

Then it was easily seen that the same word in the same case and always with the same meaning might still be written differently. Particularly striking was the use of two symbols which could be written or left out at pleasure anywhere in the word, whether beginning, middle, or end. Consideration of the Egyptian hieroglyphic writing, where in Egyptian words the vowels almost invariably are not represented, while in foreign words they may be written or not, at will, suggested at once that these two signs stand for vowels. At all events it is improbable, a priori, that spoken consonants should have been left unrepresented in writing.

But this arbitrariness in the representation of the vowels is not the only cause of the variety "of the word-figures. One and the same word may be represented in each of the following ways: I. By means of a single sign which stands for that word and for no other. 2. By means of this sign in company with other signs found also in the groups for other words. 3. By means of these latter signs unaccompanied by the first. The following scheme will explain the statements made. Suppose K is the symbol with the meaning "king;" a and b the other symbols. Then the word for "king " may be written as follows: 1. K,

2. a-b, 3. K-a-b, 4. a-b-K, 5. a-K-b, 6. a-K, 7. K-b. A word may therefore be represented: 1. ideographically, /'. e., by means of a sign standing for the idea expressed by the word, and for this word itself; 2. phonetically, i. e., by means of the signs representing sounds of this word and primarily for its consonants; 3. by a combination of the ideographic and phonetic methods, in which the latter is to be held explanatory of the former.

The ideographs prove to be very numerous. As we learn from our determining the contents of the inscriptions, we have ideographs for the names of countries, persons and gods, for titles and dignities such as king and lord, for adjectives, and so on. The numerous ideographs used for the names of gods who play an important part in the inscriptions deserve special mention. A very remarkable feature still awaiting a satisfactory explanation is the fact that perhaps all the gods mentioned in the inscriptions may be represented by a hand placed in different positions. Thus the " Father of the Gods" has a flat hand as his original hand-hieroglyph, which however was simplified later, while the "Mother of the Gods" has a fist as her handhieroglyph.

Some of the ideographs, apparently, may be added or left out at pleasure. Such are the symbols for " god," "man," "country," found before the names of gods, the names and attributes of kings, the names of towns and countries respectively. In such cases the symbols are to be considered as determinatives, specifying the category of the word which follows.

The symbols with phonetic values may be divided into two main classes, those which are but rarely met with, and those which are found everywhere in the most various wordgroups. It is at once apparent that the phonetic values of the latter must be as simple as possible, representing only a single sound, or at the most a consonant and a vowel, while the majority of the former represent combinations of more than two sounds, perhaps a consonant and a vowel and a consonant, or, neglecting the

vowels in between, a series of say two consonants.

The symbols ocurring frequently are remarkably small in number, and in at least four different instances two of them have been interchanged. As they are not vowel-signs, it follows that the sounds they stand for must have one consonant in common, while only one of them in each case can stand for a simple consonant. There are scarcely more than perhaps eight signs for simple consonants. Hence it would appear that in the Hittite tongue there were only eight consonants. This, however, seems incredible. We are therefore compelled to assume that as in the Cypriotic syllabary a single sign could represent several consonants, all belonging to the same category, of course, as e. g. k and g, d and /. Our phonetic decipherment will furnish the proof of this assertion. Moreover, we find at most three vowel-signs, one for a and o (and a ?), another for e and;', whereas it is evident from the Assyrian and Greek versions of proper names belonging to the Hittite area, e. g., Melidd-u, Syennesis, Kommag-ene, that the Hittites had more than three vowels to dispose of. Such transliterations therefore prove that they were as saving with their vowels as with their consonants.

The above will serve to show in a measure how it was possible for me to make out the system of the writing without being able to read it in the proper sense. The contents of the inscriptions, however, could in part be made out even without this. A few hints may now be given to illustrate it.

Inscriptions which we are forced to assume to belong to some king or other dignitary frequently begin with a figure consisting of a head with an arm attached, the hand pointing (not to the mouth but) to the region between mouth and nose. If we suppose the hand to point to the mouth, a reference to an analogous instance in the Egyptian writing must at once suggest the meaning " to say " or " to speak" for this figure, as was assumed by Sayce at a later stage of his decipherings: "thus speaks such and such a king." But if this supposition be ruled out, then according to all analogy, the meaning " I" favored by Halevy and others, and at an earlier stage by Sayce as well, seems about the only one in order. What else should the figure mean? Other considerations must lead us to suppose that a word following this figure, or else its phonetic transliteration, must stand for " am." After this we must expect to find names and titles of the king. Since even in the greater inscriptions such titles, etc., are also found in the middle and even at the end, always appearing in the same form, /. e. , in the same case, we cannot help concluding that at least the bulk of the inscriptions beginning with "I am " contain only titles, attributes, and so on; including above all, of course, the title "king of."

This circumstance assists us very materially in understanding the inscriptions correctly, for it appreciably reduces the number of possible meanings. By comparing the inscriptions with one another we can now establish the ideographic or phonetic equivalents, or perhaps both, for " king" and various synonyms of the same; for " son " or " child " with one synonym; for "country " and the names of countries; for adjectives like " great " and "mighty " or their likes; for the pronoun " this; " for the names of gods, which being regarded as sacred are very frequently isolated by placing before and after (that is, above and below) them the symbol which denotes the beginning of a new word; for words expressing the relations between men, mostly the king and the gods, as perhaps "servant," etc.; for names of kings; for a king's title occurring only in certain inscriptions found within a narrow radius. Thus, without being able to read a single symbol, I was in a position to explain a not inconsiderable portion of the inscriptions. Furthermore, I could make out various points which went far to determine the character of the Hittite speech. Thus the substantives have flectional endings, those for the nominative and genitive singular containing only vowels, that for the genitive plural a consonant. As for the syntax, it was plain that the genitive could

follow or precede the word that governs it.

This fact alone excludes the possibility of a connection with the so-called Turanian languages on the one side and the Semitic tongues on the other.

It is now to be noted that the word for " I" contains a consonant of the same class as one word for " this," and the ending of the genitive plural a consonant of the same class as the word for "am." Besides, a word for "great," or the like, has the latter as its first consonant and the former as its second. The last named, again, is the first consonant in two different words for " son" or "child;" while, as appears from the writing of it, a word for "king " could be regarded as a compound beginning with the word for " man." It cannot escape the Indogermanic scholar that exactly the same is or must have been the case in Armenian. Thus, before I could read a word, I might have concluded from the mere way the words were written that the speech was Armenian. For in Armenian the word for " I " is *es*, out of *eso* (out of *edzo*, or the like), while a word for " this" is *ais*; *em*, formerly *emi* means " I am," while *om* was once the ending of the genitive plural; *mets* out of *medzi(s)* or the like means "great;" *ustr* means "son " and *zav-ak* "descendant;" *ark'ay* is " king," and *ayr,* formerly *ar(o),* is "man." This could have indicated a way of arriving at the reading of the inscriptions. I found another which led to the same astonishing result.

If the inscriptions from Syria and the districts to the north belong, as we have shown at length, to the period between say 1000 and 600 B. c., then those from Hama in Syria have come down from kings of Hama; those from Jerabis on the Kuphrates, in the territory of the ancient Karkemish, from kings of Karkemish; those from Mar'ash north of Syria from kings of Gurgum, whose capital was Markash, the modern Mar'ash. In other words, these different inscriptions go back to princes of various petty states, not to the lord of a single great empire called Khate embracing all the others. Accordingly, it is vain to try to find in them a word-group or

a single symbol denoting a common expression which includes the whole territory of these kings; rather do we find in the places where such a common name might naturally be expected, i. e., in particular at the beginning of the inscriptions before the word for " king," different expressions according to the different places of discovery. It is therefore important to know from the beginning the name of which land in each case is to be expected in the inscription. Had we not been able to fix the chronology of the inscriptions approximately, did we not know, for instance, that the oldest of them can scarcely date from much before iooo B. c, while the oldest of those in engraved characters cannot be much earlier than 717 B. C, i. ?., the year of the absorption of Karkemish, it would have been difficult to determine these names with certainty. Suppose, for example, that the earliest of all the inscriptions found in Syria, — those from Hama — belonged to the year 2000 B. C, we could not in this case count with certainty upon rinding this same word "Hama" in an earlier form in the name of the district or city mentioned in the inscription.

Matters are different, however. We know that as far back as at least the ninth century there existed a state or kingdom with its centre at Hama. Karkemish is mentioned in an Assyrian inscription as far back as 1100 B. C. and also in Egyptian inscriptions of much earlier date. As for the great lion inscription from Mar'ash, it is as good as certain, that in the year 750 B. C, the approximate date of the inscription, the city was called Markash and the territory in which it lay Gurgum. We know, therefore, what names of cities important for our investigations are to be found in Syria and to the north, at the time when our inscriptions were written. Various considerations lead us to the conclusion that the old name Hamath occurs three times on a stone from the modern Hama; that the old name Karke mish is found in all the longer inscriptions from Jerabis (considerable portions of which have been preserved), but with a single very important exception nowhere else; finally, that in the well preserved lion-inscription from Mar'ash the name Markash or Gurgum must occur.

Several years ago a beautifully preserved inscription surmounting the representation of a lion-hunt was dug up in the neighborhood of Malatya, the ancient Meli(e)dia or Melitene. The style of art and the character of writing prove that it belongs to the last period of the pre-Assyrian supremacy of the Hittites in those regions. It seemed, however, unlikely on this hypothesis to assign it to a native king of Meli(e)dia, because the names of four of its last native kings appear from their length to be compound names. Certainly the last of these kings bears a compound name, while the name of the king of the lion-hunt, represented as it is by a single sign (the head of perhaps a horse or colt), cannot be a compound. Moreover, the name found on the Malatya slab is known to have been borne by no fewer than three Hittite monarchs, the one mentioned above, a king of Karkemish, and the king of the inscription found at Bor west of the Taurus. In the Assyrian inscriptions, on the other hand, no Hittite king's name occurs so frequently as the name Mut(d)allu, which is found there as the name of three different kings. The same name occurs perhaps once also in Egyptian inscriptions. It was therefore natural to suppose that the king's name in the lion-hunt inscription was Mut(d)allu. In the last years of the pre-Assyrian Hittite rule we know of two kings of this name, kings of Gurgum and Kommagene respectively, both neighbor states of Melitene. What if one of these monarchs for a time had held Melitene also? Winckler had already surmised this, but a mistake in his edition of the inscriptions of the Assyrian monarch Sargon prevented him from reaching a definite knowledge. The Paris cast examined at my request brought the needed certainty.

According to the Assyrian inscriptions Mut(d)allu of Kommagene was also in possession of Melitene from 712 to 708 B. c. Hence it is in the highest degree probable that he is the king of the lion-hunt. Considerations which shall be given later place the matter beyond any doubt. From Mut(d)allu's inscription we get the word-group for Kommagene and Khati, two names which for the period to which the inscription presumably belongs have been preserved to us in the forms Kummukhi and Khati(?).

Four inscriptions, all emanating from kings of the same realm, have been found northwest of the Taurus, while another apparently cognate with them, that on the bowl, has been discovered in the ruins of Babylon. One of these monarchs, according to his inscription, possessed at least the territory of Karkemish on the Euphrates, if not Karkemish itself; while according to the bowl inscription, another of them, perhaps the son or more probably the grandson of the former, was in possession of Karkemish itself. This bowl inscription, to judge from its character, must be one of the very latest of the so-called Hittite inscriptions. A king who bore sway at once over the land west of the Taurus and over the lands of Karkemish must have been lord of the intervening territory of Cilicia also. We know nothing of a temporary conquest of Cilicia in post-Assyrian times, to which date the inscription in question must belong, since according to it the territory of Karkemish is neither independent nor yet held by Assyria. It is therefore highly probable that the kings of these inscriptions were kings of Cilicia ruling also over the territory beyond the Taurus to the west, and that the hieroglyph for their country is that for Cilicia, the native form of which name would probably be Khilik with a vowel at the end, to judge from the Egyptian, Assyrian, and Greek transliterations.

In the first line of his inscription, one of these kings, perhaps the earliest of the series, calls himself king, not of Cilicia, but of something that perhaps has the same attribute as occurs in connection with the city of Karkemish in the Jerabis inscriptions. Unless, therefore, the kings of Cilicia, like those of Assyria, for instance, bore some general title like "king of the whole earth " or the like, we must suppose that Tarsus, the capital of Cilicia, is meant. According to the Assyrian and Aramaic writing of the name at the time to which the inscription belongs, about 600 B. C, the word must have been pronounced Tarz, or if the Biblical " Tiras" in Gen. 10 be identical with it, must have had the consonants Trds. This, accordingly, will be the form of the name in the inscription.

There is one title which amongst all the Hittite sovereigns is peculiar to those of Cilicia. In the word-group which stands for it, the first symbol and the fourth are alike. From the frequency with which it occurs this symbol must have a simple phonetic value. As it is not one of the vowel signs, it must denote a simple consonant. At least three Cilician kings are called Syennesis in Greek. Only one, the father of one Syennesis, has a different name, Oromedon. From this observation it has been surmised for a considerable time that Syennesis is properly a title. The fact that in Herodotus the father of one king is called by a different name need cause no difficulty, for Syennesis may well have been the designation only of the reigning sovereign, who after death recovered his proper name, while his former title passed to his successor. This title Syennesis (borne by the kings of Cilicia) with its four stem consonants: s, the spiritus lenis between y and e, which we and the Greek do not write, n and s, has the peculiarity that its first consonant is the same as the fourth. But as noted above, exactly the same is the case with the Cilician royal title in the so-called Hittite inscriptions, and we may venture therefore to read this latter as Sy(u)ennes.

All these readings have for the most part been found independently. If they are correct, they must check each other to some extent at least. That is to say, in spite of the peculiarity of the Hittite characters there must be many cases where in the supposed names the same sound will be represented in the corresponding word-groups by the same symbol. This is in fact the case. Take the phonetic wordgroup for Hamath for example, which begins with a breathing. It has the same sign in the first position as the group for Sy'ennesis in the second, the same sign in the second position as a group for Karkemish in the third, after the symbol for *k* and *g*, and the same in the third as the group for Khati(?) in the last, *viz.*, the sign for / and *d*. A similar correspondence appears in the groups for Karkemish and Cilicia; for Karkemish and TAR-BI-BI-or TAR-QU-*was*/*temt*, commonly read Tar-qudimme in the above mentioned bilingual of " Tarkondemos;" in those for Gurgum or Marash (with *r* as second consonant) and Tarz-(?); in those for Syennesis and Tarz-: in fact, the correspondence is as complete as can well be imagined, and the reading of a number of proper names has therefore been attained.

A foundation had thus been laid for the reading of the inscriptions. A comparison of the name-groups fixed the signs for *k(om*, *g(o)m*, etc.; *m(ak*, *m(a)g*, etc.; *r*, *k(g)*, *t(d)*, *m*, etc. Employing these results in word-groups with a known meaning, I discovered, for example, that the genitive of words in /' ends in two vowels, presumably; (or *f)* and *a* (or 0); that names of peoples have a similar termination; that the ending of the genitive plural contains the consonant *m;* that ' and a sibilant stand for "I," while two vowels, presumably *a* or *o* and *i* or *e*, and a sibilant stand for " this;" that *mi* or *me* means " I am;" that an attribute of the king and the lord of the gods, say Sanda, contains a /-sound followed by two vowels, probably *i* or *e* that a word for " son" or " child " is made up of a sibilant, a dental and *r* for its consonants, a word for " country " of a labial and a dental and r, a word for " great," or the like, of *m* and a sibilant, and so on. Before we were able to make any definite statement as to the reading of the inscriptions, we could have surmised that the Hittite language was Armenian. This is a surmise no longer; the actual reading of the inscriptions has transformed it into a certainty. For almost everything that we know in the Hittite tongue is Armenian, or better, Old-Armenian, and the corresponding forms in modern Armenia

have been developed out of the former precisely according to the known laws of Armenian phonetics.

Thus in the inscriptions the genitive of words in or *e* is *i* or *e* and *a* or *o*, to which in Armenian corresponds the ending *i* out of an earlier *to* or *ia*. To the similar ending for names of peoples in Armenian corresponds *i* out of an earlier *to*. "I "is in the inscriptions followed by a sibilant (and a vowel), in Armenian it is *es=* earlier *eso* or *edzo* or the like; "this " in the inscription is *a* or *o*, and i or *e* and a sibilant, in Armenian it is *ais*. To *mi* or *me*, perhaps with a vowel in front, meaning " am," corresponds Armenian *em* out of *emi*, = " am "; to the attribute of the kings and the supreme god composed of a dental and *i* or *e*, and another *i* or *e* corresponds Armenian *te* in *tfr*, "lord," "master," *i. e.*, *te* + *ar* (=" man "), and in *tikin*, "lady," "mistress," */'. e.*, *te--kin* (= "woman "); to the word for "son" with a sibilant and a dental and *r* for its consonants corresponds Armenian *ustr*, " son "; to the word for " country" certainly having a labial and a dental and *r* for its consonants corresponds Armenian *vayr*, = " country," with the meaning of Latin *rus*, also " place," which of course has the original meaning " country," perhaps out of an earlier form *watira*, while to the word for " great," or the like, having as consonants *m* and a sibilant, corresponds Armenian *mets*, = " great," out of an original *medzi*, and so on.

With this newly established basis to work upon I have extended my field of operations, succeeding in finding new sound-values and further meanings of words which could only confirm my thesis. Thus I have been able to read the Hittite word for " king," apparently *ar-wai* = Armenian *ark'ay*, also the word for " man," in Hittite written r, but read *aro* = Armenian *ayr*, out of an earlier *aro*, and so on.

Under such circumstances we scarcely need this additional fact that the phonetic values of the hieroglyphs, so far as these hieroglyphs are recognizable as pictures, stand in relation to certain Armenian words, thus showing that the Hittite writing was invented by the fore-

fathers of the modern Armenians.

The consonants, for which the hieroglyphs stand, correspond either to the beginning or to the whole of those words which must once have been the Armenian names for the corresponding pictures. Thus in the inscriptions a pointed shoe stands for / or *d*, while in Armenian *trekh* means a peasant's shoe; a calf's head representing the whole calf stands in the inscriptions for *po*, *pa*, etc. , while in Armenian the word for calf is *ort* from earlier *port*. More decisive are the cases where the correspondence is still more complete. For example, we find a fascicle with the phonetic value *t(d)* and *r*, while Armenian *trt'sak* means " bundle;" the head of the horse or colt, as we saw above, must be approximately read *mudal* Op *mutal*, while " colt " in Armenian is *mtruk* (mtr-u and the diminutive ending) out of an earlier form *m-d-r* or *m-d-l* with / or a after the *m*. Furthermore, the picture of a pine tree or the like, or a tree in general, is the cryptogram for *sar*-or *t(d)sar*-, meaning " king," while *saroy* in Armenian is a word for the pine or the like (hardly a Persian loan-word), and *tsar* means " tree."

In this connection we may turn to the inscription referred to above, which we took to belong to a king Mut(d)allu of Kommagene. The name of his country, *i. e.*, Kommagene (Kommoghi), is here represented by two hieroglyphs, a bull-dog's head and a boar's claw. The first hieroglyph, therefore, must probably be read as *kom*, and the second as *mogh.* Now the Hittite characters do not distinguish *a* and 0, *k* and *g* or *gh* respectively, while the Armenian word for bull-dog is *gamp'r* and that for claw *magi/.* Thus our interpretation of the inscription of Mut(d)allu confirms our thesis that the authors of the Hittite characters,/. ., of course the Hittites themselves, were of Armenian stock. And this in turn bears out the correctness of our interpretation.

It is evident from the above that the Hittite symbols or signs sometimes represented the full consonantal value of the corresponding word, sometimes only the beginning of it, and that therefore in the creation of symbols for single sounds or syllables the principle of acrophony was employed.

The knowledge acquired goes far to determine the native appellation of the Hittites, and this again, which is a circumstance to be welcomed, provides us with a new argument for the Hittite and Armenian relationship, thus supporting our hypothesis. One of the kings of Hamath, the kings of Karkemish, one of Gurgum, another who has left us an inscription found at Izgin north of Mar'ash, one king of Cilicia, the same to whom the inscription upon the bowl refers, another king one of whose inscriptions has been discovered at Kolitolu in Lycaonia, the author of an inscription from Beikoi in ancient Phrygia, and perhaps the man to whom the inscription recently discovered at Babylon refers, call themselves, or are called, X, or X son of an X, or grandson of an X. This X is differently written. When written phonetically, with perhaps two exceptions, its first symbol is a hand grasping a knife. Then may come a shoe, the sign for a dental, while the vowels following, which in nominative at least are *i* or *e* and *0* or *a*, may be left out. This phonetic writing alternates with the ideographical one: a man's head with a handle or pole attached, where the handle or pole stands for the full human figure below the head. This may mean one of two things, either a human being in general or a member of the people of the inscriptions; but it does not stand for either man or woman, the hieroglyphs for which are different. If, however, the kings mentioned above feel it incumbent upon them to call themselves in their inscriptions X son of an X, the first alternative maybe dismissed, X accordingly meaning one belonging to the people in question, whose national name has a dental as its last consonant.

It is a fact that a very large number of the inscriptions come from the country of Khate; and it is also true that just as we know of no people with a like appellation, we know in those parts of no other country the name of which could occur in all the inscriptions mentioned above, and at the same time have a dental as its final consonant. Hence it is enticing to see in the name of our people, ending as it does in a dental and *i* or *e* and *a* or *o*, a form derived from Khate with the old Armenian ending *to*, thus justifying the name Hittite to some extent. The inscriptions themselves, however, provide no convincing proof for this reading. But here the relationship of the speech of the inscriptions with Armenian seems to intervene in our behalf. We saw that in the phonetic writing of X, the shoe, which is the symbol for / or *d,* can be left out at pleasure. Hence it serves here as a mere phonetic complement; that is to say, it signifies part of the reading of the sign which precedes, indicating that the hand with the knife has a phonetic value in which a dental is the last consonant. The hand with the knife represents the idea of cutting. In the event of the character having been invented by predecessors of the Armenians, its phonetic value will therefore connect itself with an Old-Armenian word for " to cut." "To cut" in Armenian being *hatanel* (with the stem *hat),* the hand with the knife should apparently be read as *h(a)t* or *h(a)d.* The name of the people of the inscriptions accordingly seems to be *Hatio.*

When I was laying the first foundation for the decipherment of the inscriptions and had just recognized the Armenian character of the speech, I conceived the idea that the native name of the Armenians, *Hay,* in plural *Hayk,* probably went back to a form *Hatio,* according to the laws of Armenian phonetics; but this was a pure hypothesis which the inscriptions failed to substantiate. Proof, however, now appearing to be forthcoming, I am forced to declare that I hold the above views until further notice. The difference between the *Kh* of Khate and the *H* of Hay is not fatal to my theory and may be easily got over.

Nevertheless it must be stated that *h* in the beginning of Armenian words may go back to *p* or *j.* Very possibly, therefore, Armenian *hat-anel* originally began with a/, which at the time of our inscriptions does not yet seem to have become *h* as in modern Armenian. But if at the time of our inscriptions the root *hat,* meaning "to cut," was perhaps still pronounced as *pad,* the hieroglyph for " to cut" in the same way could only be read as *p(ad* or *p(a)t,* and not as *h(a)t.* In this case the name of the people of our inscriptions would be *Patio,* not *Hatio,* and could have nothing to do with the name of the country Khate and the name Hittite derived from it. Moreover it is worthy of remark that three times in an inscription we find a word with a labial and a dental as consonants which it seems possible, though not likely, to identify with the national name of the people of our inscriptions. On the other hand, however, we must not omit to mention that in two inscriptions we meet with a succession of symbols (those for ', / and ') which possibly might have been used to denote a word *Hatio.*

Be this as it may, whether *Hatio* or *Patio* is the form we are looking for, so much is certain, that the name of the people of our inscriptions has the same consonants, or consonants of the same class, as the Armenian word for "to cut " once had, *viz.,* p or h or even s and / or d, that therefore Armenian *Hay*= " Armenian," out of *Hatio,* and this again perhaps out of *Patio* or perhaps *Satio,* goes back to the national designation of the people of our inscriptions. This is a fresh confirmation of our theory that the Hittites are the ancestors of the modern Armenians.

Their history is the early history of the Armenians; their civilization, their belief, and their religion are the civilization, the belief, and the religion of the ancestors of the Armenians. What we learn of these can in future count upon the interest of all educated men.

The inscriptions and works of art discovered bear witness as to their civilization. They indicate a mastery of the technique of sculpture which in part is very remarkable. But as others have written at length upon these points, it is here unnecessary to discuss them.

Until recently all that we knew of their religion came from the study of their sculptured monuments, but now we learn something from the inscriptions as well. At the head of their Pantheon stands the lord of the heavens, the god of the sky, the dispenser of the blessings of the fields; he is called " the lord," or " the supreme one," " the great *papa* or *baba*," i. e., of course," father," — compare the Phrygian Ztvs *Tldiras* — also the " lord of Khate-Hati," etc. His consort is " the great *ma a* (= Ma)," that is, of course, " mother," also called " the great goddess." Her paramour, probably a sun-god, is one of the most noteworthy figures of the Pantheon. Beside them stands a number of other gods, some of whom are also mentioned in the inscriptions. 1 he principal figures are immigrants from Syria, and one at least, *viz.,* " the great mother," did not stay her course among the " Hittites," but with her lover passed on into PhrygiaHow from Phrygia her cult spread farther over the West is familiar to all. In the worship of the Virgin in our own day there seems still to live the same force which in a hoary antiquity was active in Svria, and which the "Hittites" in Asia Minor may well have helped pass down. Moreover, this cult also flourished, where we may at least venture to look for it, *viz.,* in Armenia. It is true that in preChristian times an Iranian cult predominated here, not without modifications however, which can be completely explained on the hypothesis that it was grafted upon a native Old-Armenian, *i. e.,* "Hittite" foundation. What in the Armenian religion is not Persian is, unless of Syrian, of" Hittite " origin.

How far back we can trace the historv of the " Hittite "Armenians is still uncertain. We do not know whether a king of Great Khate, mentioned by Thothmes 111, of Egypt about 1500 B. c, belongs to the same race or not. About 1400 B. c, in Palestine, we find two men with names which appear to be Indogermanic, and therefore may possibly be Armenian, *viz.,* Shuar-data and Wash (Yash or Ash (-data, where *data* can also represent *dato* or *doto.* The names may accordingly mean "given by Shuar or Wash (Yash or Ash) " respectively. We certainly find people of Indogermanic blood, and therefore probably Armenians, in the army of King Khate-

sere of Khate, who flourished about the year 130x3 B. c.; but whether this monarch himself and his countrymen were "Hittite "-Armenians must remain an open question. In such an event the name pronounced by the Egyptians approximately Khatesere might represent a native name Hatiseri-s = " Hati-loving," corresponding to Armenian *hayaser.*

About 1200 B. c. the inscriptions begin. The very fact of their existence proves that about 1000 B. C. at least Hamath-Hama and Karkemish were in possession of the "Hittites." But of a " Hittite" empire in Syria we know as little as do the Assyrian inscriptions of the first thousand years antedating our era. At this period there were only petty " Hittite" states. The inscriptions lead us *to* suppose that the conquest of Syria and the district to the north, with the apparent exception of Karkemish, in all probability proceeded from Cilicia, for several distinct kings of this group call themselves Cilicians, and Cilicia is spoken of in several of their inscriptions, even in cases when an actual connection with Cilicia is out of the question. The inscriptions prove the Cilicians to have been a subdivision of the " Hittites." Sargon of Assyria (722-705 B. C.) put an end to the "Hittite " rule over the country east of the Taurus.

At what date the Hittites or their kindred first appeared in the district west of the Taurus remains still unsettled. From considerations stated above it does not seem impossible that the so-called Pseudo-Sesostris in the pass of Karabel near the coast of the *JEgean* Sea dates from before 1200 B. c. Somewhere about 850 B. C. and later there flourished in Cappadocia a kingdom, perhaps called Khamani, the kings of which have left us the magnificent Hittite sculptures and inscriptions at Boghazkoi.

When the universal empire of the Assyrians, which had absorbed the petty " Hittite " states, was shattered to pieces, or perhaps a little earlier, the Hittite " nation lifted its head once more. It was led by Cilician kings under whom, perhaps 800 years before or

even earlier, it had settled southeast and north from the mount of Amanus. About 600 B. c. we find a " Hittite" king of Cilicia, the king of the Bulgharmaden inscription, whose dominions, besides Cilicia proper, south of the Taurus, include Cataonia to the west, Khate to the east of the Taurus, and the territory of Karkemish on the Euphrates to the east. He styles himself perhaps also supreme lord of the Lycaonians, just as he does of the " Hittites." Another king of Cilicia has left an inscription found in ancient Lycaonia in which he perhaps styles himself king of Lycaonia. Between Kaisarive (Ca?sarea) and the Taurus there has been discovered an epitaph of a relatively late date, belonging to a Cilician, son of a Cilician.

This expansion of the Cilician power in the final period is attested by Greek writers of later date. It explains how a Syennesis of Cilicia, in conjunction with a contemporary king of Babylon, undertook to reconcile Alyattes of Lydia and Kyaxares of Media. He of course divided the supremacy of Asia Minor with Alvattes and was the neighbor of the Babylonian monarch. It is also not improbable that the expedition of Necho, king of Kgvpt, undertaken in the direction of Karkemish, was directed not against Nebuchadrezzar of Babylon, but against a Cilician king to whom Karkemish already belonged, and whom Nebuchadrezzar came to assist.

The latest inscriptions date probably from about 550 B. C. It is in the highest degree probable that the " Hittite" characters were superseded by the Aramaic during the Persian period. The supremacy then established in those parts by Persia mav also explain why no further inscriptions ot Cilician kings have been forthcoming since that time. After 550 B. c, all that we know of the Indogermanic inhabitants of Cilicia is contained in Cilician proper names of a later date.

Some time about 500 B. C. we find Indogermanic " Hittite "-Armenians in Western Armenia. By what route they effected their entrance, or at what date, we do not know. It is not improbable that, as I suggested some years ago, the Cimmerian invasion into Asia Minor pushed them in this direction, and it is possible that their native seat of Khate was the starting point of this displacement of the Armenian people. It is equally possible, however, that as we also have found a Hittite in ancient Phrygia, these Armenian immigrants came from the west. This would confirm certain traditions of antiquity according to which the Armenians originally came from Phrygia, their speech resembling that of the Phrygians. Such traditions, however, in themselves are not too worthy of credence, and this coincidence is scarcely required.

A word may be expected as to the Hittites of Palestine mentioned in the Bible. This is a difficult question, and its solution is still to be sought. We know that according to the Old Testament Abraham found Hittites in Hebron, Hittites being counted among the original inhabitants of Palestine, while Ezekiel refers to the father of Jerusalem as an Amorite but to its mother as a Hittite. The Egyptian and cuneiform inscriptions give us no commentary upon this, unless it be the circumstance that a Philistine king's name is perhaps identical with a name found in North Syria, and the fact that the Philistines are perhaps descended from a pirate people mentioned in the Egyptian inscriptions as coming from the north.

This, however, is not sufficient to enable us definitely to pronounce upon the problem raised by these Hittites, viz., did a section of the inhabitants of Khate in North Syria really at any time settle in Palestine? Or, what is still more doubtful, are we to understand by the Hittites of Palestine merely a particular race cognate with the people of our inscriptions? As stated above, the mere name tells us nothing as to the nationality of the people. This much we may venture to say, that we find in Palestine, about the year 1400 B. c., people with names which to all appearance are Indogermanic, and therefore may possibly be ancient Armenians. But that they and their countrymen were ever settled there in great close corporations is a supposition which lacks proof. So much for the primitive history of the Hittite-Armeni-

ans.

The deciphering of the so-called Hittite inscriptions thus opens to us the archives of an ancient people, giving us authentic information as to their history, language, and religion. This is a feat remarkable enough in itself, but that this people should prove to be the ancestors of the modern Armenians makes the matter still more remarkable. Our new knowledge throws light upon many centuries of Armenian history and of the Armenian tongue which up till now had remained in total darkness. Moreover, the Hittite inscriptions must be regarded as the most ancient monuments of our Indogermanic speech, and as the oldest native documents of Indogermanic history. If the dispute be justified as to whether Asia or Europe is the original home of the Indogermanic nations, the fact that about 1000 B. c, if, indeed, not much earlier, Armenians were settled in Asia Minor, Svria, and perhaps even Palestine, must eventually influence its settlement.

GENERAL INDEX.